Ken Kesey's previous w[...]
*Over the Cuckoo's Nest[...]
Notion, *Kesey's Garage [...]
(with O. U. Levon), and [...]
His children's books include *Little Tricker the
Squirrel Meets Big Double the Bear* and *The
Sea Lion*. He lives in Oregon.

SAILOR SONG

Ken Kesey

CORGI BOOKS

SAILOR SONG
A CORGI BOOK : 0 552 14110 0

First publication in Great Britain

PRINTING HISTORY
Corgi edition published 1993

Set in 9½pt Linotype Melior by
Phoenix Typesetting, Burley-in-Wharfedale, West Yorkshire

Corgi Books are published by Transworld Publishers Ltd,
61-63 Uxbridge Road, London W5 5SA,
in Australia by Transworld Publishers (Australia) Pty Ltd,
15-23 Helles Avenue, Moorebank, NSW 2170,
and in New Zealand by Transworld Publishers (NZ) Ltd,
3 William Pickering Drive, Albany, Auckland.

Made and printed in Great Britain by
Cox & Wyman Ltd, Reading, Berks.

To Faye –
  a deep keel in the raving waves
  a polestar in the dark
  a shipmate

Grateful acknowledgement is made for permission
to reprint excerpts from the following copyrighted
works: 'Suzanne' by Leonard Cohen. Copyright ©
1967 Leonard Cohen Stranger Music, Inc. Used by
permission. All rights reserved. 'Empty Shelves' by
Ernesto Cardenal. Translation © 1986 by Jonathan
Cohen. Reprinted by permission of City Lights
Books.

And Jesus was a sailor
When he walked upon the water
And he spent a long time watching
From his lonely wooden tower
And when he knew for certain
Only drowning men could see him
He said, All men will be sailors then
Until the sea shall free them.
But he himself was broken
Long before the sky would open
Forsaken, almost human
He sank beneath your wisdom
Like a stone.

—Leonard Cohen

1
Dream of Jeannie with Light Grey Matter

Ike Sallas was asleep when it began, in a red aluminum Galaxxy, not all that far away and only a short skip into the future. It was the best of times, it was the worst of times—and that wasn't even the half of it.

He was dreaming about his ex-wife, Jeannie, and how good she looked in their duster days in Fresno—the clean, simple days, before the baby and the Bakatcha Movement were born.

Before the decade came to be known as the Nasty Nineties.

In this dream Ike has just come in from a 3-ZEE job over the chokes to find Jeannie sitting in the morning sun of their breakfast nook, naked. Out the window can be seen the megrays tending the fields, a twinkle of hoe-blades rising and falling. The flyby mist is still hanging in the silky morning air.

Jeannie is still in her platinum-bleach sexpot days, her face still able to convey a measure of contentment. The breakfast nook was her favorite spot in the whole house, she always claimed—after, of course, the sack. Jeannie, Jeannie . . .

She is reading aloud from her grandmother's Bible. The Bible is covered in soft white doeskin. Jeannie is wearing tinted reading glasses, ironed hair and one of those hats Sally Field sported in 'The Flying Nun.' Her favorite re-dish, she always maintained—after, naturally, 'I Dream of Jeannie.'

Nun's hat, tinted glasses, and that spectacular swoop of platinum hair over her bare shoulders, like a linen wimple, whiter than the book in her hands. Not a stitch else.

Ike can see her lips moving as she reads, but all he can hear is the whir of the distant crop planes and, from someplace much more distant, a thin, strangled, half-human cry.

The tableau strikes him as sadly burlesque: the all-American breakfast nooky; the religious motif; the way she cuddles the book so close she might have been following the text with a nipple. Something about the scene ludicrous and insulting, like the taunt of a thumb ribbing you.

To keep from laughing at the dream he starts yelling at his wife, something on the order of 'Either shit or get off the sexpot! Put down that stupid book and take off that goofy hat, it's all too ludicrous.'

But it seems she can't hear him either, enshrined there in her bell of sunshine. She doesn't turn her head. She licks her finger, turns a page, and her lips move again. And Ike feels that goddamn thumb. He tries more yelling, but the insults glance off her bell like little hailstones. He turns to the bookshelves where her Bible has left its recent gap. His old leather-bound edition of *Moby-Dick* is the cannonball he chooses. He hauls it from the bottom shelf and turns and puts it into the air, all in one thrifty motion. A heavy thump, and the bright tableau goes undersea-grey. The sunny nook in Fresno becomes an icy dawn in an antique trailerhouse in Alaska, long years later. Somewhere through the grey he seems to hear again that airless cry, far away and remotely woman. Then quiet.

'Ludicrous,' Ike says aloud. 'Stow it.'

He rolls to look at his alarm on the table beside the cot. Still hours before he has to meet Greer at the docks. Stow. He has just reclosed his eyes to ponder the dream when he feels something start bumping the trailer, very close and very real! Cold air fills his lungs and Ike slides his hand out of the bag's velcro seam and feels for Teddy.

Teddy is the .22 hi-standard he keeps beneath the bunk pad.

'Greer?' Breath in the still air. 'Is that you, Partner? Marley? Marley, you mutt, is that you?'

The bumping ceases. He grasps the warm gunbutt, then carefully stretches up to the window above the bunk. Far too filthy to see through. He locates the aluminum handle and cranks the glass open a crack. The bumping begins again, right outside the window.

He knees the bag all the way open and lands both feet in his mukluks, gripping the butt of the gun. 'Greer? Marley?' No answer. He sees the dark lump on the sheepskin rug in front of the propane heater. There's old Marley, still as dead to the world as the ghost he's named after. Greer's probably out carousing someplace—'shelunking,' Greer calls it. A rare recreation, these days. When the world-wide UN AIDS inoculations wiped out the disease at its source—the dirty dick—it also seemed to wipe out a great deal of such urges as give rise to spreading the disease. Male ardor cooled and never rekindled. Greer, however, was different. Either he had somehow ducked the decade of inoculation drives down in his Jamaican jungles, or had been of such lusty urges, such hard-horned goat power, that he overcame, as it were, the vaccine's side effect.

Ike eases around the sleeping dog, feeling along the cold metal bulkhead of the trailer until he finds his flashlight. He takes it off the wall charger and sticks it in the elastic waistband of his thermals. He draws a breath and jerks the trailer door open, kicking wide the screen. The .22 is ready in his right hand as he snatches the flashlight from his waistband with his left, moving smooth like an old-time two-gunned pistolero. The sight he beholds seizes him in mid-move, the light half-lifted, the gun's safety still on.

He feels the second dig of the day from that unseen thumb.

The thing had been crouched at the bottom of the aluminum steps. At the crash of the door it rears upright, standing easily waist-high to a man. The ideal size for a demon. Before Ike's horrified eyes it begins to waltz about on its hind legs, its forepaws lifted in a swaying, obscene invitation. The midsection of the thing is practically nonexistent, a dark hollow scooped beneath a ribby chest, pumping for air. Its legs look like a pair of broken sticks matted with burrs and blood. Its long slimy tail lashes back and forth for balance, like a lizard's.

But it is the cursed thing's *head* that turns Ike's breath to dry ice in his throat. From the shoulders up the creature seems to be perfectly smooth, hairless, featureless, flawless. Ike stands blinking, feeling in a remote way vindicated. This is no dream, this dirt mama is real. *Real!* The Thing itself, here at last, both hell-whelped and man-made, right in front of him . . . the unnatural spawn of meddling as Claude Rains had meddled in that horror classic *The Invisible Man* 'With Things Man Was Meant to Leave Alone.'

When Ike finds the flashlight's switch the illuminated sight is even ghastlier. The wretched thing's head is smooth all right, slick and seamless as chrome, but the light's beam reveals it does have features. Beneath the glassy surface a *face* can be discerned, pulsating in some kind of prenatal goo. A dirt-mama abomination for sure—blow it *away!* But just as the gunsights come level the creature abruptly manages to pirouette full around. On the back side of the cylindrical head Ike sees the tattered scrap of label:

BEST FOO
REAL MAYO
LOW CHOLE

'Hell, it's a cat, a cat got his head stuck in a mayonnaise jar.'

The cat pirouettes back to face the sound, still swaying upright, bottled head tipped backward. This tortured position seems to be the only way the animal has found to keep an air passage open at its throat.

12

'You're in a fix, cousin.' Ike lays the gun aside. He drops to one knee on the oyster-shell yard. 'How long you been this way? Let me give you a ha-*aagh*!'

The animal takes the offered hand in all four of his, raking Ike's forearms from elbows to fingertips. Ike curses and slaps the creature to the ground. It springs right back after him. He slaps it to the ground again and this time leaps straddle of it before it can rise. He pins it against the oyster shells with a fistful of slimy fur, the flashlight lifted like a fishclub. But the animal is limp. Slapped unconscious or emptied of its energy by those clawing fits of fury. Relenting his wrath, Ike lowers the light to gently tap the jar at the collar. When the glass finally cracks, the residue goo keeps the shards from scattering. The jar swells open slowly, like a hatching egg.

The emerging head has swollen to take on the shape of the jar, teeth protruding through lips that were flattened against the glass, ears glued to the top of the concave head. Ike pushes apart the shards with the rim of the light, clearing the mouth first, then the nostrils. The cat lies motionless during the procedure, gulping the air. When the animal's muzzle is at last cleared Ike turns loose the handful of fur to try and wipe some of the rancid salad dressing from the eyes. The instant it feels itself free the cat attacks anew, yowling up Ike's arm, this time with claws *and* teeth.

'You slime-sucking mother!' Ike slings the animal away. It rolls on its all-fours and comes yowling back. Ike kicks at it, but not hard enough. It comes swarming up his leg right into his face. He snatches it away and slings it again to the ground. It spins to come back, but this time Ike really gets his mukluk into it, sidekicking the slimy ball as though trying for a fifty-yard field goal. Across the shells the animal goes pinwheeling and yowling. When it finds its footing it keeps on going, scurrying around the propane tanks and through the fern and on up the boulders toward the pines. The furious stone Ike hurls after it wakes a trio of crows from the scrub. They flush in a whirl,

13

blaming the cat with raucous screeches of outrage. Ike lets the crows take over and leans heavily against the woodpile, waiting for his panting to subside.

Then, like the next movement in a running gag running too long, he hears the cry again. Not from the cat at all, but from the other direction, down past the dump, tiny, and strangled, and—he's certain now—definitely woman.

'Somebody oh please *he-e-elp* me.'

It sounds like the Loop girl, Louise. Ike listens, frowning. The Loop menfolk frequently disturbed the tranquility of the nights at this end of town, squabbling and fighting and grunting like the hogs they raised—especially after they have bowled some big-league victory at Papa Loop's Lanes downtown. But Ike hasn't heard of any bowling tourneys, and he can't recall *ever* hearing the girl carry on like this. Her style has always attempted to be more provocative than provoked; a little lame, perhaps, but never loud.

'Somebody help me oh *pleee*—'

The scream is abruptly throttled. Ike holds his breath. The dawn is silent. Just the whistler moaning out on the bar, and those three crows up the hill, still after the cat. Nothing else. He listens a long minute, not breathing. At last he sighs; he'll have to take the van and go check. He shuffles to the back of the trailer and sees that his van is stone gone. In its place is his roommate's old Jeep.

'Damn you, Greer.'

He crunches across the shells to the shrouded shape of the ancient vehicle and throws the tarp from the hood. The seats are upholstered with frost.

Ike starts cranking the engine. Five times, he reminds himself; then let it sit a count. Don't flood it. Five more and another count. Using the last dregs of the battery the four cylinders fume begrudgingly to life. Ike wheels off downhill with the engine still cold.

To save the feeble battery he doesn't switch on the headlights. He steers his way toward the dump by smell and smoke. Mountains of smoldering garbage begin to loom past, like miniature volcanoes still active with fluttering fires of orange and green and methane blue. The dump has been smoldering like this for decades. Townspeople thought it had finally been froze out by that crazy winter of '93, but when the June sun melted the shell of ice the fire still smoldered down in the magma of refuse, rank as ever.

Ike lifts his upper lip and tries to breathe through his moustache to filter the air. He doesn't mind the dump, usually; it makes for a kind of moat between him and the rest of the town. But lately there has been more and more confiscated drift-net to burn, mainly Chinese Molecumar. The stuff smells like dynasties decomposing.

Ike roars past the last steaming mountain so fast he almost misses the altercation that has caused the cry of distress. He glimpses the ghostly beige glow of his Honda Heftyvan pulled back in one of the dump's many little inroads, its doors all agape, its interior light silhouetting a frozen struggle of human limbs.

Ike brakes to a skid and jams the floorshift into reverse, flicking on the headlights. He cramps the Jeep around backwards until the beams fix on the tangled arabesque. Lifted high against the van's open rear door is what has to be the top half of Louise Loop. Her round white face floats vacuous as a balloon atop a billowing pair of breasts—three glowing globes, like a sign above the door of some kind of X-rated pawnshop on Meatstreet. Then the globes are dashed down out of sight and he sees the man's naked back. The muscular shoulders are white as the breasts and quivering with rage.

'Hey, let her go!'

Ike vaults out, leaving the motor idling. He charges through the litter with the flashlight held before him like a lance. It isn't until he's almost on top of the pair that he appreciates the muscular spread of that white back and shoulders, and thinks of the pistol, back on the trailer steps.

'Hey you! Let her go—!'

The man does not seem to hear. Ike can't see the guy's

15

face but he can tell he's in some kind of zone-out. Ike
realizes he'll have to grab the slimy bastard. 'Hey,' he
hooks a naked elbow, 'turn loose before you strangle
the poor twink. Turn *loose*!' The flesh in his grip feels
as slimy as it looks, but Ike holds on until the man's
trance seems to break. The shoulders relax, the quivering
subsides. Without releasing the woman's throat the man
slowly turns his head, rotating into the light a face almost
as shocking as the one hatched from the mayonnaise
bottle. It is completely smooth and white. No brows
or lashes. Lips and eyes the color of salmon eggs. A
bright porcelain brow framed by an even brighter mane
of hair, like chrome, for all the world like flowing mother
chrome! 'Jesus!' Ike staggers back. 'Jesus Christ!'

The salmon egg lips lift in a bemused purr. 'Sorry,
dunk-o, but I'm not Jesus.' Then he turns matter-of-factly
back to his unfinished task of choking the unconscious
woman, adding in a roguish afterthought out the side of
his mouth: 'And she's no twinkie, she's my wife huh huh
hmmm . . .'

It isn't the matter-of-fact strangulation that gets Ike,
it's the tone. That familiar aggravating tone within the
sniggering. He heard a lot of it in jail—a kind of shared,
one-dude-to-another tone, carrying both the sting of insult and the touch of intimacy, like 'Hey, man, we dig
huh huh huh.' Now he'll have to grab him again. Ike
lays down the flashlight and grabs both hands full of
the long mane of white hair running around the man's
neck (just like the collar of a judo jacket) pivots until
he's back-to-back, and throws. The long form of the silver
man cartwheels overhead, then whoops full-length on the
littered ground, like a wet rag doll. Ike turns loose the hair
and stands, his breath slowing. Some of the braver of
the Loop boars have come rooting out of their smoky
grottoes, curious to examine the spoils of this conflict;
when something hits the ground that hard and ripe it
usually stays there and is occasionally good to eat. For
a moment Ike finds himself hoping the guy is dead,
killed clean and done with.

The silver man rolls over and pushes himself to his hands and knees. In the shimmer of the headlights he looks suddenly fragile, evanescent as a mushroom. The muscles of his torso are shivering again and seem ineffectual looking. He rises to his knees and clasps his long white hands before him in supplication.

'Please don't hit me again, I'm okay now. You know how it is.' His mouth lifts in a smile but he doesn't snicker. 'I tweaked. You know the bit: you come back after *years* . . . you walk all the way through town fantasizing how it's gonna be; moonlight in her tears, waiting at her lonely window . . . instead you find her parked out in the garbage balling some reggae clown . . . and you tweak. But I'm cool now. You don't have to hit me again.'

'I never hit you in the first place.'

'Then don't hit me now, either. I'm cool and I'm sorry. Okay?'

The man is still on his knees, wringing his hands. Ike stares down in confusion. The remorse seems so overplayed it makes it difficult not to view the display as a kind of put-on.

'Okay, you're forgiven. Get up.'

The guy doesn't get up. He stays on his knees and continues to wring his hands in remorse. The pigs grunt from the shadows, full of sympathy. Behind him Ike hears the Jeep motor cough, choke and die, the dim headlights rapidly darkening. A crow squawks. Then from down the road Ike hears the door of the Loop house clatter open and slam, footstomps through the cans. Ike hopes that it's maybe Greer, creeping out from hiding now that the danger is subdued. But a momentary breeze in the hanging smoke shows that it isn't Greer. It's Papa Loop. There's no mistaking the bowling-alley walk. Omar Loop always trudges in a purposeful hunch, like he's about to roll that thundering strike in the last frame and win himself another trophy.

'So it *is* you, is it then?' Loop trudges toward the kneeling man, ignoring Ike. 'My boys said they heard you was back in the territory but I couldn't believe it.

17

I told them you had better sense. Well, I been wrong
before and too bad for me and this time too bad for you.
We *warned* you, you pink-eyed freak, what we'd—'scuse
me, Sallas—' Loop pushes Ike aside to better position
himself—'what'd happen if you come back and bother
Louise again. This family looks out for its *own*'—then
lets the guy have it right in the face, *crack*, a short,
efficient uppercut, thrown with all the force the squat
legs and bowler's back can muster. The head snaps and
the stranger hits the ground again with a grunt. Papa Loop
is cocking for another when Ike steps forward.

'Hey, Omar. There's no call for that—'

'We warned him, Sallas, when we kicked him out years
ago! I'm a free-thinking man, but I draw the line.'

The silver man is dragging himself to his knees again.
Omar Loop bobs from one rubber-booted foot to the other,
rolling his shoulders.

'Hold on, Omar—' Ike tries to step in front of old
Loop.

'One side, Sallas. This is a family affair.'

'Please, Papa Loop, please, please, please.' The man
laces his fingers in front of his bleeding nose. 'I tweaked
when I found her with that Rasta bastard. But I'm all right
now, I'm cool. Besides'—then, incredibly, allowing that
loose insinuating smile to show again right through the
blood—'the poor twink *is* my wife.'

Crack! Omar hops to one side and throws the uppercut.
The silver man's head snaps and reels, but he remains
upright on his knees, available for the next punch.

Ike draws another lungful of air through his teeth:
now it's old man Loop he's going to have to grab. 'No,
Omar—' Ike wraps his arms around the barrel-shaped
torso, wrinkling his nose against the reek of tobacco juice
and pork—'don't hit him again.'

'Isaak Sallas, you better unloose me!' The torso continuing to bob, measuring the head for another shot. 'I appreciate your concern, but this is Loop family busi*noop*!'

Ike has slipped his hands up under the arms and locked
the neck in a full nelson. Omar Loop twists and snarls,

threatening terrible consequences if he isn't unloosed. Ike tightens his hold and waits; the old man can't throw a punch. But there's nothing stopping his legs. He sinks the reinforced rubber toe of a boot all the way to the instep into the shirtless abdomen before him. Ike squeezes the nelson harder, wondering at the old man's strength. 'I'll keep squeezing, Omar'—though he is actually beginning to worry if he can hold the little brute—'just have to keep squeezing until you'—then an arcing beam of light from behind stops wonder and worry both. Out of nowhere it comes, knocks stars all down the side of his skull. He is able to turn just in time to see the girl Louise raising the big flashlight for another blow. Then another shower of gentle stars. He hears the squawking laughter up the hill. Just the kind of joke they love, those crows: rescued damsel opens her eyes, does she see a hero? A knight, a savior? Nothing like it. She sees a fiend in red longjohns breaking Papa's neck while hubby rolls around in the garbage drooling blood. It only follows that she just naturally . . . but never mind. Still, it does go to show, does it not, to always leave the djinn alone? No matter how it hollers, how it cries . . . to always leave it alone in the you-know-what.

Or the joke's on you-know-who.

He might have laughed along if it hadn't gone all undersea grey again.

2
Hog History Duck
Gutters and a
Rum Soaked Rag

That family of hogs had been dwellers at the dump
decades longer than any of their neighbors. Shipped
into Kuinak as piglets, they were originally housed in
a failed icehouse on the corner of Dock and Bayshore.
Like the icehouse, they were originally the property of
Paul the Prophet Petersen. 'Bacon from fish waste! Gold
from dross! I predict Petersen's Sea Pork will be all over
the territory in less than a year.'

Like a lot of Petersen's famous prophecies this predic-
tion came true, but not quite as anticipated. The failed
icehouse, for example, had been based on his prescient
vision of the forthcoming need for more chipped ice
during the summers; the visiting sports-fishermen would
surely increase as soon as Kuinak became an internationally known sports-fishing attraction. He was right.
As the takes dwindled in Ketchican and Juneau and
Cordova, more sports boats began showing up in Kuinak.
'Nightdish' did one piece, and *Field and Stream*. So
Paul's pitch was successful and the money was raised.
The resulting structure was a ninety-foot grey cube,
bereft of windows and built of pumice blocks stuffed
with flowfome to insulate the ice Paul would float in
from the glacier. 'Only stone building in a hundred miles!'
he bragged to his investors, clanging a corner with his ice
tongs. 'Last a hundred years.'

The following week a seagoing refrigeration plant from
Norway chugged into Kuinak and the Great Northern

Glacial Ice Bank went bankrupt in less than a hundred days. The Norwegian owners eventually sold out to Searaven and retired to Innsbruck.

It can get depressing for a bad luck prophet, always calling the winners but never quite getting the race right.

But Paul was not the sort to stay depressed. He liked to look at the bright side of the ledger. He still had that big grey block, for instance, like a safe just waiting for a deposit, like a—wait! that was it!—a Piggy Bank! Now *there* was something solid—pork commodities. Paul had raised pigs in Connecticut. It was a greasy business, but it always kept the wolf from the door. And it made sense. Why ship refrigerated meat all the way from Seattle when you could raise it right here on the shore on slop the town was throwing away by the tons? It was a perfect way for the investors to recoup their losses, as well as get in on the solid ground floor of a sturdy future.

The capital was grudgingly raised, the barge of porkers came noisily in. They trotted down the chute right into the big stone block and straight to the plank troughs Paul had waiting. The smell of guts and gills drew them like pig iron to a magnet. They could be heard squealing and fighting and gobbling and putting on pounds from clear up at the Crabbe Potte, where Paul had retired with his business partners to drink a toast.

'To Petersen's Pork o' the Sea! All over the whole territory!'

That night all involved parties slept deep and full. The following dawn something awoke them—a mighty sucking sound, coming, it seemed, from some huge dark maw across the bay. Boats and buoys, piers and pilings were being sucked away into the night—the very sea itself was being siphoned out, as into some monstrous bag. At length the sucking sound ceased. The bag was full. Then it came blowing back. It was the 1994 tsunami, thirty years to the day after the last big seaquake. The tidal wave came like a wolf made of water, huffing-and-puffing across the bay and the docks and the lot at ninety miles an hour, and down came the whole front wall of the little

21

pigs' house, brick-built though it was (twigs and straw and tar paper fared better, in fact), and such squealers as survived the collapsing rubble took off for higher ground. Paul the Prophet took off north.

The pigs kept running until they reached the mountainous Kuinak Town Dump up at the tree line. One boar named Prigham, young and Mormonesque, proclaimed 'This is the place,' and they dug in. The century-high piles of smoking garbage provided shelter and sustenance both. And those that lasted through the next few seasons of wicked weather and bad bears eventually became the hardy seed of the Loop swine herd. Omar Loop happened to encounter the hogs while in Kuinak scavenging. He was a professional bowler by brag but he made his money as an amateur scavenger. He ferried an old flatbed Chevy up and down the coast, hustling the lanes by night with his good luck ruby-red bowling ball, and exploring the various dumps by day with his flatbed—looking for whatever he could buy cheap and sell a little less cheap. Web, mainly. A lot of fishermen will throw away a perfectly good net rather than take the few minutes clearing and patching it. Loop enjoyed a good living, sampling various small-town bowling alleys and landfills like a surf bum sampling bars and beaches, able to wire home enough money every month to Juneau to keep the missus and kids off his hunched back. He liked floating around footloose and free and was resolved to keep it that way. But that morning when he rounded the corner on the smoking majesty of the Kuinak dump and saw those wild hogs rooting amidst the burning debris—charred, savage, prehistoric things, with hide like armor plate and bristles like eight-penny nails, swallowing salmon heads whole right along with plastic milk bottles and Pampers—Omar's resolve collapsed. Here was his kind of spread and his breed of livestock.

Inquiring around, he learned that the hog pack had become something of a protected species. They'd been written up in *True Grit*. The town was proud of them.

22

They represented survivors of the '94 quake, not to mention all the years of bears and mosquitoes and frostbite. Survived by burrowing *right into the embers*, the boogers did!

'Somebody musta owned them oncet,' Omar insisted. Someone recalled that old Paul Petersen had brought them to Kuinak, but Paul had disappeared. He had kind of fell to pieces after the quake, just like his icehouse. Last anybody heard, he was in Anchorage in a home for nervous breakdowns.

Omar Loop headed off in his truck and located old Paul the Prophet up near Willows, caretaking a string of motels that catered to pipeline roughnecks. The messiest breed of roughneckers there are, pipeline workers, producing their own bulk daily in beer cans alone, not to mention other trash. This time Paul was the one pitched to. A good flatbed truck worth three grand Blue Book, $2,500 easy, was the very thing his caretaking business needed. A fair trade for a blockhouse with only three walls. Paul agreed; twenty-five hundred was certainly fair and, sure, he'd throw in those damn ungrateful hogs, wherever they were. Hadn't thought about them in years.

Omar got a Small Business Loan on the icehouse property and used the money to make a down payment on the worthless dump and its adjacent pungent acreage. Some of this turned out to be timber; he traded half for working capital and contracted to turn the icehouse into a six-lane bowling alley. He knew of a half-dozen boarded-up bowleries where he could pick up furnishings and pin-setters for a few lies and a song; all the blockhouse itself needed was a john and a front wall and some neons. Not that he expected it to turn much of a profit—they rarely did. He had other ideas for that.

With the remainder of the timber he and his boys built a dump-side cabin that served as the Loops' slaughter- and bunkhouse both. They built it high enough off the ground so the hogs couldn't get in, yet low enough so the piglets could hide beneath the floor. In time they built a separate bunkhouse, which in time became a

23

bigger slaughterhouse. Then another and another, until the place was a maze of rooms in segments, growing out from the dump into the stumpland like a wooden tapeworm.

As usual, Louise Loop and her mother dwelt in the most recent addition; Omar and the boys still lingering in the previous segment. The recent addition was called the dining room, though it might just as well have been called the dining room living room laundry room and kitchen. The door frame between it and the other rooms was hung with partition plastic—vertical overlapping strips thick as transparent leather. The plastic was spattered with gore and tobacco spit on the gentlemen's side, and decorated with stick-on butterflies on the ladies'. Lady's, really. Mother had been absent from the gore and garbage for more than a year now, away in one of those Anchorage homes for the broke-down. Some claimed it was the hogs that caused it, others said it was the bowling. The Loop dish was rarely tuned to anything but 'Bowling for Bucks.'

The butterflies were Lulu's idea; she claimed it made the splatters on the plastic look like bouquets of red roses. It wasn't that she minded blood or chaw, but she liked blossoms and butterflies better. She liked them so much, in fact, she had continued the motif right on off of the plastic divider strips. Butterflies adorned the insulation between the unwalled studs. Butterflies were pasted over the open snarls of wiring, and across the layers of dirty Vizqueen stapled on the windows, and all the way up across the fiberboard ceiling and down into the plywood floor. By the thousands.

One tasteful butterfly each was embroidered above the open muzzles of her favorite double-barreled brassiere; she had put the garment on special, after that embarrassment out at the van. This butterfly bra was the first thing that Ike saw when he at last surfaced, blinking and gasping. The boundless grey cold had given way to a kind of bottled confinement—air so hot he felt he'd been kissed by steam. The leading lady was holding his

24

head tenderly in her lap and cooing over him like he was the hero after all.

'. . . So when you *did* finally turn and I *do* finally see your face . . . well, there couldn't anybody have recognized you even if it had been broad daylight. I mean you were a scratched-up *mess*! Still and all I'm real sorry I whacked you. My mistake. Sue me or take it out of my skin.'

Past the butterflies he saw it was Louise Loop. It seemed she'd been apologizing for a long time. She raised a wet cloth and smiled down into his face.

'Anyway what I mean to say is thank you for coming when you did—' She gave the washcloth a wring and added 'neighbor.' A dribble of liquid seared his lips. He tried to sit up but Lulu held him trapped under that twelve-gauge bra. 'Take it easy, it's only rum. One-fifty-one. I phoned The Radio Man and he said it'd be as good a disinfectment as they'd use on you down at the Rising Daughters Infirmary. Lay still—'

'Where is everybody?'

'Gone. Edgar and Oscar took that maniac ex of mine down to see if Lieutenant Bergstrom won't lock him up for insulting battery. Papa, he had to drive the tanker truck to the docks for more fish guts. The ruckus got the boars real roused up.'

'The docks?' He tried to sit. 'Shit, what time is it?'

'Time for you to lay still and rest is what. The Radio Man says I'm to stanch any bleeding wounds and keep the victim still and warm.'

Ike groaned. The Radio Man was one Dr Julius Beck, a disbarred proctologist from Sydney, where he used to be referred to as Dr Outbeck and occasionally as Dr Far Out Beck. He was now known as The Radio Man because he had a clandestine shortwave set-up somewhere in the area where he beamed out dubious medical advice and outlawed reggae and rifrap. He had a bad stutter and when his haphazard broadcasts would break into a CB band he would announce himself: 'G'dye, dunkers. This is the Fuh-fuh-fuh-Fishnet Works!'

'Also to frequently check the pupils for concussions,' Lulu added. She leaned over the cliffs of herself and probed his eyes with hers. Like her father and brothers she was squat and stout, but she had a pretty face, sweetly pink with the heat, and a honey-colored puff of wispy curls. She reminded Ike of a cotton-candy booth. She squeezed out another searing trickle of rum, laughing at his outcry.

'Listen to the big Bakatcha Bandit; for such a reputation I can't believe what a sissy!' Then added coquettishly, 'Also I simply can *not* comprehend how you let a wimp like my ex work you over so bad.'

'Wimp? I'll bet he weighs two-thirty! Let me up, Lulu; I've got to get to work.'

'He's all meringue,' she said, 'banana cream and Stanazone. You were in no great danger, I oughta know.' She shook her head at Ike's appearance and sighed again. 'I just hope he didn't give you some kind of infections.'

She turned to resoak her washrag. The rum bottle was nestled in a big snowdrift of Band-Aid wrappers, as though to protect it from the heat. As she unscrewed the lid, Ike was able to dodge free and sit up. He saw he was on a rumpled comforter, hemmed in by pillows and butterflies. A red formica table occupied the center of the room, ringed round with dirty paper plates. In some of the settings the paper plates layered down through the archaeology of a week or more's meals. Paper cups were nested and piled, stained with past drinks. More paper plates, along with orange rinds and apple cores and milk cartons and pizza boxes, were piled beneath the table. Lulu saw Ike looking at the spectacle.

'We're due to clear it out pretty soon now. The hogs like for us to let the paper age a little. I expect it makes it more tasty.'

Ike found one mukluk and pulled it on. The girl sighed and returned the bottle to its nest, giving up on further treatment. She stood to follow Ike as he kicked through the litter to finally find the other furry shoe. When he leaned to put it on Louise ran her hand under his thermal tops. 'Why you're all sweaty, Mr Sallas. You ought to ease up and scoot down a little more. Everybody in town says so.'

'God yes I'm sweaty, Lulu,' Ike panted. 'You got it like an oven in here.'

'Papa does like to keep it warm,' she admitted. 'But you ought to scoot down more nonetheless. I *never* see you at the Crabbe Potte on Free Girl Night, for an instance. Don't you like girls, Mr Sallas?'

'I like girls just fine, Louise.' In a way he felt grateful for her simple-minded baiting; it was waking him up. 'The fact is I was supposed to have a date at daybreak with Alice Carmody to do a little fishing. And I'm late.'

'I'm not certain Alice Carmody *classifies* as a girl,' Lulu said, sticking out her lower lip. 'I am certain, though, that those salmon will wait a few minutes.'

'Probably. But not Alice Carmody.' He finally located the door out, hidden behind the hot-water heater. The cool air gushed in on him. Before he left he turned back to look at her pouting in the narrow doorway. 'You'll be okay with this guy around?'

'Aren't you sweet?' She dropped the pout and smiled. 'Don't worry, he usually's in control. He just kind of lost it when he came back unexpected and caught me and your buddy Greer doing, uh, the Jamaica goat dance, Greer called it. I'll be okay. Just meringue. Edgar and Oscar was always able to bat some sense into him. I swear I can't imagine what prompted him to come back after last time; he ain't dense. Papa says he's a bad penny is why. A Jonah jinx, you know what I mean? Papa warned me from the first that they are all of them jinxes. Born that way. I didn't believe it, naturally. I was only fifteen and he seemed, you know, *special*. Now, I have to say I think I agree with Papa: bad luck is born in them.'

'Thanks for your doctoring,' Ike told her.

'Anytime. Thanks for the rescue.' She dabbed at the sweat on her throat with the rum-soaked rag. 'I hope you don't catch a virus going out in the chill so sudden. Papa insists we keep that old stove stoked up.' She stopped

27

dabbing and started blowing into her bra, first one side then the other, as though trying to cool two bowls of chowder. 'A girl could die of heat frustration.'

The van was gone. Knowing Greer, Ike had expected as much. He hurried along to the Jeep, hopping from one frosty grass hummock to another to keep his mukluks out of the melting spring mud and scattered debris.

The Jeep was stone dead. But it was parked pointed up the shoulder of the roadway at enough slant that Ike was able to roll-start it in reverse. He let it warm up awhile, then headed back up the road. As he cruised through the smoldering mountains of waste he noticed that none of the dump's famous hogs were in sight. He heard a skirling chorus rising above the peaks, furious and hysterical. Lulu had been right; the ruckus had roused them real up and they wanted their garbage.

Ike pulled to a stop in his raked oyster-shell yard, gave the Jeep some choke and left it idling. He retrieved the pistol from the steps and after a moment's consideration placed it in a planter that hung outside the door.

Inside the cold trailer the light was still grey. The old dog was lying just as he'd been left, front legs doubled back under his chin. At least the front legs could still bend; hindquarters apparently got older faster. Greer'd had Marley all the years Ike had known him, outlasting three of Greer's wives. A crossbreed of some kind of Alsatian and Border collie, but large and long-legged, with a rangy wolflike look even in his crippled sleep. People assumed the dog was named after Bob Marley, the long-dead reggae radical that Greer featured in his occasional guest stints on The Radio Man's illegal shortwave. Ike knew Marley was named after an even older ghost. The night Greer found him was Christmas Eve. Greer had been off on a lone wire run and was drifting down the coast to Crescent City where he knew a nurse blest with three breasts plus a large Fannie Mae coming mature. His headlights revealed the dog limping north along the shoulder of 101, wet and lost. Thirty feet of steel chain was dragging from his bloody collar. 'Marley's ghost!' Greer pulled over in a sliding screech. 'You be a spirit come to make me mend my ways, mon? Hop on board.'

Freed of his chain Marley soon got over his limp and turned out to be a great watchdog—though his act was really more a welcome than a warning. He would hide beneath a big salal out at the edge of the road and make a sudden silent rush at any vehicle coming into the yard. He had once been able to leap all the way over the hood of the old LeBaron Ike used to drive, grinning with toothy glee as he sailed past the startled driver. That didn't seem so long ago, but Old Leaper Marley had suddenly become just old. He couldn't have jumped over a wheelbarrow.

Ike nudged the skinny flank with the toe of his mukluk. 'Marl, you still with us?' The old dog lifted his muzzle and looked around. His eyes finally focused on Ike but he didn't give his usual wolfy grin of greeting. Instead, he growled at the face above him, the sound low and serious.

'Hey, Marley, it's me! Uncle Ike!'

He knelt and let the dog smell his hand. Marley stopped growling and grinned, the expression a bit hedged with embarrassment. Ike scratched the ragged ears until the dog's head lay back into the bag and the filmy eyes closed. He noticed a turd matted to the dog's withers and picked it loose and carried it to the garbage pail beneath the sink, then went into the little bathroom to get the stink off, frowning thoughtfully. Marley had never growled at him before. When he flipped on the bathroom light and saw his reflection Ike understood the reason. He also understood why there had been such a pile of Band-Aid wrappers on that Hide-A-Bed. She must have used the entire box. The face in the mirror was criss-crossed everywhere with bright butterfly Band-Aids. From his eyebrows up, his head was swathed like a mummy's. He felt around but he could not find the end of the wrappings. He tried pulling the Band-Aids off but they were glued tight with dried blood and rum. Splash as he would, they hung fast. He looked at his watch. He didn't have time for this. Greer would wait, but not Alice.

He hurried into his clothes and rushed out to the sputtering Jeep, his boots in one hand, a pair of scissors in the other. On the windy ride through town to the bay he was able to clip loose and unwind four or five ends to the head bandage, each several feet long, but they flapped and fluttered so much he had to wrap them around his neck to keep the cloth out of his eyes.

When he reached the dock lot he could see that he'd been right about Alice Carmody; she hadn't waited. What was fucking more, he realized, climbing out of the Jeep, the bitch had taken his boat. And what she'd left him had to be the damned leaky relic the *Columbine*. You couldn't mistake the old bucket, bobbing there by herself just past the gas pumps. A wonder it still floated.

He set off in a loping run. As he approached along the empty docks he saw the ancient inboard was already idling out a gurgle of fuel fumes and the cabin windows were steamed up. Greer had hung around. Damned white of him, Ike thought wryly. As he ran he was suddenly aware that he had an audience. All the windows of the big cannery were filled with eyes. He could imagine the spectacle he must be presenting. All those fishkids up there working or hanging out waiting for an opening, hoping for their crack at those big bucks, that big break on a boat. Fat chance. Most of them lived out at the campsite the city had provided on a damp bayside lot that was supposed to have been the site of a multi-mil tire recycling plant. The recycling entrepreneur had barged in load after load of tires from every waste management center between Seattle and Anchorage. By the time the Kuinak city council learned that the entrepreneur had no multi-mil backers he had barged away into the blue, pockets bulging with disposal fees, five bucks minimum per tire, as much as twenty-five for the big ones. The waste management centers had believed in the recycling plant, too. Nobody had imagined the indigent youths would survive out among the mosquitoes and the rats, let alone prosper. But no-one had counted on the fishkids' talent for waiting, for watching and waiting. Well, Ike thought, this impromptu performance in streaming bandages and butterfly Band-Aids is a sight worth waiting for. Look! That's Isaak Sallas, the original Bakatcha Bandit. Golly, he doesn't look too good. Must be that the hero business ain't so hot these days . . .

3
Silver Fox Wing-Sail
a Pet Blizzard GHH-ZZ

Emil Greer came ducking up out of the tiny cabin just as Ike stepped on board. At the grisly sight Greer went off like a bundle of black springs—limbs, fingers, even the coiled ropes of his Rasta hair, springing out stiff in all directions. A vise grip was left spinning in midair like a propeller without a motor. 'Aaaai!' Greer yelled, snapping into a martial arts stance. Greer had a mottled complexion and when he was alarmed, as he frequently was, his face flashed hue-to-hue like a spooked cuttlefish. The vise grip began to fall, but Greer's left hand darted out like a snake and caught the spinning tool before it hit the deck. Though he was often accused of being fearful to the point of laziness, nobody ever said he wasn't fast.

'Sacre fucking bleu, man,' shaking the retrieved tool at the apparition, 'don't *ever* be sneaking up on me like that! I thought I was in *The Mummy's Curse*. You are lucky I didn't tae kwon *do* you.'

Ike popped his duffel from his shoulder with a grunt. 'Like you tae kwon did Lulu Loop's husband this morning?'

'This morning?' Greer held his stance. His variegated complexion was still fluttering. 'Well, hey, I retreated because I'm too dangerous a dude, man,' he explained, still watching his partner warily. 'I was afraid I might commit something lethal I get involved with that big loaf of white bread. When he manifested I took the path of least resistance.'

'I see.' Ike opened the duffel and traded his Cowichan

32

vest for an orange life jacket. He began strapping the jacket on. 'Very Buddhist of you.'

'I'm glad you appreciate it.' Now that Greer was coming out of his martial arts mode his natural curiosity was piqued. He stepped over to Ike to more closely study the bandaged visage.

'Jesus Mary and Mohammed, Pardner, what were *you* doing up there all this time? Snorting wildcats?'

Ike zipped the duffel and heaved it into the compartment beneath the dash. Greer watched as his friend peeled a length of paper towel from a roll to rub the salt and grime off the windshield on top of the cabin. When it was clear that he wasn't going to get any response to his question, he opened his vise grip and bent back to the mounting nuts. The skin of his face calmed back to what could be called customary, though it was by no means ordinary. He was as dappled as the bottom of a tidepool. Born in the blackest section of the Bimini slums, Greer had been the tenth son of a golden girl of East Asian extraction knocked up by a red-bearded descendant of the Vikings—a machinist's mate on a cheese boat from Göteborg. But the union had not produced a black man, nor a yellow, nor red. Greer was like one of those Easter eggs that is a little cracked and left for last and then put in a cup of all the leftover dyes slopped together. They always come out brownish and splotchy with shifting shades of purple and mauve and terra cotta and cinnamon. People would have never guessed him for an islander at all if he hadn't affected some broad hints: he plaited his hair into bouncy dreadlocks; he salted his talk with occasional French phrases, though he'd never heard the language except in movies; and when asked about his Erik-the-Red beard he would explain, 'I be a Viking from Bimini, by yumpin' yiminy!'

The engine began to shudder less under Greer's tightening. From the corner of his eye he could see his friend had finished toweling the windscreen and was scowling out the glass at the empty stretch of dock. Greer continued to work the nuts.

'So,' Ike said at last, 'Admiral Alice couldn't wait around a couple minutes . . .'

Greer laughed. 'Whoa, man, how about a couple *hours*. She held her mud pretty good, too, for Alice Carmody. Finally she says she gots to go, that she was going to have to pull up early today anyway and she wanted to see if at least *one* of us couldn't haul in enough to pay for gas. Then she storms off.'

'Did she have to storm off in my boat? If she has to pull up early why couldn't she have done it just as well in this old tub and left me *my* boat?'

'I couldn't get this old tub running is why.' Greer revved up the throttle at the linkage, watching the rusty mounts. He had to shout over the roar. 'First, there wasn't any spark. I fix that, but she keep cutting out. Dead mice in de gas tank; took most de hour to blow dem clear. Then when she do get going, sound like she going to shake right off dem cheesy mounts. Whoa! Alice tells me, say *she*'ll take the *Sue-Z* and for me to meet her out at the grounds when I get de engine running right. Wasn't nothin' *personal* to it, mon . . .'

Greer was aware of some very dangerous crosscurrents that had been churning between his friend and the boss's wife during Carmody's absence. He hoped he could keep enough oil on those troubled waters to last until the old man got back. He spied a furry lump stuck to the gunwales and picked it up with the vise grips, glad for something to change the subject.

'Ain't it fascinating? The mice have become gas-heads, mon. I read in *New Light* that it's happening at dockside pumps all along the coast; if the pump hoses aren't screened, mice crawl up in them by de mother *wads*.' He opened the grips and dropped the drowned rodent over the side. 'Another symptom of the *Ee*-fect, is what *New Light* claims. Even the animals be committing suicide.'

'Sounds like *New Light* is still beaming out the same old bull.'

'Hey, all those beached greys in San Diego? The deer laying down on highways in Idaho and Utah? *Woo*.'

'Whales have always beached. The deer were crossing the highways looking for food . . .'

'Because the Effect starved them down out of the mountains,' Greer kept on. 'It *depresses* 'em.' Greer snatched up another wet lump of fur in the grips and held it. 'This little mice? He say, "Hey, mon, I feel de heavy pressure drop coming. I depressed, I t'ink I go drink some dat Chevron *Supreme*."'

New Light was a monthly Greer subscribed to, dedicated to networking the 'Mature Souls of Light.' The way it accomplished this chore was by publishing photos of subscribers, always in their early forties and their briefest briefs. Greer sent in beefcake photos of himself in various poses for nearly a year before it occurred to him that he had never seen any pictures of black males in the magazine. Ike kidded him that the reason must be that the publishers couldn't believe that men of the darker persuasions could ever truly be Souls of Light. Greer maintained that it was because the publisher probably thought he looked too young, that they couldn't believe a dude of color ever *reached* the ripe old age of forty years anymore.

Greer tossed the second mouse overboard and revved the engine a couple more times. 'Well, it probably won't shake off until we're a few miles out. Now, let me check the bilge pump, den I get de *ge*nerator—'

'We're casting off in exactly five minutes,' Ike said.

'Five minutes? This thing ain't been in the water for *years*. The wood needs to soak. The radio needs to dry out—'

'We'll be fine.'

'Isaak, the bilge needs bilged, for Christ's sake!'

'Five minutes and sailing, Pardner.'

'All right, all right, five minutes and sailing. Who can argue with a face out of de hunnerd-year-old horror movie?' Greer went scurrying back down the hatch.

Ike leaned back against the wheelhouse and let him scurry. Greer was stalling, it was obvious. The old Mercury was bolted down as securely as it was ever likely to be, and running smooth—probably had been running smooth for an hour, for all that talk about mechanical travails. These days, anybody but a bad mechanic could diagnose a jammed line and have the dead mice dug out and blown clear in a matter of minutes. And everybody knew Greer was a good mechanic. Not much of a sailor, though. For all of Greer's island boyhood and years of maritime service, he was still notoriously afraid of the ocean. He made no bones about it. Ike had heard him describe his misgivings about the sea often and at length. Greer could fret about every watery danger anyone had ever heard about, from the bizarre to the traditional, the mystical to the modern. The Great Maelstrom and the Bermuda Triangle were two of Greer's favorite subjects. Tall tales or hard facts, if it was something bad to do with the sea, Greer fretted about it, the weirder the better. He fretted about the old *corpo santo* or St Elmo's Fire, and he fretted about those new oddities called Tinkerbells that had been reported by some Arctic crabbers. *New Light* proclaimed these must be manifestations of insulted Undines, these Tinkerbell things—vengeful elementals rising up against seafarers for the way they had misused the Mother Sea. Who wouldn't fret?

Most of all, Ike knew, Greer worried about going out alone and tripping overboard. Greer had a slightly maimed left foot, the three inner toes missing. The three toes had been bitten off by a moray eel, Greer claimed, during a salvage dive off St Croix. Ike knew different. It was true the toes had been bitten off, but by no eel. Greer's second wife had locked him outside after an argument in their honeymoon motel in Reno, and a sudden chill had frostbitten the toes before he could persuade her to let him back in. This version came from the ex-wife herself, but Ike never brought it up and he never contradicted the eel story. The amputation of the three digits left Ike's partner with a slight limp. Greer claimed it wasn't a limp so much as a dance step. 'Gives me synco-passion, like Legba, the God of Rhythm. Very erotic to the ladies.'

Indeed, Greer was a spectacular bar dancer and frequent

winner in the native kick games. He was also a surefooted dockhand when he actually set to a task; he could shinny up a mast or out along a fouled trawler pole with a nimble confidence that assured him employment in any sailing port on any sea. Nor did bay work bother him. But as soon as the vessel cleared the bar that confidence sank like an anchor and that erotic asset became a liability, especially out alone in a bucket like this. That was the real reason Greer had waited, Ike knew.

Ike gave the bowline a quick snap, flipping the loop off the mooring post without his having to disembark. Carmody taught him the move; in the elbow, not the wrist. Coiling the wet rope, he called down to Greer. 'Come up and cast off stern. If we don't log a couple hours out there Admiral Alice will flog us for days with that scowl of hers.'

It took Greer three snaps to free his line. The boat swung stern-first out into the foamy-flecked current. Ike was at the wheel but he let it swing on its own without going into gear, watching the fragile old hull clear the pilings. Greer stuffed his rope behind a fishbox, his lips pursed in disapproval.

'You ought to lighten up on Alice, Isaak. She's been real cool about this spree of Carmody's. Slice her a little slack.'

Ike didn't answer, watching the slow swing of the stern. Carmody had flown to Seattle to size up a sixty-eight-foot steelume all-purpose he'd read about in *Alaskan Fisherman*. He said he'd be back before the Monday opening, just wanted to have a firsthand gander at some high-rent state-of-the-art. But he'd phoned the next evening to tell them he'd bought the goddamn thing and would be cruising her back up the Inland Passage—so fly the two Culligan boys down to help crew. Weather permitting, he'd still be home for opening day.

That had been almost three Mondays ago and good weather the whole time. Phone messages from ports of call on the meandering passage made it clear the old fisherman was indeed on a spree, taking time to show off his new high-tech fishing machine to every acquaintance and crony he could remember along the way. He was missing some of the season's most important runs, but no-one begrudged him his fling; Michael Carmody had been hard at it in Kuinak for decades, in all weathers on all waters, going out with purse seines and long lines and gillnets and crab pots after anything legal and edible, building up an operation that boasted a yearly harvest as big as some of the Deap co-ops. He deserved a vacation.

It had been no problem finding replacements for the Culligan boys. Some of the fishkids out in Tire City were still hanging on to the old dream of earning enough to pay their way home and have cash to spare; they still came pounding the docks instead of lying around in the truck-tire casings, sniffing glue and cutting patterns out of inner tubes.

When ten days had passed and Carmody wasn't back for the summer opening, Alice turned the smoking and canning operations over to Greer and the fishkid replacements and took over the wheel of her husband's gillnetter, the *Houligan*. The way the UN count was going, this could be the last salmon session of the season and she wanted to be sure they filled Carmody's quota. Ike was told he could get by on the *Sue-Z* without Greer's company if she could manage the *Houligan* without Carmody's.

Ike hadn't minded working the *Sue-Z* single. He preferred it, in fact. But something about the way she commanded him to do it had irritated him. All that first day it had irritated him—the way she kept her boat so close out on the grounds; the way she was always putting out her net adjacent to his, as though to keep him in sight. Maybe she hoped to bust him dealing off some of his catch to the Japanese jointers, like a lot of second partners did. Whatever it was, her dark, sharp presence had become more and more of a thorn in his butt these last few weeks, yet he had continued to lay his net and pick his haul without complaint. Then, the day before yesterday, the transmission of the *Houligan*

38

had blown up, just like Carmody had warned it was due to blow. One of the Wongs had towed Alice in and she swung wide and scraped the jetty. A nice long leaking rip opened in along the port. She was lucky they weren't far from the docks. One look at the mess and they lashed down the *Houligan* for the season.

Ike had assumed that was that—she'd go back to the cannery and let him fish. He felt confident he could fill both his and Carmody's share of the quota before Friday's closure, with just the *Sue-Z.* He told Alice as much. She had just grunted. Then the stubborn Deap bitch had dragged *this* leaky old tub down off the ways and spent all night caulking the cracks! Late yesterday Greer got the engine running enough to be able to coax the craft around to the docks. Isaak had secretly hoped the stubborn squaw *would* get the old *Columbine* running good enough to take it out to the fishery; a good strong wave might rid everybody of two nuisances. But how had things worked out? Admiral Alice the Angry Aleut was out in the sturdy, reliable *Sue-Z* and Ike Sallas was the one in the leaky tub.

When he was sure the current had swung them safely clear he shoved it into gear and gave it some gas. The screw churned and he spun the wheel seaward. As usual, the fresh breeze pulled his lips into a grin and he felt better. Greer was right: cut her a little slack. Of course, Greer said that about all women.

They had to battle a tide all the way to the bar, the engine shrieking with every bounce. Greer unpacked the survival suit he always wore at sea and began struggling into it in silence. Sallas stood at the wheel. When they cleared the bar the water settled into long southerly swells coming abeam and Ike eased back to half power. No other boats were in sight. The wind off the open sea was cold and he put his Cowichan sweater back on over the life jacket, zipping the big rolled collar up over his chin. The wool stank and the zipper scratched, but without a windbreak your chin was like the prow of an icebreaker. This was why so many fishermen had beards. Unless you had some reason for shaving, it was better to grow your own muffler. Ike was in the beardless minority at the fishery.

As soon as they were past the chop off Hopeless Rock he wheeled hard starboard and headed due north. To his left he could see the dim horizon that was open sea; in the other direction to his right the Pyrites rose like a jagged wall of castle battlements.

At last he thought he could make out the distant line of bobbing boats through the mist ahead. He set the wheel against his hip and pulled his miniature binoculars out of his sweater pocket. Yep, there they were, ghettoed up at the narrows. Everybody was working that spot where the Wong brothers had got that big bite last week. Lined up like a bunch of kids at a piñata. At the sight Ike's good feeling began to ebb. It was already hours after the opening and he didn't enjoy the prospect of having to go putt-putting all the way past everybody to the end of that line, like the kid late for the fiesta.

Bosley's big tender was anchored at the far edge of the boundary; all the rigs that weren't setting web or hauling in were queued up behind. As soon as an opening showed the first in line roared away into the prescribed area. All this wide sea, yet bunched together like that. Christ.

Ike swept the glasses for the *Sue-Z*'s blue cabin. He didn't see her among any of the working boats. He scanned back up the line and finally saw her, in the last spot, like a tiny blue bead at the end of a string. Double-loaded too, by the depth of her. Just like Alice Carmody to walk ass-deep in fish before making a pit stop. Well, that settles that, Ike decided. He was damned if he'd sit there at her rear sucking exhaust out of his own boat. He pulled the throttle back to one-third and swung the wheel one-eighty around. Greer's face poked out of the cabin.

'The hell happ'ning, Isaak?' Greer was holding two steaming mugs. 'Be a little more careful, dis de last pot of scoot in town. Be a pity it spill before we get a bit of *chat* about you and that Loop lady . . .'

'I'm in no mood to socialize,' Ike told him. 'I'm going to try for Duck Gutter.'

Greer emptied one of the mugs with a gulp and started on the other; the best way to carry precious liquids on a rough deck was to swallow them. As his tongue cooled he gave Ike a long, hooded look, and when he spoke his accent was much diminished.

'So. It's try for the damned Duck. Seems extreme but go ahead and try. I doubt you'll even find the nasty little sewer.'

'I'll find it all right,' Ike said. 'Though with the tide ripping like this it might be a little tricky getting in.'

'Not to mention out,' Greer mumbled to himself.

The Duck Gutter was a tiny, off-again-on-again stream that wriggled out of the mountains just north of Kuinak Bay, waddling its way across the sandy flats down to the sea by whatever route the ever-shifting delta happened to provide. Sometimes it came flushing out through the banks in one place, sometimes another. Some days, if the tides had leveed the shore high and wide enough, it didn't come out at all; instead it would build a little lake inland and wait until the levee burst or the channel shifted. But if you could find the Duck's mouth and make it through you could usually find fish.

Greer handed up the last mug so he could zip his survival suit. After the crabber he was working on heeled over out of Bristol Bay, Greer had commenced wearing a survival suit on all decks in all weathers—and no more crabbers. Since then the only crabs he'd caught had been while sailing the various waters of Womandom. Ike finished the tea and handed back the mug. He was feeling buoyant again, now that he'd kissed off the other boats. He grinned at his friend.

'So, the great lover Emil Greer got flushed out of his lair last night . . . by the traditional irate husband.'

'Flushed out? Hardly. The Great Greer does not flush until he is *finis*, no matter how traditional and irate. It is a code, it is a—'

Ike stopped the chatter with a raised hand, then pointed

toward a swirl of dark water ahead. Greer's face fell.

'Ahh, shit, there it is. And marked by the wreck of some fool's *previous* folly, I hope you'll note.'

The rusted ribs of one of the casualties of the '94 tsunami showed through the surf-line mist. Across the channel from the derelict was a big spruce snag driven up by the spring's storms. Greer shook his head.

'Too tight, old chum. Shouldn't advise trying to get anything bigger than a canoe through there.'

Greer knew the advice was wasted; this was to be the punishment for the van. The engine roared and the bow sprang forward. Greer zipped up the neoprene hood and took a good hold on the gunwales.

Ike had learned to work the Duck from Carmody years before, when he was still ten-percenting with the old man in this very inboard. One thing about some of these old woodies, they can run real shallow. The main thing was you couldn't be halfway about it. You had to make your guess and go full at it. Any little crosswave could toss you up on one side or the other if you weren't making some pretty respectable way when you went through. He pushed her wide open.

When they went through, the ribs of the wreck were looming a scant meter off their port side and the limbs of the snag scratching overboard. Ten meters in, the gutter jogged ninety degrees to port, then back, then spread out over a miniature bar. They heard the old Mercury engine groan as the prop found mud, but Ike jerked it into neutral. Their momentum carried them on over the bar and into a bay that had been completely undiscernible from the outside, big and flat as a football field.

'Thus the mighty helmsman finds his own private sea,' Greer congratulated with weak sarcasm. 'Rule Britannia.'

'Piece of cake,' Ike answered with a reckless grin. He realized he had been hearing the trumpets again, but the motor noise had kept them from his thoughts. Then he saw the chromium roll of a powerful back in the water, then two more. He feathered the gear into reverse and let their wake slosh past as they slowed. 'Reel 'er out, matey.

42

Let's see what our private sea has to offer.'

Greer was reluctant and clumsy in the ballooning folds of his neoprene suit. He opened the fishbox and exchanged the mugs for work gloves. With a sigh he stepped to the net drum at the boat's rear and began hooking up the leader float.

There was no PTO in the drum of the old *Columbine*. That was why Greer and Alice had been planning to double in her—one to tend the heavy nets off the aluminum reel, the other to tend the helm. On the haul-in, then, one had to crank the drum manually and the other pick the catch. Real old-time. When Carmody got the *Lady Red*, Ike and Greer had worked the *Columbine* for a couple of seasons, until Carmody fronted Ike for the *Sue-Z*, which could be worked single. Greer then went happily ashore to help around the cannery and the *Columbine* went under a tarp behind Carmody's garage, with the rest of the junk that Carmody referred to as backup. The *Columbine* hadn't been called back to duty in years, not even when the *Lady Red* went down.

When Greer had the leader floats out Ike gunned it. Greer still had to manually crank out fifty meters or more before the little engine could get power enough to let the net drag on out on its own. Ike eased back and made a gentle arc port. When all the net was laid out and the last floats over, he disengaged and circled back to the first bobbing orange ball. He could tell by the roll of backs on the water there was no need to wait. He backwatered up to the float and Greer hooked it. Ike left the motor idling in reverse and went back to help crank. The web came in heavy, shuddering with life. The first salmon to appear was a prime king, as long as a man's leg, worth four or five hundred dollars on the lox market if you could get it there fresh.

'I guess it's true what they say,' Greer conceded when he saw the prize. 'God looks out for fools and niggers.'

On the first set they hauled in twenty-one reds, three kings and a flounder so big they couldn't crank it up. 'Fucking freak,' Greer cursed as they struggled with the big fish. Greer disliked flounder beyond all the other distasteful denizens of the deep. It was that migrating eye. He finally drew his knife and sliced the strands of monofilament binding it. It whacked back into the water upside-down, broad belly rolling white.

'That was a two-hundred-dollar web you just cut,' Ike said.

'Don't even think about it,' Greer told Ike. 'I'll patch it tonight. We could buy another one with the money we saved not wasting time picking that nasty mother.'

The next haul was even bigger, four more kings and so many reds they quit keeping count. The third was bigger yet. They worked steadily, without talking, the way Ike liked it. The radio woke up and began crackling the usual fisherman gab. The two men paid little heed to the reports. Fishermen never honestly broadcast great luck for fear of attracting competition; nor great lack, either. They tried to conceal truth from all but their quota partners, broadcasting in private codes that were both secret and transparent. The Wong brothers, for instance, kept telling each other that their take was 'spotty,' which most eavesdroppers knew was a double switchback; 'spotty' was too obvious a signal for 'good,' so everybody knew it really did mean 'spotty.'

A few times they heard Alice Carmody asking if any-body had seen sign of the *Columbine.* 'Negative,' came the assorted replies. Greer attempted to answer but the rusty mike transmitted nothing but painful buzzes. Ike told him to let her sweat. 'She'll see us when we unload at the tender. Her damn eyes are going to fall out.'

By mid-afternoon they were too full to chance another set. The radio had quit altogether. The tide had turned and was rising again. Greer suggested they drop the hook and let the tide come on up before they tried the little bar. But Ike grinned and gunned the boat around.

'A fucking hot-dog,' Greer accused him. 'You just want to make a grand show of our load.'

'Fucking A,' Ike shouted back, shoving the throttle. He could see the coffee-colored V rushing in strong past the bones of the derelict. It wasn't quite as deep as when they had entered and he eased back a moment in debate. He knew Greer was right. Still, it *would* make a grand show. All these kings. The bastards must have been landlocked in there since early spring, waiting for Duck Creek to rise. Kings this big were front-runners, usually, long gone before the opening. He gunned the throttle. 'Hang on!' he shouted over his shoulder. 'We'll make it.'

They didn't. The keel scraped hard and the prop mired. Ike tried to pop into reverse, but this time he was too late; the motor gulped and died. He put it in neutral and tried to restart, but the battery hadn't been charged enough since the resurrection. He threw open the housing and went to yanking the pull-rope; the motor would only cough and whir.

Greer's speckled face peeked down at him. 'Spot of trouble?' he asked innocently.

'Come on,' Ike commanded. 'We got a chance if we get it going right away—catch a wave, maybe.'

'Right-o,' Greer said, lifting his brows.

They both tried yanking. The motor coughed and whirred, coughed and whirred, until fuel was spitting out of every coupling and they were both giddy from the fumes.

'I say, Mr Sallas. I think she's flooded.'

'Of course she's flooded!' Ike felt light-headed. All this heavy breathing had made Greer's tea kick in hard. Ike wasn't a steady scooter so it didn't take him much. 'We'll have to pull the plugs and blow it dry.'

'We it is, sir!' Greer began peeling out of the heavy neoprene; no need for a survival suit when you can feel the ground under you. Besides, it hampered a good mechanic.

Greer had to take out the plugs and dry them twice before they were able to coax the engine to life again. By this time the bow had raised in the rushing tide and they were listing to port. Ike took the helm and gave it a careful try, easing the gear forward. Muck and mire churned up aft, but the boat didn't move. He put it in reverse and gave it the gas. It strained a few yards backward, then the prop pin sheared with a sharp ping and they were still. Ike cut the motor and the trumpet blew a dirty sarcastic told-you-so: wha-whah-h-h! Not only were they beached fast, they were beached right on the shore of the main channel back from the fishing grounds. They would be in full view of the whole fleet. *Another* show! You're racking 'em up today, aren't you, hot-dog?

It was still. The wind had let up and the surf laid down a gentle chop along the cluttered beach. Ike cursed awhile, without much heat. Finally Greer's brows lifted in their innocent arch. 'It's hard to know what to say to a mummy with fish scales all in his windings. Let's go below decks. I'll bet I can find something capable of soaking the adhesive off those filthy bandages and taking the edge off this wicked scoot both.'

Nobody was exactly sure what scoot was or why it worked, not even the DEA. The final brew always had to be acquired in two parts, from separate dealers. Customarily these were two bags of different tea, black and herbal green. The bags had to steep together for ten or fifteen minutes just below boiling before their ingredients combined to make the active drug. Even then it was difficult to isolate; the brew was masked by so many other alkaloids natural to the real teas—caffeine and spearmint and skullcap and chamomile—that none of the world's leading pharmacologists had been able to duplicate the formula. It made for the ideal seller's market.

The drug was reportedly another miracle product of New Germany. There had been a lot of wonderful new over-the-counter compounds designed by the reunited German scientists. It was only natural that they should come up with some wonderful new under-the-counter ones as well. The Third Reich invented speed, remember? Hitler developed a taste for cocaine and feared the trade routes from Peru might be jeopardized should a war, perish the thought, eventuate. He wanted a substitute just in case. Methamphetamine was as close as his chemists could come. Until scoot.

Each half of the formula was reportedly developed in separate and secret laboratories—one in Frankfurt, the other in Berlin. Some of the Kaynak tribesmen from across the Aleutians claimed to have seen one of the laboratories, somewhere in Siberia. Probably the east German branch. The other lab was rumored to be beneath a fireworks factory in Taiwan. Since the genetic termination of all the vegetable psychogens, scoot was hands down the major drug-abuse problem in Alaska. A lot of the young highliners did a lot of scoot during the grueling salmon sessions. Decreasing runs were being fought for by increasingly fierce fishermen. These were the hotshots with the souped-up race-boat motors and side arms over their rain pants. A haul of salmon worth ten grand or so needed a display of protection.

Isaak Sallas and Emil Greer were of an older and less aggressive sort. Ike had all but stopped using the stimulant. Greer might nurse one pot all day like a pot of strong coffee. Only it was better than coffee; you could work hard, then lay back when it suited you and sleep, and wake up rested and refreshed. You just didn't dream. That seemed to be the severest side-effect. And when you turkeyed out the only withdrawal symptoms seemed to be a runny nose and slight nervousness, and the need for a few days' deep sleep. The runny nose could be easily endured, and the nervousness as well could be smoothed off with a little booze.

Below decks, Greer located a bottle of recon Seagram's in one of the tiny cabin's tilted drawers. Ike came up with two cans of Dr Lite for mixer. They drank the warm cola and bourbon while Greer cut free the last few strands of Ike's bandages.

'Foo, man. Dis ain't any concussion. Dis nothing but your run-of-the-mill knot on the head. I thought you was hurt.'

The butterfly Band-Aids came off the same way they had been glued on, with liberal dabbings of alcohol. When he had finished, Greer stepped back and studied the scratched cheeks and neck, sucking through his teeth at the sight. 'Snorting wildcats, was it then? Looks like more than *that* went on. *Tell* yo' man, Emil, eh?'

'First I want to hear what went on in my van *before* I got there.'

'What? Whoa! *She* was the wildcat scratch you to ribbons? Louise Loop?' Greer swirled the drink in his mug and settled into the single chair, glad he'd waited for the story to come out on its own. 'Whoa-*ho*! Lulu ze Loop.'

'No, she was the one who patched me up,' Ike told him, 'and gave me the knot on the head. A real cat scratched me.'

Sipping the whiskey and soft drink, Ike related the events of the morning, from the bottled animal waking him, to the strangled cries in the night, to the strange silver man. Greer loved it, sucking his teeth and nodding his appreciation of the tale.

'Rode to the rescue with bugle blowing. Isaak, you make me wish I'd stuck around to observe this exotic silver man,' Greer wished. 'It would have interested me enormously.'

'Try coming to the front door instead of ducking out the back; you'll encounter a lot of interesting men.'

'I just want to *observe*, Isaak, as a scholar and scientist. I leave the encountering to paladins like you. So,' Greer squirmed on his stool, his excitement growing, 'where do you expect he came from, this sudden spouse of Lulu's?'

Ike shrugged. 'Up out of the ground like a toadstool, for all I know.'

'There was talk at the Underdogs last night that a major movie shoot was coming to Kuinak. Perhaps he's a Hollywood scout. What did Lulu say?'

'Lulu said he was a Jonah jinx.'

'A Jonah jinx? What the hell is a Jonah jinx?'

'A bringer of bum luck, according to Lulu's daddy's religion.'

'Shoo! What*ever* kind of religion could old Omar Loop believe in?'

'The Tenpin Commandments.' Yeah, he was a little

48

high, all right. 'Everything is bad luck except for red bowling balls and black boars.'

'A full-blood albino man, you say? I never had the opportunity to study one of these all-whites.'

'There was one in the Sheriff's Honor Camp,' Ike recalled. 'A scrawny little dealer punk who wore prescription shades with opalescent lenses to filter the light. Drove the guards nuts they couldn't confiscate them.'

Greer was fascinated. 'Did he bring bad luck?'

'No, just a lot of nuisance and noise—the way big-talking punks will. He saw himself as the camp joker—whoopie cushions and squirting rings and like that. Once he sprayed super-glue on the teeth of the camp dog because the dog had nipped him. For a runt in jail, not too wise a move. He could have got himself snuffed over that but for some of the big Bloods took to watching over him. They called him St Nick.'

'He looked like Santa?'

'He was always signifying, promising gifts. But about a week before my stretch was up I noticed the Bloods started calling in the markers.'

'Calling in the markers?' Greer loved to get Ike reminiscing about his jail time. 'What awfulness did this entail?'

Ike sipped his drink and looked out the sweaty window. 'The kid had a camp job, latrine duty. I was on the road crew. One afternoon they brought me in early because my lawyers were coming up—to counsel me about divorce proceedings. The rig dropped me off at camp and I couldn't find a soul. Dorms, dayrooms, mess hall, everyplace—completely deserted. Finally I heard a lot of laughing down by the iron pile. I walked down and there was a whole gang of dudes lounging around the weight-lifting apparatus, guards and trustees and everybody. In a kind of line.'

'Eek,' Greer said.

'Exactly. Pretty soon I saw the punk come draggling out of the shower with his legs all bloody.'

'What did you do?'

49

'There wasn't anything *to* do. It had been done.'

'Did you tell somebody?'

'Tell who? All the camp brass were already in on it. I didn't figure the poor guy needed me advertising it to the noncoms too.'

'What finally came of him?'

'He was still there when I transferred to Halfway. I heard he finally mouthed off once too often and got pillow-snuffed.'

'Far out. Maybe that guy last night is the spirit of the same poor freak, back from the dead.'

Ike shook his head. 'If so, it was a spirit about three times the size of the original. No, last night's freak was just some pissed-off husband with a pigmentation problem and hostile in-laws.'

'You never know,' Greer said. 'Spirits can be pretty tricky.'

The boat teeter-tottered gently and the butane burner hissed; the two men sipped their drinks and speculated about Louise Loop's strange and sudden husband. Ike was feeling fine. He didn't even mind being marooned out here like a sore thumb. This was fishing the way he liked it, looking for new waters, taking some chances. So they were going to have to be pulled free and towed in like fools? Those hot-dogs would know who had balls to at least still *try* the Duck. And when they got a look at these kings back dockside . . . well, it was worth looking a little foolish.

His sense of equanimity was not even shattered by the sight of the *Sue-Z* churning past still hours before closing. It slowed enough for the black lump of Alice at the wheel to study them through binoculars. Ike waved her on.

'She would have sunk us both,' he told Greer. 'We'll wait for one of the Wongs.'

'Suits me,' Greer said. He got up to try the radio again. 'I would like to know where she's going in such a hurry. Maybe Carmody's back.'

'Let us pray,' Ike said.

They stayed in the cabin and drank and dozed until nine when the closure whistle blew. Then they went out on deck, watching the boats streaming wearily for port. There weren't so many; a lot of the others must have pulled up early as well. When Norman Wong hove into sight they waved for a line. He cast a weight to them with a spinning rod, then reeled in their attached bowline. His big diesel had them off the bottom in minutes. They wallowed behind him, pitching and rocking in his wake.

Wong dropped them alongside Bosley's old tender so they could unload. Bach was booming from the tender's speakers. Bosley always played Bach. Or the Beatles. While he figured their take and counted out the cash Greer went forward to gab with Bosley's daughters. He wanted them to admire the size of his *king*. They were keeping this one, he told the girls, for brag. They helped him gut and gill the fish and he handed it back down to Ike on the *Sue-Z*. Bosley let their line out so he could tow them the rest of the way.

When they rounded the headlands and swung toward the bar, they were both astonished. Towering high above the masts and spars of the other boats was what first appeared to be an enormous dorsal fin, blue-green and silver-white, gleaming a good hundred feet high in the setting sunlight. It looked like the fin of a giant killer whale. Greer grabbed the binoculars from Ike's pocket and leaned into them.

'Sweet Jesus in drag, Isaak; it's the *Silver Fox*!'

The name was familiar, but all Ike could do was shrug.

'The *Silver Fox*, the hottest yacht afloat! A wing-sail. Man, don't you know what am *zam*?'

Ike told him he hadn't known what was zam since leaving California years ago.

'It's Gerhardt Steubins' world-famous floating studio is all.' Greer was dancing with excitement. 'Gerhardt *Steubins*!'

'The movie director?'

'The world-*famous* movie director. Those rumors are

51

true; we *are* going to have a major shoot here. Whoa! Forget these fish.' Greer kicked the gutted king across the deck. 'Full ahead, Bosley. Stardom awaits!'

Ike took the glasses back from Greer. Through the buck and spray he could make out the chromium gleam of a three-tiered flying bridge beneath the big wing-sail. 'Must have come as a big letdown to poor Alice, rushing in to see her old man's new rig.'

But he was wrong again. It had been getting worse all day. As they chugged toward the repair slips he saw Alice Carmody on the dock, and she was grinning from ear to ear. She was standing alongside the yacht's gangway with the rest of the crowd, her head hatless and her dingy gob of hair washed bright and brushed down her back in a luminous coil. He zoomed the lenses in, amazed. She was wearing a native blanket dress replete with mussel-shell buttons and puffin-beak fringes plus brace-lets and beads and baubles—*with dark hose and high-heeled dress shoes!* More amazing still, she was drinking. No-one had seen Alice Carmody drink in years.

'That's Dom Pérignon!' Greer exclaimed. 'Come on, Bosley! Give it some gas.'

As they coasted past, Alice caught sight of them and waved. 'Hey you, Sallas! Greer! Where you boys been, duck hunting?'

This got a big horse-laugh from the crowd.

'Tie that old tub up or sink it!' she yelled again. 'Haul your butts on up here and socialize.'

Greer arched his eyebrows at Isaak. 'First it is a nasty message in a mayonnaise bottle, then it is Lulu Loop with a surprise spouse, now it is Alice Carmody high-rolling with the Hollywoodies. *Très* interesting, ees eet not, how the simple surface can conceal such mysteries?'

'*Très* indeed,' Ike admitted.

They secured the *Columbine* under the deserted mech-anic's shed and headed back up the dock on foot. Alice met them, her face glowing with the champagne and the last rosy rays of the ten o'clock sun. She handed Greer the bottle, then spun grandly around in the clicking, tinkling dress. 'How about this getup, Sallas? Is this classic ethnic or what?'

'Like an Edward Curtis portrait,' he answered.

Alice started to frown at Ike's response, then laughed it off. 'Come on, you bozos,' hooking both men by the elbow, 'somebody here I want you to meet.'

She escorted them toward the little crowd on the dock—a couple of the Wong brothers, the Bosleys, various gillnetters and a half-dozen or so assorted fishkids. They were all drinking Labatts from twelve-gauge popcans, listening and nodding to a man with his back to them—tall, wide-shouldered, his head hooded by a fur parka. Ike reasoned it had to be the famous director, by the way he was holding court. Alice walked right up and slapped him in the middle of his back.

'Mr Sallas? Monsieur Greer? My son, Nicholas Levertov.'

The man turned and tossed back the hood so it fell around his neck like the collar of a clown's oversized costume. But this clown's fright wig wasn't kinky red, it was straight white; it swirled and buffeted about his face like a pet blizzard.

'Don't call me Nicholas, either,' the man's white hand reaching to Ike's. 'Call me St Nick.'

Ghh-zzz! Ike jerked back, crying out. The purple lips spread in a grin as the white hand opened to reveal a joke buzzer. Everybody laughed—Greer, Alice, the fishkids, everybody. The crows even took it up, circling and squawking. Ike joined in. But beneath the laughter those questions reverberated dismally in his tired mind: Why here? Why now? Why Kuinak?

4

Damsels in Distress Demons from the Past Yachts from the Future

First you should know why Alaska. Because Alaska is the end, the finale, the Last Ditch of the Pioneer Dream. From Alaska there's no place left to go. There used to be Brazil, but they cut it down to pay their Third World debt to the First and Second, who fed it to McDonald's. Over ten zillion sold.

There was hope for a time that it might be Australia, but that hope proved to be just another Victorian whimsy, riddled with white ants and racism. Africa? Africa never had a chance; the wheel was rigged before it was even invented by riggers of every persuasion. China? The legendary Sleeping Giant woke up in economic chains and smog. Canada? Nutted by resourcers while the hosers watched hockey and drank beer. The moon? Mars? The Fractal Farm? No game, sorry. The planet Earth is the ball we were pitched—it's the ball we have to play.

So it came down to Alaska, the Final Frontier as far as this sick old ballgame goes. Top of the ninth . . .

For one thing, Alaska is a field vast enough to still be relatively unpolluted, for all the oil spills and garbage dumps. It has a land area of five hundred eighty-six thousand square miles, or three hundred seventy-five million acres. Even now, in the twenty-first century, most of this acreage is still utterly untrod by the foot of White Man, or Red or Black or Yellow Man; or any mammal's foot at all for that matter, when you get down to the inch-by-inch. It's empty. Life flourishes essentially along its stretch of shoreline, of which there is more, mile-by-measured-waterfront-mile, than there is along all the other waterfronts circling all the rest of the United States, including the Eastern Seaboard, Hudson Bay, the Gulf of Mexico, and the beach north from San Diego, California, to Vancouver, British Columbia—combined! A stretch still very unsettled, historically and geologically.

The Aleutian Trench is one of the most seismically active areas in the world. It is the haphazard trail of cracks and crumbs left in the wake of the breakup of the Supercontinents twenty million years ago. It still can't seem to rest easy. The sea creates weight, then pressure, then the racked beds of graywacke and sedimentary shale heave up and crack open—like old books freshly discovered. Here are the deepest stacks of the library (see appendix for details). In these stacks are the earliest known issues of *Time* and *Life* and *True Stories* and *National Geographic*. Such stories. Some long and slow, like that million-year-long saga of the Supercontinents' heart-breaking breakup; some of them quick cryptic puzzlers, like why should the molecules in a certain stratum of clamshell fossils (circa twelve thousand five hundred years ago), after eons of pointing their little negative molecular tails one direction, north, all of a sudden in the very next layer above, turn and point negative south? Solid facts in these stacks, maybe, but slippery. And the higher up the stacks you go, the more slippery it gets, especially when you get into the *historians'* histories. Printed histories have a disturbing habit of leaning along the party line of the parties that own the printing press. In fact, the best way to get an angle on the history of the Kuinak area is to give up on the facts and look for the legend.

Picture in your mind that elusive Holy Grail of the New World, that Pass to Xanadu, that Rainbow Bridge to Asgard's Pot of Gold: the famous Northwest Passage! This whimsical waterway of the eighteenth-century imagination was supposed to traverse all the way across the mysterious top of the uncharted American continent, Atlantic to Pacific. On the Atlantic end, all the experts agreed, the passage had to begin in that swampy filigree of trickling possibilities at the west end of the huge Hudson Bay. It then would flow through the far north wilderness, past the savages, somehow *over* the nuisance of the Rocky Mountains, to finally emerge somewhere, was every expert's guess, between the Golden Gate and the Arctic.

That famous and wonderful and impossible whimsy—the Northwest Passage. O, how they wished it—to sail *across* the continent, from one ocean to the other, without that soul-killing swing around the Godforsaken Devil's Horn of South America! This was a dream dreamed so devoutly, for so long, that it became an obsession. For more than a century it taunted mariners and merchants alike—by the saints it *had* to be there, this river flowing up and over the Great Divide—and they broke their hearts hunting for it . . . Rogers and his ragged Rangers in the Quebec marshlands—lost, crazy, finally actually eating each other in order to continue the quest . . . Captain Cook . . . Vancouver . . . countless lathered Spaniards, sailing up and down the West Coast checking every river and bay they could locate in the misty drizzles . . . seeking the Northwest Passage.

The wide, flowing mouth of the Kuinak Bay must have raised many a mariner's hopes.

Vitus Bering was the first man to set spyglass to this bay, tucked away like an elephant's mouth up under the curving trunk of the Aleutians—July 20, 1741—but he sailed on when his men rowed back with reports of no ermine sign. Always the explorer, Bering would have relished a sail inside the little bay—just a peek—but he was working for the Russians, and Russian royalty made it clear they were interested in furs, not fantastic waterways.

Forty years later Captain Cook dropped anchor off the sheer jut of rock where the Lighthouse Museum is today. Unable to climb the rock for a higher view, his crew turned the dinghy shoreward and rowed in to interrogate the Kuinak natives.

The beach reeked of fish in various stages of preservation or decomposition, it was hard to say which.

The steep shelf of sand was cluttered with boulders and bones, empty shells and naked kids. Flies and mosquitoes and, gradually, human beings swarmed forward to greet the hairy men from the marvelous boat. The expedition's linguist, a lay priest named Perkins, known shipboard as the Jabbering Jesuit, jabbered. He kept jabbering and making sign language with one hand and slapping at insects with the other, until the main question was communicated.

No, none of the tribe had any idea where the river flowed from, but they didn't think it was from Another Great Water Beyond the Sun Coming Up.

A sailor with a glass shimmied to the top of the village's lone totem pole. He called down that he could see easily the headwaters at the far end of the little bay. 'Less than five league inland I makes it . . . river falling into bay from a glacier . . . considerable steep ice, rock cliff to starboard and port. There be na passage here, sir; nor scant elst of importance to *me* eye.'

So Cook rowed back out to the *Discovery* and, as was his custom when there was little of importance, set about the task of naming everything in sight.

The precipice on the northern mouth that his sailors could not scale, he christened Hopeless Rock. The snowy crag leaning out of the clouds became Dover Peak.

The plunging glacial cataract was baptized Prince Richard River, after George III's second son. The bay became naturally Prince Richard Bay, and the settlement—should one ever emerge in the clam shells and the fish bones—was to be called Prince Richard Fort. But alas, that very year poor little Prince Richard took a chill during a ceremony on the foggy steps of Buckingham and died of the ague, and the potential town of Prince Richard slipped back to the less regal but more ancient name: Kuinak.

Cook was followed by a second wave of Spaniards hoping to have their names added to that long flotilla of Spain's sailing immortals, but this truncated little bay beneath the Aleutians was obviously no Straits of Magellan. Nobody else even bothered naming it anew.

Thus the original name survived. The tribe did not. After a particularly long run of cruel winters and fishless summers—topped off with a devastating dose of the Russian clap—the surviving natives began to die or defect in droves, joining clansmen and relatives in other moieties, on other bays.

As years passed and the salmon runs returned, so did some of the old inhabitants. They found out quickly that it was no longer their land. They did not complain. They knew they had somehow betrayed their heritage by leaving it in the first place. Forsaken their birthright. The village still had its old name, but most of the villagers didn't even have that anymore, calling themselves Haidas, or Tsimshians, or Tlingits or Yupics or Aleuts. They would have continued thus but for an unexpected legality: after the Native Land Sales Moratorium came to an end one of the legislative riders declared that by century's-end, all so-called natives must agree to an appellation by which they could be referred to collectively *legally*. The President himself explained the wisdom of this rider at a private luncheon of the DC Bonies.

'They're all so *sensitive*. They go into a thundering funk every time one of our legal staff makes the mistake of addressing them wrong. Inuits, for instance, don't like being called Eskimos. Eskimo means "eater of raw fish." The Inuits want it known they eat stuff besides fish, cook a lot of it, too.'

He had just flown back from a two-day convocation of tribal leaders in Juneau, and was letting his beard grow.

'What's "Inuit" mean, then?' the Georgetown Bone wanted to know.

'"Inuit," like most of the names of tribes, means "The People." The tribal name "Tlingit" means "The Real People," so the Tlingits object to being simply "The People." *None* of them like being called "American Indians." Or "Native Americans" either. Even "Early Peoples" didn't please everybody. They make the point that they in fact aren't the Early People, but the Early People's descendants, the "Current People." Technically, they are correct, but I dinged that real quick. Sounds like a gay choir. After a full day and night of argument they decided on "Descendants of Early Aboriginal Peoples." I know the acronym is a cut-hair pretentious, but at least now, up in Ay Kay, when you see a tall, or short, brown or beige or devils-food-hued person, with eyes from Tibet and a jaw from Samoa and a mouth from sunken Mu, you can get away with calling him a Deap. Or her. Maybe . . .'

And why Kuinak? Because if Alaska is the Last Ditch of the American Dream, then the town of Kuinak represents the Last Gasp in that Ditch. Due to its uniquely protected location, Kuinak has remained remarkably untouched by the ravages of the twenty-first century. The temperatures are still much like always, average thirty-seven to sixty-five degrees in summer, and seven to thirty degrees in winter, extremes varying from a record forty-five below zero in the winter of '89 to a not-uncomfortable ninety-nine on the famous Firecracker Fourth when the mercury reached 119 in DC and all the cherry trees died.

The outlying sea is not generally rough. Although the fetch of open water over which the winds can blow is great, the building waves are so chopped up by spits and reefs that they are tumbled into the bay more like a coleslaw than a surf.

The bar is steady and smooth enough to accommodate container barges and tankers on a regular schedule, but not deep enough for the high-collar cruise ships like the *Island Princess*—besides, whoever could imagine why the line should ever wish to add this grimy little puddle to its Love Boat Ports o' Call?

Across the bar inside, the bay shore circles like a rusty horseshoe—the ash-grey glacial river at the rear, rotted piers and rotted pilings along both sides like bent horseshoe nails.

The town proper stands just inside the mouth on the southern shore. Squats would be more like it—the tallest building being the new three-story casino-hotel built by Searaven, the local Deap Ink Council. The container barges that steam in from Anchorage or Seattle are piled higher than this. Without connecting highways to the interior, the bulk of the town's fungibles are hauled in and out on these floating freight cars—foodstuffs coming in along with TV sets, cars, snowmobiles, prefab double-wides; canned or frozen or filleted fish going out.

The only paved road is the three-mile four-lane stretch from the tiny airport. When this highway reaches the town where the federal funding ends and local levying begins, the four paved lanes become five gritty fingers. The westernmost digit, the thumb, cul-de-sacs abruptly down into the crowded boatyard, as though trying to hitch a ride out on one of the crafts being serviced and fueled.

The index finger points straight into the industrial heart of the community: the docks and canneries and high-heaped barges; the tin-sided freezing plants; the tangled lots where forklifts empty and load the cabless semi trailers that come in and out on the barges; the reeking stacks of web and line and day-glo floats . . . towers of crab traps . . . crates . . . and an unbelievable collection of cast-off hardware commonly referred to as 'crap.'

The middle finger waggles brokenly through the com-mercial district, the downtown, past Herky's Merkentile & Pharmacy, past the Honda dealer where towers of snowmobiles wait like uncrated virgins . . . across Cook Boulevard where Deaps and dunks sleep it off on any or all four corners, any hour of the day . . . past LOOP LANES where Omar waits like a pool shark with his ruby red ball . . . past the Searaven Inn and adjacent bingo casino . . . past the Crabbe Potte and the Sand Bar and the Bear Flag Inn and Cannery Row Cannery (the Bear Flag and Cannery Row Cannery were so named as a tongue-in-cheek tribute to John Steinbeck. None of the patrons were ever literary enough to appreciate the jest. That was the point of it.) . . . crossing then the ring-finger and the rundown radiance of the Russian Orthodox church where the faithful still pray and Father Pribilof's lilac bushes still flourish untended . . . ending finally at Kuinak High School. One whole side of the school gymnasium is a blue, green and red Haida Thunderbird design of ancient origin; prehistoric; yet, in the all-but-empty halls and corridors, stepped-on samples of all the modern mixtures are available on any school day, eight to four-thirty.

The last little finger of this dirty down-hanging hand is barely a road, just ruts and dust in the summer, a toboggan run in the winter. It crooks daintily east, around the steelume tower and tank that holds the town's drinking water, then past the Loops' slaughter- and bunkhouse at the edge of the town's world-class dump. After negotiating the canyons of garbage the road dwindles on up into the fern and salal where it finally ends at a lone trailer house.

The tires are flat, the windows are taped with Vizqueen, the siding and roof painted cherry red. It comes as something of a surprise, this blurt of color. Like a painted nail at the end of a filthy finger. But there is something valiant about the old trailer—noble—as though this particular pile of junk had managed to crawl this much farther from the dump than the rest of the crap before expiring.

Valiant and noble and more than a little lifeless looking.

Yet Isaak Sallas has lived here for the last fourth of his more than forty years, usually alone, contentedly if not exactly happily, and would have lived on much the same way for the next forty if he'd had his choice . . . if such interruptions as deranged cats and damsels in distress and demons from the past and yachts from the future and Alice Carmody would just have left him alone. Especially Alice Carmody.

5

Strip of Worthless Mud
Crossways in Her Craw

Alice Carmody was a Deap. She was known as Alice the
Angry Aleut but she wasn't an Aleut. She was one of
the last true blood Kuinaks. Her grandfather had been the
tribe's shaman for fifty years before siring her mother, and
her mother was just getting a good grip on the practice
when a shambling but handsome Russian émigré oaf
persuaded the poor pagan to forsake her unholy ways and
hook up with a devout Christian. He was devoted to Virgin Mary all day every Sunday and to vodka martinis all
the other days. His name was Alexis Levertov and he had
a history of misfortune that made him surly and thirsty.
Was his drinking a result of his misfortune or the other
way around? Alice's mother must have pondered this
puzzle—she was a woman of some intelligence if perhaps not much wisdom. All she saw for certain was that
the puzzle was indeed handsome, and available, and the
shaman trade had been a trifle slow with only a couple
dozen of the old tribe left. So the last of the Kuinak
shamans abdicated her heathen heritage, forswore her
trances and her dances and her dreams, and traded
her bag of roots and toadstools for a rosary and a cocktail
shaker.

Baby Alice was baptized in that aforementioned
Russian Orthodox church, that rundown jewel set on the
ring-finger of the ramshackle town. When Alice was thirteen her mother died (of mushroom poisoning, the clinic
concluded; was the old woman backsliding on the sly?)
so the dark-eyed teenager took up the old lady's place
alongside the father, in the fishing boat and the church.

She even learned to shake the vodka and vermouth just the way surly Russians like it.

She was elected class president her freshman year at Kuinak High and was the Sophomore Homecoming Princess the following fall. She was a beauty, black eyes crackling with just a touch of Baltic blue—full bosom, wide lips and broad shoulders and hips. But unlike any of her other budding blood relations, Alice Carmody had a wasp-thin waist. 'That won't last,' muttered the female fans when she stepped out of the Camaro convertible in her eye-catching hourglass evening gown at the homecoming parade. 'Not if we can help it,' thought the males, looking hard and breathing heavy.

It didn't. By Christmas vacation the waistline was expanding fast. By spring finals she was able to use the hard bulge under her smock like a little writing desk to prop her clipboard on, scowling like a bakestove as she filled the bluebooks.

She never offered any clue as to which of the heavy breathers might be responsible for the bun baking in her oven, and that scowl stopped anybody from asking. Not even Father Pribilof knew, and he knew just about everything there was to know about his flock. All summer when Alice gave confessions there was never a word about her condition, yet the old priest was the first person she took the babe to. As soon as she could stand she pulled down her dress and carried the child past her passed-out papa to their pickup. She drove the pickup right across the churchyard lawn to the door of the rectory in back. The old priest stepped out, chewing toast and cream cheese and lox, sniffing and blinking in the hard sunshine. He was color-blind and cataract-prone but his nose was sharp. He smiled when he smelled it was dear young Alice, poor young Alice, O brave young Alice; no quick-fix abortion for her! She held out a bundle for him to look at.

'Help me, Father. This is more than I bargained for.'

The priest stopped chewing and leaned close. Even color-blind he could tell the baby was white, white as

63

the cream cheese on his toast—with eyes the color of the
slivers of salmon meat.

They cleaned a tool room and the young mother and
child moved in. At the priest's urging Alice returned
to Kuinak High that fall, thin-waisted as ever and even
fiercer-eyed. It would have been a pity for such a good
student not to go ahead with her education, and there
were plenty of babysitters available for the infant oddity.
Sometimes Alice brought the baby, wheeling the stroller
through the hall crowd between classes, her face daring
and defiant. Sometimes she stayed home in the toolshed,
rocking the quarrelsome child as she browsed through
Father Pribilof's collection of religious art books. She
tried some copy sketches, using the crayons from the
Kiddee Kare room. The results were a troubling amalgam
of styles. Van Eyck's *Adoration of the Magi* looked like a
Kwakiutl box print. Holbein's *Christ on the Cross* looked
like a Bela Coola totem pole. But she had time to work
on these problems; often the baby was away for weeks at
a time with a church social worker, at the eye center in
Anchorage, at the allergy clinic in Victoria. For special
treatment. Young Nicholas Levertov was what they called
an *especially* special child. Alice had been right: she
needed help. This was more than she had bargained for.

She completed both her junior and senior years in
those next three terms and graduated on that truncated
football field, receiving special mention for her grades
and her talent. She had progressed from Kiddee Kare
crayons to latex house paints. She was the one that
painted the Thunderbird on the side of the gymnasium. It
won her a blue ribbon in a nationwide mural contest and
prompted the Alaskan Arts and Humanities to award her
a full scholarship to the college of her choice. Everybody
naturally assumed it would be the University of Anchorage. The church maintained a dorm-and-daycare right on
campus, for hapless young Deap mothers just such as she.
The AAH told her the University of Anchorage would
be perfect. Alice told them to go suck. She'd had her
fill of the squalid mudhole called Kuinak, of defecting

Deaps, of her drunk and clumsy father, of her especially special kid and her hometown sympathy and all the rest of the State of Alaska, thank you. She would go to the San Francisco Art Institute. She would be a California Girl, she haughtily informed her old school chum Myrna Hoogstratten. The kid? The church could keep the kid.

She painted and she partied in the San Francisco whirl. When her scholarship ran out she took work in a big Castro Street gallery. Her boss was one of her previous life-drawing instructors, a gruff old man with a handlebar moustache. Soon she was rooming above the gallery with him, seeking to learn more about the love of art and the art of love. But when her boss tried to bring another man to bed with them—a smooth-skinned young artist from Wyoming who painted manly scenes of cattle-branding and horse-breaking and wore spurs with his ostrich boots, and without—Alice took her clothes, her paintings and all the money from the gallery safe and hailed a taxi for the airport. The paintings she air-freighted back to the church in Kuinak; she flew off in the other direction, to San Diego. She didn't know anyone in San Diego, but she was damned if she was returning north. If she had to pull stakes again it would be to Guadalajara.

She got a job teaching Pacific Northwest Ethnic History to teenagers, most of whom didn't speak anything but South American. She moved into a motel, long-term and low-rent. She began to let her art and her waistline go and took up drinking and cursing. She feared she was finished with painting. She was *certain* she was finished with men. Leave the bastards, the pricks with spurs and the assholes with moustaches and the clumsy surly Russians with their martinis, *to each other*—they deserved it.

She kept to her job and her room. She wouldn't even fly home when the priest wired her that her father had finally fallen overboard for good. It was the lifting of the Land Act Moratorium that eventually necessitated her return to her birthplace. Grubby little mud-hole though it was, it was now real estate ready for the deal.

Back in Kuinak she intended to sell her parcel with as much haste as possible and get the hell out, but there was something about the lawyer the tribe had hired that got crossways in her craw. Maybe it was because he was a Deap Made Good, a Yupic Yuppie with a briefcase of dappled sealskin; maybe it was because he reminded her of the smooth-chopped artist from Wyoming. Whatever, she refused to sell out or throw in with their consortium. She held on to her strip of worthless mud out past the airport and leased her father's acreage into escrow (a mandatory seven years had to pass before it was legally hers, to make sure the sodden old Russian sponge didn't pop up out of the briny again). With the cash she bought a two-fifty-by-two-fifty block corner with a rundown motel and a closed-down smokehouse on it. She was the one who named the enterprise the Bear Flag Inn and Cannery Row Cannery. Taking lit in college can tempt one to do that sort of thing.

After deals were firmed up and contracts signed, most of the other Deap litigants quickly departed, leaving Searaven Enterprises in the care of the Yupic lawyer and the Searaven corporate executives. The litigants went back to what they had been doing before —namely, drinking alone in front of dish soaps in Searaven Retirement Centers around Anchorage and Sitka, peacefully dying. Alice contacted her kid at the church school in Fairbanks, to tell him of her real estate investments, but he didn't seem to have any more affection for Kuinak than she'd had. He told her he had a couple of foster parents already nicely trained, and friends in Fairbanks; maybe he'd come be with her during vacations. Got to scoot. Later.

Alice soon learned that her outspoken distaste for native-owned gambling corporations had not won her any friends among her Deap neighbors. They kept inquiring as to her plans. If she didn't want dealt in why didn't she butt out and go back to—to wherever she'd been? It pissed her off, just like that Yupic shyster. Finally she announced that her plans were to *remain* in her beautiful birthplace, out of respect for her roots. It was really out of orneriness, her neighbors were heard to opine, behind her back. She made it clear she didn't give a wrinkled rat's ass what the opinions were. She was staying.

So Alice stayed on in Kuinak out of blatant spite. She would run her *own* goddamned business, she didn't need any heirs or any ancestors or any cut-of-the-card action. She wouldn't buy one of those super dishes to hole up in front of and get respectably shit-faced in private, either. Any drinking she did she was going to fucking do right out in front of God and everybody, god*damn* it!

That was the period that earned her the name of Alice the Angry Aleut. To old acquaintances like Father Pribilof it was almost as though there were two people. One was still the soft-spoken, eager-eyed student of Creation's Palette; just her simplest rearrangement of a flower, a candle, could change the way the whole church looked. But as soon as the soft-spoken Alice Levertov got drunk—which began to happen very fast, and very frequently—she was transformed into a raging, red-faced harridan with a tongue like a harpoon. Her voice didn't slur with alcohol; it got sharper. It stabbed and stuck, and there was no getting loose from it if you happened to be the target, not until unconsciousness cut her harpoon line. When she awoke she was mild-mannered and contrite.

But the onset of Alice's angry alter ego seemed progressive. Year after year the raging harridan needed less and less alcohol and only the slightest trace of an insult to activate it. The roots of Alice's anger began seeking new soil, branching out underground in all kinds of directions. She could be angry with the government as well as the governed. She was always angry with the whites—her people had been screwed just too goddamn much by the round-eye fishbelly bastards—and she was just as pissed with her people that they had sold out so cheap. She could be furious with the whole human race in general, for the way they had fucked things up so bad, while at the same time contemptuous with any idealistic lint-head naive enough to think things would ever be fixed. A few seven-and-sevens and Alice Levertov could become outraged at anything.

After the first drink it might be the barkeep, or waitress, or *what*ever son-of-a-bitch it was selling the bland recon piss they called bourbon nowadays. After the second she was down on every lamebrain in the establishment that was dumb enough to drink it. After the third Alice might enlarge her rage's range to include the whole shithole town and everything about it—the dirty sea, the scratchy sky, the evil wind . . . the long, dark nasty night itself. The day after, head hanging in a shy scowl, she was once again soft-spoken and halfway social.

But a bar with Alice drinking even socially in it was at best only a dormant battleground, an impending pit, because it could quickly become a bar with that other Alice drinking in it: Alice the Angry Aleut. Such a bar could find itself emptied of all patrons in a matter of minutes. It usually remained empty until the management either closed down or kicked her out.

Closing down was easier. You could always wait fifteen or twenty minutes until she reeled off on her way to her next outrage, then open back up. If you kicked her out you ran the risk of giving her anger focus. She might be right back, a snowclod through your window, shit in your pickup seat. After being ejected from the Sand Bar into a ten-below midnight, she stacked the garbage cans into a precarious scaffolding at the rear of the place so she could climb up on the roof. There she was able to kick off the galvanized stove-pipe and pee down into the oil-drum stove. Within seconds the street was full of customers, eyes weeping like they'd been gassed.

If you called the police number and Lieutenant Bergstrom got around to actually ordering his lazy Wasp cops to haul her off and lock her up for a week, you could expect trouble from some of the other Deaps. Unpopular as she was among them in gossip, many secretly admired her spirit. One December, after she had been eighty-sixed from the Crabbe Potte and sentenced to a week in the D&D tank, some of Alice's secret admirers slyly pried all the nails almost all the way out of the aluminum panels that sided the building. Nobody inside was aware of a thing. The Lobo Ladies was banging out loud salsa swing that evening, and the lead guitar was a Matamoris frostback that played bad bottle-finger electric, so it sounded like nail-pulling anyway. At midnight the tide turned and a little circle blow started spinning in off the sea. It increased in velocity until it peeled the Crabbe Potte Grill and Lounge like an Almond Roca, slinging the wrapping all the way to the water tower. Glass wool and foil insulation draped all over town, like tinsel and angel's hair for the coming Christmas.

When the siding was replaced and the Potte repaired Myrna Crabbe sent old school chum Alice an invitation to the grand re-opening, just like the rest of the town's important movers and shakers. Alice bought a pearl-grey two-piece suit that she hoped would emphasize her serious side and at the same time camouflage the inches she had put on around the waist. This new recon booze might be easier on the liver, but all the additives made it harder on the waistline.

She took a stool at the end of the new bar and ordered a lite draft, serene as the eye of a hurricane. She comported herself with daintiness and decorum all evening, resolved to disappoint the bunch expecting a row. Almost all evening. She even smiled it by when Dan Crabbe asked that joke what was the difference between a lesbian and a beluga whale—'two hundred pounds and a two-piece suit, yee-*haw*!' But when Myrna Crabbe got a little too oiled and evangelical about the sins of the fathers not being visited on the sons but that many a poor kid none-theless was made to pay for his mother's bad *jeans* . . . it was too deep a dig to let slide. With a bloodcurdling whoop Alice snatched an ulu from her shoulder Gucci and was behind the bar before Myrna's pun was under-stood by the general clientele, let alone appreciated. The razor-edged squaw knife was the finest made, ordered from Tribal Tools in Anchorage. It was to have been a peace offering for the occasion and was engraved 'To

69

the Crabbes . . . When Tide Is Out Table Is Set.' Now its chromium crescent flashed viciously in the barlight among the hanging wineglasses. 'Bad jeans, huh?' she foamed. She had come over the bar so fast that beer froth still clung to her upper lip. 'On your knees! On your knees *now*!' The Crabbes knelt like condemned royalty in their quivering crowns. Alice let them quiver a moment, then turned and calmly sliced the push-button spigots off all three drink-makers. She left the hoses whipping about in high-pressure frenzy, spewing booze and water and soda and mixer like decapitated serpents.

After that Myrna talked of having her drowned. A secret collection was even started among the Crabbe family to raise the wherewithal. Luckily, that was when fairer breezes blew old Mike Carmody into Alice Levertov's foamy fetch.

That particular winter, while the big boats were off on the tuna grounds for a couple of months, a family of bears took up residence in Mike Carmody's house out on the bay. They wanted to even up that Goldilocks caper. They couldn't find any porridge, but they managed to claw their way through the kitchen floor to the freezer in the basement. They made themselves right at home. Appraisers told Carmody that to repair it would cost as much as he had made out on his tuna run, and take just about as long. Longer, if he stayed around to bother the repairmen. So Carmody packed up and left the place to the carpenters and the bears and took a room at the Bear Flag Inn.

Alice knew him, of course—everybody in Kuinak knew the pot-bellied old dunker. Round and red-nosed and fringed about the ears with fuzz that must have once been red, he was one of the town's most popular characters. A cross between the Ancient Mariner and Friar Tuck, was Alice's opinion—as played by the Pillsbury Doughboy. She shrugged. More damn white bread, just staler and crustier. But when he slid the key out of her palm there was something in his touch that made her eyes leap up to his. Damned if the bald-headed old rubber ball didn't *wink* at her, so quick she didn't really believe it until he was gone up the carpeted hall. Then she laughed—one silly yip. It had been a long time since anybody had made her laugh like that.

Carmody was a good tenant. His ways were easy and his needs simple. He ate Kwikhot food from the machines and listened to the CB. He liked his pipe, his Irish recon and his Irish coffee. But it had to be good coffee. He'd finished enough albacore seasons off the South American shores to develop an appreciation for good coffee, a rare thing for a British-born palate.

Alice had barely given the man a look when he first checked in—just another dunky to have to clean up after. In point of fact, though, Carmody was something of a rarity—a dunk that had actually made a success of it, by staying on top of the market as well as the ever-changing waters of the region. Carmody could find fish when everybody else in town was pulling up waterhauls, then he could find top market for them. And he didn't run off to Maui to spend the take. He picked up loose quotas. He invested. He owned a small cannery that specialized in canned smoked salmon, in salted salmon, in salted salmon eggs. He also owned the smokehouse. He was an old-time salt who had always made Alice think of an old-time rubber doll: round and pink and bald. But there was that merry wink . . .

Then, the next morning, when she looked up from her desk and saw him grinning in her office doorway—a fifty-pound bag of gourmet coffee under one arm, a kettle and pot and package of filters under the other . . . and a huge hot plate dangling at his throat, power cord chomped in that goofy grin . . . well, there was something about him that made her grin back. It was the way he *carried* things, she later theorized. Especially that belly of his. Peeking between the buttons of his plaid shirt, Carmody's belly looked heavier than the coffee bag under his arm, and harder than the hot plate. A real dunker gut if she ever saw one, but he carried it with, well, with an air of bemused pride. He made Alice think of Ho Ti, the laughing Buddha.

'Joint knee?' he asked. Alice gave him a blank look. He unloaded his paraphernalia on one of the washer-driers and took the cord from between his teeth. 'Won't you join me? In a cup of mud, fresh from Bogotá?'

She knew what he was really after was a 220 plug-in for his hot plate, but the coffee *did* smell fresh, and better he plug in here than try to jerry-rig something in his room.

Prattling away, he bustled among the washer-driers, setting up his coffee. Alice realized the old pot-gutted Englishman was actually quite nimble and quick, moving the way a bear could, speed disguised inside the slow-seeming ball of flesh. Carmody finished grinding the beans with his own hand grinder just as his kettle boiled. At his teasing she had to admit he brewed one of the best cups of coffee she had tasted since San Francisco. Talked one of the best lines of bull, too; nothing pushy or fishy, like most Alaskan man-to-woman talk, just your basic top-o'-the-mornin' blather, to fill the space between sips. Yet it was nice. It was easy. It made her grin.

After a half-dozen mornings sitting among the tumbling driers and surging washers, sipping coffee and listening to this old sea lawyer spin yarns and talk blarney, Alice Levertov began to notice that the fire of Alice the Angry Aleut seemed to be cooling down. After three weeks she went out to help him put the new linoleum on his kitchen floor. After a month she joined him in a ceremony at the same church where she had been baptized, blushing alongside until she was as pink as he was. She knew it was a match made mainly out of the moment's practical necessity—old Carmody needed an American spouse to keep him out of the grip of the Migres. His trip home to Cornwall had somehow triggered some government computer somewhere to the fact that Michael Carmody had become practically a North American landmark without ever becoming a naturalized American citizen. The marriage made him a full citizen. On Alice's part, she became half-owner of a thriving enterprise including buildings, boats, quotas and real estate, and full owner of a grandly elevated social position in the town. She was Mrs Carmody. She hadn't been so looked-up-to since high school, after her art awards . . . before her ivory babe.

Alice stopped drinking that spring, and started shedding the angry armor of fat. She retrieved her old paintings from the church and hung them around the mansion Carmody gradually built for her around his shack out on the bay. She bought a pair of budgies, even took to cooing back to them like some old blue-haired biddy from Bella Coola, until one of the Wong brothers' roaming dogs roamed into the mansion's living room one dawn and crashed down the cage and ate the birds. Alice came downstairs with Carmody's double-barrel and found the dog curled up comfortable in front of the fireplace, feathers on his lolling lip. Much to her surprise, Alice did not shoot the murdering mutt, just booted him out the door with her bare foot. This badly jammed her toe, and while she was hopping around holding it the dog rushed back and nipped her on the other foot and she *still* did not shoot him. That was when she knew the angry fire inside was dwindling away at long last. In the half-dozen years since that marriage she had watched with relief as it steadily shrank to nothing more than a memory, a joke, a spark. She had thought it gone out for good until tonight, on the docks. That damned Sallas.

It wasn't just the champagne, either. It wasn't even what he said, it was the way he said it: 'Why here?'—forlorn and self-centered and most of all long-suffering, as though his holy fucking solitude were being unjustly threatened—'Why *Kuinak*?'

'Why the hell *not* Kuinak,' she heard herself flare back. 'Sallas, you're worse than my damn cousins. You don't believe this place is worth shit, do you? Certainly not worth rich Hollywood shit.'

He had looked away without responding. Alice immediately regretted lashing out in front of all these people. It surprised her, her fierce reaction. That little dab of champagne? Maybe she was more of a wino than she thought, if a couple of glasses could set her off so ferocious. Put cork in bottle, she tried to warn herself, before it bubbles out all over everybody.

'I don't think that's what Mr Sallas meant, Mother.' Nicholas Levertov had made an airy attempt to mollify the situation. 'He wasn't wondering why *Holly*wood had wended its way up here into his citadel; he was wondering why *me*. You see, Mr Sallas and I have enjoyed a previous encounter—'

'Two times,' Sallas said, still looking out across the grey-green water.

'—and I believe that I *almost* had the honor of making the acquaintance of Monsieur Greer.'

He extended the long white hand to Greer, careful to show that the buzzer had been removed. Greer gave him a cautious five, then turned to Alice. 'Your *son*, Alice? I never knew you were married before—'

'I wasn't,' she replied.

Greer wisely chose to overlook the implications. '*So!* That's Gerhardt Steubins' boat.' He rubbed his hands. 'I deduce he's come to shoot another mighty outdoor epic, right? A little Eskimo boy loves his father's giant malamute lead dog. Dog save de kid from a Kodiak but lose his front paw. Vet say dog'll never race again . . . but de boy carve him a *ivory* paw. They take the Iditarod, fastest time ever, and the Eskimo boy goes on to become zee senator.'

The silver man pursed his bruised lips. 'You're a quick study, Greer, for a Frenchman. In essence that's close, very close. Only this is a little Eskimo girl that falls in love with an *animal* spirit—'

'*Shoola and the Sea Lion!*' Greer exclaimed with a loud clap. 'The Isabella Anootka classic!' He turned to enlighten the others. 'The story is a thousand years before de white mon, right? What happens is our little nubile native and her friend dey down at the beach one day—the friend's a carver of spoons or some shit, crippled—when dey suddenly *see*—'

'We've all read the Shoola stories, Emil,' Alice said.

74

'Yeah, Greer,' one of the Wong boys put in, 'even us.'

Greer lowered his brows, unhappy at being cut off.

'To be honest,' the silver man confided, 'I like your story about the crippled malamute better. The ivory paw angle is hot.'

'We call it *Moby-Dog*!' Greer exclaimed again. 'I will whack out a treatment just as soon as I have a little more of dis Dom Pérignon of Alice's.'

Greer tipped the bottle, looking up the gangway. At the top of the rope-railed plank an enormous Asian was positioned at parade rest. Beyond him Greer could make out the splash and squeal of ladies at play in a swimming pool. He arched his eyebrows at Alice's son.

'Is Mr Steubins on board at the mo', mon? To talk options? I like to move on dese creative projects while they're still sizzling in de brain pan.'

Levertov laughed and pointed toward the below-decks aft. 'He's in his cabin this very mo', mon, *resting*, after his *ard*uous journey.' The purring voice insinuated all kinds of hanky-panky. '*Quite* arduous, if you knew our dear director. That's why I flew up in advance.'

'What's your position with Steubins, Nick?' It was the first words Isaak had spoken since the handshake. 'Best boy?'

'Right gender, however, wrong adjective.'

They studied each other's ruined faces for a moment, an obvious tension gathering. The swimmers splashed and squealed.

'Well, I've got to go secure a boat,' Isaak said at last. 'Good to see you again, Nick.'

'You, Greer,' Alice said. 'Give me back my bottle and go help Sallas.'

'I can handle it, Alice. Let Monsieur Greer enjoy this Hollywood shit while it's still hot.' He gave her outfit another quick look and headed back down the dock. 'I've enjoyed about all I can stand.'

'Have it your way,' she muttered, turning fiercely to Greer, 'but I do want that damned bottle back. It's my first Mother's Day present in twenty years. Pop one of those

75

beers out of the cooler if you're thirsty.' Then, raising her voice, calling down the dock after him, 'I'm the only one here *dressed up enough* for Dom Pérignon.'

Everyone laughed. Alice let the men take over the talk while she brooded. She'd been a damned idiot as usual, wearing this ridiculous costume. What had he said? 'Like an Edward Curtis portrait'? She should have known; try to parade a little bit, just a rare little bit in honor of a rare special occasion, and some has-been hero jealous about having to stand on the sidelines will find a way to bring the rain down on you.

The men popped their beers and shot the breeze. She pulled on a smile and kept quiet. The huge rigid sailwing wagging back and forth in the sky above reminded her of Father Pribilof's scolding finger—'Ah-ah-*ah*, Alice, remember what I always tell you: first one gets mad; then one *goes* mad.'

When the beer was gone Nicholas volunteered to take them on board for a tour of the yacht's larder, 'for a little preview of our upcoming press conference extravaganza!' Alice respectfully declined.

'You guys go ahead. I've got some stuff I should see to at the Bear Flag.'

'Mother.' Her son bent and gave her a quick stagey kiss on her head before she could object. 'You work too hard.' To conceal her fluster she stalked away, just as stagey, swinging her champagne bottle and her puffin-beak dress, her nose in the air. As soon as she was across the lot out of sight, she leaned against a stack of empty power-line spools and vomited on the tarmac. She retched so hard that little neon fish came swimming to her clenched eyelids. When she was finished she washed her mouth with the Dom Pérignon and squirted it against the spools. Then she said 'Oh fuck-a-bunch-of-shit' and swallowed the last mouthful. It was, after all, her Mother's Day gift.

She was still carrying the empty bottle when she reached the town's main intersection. The anger that had been sparked back on the dock continued to smolder, but she was keeping it contained. She nodded pleasantly to the pedestrians. If there was a comment about her attire she made herself remember that wagging finger—'Ah-*ah*, Alice . . .' and walked on by, cool. When she passed the open door of the Crabbe Potte and heard a raucous chorus of bullshit laughter that might have been about her, she walked on by. She walked on by when the two Wasp cops went into the antique beer song at the sight of her costume—'From the land of sky-blue wah-ah-ter . . .' She walked on by when one of the Loop twins sitting in the cab of their bigfoot pickup spit pistachio seed hulls in her path—well, *almost* walked on by—would have, anyway, if that big damned steranoid husky they kept chained in the back hadn't decided to attack her.

He hit the end of the chain with his fangs about six inches from her face—ninety pounds of nasty noise!—so she brained him with the Dom Pérignon bottle. He dropped back into the cluttered pickup bed like a big fuzzy toy. The Loop twins came boiling out each side of the cab, spitting beer and pistachio shells.

'Alice, you cunt—!' 'Alice Carmody, you *cunt*—' '—if you hurt True—' '—if you hurt Old *True*—'

'Hurt him how? By conking him on the head? There's nothing *in* there but grease and gristle. I just calmed the hyper son of a bitch, is all.'

The dog was stretched out on his side in the trash with his eyes open, breathing comfortably. Alice still held the bottle cocked back over her shoulder.

'See? He likes it.' The anger was gone, but she was still enjoying the feeling of mischief. 'Maybe I ought to conk him again. . .'

'Alice, you cunt—' The twin on the sidewalk stepped toward her. '—you better let me have that bottle before I by *God*—'

She let him have it before he revealed exactly by God what. He went down as politely as Old True. The brother came rushing around the tailgate and had her from behind before she could turn. She struggled, smelling the swine on his clothes, fearing that she would begin retching

77

again. She was glad the two Wasp cops were close enough to hear her cursing and come to the rescue.

After they all finished completing their various statements at the station, they struck a bargain: Alice wouldn't bring vicious-dog charges against Old True (which could require as much as a six-weeks quarantine) if Edgar and Oscar wouldn't bring Disorderly Deap charges. That way the Wasp cops wouldn't have to fill out any lengthy reports and the desk sergeant wouldn't have to wake up from his nap back in the spare cell. Everybody parted amicably at two AM just as the sun was rising from its brief rest. Alice resumed her walk on home, barefooted, tousled and rumpled, but with her beribboned bottle still unbroken.

She had just passed Herky's Merkentile and was wondering where she could duck out of sight to be sick again when the white Heftyvan pulled alongside.

'Get in, Alice. You look like you could use a ride.'

She got in. She couldn't think clearly enough to come up with a reason not to. When the van was moving she asked why he was still cruising around. 'I thought you went home.'

'I went down to clean the boat, remember? I'm on my way home now.'

'Conscientious prick, aren't you?'

He didn't answer. She hated it when anybody did that, especially this curly-haired Greek prick, but she rode on in silence. Even if she had wanted to make small talk she couldn't think of anything to talk about except her recent altercation with Edgar and Oscar and Old True.

'You headed to your motel?'

She just grunted. See how he likes it. They jounced and rocked along as he negotiated around the ruts and chuck-holes of the run-down street. The puffin beaks hanging from her hems clattered and chittered. All the evening's incidents hung the same way, dry and separate and chittering. On just one goddamn bottle of champagne! Injun agents had been right all along: Firewater no good for Injuns.

They bounced along until she finally had to holler, 'Stop, damn you!' He pulled over and let her out. This time she made sure she was empty. When the neon fish stopped swimming she got back in the van. She leaned forward with her arms wrapped around her knees, shuddering as he put the van in gear and eased it back on to the pavement.

'Hey you Sallas?' Her face turned toward him without lifting. 'I want to know what it is about me sticks in your craw? Why you always on my case? Uh? That shit back at the dock about my native dress, for instance, the fuck was that about?'

Sallas didn't answer.

'You jealous I'm having a little bit of a good time? That now I got me an influential son and husband *too*? Uh? Well, whatever, I'm sick of it. Stop the car.'

Sallas swung the van off the road again, so suddenly this time that Alice had to laugh.

'Haw, you're scared I'm going to soil your precious bus, aren't you? Well, I'm just getting *out* this time, thank you very much, not sick.' She slammed the door and reeled away without looking back. 'Nighty-fucking-night.'

Up a gritty roadside embankment toward a weedy lot she reeled, walking stiff-kneed, like a doll. Like a doll ridiculously robed in ethnic attire, going chitter-chitter-chitter as it walked. If she didn't try anything fancy she felt she just might negotiate a crossing of the heaving lot. Then she'd be at her motel. Her good old good old good old motel. Ace in the hole. She didn't object to poker, just casinos. Poker's a good teacher. Keep your cards close to the vest, always have that old ace down in the hole. It's one of the main reasons Carmody had taken to her, she always thought—he liked the way she played her best cards close to the belt. She was a good conservative poker partner. Carmody was a plunger and plungers need conservative partners. Helps trim the load.

Alice felt better as soon as she entered the little semi-circle of cottages. It was her only home, really; she had spent more time around these little cottages, child and

79

woman, than any other place in town. Except, perhaps, the church. You couldn't count the church. A church wasn't a private place. It was the most public place of all, being God's. But these crude cottages, circled against the swirl of nuisance, offered both privacy and protection.

Most of the units were still lit, though the sun was already rising. She made it to the utility room door and up the spiral staircase. The key was still in the works. She sat on her frameless mattress on the floor, swirling. After a few minutes she got up and drew the shades against the light. Maybe that would calm some of the jumble down. Not a chance. The room kept swirling along at high flood, shore to shore. And it wasn't just the LA excitement or the champagne. It was—she let her dress fall chittering and stood before the mirror —the rhythm of the images. That bottle. The thin, proportional rhythm, swooping in from the breast so the thin waist really gave you something to flare out from, then nice and narrow again. Thin rhythms. Modigliani. Rhythms restrained. You'd think a girl from a blood inclined genetically to go broad would have had the sense to let go and lay back for old Master Rubens . . . but no, not Angry Alice . . . Alice, she's always got to go against the grain, walk to school, no thank you, no ride necessary, no movie after, no help needed, no gummy-bears in the balcony, no butter please, no hands there, thank you . . . no urban sprawl, thank you . . . no brown map to be rolled out, no graphic sweep of the glorious heritage of the famous Alaskan Trail tail so widely appreciated . . . no, no letting it spread, not even after she got it spread in spite of her best resolutions . . . because getting it spread and letting it spread are different . . . rape and seduction . . . one done, one allowed . . . the second the greater violation . . . so play it close to the belt and keep it tight, tight and light and trim of line—because *that's* what sticks crossways in *their* craw!

Alice dropped back to her mattress and pulled a blanket over her. The swirl calmed after a while but she still couldn't sleep. Her head ticked. Bird sound announced the day. She got back up and pulled the curtains open

80

at the big window. In the vacant lot below three devout crows and a dozen skeptical gulls were already assembled on a power line. They were watching the crazy raven in the Caterpillar tractor guts. Even asleep the raven looked crazy. The angles were all askew. Feathers poked out erratically, as though stuck into a gob of restless tar. Sometimes when the dawn light shocked him awake he would totter around the engine parts with his wings spread and his head crooked back, screeching like a seer in the throes. This morn he was still sleeping—a nappy, disreputable black gob.

Out past the lot she saw the gentle sea, the boats jiggling at high tide . . . and, over all, that high sail wig-wagging like a metal finger. She closed the curtain again. Forget that crazy shit.

6

Bark Us All
Bow-Wows of Folly

Far down to the south the sun was westering wearily along. It had begun its journey ten hours earlier and would continue for about that much longer, swinging north when it got over the ocean. Far up toward the pole it would dip out of sight for a quick few winks, then be back in harness over to the east for another low, long circle. A house sitting on these latitudes can watch the cheery rays of morning beam in its northern windows, then see the somber rays of sunset come through the same window later the same day. So these are long hours for Apollo and his team, toiling these summer fields this high up on the tilted globe.

By first light that morning most of the town already knew about the arrival of the famous director and his yacht; the sail was visible from any window. All morning a steady stream of citizens had journeyed down to the docks to get a closer look at the wondrous metal airfoil upraised from the deck of the ornate vessel like a sword blade from a jeweled hilt. After gaping awhile in reverent silence they went back to their breakfast tables for more coffee. Brisk speculation went on in every bar and cafe and kitchen. How big was this upcoming epic? What size budget? Would there be jobs for the locals? And, what soon became the most urgent question, how did one go about finagling a place on the guest list for the big yacht party and reception tomorrow night?

Nowhere was this speculation brisker or the questioning more urgent than on the front porch of the Underdog House. By noon the little wooden platform could not contain the crowd; club members and mascots spilled down the steps across the sidewalk and into the street. They milled around in the town traffic, endangering dogs and drivers alike. The front door to the large house was open but none of the crowd moved to enter it. One of the oldest and strictest laws of the organization clearly stated: 'On the Day of the Howl Nobody Enters the Den Till Dark.' Otherwise you would have lazy mutts lounging around in there all day long just like usual, scratching and farting and drinking beer. The Sacred Moon would be wasted and the Sacred Den become just another mongrel hangout —lose all sense of what the members called Dognitty. This law was even written into the terms of a joint ownership contract: the Underdog House, half owned by Searaven, could be reserved by Deap Inc poker parties or blackjack nights, any night of the month save one: the night of full moon. On that night it belonged to the Underdogs.

The Loyal Order of the Underdogs was an organization of some considerable power in the region, for all its raunchy reputation. It was the Alaskan equivalent of the Friars Club, if you can imagine the Friars Club composed of an elite selection of fishermen, highwaymen, longshoremen, teamsters, bush pilots, Merchant Marines, hockey fans, party animals, recanted Jesus freaks and rejected Hell's Angels. This august fellowship had come into existence during a weekend-long Dreadful Great concert at the University of Washington football stadium. Fans from Kuinak were so numerous they had chartered a ferry to take them to Seattle, bringing beer and jerky for the trip. And sleeping bags and scoot pots and pop tents so they could sleep on deck. And their dogs. Lots of Alaskans still fancied dogs. Big dogs. So many big dogs that a special cyclone fence compound was constructed under the bleachers. When Greer was told that Marley would have to spend the concert in this compound, Greer moved right in with him. When Ike Sallas and his setter, Penny, joined them, the whole Kuinak contingent followed, tents and coolers, pedigrees and mongrels all. They spent the whole weekend behind wire.

Once all the dogfights were settled and the unruly dogs spranqued, the pound turned out to afford the Kuinak contingent the best seats in the place. The Effect was heavy that summer and the mercury in Seattle reached temperatures in excess of one hundred. Hotter, still, in the middle of Evans Field. But it was mercifully shaded under the bleachers, dusty but cool. The heat rising from the swelter on the Astroturf sucked in a pleasant draft off Puget Sound; the earsplitting shriek of tortured speakers was nicely baffled, and if you couldn't see the stage you nevertheless could enjoy the view of the swirling tie-dye skirts above.

Such a good time was had by the Kuinak contingent that they formalized the club when they returned home: the Loyal Order of the Underdogs. They devised rules, rituals and a copyrighted trademark—the club's full name rainbowing over the red silhouette of a fire hydrant with the four first letters of the name spewing up from it like a blare of sound: L-O-U-D.

And loud was what they were, loud and loose. The following spring the Underdogs entered a float in the Kuinak Day-Before-Opening-Day Parade—a twenty-two-foot papier-mâché old-fashioned fire hydrant built to conceal four kegs of Henry's Draft. No-one thought to arrange for glasses or plastic cups. It was best so, Ike pointed out. Glasses would have drawn the attention of the parade patrol, and possibly expulsion. The open-container law was strictly enforced on this important day, in the event of any national dish coverage.

So the beer was sucked straight. The four tap hoses passed surreptitiously from man to man as the club members stood in a great circle around their teetering altar, arms oafishly over each other's shoulders, swaying and singing in husky-voiced camaraderie. A visiting primal anthropologist from Sweden on the curb corner was expounding ecstatically that it was the most beautiful manifestation of male-bonding brotherhood chant one was likely to find in the modern world! Until an onlooker pointed out the Boswell girls and Herb Tom's wife. Some of the brothers were bitches?

The Day-Before-Opening-Day Parade passes through the town four times, north along Main, south back along Main, east up Cook, then west back down Cook, finally to the carnival in the boatyard parking lot. Thus, as the Dog Brothers paraded, howling through such canine anthems as 'Old Dog Tray' and 'Bark Us All Bow-Wows of Folly,' they developed a scorching thirst. They managed to drain the hydrant during the first half of the parade and then drench it during the second—even the three bitch Brothers joining in. When the float wobbled into the boatyard the papier-mâché was disintegrating and the hydrant listing hard to the lee. A gusty breeze set it rolling and it rolled over the Kuinak High School Band Bake Sale, through the pony ride and into the bay.

The success of the Loyal Order of the Underdogs was sealed after that. They were in demand at every local function and soon became frequent visitors to other venues. They rented a RO/RO and barged down to Skagway for Gold Rush Days and did their melting hydrant act. When no accommodating breeze provided them with their boffo finish they pushed the hydrant over manfully. It fell like a warm sponge, right on top of Skagway's Bigger Hammer Construction Company Marching Band marching right behind. A grand fistfight ensued. Skagway's band of rowdies far outnumbered the visitors from Kuinak, but many of the Underdogs were actually dogs, huge Alsatians and malamutes and Siberian huskies suckled on stanazones and trained to pull sleds, pant legs, shirttails or anything else they could get hold of. Following this debacle the Skagway parade committee passed an ordinance disallowing any four-footed entry weighing more than fifty pounds, a rule Ike eventually convinced the Underdogs themselves to adopt: 'especially these steranoid has-beens from the big sled marathons; they're like punch-drunk prizefighters. We'll build 'em a place under the porch . . .'

With the exclusion of the Beast Element the Doghouse came under the influence of the higher powers of the psyche. The Home for Lost Puppies was established and extensive funds raised by the HLP newsletter that scribe Wayne Altenhoffen put out. A scholarship to the Veterinarian College in Norman, Oklahoma, was endowed and awarded yearly to a deserving local youth. A Doghouse house band was formed called the Silver Beagles: John, Paul, George and Fido. They even had one of their cuts make it to the networks for a few weeks—'I Want to Hand Your Hole.' Greer on the bongos and nose flute was Fido. For a few years a soapdish venture was pursued, a low-budget daytime that would star real animals as real animals, with human voices dubbed in to carry the modicum of plot. A pilot was actually produced and presented to various pet-food companies—'A Program for Those Loyal Friends Left Guarding the Home While the Master's at Work,' was how it was pitched. The show was to be called 'One Dog at a Time.' Purina showed some interest, but before anything could be firmed up, the female lead—played in the pilot by Penny, Ike's glamorous red-headed setter—got salmon poisoning and died.

Ike Sallas seemed to lose interest in the Loyal Order after that. He started skipping meetings. Everybody could see he was heartbroken; the setter had been like his old lady. He was offered a number of other comely bitch pups but he turned them all down. Secretly, he was glad for the excuse to withdraw from his club presidency; he hadn't made the move to this remote fishing burg in order to become a civic leader. There'd been enough of that in the lower forty-eight. When he abdicated his office Greer was installed as president, but while Emil Greer certainly was a better-than-average example of Underdogdom, he had no flair whatsoever for leadership and he relinquished the honor forthwith to Billy the Squid Bellisarius, the town's resident genius and scoot dealer. Greer stepped modestly and thankfully down to vice-president—a position that both his reputation and his inclination better qualified him for.

Billy the Squid was a disagreeable and pompous little prick, but he made a good president. He had the capacity to pour a lot of creative energy into a project, then back it up with chemicals. He was the one, for example, that got the city to turn over the Fourth of July fireworks display to some real *experts.* Billy turned out a stupendous pyrotechnic spectacle, picked up on Sky Eye. After that all the club's revenues went toward bigger and better pyrotechnics. Homeless puppies would have to look elsewhere.

Attendance had begun to decline at the monthly meetings nonetheless. The wild excitement seemed to be gone. Even the upcoming Midsummer Full Moon Howl had lost its bright wolf-eyed luster. No special festivities were planned, no events looming. President Bellisarius was away south, looking to score fireworks and replenish the club scoot stash. Until that action got consummated, none of the members cared whether this Full Moon meeting was called or not.

Then, out of the blue itself, that fabulous yacht had arrived, and the old Underdog electricity was suddenly jump-started. Ever since breakfast the voltage had been rising out on the porch of the wooden hall. A little past noon Dogmember Mrs Herb Tom dropped by with a piece of news that turned up the juice twice that high. Her husband, Herb, had rented out the town's only stretch limo and it was cruising the streets delivering invitations. It had stopped first in front of the library and let out one of the movie twinkies, a girl of sturdy Slavic proportions and robust energy. She ran up the library steps with tan legs flashing, Mrs Herb related, carrying a little black fan of playing cards. Each card had an embossed silver fox on one side and on the other there were engraved invitations for all the town dignitaries—the mayor, the police chief, the high-school football coach and the city's two councilpersons, Mr and Mrs Hiro Wong. The names of these dignitaries were embossed in real raised gold, Mrs Herb Tom claimed.

She'd seen the one to the football coach and copied it on her copy board. She passed the board around:

> to
>
> ### Coach Jackson Adams
>
> *Foxcorp Studios*
>
> *humbly requests*
> *your presence*
> *at a*
>
> ### Sunday Soiree
> *aboard the*
> ### Yacht Silver Fox!
> *six p.m. till midnight*
>
> *signed:*
> *Gerhardt Steubins*
>
> *(please present this card to dockside watch)*

The Brothers were outraged and amazed. How the weird hell did Gerhardt Steubins know the name of the Kuinak Cohos' football coach? Weirder still, how did he know that the coach shared lunch at the library every Friday with the goddamn mayor, police chief, librarian and *coun*cilpersons? They'd just have to sit tight and stew until their invites came, the brothers guessed.

The limo roamed the rutted streets and roads of the little town all afternoon, making its deliveries. People could see it wasn't Herb Tom driving, even through the tinted glass. Herb Tom was so short that he had to pull himself half upright to see over the dash of his huge machine, like a jockey standing up in the stirrups. This driver was an enormous silhouette, and slope-shouldered and nude-browed. Some people swore it had to be the giant that guarded the yacht's gangplank, but others vowed they had just been to the docks and the giant was still at his post. This had to be another Jap giant.

Other silhouettes could be discerned in the car's cavernous interior—four or five others—but the only one that ever got out was the long-legged blonde. She dealt out the precious cards all afternoon, with spectacular flashes of leg and tooth, yet never a word of English—just a husky and mysterious *'danke schön'* or *'auf Wiedersehen,'* no-one was sure which.

There was one thing about which everybody became gradually and completely certain, however: not one invitation had been awarded any members of the Loyal Order of the Underdogs. At first it was assumed by the Dog Brothers that they were not as easy to locate as shop owners and city officials. That was one of the reasons the members kept ranging off the porch of the meeting hall, to give the cruising limo a better target. But after it had cruised past the crowd several times without so much as slowing down, an angry grumble began to arise around the porch. It had been rising steadily for hours.

Isaak Sallas and Emil Greer were among the few citizens who remained ignorant of this rising excitement. Greer had yet to make an appearance on the deck of the vessel that had swallowed him down the night before, and Ike had skirted the downtown. He had driven straight from a skillet lunch of eggs and smoked salmon to the crippled *Sue-Z* in the boat shed. He was glad to find the shed deserted, and the parking lot empty; the only other vehicles were parked way at the other end of the floating docks, where that wing-sail rocked its gleaming come-on. In the distance he could see cars jammed around it like bugs around a porch light. There was at least *that* to be said about the damned thing, Ike conceded—it kept fools out from underfoot. He was even glad Greer wasn't around, handy mechanic though he was. Let the poor frazzled peacock sleep; he could use the rest. Ike could use the solitude.

Not only was the pin of the *Sue-Z*'s prop shaft sheared, one of the blades had been bent, probably while they were being towed off the mud. Ike found this out by peering around beneath the boat with the Wongs' fiberoptic snake. Ordinarily a job like this would call for slipping a steel-web cradle beneath the hull and raising the boat, but neither of the Wong brothers in charge of the shed was around to work the winch. They were probably with their brother Norman up in town, drinking saki from snuff tins warmed over a butane lighter. None of the Wong boys were Oriental by blood, but their adoptive parents were; and they all had acquired certain Eastern sensibilities.

It was just as well they were gone, too. Ike never liked to raise a craft, especially a vulnerable old wooden ark like the *Sue-Z*. He drove back to the trailerhouse for his wet suit and faceplate and had the screw off in three dives, less time than it would have taken to rig the cradle.

One of the brass blades was also badly nicked on the tip —an old wound, it looked like by the verdigris on the nick. This was what had made the motor shudder so. Ike drove the screw to Mowbry's Welding but Bob Mowbry was also away, probably groveling around up at the Dog House. Bob was a Prospective Pup who wanted to be a full member so bad it made him cringe every time he passed the club. Thirty-four years old and six-foot-six, but you expected to see him squat and piddle at any moment.

He had a good welding shop, though, and the back door was unlocked. Ike brazed a gob of brass into the nick, then held the screw in the vise while he ground it smooth. Back at the dock shed he got the prop back on the shaft in the first dive—he'd emeried and greased it good—and the nut and shear pin on in the second. Before removing the suit he started the engine and revved it hard. It churned smooth as butter, the way it used to. He cut the engine and dived back under with a wrench. The nut was secured, the pin seated. When he splashed back to the surface there was Greer standing on the

90

shed's grimy floor. Even through the foggy faceplate and the engine fumes it was clear to Ike that the poor peacock had received no rest at all.

'Good God, where did you come from?' Isaak held up a hand for assistance.

'From that tall-sail Love Boat down there, mon, where else?' Greer answered. His face looked like a limp dream. When he made no effort to reach down, Ike floundered on to the dock and removed his faceplate. Greer's eyes were so red and sunken he probably hadn't even seen the hand. His patchwork trousers no longer looked rakish, just ragged. His long arms and his matted locks dangled like grimy ropes.

'Damn, Greer,' Ike shook his head, 'you look like something a sick bear threw up into a gulch.'

'Perhaps, *mon ami*. But whoa! What a gulch. Two of them, *actuellement*—grand and glorious gulches. I am grateful to zuch a bear.'

Ike sat down on a toolbox and began peeling out of the wet suit. Greer continued to stand, half in and half out of the shed's shadow, swaying and smiling. 'It was a night *magnifique*, mon, wait'll you hear.' He was just easing into a humid description of the evening's delights when Carmody's pickup swung to a stop up on the pier and Alice got out. She was back in her overalls and black rubber boots. Carmody's big army-surplus binoculars swung from her neck as she came thumping down the wooden ramp. She gave Ike a surly nod, then frowned into Greer's face. 'Hey, you, Mr Vice-President! You better shake it awake. They been baying for you up at the Dog House.'

Her eyes were flat and hooded again, and her hair retwisted at the back of her head in a severe knot. Before Greer could answer she thumped on past them to the dock's edge and raised the heavy glasses .

Greer went on rocking, as though not having heard. Ike pulled on out of the suit and ducked behind the winch housing to dry himself with one of the Wongs' dirty towels. 'Still nothing from Mike?' he called.

'Mr Carmody has never been one for radioing ahead.' Alice continued sweeping the sea with the glasses. 'I'm not worried—if something'd gone wrong we'd have heard—I'm just curious to know what that old pirate has been up to, all this time.'

'You say "*baying*"?' Alice's announcement was beginning to penetrate Greer's foggy bliss. 'What would they be baying for *me* about?'

'I didn't ask. They sounded pretty salty, though. Sallas . . . ?' She still didn't turn from her examination of the horizon. 'I want you two to batten down the *Sue-Z*. The *Columbine* as well. Secure and batten them both completely.'

Ike frowned, pulling on his Levi's. 'What the hell for? We'll be taking them out again first thing Monday, gillnetting—'

Alice swung the glasses to the southernmost finger of headlands. 'Maybe,' she said. 'Maybe not. I'll bet Carmody's here tomorrow, or Sunday sure. And I'll bet the first thing he does with his new toy won't be some rinky-dink little gillnetting. King crabs, maybe. Or tuna. You guys will probably have to go out with him.'

'You could still net with the *Columbine*, couldn't you?' Ike insisted. 'You sure did today.'

'I've been given a position on this forthcoming film,' she explained in a matter-of-fact voice. 'I'm the art director.'

Before Ike could comment Greer suddenly slapped his hands to both gaunt cheeks. 'Jesus H Christ, I know what it is, it's full moon!' He grabbed Ike's arm. 'It's the Midsummer Howl, Isaak!'

Ike shook his arm free. 'I don't get it, Alice,' he continued. 'I never knew you to waste so much as one day of a session. What do you know about being an art director, anyway?'

Alice turned from the sea, bristling. 'I know I'll make twice what I could out there wrestling a bunch of runt fish. They want me to help design a longhouse. I *do* know a thing or two about that.'

Greer grabbed Ike's arm again. 'Please. With Billy away I'm Top Dog. Ride shotgun with me on this, Pardner. You, me and Old Marley? We're going to have to deal with some very important 'Dog business tonight.'

'*What* important 'Dog business? This story's about a sea lion, if I remember right. Not about a bunch of mangy mutts.'

'Any story to do with Eskimos is going to require dogs, is it not? Numerous *stand*-ins and extras? That makes it a union issue, *mon ami*; all these mangy mutts are members in good standing.'

This was so. One of Ike's early club efforts had been to draw up a union charter for working dogs. This was initially done to protect old Iditarod racers from becoming penniless pound hounds in their decline, but the idea had rapidly spread to include other animals—racehorses, circus lions and tigers, even fighting cocks. Animal handlers were pressured to unionize their bread-winners or be picketed by Animal Solidarity packs, and the union prevailed. Out of every dollar earned by an animal two-and-a-half cents was paid into a pension fund toward that animal's retirement.

'Okay, it's a union issue,' Ike agreed. He didn't like arguing this stuff with Alice Carmody five feet away. 'But you and the union will just have to handle this important business by yourself. Old Marley and I are going to stay home tonight. I'll read him *Call of the Wild*.'

'Crap in a paper bag,' was Greer's opinion.

'Yeah, what's happened to you, Sallas?' Alice lowered the glasses and leaned against the rail. 'I can remember when you would have been foaming at the mouth to get in on this kind of action.'

'So can I. That's why I read paperbag crap. Just as filling and far less likely to start you foaming at the mouth.'

Greer turned to entreat Alice. 'Isaak thinks he's out-grown us, Alice. *Talk* to him, would you? For Old

Marley's sake? The poor miserable old fellow's up there in that trailerhouse alone all day. Don't you 'gree it do the old guy good to get out and rub a little elbow with his own kind?'

'Nobody can be a pup forever, Greer,' Alice said. 'But hey, what the hell, Sallas? Maybe you ought to consider going. Maybe be good for you, as well, to rub a little elbow.'

'Thanks, Alice,' Ike answered. 'I'll consider it.'

'Not that I personally give a damn one way or the other,' she added. 'Just be sure that whatever you two Dogs decide to do, get both of these boats battened down first. And be sure you keep your calendar clear for sea duty next week.'

'Oooh,' Greer groaned, rolling his eyes.

'I'll be sure,' Ike said.

'Well, if you gentlemen will excuse me, I got work to do.' Alice flipped up the collar of her overalls and went thumping back the way she'd come, the wooden planks slapping water beneath her. '*Art*work,' she flung back, her voice slapping just like the salt water.

'What do you think of *dat*?' Greer lamented when the pickup was gone. 'The first real action in this hole for years and she want us to pull *sea* duty?'

'I think—' There was just something about that slapping voice, that upturned collar, the mean and arrogant knot of hair in the pickup's rear window, '—that Old Marley and I might consider going to that goddamned meeting with you after all. C'mon, help me pull this bucket clear. . .'

It was after nine by the time they had secured both boats up the gutter near Carmody's mooring. They hiked back overland, taking care to stay on side roads when they came through town. Greer wasn't ready to pass by the Underdog hall. Alice had been right; even from a block away they could hear the grumble of the mob around the porch, like the rumble of a possible storm. It was still a sound more ambiguous than angry, Ike noted. Unfocused.

94

It reminded him of the sound he'd heard the migrant workers make, clustered around the misty bus roads in the Fresno vegetable fields, grumbling among each other whether they would obey the morning's assignment . . . the threat still unfocused, in the mists.

The two friends crossed the parking lot as the long day was at last fading. In silence they drove the van back up to the trailerhouse. Greer had been growing less talkative and more jumpy by the minute, and Ike knew better than to do anything to make it worse. The jittery Jamaican had been known to bolt from responsibilities far less threatening than this.

The trailer's little butane water heater only held enough for one warm shower and Ike let Greer have it. 'You're the one that's going to have to be in the public eye.'

Greer chose the lime-green see-through that he'd worn at his most recent wedding in Kingston. It still smelled of dark rum and ganja. His long black fingers were shaking as he worked at the tiny shell buttons.

'Put a little cool on it,' Ike told his friend. 'It's not like this is a UN assembly you're chairing.'

'Like hell it isn't! The whole mother town is going to want to know where the club is on this movie business. I don't just mean the Dogs, I mean mother *ever*-body. If we don't get a righteous bite out of a pie this juicy, mon, then ol' Vice-Dog Greer he might as well turn in he teeth an' testicles.'

Ike laughed, but he knew Greer was right in a way. The Loyal Order had made its reputation by getting the best seats at any event worth attending—inside track at all the snowmobile races; backstage at all the rock concerts from Anchorage to Victoria. They were even allowed to wear OFFICIAL badges at the Iditarod finish in Nome, so they could examine each license of the top twenty teams. They compared noseprints with those on the union record to make sure none of the members were getting shorted a share of the prize money. For nearly a decade the Underdogs had managed to have a paw in every pie the region cooked up—two or three paws if the pie was particularly juicy—and now what was likely to be the biggest plum pie in the town's history was about to be served up. If the Dogs couldn't devise some way to get an honorable slice of it, the status of the entire Order would be damaged.

Marley had unstiffened enough to walk out to the van on his own, but Isaak had to help him lift his emaciated hindquarters in the rear door. The old dog grunted his appreciation and climbed into the van's low bed so he could hang his head out the porthole.

'Look at the old bastard grin,' Ike said, hoping to ease his friend's anxiety. 'It's been a year at least, but he still knows he's going to an Underdog howl. He's the one should have got the shower, don'tcha think?'

Greer said nothing. He was perched on his heels in the passenger seat with his arms around his knees. The lines of his speckled face were constricted into a scowl and his lips were drawn back from his teeth in such a stiff grimace they were incapable of forming words. Greer could get himself in a state about any number of favorite fears and phobias, but rarely in such a state he couldn't speak.

It was past eleven by the time they reached the Dog House. The crowd had stopped its grumbling and was standing silent, faces turned toward the extreme northwest. They were watching the sun squeeze out of the belly of a tight little black cloud nesting on the horizon, like an egg squeezing out of a hen. The faces all turned when the van pulled into the president's parking space alongside the packed porch. No-one spoke, but a strange whimpering started up as the vice-president got out. Greer took the first glass held out to him and gulped it down without tasting what it was. Ike could not believe the size of the crowd. Men he hadn't seen around town in years were pumping Greer's hand and giving him the high paw. It looked like every dunk and duffer that had ever shelled out the fifty bucks for the membership card had made his way to the meeting. He saw some that must have flown in from chapters as far away as Anchorage to the east and Unalaska to the west.

Greer slipped alongside of Wayne Altenhoffen. 'Still no sign of Billy?' he inquired in a hollow whisper.

'Nary a yip,' Altenhoffen whispered back. 'The Squid isn't one to cut short a shopping trip, even if he's heard of this movie shindig. So you're our prez tonight, Emil. You're the man with the plan. What are the Dogs going to *do*?'

Greer lifted his bony shoulders in a feeble show of nonchalance. 'About what, Poor Brain?'

'About us getting sniffed over like this! Not Dog One has received an invitation to this high roll on the yacht tomorrow. That constitutes a gauntlet slap to our collective muzzle, wouldn't you say? Underdog honor is at stake, Brother Greer, and as fate would have it you are the man. So what's the plan?'

Other members were pressing close to the whispering pair.

'The plan is,' Greer put on his shades and turned toward the horizon, as ceremoniously as he was able, 'to wait until the sun goes down, then have our meeting. Just like always.'

The sun neared the horizon and the crowd began to quiet. Even the desultory whimpering ceased, except among some of the mascots. These malcontents were dragged away to their respective pickups and tethered there, downcast and ashamed but still unable to curb their whining. The smaller, more civilized dogs were herded beneath the porch, where they watched in decorous silence through the latticework. As the sun touched the distant line of water, even the whiners in the pickups became completely silent. When the last red blob spread out and blinked to green, a terrific howling ululation commenced, perfectly on cue. The effect seemed somewhat burlesque at first, self-mocking and more than a little shallow, but as the howling lifted there were heard notes of true pathos beneath the parody, of honest achings and deep animal despair being given throat, and the self-consciousness and the burlesque melted, and the shallow was swept into the deep. The obedient and the civilized beneath the porch joined in with a sweet tenor, then the heartbreaking baritone from the pickups. These notes spun and twined and plaited into a line of surprising strength—a single sobbing wail: the Call of the Underdog. This wail continued until it lifted above the town and rebounded off the face of the little glacier across the bay and came echoing back, reweaving with itself like the chord of a pipe organ in a vast cathedral. When the echo died away the men began to file into the hall, leaving cans and bottles and fruit jars outside in the brimming trash barrels—another rule learned from experience.

Not a word was spoken as card tables were swept clear and folded against the walls. Wooden chairs were dragged from closets and unfolded in uneven rows around the wooden floor. When every member was standing in front of a chair, Greer walked stiffly to the big cutout of the hydrant logo that served as the podium. He raised the polished bear femur that represented the chief's gavel and with his other hand pointed a finger at the floor. 'Sit,' he commanded. They sat. He held the hand up, palm toward the multitude, and bade them 'Stay.' His voice was steady. They stayed. 'This Midsummer Night's Full Moon Howl of the Loyal Order of the Underdogs is now in session. Have a care and govern yourselves accordingly. Faithful Scribe, Poor Brain? Is there any old business?'

Wayne Altenhoffen stood up with a black ledger and opened it with a flourish. Altenhoffen was a substitute teacher at the high school when he wasn't fishing, as well as the editor of the *Kuinak Bay Beacon*, the town's weekly or biweekly or sometimes bimonthly news rag. Long-nosed and wordy, he was nonetheless a valuable asset to the town and the club both, a bright and eager citizen who was often so full of plans for community productions and projects that he would begin a conversation: 'My poor brain is simply *pul*sating with possibilities.'

'The previous meeting of the Loyal Order ended on a sudden and dramatic note,' Altenhoffen read. 'The matter

98

before the members was the court order to cease and desist the practice of setting off fireworks in the meeting hall. When informed that Thomas Toogiak Senior and the Searaven council had threatened to evict our organization, President Squid stated, and I quote, "Fuck Tommy Toogiak and his whole band of beer-barrel savages. If they mess with the Dogs I'll cut off their tea cold turkey. We shall set off firecrackers when the spirit moves us." Unquote. Members agreed with a unanimous woof except for Tommy Toogiak Junior, who objected to his father being cursed, and Charlie Fishpool, who objected to some of the other wording. "Beer barrels we may be but savages we ain't. We are *descendants* of savages." Norman Wong responded, and I quote, "Then descend back to your seat, Charlie; your beer barrel's showing." To which Charlie Fishpool responded, "At least I descend from somebody, Wong." At which point Brother Norman Wong struck Charlie in the back of the neck with a rolled-up *People* magazine, knocking the aforementioned Charlie to his knees. Then Brother Clayton Fishpool struck Brother Norman Wong on the back of his neck with a rolled-up copy of *Atlantic Monthly,* knocking him to his knees. Then the meeting broke up.'

He closed the book and raised his bright face. Greer nodded his approval. 'Thank you, Scribe Altenhoffen. Does the pack concur with the record?'

The room answered in unison, 'Woof woof!' Altenhoffen sat down.

'The minutes stand approved as read. Any further old business?' Greer peered around fiercely, feigning confidence. Charlie Fishpool raised a thick hand.

'I'd still like to get an apology on the record, but maybe this ain't the time—'

'Woof woof!' the members agreed and Charlie took down his hand.

'Any reports from any committees?'

A deep negative growl answered.

'Excellent.' Greer gaveled the podium top in a neat rim-shot conclusion: thump-a-bam! 'Is there any *new* business, then?' The big white bone was held high, waiting. 'Eh?' Nobody seemed able to think of any new business.

At the rear of the room near the door, Dog Brother Isaak Sallas let his chair tip back to the wall and relaxed. Greer was going to do just fine, he saw, for all that trembling and trepidation. That was one thing about the Underdog ceremonies: they could be counted on to keep the members from taking any business too serious, old or new. Finally, Wayne Altenhoffen placed his ledger on the floor and raised his hand. Greer sighed heavily.

'The chair *again* recognizes Scribe Altenhoffen. What's on your mind, Poor Brain?'

Altenhoffen stood amid low growls. He raised a finger. 'I shall be brief,' he promised, then drew a deep breath. 'Mr Vice-President . . . Dog Brothers . . . fellow citizens . . . I wish to raise the question for discussion, with consideration for the Order's historic involvement in so many memorable events of the glorious past—'

'Grrrr,' warned the members. They were all too familiar with Poor Brain's wordy preambles.

'—the question being *this*,' he hurried on, '*how* do the Underdogs go about getting their righteous bite out of this forthcoming action film?'

'Woof *woof*,' the members seconded.

Greer stroked his frizzled chin. 'A very interesting question, Scribe. Is there any discussion? If not—'

'I got a even more interesting question!' someone interrupted from the other side of the room. 'How do we common Dogs get a invitation to this party tomorrow night—like certain *other* brown-noses got?'

'You're out of line, Dog Brother—' Greer gaveled. He couldn't see who had spoken.

'Where do we get *in* line, Mr Vice-President?' another growled. 'Out at Loop's pigsty?'

Greer tried to slide it past with his Gallic shrug. 'Zuch is zee movie business—' but the members were no longer in the mood for comedy. Mrs Herb Tom stood up, her red-nailed finger aimed like a pistol.

'Greer, so far you are the only dude in Kuinak with suck enough to get on that floating smorgasbord. Don't say different, the whole town knows. What *we* want to know is what you've done about getting your loyal Dog Brothers a little nibble, damn your skimpy black ass! Is this a first-class club or what? I for one didn't pay five hun 'hun to sit home and watch the rest of the world ridin' first class. I could've given the money to Herb if that was what I wanted; he could've bought a new dish. So—' Mrs Herb Tom raised a black leather purse and poked the red-nailed hand inside, very pointedly. '—what about it?'

Greer was looking a little worried. 'Mrs Herb . . . Dog Brothers . . . I swear to you I *asked* about getting the club passes on board. But the couple that entertained me did not speak one word of English—just Russian or something—and I never did see Steubins.'

Mrs Herb was not appeased. 'What about your albino buddy? He sounds like a understanding sort, catches you humping his wife, then provides you with a couple of replacements?'

'Vanished below decks, Brother Mrs Herb, right after he turned us over to the Russians. Vanished below decks. I haven't seen him since. Dog's honor.' The knot had returned to Greer's brow and his hands were beginning to shake. 'I don't know this albino dude hardly any *any*way. Listen, everybody; Alice Carmody's the one you ought to hit on. She *is* his mother . . .'

They didn't even honor this suggestion with words, just the low growl.

Ike let his chair tip back to the floor. Silly kidsclub business notwithstanding, you always had to keep in mind that the kids at these meetings were fully grown and usually drunk and frequently strung out and, more often than not, armed. As president, he'd more than once had pistols pointed at him over some silly kidsclub business. And the previous year the peaceful little town of Kuinak had chalked up the third-highest handgun fatality per capita in the nation, just behind Houston, Texas, and Washington DC.

'Then hit on Ike Sallas!' Desperate, Greer pointed with his bone. 'Ike spent time in *jail* with the son-of-a-bitch; all I do is spend time with his mother *wife . . .*'

The faces turned, flushed and twitchy. The first signs of scoot withdrawal. Even the women. Ike found himself remembering why he'd stopped coming to these fun-filled monthly meetings.

'What about it, Sallas?' Mrs Herb Tom demanded.

'Don't look at me. You didn't see any Slavic twinkies bringing me a silver card with *my* name on it.'

'My name isn't on mine, either!' Greer cried. 'I mean, I don't *have* no stinkin' card.'

The Dogs were not placated. Some continued to glare at Isaak, some at Greer. The growl kept rising. For the third time in two days, Ike regretted leaving Teddy at home; then, as if the thought itself had touched a trigger, a gunshot boomed in the room. Norman Wong waved a .44 Colt revolver over his head, the fourteen-inch barrel drizzling smoke. The piece was an antique Civil War weapon, property of the Order. It was issued to the sergeant-at-arms at his inauguration, and was to be passed along. Norman had held both post and piece since the club's formalization. Luckily, he was the coolest-headed of the Wong boys, and had never used the weapon except procedurally.

'Order in the den,' Norman spoke into the blast's after-math. There was order. Firecrackers and Uzis were one thing, but a big .44 had the ring of historic authority. 'This is a formal meeting. Have a care and govern yourselves accordingly!'

The crowd settled muttering into their wooden chairs, turning back to the podium. Greer showed his teeth and tried to arch his eyebrows into some show of Jamaican cool.

'The Squid will be back in a couple of days, O my Brothers,' he reassured them. 'He'll take care of us.'

The low rumble commenced anew. 'Billy the Squid don't have friends inside on this one, Mr Vice-President,' Mrs Herb pointed out. '*You* do.'

'Woof *woogh-h-h-f*.'

Ike heard the rumble rising—questions, demands, accusations. He was reminded again of the sound he used to hear from the field workers, and from other places—in the barracks at El Toro, in the cells full of unsleeping men at the Sheriff's Honor Farm. The sound came from an ache so common that any low-rung group might have produced it, from the bottom of any social ladder. This wasn't any melodic howl of mutual Underdog blues; this was the dark and dangerous complaint of the *mad* underdog, of the left-out, the cheated, the long-toothed and empty-gutted. This was the universal growl of guys who had purchased the centerfold but didn't get the girl, of wives that had bought into the bubbles of daytime soap operas while life just got dirtier—this was the grumble of dreams being disappointed and glands being denied. What the crowd might do if that grumble kept growing to its uncharted end was anybody's guess.

Trapped at the front of the hall, Greer kept stammering one-liners and reassurances, but the growl kept getting louder. The Boswell sisters had joined Mrs Herb in a shrill caucus. Sergeant-at-Arms Wong waved his big pistol and called again for order, but it was clearly past that. More members were beginning to rise wild-eyed from their chairs. Norman Wong waved his pistol; Greer hammered the bone gavel; the growl got more thunderous. Then, at the peak of the turmoil, all of the lights in the hall flared to sudden dark—as though by a signal—and the growl was overwhelmed by an ear-splitting crack of actual meteorological thunder.

That little black cloud had apparently moseyed on into town after finishing with the sun, to see what was up. It had actually considered the uproar at the Underdog hall for a few minutes, before the town's power station had captured its fancy in the next block. All those wires and insulators and diesel-driven generators! It tossed its single bolt into the seductive spread of machinery with a passion that made the earth move and welded a wheelbarrow against a metal piling. Satisfied, it began

103

to unload its little load of rain before turning back out to sea.

The members had of course gone immediately still and respectfully silent. One thing you do learn, living on the low rung: respect such manifestations as come from on high, beyond the ladder—like the weather. High-rungers could afford insulation from such annoyances, but not low-rungers. They were at the mercy of such mysteries.

And they remained motionless and silent as the rain hammered down and the real dogs whined under the porch, for a shared mystical moment. Then the reserve generators kicked in and tame electricity returned to the light bulbs. It had taken no more than a fraction of a minute, but the effect on the Underdog meeting was enormous. The tension in the hall was reversed as instantaneously as switching a toggle from negative to positive. Nobody questioned it. Everyone was on their feet, laughing and jostling and pounding each other's back and giving the high paw. Ike found himself swept up in the surge of relief with all the rest.

Greer tossed the gavel into the podium and hopped down the stage, headed for the door. As far as the presiding prez was concerned, this meeting was undeniably over. He was stopped in his tracks before his hand found the door handle. There was someone on the other side of the gritty screen. And he stood there so paralyzed, with such a look of abject surprise and dismay, that the celebrating members took notice and began to calm down. When they at last quieted, a friendly purr came through the screen: 'Hi, guys. Can a stranger enter the sacred den?'

Ordinarily, the Underdog Growl of Warning would have answered such a request, but the members were too spent; they could only stare at the shape beyond the screen. Greer finally shook himself from his trance.

'Sure, hey, why not? The meeting's adjourned, mon. Come on in.' Greer flipped the latch and swung open the screen. 'Dog Brothers, this is Nicholas Levertov.'

Nicholas swept through into the glare of curious eyes. He was wearing cream-colored slacks and shirt, with a pastel peach overcoat draped over his big shoulders like a cloak. The prescription lenses covered his eyes and a thin chain held a gold crucifix at his throat. He's dressed to look like a stereotype of some Italian film mogul, Ike realized, right down to the floppy Fellini fedora.

'Gentlemen, I hope you will forgive this unseemly intrusion—hello, Isaak, don't I look spif?—but I could think of no other way to catch you all together.'

'So, now you've caught us,' Norman Wong said. 'So now what?' Norman didn't like the way Greer had flipped that latch so fast; it was the sergeant-at-arms's duty to decide when the den was open to the public.

'So I was just dropping this by, Big Fella.' The white fingers flickered and a black card appeared. 'That's what.' He put it in Norm's holster, alongside the .44. 'Also, these.' A fan of cards fanned out from each hand. 'Be so kind.'

The cards were all generic, inscribed only 'Noble Underdog'—but they were official invitations nonetheless, and for everybody. The very last card of the fan was handed with a flourish to Ike Sallas. When Ike started to protest that he wasn't much on parties anymore, the man leaned close, said a brief something in Ike's ear, then swirled back out the screen the way he'd come. The Dog Brothers stood on the porch and watched the limo bounce down the rutty rain-slick street.

'Who was that masked man?' Scribe Altenhoffen was the first to speak. 'The Lone Stranger, or the Tooth Fairy?'

'I think it was the Tooth Fairy,' Mrs Herb Tom judged. 'The Lone Ranger wouldn'a kissed Ike Sallas on the cheek like that.'

'It was no kiss,' Ike protested. The members waited. 'It was more on the order of a royal command,' he went on with a deprecating shrug. 'Nick said His Majesty Mr Steubins wished to see me, was all. Personally. Let's go home, Greer. I bet Old Marley's rubbed enough elbow to be ready for the sack. I know I have.'

7

By Thy Long Grey Beard and Thy
Glittering Eye
Whyfor Thou Stoppest Me?

Early Mass at the Russian Orthodox Church found
Father Pribilof addressing a bigger flock than he saw
on Christmas and Easter combined. The pews were
packed and there was standing room only when the
bells in the rickety old steeple started chiming the
call. They came like pilgrims, to offer up their grati-
tude for the bounty befalling.

Most of the multitude were, like their house of worship
and their Good Father, also old and rickety. Derelicts of
better days; fishers of forgotten runs and their rundown
fishwives; old Deaps. Considerable many old Deaps.
There were present more mossbacked old Deaps than
anybody had imagined were still alive in the area. They
had thronged forth as though to celebrate the capture of
a great whale. Maybe they didn't have an engraved card
to the inner circle of the whale feast, but with a catch
this big the blubber was going to be flying.

Father Pribilof had chosen his text three days previous
to that big metal-sided whale's landing, but everyone in the rapt congregation was certain the sly old
priest had tailored the sermon especial. The theme of
his loosely woven sermon was the Evil Net, and the
book was Ecclesiastes. Only the Good Father knew
that the sermon was a work of fate, not fabrication,
and better than tailor-made—that it was the Needle of
God Almighty that had stitched this sermon. Father
Pribilof was only the lowly thread of reason. And if

that thread tended to run more toward the oracular than the orthodox as time spun on, that was fine with the flock; a twisted line was just as good as a golden braid for stringing words together.

'For O, man knoweth not his time!' The Father was booming toward his finale, as much as he was able to boom with his reedy, ninety-four-year-old voice. 'And as fishes that are taken in an evil net, and as birds that are caught in the snare; so are the sons of man snared in an evil time.'

The congregation wiggled with anticipation on their crowded cedar seats. Hot dog, an evil time! Let's get at it.

'There was, O, a little town,' the Father went on, encouraged, 'with a few men in it. And O, a great king came against the town and besieged it. But there was in this little town a good man, a man poor but wise; and he, by his wisdom, he delivered the town. Yet did *anyone* thank that poor man? Did *anyone* in the entire town remember him in their prayers?'

The crowd shook their heads in happy negative: shit, no.

'But I say, O, that wisdom is better than might, though the poor man's wisdom is despised and his words not heeded. I say the words of the wise are better than the shouting of a ruler of fools. *Dead flies make the perfumer's ointment give off, O, an evil odor!*'

Noses wrinkled and nostrils flared, ready for more.

'Thus I say unto you,' he concluded, his veined hands fluttering against the gold brocade of his cassock like blinded birds, 'cast your bread upon the waters but not your pearls before swine. Thus I beg you all to remember: "Blessed are the poor in spirit though they have *not* an invitation to the rich man's hall." Blessed, O blessed indeed. A-men!'

'A-men!' they answered, fast, ready to get on to the bread and pearls and swine. 'O Amen a-*men*!'

Outside afterward in the thin sunlight, accepting congratulations for his stirring sermon, the Good Patriarch

107

had to confess that yes, he himself personally had received an invitation to the evening's event, and that yes, of course he was going—Gerhardt Steubins had scribbled a specific request. He was going in his capacity as a priest, though, to bless the event—not as a local bigwig. Even great whales have need of a little blessing, and it wouldn't hurt swine, either.

'But blessed are the poor in spirit nevertheless!'

By Sunday dinner the whole town knew which local bigwigs had been awarded invitations and which had not. Some citizens had heard the news by phone, some by the local Fishnet radio. Some read it in a special edition of the *Bay Beacon*, pasted up by Wayne Altenhoffen during the night; and some heard it from the *Beacon* readers. But most of the citizens heard it outright, by means of an acoustical phenomenon peculiar to many Alaskan coastal towns. Contained on three steep sides by swooping peaks and a glacial cliff, the sound of the town feeds back on itself. It can't get away. It swirls and circles like prayers imprisoned in a dome. Most days this phenomenon was just a mass of muddy noises, but on a Sunday, when boats were serviced and secure and the metallic protesting of the canneries finally hushed, that circling swirl unmuddies and those sounds separate into clear voices. Anybody who bends an ear to listen can hear anybody else, up close and personal. There is no anonymous highway roar, like you might have in the more metropolitan south. Up in these little trapped towns each vehicle's movement becomes individual—identified and interpreted from any front porch in town:

'That's Leroy Danestron's old lady peeling out to go crying to her mommy—and that old Malibu won't take too much more of *that*!'

Any debate in front of any one of three bars could be heard and judged by the juries loitering in front of the other two:

'That's Leroy down at the Potte saying his old lady is deeply wounded that they never got a ticket. He says she says that as the town's sole chiropractors they should have been invited. *I* say who gives a big bag of fish shit? Leroy's old lady'll be there just like the rest of us suck-ups, right? Ticket or fuck-it.'

There was some bickering between the havers of tickets and the have-nots, but nothing serious; everybody in town was going whether they had received invitations or not. They knew there would be plenty of action dockside. Preparations had been going on since first light, anticipating the crowd of suck-ups. Searaven had set up their bingo tent and beer garden. The local Eagles Aerie had pieced together their plywood dance floor and were already calling clog dances. At least a dozen ninety-watt fender boomers were booming out a selection of rhythms; every clopping clog could always find a beat to stomp to.

Omar Loop was one of the few that had refused to have any part of any of it; he was still so outraged that Bergstrom had refused to lock that freaky son-of-a-bitch-in-law up that Omar had bolted the front door of his bowling alley at noon. He would bowl alone in protest. But his two sons had been won over. They had rigged a spit in the back of one of Omar's pickups and filled the bed with charcoal briquettes; they were cooking and carving and selling slices from the carcass of a huge brood sow that a bear had mauled the week before: tenderized pork and a scoop of beans—twenty-five bucks a plate.

Float planes had been sailing in in a steady stream, mainly bush-hoppers from towns nearby, but there were also exotic arrivals. At six PM straight up, two Lear Seahawks swooped down, taxied across the bay, unloaded technicians and aluminum equipment chests at the yacht's fantail lift, then swooped away again, wingtip to wingtip, like a pair of metal-feathered water-fowl. A little later a shuttle chopper whirled down and let out a half-dozen squealing girls with hair like red road flares. A cheer went up. This *had* to be the Cherry Tarts, a group out of Anchorage currently making a name nationally with their Fourth World renditions of Golden Oldies. They were six real natural redheads and were famous for wearing outfits cut to cleverly prove it. They came scampering from beneath the whirling rotor and up the gang with curls flying and onlookers applauding and shouting—'The Cherry goddamn hell bitch *Tarts*! Big time.'

The giant at the top of the gangway stepped aside and let the girls on board.

A few minutes before seven an iridescent green-and-yellow shimmer appeared above the horizon in the west. This gleaming chimera came in very low and very fast, borne on an earsplitting whine of smoke. Above the parking lot it suddenly swooped its beak skyward and hovered in midair like an enormous hummingbird; then it leveled off horizontal again and lowered itself to the bubbling asphalt of the parking lot.

When the smoke cleared the word *MITSUBISHI* could be seen in black letter-strokes. Three Asians in dark blue suits climbed down the wing steps and were handed three briefcases. The man handing down the cases was not Asian. He was Beach Boy all-American, wearing white deck shoes and surfer trunks and a Hawaiian shirt with bird-of-paradise print. A blond fuzz of close-cropped hair flashed in the jet wash as he hopped to the ground. He grinned a sunny smile and waved to the circle of onlookers, then hurried after his three grim traveling companions. When the four passengers were clear, their craft rose again into its screaming hover, canted the engines, and was out of sight back over the sea before its passengers had crossed the lot to the yacht. Wayne Altenhoffen shook himself from his awe to write, 'After the jump jet's appearance nobody would have been surprised to see a nuclear sub surface . . .'

A few minutes past eight that all-American corn-fed face reappeared at the rope gate, smiling cheerily into a hand horn. Nicholas Levertov was with him, in fedora and tinted glasses. The smiling all-American beamed out on the crowd, nodding this way and that while the chatter quieted and the fender boomers were turned down, then began to speak through the horn.

'Hey, gay-*ang*!' He sounded like a game-show host greeting his studio audience. 'How's *fishin'*?'

Laughs and catcalls answered him. When they subsided he triggered the horn back on.

'Allow me to introduce myself, people. My name is Clark. Clark Clark. Clark *B* Clark. Now dig: I don't care if you forget my first name, I don't care if you forget my last name—but that *middle initial* is something I can get pretty sensitive about. So here's a little memory trick I find helps folks to remember. Repeat after me, Clark-as-in-Kent—'

They repeated this tentatively.

'—B-as-in-bullshit—'

This they echoed with more enthusiasm.

'—then Clark-as-in-the-first-name. Clark B Clark. I think my mother had a speech impediment after her labor. Not me, though. I am the Mouth from the South and the official speech man for Foxcorp, and first off I want to take the proper-tune-ditty to *thank* you one and all, citizens of Kuinak, from the bottom of our corporate heart for the warm welcome your wonderful community has afforded us. B-as-in . . . ? You got it. Come closer, come closer. It's also my joyous task to welcome you to the *Silver Fox,* folks, because, and I'm shooting straight here, *you* got something *we want.* What is that, may you ask? You may. And I'll tell you. You got what is called in the biz a location, a *spectacular* location with scenery *still* un*trammeled*—everything south of here has been just about trammeled to shit, if you haven't noticed—but your sky is still clear and your air still sweet . . . if one overlooks the smell of fish guts . . . and *we* got something *you* want. Namely, *big bucks*, folks, let's tell it like it is—big *bucks*, hot *deals* and high *times.* All you have to do is let us use your location. Clean deal or what? So think it over. And while you're thinking, folks,' he unsnapped the braided rope with a flourish, 'come on aboard, let's party down and get acquainted. I would like to say *all of you* come on board, but I can't. Because Big Joe here has orders to let

111

no-one pass without a pass, and being unable to speak Giant, I cannot tell him otherwise. But I can tell you *this* . . .' He darted a look both ways, then whispered into the horn, '. . . the big goon never *takes* the card, dig? All you have to do is wait until someone comes back *off* with *his* card, and—' He winked conspiratorially, 'who's to know? Certainly not Big Joe. We all look alike to Big Joe: short. So trust me, people; if everybody will be a little bit patient, everybody will get a turn on board and we won't get sunk like we almost did once in Brazil. On the Upper Amazon, it was. Okay, Clark B-as-in-bullshit, that's enough, shut your hole. It's time for a little moo-zak and moo-zam. Bring 'em on. The Cherry Flaming Tarts! Do it, darlings. . .'

The girls swept on deck with wireless guitars and chin mikes, screeching 'North to Alaska' in a throat-ripping falsetto, shrill beyond belief. The guests thronging up the gang had to battle their way straight into a gale of amplified sound. All other sound was obliterated. Those in the parking lot with fender boomers folded them up and put them away.

By the time Ike and Greer arrived an hour later, the main deck of the big craft was jammed to the rails and spilt champagne was running from the gunwales. The Cherry Tarts had climbed to the top of the flying bridge and were screeching their hit 'Parsley, Sage, Rosemary and Newsweek' with a raunchy backbeat and lots of body drum. It was still bright day, but the ship's spotlights had been turned on and trained on the magnesium sail. It looked more like a blade than ever, and the long black shadow of it fell all the way across the crowded parking lot to the Heftyvan.

'Don't pull down into that mess, mon,' Greer told Ike. 'We'd never get out if shit gets sticky. Park here, the walk'll do us good.'

The last two nights had taken a lot of wind out of Greer's sails. His face was puffy and his eyes looked glazed, even after spranquing himself unconscious for eighteen hours. He had borrowed Ike's binoculars and nervously kept adjusting and readjusting them to his eyes as they drove, as though looking out for ambushes.

Ike stopped the van along Front Street at the bottom of Cook and got out. Greer hesitated, scowling through the windshield with the little glasses. He was trying to spot Billy Bellisarius' fire-stripe Mustang in the lot, still hoping relief would show up and take the heavy mantle of responsibility from his narrow shoulders so he could enjoy the party. But there was no sign of the Squid ragtop. He was gratified, however, to spot the Cherry Tarts on the bridge roof, jumping and bumping and screeching. When he saw for himself the evidence that red was indeed their natural hair color it gave him courage. 'Mmm, thank you, Lawd. I needed that.'

'See anything you recognize?' Ike asked.

'The Cherry Tarts, man; I recognize *them*. Whoa. I also see about a thousand drunk Underdogs.'

'We don't have to do this,' Ike suggested.

'Ah, but we do, my man. We must.' Greer sighed, unfolding down from the van. The stress was transporting him into a kind of philosophic calm. '*Très amusée*, eez it not? One's wildest party dream, or is it *ze night*mare? Shall we?'

As they were getting out of the van Omar Loop stepped from the door of his bowling alley across the street. The ruby bowling ball hung at his side like a battle mace. Backlit by the neons, the humped form reminded Ike of one of those hogs coming out of the embers.

'You'll see, Sallas,' Loop called across the street. 'He's come home for his getbacks, like cholera with a grudge. You shoulda helped me break his neck, not stopped me. You'll see . . .'

Ike didn't answer. Greer called something back but it was lost in the skirl of amplified music blowing across the tarmac.

They strolled through the lot, stopping at tailgates for a word or a handshake. Lots of mellow kidding. Not a thing about invitations. Everyone was in too festive a mood to feel envious, even if they didn't have a pass

113

to the festivities. Ike followed Greer up the gang and the giant waved both men through the gate without a glance at their cards. They were still blinking about in the glare and the blare when Wayne Altenhoffen scurried across the deck to them. His eyes were glittering.

'Some blow, huh, Brothers? High-tech and I do mean very. And the goodies! Mmm! You want? If you do, you see that cute little cabin boy?' Altenhoffen fluttered his ragged notebook at a young Asian with cerise hair in a samurai knot. The boy was carrying a steelume case held flat in front of him like a serving tray. It was arranged with filled champagne glasses to one side, saki and cups on the other, and an elaborate cloisonné teapot steaming between.

'One side makes you larger,' Wayne Altenhoffen sang, 'and one side makes you smile. He even claims they've got original Purple Haze in the private reserve below deck. The poor brain shudders.'

'Better take in some sail, Poor Brain,' Ike warned. 'Greer still hasn't recovered from that private party they gave him Friday.'

Poor Brain paid no heed. 'Look!' He pointed at another man with a notepad, coming up the ramp. 'There's Mr Clip What's-His-Face, the entertainment editor for the *Anchorage Sun*. Oh, boy! He must be fucking green, such a big bash outside his bailiwick. I'll go bug him—no, wait.' He stopped, frowning to recall the reason he had accosted the pair in the first place. 'Oh, right. I was supposed to tell you that Nicholas Levertov has been asking after you. One flight up, opposite end from the barbecue pit. Russian caviar and Nordic tits. Enjoy.'

'Nicholas Levertov will have to wait a while longer,' Greer said after Altenhoffen and his notepad had fluttered away. 'I need a pick-me-up.'

They pushed through the throng to the cerise samurai with the steelume tray. 'I'll have some from Mother,' Greer said, nodding at the cloisonné teapot. The boy made a brief bow and waited. Greer realized he was supposed to fill his own cup. 'Ike?' he asked. 'Spot of?'

Sallas shook his head and took a bottle of Corona from the ice in the bar sink. They sipped their way through the crowd, nodding and smiling at acquaintances. The music was too loud for conversation. The Tarts themselves might have been way up on the top of the bridge, strumming and screaming, but their amps were located in the lower decks. It was this din that finally drove Ike and Greer up the teak steps to the party above.

This was the first time Ike had any idea of just how big the yacht really was. Before the mast was the domed roof of a flying bridge, now a stage for the singing Tarts. The sail was unbelievable. It telescoped up in eight stream-lined sections of magnesium, polished like pewter. The second section from the top was painted with the Foxcorp emblem: a silver fox head in a black circle ten or twelve feet in diameter, glistening high in the spotlights. It had to be the tallest mast in the history of the sea.

'I wonder how they paint the damn thing,' Greer wondered, having done a bit of high-mast painting.

'They lower it.' Ike pointed. 'See the segments? It must telescope down inside itself like a car aerial. Those pontoons along each side of the hull must do the same, like retractable outriggers.'

On the seaward side of the metal sail a barbecue pit was ablaze, a long line of people waiting with plastic plates; on the other side, out of the sun's low glare, a half-court basketball game was in full swing. A team of Underdog Deaps was battling a team of Underdog Round-Eyes. The hoop was mounted at standard height in the middle of the bottom section. The sail's base was big as the end of a basketball court. There was no keyhole and the free-throw line was a painted semi-circle; this was because the vessel's computer continued to automatically feather the big blade into the wind, thus the basket and the backboard—the whole hoop-end of the half-court, in fact—pivoted smoothly back and forth.

A voice yodeled from the afterdeck behind them. 'Yoo-hoo, odd couple.' It was Clark B Clark, waving from

115

beneath the billowing canopy of a tie-dyed parachute. The chute was lashed between guy wires running from the raised poop to a pair of booms forward. Rainbows of silk swelled and sank in the easy breezes. A traditional spoked captain's wheel and compass binnacle stood on a raised cockpit, varnished and shining. Both wheel and binnacle looked like priceless antiques. A crowd of revelers lounged on pillows and life jackets piled around the cockpit.

'Come on back, gentlemen. Nick wants to introduce you around.'

Nicholas Levertov was propped up in a pile of puffy orange life jackets with a bunch of girls and one big black Labrador. The Lab looked to Ike like Louise Loop's dog, Nerd, except the dog seemed to belong to the girl nestled nearest to Nick—a breasty brunette in a one-piece see-through pajama-thing. The dog kept nudging her with a wet nerf ball.

Only a few other males were present—some fishermen, and Chad Evert, the Honda dealer, and Norman Wong; Norm was trying to keep as far from the giant-that-was-taller-than-Norman as he was able to get. The other dozen or so were female. One of these, Ike realized, was Alice. As Nicholas' mother, she stood on the raised cockpit above the lounging harem pile, dressed even more ethnic than the other day. For this occasion she had put on her grandmother's old ceremonial blanket robe, red with black wool appliqués in bird shapes, and big mother-of-pearl buttons following the designs. It was a nice robe, but to top off the outfit Alice had added, in her defiant fashion, a leopard-skin pillbox hat. Hovering at Nicholas' shoulder, she looked to Ike like the queen dowager of some pampered Third-and-a-Half World potentate. After they had said hello, Nick made other introductions.

'Isaak, I'd like you to meet Tatiana.' The white hand fluttered, the way it did with the cards. 'And this is Ingrid—Mr Greer has already whiled away a few idle hours with Ingrid, as I recall—and this is Gretchen. Suffice it to say you have come to the *strudel* section of the

116

ship, Slamboy; if you prefer sushi you'll have to go below decks.'

The girls shook hands and smiled husky hellos—as uninformative as Greer had claimed they were.

'You both of course know my mother, Mrs Carmody, and—oh my, yes—and *this* generous helping of devil's food—' he pointed with a long white toe at the brunette in the see-through '—is Mrs Louise Levertov, in case you perchance overlooked the new her.'

'Mrs Louise *Loop* Levertov,' Lulu corrected, arching back to give Isaak a good look at the new her.

'I knew I recognized that black Lab,' Ike told her.

'Lookin' good, Lulu,' Greer nodded.

'Feelin' good, Emil. How about you, Ike? Feeling good yet? Maybe you don't know this about your old Slamboy, Nicky, but Isaak Sallas doesn't like to get feeling too good too fast. I believe he thinks it's bad for his reputation.'

'I remember that from the time we did time together, Louise. Here, dog; give me that!' Without warning Levertov snatched the soggy ball from the Lab's wet muzzle and flung it over the seaward rail. The dog sailed right over after it, a good thirty feet down to the water. Greer rushed to the rail in time to see the dog splash out of sight below.

'He's all right,' Norman Wong said glumly. 'This is about the sixth time they've done it. He swims around the fantail with the ball and my brother Lloyd helps him on board. Maybe seven.'

'Takes him for*ever* to find his way back up here,' Lulu giggled. 'Gives us all a break.'

Nick had completely dismissed the dog. He was peering down the deck forward. 'Oh, good. Here comes the photog. Mother . . . Louise . . . Tatiana—cuddle in close.'

A man came struggling up the stairway amidships, carrying a huge old-fashioned eight-by-eleven plate camera on a tripod.

'Isaak, this is supposed to be a family portrait,' Nicholas smiled, 'but you and your friend are welcome to cuddle in. Both of you have earned a place, in my estimation. . .'

'I'll Pasadena, thanks,' Greer said, hopping out of the photographer's way.

'Me too, Nick. It'll be a better portrait with just you and your harem and your queen.' Ike shot a look at Alice. 'And of course the *royal mother*.' He saw her neck stiffen, but she didn't answer back.

Ike and Greer waited to the side with the other men, sipping their drinks. Norman Wong edged close, his big forlorn face lowered. 'We heard from the Squid.'

'You *did*?' Greer grabbed the other man's arm. 'Where is he? What happened? Why isn't the boy genius here taking care of business? I be *weary* of these burdens of state . . .'

'He's in the Skagway Clinic. Got in a argument and kind of got laid up. A busted tailbone, he said. And he says they won't check him out unless somebody goes down there to take responsibility. He wants a couple of members to fly down.'

'Down to *Skagway*?' Ike laughed. 'He's crazy. Somebody must've busted more than his butt.'

'*We'll go*,' Greer volunteered. 'Ike'll rent a plane and we'll go in the morning. Absolutely.'

'That's what he was hoping,' Norman said. 'You and Ike.'

'Wait a minute,' Ike said.

'He's our Dog Brother, *mon ami*. Our *president*! Remember: "Bros in the bone, never alone."'

'Who beat him up, Norm?'

'Remember that ex-Bear linebacker that saved Greer's ex-wife from the fires of Hell? Thump Greener?'

'Bible-thumper Greener!' Greer remembered with a look of horror. 'Six-two, two-ninety, all-Asshole black Mormon. God's own turd!'

'That's him. I guess he married your ex.'

'He already had a wife,' Greer recalled. 'How does he get away with another one?'

'Another five,' Norman Wong corrected. 'Billy said Greener claims to have special dispensation from Heaven about a lot of stuff.'

Greer was impressed. 'Five? Mmm! How do one *get* one these special dispensations?'

'I remember Greener,' Isaak nodded. 'He came soul-saving after me during one of our Gold Rush Day parades down in Skagway. God's own turd is right. I wouldn't think he and Bellisarius would be running in the same circles.'

'The Squid's got a little girlfriend runs a burger stand in Skagway. He says he had just dropped by for a quarter-pounder and a little skin talk when Greener showed up. I guess Greener had been working to add her to his collection of Soulmates Saved from Hell. Billy objected and I guess Greener broke his tailbone.'

'*Zut alors.*' Greer shook his head. 'What a mortification for the poor Squid.'

'Worse than you think. He took all Billy's fireworks and threw them in the Skagway River. Billy said the big turd would have thrown in his mulecase, too, but it's shackled to Billy's wrist.'

'Exploding shackle too, I bet.'

'No fireworks, no *scoot*?' Greer turned loose Norman's arm for Ike's. 'This is more than a fraternal affair, Isaak. This is a regional emergency.'

Norman nodded solemnly. 'Billy said if you two couldn't make it he wanted me and my brother Irwin to come get him. We can't. Tuesday is the folks' fiftieth wedding anniversary; Wongs are gathering from as far away as San Francisco.'

'Alice wants us on hand tomorrow.' Ike tried to free his arm. He was beginning to feel hemmed in again. 'In case Carmody gets back . . .'

'Carmody won't be back for days, Isaak,' the big man said. 'He's off goofing. Look out. Here comes that poor damn dog . . .'

The black Lab came straggling up with the sponge ball. His head hung and his tail was tucked between his legs as though he were ashamed at the long time it had taken him to return. He was shivering so hard that he could not shake himself dry. Nicholas looked at

119

the dripping animal and decided that the photography session was finished. 'It's a wrap, chaps. I don't think we need any drowned hounds in our family portrait. Photog? Go away. Isaak? Folks? Come on back over. The photo-op is finished and the drinking lamp is re-lit.'

Ike was relieved. He broke away from Norman and Greer and headed for the bar. 'I need a gin-and-tonic, Alice, if you would? I think I feel a touch of the malaria.'

His relief was short-lived. He'd barely taken a sip from the big tumbler Alice had prepared when Clark B Clark came ducking up the teak hatch aft of the raised poop. He bustled across to Nicholas Levertov. Pointing at Ike, the man whispered an urgent message in Levertov's ear. As he whispered, the albino's bruised lips spread in a wide grin. He turned the grin on Ike.

'My, my, Slam. The great Gerhardt Steubins requests the honor of your company in the big conference room below. Just follow Clark B here. You better take your drink. Face to face with greatness can give one the dry mouth. *Mean*while—' He suddenly grabbed the dripping sponge ball from the Lab's muzzle and sailed it once more over the railing. 'We will carry on.'

The big black dog sailed after the ball.

Ike followed Clark B's crewcut down the polished teak stairwell, scowling. He wasn't sure why he responded to the summons from Steubins so obediently. He couldn't care less about legends. And he certainly entertained no desire to be part of the upcoming filming. He knew there was nothing down in the belly of this mechanical whale that he wanted, nor anything that was likely to do him—or anyone else—any good. Curiosity, perhaps that's what it was.

A porcelain passageway led between a series of small rooms with doors ajar. For ventilation or for effect? A visitor could not help but be impressed by gleaming arrays of equipment. They could have been comrooms outfitted by NASA or the US Navy. One room held an actual three-screen flatbed Keller Editing Machine for 70mm film with computerized video interlock. Another displayed a miniaturized laboratory with ranks of tiny, toy-like bottles and piping and beakers. No wonder those caterers could offer such a collection of goodies.

Clark B stepped to the wall to let Ike pass. 'Yonder,' he beamed. The door at the end of the passageway parted noiselessly in the center, revealing a crowded room. It was the grand salon. Once, while waiting for a root canal in Monterey, Ike had come across a twenty-five-year-old copy of *Fortune* magazine. The main story and center spread was a pictorial essay on Saudi businessman Adnan Khashoggi's 280-foot yacht, *Nablia*. Photos documented the sleek lushness of the vessel's opulent interiors, pointing out king-sized waterbeds beneath mirrored ceilings, with bedside control panels to adjust mood lighting and television replay. The magazine had a centerfold of the Nablia's main salon, furnished with suede-covered ottomans and draped with Thai wall hangings. The effect was of some grand pasha's tent prepared for a meeting of all the desert's mightiest sheiks. Photos showed tables of lapis lazuli heaped with platters of figs and pomegranates; hookahs and samovars smoking; a golden sphinx spouting champagne into a marble bowl between its paws. He recalled the title of the article about Khashoggi's yacht: 'Never Again Such Floating Grandeur.'

The writer clearly had never anticipated the. *Silver Fox*.

Bulkheads and ceiling were constructed of the new glowloy paneling, making the long room look as though it were carved in the interior of a glacier. A milk-blue fluorescent light illuminated all the crannies and corners. The furniture seemed to float above the carpeting, like orbiting leather satellites. Even the room's occupants looked levitated in the unearthly glow, standing or strolling on air, like a collection of ill-at-ease ghosts.

Ike recognized a selection of the town's leading citizens. There was Father Pribilof, the requisite relic. Bank manager Jack McDermitt and Mayor Saul Beeson of the Bering Hotel were puffing on ludicrously long cigars and sipping brandy as they listened patiently to high school principal Jorgensen's explanations of the working of an antique brass astrolabe displayed on a sideboy. The two oldest Wong brothers were wedged ham-to-ham on an elegant English settee, paralyzed with concern for the tiny brandy snifters in their big pink paws. Opposite them, cross-legged on real Babi pillows, their elderly parents were drinking what was probably real Chinese tea from real China teacups. Police Chief Gilstrap was teasing his father-in-law, the Reverend Winesap, with a medieval chastity belt he'd discovered in the collection of rare weapons.

Tommy Toogiak Senior was hunkered on his heels to one side, his eyes unfocused, his back against the bulkhead. As board president and major shareholder of Searaven, his presence represented hundreds of Deaps, as well as the local FM station. The station, KDEAP, boasted five call letters instead of four and regularly interrupted network shows to air local bingo winners or Yupic talk shows intended to thwart the rise of Deap suicides. The FCC never pursued the infractions. 'It is, after all,' the FCC once explained, 'their air.'

Tommy Toogiak Senior also held one of the long cigars and a snifter of brandy. It seemed to be the standard issue of the eve. Before Ike could decline he had been issued his own imported panatela and crystal snifter. He lit the smoke and waited, looking around. This selection of citizens had been summoned with obvious consideration to be honored with some kind of announcement important to the community. But why was he here? What did this Steubins want with him? While he was pondering this Clark B Clark walked over, beaming and loquacious, and took a seat alongside. Ike was elaborately informed that ol' Clark B used to be something of a Bakatcha Bandit himself:

'Yeah, keep it under your hat, but ol' Clark B was *expelled* from San Jose State for dynamiting the outlet of their greywater shunt that *I* found out was running directly into the bay. Best thing ever happened to me;

Lucas heard about it and awarded me a scholarship to USC. I majored in film-flam. Well, nice talking to you, but—' Clark B patted Ike's knee and stood back up. 'I think this briefing's about ready to roll. I better go jump-start the cap-a-*tin*.'

The man glided away through the chatting clots of townspeople like an eel through kelp, then disappeared into a thin door at the narrow rear of the salon. Ike sipped at his brandy, feeling more and more puzzled. Those invitations, for instance; it must have taken quite some time to come up with these select names and get them engraved. Coming to Kuinak hadn't been some snap, from-the-hip decision.

Clark B Clark reemerged from the narrow door. A gaunt figure could be seen standing in the passageway behind him, head lowered in what appeared to be momentous thought.

'Gentlemen and—' Clark's solicitous gaze sliced back and forth until he located Mrs Wong. '—and lady . . . if I may say at the outset, in all sincerity, that all of us aboard the *Fox* are profoundly grateful for your kind patience, not to mention indulgence—responding to our spur-of-the-moment—ah, let's see—how shall I call it?—'

'How about callin' it quits—'

The drawl was so countrified, so rednecked raw, that people thought at first it had come from one of the locals.

'—and gettin' outta the way.'

Clark B Clark sidestepped a few inches, genuflecting. 'Gentlemen and lady, may I present our commander-in-chief, Gerhardt Luther Steubins, recipient of four Oscars, five honorary doctorates, six paternity suits—'

'Let me pass, you damn puppy, I'll paternity *you* . . .'

Clark B Clark hopped away from the door. 'Folks, the great Gerhardt Steubins!' A very old man with pewter-grey hair and black eye patch stepped into the room's silent gape. If Ike had hoped to find some sinister foreign mastermind at the center of this glitzy web, he was vastly disappointed; this mastermind had a drawl from the Ozarks and a grin like what was left of a baked Virginia ham. The internationally famous Gerhardt Luther Steubins was a big, bony, turkey-necked shambler from the All-American South. Ike imagined that in his prime he had probably carried another couple dozen pounds of working muscle on that gnawed frame, but the old man still looked amazingly fit. The tan arms were still cabled and the gnarly hands looked like they'd seen a lot of rough use.

Steubins drew a breath and exhaled, a long, private sound humming from deep in his ribcage as his solitary eye appraised the room. Finally he raised a big cut-glass tumbler of amber whiskey and drank to his guests, the eye still open. He was still drinking when the salon door opened and Nicholas Levertov entered at the other end of the room. Levertov was flanked by a chunky man wearing the dress whites of a naval officer and the dark sensuous simper of a minor Hindu deity. Steubins' smile got broader at the sight.

'Almost forgot all about you, Snowball.'

'Mustn't do that, Captain Steubins.'

'Oh, I shan't, Mr Levertov. Nor Mr Singh there, neither.' He raised his tumbler and spoke to the room. 'People, some of you probably already met Nick Levertov. This invasion on you is all mainly his fault. It was him convinced the bigwigs that his home-town of Kuinak had all the peculiar qualities required for the Shoola project. Ain't that right, Nick?'

'That's right,' Levertov nodded.

'That's right, Captain Steubins,' Clark B echoed happily from the other side of the room.

'And the dapper dude alongside him is the *Silver Fox*'s first mate, Mr Singh. Mr Singh's the dude really *runs* this seagoing Radio Shack; I just drive it.'

Mr Singh didn't even nod acknowledgment. Ike began to get the feeling that this might not be what one could call a happy ship.

'Anyhow, very peculiar qualities, as I was saying. That's why we decided to take the bull by the balls and lay our cards on the table.'

'Right. By the balls,' Clark echoed.

First Mate Singh found a seat but Levertov remained standing. He nodded at Steubins to continue.

'Right. And I guess the best way to start is to let you folks know what's in the pot. What's the real marbles. Somebody want to hazard a ballpark guess first? Anybody?'

The blue eye raked the room. It was Mayor Beeson that finally hazarded. 'Well, I got some previous input, folks,' he grinned. 'Last fall in me 'n' Mr Clark—CB's—initial talk, there was talk of a budget somewhere in the area of ninety million? Now I call those real marbles.'

'That's just the ante,' Steubins said. 'Just openers. Mayor, if the cards are decent to us, even *halfway* decent—we're talking a pot of ten times that.'

'That's right, ten times, and that's *liquid* assets,' chirped Clark. 'Flowing into Kuinak like a tidal wave.'

'A *green* tidal wave, people. Because here's the pitch, plain and simple: the real ante.' The old man glanced at Levertov, then continued. 'We want to make this town *partners*, partners with us in this venture. Shareholders! We ship together, share and share alike. Or sink together. Because we want it *crystal clear* on this, folks, that we ain't here to rip you off; we're here to make you rich, or the whole lot of us bust. So, Burrhead—? Let's show them the maps.'

Clark B Clark hopped back past Steubins and from the passageway wheeled forth a draped display easel. He rolled it into position at the head of the long oval table. It was suddenly clear that this was the point in the meeting when all the future shareholders were to find their seats. Ike located a place as far back as he could on the long oval table. There was a little memo pad with pen attached, an ashtray and a coaster—all playing card-shaped, like the invitations, with the *Silver Fox* logo in the center. He put his gin-and-tonic on the coaster and swiveled his chair forward.

'Anybody want to freshen up just raise your hand,' Clark B told them, waving for a boy with a rolling bar.

'Gerhardt here likes his listeners to be as comfortable as he can get 'em.'

All the Searaven clan took a refill, and the Wongs. Their parents continued to nurse their tiny cups of tea, like effete hummingbirds. When the boy with the bar reached Ike he covered his tumbler and shook his head. He heard a muffled clatter of buttons beside him, and a whisper.

'That one of mine was double enough, eh?' Alice had eased into the chair next to his. She must have slipped into the salon unnoticed in her son's flamboyant wake.

Clark B hustled around, getting the rest of the Deaps into seats and divans. Steubins waited patiently at the head, hands behind his back, deck shoes planted firmly apart as though braced against an unexpected wave. Nicholas had worked his way around behind him and lounged on an elbow on one of the round settees. His white overcoat was spread beneath him like a fur.

'Okey-dokey,' Steubins drawled at last, then whipped the drape from the big display easel. The display was a detailed cartoon hologram of Kuinak and its environs. Everything was there in caricatured 3-D, brighter than life—the glacier, the bay and docks; all the stores and streets with their quirks and corners rendered humorously but accurately. The map covered everything from Carmody's place way on the far side of the bay to the dump and the pigs and the water tower in the foothills. Ike even located his trailerhouse; it had a cartoon dog sleeping in the yard.

'Some piece of work, huh, Sallas?' Alice whispered. 'Even you got to be impressed . . .'

The five-foot-wide hologram accurately depicted every feature of the area—geographical, social, mythical. The south jetty had a grinning channel marker, for example, but in its proper place. The light on Hopeless was on the rock's eastern face, exactly as it actually stood, except a little cartoon lighthouse keeper had his head out the top window of the tower and he was holding a hurricane lamp. The little glacier swooped up from the bay at the proper location, though it had a cartoon brown bear

126

skiing down the swoop, wearing ski goggles and a flowing red scarf. The distant Pyrite peaks were guarded by a cartoon Dall ram and his herd. Puffy cartoon clouds with big blue eyes floated in the clear blue sky.

'Okay, so *now*,' Steubins drawled when people had gawked long enough, 'you see your noble village as it stands today. Any questions?' Ike's mouth suddenly did feel dry, just as Nick had predicted. Nobody had any questions.

'Good, good,' Steubins continued. 'Now,' he gestured at the map, his eyes twinkling with a merry, boyish innocence, 'here's how you might look *next* week if you all go for the deal. Burrhead?'

Clark B leapt to the map and pulled a new hologram sheet down from a roller. It was a transparent overlay of the first map, with changes and additions in the same cartoon motif. Now the establishments were spiffier. A rugged cliff had replaced the rundown cannery. And near the glacier's base stood a beautiful Northwest Indian longhouse with lofty totem poles on each side. The front of the house was a great stylized raven's face, the top of his head in the roof beam. In his beak hung a goggle-eyed frog with frog legs aspraddle. The door into the house was through the frog's oval crotch.

'Tribal sign of the Sea Cliff Clan,' Alice whispered to Ike. 'Never existed. Total fantasy. The Frogbird longhouse only existed in the Shoola tales.'

Steubins overheard and turned to the whisper. He focused his blue eye. 'You're Nick's mama, am I right?' he asked for all to hear.

'That's right. Mrs Michael Carmody.'

'Mrs Carmody, I *thought* so,' he chuckled. 'I heard you was bright, beautiful and outspoken, so who else could it be? And of course you are absolutely correct, ma'am. Total fiction. Fantasy. But right there is exactly why we all love Shoola and her world. Because it's a world that *don't* exist, and *never* did, only in those books by Isabella Anootka, born Rachel Ruth Ostsind, incidentally, from New Jersey. Total make-believe. But tell me. Which place is more real in you folks' mind: the Emerald City of Oz, or New Jersey?' He raised the eye to the rest of the room. 'That's why we know we got a hit combo here, folks. That old make-believe story and your new make-believe town. You know what the temperature was in New York yesterday? One-twelve. It never dropped below a hundred until just before dawn. Read the paper. No offense, but you guys have got a grubby little paradise here and don't have a mother clue. We'd like to show that paradise to the rest of the poor panting populace, first a full-screen, then a worldwide dish special. And we've got international interest in a Shoola series. *Big* interest out there. So. Any interest so far?'

Nobody so much as nodded, so mesmerized were they by the old man's deep voice and rich promises.

'Okay, then. Here's how we'd like to get it rolling. We're gonna need spaces—production offices, crew quarters, warehouses for interior setups, mess halls for the crew, crap like that. I mean, you can't *imagine* the crew a venture like this takes. The contracts . . . the goddamned Teamsters have it in their contract now, for instance, that a weight room and a sauna must be provided or no show. Renting space like this runs into big bucks real quick. Take my word.'

'Take his word, folks,' Clark B nodded emphatically. 'Dear old Ger went so far over bucks in his last fiasco that the creditors swamped us before we made it to the theaters. A disaster! The whole studio would have gone under but for a bailout from our Asian shareholder friends.'

Three men in dark blue double-breasteds bowed back at Clark B's grateful grin. It was the trio from the UTO.

'So . . . what we propose *this* time,' Steubins continued, 'is a kind of partnership. To put it dirt simple, as my grandpa used to say: you folks can either rent for cash or you can lease for points. You all can become shareholders yourselves. Our people will lay it out for each of you at your private convenience. Some of you

128

we've already spoken with. Beeson's gone for it with his hotel. Toogiak and the Searaven people have told us to count them in with the Searaven Inn.' He took a slip of paper from his pocket and looked at it. 'Herb Tom says his rental business is up for it. Lotsa others. But listen: nobody has to make any decisions tonight. Circulate. Talk it over. You'll find Foxcorp very accommodating, whichever way you choose to go.'

The room didn't move. The muted thump of the Cherry Tarts' amplifiers could be heard through air conditioning vents. Steubins finally swung the blue eye to the settee where Levertov was reclined. 'Anything else?'

'Not tonight, Captain Steubins,' the man purred pleasantly. 'You did first-rate.' Levertov rolled to his feet in a fluid motion. 'Did he not, folks? How about a hand for one of the twentieth century's greatest directors, Gerhardt Steubins.'

Applause followed the bony back as the old man returned to his room and shut the door.

Alice cast a glance at her wristwatch. 'Well, at least they seem clear about what they want, don't they?'

'Except for what they want with yours truly,' Ike answered. 'I don't own any motels or car rentals—what do they want with me?'

Before Alice could answer a call came from the other end of the salon. 'Ahoy! Isaak Sallas.' Clark B Clark was waving an exuberant hand. 'Mr Steubins would like to say howdy if you've got a sec.'

The captain's quarters were as nautically old-fashioned as the rest of the yacht was modern. Hanging lamps lit oak and brass and leather. Framed pictures of historic ships lined the port and starboard bulkheads, and a warm carpet covered the floor. There was an orderly display of map cases beneath a navigator's table. A brass telescope stood on a tripod beside a sea chest with ivory inlay. In the room's center beneath a stained glass lamp was a poker table, cards and chips stacked and waiting.

Steubins was mixing a drink at a walnut sideboard. He turned with a broad smile when Ike entered.

'Isaak Sallas! Come in, shut the door.' The old man crossed the room in a rolling walk and thrust out a big hand. 'Son, it's an honor and that's the truth. You've been one of the only bona fried heroes I ever had. I've been pestered two-thirds of my life by fans and it's nice to have the opportunity to do some pestering back. Glad to finally meet you.'

Ike could only mumble and nod. The palm in his was calloused harder than anyone could have expected, especially in this automated luxury. It had hauled some rough ropes, through some long rough times.

'I been a fan since that first strafing run you made over the—was it the State Fair in Sacramento?'

'Madera. The County Fair.' Ike felt himself blushing like a kid. 'I didn't do the State Fair till a couple of times later.'

'Whichever it was, it got a lot of us in trouble, you ornery bastard. I blew a very lucrative KFC endorsement. I was so pumped when I heard it on the news I went right down to the studio and threw a bucketful of giblets and gravy all over this asshole child-prodigy director. Kicked my ass clear off the account; it was months before my agent could get me another contract.'

'Sorry about that,' Ike told the man. 'A lot of guys got kicked off their jobs because of me, according to the DA.'

'Sorry?' The old man clapped the big hand on Isaak's shoulder. 'Good God, don't be sorry. Not for us old cobs, anyway. Probably the only righteous kick a lot of us old sleeping dogs ever got. You were our hero—still are—and *every*body needs a hero. If you got to be sorry for somebody, be sorry for yourself, I always say. It's more satisfying. Anyhow, it's a honor to come up here and meet you, boy. Can I give you a slosh of the Four-Star? Real *Hennessy*? A Havana?'

Ike thanked him but said he had friends waiting on deck.

'Fair enough. But do let me give you this, son; a little advice, just between you, me and that bulkhead yonder:

130

steer clear of this shareholder deal . . . unless you want your *holder* sheared, as they say in the trade.'

'I thought you said it was the best deal we were ever likely to get.'

The old man flipped up the black patch so both eyes could twinkle with boyish merry innocence. 'A gig's a gig, son. This is show biz. Another thing, watch out for your slam buddy. He's got a *thing* about you, and he's not known as the Great White of Westwood for nothing. But not a squeak, you hear? I'll deny I said Jimmy Jack Shit. I can lie like a sailor if I have to. You play poker? Simple American stud, one-buck ante, three-raise limit?'

'Played plenty in jail, but that was a *one-smoke* ante.'

'Pot's not important in good poker. Players are what's important. *Personalities*. You must know some doozers roundabouts?'

Ike smiled. 'My boss Carmody would rather play poker than eat . . . and he *loves* to eat. And my partner claims he used to deal professionally in Port-au-Prince.'

'Just my meat. You boys name the night.'

'I may be out of town a few days.'

'When you get back, then. Any night. I'm eager to see how this famous bandit can stand up to a stiff bluff.'

The black patch flipped back down, like a door closing.

Back outside, Ike managed to avoid meeting any other eyes all the way through the salon and back topside. He didn't see Greer but he located Alice back at her bartending post by the binnacle.

'I'm ready for another double, Alice. And if it's all the same to you, I'm going to take tomorrow off.'

'Oh yeah? Why . . . ?'

'Greer needs me to fly him to Skagway.'

'Emil can't fly alone?'

'We need to rescue an injured friend.'

When he didn't elaborate Alice shrugged. 'If Carmody doesn't show, sure, why not. Maybe you can locate the old pirate and rescue him in the bargain. Kill two birds with one heroic flight.'

Ike let the dig slide. But she was lucky she didn't ask what he and Steubins had talked about. He wasn't sure he could have respected the old man's request for discretion, especially about Levertov. And what mother needs to hear her son called a shark?

8

Keep Flying Speed
Jook 'Em Blindside

Ike was up at dawn, securing the boats and gear. When it was ten AM and there was still no word or sign of the wandering Michael Carmody or his new boat, Ike drove back up to the trailerhouse to awaken Greer. It was hard for him to say just why he was making this rescue run. He had little interest in some flying mission to rescue Billy the Squid. Not that the little hustler didn't have his points. Billy was every bit the genius he cracked himself up to be. Ike had seen him win bets by doing lengthy square roots in his head faster than the challenger could key the problem into a wrist calculator. He had heard him in argument with a touring professor of virtual hydraulics from Woods Hole, punching holes in the professor's theories until the poor man went into what Billy later referred to as Acute Unearned Tenure Shock. Billy Bellisarius could talk the talk. The drag was he could talk it too much, in a voice like a sulky hornet.

On the other hand it was an excuse to get out of town, coming at a time when, for the first time in years, Isaak Sallas found himself wanting to get out of town.

Greer was hard to wake. The teapot was dry and Greer was getting the scoot zees. The most serious charge yet made to stand against the prolonged use of scoot was that you needed a lot of sleep during the first week of your scoot withdrawal, needing the dreaming more than the sleep, it seemed. You could sleep on scoot, but you got no REMs. No clearance for dreams to come in. It was as though the dreams were airplanes piled up waiting for the airfield to become unsocked, circling and circling and

piling higher and higher. When he was first out of jail and
the brew had just come on the streets, Ike would spend
days drinking it—not for the sustained rush of simple
energy it delivered, nor for the sweet dreamless rests,
but for the scoot withdrawal itself, for the dreams that
came crash-landing down during those first long sleeps
off the drug. Sometimes they were good clear dreams,
sometimes they were brain burners, but good dreams or
bad, clearheaded or tongue-gnashing crazy, the dreams
were at least your own. In jail, you dreamed everybody's
dreams.

'Get in the shower,' he told the swaying, naked Greer.
'I'll put Marley under the trailer.'

'Marley likes it *in* the trailer.'

'Marley shits in the trailer.'

'Something might come by and get him under the
trailer, mon. One of Loop's boar hogs might try to go
him hoggie style. Marley couldn't get away.'

'Okay, I'll leave the door open for him. He can even
invite the hog in. But let's go if we're going to do this.
Herb Tom is gassing us up right now.'

'What did we get?' Greer called from the shower stall.
'The Piper, I hope.'

'The movie bunch has the Piper rented, full time. And
all the other turbos. We got the Otter.'

'That old banger?' Greer was waking up. 'That'll take
mother *forever*!'

'You call Alice, tell her we waited and we went. And
ask her to come by and check on Marley.'

'*Me* ask her?' Greer came out of the shower, shaking
his dreadlocks like a poodle. 'I'm in no shape for that
action. Why not *you* ask her?'

'Because he's your dog and you're the one that's the
acting president of the Loyal Dogbrothers and you're the
one who wants to make this run. I'm just driving.'

Ike helped the big Border collie down the metal steps.
The old dog seemed to be moving a little better; maybe
that outing had helped. He let him wobble by himself to
the edge of the oyster shells for a shit. Water dribbled

around his paws as he squatted. Ike sighed. Yeah, he might be moving a little better, but he still was unable to lift a hind leg. Those days were over. When Marley came back grinning, wagging his tail, Ike rubbed his ears and let the filming brown eyes stare into his.

'How's it hanging, Marl; what's the old dog report?'

The dog grinned a silly wolfish grin in answer. Ike put the dishpan full of dry food under the trailer and Marley followed it. Ike filled the big plastic bucket at the tap and poured a little on Greer's sad little bonsai hemp. Greer had raised marijuana in the days before genetic pollination, and loved it. Now, even though there was nothing left but the feeble little impotent males, he still tried to keep a little growing; for sentiment, not for smoke. The active ingredient had all but vanished, like the species.

Ike saw the dismantled .22 pistol in the window box and considered for a moment taking it along. He'd heard of some pretty rude stuff this Greener had pulled in the name of his Latter-Day God. But stats continued to reinforce the point that you were more likely to encounter violence when you were packing than when you weren't. Besides, there shouldn't be any reason to have to confront the Greener at all. They could check Bellisarius out of the clinic, stash him straight on board and fly the hell out of Dodge. He knew a bootleg pump where they could gas up first on the sly, and be ready immediately. If Billy the Squid wanted to settle any accounts he could by God do that on his own time, over the phone. By not having a gun along that point could be more easily made.

He filled the bucket again and lashed it to one of the trailer blocks, so the old animal couldn't knock it over. Then he pounded the trailer side, shouting, 'Off we go, Greer!' Greer came down the steps carrying a big Mexican bolsa. The shower had brightened him up. He shook his dreadlocks, singing in time to the spangles of water in the morning sunlight. 'Off we go . . . o . . . o . . . into the wild! blue! Won! Der . . .'

'*Wide* blue *yon* der,' Ike corrected as he clambered into the driver's seat of the van. 'Get in.'

'Hey, das right, mon. I sometimes forget you were also the big *war hero* pilot. "Fly-ing! into the sky . . ."'

Ike drove and let Greer sing. Sometimes he forgot, too. As much as he was able, in fact. But as they pulled into Herb Tom's RentsaLot, the look of the old Otter he had rented brought a jolt of it back. And when they were loaded into the vintage seaplane and roaring over the waves in a slow shuddering takeoff, he couldn't help but be reminded of his old Nightmoth—all those clandestine launchings in the offshore mists, all those heroic missions. Of course, the Moth didn't roar. She hardly hummed, with her big muffled prop and blimped engine. It was the slowness the two planes had in common. The Moth's top airspeed wasn't much greater than this old Otter's, but the speed at which she could remain aloft was far lower. That was the aircraft's great innovative advantage. A Moth could keep flying speed at six-and-one-half mph, about the pace of a fast-walking man. Once the Navy began to realize that the modern mission didn't need the traditional big bomber launched from the deck of a huge carrier, that smaller planes could be boom-yarded up out of the hold of a cargo ship and set down alongside for takeoff, swaddled in darkness and silence, with the black sea for the runway and infra scopes for their eyes, then the Nightmoth was the next logical step. It could hum in beneath the radar, put a timer on a precise target, and be humming home before the enemy below awoke. Or didn't wake, depending on the payload. Usually it was just pamphlets, or bogus currency. Ike had dropped many a queer million into various Central American states on covert destabilizing sorties for the CIA . . . as though *any* South American state ever needed assistance destabilizing.

Nightmoths were difficult to detect and as hard to hit as bats. Even if one was spotted by ground-to-air sentries, the heat-seeking missiles found no jet trail to home in on. Anti-aircraft was useless because they flew beneath the ceiling of altitude shells. Rifles were the most dangerous, because the Moths were slow targets with a lot of unshielded fuel-tank exposure—easily punctured; but even when hit they rarely crashed. They could set down on a small river or a pond, or even a meadow as long as there was enough damp grass for the teflon to skid on. One of the squadron's follow pilots could easily pick up the downed comrade with a quick touchdown—a catch cradle was dropped between the pontoons for this purpose—and be back in the air before hostile ground forces arrived. Ike had scooped up three downed pilots this way, one from a narrow slough near Zaire, another from a sand dune outside Alexandria, and one crippled kid from the end zone of a football field in the center of Jerusalem. This kid had been a track star from the University of Missouri, and he was sprinting across the field in world-record time. A rip of lead up through his left heel ended that. He couldn't even stand for the catch cradle. Ike had to land between the hash marks, get out and carry the bleeding boy to his idling Moth, then take off from the fifty with assault slugs skipping viciously across the wet turf all around them. They cleared the goal posts just as the kid's downed plane self-destructed in a flash of green magnesium. Ike could see the enraged faces of running Israelis on his rear zoom monitor, and hear the machine-gun fire. He got the Navy Cross for that one but was never allowed to wear it in public or reveal specifics about the mission; the US was never officially at war with their old ally Israel.

Oddly enough Greer didn't have a bit of fear of flying, though statistics yearly made it clear that bush-hopping was far more dangerous than boating, especially in rural Alaska. Greer was so at ease with flying, in fact, that the moment the Otter was airborne he fell asleep without another word. Ike was glad; these old prop jobs were hard enough on the ears without having to strain to hear small talk.

After gaining altitude into the northeast wind, Ike banked around south at about a thousand feet, back over the town. He'd forgotten how much he enjoyed the world from this altitude: not so low as to need to be on alert, not so high as to lose the character of the place beneath. The

137

town looked like a big toy—toy houses and toy streets, toy pickups and boats and water towers—crisp and clean as pictures in a pop-up book from your childhood. Sharply familiar. Then he realized with a start that the town looked an awful lot like that cartoon map, was what it was! Duck Gutter with its little inland lake looked like a miniature golf hazard. The church and high school looked like mock-ups for a pageant. The tin-roofed Crabbe Potte, there, for instance, could be the set of one of the farnorth dish sitcoms—enjoy the antics of hard-livin' hard-lovin' farnorth characters in an authentic Alaskan fisherman's bar. Old Steubins was right: Kuinak had a valuable quality that the townspeople were still largely ignorant of. Kind of neo-retro. They had been in the backwash so long that they had become the forefront without realizing it.

He tilted a wing low over the trailerhouse but saw no sign of Marley. The old dog had probably gone back inside to finish his morning toilet. Ike banked the airplane on around and began a gentle droning climb into the sun, east. It always felt strange to him, having to fly east to get to places that one just naturally assumed lay south, toward the forty-eight. Like it always seemed that Los Angeles, say, lay almost on a straight line toward the South Pole. But if one were to fly due south from Kuinak, intending to land in LAX, one would miss the California coast by hundreds of miles and be headed for Tahiti. If you missed Tahiti you could end up at the very bottom of the world before sighting land.

They had a six-hundred-mile flight ahead of them to Skagway. In this old droner it would take the better part of a day and most of his fuel. He'd told Herb Tom to call him in a flight plan that would loosely follow the coastline by sight, but he had not checked it in over the radio. The Air Traffic authorities wouldn't be alarmed: radio contact was too jammed up unless you had the latest secure channels. He preferred it like this anyway, unscheduled in the wild blue wonder. If they ran into trouble they could always baby her into some little cove. The motor sounded reliable but you could never tell about the weather, not these days. Like the old Vikings who always sailed with the land somewhere in sight, he preferred to fly with a body of water close by. It was a holdover from the Nightmoth runs.

Prince William Sound shimmered into sight off to his left, looking perfectly healthy from this height. The only thing that revealed the blight beneath the surface was the paltry number of boats. Just a couple of crabbers, some longliners, and a few gillnetters still making desultory sets along the once-vigorous fishing grounds. Barely a dozen. And this wasn't even an odd-number year, this was an even-numbered year. For a while some good runs had come in on the even-numbered seasons—seasons not affected by the two- or four-year cycle since the '89 spill—but lately those runs had diminished even with redoubled efforts at the hatcheries. There weren't even many tankers in sight. These days the Dutch preferred to make the longer but surer trip through the Bering Straits to take on oil at the source well; the pipeline to Valdez was still judged unreliable, even after this long. There hadn't been any real documented bandit hits in ten years, but for a while it had been fierce and Big Oil was still leery about Prince William. There had even been bandit strikes on the tankers themselves that came steaming into the sound—minor computer-jamming usually, by radical hackers with virtual dish-ins—but some Big Oilers had been torpedoed outright. Unmanned outboards were loaded with plastics and aimed in collision course through the dark. You grease us, we grease right back atcha.

Of course, these militant acts weren't all the spawn of his summer of vengeful folly, Ike knew—it had been going on long before he got into it. But he had to admit that he was the one that had given them the flag they rallied around. He was the one that had created the Bakatcha logo, little suspecting that it would become so universal that for a season it was the third-most encountered emblem on the globe—a simple, single splat of black in the middle of a yellow-and-red bull's-eye. It turned up as graffiti spray jobs on freeway abutments, then on T-shirts and stickers and even balloons. Sometimes the black blot on the bull's-eye had the word BAKATCHA! printed in white, for the symbol-impaired, but gradually the printed word was dropped. It was no longer needed, any more than the word STOP or ALTO was needed in the hexagonal stop signs anymore.

Ike couldn't remember ever writing the word himself. There hadn't been time, or room. The bull's-eyes were the business cards of the spray service he worked for and only about three inches across: a stiff paper disk of concentric yellow and red circles with the company name in small blue letters in the center—'Bull's-Eye AIRIAL SPRAY. Call 1-800-AIR-SHOT For Terms. A Cog Weil Inc Subsidiary.' The black splat covered all that. Maybe he had penciled in the word on a few of the first cards, he couldn't remember. Whatever, it had been enough. The press had seized on the phrase and welded it to the bull's-eye-with-black-splat symbol forevermore. It could be found illustrated in all the modern dictionaries, sometimes under S, sometimes under B, sometimes under E for eco-terrorism. Often under all three.

It wasn't something he had intended or anticipated. There had been no planning at all on his part, no conspiratorial deliberations, nothing—unless you count that vague seething that had smoldered for almost a year, like a buried fuse, before the blow-off. Almost a year exactly. The blow-off had been less than two days before the Sunday that would have been little Irene's first birthday. It was a Friday noon. Ike had cashed his check at the airport bank and was driving home in his LeBaron. He had knocked off early in case any of the doctors wanted to talk to him. Workers were still toiling in the heat waves rippling the vegetable fields. The big picking gantries were chugging along with pickers stretched out belly-down on the booms extending from both sides. He could see the ripe tomatoes flowing like ribbons of blood as they were plucked and placed on the booms' ribbed belts. Other workers sorted and crated the ribbons' red flow. When a gantry reached the field's border the crates were off-loaded on to a flatbed truck and the big spidery-looking device was wheeled about to begin another slow pass through the crop. It could harvest twenty rows of tomatoes at a pass, and haul thirty migrants—one picker over each of the ten rows on each side and ten sorters and craters in the middle. The pickers were men, the sorters and craters usually women and children. The driver was always a gringo Teamster, high up in an air-conditioned cab with glass on all sides so he could keep an eye on the operation and slow down or speed up according to how that section of the field looked. An experienced driver could increase his machine's daily harvest by as much as twenty percent.

Carlos Bravo, the UFW picket, woke from a deep sleep when the LeBaron pulled under the mimosa and into the yard. He had been napping in the porch shade of Ike's triple-wide. It was Carlos' assignment to harass this *pesticido* pilot. He was supposed to march in front of the Sallases' home with signs protesting the policies of the truck farmers in general and the Department of Agriculture in particular; but since Ike was generally working most of the day and Jeannie was either usually in town at the clinic or at her sister's place in McFarland, there wasn't much for Carlos to harass. So Ike told him he could wait in the shade in the porch swing.

Carlos stood up from the swing and came forward unsteadily, pumping his sign up and down as Ike eased the LeBaron into the tin-roofed carport. He and Carlos had built the carport on a weekend the summer before, before the picketing had started. They were old poker amigos and joined with other penny-ante friends every other Wednesday night. It was why Carlos had been given this particular assignment; Carlos had been an active member of the United Farm Workers for nearly half a century, and was not in the best of health. His breathing often became troubled and he was subject to spells of dizziness. Especially when conflicted. So he had requested that he might be given the duty of harassing the

141

pilot Señor Sallas, as they were already compadres and conflict would be less stressful. He had been picketing and harassing the triple-wide for months without a dizzy spell.

'*Pon un cuño a la cabeza, hombre!*' Carlos insulted, pumping his sign. '*Tu madre es puta.*'

'Hello, Carlos,' Ike said, hauling his sweaty flight suit out of the back. 'How are you feeling today?'

'Ah, pooty good, Eye-zack. They prescribe for me some new inhalers, helps me sleep better.'

'I noticed that,' Ike grinned. He tossed the zippered suit over an oleander bush to air it dry. The suits were supposed to be laundered every night, but the washing machine at the hangar was on the fritz again, and the oleander was dead anyway. 'How long has Mrs Sallas been gone?'

Carlos shrugged. 'I don't know, Eye-zack. I did not see her leave, but some long time I think. She was gone when I wake up for my lunch break.'

'Right,' Ike said. 'Some long time.' Jeannie had been spending more and more time at her sister's on the way back from the clinic, drinking wine and smoking black rock and praying. Sometimes he had to drive over and bring her home.

'Looks like it's just us hombres again, Carlos. How about a beer and some nachos?'

'Sure, you bet.' The old man pushed his sign beneath the triple-wide's porch. He had been storing it there so long that dirt and mildew had all but obscured the original lettering. Only three words were still clearly discernible: 'DOLLAR' and 'CANCER' and 'MOLOCH.'

Ike handed Carlos a Corona and drank one himself while he showered. When he was dressed he carried out two fresh beers and some tortilla chips and took a seat in the porch swing. Carlos had relinquished it for a place on the steps. Across the road in the choke field the crew was knocking off for the day; they were singing 'Yellow Submarine' in Spanish and the old man was humming along. He took the bottle from Ike and sipped thoughtfully.

'And so, Eye-zack my fren',' Carlos said at last, 'how is the little Eye-reen?'

'Lots better,' Ike told him. 'Chipper. The new shunt they put in drains more effectively, so her earaches have stopped.'

'Still smilin', I bet?'

'Still smilin',' Ike answered.

'I am glad.' Carlos started humming 'Yellow Submarine' again.

Irene had been born a spina bifida baby, with enlarged cranium and a section of her lower backbone exposed. Numerous operations and skin grafts had covered the flaw, but the fluids in the cranium still didn't drain properly. The shunt would plug, the head would swell up, and the little girl's bright blue eyes would burn even brighter—febrile, the doctor called it. They were told to bring her in whenever her eyes looked feverish, especially if she complained of earaches or was holding or rubbing her ears. These were the only signs they had to go on, because the child rarely cried; she kept up her brave little smile even during the most feverish periods of fluid retention. Nothing seemed to daunt her but the earaches, and Jeannie said the doctors were confident these would diminish as the cranium grew.

Ike was glad that Carlos was there at the triple-wide, even in his capacity as adversary. He was also grateful that Carlos Bravo had never tried to implicate the baby's birth defect in the Farm Workers' campaign. A more zealous union member would not have let the opportunity pass, even though researchers had assured the farm workers over and over again that there was absolutely no connection. A zealot would have jumped on the chance. But Carlos was of a more philosophical nature, like Jeannie. 'Believe in blessings,' Jeannie enjoyed saying, 'not in blamings.' In fact, after the birth, when Ike was fretting if the defect might not have come from *him* (all those runs over the coke slopes in Ecuador, for example? spraying those botanical recombinants?), Jeannie had been the first to reassure him otherwise:

143

'Hey, man,' tossing back her hair with a bright smile, 'like Job says: shit falls on the saint and sinner alike.'

He went in the triple and brought out two more beers. The workers in the choke field had piled on to the flatbed and were jouncing off along the dirt dike to the field house to turn in their time. The sun had dipped down into the heat waves and was spreading out, red and misshapen, a bloody egg. Ike had just finished the third beer when the phone rang.

'Jeannie's drunk sister in McFarland,' he predicted to Carlos, rocking up from the swing.

It was Jeannie's drunk sister all right, but they weren't in their kitchen in McFarland. Where were they? She was calling from the clinic in Fresno; Ike should come right away. Could he speak to Jeannie? No. And no, she couldn't tell him more than that. Just come.

As the phone buzzed in his hand he saw the sun split open. Something was coming out. Then he felt a cold wind take hold of him, like a hand gripping the back of his neck, pushing him to the eyepiece, making him look. It was blurry for a moment, then he saw it all. Like a thing on a slide under a microscope. Not a new thing. It had been there all along for the seeing. One would have only had to bend down and put eye to the experience. The clandestine flights in the venomous little Nightmoths; the *pesticido* planes; the subversion of a natural process in the name of a Bug-Free Drug-Free Thug-Free World. And it works—infinitesimal alterations at the genetic level. And why not? It makes sense, it preserves personnel, it saves money and it keeps the collateral damage at a minimum. Of course, there was always the possibility that if you mess around with it long enough you might get some of it on you.

The little girl had been dead more than two hours when he arrived at the pediatric ward. Complications, the nurses said. The shunt failed, the wastes accumulated, the pressure popped. Something somethinged something, the doctor said. Ike begged to see her despite

144

warnings from the doctor and Jeannie's sister. They said he should go see the mother instead. But Jeannie was asleep, sedated, zoned out. And Ike wanted to see his daughter. He kept pushing. They gave way. The child was already on a slab in a cooler drawer when they took him to her. She was naked under the sheet, lying on her back with her legs frogged out, the way she used to lie while she waited to have her bottom powdered. Her little fists were clenched tight. Her mouth was still in the smile, eight-toothed now, not at all unhappy-looking. But her brow and temples were swollen huge, purple as an eggplant. She looked like a thing on a slide.

He assured the doctors he was fine and drove home and parked under the mimosa. He went inside and sat down in the breakfast nook. It was dim at this hour, but he didn't turn on the light. The dimness was cool. As his eyes adjusted he saw Jeannie's little pipe on the tabletop and he lit a candle and fired it up. One jolt was all he needed. He had always been that way. One jolt of anything and he was off, like a toboggan over the edge. A drag off a cigarette could do it as well as off this fetid pipe. He always figured that was why he never got hooked on anything. One jolt was enough.

When he opened his eyes he saw the open book on the table by the candle. Jeannie must have been reading here when she was interrupted. He expected to find a Bible, but saw it was a book of poetry, folded open at a piece by Ernesto Cardenal. A South American poet, he thought. Last century. In tiny print. Gradually, he was able to read the words:

*Yesterday I went into a supermarket and saw shelves
    bare-empty;*
most of them empty; and I felt a little
of the melancholy of the empty shelves,
*but more than that, a happiness about our people's
    dignity*
that's plain to see on the empty shelves

. . . It's the price we're paying, a small nation fighting against the Colossus, and I see empty shelves completely full of heroism

His face came up from the page. The melancholy of the empty shelves. The dignity, the *hero*ism of the empty shelves. He remembered watching the news coverage of the Mothers' March on Sacramento—thousands of women, balancing on their heads buckets and jars and pots of Central Valley tap water. They were shown lined out for miles along the shoulder of the highway, barefoot and bleeding like medieval penitents, with their watery offering to the state legislators. They carried only one sign: 'If it's so pure—you drink it.' That was enough to get them arrested for unlawful demonstration along a public thoroughfare. They were hauled off by the busloads. None of the sardonic gifts of water ever made it within ten miles of Sacramento, and buckets and jars and clay pots were left to drain dry in weedy stretches of ditch. The heroism of the empty. When he had watched the program two years ago he felt sorry for the women. Now he felt ashamed before them.

The trailer was too dark to read more, the candle too fluttery. He went into the bedroom and lay down on the unmade waterbed, still dressed, his eyes clenched. The bed folded around his shame, dark as a wallet, comfortable as a cloud. Small wonder he had never wanted to lean his eye to that eyepiece. He had always feared that the casualty he found there would be wrapped in the Stars and Stripes, in a cheap, lying, dirty banner made in Korea. He would see through the magnifying lens the flaws in the flag's fabric, the signs of irreversible unraveling. A faulty equation must have been allowed to creep into the intricate formula of warp and woof at the Korean flag factory. Or had been planted there on purpose like a recombinant virus. Small wonder you didn't want to lean down and look close—it was your flag unraveling, the one you'd fought for. Invested in. Life savings. Small wonder you shouldn't want to watch the flaws grow monthly more obvious. Childhood cancer in McFarland four hundred percent higher than the norm just for example. He remembered reading the statistic, back page, one column. No connection proven of course. No connection? What the shit, were we blind? So many kids from around McFarland go to Fresno Clinic that they use car pools. Car pools! The water rocked him and the cloud took him and he slept. He awoke at seven in the morning and had muffins and coffee in the nook, then drove to the hangar as usual. The flight jobber told him to take the day off and rest, for chrissake, but Ike begged to be allowed to work.

'They told me at the clinic it was best to go on about your business. I need to fly, Skip. I'll take it slow. Don't worry. You go on to the office, tell them I'll be ready for the noon run.'

The jobber shrugged and left and Ike sat down in a swivel chair and stared at the spread of assignment sheets. Some of the pilots dropped by for a few muttered words of sympathy on their way to the field. He nodded at them and said he was all right, be along in a bit. Soon.

He sat in the deserted hangar for a long time. He had no idea what he was going to do, no plan whatsoever. When the field outside was empty of the bustle and roar of tank-ups and takeoffs he walked to his old Cessna and looked at it. He had always loved the look of his airplanes. There was something both predatory and gentle about these old prop jobs, like fat old hawks. The leaky hydraulic seal hadn't been fixed, he saw. The engine was still dripping oil on to a pile of newspaper, one drop every ten seconds. No big problem. It didn't leak in flight, only when it had been sitting long enough for the seals to cool and shrink. Then it was regular as a clock, one black drop every ten seconds, six a minute. He watched it drip awhile and then went back to the hangar office. He took a roll of the round business cards from the phone stand and returned to the dripping airplane. In half an hour he had a drop of dirty grease in the center of every bull's-eye. One hundred and eighty, six every minute. Regular as a clock.

He still didn't know what he was going to do, not

until he saw the sucker truck drive past the hangar's open door on its way to the workers' facilities across the field. When the truck came driving back from its chore Ike met it, waving his arms.

'I need to borrow your truck, Ojo.'

'What for?' The driver stuck his head out the window, suspicious until he recognized Ike. Ojo was a kin of Carlos Bravo, a grandnephew or something. He was about twenty years old with a fat face and a silly moustache elevating the corners of his mouth.

'For about a half hour, hombre. For twenty bucks?'

'Hey, for *chure*, Isaak. Just don't try to go to no fast-food drive-thru. They don't like it.'

Twenty minutes later Ojo had his truck back and Isaak was in the air, winging toward the Madera County Fairgrounds. Madera was the best he could hope for this time. He wasn't sure he had the fuel to make it all the way to Sacramento with this load.

He reached the park just before noon. He made one reconnaissance pass to study the wind and wires, staying at about one thousand. A gaudy swirl of happy young families could be seen flowing through the gates into the midway below. It was Under Ten Day, with the Dairy Queen Special. An empty DQ Banana Boat Sundae cup got you a free ride on the Under Ten rides. The kids were hauling in the used cups by the bagfuls.

Out over the packed parking lot Ike banked the Cessna sharply back around and down. The fairgrounds came up fast and clear. Piece of cake. The Ferris wheel was right on the near border of the fairgrounds and lit up like a marker pylon. Ike grinned as he bobbed over it, tail wheel nearly in the seat of the screaming topmost car, then he nosed down and hit the flaps and the spray cocks. All he could see in his rearview zoom was an elongated scroll of panicked faces streaming away horrified behind him. He throttled up over the rodeo stands and jammed the cocks closed. The gauges showed he was still more than half full. He banked around. This time the swirl of families was no longer happy and gaudy. The midway

148

looked like an anthill after a squirt of Raid. And this time he was able to see the faces head on. The horror was still there, but the panic was subsiding. He emptied clean as he bobbed over the Ferris wheel, feeling the satisfying rush of lightness, of emptiness. On the third pass over—leisurely now, to dip the wings and drop the cards—he saw that the crowd now knew what they were being sprayed with. Their initial expressions of panic and confusion were now entirely purged by a new phenomenon, a new face: outrage—fist-shaking, rock-throwing, finger-giving outrage. Brown-stained mamas and papas, carnies and kids and all, were bobbing up and down beneath him like turds in a turbulent cesspool. His dispersal had been beautiful; not a one but was somewhere besmirched. He just wished he'd made more cards.

He was home in the triple-wide again, asleep in the unmade waterbed still fully dressed again—only with Jeannie beside him this time, also fully dressed in her sedated state—when the Fresno sheriff and about a dozen deputies came knocking. Jeannie woke up enough to open one eye as they were leading him out in handcuffs.

'What is happening?' she managed to inquire.

'Go back to sleep,' one of the crisp young deputies told her.

'What is *happening*?' she screamed.

The deputy grinned. 'Unknown County Fair Terrorist captured. Details at eleven.'

It turned out to be a lot more than details. And by eleven Ike Sallas was no longer unknown; he was well-known. A local TV crew had been covering the kids' day special and the fly-by footage played big. Lurid close-ups showed the screams and panic of the first fly-by, the disgust and outrage of the second, then the final insult of the calling cards. The conscientious TV crew had traced the plane's number and had arrived at the vegetable fields while the sheriff was still interrogating Ojo Bravo.

'*Choor*, I savvy,' Ojo had told the TV cameras. 'I know what Ike Sallas wants with my truck, from in front! Hey,

149

his little baby choost died? He got pissed off, choost like us. Do I think he is a terrorist? No, Ike Sallas is maybe what we call a bandit, but he is no terrorist. Choost a bandit who got pissed off. Anyhows, what was it that he did that was so terrible, eh? Got a little ca-ca on some upper middle class? I get the same thing on me every day for under minimum wage.'

Ojo's eyes were crackling and black when he spoke, and his silly moustache quivered with passion in the close-ups. The interview was so effective that it played every time the spray footage ran. By the time Ike was out on bail two days later he and Ojo Bravo were both world famous and out of work. Not that this kept them from repeating their smash act; it just meant they had to wait for the signal from other migrants that the coast was clear and the Cessna and the honey wagon available. Ike was able to hit the Stockton County Fair a weekend later, with the Cessna's ID number taped over, and the State Fair in Sacramento the next Friday before they hauled him in again. They didn't bother with Ojo Bravo this time. Just Isaak Sallas. And this time there was no bail. The Bakatcha Bandit would await trial with his wings clipped and his ass incarcerated. By then, however, a legion of similar bandits had arisen to carry on the effort. It was an exciting summer.

The old Otter droned steadily on over the Mandelbrot Set of the coastline, and the fair weather held, smooth and clear. The skies didn't start hazing up until the Chilkoot Pass came into view a little past two in the afternoon. It thickened rapidly until there was no visibility. Ike raised the Skagway airport to try to get a beam-in through the curdled yellow murk. The comeback squawk of the control tower brought Greer pawing wildly from his six-hour nap. His dreadlocks whipped his cheeks as he stared pop-eyed about the droning cubicle. When he realized he was in an airplane he sighed thankfully. 'Woo! Thank de Lord. A minute there I thought we was in a submarine.'

'Not quite yet,' Ike reassured him, 'but if it stays this soupy we damn well could be. I can't see a damn thing and there's no landing beam coming in.'

The radio advised him that sun storms had temporarily disrupted the beam transmission but they had his aircraft on the radar and he was coming in just fine, just a few miles off-course seaward—which was his best approach in a yellow-out anyway. It kept him clear of commercial routes.

'Limited visibility up top,' the speaker squawked. 'Swing east-by-northeast twenty degrees and drop to fifteen hundred. It opens up. And please identify. Hello? We need your name and wing number . . .'

Ike kept quiet and nosed down tentatively. In a few minutes the little airplane emerged from the yellow underbelly of the sky and he had all the visibility he needed. The town of Skagway lay dead ahead of them in its tiny crack. Two big tour liners were moored at the dock, all rigging lights ablaze. There was a crowd of tourists around the huge gold-plated gold miner statue on Skagway's waterfront. The statue was also illuminated. The whole town, Ike saw, was lit up like a carnival at twilight, though sundown was hours away.

He saw the blue lights of the new landing strip that ran along the Skagway River. The strip had been extended on cement pilings out over the water of the bay like an eight-lane freeway that ended abruptly, above nothing. An Air Israel jumbo jet was just booming off, taking a load of Jewish tourists back to their besieged Holy Land. The jumbo had all of its night lights on, too.

The controller instructed Ike to set down south of the town and taxi across the bay to the pier to be safe, then report immediately to authorities with identification and explanations.

'Will do,' Ike lied and flipped off the radio. He tilted steeply for the water below and headed straight for the town, riding the groundswell and keeping the tour boats' smokestacks between the Otter and the control tower. He was damned if he intended to hang around some pencil-pusher's office filling out forms and making explanations.

He put down just off the pier where the railway ended and found a cozy spot between the two huge liners. Greer hopped out on a pontoon and tossed a coil up to the crowd of young tourists beaming down at them from the pier. They were a tour group of German psychology students and they all had sunburned knees and noses.

'But there is no *ladder* here,' the young blond who caught the line felt obliged to call back. 'Nothing up which to climb . . .'

'There *weel* be, my mon, you just tie dat line to something solid.'

To the delight of the crowd the wild-headed black man scrambled immediately up the twenty feet of rope, like a monkey up a vine. Then his white friend followed, looking in a way even wilder, his face a snarl of scratches and scabs. Now *here* was some of the rash and reckless old Alaska they had paid to see.

Ike declined the Germans' invitations to share their mule-drawn wagon ride into town; it was only a few blocks to the clinic. They would walk.

'Though we surely might be take you up on you offa on de way back,' Greer added. 'We might need a wagon by then, for to haul de wounded.'

But at the clinic they were informed that patient Bellisarius, William A, had already been hauled. 'Hours and *hours* ago,' the male nurse at the admissions desk told them, 'by his *pretty little woman* . . . or so she claimed when she paid Mr Bellisarius' bill. She and one other *very* pretty little woman wheeled him out and loaded him on a dirty mattress in the back of a beat-up pickup, assisted by the *very big black man* . . . none other than, I fear, the Reverend Thaddeus Greener. And there you have it.'

'Do you have perhaps the *very smallest notion* where they took him?' Ike asked.

'Of course I do. They took him where the Reverend takes all his little lost lambs—to his *Beulahland* Farm on the shores of *lovely* Lake Bennet. I hear he has quite the flock up there, tilling the fields of the Lord.'

'Now let me get this straight!' Greer was shocked and indignant. 'You let them drive a injured man up the White Pass in the back of a beat-up pickup? Some nurse *you* are.'

'Oh, they didn't drive. Gracious no. The White Pass highway goes nowhere *near* Reverend Greener's Beulah-land. They took the Gold Rush Historic Tour Train. The train of course is scheduled for Dawson, but the Reverend has an *agreement* with the engineer; if the engineer agrees to stop and let the Reverend and members of his flock off at the Bennet siding, the Reverend agrees not to cave the engineer's skull in. It is the only way to access the Reverend's little Shangri-la . . .'

'When does the next tour go up?' Ike asked.

'Oh in about, I should say—' The nurse looked at the watch pinned to his white shirt pocket, thick lips pursed, '—six days and four hours.'

'A *week*?' Greer cried. 'Jesus Flying Christ, we can't wait that long!'

'Even Jesus would have to wait, I'm afraid. Or fly. But He can *do* that, can't He?'

Ike held Greer back. 'This place is on the lake, you say?'

'Not the *main* lake; on one of the little upper pools. It's quite a lovely little puddle from what I hear. Spiritually therapeutic. You gentlemen might benefit, honestly you might . . .'

Ike had to drag Greer away down the clinic aisle.

'I got a little therapy for that simpering asshole,' Greer protested. 'You shoulda let me minister it.'

'Forget him, let's go. Back to the plane—'

'And leave our poor prez?' Greer gasped in disbelief. 'Mon, I can't be*lieve* you'd do that . . .'

'Mon,' Ike said, 'I can put down in *any* puddle—I don't care how little and lovely it is.'

They got a German tourist to cast them off. Ike paddled the plane end about before starting the engine. They idled out from between the two liners and took off north, skimming low over the water. Ike knew an unlicensed float station in Dyea where they could gas up. He skimmed along just above the surface of the ten-mile fjord, until he sighted the houseboat moored near the mouth of the Chilkoot. It was part of a network of secret filling stations sprinkled along the coast from Anchorage all the way down to Crescent City. Ike had used it on the occasional mule flights he used to make.

The same toothless old sourdough still ran the station. He came out on the spongy deck buttoning his pants and squinting at the plane puddling toward him on the scummy water. He recognized Ike, but said he couldn't pump him any gas, not right off anyhow. He'd heard talk over the tower frequency about an unauthorized Otter flying his direction, and reckoned there'd be a spotter along any minute.

'Just keep puddlin' on that ways yonder and park 'neath them willows—they bend right down over you like an umbrella. It'll take about a half hour for the bear in the air to come and go. I'll fire a all-clear signal. Here's two big beers. By-the-by, I no longer accept cash . . . just credit cards.'

The branches folded down over the parked plane with the easy pull of habit. There were even cords attached to tie them in place. When they were sure the plane was hidden Ike and Greer took the two half-liter cans of Australian beer and waded ashore. They found an ancient wooden gate across a grass-grown road.

'I *know* dis place, mon!' Greer exclaimed. 'This is the entrance of the Dyea Avalanche Cemetery! When we was first in Skagway Wanda she like to come here and ball on the graves. She say she can feel de spirits still in*fluencing* the whole area. She say she can feel them in the ground callin' "I want love, I want *love*." Made her horny, whoo!'

The cemetery was a little cluster of faded white head-boards all but lost in a thicket of cottonwood and ash. Fern and tiger lilies and tall, nodding daisies choked the grave sites. Many of the trees grew directly up through the center of the grave plots themselves, some with trunks as thick as oil drums. Greer gaped at the jungle.

'These damn trees *twice* as big as when Wanda and me were here! Talk about the power of the spirits.'

'More likely it was the roots finally making it down to the nutrients below,' Ike reasoned.

'Damn, Isaak, you are totally void of any romance and that's de truth. Listen!' Greer held up a hand. 'I hear the UN plane, I bet.'

It was a single-engine turboprop, making a low pass over the fjord just like the old man had predicted. It passed overhead, up the Chilcoot. The two friends sat down in the grass among the tree trunks and headboards and opened their beers.

'Some spot, hey? If you look close you can still see some de dates, ya know . . .'

As Ike's eyes became accustomed to the leafy gloom he saw that the cracked boards had once been white-washed, and many still bore the faint hint of painted names and numerals. 'They all look like they have the same death date,' he observed.

'March 3, 1898,' Greer nodded. 'These unfortunate souls were part of that first wave of stampeders to try the Chilcoot. Something—all dat spirited Gold Rush rejoicing, maybe?—brought a damn *avalanche* down on them! Killed dozens. March de third, eighteen-hundred and ninety-mama-eight. Mon!'

Gradually Ike was able to make out some of the names and dates and hometowns. From all over. Just kids, mostly . . . twenty-one . . . twenty-six . . . nineteen . . . from Akron . . . Muncie . . . Hoboken . . . wild-eyed kids from all over America on their way to the Klondike gold fields to strike big, or at least to strike *at* it big. They didn't even get to first base.

The UN spotter plane came whining back, higher this time. As it faded out of earshot a reverberating blast shook cotton and ash leaves loose and Greer jumped a foot.

'Jesus Booming Almighty God *Damn* Bleeding Christ,

that was your old buddy's signal shot? Or has he installed antiaircraft?'

Before leaving the little thicket, Greer insisted Ike check out a particular grave. If Greer could find it. After fighting back and forth through the brush Greer finally located a strange wooden pylon. He explained that this was the infamous centerpiece and puzzling mystery of the place. Ike had to push the flowers aside to see the marker. It was taller than any of its neighbors—not out of reverence, it seemed, but out of an attempt at some kind of reverse emphasis. This pylon was no cross. No simple, seemly curve-topped headboard. There were no religious symbols or sayings on this monument. Not even any birthplace. And the resident buried beneath had been allotted one name only, defaced but legible still:

M O N T I A C
Shot In Mountains
March 7, 1898

'Uh-huh? You dig that? Four days *after* that snowslide make cold cuts of all these other dudes! What was Mr Montiac doing up here that was so *anus* they shoot him den give him the biggest monument in the neighborhood? Mm?'

The pious white of the daisies suggested what a splendid sight the marker must have been, more than a century ago. A whitewashed edifice to some supremely dark deed. Now it was only faded flakes and peeling slivers here and there on the old pine boards. Except for the side of the pylon opposite the inscription. When they had pushed through the fern and flowers the two men discovered that this pine board had been painted white anew, not so long before. A spray-marker face of Elvis occupied the middle of the restored surface. This skillful likeness of the singer was from his corpulent white-suit period near the end. The inscription below was in quotation marks—a familiar graffiti and bumper sticker:

I WANT MY
PORK LIPS
NOW!

'So much for what the spirits want,' Ike said.

The old man apologized for the unseemly blast when they taxied back out to his floating pump house. 'Discovered I didn't have no cartridge for my signal pistol,' the toothless mouth explained. 'Had to make do with a bundle of old blastin' sticks. Didn't want to jostle 'em apart 'cause they looked a trifle unstable. Sweatin'. So I shot the whole dozen. You figure I should check your oil while I'm at it?'

Fueled and ready, Ike powered her up in a steep bank to the right, over the low northern peninsula and out to sea. This was so he could come in on Skagway Gorge from the south, as though arriving from Juneau. He took care to stay just inside the jaundiced bottom of the overcast. He didn't turn the beacon on at all, following the gorge by sight. Down through the peculiar light the White Pass was easily visible, winding and climbing. The new highway followed the slopes to his left, the old narrow-gauge railroad to his right. Straight down below the river crashed and writhed, like a stepped-on snake. As the pass rose higher the slopes on each side grew steeper, but the hazy ceiling remained just as low. Ike soon found himself having to fly right down in the crack to keep the river in sight, granite and green flashing by close out both side windows and getting closer.

He flew without comment. He didn't let on to Greer that they'd got themselves into a predicament from which there was no turning back. He couldn't speed up enough to get into a hard climb and he couldn't bank out of the gorge. Without instruments to warn him he might bank straight into any sudden unseen jog of the canyon.

At last the ocher haze began to thin and they broke through into the sunlight. The sky was blue and hard as a diamond, and the saddle of the White Pass summit gleamed sharp ahead of them. Huge Lake Bennet unrolled off to the summit's south ridge like a bolt of deep purple silk—a bolt already cut into patterns and laid out for the stitching on a dark brown table.

The commune was easy to locate; it was the only part of this ten-thousand-foot-high tabletop that wasn't deep purple or dark brown. Orderly green rectangles were lined up along the landward side of the little railroad. These fields were glowing with vegetable health.

'Look like Reverend Brother Greener must be doing *some*t'ing right,' Greer said, 'besides whippin' on women and wimps. That's a thriving garden down there if I ever see one.'

Ike didn't say so, but he suspected that those neatly kept vegetable plots were probably the direct product of that very whipping. He'd seen these kinds of zealous agriculture operations before; you didn't come up with fields like that without a good deal of traditional ass-busting labor, especially when you didn't fertilize. And way up here you were going to have to haul a lot of dirt or humus or something for planting mix: these tundra soils were only inches thick at their deepest.

Ike forced himself to drop the plane into the narrow pool on his first pass. Whoever this damned Greener was, Ike didn't like giving him too much warning. He taxied near a rocky bank and Greer put out a back anchor and waded in with the line. Ike waded in with a second line. The boulder he tied off to was porous lava, so abrasive his hand was bleeding when he finished the tie. All the rocks were the same, jagged and abrasive as slag. Raw and weird. As they were stumbling across these jagged rocks he realized why: the tundra that had covered and softened the terrain was gone, stripped as clean as the patch around a hill of red ants. That's where Greener had got his planting mix, scraping ten acres of moss and bayberries to make one acre of green peas.

They reached the tracks and the siding and crossed a graveled lot full of rails and railroad equipment, rusting away among stacks of creosote-treated ties. The only machine that looked like it had been manufactured for something other than rail work was an ungainly shape covered with Vizqueen and bird net, like a camouflaged war machine. Ike couldn't make out much more than its tarnished gold color through the cloudy plastic, but the size and spread of the thing reminded him of one of the picking gantries that worked the California vegetable fields. Evidently even the born-again had to work on their bellies to bring in the crops.

Smoke rose from the chimney of a long tin-siding house with a loading dock fronting the spur line. The spur hadn't been used in years. An antique hand-pump crew car stood forlornly alone on its rusty tracks, wild berry vines twining through the floorboards and up the pump handles. Beyond the siding yard was a field of bush beans, lush and thick and immaculate. A line of sweating workers were chopping away with their hoes, though not a weed was in sight. An indistinct cadence arose as they chopped. And Greer had been right: women and wimps, mostly young and mostly black. They were all naked to the waist.

'Beulahland, I *guess*,' Greer whispered, not wanting to disturb their taut rhythm. 'You think Boss Greener he keep all this young blood in line with just one stick? I wonder if he could use some *backup*?'

'*Mr Sallas!*' There was a hiss from the methodic chopping activity in the beans. '*Mr Greer!*'

It was Archie Culligan, one of the two brothers who had gone south with Carmody. He continued to chop at invisible weeds, his eyes pleading.

'Archie, what are you doing up here?' Ike crossed the spur and started down the row toward the boy. This agitated the whole line of choppers into faster chopping and chanting. He could make out their murmurous chant now—'*Take* me Jesus, *take* me Jesus . . .' over and over, like so many sewing machines.

'Archie. Where's Carmody and Nels? Where's the new boat?'

'In Juneau,' the boy whispered, chopping. 'Getting the keel welded. Mr Carmody was showing off to the Inland

159

Ferry and run aground. Nels and me had an argument and I split for Skagway. O, Jesus, take me *outta* here . . .'

This stirred the muttering chant around them yet louder—'*Take* me Jesus, take me *now*.'

Greer had reached them through the rows. 'Shitfire, Archie, look at you! Put a shirt on. Your back is fried like bacon.'

The boy continued to chop along with the others, his head down. Ike and Greer had to shuffle to keep up. Ike spoke gently.

'Where's Billy the Squid, Arch? Have you seen Billy?'

'He's in the cloisters—' A slight jerk of his head indicated a windowless refrigeration car next to the siding dock. '—getting saved. *Save* me Jesus, save us all.'

'*We* came up here with that in mind, Archie,' Ike said. He could feel the heat stirring in his ribs, burning away the last of his reservations. And he seemed to hear music, as from faraway trumpets.

'In the cloisters, Ike. But watch out for *Him*,' the boy said. 'Don't let Him eyeball you, it does something awful—'

'Who? Billy the Squid?'

'No, keep me Jesus . . . *Him*.'

This time the tiny twitch of Archie's head indicated something directly behind them. Ike and Greer turned and beheld a sentinel form atop one of those jagged boulders at the edge of the field, like a carved and polished pillar of black granite. It took several moments to convince the senses that this obelisk was actually a man. He was wearing a pair of bib overalls without a shirt, carrying a long-handled digging fork in one hand, a book in the other. He was barefoot and bare-scalped with a full curly beard. The fork could have been taken as some pagan god's trident, but the book could be nothing but the Bible.

'Come to Jesus,' the form called, a sound so deep it might have issued from a crack in the ocean floor. 'The three of you . . . come now.'

Archie obeyed without a word and the other two followed. Ike discerned immediately that this was not your

160

run-of-the-mill power-tripping steranoid holy man. As he came closer he saw what Archie meant about the man's eyes, though it wasn't what he expected; they were long-lashed and gentle, almost feminine beneath the sympathetic brow—not at all the penetrating instruments of persuasion that one had become accustomed to seeing in the faces of the recent rash of these cult leaders that kept making the news. There was a quiet certainty in this soft brown gaze that didn't seem to need any of the fanned flame of fanaticism. The man tucked his Bible in the bib of his overalls and stepped down from his rock, holding out his hand.

'You must be Isaak Sallas. Mr Bellisarius said you would come. We are honored that you have chosen to visit our little farm. I am the Reverend Thad Greener, your humble servant.'

As Ike shook the horn-hard palm he remembered what the boxing pundits had claimed about Greener when the man left the gridiron for the ring: 'Never a scratch in thirty professional bouts. Hide like a rhino. Couldn't cut him with a meat cleaver.' He noticed that the rock Greener had been standing on was of the same igneous composite that had shredded their shoes on the walk from the plane.

'Reverend Greener,' Ike nodded. 'This is my partner, Emil Greer. We come to get Billy.'

'Of course. We will go see how Mr Bellisarius is feeling. And I swear before God, brother,' he was still speaking to Ike, completely ignoring Greer, 'I had no intention of harming the little man. None. It was clumsy of me and I am deeply sorry.'

The eyes verified the truth of this. Ike nodded again. The man turned and went crunching barefoot across the cinders toward the boxcar, Ike and Greer and Archie following in a silent single file.

Billy was around the other side of the car from the rail yard, on a porch that had been built out at floor level. A sign at the bottom of the whitewashed steps said 'Infirmary.' The porch had been roofed with odds and ends

161

of corrugated siding to shelter convalescing patients, but the sun had sunk beneath these mismatched eaves. It came shining hard across the layer of yellow haze above Skagway, right into the whitewashed porch, stark and remorseless. Billy lay on what was apparently the same short-legged cot that he'd been carried out of the Skagway Clinic on, facedown, or, more accurately, ass up. A small pillow under his pelvis elevated his rear, which seemed to be enclosed in a kind of plaster pamper. One arm hung over the cot's edge, shackled to a steelume briefcase.

'I unintentionally sat him down too hard,' Greener explained. 'Broke his coccyx. All I wanted to do was discuss a certain theory about which he was patently wrong but infuriatingly stubborn. Billy? You got friends here to see you, Billy. Awaken.'

'I'm awake, Asshole.' Billy's face was turned into the sun, his eyes closed. A little puddle of drool had puddled from his lips where his cheek pressed against the sheet.

'Is he all right?' Greer whispered.

'Just zeed out. Zeed out and scootless and can't get no help outten that devil bag he is chained to.' Greener fixed his moist eyes on Greer. '*You* must know how it is, Homeblood? When the drug stops and the dreams begin? How weary it gets holding your eyes open? As a matter fact I see that you look a little weary yourself.'

Greer nodded beneath the soft understanding gaze— weary, weary.

'Perhaps you men would like a glass of tea while Mr Bellisarius is awakening up. Sit, please. Gretta? Where you hiding, girl . . . ?'

A young Hispanic girl ducked instantly out through the curtained boxcar door. She was wearing a dingy nurse's uniform and cap. 'Yes, Revren' Greener?'

'Would you go to the kitchen and bring a pitcher of herb tea to serve our guests?'

'Yes, Revren' . . .'

She started down the wooden steps, but he called her back. 'Oh, and Gretta?' He put a hand on her shoulder. His next instructions were pitched beneath Ike and Greer's hearing. Gretta said 'Yes, Revren'' again and hurried on around the car. It made Ike wonder exactly what kind of herbs they were to be served.

'What theory were you and Billy discussing, Greener,' Ike asked, 'that you had to sit him down so hard?'

'A teleological point, Mr Sallas. Concerning the End Times. Seem like these days *every*body is a expert on the End Times, talking a lot of dangerous trash with no thought for the consequences. And Brother Bellisarius, he was making some very irresponsible assertions, right in a public eating establishment full of all sorts of impressionable youth. Some ex*tremely* irresponsible assertions.'

'The fuck I was,' came a slurred voice from the cot. 'All I was asserting was that ice'll suffice.'

'What's that, Squid?' Greer asked.

Billy's eyes were still shut, but he licked his lips. 'Ice will suffice,' the voice repeated.

Greener pretended he hadn't heard a thing. 'Please, my brothers,' he said. 'Sit.' He pointed the digging fork at a wooden church pew against the side of the car. Archie and Greer obeyed at once. Ike continued to stand, squinting in the sun. He didn't know what was up, but he knew he didn't want to sit in a church pew with this suspicious pillar of granite standing between him and the steps. He was feeling hemmed in enough as it was.

When it was clear that Ike was not going to take a seat, Greener turned his attention to Ike's sidekick. He leaned the fork against the wall and pulled a folding chair from beneath the pew. He opened it and placed himself directly in front of Greer's apprehensive face.

'So, let me ask you, my fretful brother—' He laid a heavy hand on each of Greer's skinny knees. 'Why have you not accepted the Lord Jesus Christ as your personal savior?'

'But I *have*, Reverend,' Greer answered emphatically. The fact had never occurred to him before, but now he was sure of it.

'Praise the Lord, I am glad, glad in my heart. For we both know that one as weary as *thou* must needs have a haven in which to rest. End Times is tired times, ain't they little brother? But thy voyage through folly and filth is almost finished. The harbor light beckons, the good light of the cleansing flame beckons, just over the bar, the good, sweet, promised light of the Fire Next Time—'

'*Ice* Next Time,' interrupted the voice from the cot. 'Ice Next Time, slimebrain. I can prove it mathe*matically*!'

Still the man gave no indication that he had heard Billy's slurring contradictions. He remained motionless on his folding chair, coolly smiling into Greer's agitated face. Ike could feel the heat building despite that cool smile, like the orange sun on his cheek.

The soft voice continued. 'But thou knowest, Brother Emil, how the sick dog is like to return to its vomit? How the bathed sow is like to go rolling in the mire? Thou *knowest* this to be so, ain't I correct?'

Greer nodded emphatic agreement; he'd seen his share of dogs and sows.

'Then I *beg* you, Blood, leave the company of them beasts. Rise up. Rise up with us here in Beulahland. Leave them. Come to us. We have been shown the way. The route to salvation is charted in simple tradition—sweat of the brow . . . fruit of the fields. Doesn't thou believe in tradition, little brother?'

'You bet,' said Greer.

'Look about you. We have raised ourselves a home above that filth down there. Join us. The choice is yours. You can till this clean land here in the sanctuary of the clouds or you can perish below in the flaming filth, in the final, terrible, horrible, inescapable fire fire fire!'

'Ice,' said the voice from the cot. 'Ice ice ice—!'

'*FIRE!*' Greener suddenly thundered, standing. '*Fire*, you blaspheming peace-o'-shit faggot! Fire and tribu-*lation* such as was not since the beginning of the motherfucking *world*! I know your kind —the Spirit of the Antichrist is the mystery of iniquity—*all* of you asshole faggots know the world is looking for a man! to show them the way *out*! of these difficulties of your own iniquitous *brew*ing! And one *day* in the *future* it cannot be fucking much further off the diseased *Spirit* of the Antichrist shall *fill* the houses of God and make in them such *dins* of iniquity that every babe's heart shall be infected with the poisons of the Babylon!'

He began to stamp about the plank porch, pounding his fists together.

'Troubled water? Shit, man, you kidding? It's a sewer—a fucking flaming *sewer*! And for a bridge over it where shall you look? Into the churches? Nay, for they are filled with blasphemy and blackjack tables. Into the human heart? It has become a cesspool, a swamp, the mire that leadeth to madness. Into Heaven then? Through the almighty mystery of the gates into sweet Heaven above? Shit a mother brick no! We can't hardly get through the *air* plution let alone the mystery of the gates. Nay, there won't *be* no place to look! No place to turn. The seas'll be boiling, the rocks burning, the moon bleeding like a *ho'* ripped up by some cheap abortionist. The heat be *on*! Credit cards *canceled,* real estate deals going *up in smoke.* Bank accounts on fire! On *fire fire fire*!'

Greener was silent, breathing hard. Ike was glad Billy didn't say 'ice' again; the way Greener was stamping around he might have ground the little man beneath his heel. Ike kept his cheek turned to the setting sun and let the man rave.

'All three of you dumb faggot fucks are the pimps of the whore Babylon! I *dare* you deny it. You have drooled after her delights! You have drunk the wine of her fornication like it was Diet fucking Pepsi! But I say unto you: God's judgment proclaims that this whore must be swept away—*swept* away—with the Broom of Annihilation . . . and I believe I am that Broom!' The thought of this seemed to calm him. 'If I'm not I'm a tall post on a high road on the *way* to being that Broom, you got to admit.' He smiled around at them, a little sheepish. 'But one thing I damn sure do know—we *all* know, my brothers—is that the whorehouse has got to be swept clean. Purged with the cleansing fire. Can any of you look me in the eye and deny what I'm talking about? That this world *got* to be purged with fire?' His voice went humbler still. 'Isaak Sallas, we warriors in the same battle, you and I. Why do you keep your face from mine? Please, man, I just want to talk . . .'

Greener stood, his silence demanding an answer. Ike didn't turn to respond, though he could feel the man's eyes on him. He glanced up into their brown glare and in an instant was reminded of a scene that was somehow similar. He remembered seeing a teenage Mexican boy hypnotize a chicken, on a wager, behind a Salinas truck stop.

The truck stop proprietor was a gamecocker with forty or fifty training coops on the bare concrete apron behind the station. 'I like to tether them out on that hot cement, keeps 'em hopping.'

The cocks had to hop up a day-glo road pylon to peck a little sip of water from the cup the cock trainer kept in the peak of the pylon.

'I put a little scoot in the water by way of more incentive. My chickens never hold still. So it ain't that they win so much as it is they don't lose. They keep moving. Courage is an admirable trait, all right, but give me movement. Ain't that what decides which one wins the most high-dollar fights? Which one moves the last? Not a one of my birds *ever* holds still.'

'I can make one of 'em hold still,' the Mexican boy said from the shade of an empty stock truck. Remembering, Ike realized this was Ojo, back before the moustache. Ojo Bravo had been more of a *brujo* than Ike appreciated. Ojo had taught him how to thumbnail-mark a card deck, he remembered, and it was Ojo who had instructed Ike in the various pachuco sucker swings, to help him through his jail time. It had proved more useful than his Navy karate training.

'Not without knocking him in the head or poisoning him you can't,' the proprietor answered.

'I can hypnotize him.'

The man had been obliged to catch his wildest champion, a purple-and-green cock of Filipino stock. The bird was darting this way and that to the ends of its nylon tether like a tiny electrical storm. After some effort the owner caught the cord and reeled it in. He untied the cord from the weighted pylon and handed the chicken to Ojo. The boy dropped to his knees on the scorching pavement and pinioned the bird between his thighs. The cord lay on the ground, running back beneath the struggling bird.

'No tying him up,' the owner said. 'If you're going to tie him up the deal's off. That ain't what we're betting about.'

The other bettors muttered agreement. Ojo paid no attention. It was obvious from his concentration that he had something more in mind than the mere trussing-up of a scrawny frier. He was becoming very still. The cock still thrashed between his knees until he caught the combless head. Gently, he forced it down to the dusty concrete, neck parallel to the nylon cord, beak aimed straight out from between Ojo's patched knees. With the other hand he pulled the cord straight so a dingy white line ran from the point of the beak straight out about twenty inches. Ojo held this end taut against the concrete with a stubby thumb.

'First, *tu sabes*, you got to get them to get in their little *minds* the *concept* . . . of the straight line—'

He twitched the cord. The orange eyes converged. Ike saw the cock get the concept.

'—then you let them see that there is an *end* to it . . .'

He raised the thumb, carefully. The rooster's eyes were crossed and locked fast, on the place where the white line stopped, twenty inches from the tip of the beak. Ojo spread his knees and stood and tiptoed backwards, his finger to his lips.

'Hypnotized. He'll stay in that trance until something breaks it. Or he falls asleep or passes out from sunstroke. Pay me.'

The bettors paid up without a grumble, so impressed was everybody with the phenomenon. They began making whispered side bets about how long the trance would last. The rooster remained transfixed in the sun, completely motionless except for the occasional shutter-flick of his eyelids, for twelve minutes and forty seconds. Then the draft of a passing eighteen-wheeler blew a styrofoam cup across the lot. The rooster stood up, wobbly and blinking.

This guy Greener had somehow learned Ojo's trick—get them to see the concept, then get them to take a long, hard, honest look at the fact at the end of it. The absolute end, guaranteed to entrance. By some quirk of fate or accident of chance—a bolt from the blue or a left hook to the right temple—Thad Greener had been given the ability to reveal that stupefying fact. Somehow the fact cried forth, like a rock-hard announcement from behind those soft, brown eyes. It was all the mojo the man needed. He didn't need the withering stare cultivated by most of these modern Rasputins. He didn't need charisma or chutzpah. He didn't really even need Christ. Not as long as he had the end of that goddamned string dangling from his face.

With all his resolve Ike wrenched his eyes free and looked back out across the barren landscape. He heard Greener's feet hiss across the porch; then the man was standing next to him, side by side, facing the dropping sun.

'Forgive me,' Greener said, 'I got carried away with my rap. I forgot who I was talking to. What you thinking about, looking out yonder? Ike Sallas is not the sort that looks away for no reason, is he?'

Ike smiled and glanced sideways, just long enough to assure the man that he was not, that he'd looked at the end of the string before, more than once; then he turned back to the denuded White Pass. He was already resolved. He knew what had to be done.

'You know what it looks like to me, Greener? Like you guys sure tore up a nice piece of tundra for a few vegetable salads. It looks like the face of the moon out there.'

'The stuff was already dead,' Greener protested. 'Cooked brown as breakfast food. Tundra can't survive in temperatures like this Effect been giving us.'

'It might've come back when the weather straightens

168

. . . if you'd left something for the spores and seeds to get a purchase on.'

'The weather is *not* going to straighten,' Greener's voice snapped, absolute and terminal. Ike saw that the man could also crack the end of that string, if he had to.

'It might.'

'It won't! Even if you forget the word of God and just read the weather report you know it is getting hotter! We have built our own pit and we shall perish in our own *fire.*'

Ike was glad there was no rebuttal from Billy. The Squid seemed to have drooled back to sleep. Greer's eyes were closed. Greener continued softly, careful not to wake them.

'You won't be taking your friends back, you know. Everyone has the right to an education, even dope dealers and fornicators. This is the University of the Motherfucking End, Sallas, and these students are up here for a crash course. They got no time to play around down in Hollywood, they got to *cram.* You know it and I know it. They got to stay. And so should you, man. I wish with all my soul I could persuade you . . .'

Ike drew a deep breath. He crossed his arms as he let it out.

'You want to know what I was really thinking about, looking out at that sun going down in the smog? I was thinking about this little dude I knew in California that could hypnotize chickens. Mexican kid with big round cheeks. See the way the sun's bulging out? Kid had cheeks like that . . .'

As they stood side by side looking at the horizon, Ike told the whole story of Ojo and the Filipino rooster and the piece of string, taking care to pitch his voice intimate. A shared secret, just between the two of them. When the story was over Greener merely grunted —'Cute trick'—but he was clearly fascinated.

'He taught me a lot of cute tricks. One especially, the sunset trick, works on people. One guy folds his arms and watches, like me, see? The other guy—he's got to

169

be standing alongside, like you—raises his arms above his head and watches. No, you got to turn your palms forward so the sun shines on them—that's it. Then the guy on the left—me—puts his *left* hand on his right bicep and—without warning as he stands there, *shoves!*'

He had never tried it before, except on the heavy bag in jail, but he knew precisely how it would feel. The right forearm hinging out swinging level across his chest, the shove from the left hand accelerating the action like a flail or an atlatl, the heel of the right hand striking the unprotected midsection of the victim alongside with compounded velocity, right where the ribs opened up to the viscera. The bread basket. The only thing unexpected was the hardness of this particular bread basket. It was stiff as a board through the heavy denim of the bib overalls. Christ, the Bible! Greener did not move. Ike thought for a panicked moment that maybe he had gone to Ojo's well of tricks once too often. Then the upraised black arms fell to his sides and the man crashed backward at full length on the porch planks.

This brought both Billy and Greer from their respective trances, and a trembling Archie Culligan crept from behind the weedy end of the rail car.

'Zowie, Ike! I can't believe it. You cold-cocked the big stud.'

'He blindsided *and* cold-cocked him,' Greer said proudly. 'Formidable. He isn't even breathing.'

'Tie him!' Billy Bellisarius hissed from the cot. 'Tape him! He isn't breathing, but his eyes are still open . . .'

The man's brown eyes never closed throughout the elaborate taping. Billy insisted they use all they could find. Archie even dashed to the office tent for strapping tape. Greer used a whole roll of athletic tape on the man's thick mouth alone. When Greener caught his wind and started breathing again, Billy tried to talk them into taping the nostrils shut. The eyes as well. Greener was blinking toward the sun. Ike rotated him instead, so he was looking at the peeling red paint on the old boxcar.

With Ike in the lead and Greer and the Culligan boy

each holding a handle at the rear, they started across the rail yard with the hospital cot, moving as fast as they could without spilling Billy into the cinders. But nobody seemed very interested in them: the men continued to grind rocks; the women and kids to worry the little fields. Except the bush-bean field was empty. When the trio had carried the stretcher to the top of the stony knoll they saw where the bush-bean crew had been dispatched. They were chopping away at the float plane as though it were covered with invisible weeds. One pontoon was sunk and the drooping near wing was completely shredded. It reminded Ike of the foil frozen-food trays around the dump after the hogs and bears had gnawed and clawed them clean. Some of the women had tucked up their long skirts and were wading around to start on the other side.

'That's one kilt Otter,' Greer said. 'Suppose they'll skin it and try to tan the pelt.'

'They'll skin *us*,' Archie said, 'when they find out what you-all done to the Reverend Greener—'

'What *you*-all done?' Greer said. 'How about *we*-all, white man?'

'We're in thick shit,' Billy said against the cot. 'You can't believe how he runs these people, Isaak. If he ordered them to make compost out of us, all they'd ask is which pile, base or alkali.'

Greer nodded in urgent accord. 'Billy's right, Ike. We're gonna have to off him before he gets unwrapped. In fact, I'll do it. I'd rather face a murder rap than a week up here with that black timebomb. I'd crack like a Easter egg.'

'What about that handcar back at the yard?' Ike asked Archie. 'Does it work?'

'I never seen anybody—you mean all the way to *Skagway*?'

'It's downhill, isn't it?'

The man on the porch was now fully awake and active, rolling back and forth and contorting like a pupa trying to break its wrapping. Billy couldn't resist hissing a parting taunt—'Ice, asshole!'—then they ran with the cot, all of them bent forward as though running through

171

gunfire. The shackled suitcase was dragging and bumping along at the end of Billy's arm.

The cot was too high for the cart—the pump handles would have been pounding at Billy's head and heels— so it was cast aside and Billy was arranged on the cart's wooden floor, belly down with his head forward and his arms around his suitcase like an alloy pillow. Greer and Archie Culligan took the handles forward and Ike began to push as they pumped. The ancient machine pulled free of the vines and began creaking stiffly along the rusty track. The bearings moaned and the old wood popped and cracked, but gradually it began to move. When it was going at a fast walk Ike jumped on board and took his end of the pump handle. It moaned to a stop and he had to hop back off and push again. They were still going slightly uphill, through the scabrous boulders. They didn't connect to the main track until almost at the top of the rise. By then Ike was seeing stars. When he was sure they were finally going fast enough he hopped back aboard and grabbed his end of the pump handle.

'Goes pretty good.' Greer grinned. 'I ain't even sweating.'

'I'm shaking too hard to sweat.' Archie Culligan was pumping hard, veins and eyes bulging.

Except for the sharp protests from the ancient wooden floorboards, the cart seemed in fine shape. The pulsing whine coming from the fulcrum motor sounded sturdy and well greased. And the hub bearings had stopped howling in all but one of the iron wheels. Almost as though it had been kept greased for just such an escape. Even Beulahland had to have a back door ready, it seemed.

Ike settled in on the pump, glad to have something physical to attend to, his ears still ringing with the adrenaline. Knocked the big motherfucker *out,* he grinned.

The car was moving at about trotting speed now. Nobody said anything. Greer and Archie, riding backward, were involved with looking back down the tracks more than pumping. Ike felt he could pump the thing by himself, but didn't know for how long.

'Come on you two, stop gawking and pump. *Pump!* And it isn't the downpush, it's the *lift*—'

'*Here they come!*' Archie shrieked. 'O, Jesus, take me now!'

Ike twisted to look. There was indeed some kind of tumult back down that little spur, of sunburned bodies and flashes of foil, but it looked more like a recess of kids let out to play than a pursuing mob of zealots. Billy raised up on one elbow to look back and had the same opinion.

'They haven't found him. They're going to be like a knocked-apart wasp nest when they do, though. So pump hard. Incident'ly, I want to thank you fine gentlemen for the rescue. The Reverend was beginning to *pressure* the Squid a little, I'll admit. The son-of-a-bitch doesn't know much about physics or meteorology, but he does understand pressure.'

They were going fast enough that Ike let himself ease up. 'How the hell did you get tangled up with this guy, Squid?'

Billy had scooted back a little to be away from Archie's ragged deck shoes; he was able to recline over the suitcase on his side. With his thinning locks and hospital gown he had the air of a rich Roman in his litter.

'It was him came to me, Isaak, like a magnet. I think I represent some kind of doppelgänger to him, only with brains instead of brawn, so he wanted to mind-fuck me. I wasn't worried; I figured I can mind-fuck with the best of 'em, right? Head on. That's when I found out he wasn't into seduction, he was into forced entry.'

'He's one gnarly monster, Mr Sallas,' Archie said. 'I can't be*lieve* you iced him like that. Ka-FOOM!'

'That's because my main mon here, he don' take the mother-fucker head on like Squid did.' Greer was beaming proudly at Ike. 'Jooks him out of his jockstrap and blindsides him. Mm! "S'cuse me, Reverend Greener, sir, look dere; you shoe's untied," then ka-FOOM! Jooked him and ka-*FOOM*. The champ.'

173

Ike had to grin at his friend's call of the action. He did feel like he'd been in a prizefight—not on a rickety wooden porch, but in a ring, under the lights. 'I'm lucky Archie warned me about his eyeball thing.'

'Bird-and-cobra thing,' Billy said. 'Fascinating. I only saw eyes like that one other time,' the little man reminisced from his supine position. 'On an acidhead Buddhist from Boulder. This Buddhist ate butter for seven months, then torched himself. He didn't need any starting fluid, either.'

'You couldn't *get* Greener to burn,' Archie said. 'He's made of some kind of fireproof rubber or something. That's why he's so happy about this Fire This Time thing—*he's* not going to burn. God *damn*, Mr Sallas, I still can't believe it—'

'What was this "fire or ice" routine you two had going, Squid?'

'That was the bone of contention. Poem by Frost. "Fire and Ice," I quoted it at him in the course of our colloquy. "Some say the world will end in fire and some say in ice—da da da du da something something . . . But if I had to perish twice, I think I know enough of hate to say that for destruction ice—is also great—and would suffice." Say, chaps, I think we've achieved escape velocity. Ease up on the pistons.'

The three released the handles and let them pump away with the car's momentum. Greer and Archie turned around forward and sat down at the car's front. Greer sat cross-legged, holding his knees. Archie Culligan was stumpy enough to let his legs dangle. Ike hunkered at the rear to catch his breath. The rails swooped brightly ahead, banking into the blood-orange glow.

'Look at that sunset, my brave compadres,' Greer said. 'We ride into it like great western heroes of old. It has been a glorious day for the Underdogs.'

Greer and Billy lifted their voices in the club howl and Ike joined in.

'How long do you think it will take us to roll down to Skagway?' Archie's horizons were suddenly opening up.

'If we make it by eleven we can hitch on the tour boat back to Juneau.'

Billy looked at his wristwatch. 'It's ten-thirty now and thirty miles to Skagway—let's hope to God we don't pick up that kind of speed. I don't see any kind of brakes on this thing.'

'You probably brake with the pump some way.' Greer turned around, concerned. 'It would have to have brakes to work in hills like these . . . wouldn't it?'

'Maybe it wasn't made to work in hills like these,' Ike said. 'Grab hold. Let's see how much we can slow it by resisting.'

After a minute straining against the teeter-totter motion of the pumps Greer let go his end of the handle. 'None whatsoever is how much. We're going to have to jump.'

'Screw that,' Billy said. 'Look at those rocks whizzing by! Even if nobody breaks a leg I still got a cracked coccyx.'

'Billy, I don't know,' Ike said, 'this mama's highballing. And we've just started.'

The steady ringing roar of the metal wheels had grown louder, and the whine of gears in the motor higher. The handles were going up and down like a sewing machine.

'Yeah, Mr Bellisarius. Nels and me hiked this track one summer. It gets pretty hairy.'

'This track was built to handle it!' Billy laughed shrilly. He was beginning to crack a little all right. He didn't want to jump and he didn't want to be left alone, either. 'You think these old steam trains could have been running up and down this pass since 1899 if they hadn't banked the turns adequately? We can ride it out.'

'We better all get down, then,' Ike said, 'get our center of gravity as low as possible. Because, my Brothers, I think we are now past the point of jumping.'

The rail banked suddenly the other direction to follow the side of the mountain. A wild torrent that was the beginning of the Skagway River crashed through the dynamited rubble to their left. On their right a black rock wall rose almost perpendicular from the railroad bed. The three had to belly down to crawl beneath the hammering blur of the handles, Ike with his head forward facing Billy on the other side of the pump housing, Greer and Archie crawling toward the back. They had just got settled when the car veered hard left and thundered across a covered bridge to the opposite side of the narrow ravine. All four men screamed, like kids on a roller coaster. Ike found himself laughing face-to-face with Billy.

'I say, Isaak,' Billy shouted, 'this doesn't look like your ordinary E-ticket ride, does it?'

'No, Squid, it doesn't,' Ike shouted back. 'We better see if we can't get a hold on each other. You sure you can't get this damn case off your arm?'

'Positive.'

Ike was able to reach one arm to Billy's and the other across Greer's ankles to the car side. 'Latch on, back there!' he shouted over his shoulder. There was no answer, but he felt Greer securing his ankles in the same way. He could feel the gears in the housing humming against his ribs and the water drops from the rocks above stinging against his forehead. When they banked hard again into the next switchback he felt the centrifugal force press him into the floorboards. Maybe Billy was right: these old tracks had to be banked accurately to have lasted this long.

Then they thundered back into another covered trestle and they all screamed again. Archie screamed, '*Jee*-zus take me, *please*—' Greer screamed back, 'Too *la-a-ate*!' and everybody laughed. Dipping, careening, banking, screaming. The clickety-click of the rail sections coming faster and faster beneath the steel wheels made a whine so shrill the men had to scream along or go mad; then the car would level out and slow down a little so everyone could catch their breath and get ready for the next plummeting dive or nut-sucking switchback.

'This thing could become more famous than the Rattler Coaster in Arizona,' Greer shouted during a leveling lull. 'All it needs is a loop-the-loop.'

The difference, as they soon came to understand, was a ride in an amusement park comes to an end after a certain logical period of time has elapsed—a coordination of how many thrills and chills can be coaxed from the kinetic energy banked by the first climb. Usually only a hundred feet or so high. But this kinetic bank had a deposit of thousands of feet of unchecked foot-pounds back to sea level with none of those second and third and fourth rises up inclines to catch your breath the way you can in amusement parks. This wild ride just kept going, down, down, down, around slashing flares of fern and salal, along sheer cliff sides and murderous switchbacks of rip-rap, over cracking wooden trestles and through blasted stone tubes where bears and raccoons pressed terror-stricken back against tight tunnel walls to let the insane business go screaming past.

The torrent became a roaring stream, the mist warmer. And the sky grew thicker, rusty-dark, until they could see the trail of sparks they were leaving behind them on tight turns. The screams and laughter turned to groans, '*O*, shit . . . *no* more . . . let it *stop*!' But it kept going. After a bombilating crash-dive through a snaggle of fallen branches, Archie Culligan declared, 'I can't stand no more,' and started to get to his knees to abandon ship. The pump handle caught him right between the shoulder blades and flattened him again. Ike found himself half-hoping the rail did have some little flaw in its banking system, some engineering miscalculation that would fling them off the high side and put a merciful end to their deafening descent. But the little car never so much as tipped up on two wheels. It just kept plummeting and booming. Well, Greener, here's one thing that still works, he thought. The sky may be a-bleeding and the sea a-boiling, but gravity still works. All this Einsteinian stuff is interesting—titillating—but if you want to put your money in some reliable old blue-chip stocks, buy Newtonian. He noticed that the shaking and banking was working some of the screws through the wooden

177

platform, though. It might shake to pieces even if it didn't leave the track.

The first lights of approaching civilization appeared down the tracks ahead of them at last. It was the White Pass RR and Historical Graveyard, where Soupy Smith and a few of the other old stampeders were planted at the edge of town for the benefit of the Skagway tourists. A girl in a ranger hat was sitting on the museum loading dock as they flew by. She was holding a can of Coke and a copy of *Vogue*.

'Call ahead!' Ike shouted. 'Switch us through.'

'Through to *where*?' she shouted back.

'Right. Through to where, old chum?' Billy, at his sardonic best, asked Ike. 'To Liverpool? Frankfurt?'

'No. The line turns at the Skagway yard on to the roundabout, so they can get the engine headed back up.'

'Where does it go if it doesn't turn?'

'It goes straight,' Ike told him. 'To the docks.'

They came into town screaming again. They had saved that much. The girl had called. The stretch past the station had been cleared of cars, just in case the runaway she had reported turned out to be real. A switchman in early-American railroad regalia stood with his hand on the switch, looking more disbelieving than authentic. He stood petrified at the sight of the car screaming toward him until the yard boss's voice shrieked at him from a breast-pocket radio—'It's real, it's real! Do it!'

The switchman heaved the lever and the straight-ahead opened up, right across the festive expanse of lighted dock where vendors hawked Goldburgers and Nugget McNuggets; through a flock of fat ravens being popcorned by Elks from Elko, Nevada; straight past Silent Land, where town ordinances had sent the overflow of mimes that always showed up during tourist time, like anonymous flies following shit . . . straight ahead for the end of the line at the edge of the dock.

The Germans were just returning on their mule-drawn wagon of straw, satiated. They had dined on king crab legs and oysters barbecued on the half-shell in butter and lemon and garlic. They had drunk beer served by the can-can girls from Dawson Creek with their canned cans. They had gambled with Gold Rush Dollars at the Eagles' Days of 1898 Revue and they had cheered halfheartedly when the evil con man Soupy Smith succumbed before the trusty ax blade of young Jack London. They had seen the box that enclosed the urn that held the ashes of Sam McGee and the Plaztex vault containing the BIGGEST NUGGET EVER FOUND. But the memory that all of them would carry home, enshrined like an extinct insect in the amber of their beery brains, was the spectacle of four men——auth*entic* Alaskans—on a full-tilt yellow handcart going like a blitzkrieg from hell across the wooden dock, through a wooden gate, beneath a chain that ripped away the pylon, handles still pumping, straight into the sandbagged abutment at the ocean's edge.

The car stopped stone-still and sudden, but the car's wooden deck kept on unchecked with its four screaming authentics, out into space, twenty, *thirty* meters through the air before it struck water and went skipping along like a seagoing toboggan. The Germans were remarkably impressed, and their cheering was not the slightest halfhearted. This was worth the whole Only in America tour ticket price.

Billy Bellisarius would have drowned—he was one of those solid-state cooked-down sorts that refuse to float—but for the suitcase cuffed to him. Archie Culligan managed to pull the little man's head up so he could cough and sputter over his aluminum lifebuoy until a rowboat from the pier found them. It was being rowed by Billy's ex-wife and captained by the big hairy-armed nurse from the clinic. They seemed to have been waiting. They pulled the four adventurers on board, then rowed quickly back beneath the piers out of sight of the cheering Germans and the converging railway authorities.

'The Reverend Greener forgives you, Billy,' the woman explained in a tender voice. She had a glow in her eyes

179

and golden crosses painted on each long fingernail. 'He forgives you all. He's on the way now to take you back.'

'On the way *how*?' Ike wanted to know. 'Did he have another handcar at the ready?'

'Oh, for heaven sakes!' The nurse laughed at the very idea. 'The Reverend has his own private *heli*copter!'

'So much for tradition,' Ike said, already casting about in his mind as they bumped along in the oily dark beneath the docks. The nurse would be easy. Billy's long-nailed ex with the holy fanatic glow was going to take a little more thought. But he felt calm. When it came to to-it time he could handle whatever. He had resurrected something long forgotten. Jook 'em then blindside 'em, let the shits fall where they may.

9

Here Is Potlatch for One and All
Into the Firepit and Gone for Good

Alice saw the guy slip past her window before she was awake—saw the yellow flash of his vest, to be precise. She knew exactly the kind of vest it was—one of those sleeveless Levi look-alikes that a lot of tribes were ordering, with traditional or personal totems embroidered in glosilk on the back. They ordered them by the gross from Korea.

She slid from beneath her comforter, but didn't stand for fear of being seen. She crawled across the office floor on her hands and knees and peeked over the windowsill, like a cautious cat. The embroidered totem she beheld was a purple penis with thunderbird wings.

'I see,' she whispered to herself. 'It's that nasty old sonofabitch Daddy-daddy, fresh from a cowboy-and-Indian show.'

Daddy-daddy was, she thought, of Tlingit descent. He never said specifically, and certainly no tribe was about to claim him.

As well as his glosilk vest, the decadent old Deap was decked out in new rodeo regalia. A blue Stetson with rhinestone band was jammed on his matted hair, and stiff new Lee jeans were stuffed in the tops of his boots. In one hand he held a kid's stick horse that looked like it had a real horsehair mane. The mane and the broomstick were dyed to match: royal penis purple. She saw that over his shoulder Daddy-daddy carried a plastic shopping bag with a maple leaf printed on it. That meant the nasty old sonofabitch must have come over from Calgary, the winner of one of those stupid Indian events.

Like the Pendleton Round-Up, the Calgary Stampede still staged some traditional events open only to Deaps with full-blood verification from the Bureau. He'd probably won the buffalo hunt or the blanket relay—probably because the poppers he sniffed kept him sober enough to be the last to fall. The events were staged mainly for comic relief, and were affairs emphasizing attrition more than tradition.

The old fool was skulking through the fireweed at the back of her cabins, with his sacks and stick horse, like some kind of guilty Santa. Daddy-daddy made Alice think of her own father, Alexis. Not that they looked at all alike. Old Alexis Levertov had been an angular scarecrow of a skulker, whereas Daddy-daddy was a muddy brown lump. She couldn't make out much more than the lump's rounded back scurrying through the dry weeds, but she could picture his face: round as a pie and the color of last week's coffee; scummed-over eyes; toothless mouth in a guilty grin. No, not toothless, not completely. He still possessed several rotting snags. Once, when Carmody had queried Daddy-daddy about how he lost his teeth, the old native had asked, 'Would you like to know one at a time?'

'I reckon I can do without the miniseries,' Carmody had answered. 'Give me the *TV Guide* summary.'

'Some I lose to candy and cake, some I lose to alcohol and argument.'

Now Big Chief Sweet Toothless was peeking around the rear corner of the Bear Flag Inn, bent over like a fat ape, the seat of his trousers stained a dark maroon blot where he'd set in something, probably Mad Dog 50-50. And split open to boot, Alice observed; a coffee-colored butt flashed obscenely through a wide rip as he crept out of sight around the corner.

'A credit to the whole bare-assed blood,' Alice remarked aloud. Then she remembered her own naked rear and crawled back from the window to look for her clothes.

She would have to go down and deal with Daddy-daddy, she knew, before he got too dug in and drunk down at his wife's unit —before he reached the punching-somebody-in-the-family stage. But she knew this usually took a while, so she dressed leisurely and took time to nuke a cup of yesterday's Colombian. Then a second cup. She would need the extra zoom to deal with a Daddy-daddy this early, this loaded with gifts. He could be frisky. One morning Daddy-daddy showed up with a live wolverine on a leash. He had traded a saddle for the beast in Missoula. She warned him that wolverines were hard to gentle, but he reassured her it was guaranteed to have been bottle raised. After it bit one of the daughters, then the mother, then him—on the dick—Daddy-daddy dragged it out into the courtyard on the end of its leash and tied it to a post, thrashing and snarling, and executed it with an Uzi. And kept executing it, with clip after clip and a disturbing look of relish. This damn execution stuff was getting *good* to him, he proclaimed to the worried witnesses. By the time Alice had got the Arvas Patrol to the scene Daddy-daddy had the gun turned on the bitten daughter and was accusing her of *provoking* the poor unfortunate creature. He could be that kind of drunk.

Daddy-daddy must have come in last night on the ferry jet from Eyak with that big crowd of Deap relatives and spent the night at the casino. Deap relatives were flocking in thick and fast, from distant and dubious moieties all up and down the coast, homing in on the news of Kuinak's recent windfall of movie money and casino action. That's what had lured him back so soon. Usually it was at least six months.

One of Daddy-daddy's many wives lived in Unit 5, with two or three of the old chief's daughters. Or four—Alice was never sure of the exact number. They always managed to make the rent. The girls worked occasionally down at the cannery with the rest of the fishkids, and the mother whittled out little argolite trinkets that she commissioned out of the Artifactory up in Sitka. Her pieces were the customary pseudo-native crap—bears and whales and seals; pseudo-Huna—but Alice had seen some of them that did have a touch. Occasionally one of the woman's carvings still showed that strict, clean line that had been Huna. The Hunas had never worked in argolite, of course, not traditionally. They were traditionally cedar weavers or boxmakers, but what sensible tourist wants to sleep under a coverlet made of splinters? Or haul around a big wooden box? Tourists wanted something compact enough to sit on the coffee table and say to the neighbors, 'Look at me. I am an authentic collectible.' Argolite figures were the acceptable items, from whatever tribe.

Daddy-daddy's wife was able to turn over about three of these black carvings a year. They had touch enough to bring high dollar at the equinox artifact auctions. Usually, around about auction time, Daddy-daddy could be counted on to show up and claim his chiefly share of the sale—and to go on his chiefly bender. After a week or so of drink and domestic abuse he would finally get kicked out and go scuttling and shuttling on up the coast to another of his families, like a crabber checking a line of traps. But Alice didn't think she could abide a week of him at this particular time. There were issues of greater import.

When she had finished her second cup, Alice checked her phone tapes in the little office below. Not a goddamned word from Carmody, or from those knight-errant clowns in Skagway, either. The only messages were from an official of the Daughters of the Deap. Nearly a dozen repeated calls were logged to remind Alice that this was Native Pride Week and the Daughters expected all ladies of blood to take part. At the end of these lengthy naggings was a message from her son on the yacht, a callback code; Alice punched it in and the machine on the other end answered.

'Hi, Mom-o!' the recorded voice purred. 'Ten AM You still aren't up? My my. Well, I still *am* up and I just wanted to remind you that our esteemed cast is arriving today. Early afternoon. They'll need at least two units, three would be better. Kissy-kiss.'

Alice stared at the machine. Our esteemed cast? Two units? What the hell was he talking about? She vaguely remembered Nick saying *some*thing about the movie company reserving some of her suites—months ago, had he said?—but she had dismissed it as just more of his Southern California sarcasm. No movie company had reserved jack shit as far as *she* could recall. She flipped through the notebook on the little rolltop into the scribbled past. Uh-oh. Three months ago a company named Foxworks had sent a little note and a check to reconfirm their phone call. The deposit check was folded in the book with the note, still uncashed; the note made it clear that a family of Johanssens was due to arrive the first of the month. In the journal Alice saw her own before-coffee handwriting: 'Party of eight, perhaps more, confirmed.'

Alice looked at her watch. It was the first of the month all right, and almost noon. She rubbed her face. She never slept till noon. She wasn't zoning off scoot like a lot of the town, so why was she sleeping so late all of a sudden? She had always been able to hop out of bed on cue, with nothing but her inner alarm, even when she wasn't on cannery duty or taking a boat out. But this last week or so, since taking this set-design assignment, and with Carmody gone and without Sallas and his Rasta henchman to keep on the hop—that alarm seemed to be on its own sabbatical.

She cleared the machine of messages, turned the chip over and hurried back up the little spiral staircase to nuke the last of the pot. She then called up her horseshoe-shaped unit board on her laptop and leaned toward it through the coffee steam. Okay, one unit would be easy—Old Norway in Number 4. Norway was overdue by at least a month, not just on his rent but in his little bowpicker. He had putt-putted out of the bay months ago claiming he was bored and was going to Nome for the dog race—'Joost be gone a couple weeks, then I be back for gillnet opening.' Calls to Nome shed no light on his whereabouts. There was talk that the old Scandinavian was *bound* to have drowned this time, and that his gillnet

185

quota should be put up for auction, but nobody really believed it. Norway had been many times missing and always eventually turned up in his tiny inboard from all over the map—Seattle . . . Lima . . . Puerto Vallarta . . . and once as far away as Hawaii. Nobody knew how he could do it, drift so far without instruments, and return. 'It is the new Japanese Current,' Norway explained. 'You joost keep with the flowing.'

And the second unit would have to be the young frostback couple in 7, the Navidads. They were two kids from Mazatlán who had slipped in by way of Canada—'for to buy a place to put down new roots.' But they were too shy to pound the docks and fight for the work to make the money to buy that place. They hadn't paid their rent in eight weeks. The boy seemed capable and ambitious enough; he had photos of himself working the tuna pursuit boats off Manzanillo, so he had to be a sailor with energy and skill, but he was just too timid about his faulty English. He couldn't force himself to go out and ask about work. He couldn't even go out and ask about firewood. So the pair spent most of their time in bed in front of the Bear Flag soapdish, under piles of bedding.

Alice felt sorry for them, but extending their rent would just be putting off the inevitable. Southern blood was always coming up here for to put down new roots, but they rarely took. Greer was the only successful transplant from the tropics that she could think of, offhand—he'd been ten years in the area—and even he was still pretty rootless.

The third cottage was going to be the hard one. Alice spread her reservation calendar out on her desk and sipped her coffee. She was just beginning to riffle through her choices when she heard gunfire—a goddamn *pistol* shot, almost directly below her—ka*rack!*—followed by a high, girlish shriek. Then two more shots and more shrieking. It had to be coming from the domicile of Daddy-daddy's wife and girls.

Alice stepped into her rubber boots and grabbed up the shotgun Carmody made her keep behind her rolltop.

It was an old ten-gauge double barrel, sawed off just a few centimeters long of illegal. She had used it a number of times, but never fired it. Carmody had told her she likely would never need to. 'You'll find there's something about looking down them two big bloody black holes that'll discourage most of your run-of-the-mill desperados. So don't be shootin' it unless ye bloody well have to,' he instructed her, 'and if ye *do* shoot it, ye try not to pull both triggers at oncet. These ten-gauge shells are impossible to get more of. Plus you'll bust your collarbone.'

She stepped out into the bright courtyard holding the weapon and feeling bloody well ready to use it. Her shadow on the raked shells reminded her of one of the imitation cave paintings the tourists liked: warrior with spear, a trite-and-true favorite. And that made her feel ridiculous. Nothing made her feel dumber than looking trite-and-true. Then she heard the sharp crack again and hurried on, ignoring the shadow. This time the pistol crack was followed by whimpers and a stifled groan. It was coming from Unit 5 all right. She ran across the shells to the cottage's front. There were no curtains on the windows but she still wasn't able to see in. Like a lot of the tenants who had to supply their own fuel, Daddy-daddy's family had stapled layer after layer of Vizqueen over the windows to keep out the cold. Nothing could be seen through the plastic except murky, jerky movements. She tried her pass key, clashing it loudly in her haste. No-one inside seemed to notice. The groaning continued, and the whimpering and some wheezing. Then there was another sharp volley of cracks. It sounded like a little target pistol loaded with shorts—probably a dinky little .22. Somebody was going to be very surprised to see Carmody's big ten-gauge. The key finally worked and she booted the door open and stepped through crouching like a swatter.

The smell struck her first—a rank, nauseating combination of organic and inorganic odors. It jarred her nostrils and stung tears from her eyes. All she could do was cough and blink. When her vision cleared she gasped in amazement at the scene carrying on uninterrupted before her. On the coverless box springs there was Daddy-daddy, teetering on his knees, his brown bottom now completely bare and redly welted. In one hand he gripped the bedpost and in the other he held the broomstick pony. The purple mane was flying, and the plastic purple nose was buried up to the bit in the wool of one of Daddy-daddy's roly-poly daughters—the eldest, Alice thought. The girl was reclined on the mattress wearing a swollen smile and a peach-colored cowboy hat. The middle daughter was alongside her sister, up on an elbow smoking a cigarette. She had on a suede vest and a bolo tie. The youngest of the girls wore a feathered headdress with bells on the band. She was on all fours at the father's front, groaning through her nose and jingling like a reindeer. Alice had to fight to keep her three cups of coffee from surfacing to join the action.

Standing at the foot of the bed was Wifey-wife. She had a new cowboy hat, too, and a pair of boots to match. The design was maple leaf. Daddy-daddy had just come from the Calgary Stampede all right. The Canadian promoters still preferred to reimburse their Indian participants with trade goods whenever possible. Some things never change.

The old woman also had a special souvenir—one of the little green buggy whips they sell at the gift stands. That was what had produced the pistol cracks and the red welts.

The wheezing and whimpering was coming from the open door of the bathroom. The whimpering came from a fluffy half-husky pup. A big red bandanna had been tied around the little animal's neck, cowboy style, but the kerchief was so big he was tangled in it and was trying to chew free. The wheezing was coming from another plump girl—so there *were* four daughters—dressed in an old sweatshirt and thermal pants. No rodeo gifts for this neglected waif? Then Alice saw something yellow shoved up each wide nostril. Amyl nitrite ampules. *That*

188

accounted for the inorganic smell. Thoughtful Daddy-daddy had brought home something for everyone.

'Out!' Alice's scream shattered the tableau. She was shaking violently, as much from fear as from outrage; she sensed that she was right on the shaky verge of eradicating the whole filthy frieze, collarbone be damned. 'The whole rotten dirty lot of you *out* . . . right fucking *now*!'

'Ah, now, sister,' the old man clucked, grinning his three-toothed grin, 'ease down, let's discuss this. Everything is okay. Everybody's copacetic. You want a popper?'

'I want you out is all I want! Now! All of you! Immediately! Go on up to the dump and fuck the pigs, if that's your style, but go *now*! I'll send your shit along later—'

'Now, Mrs Carmody, sister,' the woman echoed her husband, 'don't be so upset. This is not no big thing. As a matter of historical fact, you know, a *lot* of the old chieftains used to enjoy relationships with their—'

'Out! Out! Out!' Alice shrieked. They must have noticed her shaking fingers on the shotgun triggers because the frieze suddenly came apart in panicked movement. Without another word of discussion they were all scuttling away, wrapped in ragged towels and robes and blankets, back around the corner and into the sunny fireweed, the way the old man had come. The crows reported their progress across the vacant lot.

They had been out of sight a long time before Alice lowered the weapon and sagged against the windowsill. She let the bitter brown juice retch out of her, she didn't care where it landed.

When she felt better she rinsed out her mouth and set about chucking the household's fetid clutter out the door—tennis shoes, magazines and makeup boxes; dirty laundry and dishes and silverware; the hot plate that had been hidden in the closet; an expensive Slitman and a box of the latest and vilest Meatstreet slits. She chucked the big crap out until she was panting, then attacked the little stuff with renewed disgust. Even *pigs* would not have amassed such worthless clutter; pigs would have trodden it under their sharp little trotters.

The bathroom was the only room that didn't completely disgust her. To her surprise there were no cheap cosmetics or oils or hair-pieces piled about on the draining board. These had all been out on the little vanity table in the bedroom, as though to protect the precious unguents. For the bathroom countertop was thick with black grime and strewn with carving tools—knives, chisels, emery wheels. The tile floor was completely covered with chiseled chips, and argolite dust was everywhere, like shiny black snow. The old wife had obviously claimed the bathroom as her carving studio; she must have worked sitting on the commode, under the glaring fluorescent, while the girls watched soaps on the dish in the other room. The poor Deap twinkies. They weren't bad looking, just roly-poly. In a natural past they would have been courted by boatfuls of roly-poly braves. Now it looked like they had to make do with Daddy.

Alice found the piece the woman had been working on—almost ten inches long and almost finished. She cradled it in her palm and ran a finger along its ebony length. It was intended to be a raven, or perhaps a loon. But the carver had started with the head too large for the piece of material, so the form had been forced to narrow down abruptly. There were no wings or feet, just beak and head and folded wings running smoothly back to the tail in a graceful crescent, like a slice of black moon. It reminded Alice of Giacometti's *Bird in Flight*. Giacometti's spare crescent was far superior, of course— the essence of the essence of soaring flight, captured in wingless abstraction—but this sad old cow had come pretty close. The piece had a touch of that essence, a palpable touch.

She put the carving back on the countertop and swept the whole collection into a pillowcase.

After she finished with 5 she went on to 2. The young Mexican couple must have been watching. They were already packed when she knocked on the door, standing amid their belongings with downcast faces. As they left the boy insisted on giving Alice a check to cover the rent

owed. *'Por favor,* Mrs Carmody; you been to us kind of.'
Alice took it with a grunt; she saw it was from a bank
in Mazatlán. When the kids were out of sight she tore it
up.

The Old Norwegian's quarters she took more time
with, packing his books and photos and collection of
pipes carefully away in cardboard boxes. He'd show
back up someday. Even if he didn't his goods at least
deserved some little portion of the respect he'd obviously
paid them. She stacked the boxes in the storage off the
laundry room, taking care that the one with the old framed
photos was on top. Then she went after the windows.

Clean windows were important to Alice. She detested
stapled Vizqueen. 'If you want storm windows buy storm
windows,' she would tell her tenants. 'Windows are to
see out of. You wouldn't tape a bread wrapper over your
eyeglasses just because you wanted to keep your eyes
warm, would you?'

It wasn't just the sheets of shitty plastic—though these
were adequately disgusting—it was also the dirt they
harbored. Spiders made their snares between them, and
the carcasses of flies and moths and other spiders that
got snared were laminated by the next sheet. The windows on the Daddy-daddy unit were like entomological
exhibits.

She was ripping down the last of these murky mem-
branes when the delegation from the Daughters of the
Deap showed up. They told her they were there for
the belongings of Daddy-daddy and family. They had
heard about the pitiless eviction. Alice pointed them
toward the pile of clutter in front of Unit 5.

'Alice, as a Bloodsister you could have been more
careful with that unfortunate family's possessions,' the
leader of the group chided. 'A family's possessions are
part of their spirit life.'

'Crap's crap,' Alice answered, snatching at the remaining pennants of Vizqueen. The leader was Doreen Eagle,
a hot-faced scowler with huge pockmarks on her flat
forehead. Carmody had once said that if Doreen Eagle

191

was Siamese twins she could have served as a waffle iron. It had been Doreen's voice on the answering machine nagging Alice about the upcoming Deap Pride Week.

'Besides, that wasn't a family,' Alice felt obliged to add. 'That was a freak show. They could go up to Anchorage and make good money demonstrating their talents.'

'This is cruel from you,' Doreen admonished, 'and is not good for the solidarity of the Bloodsister Movement. We all must keep kind and tender souls to each other. We must keep at our solidarity.'

Alice kept at her window-cleaning chore and kept her mouth shut. Some comments about what they could do with the whole air-brained Bloodsister Movement went through her mind, but she kept them to herself.

It wasn't until the women had left with the family's precious pile of possessions that Alice went back into the unit and discovered none of those kind and tender souls had thought to take the pup. It was cringing behind the overturned laundry hamper, the tatters of the kerchief still knotted around its throat. She picked it up and untied the rag and saw it was a female. It weighed practically nothing; the little ribs felt like a washboard beneath the fur. 'Pup, you're nothing but fluff and bones.' The pup whined and trembled. Alice had never been fond of dogs, but this little wretch was so skinny and shivering and pitiful—Christ! How could people get so fat and let a puppy get so skinny?

'Come on, Worthless. Let's go up to my place and see what we can find for you to gnaw on.'

There were scraps of a Chicken Lickin in her refrigerator. The puppy fell on these in a slobbering frenzy. When Alice tried to pull away the larger bones for fear the animal might choke, she got a good snap. Alice laughed and opened a can of tuna and coaxed her away from the bones. The pup gobbled the canned fish as Alice brewed fresh coffee. It was while she was sitting at the table watching Worthless gnaw the empty can that Alice remembered her promise to check in on Ike Sallas' old dog, Marley. 'Damn, Alice.' She slapped her forehead. '*Now* who's air-brained!' A minute later she was rushing out to her Samurai, carrying a box full of tossed-together canned goods under one arm, the pup under the other. What else could she do with the damned thing? If she left it inside it would shit and piss all over her office; if she left it outside some of the roving Rottweilers would rip it to ribbons for sport.

'Damn all dogs and damn all dog owners; I don't know which is the bigger nuisance. Get in back, Worthless. I'm afraid you're about to attend a funeral for one of your distant worthless relatives.'

But Marley wasn't starved; he wasn't even very hungry looking. He came stiffly from beneath the trailer, grinning to greet this first human company in days, whoever they were. Tracks in the mud around the trailer showed that his only other visitors had been four-footers of the smaller, varmint variety. Marley even managed a little stiff-legged romp to impress the pup. The vacation from Emil Greer's night-owl adventures and Ike Sallas' brooding presence seemed to have done the old dog some good, Alice thought. Foxes and raccoons and wildcats probably were a welcome relief.

There was still plenty of Purina Chow in the bottom of the fifty-pound sack, for all the varmint sign around it. And the five-gallon plastic bucket tied to the wheel was still more than half full of water. The pup was enormously honored to make old Marley's acquaintance. It rolled on its back and wriggled and whimpered while Marley rumbled big bad Papa Wolf warnings deep in his chest. Alice shook her head. These macho male ceremonies always amused her, whatever the species—the way elk racketed their horns together in the spring meadows, like little boys with wooden swords; the way roosters crowed and cock-walked after the conquest of some dizzy pullet; even the way sugardudes came prancing up to a twinkie in a bar, all sucked in and shoulders rocking and eyes lidded like bedroom windows with the shades almost drawn, but *not* quite. Their barroom prancing was

193

like this old dog's rumbling—too primal to get pissed at, too ridiculous to take seriously.

'Snap him on the snoot, Worthless, if he gets too tiresome. Your snappers are sharper than his.'

But Worthless was happy to keep groveling and whimpering. After living with Daddy-daddy's litter this menacing old growler was probably a welcome relief, too. The dogs growled and groveled until Alice finally laughed aloud and kicked shells at them.

'Okay, that's enough. Don't talk it to death. How about some of this canned Boyardee Spaghettios? I'll find a can opener . . .'

As though dismissed from ceremony by her tone, both dogs began to romp in the shells. Carrying her box of cans Alice followed the muddy trail of raccoon tracks up the metal steps and through the open door.

The trailer was a shambles—torn Oreo boxes, scattered cornflakes, elbow macaroni everywhere; a broken bottle of cooking sherry; a chewed-apart deck of Nudie Cutie poker cards—a worse mess than the Daddy-daddy digs, really. Over the whole interior, like a miniature snow scene, was a dusting of goose down from a ripped-up sleeping bag. She also noticed various deposits of lumpy turds arranged here and there, judiciously—in a sake cup on the countertop; in the silverware drawer; atop the North Pole on a little world globe table lamp by the bookcase. Alice found herself grinning anew. Yep, Old Marley had had some of the boys over all right—eat a little pasta, play a little poker and drink a little sweet wine—and had let things get a little out of hand. Or paw, as it were. If she'd waited another night she probably could have caught them with a stag film: *Bambi Does Dumbo*.

She found garbage bags beneath the sink and a broom in what had to be Greer's closet. The wardrobe looked like an exhausted Mardi Gras—smelled like one, too: Blackrum and Brut and Koolspice. The broom had been used as a make-do tie rack, leaned upside down and the ties strung between the broom straws. She hung the ties around the collar of a mauve sports coat and set to sweeping out the marauders' mess. She did feel she was somewhat responsible. If she'd been up here regular like she promised, this debauchery never would have happened. These primal animal rituals could get a little messy if not properly monitored.

It was Greer's area that needed cleaning the most—most of the Wild Thing action seemed to have taken place around Greer's tousled cot. The animals must have been attracted special to his flowery funk. Ike's area, on the other hand, had been left comparatively clean. His sleeping bag had been ripped, but mainly for decorative purposes, it appeared. There were no Oreo cookies rubbed into his pillow, no little nosegays of turds on any of his personal effects. Here was a male critter, it seemed, that other male critters gave a cushion of respect. Or didn't notice at all. Maybe Sallas had achieved a state of odor-free enlightenment with all this denial of the flesh, like certain hermits and holy men were said to achieve. As well as certain women she might name, not so holy.

Once the goose down was vacuumed away and the tipped-over pictures uprighted, Sallas' little niche was a study in neatness and economy. It was arranged a good deal like a stateroom, she realized, or a cell . . . an area where one had to be compact and efficient because it was all you were going to get until your time was up. A holdover from Navy days and jail time.

On the bedside bookcase there was a clock and a goose-neck lamp. The clock was an old-fashioned round face and the lamp still used the old inefficient incandescent bulbs. Not only spartan, Alice noted, but a bit sentimental. His only piece of wall art was a comic postcard common in a lot of souvenir shops: a black-and-white aerial photo of Kuinak and its ragged environs, with the joke line in big red capitals: GREETINGS FROM THE END OF THE WORLD!

Moving closer, she examined the offering in the little bookcase. The first shelf was for the framed photos she had uprighted. Now she looked at them. This must have been the famous platinum-blond wife, in a lawn chair

195

wearing halter and shorts, a fruit jar full of iced something balanced on the chair's aluminum arm rest. And this, the young couple on striped donkeys in classic Tijuana black-and-white. Maybe the honeymoon. And his Navy group wing photo on the deck of one of the Nightmoth carriers. And a shot of the crew from about eight years ago, on the deck of the *Sue-Z*: Carmody grinning, horsing around, pointing a hose at Greer sleeping on a pile of net. The payoff photo must not have come out.

There were more shots of the blonde and Sallas together —at a table in a nightclub somewhere . . . out in front of a mobile home not unlike this old red-roofed relic—but no shots of the kid; nowhere any photos of the famous kid.

The bottom two shelves were books, old books, hardbound. She eased her hip on to his bed to read the titles. Her eyes widened as she read. After a minute she said, 'Okay, Sallas, I'm impressed.'

It wasn't just the selection, though that in itself would have been impressive; every volume was a carefully considered American Classic—*Moby-Dick* . . . *As I Lay Dying* . . . *The Sun Also Rises* . . . *The Grapes of Wrath* . . . *On the Road*. It was also the books that *weren't* there. No lightweight travel novels, no how-to's or bios or gonzos. Sallas, it seemed, didn't have room for anything except the essential heavies. Then she saw the plastic box on the bottom shelf.

It was one of those Treasure Troves of Literature you ordered from late-night TV by punching in your Visa number—'Get the Condensed Classics in an Attractive Vizboard Box with Matching Laser Disk . . . Reader/Viewer edited.' It seemed completely out of place with the other bound tomes. She pulled it out and looked at the lettering on the side. This was the Children's Classics edition. In all the cramped and considered little bedside display this little box of books was the only indication that this past had ever known a child.

The seal on the box had never been broken and all the little books were still in their film package. She split it with her thumbnail and peeled it open. The spines

196

revealed *Hans Brinker and the Silver Skates . . . Peter Pan . . . Shoola and the Sea Lion*. After a moment's consideration Alice ran that thumbnail along the shrink film and withdrew the *Shoola* volume.

It was the same edition she'd known as a child, only shrunk to about one-third its original size. This was what these Treasure Trove houses did with most of the works they scavenged from the public domain. Still, the beautiful old print was the same, however shrunk, and the wonderful wispy illustrations that strayed in feathery half-tone in and out of the print were still rich and poignant. How she had loved these Shoola books . . . just the look and feel of them. Christ, how they had sucked her in. The stories were always complex enough to challenge a modern young reader, yet they seemed to have some drumbeat of authentic mythology pounding at the core. The pictures were suggestive enough to lure the mind, but spare enough to leave places for the imagination. Nice watercolor work. As a girl she had assumed that the mysterious old Eskimo storyteller, Isabella Anootka, had done the illustrations herself; now of course she knew better. Everybody now knew that Anootka was a total fraud, not an Eskimo of any blood, but a retired math teacher from New Jersey who had scrounged her stories together out of the ethnic wing of the public library. Maybe the artist they had hired had been more authentic. The illustrations had always had a nice touch to them, like that carving in the motel. Alice hoped she had been at least a Deap, this illustrator, not just another round-eye, faking it. She flipped to the credit page. It was full of printing history and renewed copyright claims, but no mention of any artist. On the title page, though, twined in with the smokey lines of the establishing picture that always led off the Shoola stories—seashore, longhouse in the distance, Shoola seen from behind with her trademark blackberry hair flying as she looks across the rocks and cliffs toward her tribal home—Alice finds a name. It takes her a moment to work out the letters: L . . . I . . . E . . . B . . . O—shit. Joseph

Adam Liebowitz! Shit a fish. Not only a round-eye, but a Jewish American *man* to boot. Shit a big dead fish; some charming illusions are better left unshattered.

Nevertheless she found herself longing to read the old story again, if only to see what had sucked in a young native girl that should have known better. She got up, her finger between the pages, and walked to the refrigerator at the kitchen end of the trailer. There was a half six-pack of real Corona, probably Greer's. Just like Emil Greer to insist on imported beer. She opened a bottle and carried it back to Sallas' bed. She took a quick swallow and set the bottle on the bookcase beside the clock, arranged the pillow against the wall, and began to read.

SHOOLA AND THE SEA LION

A Shadow Dance

Isabella Anootka

Our story this time is not so much about Princess Shoola as about her friend Eemook, and how he dealt with the strange spirit that came one night to entrance the Sea Cliff People.

The boy Eemook was the Sea Cliff tribe's spoon-maker. This job was usually assigned to one of the old people who could be better spared to crawl about on the beach, scavenging for washed-up shells. It was not the proper task for a young brave.

But Eemook was a cripple, as well as the son of an um-onono—meaning 'Slave Woman.' Um-Onono had been captured as a child when the Sea Cliff People still made raids on the Copper People, far to the south. Like Eemook, it had been her lot in life to do the tasks none of the others wanted. On the day that Eemook was to be born, his mother had been gathering sea urchins from a dangerous tidepool. Without warning, a sly wave caught her from behind.

The wave carried her to the cliff rocks and mauled her cruelly. When it was done it cast her up on the beach with the driftwood. The netsmen pulled her from the surf and pounded the water from her lungs. When her breath began so did her labor. After the child was born, the unfortunate young mother died on the pebbles, barely a woman.

Her death left her poor offspring nothing but a cocked backbone and a shrunken leg. Chief Gawgawnee decided at once that the baby should be left on the low rocks, the way the girl babies were usually disposed of.

'It will be best to send this broken moonfawn along with the doe that bore it,' the chief maintained. 'Let the Sea Spirits finish what they have begun.'

Most of The People agreed. But Um-Lalagic, the ancient root woman, who slept alone because she was barren and produced only foul winds, spoke up for the babe:

'I shall keep him,' she said. 'I shall raise him and make him strong with clam nectar and honey. I shall call him Eemook, The Broken Gift, and he shall call me Grandmother. If you do not do this thing for me,' she told the chief, her eyes sharp as flint, 'I shall take the Slow Walk with him myself. I swear it.'

So Chief Gawgawnee took back his sentence and told the old woman that she could keep the child. In truth, he was swayed more by Um-Lalagic's ability as child-watcher than root-finder. Her skill at the shadow drum had quieted many an annoying crybaby in the longhouse.

Some of the clan muttered against the chief's change of mind; they claimed that the spirits were often known not to favor unsteady leaders, or deformed orphans, either.

The old woman paid the mutters no heed. She raised the boy in her corner of the longhouse and protected him with her flinty glare. She worked hard to coax his shrunken leg to grow. She rubbed his back with special oils and sung many healing chants. But his bones never straightened. With his walking stick he could keep up with the smaller of the boys; without the stick he could only move himself along in a kind of floundering hop, like something from a bog.

Still, as though to make up for these defects, the Great Giver-and-Watcher had also given Eemook long, smart fingers, and a tongue clever at story singing, and sharp, proud eyes like Oorvek, the osprey, who can circle higher than the sun and still see the perfect twig to finish the nest.

Young Eemook had always been satisfied enough with these gifts. He liked making spoons. He didn't mind that boys younger than his years were already out on the rocks, assisting the spearmen. Sometimes Shoola slipped away to keep him company; and when she didn't there were always the little animals that crept out on the rocks and bushes to join him. So he had attended to his solitary task over many long seasons, cheerfully and without complaint; and he was happy.

But one fall afternoon this all changed . . .

He was on the beach beneath the grassy bluff, at the big smooth stone where he did his work. The waves were quiet. He had already scavenged the high water line to see what last night's tide might have brought in. There wasn't much; the sea had been calm for many weeks, too lazy to stir up anything interesting.

Eemook knew this was soon to change. It was late in the season. The drooping sun showed the bellies of many clouds swelling to the north. Eemook was busy with his bow drill, making holes in the shells he had collected so the notch handles could be tied secure. When he would raise his eyes from his work he could see the other men on the rocks intently hunting the foamy currents. They could sense the coming as well. They danced from rock to rock with their young helpers, holding their three-pointed spear high, singing as they danced. They were singing their wish for the one last prize they each hoped to capture before the gathering season ended.

The women also sang, hurrying back and forth along the path above with their baskets on their shoulders.

As he watched the men and women singing and working together, Eemook began to feel sad. He pictured how he must look to them, propped against the distant stone. For the first time in his life he saw how small he really was—how inferior—and it made him very, very lonely. He found himself wishing he also had a helper to sing and work with. He was hoping his playmate Shoola might slip away and come help him hold the shells for the drilling when, as if in response to his wish, he heard his name called:

'Yi, Eemook, yi!'

It was the princess herself. She had stepped from the path to wave to him. Her cedar skirt was tucked high and her long hair was flapping about her shoulders, like the blue-black wings of a raven. She was waving her basket to him so he could see. It was a woman's basket; the weavers had presented it to her that very morn.

Eemook waved back, clacking his bow and bit together above his head. As he was waving, Shoola's father, Chief Gawgawnee, came blustering along, wrapped in his royal robes and fat. He saw Eemook waving to his daughter.

'You worthless jellyfish!' the chief shouted. 'You crippled slaveboy *frog*! You do no worthy work and you offer no respect to your superiors. You do not even know how to be a good slave. Spoonmaker? Paw! You would make better crab bait.'

It was not true that he did no worthy work, but respect had never been an easy offering for Eemook to make—especially to this blubber-faced old blusterer. For this reason the boy had suffered many harsh scoldings and beatings. But his proud eyes never lowered. Even now he glared back at Chief Gawgawnee, reaching as he did for a piece of driftwood.

The chief took a quick step back. For all the little slave's handicaps, Eemook had very strong arms and a history of hurling things when angered—with alarming accuracy!

'Shoola! All of you dawdling girls! Ignore this frog-boy slave! Back to work, back to work.' The chief blustered on, shooing his daughter and the others ahead of him, over the slopes . . . leaving the disrespectful orphan behind in the little cove.

The waves went quieter still. The barnacles clicked and the mussels hissed. The wind cried its mournful cry in the ribbon grass—'Lonely . . . O, loneleee-e-e.' Eemook's eyes filled with sympathy with that wind. He felt smaller and lonelier than ever. At length, he put aside his drill and bit and spoke out loud to himself:

'I do not wish to be a frog boy forever,' he said. 'I wish . . . I wish I could *change*. I wish that at least I could turn into a frog *man*!'

What he truly wished, though, was that Shoola would keep him company again, the way she used to. Perhaps the two wishes were the same wish. He did not know. He did know that neither wish was very likely to come true. Shoola was the chief's only living child. Though Chief Gawgawnee had fathered many offspring, they had all been girl babies, and at his practical command their cradle had been that cruel surf at the bottom of the big cliff. But on the day that Shoola was born it happened that the chief had enjoyed an exceptionally fine day at his fishing weir. Forty red salmon and a fat seal calf in the stone maze! The chief ventured that perchance this new baby might be the bringer of such good fortune, so he called her Shoola, Luck Bringer, and let his wives keep her.

Eemook and Shoola were the only children of that season. Shoola grew to be Eemook's only true friend, and he hers. Now she was gathering with the women, with her skirt tucked high. Eemook looked at his own bare legs.

'This wishing will change nothing,' he sighed. 'While a tadpole can become a frog, a frog will never turn into anything more than a frog. Things are what they were made to become.'

He set his jaw and bent back to the bow. As the twine whined and the drill spun, he heard the men singing on the rocks. The chant they sang was a song in praise of the sea. It called the sea an adversary that should be ever battled, a 'Great Warrior' from whom the victories of food must be won.

The women hurrying along with their baskets of crabs and clams—and seagrasses and fernroot to grind for The People's bread—sang back. Their song claimed that the sea was a Mighty Mother that should be feared for her ferocity, and honored for the care and nourishment she granted her children.

'The sea is neither a Great Warrior nor a Mighty Mother,' Eemook said to himself. 'The sea is nothing but a great big bowl of fish stew! And I, Eemook, shall honor it as a spoonmaker should— with a great big *spoon*.'

And with that he reached into the bottom of

his basket and took out a roll of woven cedar. After looking both ways he began to unroll the bundle. From the wrapping he produced a gleaming wonder—a carved bone, ivory white and gently curved, like the slimmest crescent of the newest moon . . . and longer than the boy's good leg!

It was the rib of some colossal beast. Eemook had discovered it after a storm, long ago, and he carved it secretly over many seasons. No-one had ever seen it, not even Shoola. Eemook had fashioned the length of the white crescent into all the little animals he had come to know and love in his lonely life: the sandrunner and the shy rock crab; the tree peeper and the pine squirrel and the puffin. All the denizens of the cliffs and shore were perfectly entwined down the length of his creation, each flowing into the other and linking firm, like links of a living chain.

The hilt of the fossil was already drilled and slotted, where the big shell must fit. Eemook had been waiting for such a shell almost from the day he had discovered the great bone. He had never found anything nearly large enough or beautiful enough. Or perfect enough.

'But the longer the wait,' he said to cheer himself up, 'the more perfect my little family will become!'

And he set to polishing the intricate creatures with wet sand and moss, singing as he worked:

Here I have a chain, of family I think
They link! They link! They link! They link!
Each to each, each to other
The frog to the mouse to the weasel . . .
And they wait. They wait! They wait! They wait!
To find the great shell to make the great vessel
Then they will shine together ah hee!
Like the Spoon of Stars that wheels
About the Star That Never Moves.
Ah hee hi yi! Ah hee hi family family family.

His spirits lifted as he worked. So intent on his singing and shining did he become that he did not notice the girl, Shoola. The young princess had come away from the path after all. She was creeping down the little cliff behind him, her basket full of seagrass and her eyes bright with mischief. Closer and closer she crept, until she was right behind him. Then, with a wild laugh, she dumped all the wet brown grasses over Eemook's head!

When he saw who it was that had tricked him, Eemook lunged standing with an angry shout. He tried to catch his friend, but of course she was too nimble. She danced out of his reach around the big rock, laughing and pointing. When Eemook saw the shape his shadow made on the sandy cliff, he laughed also; the sea grasses hung down his shoulders like the mane of some ragged animal. Laughing, he fell to his all-fours and began to rock his head to and fro, mooing, like the little rock seal bull mooing its song of courtship to a young seal heifer.

'Hah-*moooo*,' he mooed. 'I am the Dancer of the *Deep*. I will dance you into sleep, I will take you to my keep . . . Hah-*moo-o-o*!'

The girl shrieked with delight and fell to her knees to join her playmate. She shook her hair down over her face.

'Not *me-e-e*!,' she chanted back. 'I am fast and free. I won't sleep beneath your sea . . .'

Thus were the two friends chanting and rocking when the boy's grandmother, Um-Lalagic, came along the path from her root gathering. For a moment she was filled with fear by what she beheld on the beach below. When she saw it was only Shoola and Eemook, her fear changed to anger. She began to throw the unwashed roots down on them.

'Foolish children,' she scolded. 'Scornful, disrespectful children! Would you mock the spirits? *Tshh!* Very foolish! Very dangerous and foolish.'

'It is only play, Grandmother,' Eemook called back.

'Then it is foolish play, even for children. Stop at once and get back to your tasks. And *hurry*. For

I have just heard that this is the very last day of fall. Winter is on its way this very minute.'

'And where did you hear this from, Old Grandmother?' Shoola asked with an innocent smile. 'Perhaps from one of the "Little Winds"?' The princess had always enjoyed teasing the rootfinder about her bloated condition.

'More mockery!' Um-Lalagic screeched. 'Mockery and scorn!'

She tossed more roots. Shoola squealed and took shelter beneath her basket. For an old woman, Um-Lalagic had a very keen throwing hand. It was she who had taught Eemook. She finally ceased her barrage, breathing hard:

'If you must know, you wicked girl . . . I heard it from Tasalgic the Crow. He told me that storms will strike this *very night. Bad* storms. Look—' She pointed to the mountains. 'See those pine tops dancing in the purple clouds? Tasalgic told me that's how it would begin. The Sea Cliff People must finish our gathering this very day, or there will be many loud bellies in the longhouse this next season. So make haste! And no more mockery.'

As soon as the old woman waddled away up the hill toward the longhouse, Shoola burst anew into laughter. 'That crow is a famous liar,' she said. 'And that root woman's belly is loud in *any* season.'

Eemook laughed along. The People had always

joked about the nether noises of old Um-Lalagic, calling her Root Rumbler or Bladder Sack. Or Spider Squaw—for indeed she did look like a spider with her skinny limbs and her big belly. But Eemook loved the old woman and knew that for all her growling and windbreaking she was very wise, and he set about helping Shoola refill her basket.

When the last tangle of grasses was lifted from the stone, there lay the beautiful carved bone. Eemook had forgotten his carving in the play. He tried to roll it from sight, back in the cloth, but the girl begged to see it.

'Have I ever,' she asked somberly, 'in all our lives, kept from you even one secret?'

He knew she had not. Slowly he unfolded the wrapping.

'Oh, Eemook!' she exclaimed. 'It is a *handle* . . . the grandest I have ever seen! Never has anyone carved a more wonderful spoon-handle! But *where* will you ever find the shell to finish it? There is no such shell in all the sea.'

Eemook was so proud he could hardly answer. 'My grandmother says . . . that for every hook there is a fish; and for every spade a hole. Something will come.'

He started to return the carving to its wrapping, but Shoola stopped him.

'I must hold it, Eemook,' she begged. 'For only a little while?'

Eemook was reluctant. No other hand had ever touched it. The magic might leak out. 'Yes, you may look at it,' he said at last, 'but I must hold to one end.'

He held forth the bone and allowed Shoola to run her fingers along its length. As she did this a very strange thing happened. Everything seemed to become very still. The wind stopped and pine tops became still. All the shore-side bustle ceased as well. The men on the rocks and the women on the bluff went stiff, frozen in their hurry like carved totem poles.

The sea itself was the only thing that had not gone completely still, and it had slowed considerably. The waves rolled as leisurely as summer clouds, and much brighter, though the sky was dark as clay.

And when the two friends squinted out into the brightness, they saw, moving from crest to crest, as though from gentle hand to hand, a gleaming round object, being passed shoreward, slowly . . . carefully . . . until it was laid in the sand at the feet of Princess Shoola.

It was a beautiful shell, larger than any clam or mussel or scallop, larger even than the abalone, and far more brilliant! It was so bright that to look into the center of it made the stomach spin like a whirlpool.

'Oh, Eemook! Your grandmother was right!' the

211

girl cried. 'For every footprint there must be a foot.'

And so saying she picked up the shell, which was bigger than both her spread hands. It gleamed between the young pair like a pool of moonlight. She held it out for the boy to try to handle. The scalloped rim perfectly fit into the carved notch.

'Now, truly, it is the most wonderful in all the world,' Shoola said softly.

Eemook beamed with pride. 'The People will be very impressed,' he declared. 'All the women will gape and pluck at their throats. All the men will say that Eemook is the most marvelous maker of spoons in all the houses on all the shores! Perhaps your father will even stop calling me a worthless slaveboy.'

'Perhaps your grandmother will stop pelting me with roots!' Shoola added, joining her friend in his excitement.

'I will present it to The People on the first winter feast. I will bring it forth to dip from the Feastnight pot! Your father will be very envious.'

'Oh!' Shoola cried, suddenly alarmed. 'Then you must not show it! For you know my father. If my father envies something he cannot have, he always declares potlatch. Then you would be forced to throw your treasure away.'

When potlatch was declared each grown member of the tribe had to give up his most prized possession. Potlatch could not be denied; it was a way the Watcher-and-Giver kept The People from growing too proud over each other.

Eemook knew Shoola was right. Whenever one of the men made a better spear than the chief's, the jealous old man declared potlatch; he could always order himself another spear. Yes, the chief would have the marvelous spoon destroyed if he could not possess it.

Then Eemook's eyes brightened.

'We will have our *own* Feastnight, here and now, and no fathers or grandmothers. We shall invite all my family to the feast!' The boy held the carved bone aloft. 'They can see how I have honored them with my carving. They will come, one by one, and I will introduce you. I will say, Mr Squirrel, this is Princess Shoola, Bringer of Good Luck, and my lifelong friend. Princess Shoola, this is Mr Tsick-tsick, the squirrel!'

And from behind the rock came the product of their play, a bone-white squirrel with his bushy tail held waving and his eyes shining. He bowed gracefully to the girl and she bowed back.

'And this is Miss Loon,' Eemook continued. A young loon appeared, wearing a bead necklace. 'Miss Loon, please say hello to Shoola, who is also becoming a woman.'

'You are very beautiful,' the loon said.

'And you,' Shoola said, blushing.

'And this is Mr Ouzel . . . and this is Mrs Puffin . . .'

One after another the creatures appeared and joined the young couple in their fancy, dancing around them in the sand. As they danced, the boy's leg straightened and the crook released its lock on his back. He threw aside his pine cane and joined the dance. Round and round the rock they all danced, hand in paw in fin in wing.

They danced for what seemed hours; and the hours might have become days if Tasalgic the Crow had not suddenly swooped down from the dark sky, cawing an ominous warning.

'Storm claw!' the black bird called at the dancers. 'Bad storm claw! claw! claw!'

No sooner had he passed than a furious flash of lightning shattered the children's fantasy. The animals vanished. The wind was once more whipping the pines. A towering wave smashed the rocks and sent the men scurrying up the cliff with their spears. The women rushed to gather the last of the fish from the drying racks.

'This time that lying crow was speaking the truth,' Shoola shouted against the wind. 'Winter has indeed arrived.'

Eemook grabbed his tools and stick and hurried for the footholds cut in the cliff. Shoola hurried to get her new basket. Stinging hail began to pelt down. Eemook had reached the top of the bluff before he suddenly remembered their wonderful prize. He saw it gleaming like a little moon on the beach stone below.

'Shoola!' he shouted against the rising gale. 'The shell! The shell!'

The girl leaped back to the beach, but a second giant wave was already rolling toward the big stone. When it rolled back the girl was drenched and the stone swept bare. The sea that had so gently bestowed the gift had just as cruelly reclaimed it.

Alice realized the Corona bottle was empty; she'd slugged it down without tasting a drop. And she was only about a third of the way through the silly book! Grinding her teeth, she walked to get the other bottle. The rage that had been touched off by the scene in Daddy-daddy's cottage was still smoldering unabated, like the burning garbage. Hotter, if anything. Because this kid's story, with its unstained cartoon caricature of mythic native life, only emphasized what was happening in *real* native life . . . namely dirt and despair and perversion.

She returned with the second beer, and this time placed the bottle of amber liquid farther from her hand, where it wouldn't be so easy to swill down unconsciously. She picked up the book and resumed reading.

Inside the longhouse there was a tempest almost as furious as the one outside. All the confusion and turmoil and last-minute frenzy to batten the holes and windows against the storm. The fire-maker was building up the center fire as fast as

215

he could break sticks. Blue smoke swirled and billowed. The small children were hugging each other in fright, and the big children's eyes were big when the lightning flashed through the cracks in the cedar planks.

The fire was beginning to roar when, suddenly, the chief held up his hands.

'Where is Shoola?' he demanded. 'Where is my daughter?'

'And Eemook?' the old grandmother cried. 'My little Eemook, where is he?'

'Perhaps the tide has finally claimed the slave-boy,' said one of the chief's wives. 'And our poor daughter in the bargain.'

Just then there was a pounding on the big door of the longhouse. The men rushed to undo the thongs. The young couple staggered in, drenched and gasping.

'Troublesome toad!' the chief cursed, kicking Eemook. 'You'll be the poison of us all!' He kicked Eemook all the way to the darkest end of the longhouse, where his grandmother wrapped him in a blanket.

When the door was once again lashed fast and the cracks caulked, the preparations for the evening's meal resumed. The heating stones were dug from the firepit and dropped steaming into the cookpots. The women began to grind the roots and fish eggs together on the family stones to make their cakes. The men smoked and rocked on their hunkers. The old grandmother chanted her soothing songs to calm the tempest without.

But the chants went unheeded. The storm grew wilder. The wind began to shake the house so terribly that all the children, little or big, were soon crying and calling their mothers from the cooking.

'Make a show, Wind Widow,' the chief commanded. 'Quiet these puppies! What are you here for?'

So the old grandmother arranged her oil lamp to cast a bright beam against the elk bladder drum. She began to make shadow figures with her hands, singing as she did:

Then here *is the chick,*
The child of the sandpiper,
Lost on the beach, crying in the storm
Afraid of the wind, the terrible sea . . .
'Ai-yee! Ai-yee! What will become of me? of
me?'

The frightened children quieted a little. They began to creep toward the old grandmother's show. Her dancing fingers produced another shadow:

Now here *is the mother piper,*
Circling down, down from the blue

To spread her wings over her child, piping
'Kee-loo! Kee-loo! Nothing will happen to you! to
  you!'

The wind outside seemed to quiet a little as well. The children settled down around the old woman. The mothers resumed their chores. At the firepit Shoola had removed her doeskin blouse and was drying her hair. When she looked up and saw Eemook watching she smiled and tossed her head as she had on the beach. Eemook blushed and turned quickly away to watch the shadow show.

Now here is the otter pup.
Tossed in the storm's terrible eye.
'Ee-yi! Ee-yi! I will drown, and die! and die!'

A larger shade came bobbing along.

Now here comes mother otter.
'Climb on my breast. Rise to our den.
It is warm and safe, within! within!'

The children all laughed to see the small shadow leap to the tummy of the larger and go bobbing away. The fear was ebbing away also.

The grandmother had just started to make the next shadow creature when, to the astonishment of all, another loud banging was heard at the longhouse door—-Boom! Boom! Boom!

Everyone stared. All the tribe was inside; who could it be, outside in this fury? The banging continued, but no-one moved. Boom boom boom! Boom boom boom! All eyes gradually turned to the chief. Finally the chief cleared his throat and called at the booming door.

'Who is there, booming in the night? Speak!'

'A traveler,' the answer came back in a voice polite, but deep with echo, as from a cave. 'A simple traveler, seeking shelter and a bit of food.'

'Do we know you?' the chief called.

'I am a stranger.'

'How do we know you are not an enemy?'

The chief motioned for one of his wives to hand him his fish spear from the wall.

'How do we know you are only one and not a tribe of enemies, come to take our winter's store and our women? How do we know what tribe you are? How do we—?'

Before the chief could finish the question or the voice make an answer, a mighty gust of wind broke the latch and blew the door wide. A thundering flash revealed the stranger, standing silhouetted, as tall as the big doorway itself.

'I am my own tribe,' the silhouette said and stepped over the threshstone into the light of the firepit.

All the Sea Cliff People gaped at this apparition, spellbound, especially the women. For he was majestically handsome. His eyes were green and his hair gold and he was taller by a head than the tallest of the tribe—and clothed like a king! He was wrapped from shoulder to foot in a long robe of fur that was the same rich color as his hair. On his forehead sat a peaked fur cap studded with stones that glittered more brightly than any of the tribe had ever seen. On his wrists and ankles rattled bracelets shinier even than those of the Copper Clan. But most impressive by far was the amulet that hung around the stranger's neck, like the moon on a beaded leash.

Eemook gasped when he saw it. It was the great shell they had found on the beach! It could be no other. He glanced quickly to Shoola to see if his friend recognized the shell. But her face showed that she was as spellbound as the rest of the women by this wondrous stranger with his royal garments and his long, glowing mane. Eemook began to have bad feelings about this visitation.

'I beg only a bit of food,' the stranger said, his sea-green eyes darting about the longhouse at the young women. 'If your maids can spare a few scraps . . . ?'

Shaking himself from his amazement, the chief ordered the young women to give the visitor all he could eat. He asked if there was anything else he wanted.

'Only a bit of hard floor, perhaps,' the stranger

said, his eyes still dancing from face to blushing face, 'to sleep on.'

'And a soft maid to share it with, I warrant,' the old woman muttered from her shadowy nook at the other end of the longhouse. Eemook saw that his grandmother did not feel at all good about this intruder, either.

Though she barely whispered, the stranger overheard. He turned straight to the old woman, his eyes blazing. She met his gaze, and for a moment the air between them crackled and smelled of flint. Then, without a word to the chief or anyone else, he began walking down the longhouse toward the old woman.

'So, Grandmother,' he said, 'I see you have a lamp and drumskin. Do you make shadow dances?'

'Sometimes,' she growled. 'During stormy times, to soothe the children.'

'Make for us a dance, then,' he bade her. 'We will see if there is magic in your shades.'

'*Tsssh!*' she hissed. 'Who are you to order me? I am not your squaw!'

But the chief called to her, 'Do as he commands, Dung Sack. Any eye can see this brave is of royal blood, perhaps a chieftain king. Obey him.'

Reluctantly, the old woman turned back to the light from the lamp. 'Then *here* then,' she chanted, 'is the frog . . . jumping and singing because

221

the rain does not worry him. "Jum-bump! Jum-bump!" Because the rain does not trouble him—'

'Then *here* then,' the stranger interrupted, casting his own hand shadow on the drumskin, 'is the Hellbender lizard that *swallows* the frog. "Ga-lup! Ga-lup!" And *no*thing troubles the frog.'

The frog disappeared into the jaws of the big salamander. The children all applauded with glee and the people laughed. Eemook could tell that his grandmother was not pleased.

'Then *here* then,' she sang, 'is the big blue heron that swoops down on the salamander. His beak is like a flint arrow. His neck is like a drawn bow. Down he swoops . . . down, down—'

The bill of the shadow-bird was cocked to stab the lizard, but the lizard changed instantly to a bigger shadow, with long teeth and sharp ears, and a bristling tail.

'Then *here* is *Kajortoq,* the fox,' the stranger said, quite pleasantly, 'to snap the heron's poor thin neck, kah-*rick*!'

And it was done.

'Then *here*,' the old woman hissed, 'is Skree, the bobcat, to rip the fox's belly—'

And it was done.

'And *here*,' the man countered, 'is *Amoroq,* the wolf, to crush the bobcat's back.'

And this, too, was done.

'Very well,' the old woman said. 'Then *here*

then is the great *she*-bear . . . the great *white* she-bear, from the far white north . . . to slap the wolf's head all the way *off* with her she-bear paws!'

She said this triumphantly, for she knew there was nothing on earth could best the great white she-bear from the north.

The man only smiled. 'But *here* then,' he said, 'is Kaw*too*lu, the Surf Dragon from the shore across the burning sea—!' and from the darkness he fashioned a huge and awful thing, a creature none of the tribe had seen before, even in their most frightful mushroom sleeps. It had long curving claws, and horns all down its spine, and cavernous, yawning, jagged jaws. These jaws opened over the she-bear shadow.

'—Kaw*too*lu, the Surf Maker, that comes up when the foam is blood-red from a baby girl and gnaws the middle from *all* the bears, black, brown, or white, and leaves behind the empty pelts.'

The terrible jaws crumpled the bear shadow.

'And then *here*,' he kept on, before the old woman could overcome her shock, 'is *Ahk-kharu* the double-headed Water Omp, who walks the ocean bottom upright like a man and never sleeps, one head awake by day, the other by night. And then *here* then is *Tsagaglalal,* She Who Watches Around Corners with eyes on stalks and has poison in her step like the centipede. And *here* is *Payu*, the Pool Crawler, whose face is rotting entrails and whose out-breathing spawns maggots and whose in-breathing sucks the mocking hearts from little boys that would be men, but have not the power . . .'

It seemed to Eemook that these last words were spoken to him and him alone. When he turned from the drumskin to the man's face, the green eyes were two whirlpools, spinning the boy's stomach, dizzying his head, sucking him down . . . down, into a deep green chill. When he ceased spinning, Eemook found himself in a forest of waving seaweed. The water was thick and sad. Dark forms swam slowly, this way and that, around a great white throne. The throne was shaped like the shell.

Eemook knew then that this strange visitor was not a human at all, but some kind of God-spirit in a man's body. This cold and silent place was the spirit's domain and the mournful forms were the minions of his court. Somehow Eemook knew as well that he was the only one that perceived this dreadful vision—that the rest of the tribe saw only shadows on an elk hide. Why had the stranger revealed this to him alone? Was it because he had mocked the spirits in his play? And why had this being concealed his true identity from the others? Then he saw the columns of seaweed part, and a huge shaggy beast come swimming toward the throne. It looked as large as Ooma, the Killer Whale. As it swam closer Eemook saw, to his horror, that someone was riding the beast. It was Shoola! Her long hair was waving sluggishly about her bare shoulders. She seemed to be laughing in some kind of dreamy stupor, soundlessly.

'No!' Eemook screamed. 'Stop!' The vision evaporated. He was back in the longhouse, at the shadow-skin. Everyone was staring at him. 'He's not what he seems!'

He struck out with his cane, but the stranger stepped aside, laughing. Eemook hopped around to swing again. This time he flopped to the floor, so hard it knocked the breath out of him. He lay there, rolling and gasping.

'I see the frog boy's legs are not properly formed.' The stranger made a shadow of a half-finished frog. 'Perhaps he has not properly learned when to get on his knees.'

'He will never learn!' the chief exclaimed. 'Though he is the whelp of a slave and a cripple to boot, he has *never* shown proper respect!'

And the shadow on the drumskin became a tadpole, wriggling helplessly out of water.

Everyone in the longhouse applauded the shadow play. The children squealed with delight and mimicked Eemook's wretched rolling on the floor. All the men puffed and nodded, and the women laughed and pointed and pounded their sides. Even Shoola.

By this time the stew in the chief's cookpot was done. The chief dipped out a bowl, making sure to get the biggest pieces of meat, and handed this bowl to Shoola.

'Give this to our guest,' he told the girl. 'For it is clear to me that he is not only a great chief, but a powerful shaman as well. Our longhouse is honored by his presence.'

As she handed the tall stranger the food, he smiled into her face. When Eemook saw how she smiled back at the stranger he felt the basket of his life go empty.

Heartbroken, the crippled spoonmaker slunk back to his corner on his hands and knees. There he found his grandmother behind the shadow screen. She was rocking back and forth on her heels and humming. She was humming the Slow Walk Song, the chant that old people sing when they are ready to take the path to the cliffs for the last time.

'Why is it you that sings the Last Walk, my grandmother?' the boy asked bitterly. 'It is *my* middle that has been gnawed away, not yours. It is *my* seasons that have been emptied, not yours. Why do you wish to end your life?'

The old woman slowly raised her eyes. They no longer twinkled; they were dull and smudged, as though by defeat itself.

'When the house stinks and the chimney is

clogged,' she said, 'it is usually time to get out of the house.'

The storm passed and the longhouse grew still. It was late. The firepit had burned very low and the shadows were long. After the excitement everyone was sleeping deeply. The longhouse was so still it half seemed empty.

Eemook was in the corner where he had crawled, his cedar robe drawn over his head. He had not slept all night, so tormented was he by despair. So this was what wishing brought— more bad bargains! He knew now that the pompous old chief was never going to accept him as one of The People. His playmate was never going to be his true mate, any more than his legs were going to turn into true legs. He felt that there was but one path left for him. His grandmother had hummed this way for him before she dropped into a murmuring sleep. Now it was time.

Careful not to awaken the old woman, he slid from beneath the robe. He untied the lashes on the firewood door near their dark corner. He crept through, dragging his basket behind him. He hobbled through the mist until he found the dark path to the cliffs.

He could hear the sea ahead of him, snoring softly between tides. The full moon strove to part the last of the storm clouds, and some stars could be seen. As he walked an owl swooped near his head and perched in a pine top, calling. 'Go *you*? Go *you* . . . ?' Eemook knew the meaning of the owl's call.

'Yes, kind bird of the night,' Eemook answered. 'This is my Slow Walk, and you may sing my song. I have no heart left to do it myself.'

The owl was still singing when Eemook reached the big cliff.

The boy closed his eyes and wrapped his arms about his basket of tools and carvings, waiting for the owl to finish. The sea crooned from the dark rocks below. He stepped to the edge. But just then he heard another sound coming from back toward his little beach. It was a strange muffled bellowing sound, like the voice of something neither beast nor man nor spirit, but something struggling between all three. Eemook hobbled through the grass to the bluff and beheld a fearful sight.

There on the beach lay all the tribe's maidens, tumbled on the sand in sodden sleeps, like piles of wet rags. All of them! Rocking on the sand in silent trances! No wonder the longhouse had seemed half empty.

The only girl that wasn't soaking wet was Shoola. Though she was on her feet she appeared to be as much entranced as the others. Like one who has eaten speckled oot-oots, she was walking across the moonlit sand—her skirt

228

tucked high and her arms held wide. Her eyes were fixed straight ahead, like a baby transfixed by the lamplight. But this light came from no candlefish oil wick; it came from the throat of a shaggy hulk—the very monster Eemook had seen in his spinning vision! The glow was made by the shell! The enchanted shell! Swaying back and forth, back and forth, as the big creature rocked from side to side in the shallow surf.

And Shoola was about to straddle the beast for a ride in the waves. That was why the other girls were already nearly drowned. The monster had saved the best for last!

With another shout of outrage Eemook started for the sandstone steps. The monster's head swung. When it saw the boy it bellowed with amusement. But Eemook knew better than to repeat the impetuous attack he had made in the longhouse. Balancing on one leg he hurled his pine cane, as the grandmother had hurled her roots. It struck the monster, butt first, on the side of his hairy neck. The thing bellowed again, but not with amusement. Then Eemook snatched his adz from his basket and threw it with all his might. It struck the monster full on the nose. Eemook hurled his heavy stone hammer and heard it thump hard against the creature's ribs. This time when the monster roared it reached up to touch the swaying shell with its flipper.

It reared upright and its hairy mane fell away. As Eemook watched, the monster turned into the stranger, standing naked save for the shell glowing about his neck. Bellowing, the giant started for the sandstone steps.

The only other heavy thing that Eemook had to throw was his curved rib. He pulled it from his bag. The stranger appeared to hesitate. Eemook raised it above his head and the stranger retreated back down the steps. Eemook could feel the carving throb with power.

Back on the beach, the man turned to the enthralled maidens. 'Go!' he bellowed. 'Chase him! Catch him! Rip him apart! We will feed the pieces to the crabs.'

The girls came up the bluff, howling.

Using the bone for his cane, Eemook turned and fled for the forest, running as he never had run before in his life. The carving not only supported him, it seemed to guide him in the dark— Behind this rock! Beneath that huckleberry! The girls came on like a pack of wolves, but they could not catch him for all their strong young legs. And the farther from the sea they pursued him, the less they howled. As the chase wore on, one by one the maids stopped, and turned, and began to drift back toward the longhouse. In silence, like dreamwalkers.

Shoola was the last to leave. From the hollow

cedar stump where he hid, Eemook listened to her thrashing in the salal nearby. She was whimpering in confusion. Once he thought he heard her whisper his name, but he didn't move.

When she was gone he lay back in the wooden bowl of the big stump while his breathing slowed. He looked at the circle of sky above. The clouds parted and the moon came down and shined into his eyes, which were going sharp and hard, like the eyes of Oorkek, the sea eagle, when she is angry—

Alice's head came up with a start. The bottle was empty. Damn it all, sucked in again. The spinster from New Jersey may not have known much about northwestern culture and its heritage, but the old girl had struck some kind of primal wellspring, funky and Freudian though it was. But wasn't it still going on! Was Daddy-daddy any less a beastly god, with his bag of goodies and his purple-maned hobby horse? Were the roly-poly sisters any less vulnerable and voluptuous? The only difference was there was no dignity in Daddy-daddy's sordid drama. No damned *class*. The kids' fairy tale may have been as phony as the Easter Bunny, but it still conveyed at least some dim sense of class. Except . . . what in hell was an oot-oot?

There was about a third of the book left—she might as well have that third Corona. But she found the last bottle was a trick—an empty put back in the six-pack. She located a wine spritzer behind a plastic bag of moldy lettuce. She screwed the top off and wrinkled her nose at the flavor: phony huckleberry. She returned to the book, but somehow no longer felt comfortable on Sallas' bed. The compact alcove had become a little too compact. She carried book and bottle outside and sat on one of the aluminum steps. The afternoon was still. Smoke from the smoldering dump hung in the tree limbs like strips of dingy bunting. Across the yard the two dogs had finished their pasta and were curled up together under a salal bush. The pup was nuzzled into the old dog's ribby chest, dreaming about the good days when there was a mother and mother-made milk. Marley was still awake, lying patient and empty-eyed, like an old uncle baby-sitting.

Three crows were waiting in the boughs of the hemlock overhead, very still, as though to keep from waking the poor sleeping orphan. Alice knew they were really waiting for Marley to drop off to sleep so they could swoop down and pick through the stray Spaghettios in the oyster shells. She took another sip of the spritzer and turned to the ending of the little story.

In the longhouse all was still with the approach of dawn. The maidens were tucked again in their family robes as though they had never moved. The men were snoring in ignorance. The stranger was seated on the chief's painted treasure box as though he already owned it. He was wrapped tightly in his long robe, facing the longhouse door.

No-one else was awake in the longhouse, except the old grandmother. When the stranger came in she had awakened and resumed her gloomy chant. She rocked to and fro as she hummed, glaring at the stranger's back. He paid her no mind. He continued to watch the door, waiting. Very likely he was expecting more soldiers from his army of shades, she thought. Tssh! She no longer cared. Her time was over. She was old. Her magic skill with the shadow play had been her only value for a long time now, and now that magic was smashed. Soon, she would be smashed as well. She rocked harder and knotted her face to hum louder, but a sudden banging froze the breath in her throat.

Boom! Boom! Boom! Something boomed at the big door. All the braves sprang to their feet and leapt for their spears. The maidens were holding each other, shivering. Boom! Boom! Boom! and the door boomed wide.

It was Eemook. He was beating the door with a great carved bone. He hopped into the startled house, dragging his basket and singing. He was singing the Potlatch Song:

Then here is the finish, here at last!
Here is potlatch! Here is the leveler!
The torch on the grass,
The toadstool on the carrion,
The sprout on the grave.
Come high and low, come empty or full,
Come rich or poor or servant or slave—
Here is potlatch, for one and all.
Into the firepit and gone for good.

He snatched his bow drill from the basket and flung it into the firepit. Sparks leaped and the fire began to blaze.

He took out his flint-tipped drills and clacked them together:

233

Then here *are my tools,*
My third and fourth hands—
Into *the firepit and gone for good.*

A puff of sparks welcomed the shafts. Eemook dug again into his basket.

Then here *are my spoons and dippers and cups*
Spoons, spoons, that were to be.
Spoons for men and women and all—
Into *the firepit and gone for good.*

By this time the people were crying out that he reconsider. These were utensils—needed for the winter ahead. 'Stop!' shouted Gawgawnee, the chief. 'You cannot do this!' But Eemook continued to fling his creations into the fire.

'What is this?' the golden-haired stranger demanded. 'What is he doing?'

'The fool is trying to declare *potlatch*,' the chief explained in an angry voice. 'It means nothing. Only a man who has a great treasure to sacrifice can do such a thing. Stop, slaveboy! You waste your goods . . .'

The young man hopped out of the chief's reach and began tossing his carved dolls into the fire:

Then here *is the pineknot beaver*
With real beaver teeth for the scraping of bowls.
And the drinking duck with agates for eyes

Into *the fire and* into *the fire, and see?*
There is *no other man like Eemook,*
There is *no other man like me . . .*

The boy tossed in the empty basket. Now nothing was left but the carved rib bone. When he held it aloft, all The People were indeed impressed. They saw the little animals shimmer and twist with life in the leaping firelight.

Now here *is my treasure—*
Who has carved better?
From antler or cedar, from bone or wood?
Into the firepit and gone for good!
And who *is like Eemook? Who is like Eemook?*
Who here is greater? Who? Who?

Once more the chief cried for the young man to desist, but it was too late. The carving he cast into the flames was more wonderful than any of the Sea Cliff People had ever seen, and their blood was stirred. With a cry, another young man accepted the challenge. He pulled his leister spear from the soft earth and threw it in after Eemook's treasure—'*Into* the firepit and gone for good!'

Then a netsman cast his net, as though to snare the leaping flames. And a weaver his basket. The chief's own brother set fire to his feathered drum and beat it while it burned. The voice of the tribe rose up to join Eemook in the Potlatch Song:

Then here *it is, then* here *it is.*
Here *is potlatch, here the leveling.*
There is *no chief. There* is *no brave.*
There is no master. There *is* no slave . . .
Into the firepit and gone for good!

Soon all of the men were dancing about the firepit, each trying to match his neighbor's sacrifice. With a groan the chief removed his woven crown and sadly placed it on the rising fire.

'We must all do it now,' he explained to the stranger, 'or the Watcher-and-Giver will be angry with us. It is our law.'

The stranger reluctantly removed his own peaked headdress and followed the chief's lead. The chief threw in his doeskin boots and the stranger did the same.

The drums pounded, the fire leaped. Soon all the women were weeping and rubbing sand in their hair in grief at the loss of so many prized possessions, and all the men were dancing naked in the firelight.

'Look to our visitor, my chief!' Eemook called. 'Shall he not give of *his* treasure?'

The chief saw that the stranger had not removed his magnificent shell amulet.

'You must throw in the necklace,' he said. 'Every man must throw in his riches—even a chieftain king.'

The stranger stopped dancing. 'I will not,' he said. 'It is a trick on me by that cripple. I will not sacrifice my amulet.'

The other men stopped dancing. They looked at their chief and the big visitor. The fire showed the anger in their faces.

'You must,' the chief told him. 'It is the law of The Sea People. You must throw in your treasure or we must throw you from the high cliff. It is our law.'

'I will not,' the stranger said again. 'I must not and I shall not! I am more powerful than your law.'

Some of the people muttered angrily and began to take up the boiling stones. The stranger raised his fingers to touch the magical shell. From the shadows flickering against the walls came once again his army of dark demons. They advanced on The People, shrieking furiously and waving their claws. The tribesmen fell back in terror, understanding at last that this handsome stranger must be some kind of invading spirit. But Eemook hopped to the pit and drew out a blazing spear. He thrust it into the black form of the Surf Dragon. The creature squealed with pain.

'They are made of shadows!' he called to his

tribesmen. 'Nothing but shadows. Drive them into the light!'

Grabbing up burning brands, the tribe charged the demon army, driving them out the longhouse door into the dawn. One after the other they melted in the morning sun.

Of all the unearthly beings, only the stranger was left when they reached the cliff's edge. He was bellowing like a wild beast and his handsome face was contorted by rage. With stones and torches they forced him to the edge, then over, into the rushing tide below.

With a roar he disappeared beneath the waves, only to surface moments later in his true form as the huge hairy-maned Lion of the Sea. The shell necklace could still be seen about his neck as he swam toward the horizon, bellowing his fury and frustration.

The women began to creep from the longhouse to peer over the edge. Shoola ran to stand by Eemook's side, her eyes full of pride. The spell was broken.

'Oh, Eemook! You saved us from an evil god! You were so brave and clever.' She turned to the chief. 'Wasn't he, Father? Clever and brave . . . ?'

'Yes,' the chief was forced to admit. 'He was clever and brave, for a crippled—' The chief paused, feeling the eyes of his tribe upon him. He knew he looked very fat-bottomed and foolish without his beautiful chieftain's robe. He finished his sentence in almost a whisper: '—spoonmaker.'

Eemook met the chief's eyes and was silent. A cripple he would always be—things are as they are—but no more a slaveboy.

Some things, not even the Great Giver-and-Watcher can make to be.

Just then, The People heard an approaching chorus of muffled toots and whistles. They looked up to see old Um-Lalagic hurrying down the path. When she reached the cliff she leaned over and spat into the surf below.

'So, my grandmother,' Eemook smiled, 'you no longer sing the Slow Walk. Perhaps you have decided not to vacate the smokey house . . . ?'

'Sometimes it isn't a bad chimney after all,' she growled. 'Sometimes it is only gas.'

The following spring all the maidens except for Shoola gave birth to babes with golden hair. The chief ordered them all thrown into the sea. But they did not drown. No matter how rough the surf, they always bobbed up and swam away, bellowing. This was the beginning of the Sea Lion People, and they have been bellowing ever since.

When Alice finished she stood up so abruptly that the crows flushed away squawking and the puppy awoke. She returned the book to its container in the bookcase and closed the trailer door behind her. She considered leaving the pup in old Marley's care, but a bear would probably eat it, or a raccoon rape it. After refilling Marley's water

239

bucket she scooped up the now bloated ball of fluff and carried it back to her Samurai. She held it in her lap.

'Wake up, Worthless. Help me drive.' She was grinding her teeth worse than ever, and her hands were shaking so hard she couldn't work the ignition card. It galled her, the way that Shoola tale had misted her eyes with emotion. Crap! she told herself, crap to the high heavens. No wonder Hollywood wanted to come up here and shoot this nauseating pile of nostalgia! Where else could the Dream Machine find better raw materials? We are such crap as dreams are made on—cheap!

Before she could start the engine she heard a scrape at her door. She looked out to see old Marley seated on his haunches in the shells beside the van. He had one imploring paw lifted and was grinning up at her like a hopeful hitchhiker. 'Oh, for Chrissakes!' she said. '*Every*body thinks just because a poor girl is from the country she's easy.' But she got out and lifted the old animal in the slide door, while the pup yipped and frolicked.

She drove back through town this time, instead of taking the outskirt road. It had been less than a week since she had come this way, but the changes that the Hollywood Dream Machine had wrought were everywhere. Lydia Glove's dainty little sweet shop no longer advertised Mice Cream Bars in her window; now it was Fox Cream Bars. The Crabbe Potte was offering a new drink on the liquid crystal marquee: 'The Shoola Shling.' And she saw that in the cobbled entranceway that led from the street to the National Bank of Alaska old Ernie Patch had been once again coaxed from his cocoon of daytime dish operas and fuzzy navels to resume work on his neglected totem pole. Under the canvas awning Ernie was chipping at the cedar log chocked on sawhorses. Ernie had been at it off and on for three or four years now, chipping and chiseling from the base up. Alice had followed his progress. He was still one of the best pole makers around; some of his figures still had the touch. That bear on the bottom especially. There was in the bear's stylized wooden face something long-suffering and touchingly heroic—like the way his cedar eyes were rolling just the slightest upward to regard the carved column of creatures that his big bear back was being sentenced to support. And the beaver above was good, too, his buck teeth at just the perfect upward angle to form the bear's long-suffering eyebrows. Clear, clean, vigorous angles. But the closer Ernie got to the top the more that vigor had waned. For years the Searaven Bank board had been badgering the old man to crown the piece, before the cedar or the carver—or both—cracked with age. He'd put them off by claiming the Spirit had not yet revealed to him what to put up there.

'Up to the top the carving goes along; but the top hisself he has to *come* along.'

Now Ernie was bent furiously to work at the topmost figure, in a blizzard of tobacco juice and cedar chips. Alice eased to the curb and leaned across to roll down the window.

'So what did you finally decide, Mr Patch? What came along?' Realizing the question was foolish, even as she asked it. 'A raven? A thunderbird?'

'No, Alice,' the carver called over his shoulder, grinning and spitting sawdust. 'A sealion, a gahdamn *sea* lion. I don't know *no* pole from Bela Coola to Nome crowned with a *sea* lion. Do you?'

Alice admitted that she didn't. Driving on, she wondered why. Since the arrival of the round-eye totem-pole historians in the 1700s, the damn things had been tipped with just about every other varmint, indigenous or not. She had seen old photos of one pole with a macaw for a top—probably the pet of some sailor. And a number of famous poles had Abe Lincoln on top of them, stovepipe hat and all, sitting like some judicious and lovable uncle. But never a sea lion. Perhaps because there was absolutely nothing lovable about sea lions. Alice had stopped to visit the world-famous Sea Lion Caves on the Oregon coast north of Florence once, when she drove her old Volksie up from San Diego, and had been absolutely

241

amazed—at the scene and at her unforeseen reaction to the scene as well. It had been late in the day in the middle of a dismal February drizzle. Alice was about halfway through a fifth of Yukon Jack and needed to clear her head. The tourist-attraction parking lot was practically empty was the reason she decided to stop. The other times that her coastal wanderings had taken her by this way had been during the heavy tourist season. Now the two blond teenagers in the gift shop were already getting ready to close. Dressed in their Sea Lion Caves shirts and skirts, they looked like twinkie twins—except one was buck-toothed and the other flat-chested.

The buck-toothed one advised Alice to come back another time, that it was almost night and no artificial lighting was used in the grotto. The only illumination was what came through the cave's seaward opening. Alice told her she understood, she didn't use artificial lighting in her grotto, either, and put down her ten bucks. The girls gave her a slip of paper and pointed her down the steps, not a word about the Yukon Jack bottle though a sign on the wall clearly stated NO FOOD OR DRINKS IN CAVE. Twinkie blond twins don't like to argue with dark-locked old Deaps, even when they outnumber them.

She was the only one in the elevator as it dropped smoothly down the two hundred eighty feet to grotto level, and the only one at the approach tunnel. The smell and the sound hit her first, as though they were one blast—a reeking roar of noise right out of the spermy, cunty, sea-slimed crotch of the underworld. Alice reeled back from the force of it, coughing. At the viewing shelf that opened out on the grotto the light was fast fading. She couldn't see much of the creatures moiling on the dim rocks, but her ears and her nose told her more than enough to make up for what her eyes were missing. It sounded and smelled like—and she couldn't think of anything else to compare it to—like a very Hell.

'Hell itself,' she said, and at that moment the winter sun cracked beneath the lid of overcast somewhere far out on the horizon—the way it often does at the end of the dreariest Oregon days, to tantalize you—and came bowling through the grotto opening on the foam-topped waves. It lit up the enormous cavern like a phosphorous bomb. Alice saw then it also looked like very Hell. Big as a football dome, snarling with driftwood and broken kelp, the cave was like an arena, a stygian amphitheater that had been specifically designed to show off the spectacle of animal brutality at its gamiest. The arena's field was divided into a dozen or so battle zones; some were great rock islands in the surf; some boulder piles; some sea-carved shelves in the grotto wall. In these zones the champion bulls made their cruel court. As her eyes adjusted Alice saw how truly ghastly these behemoths were: bigger than her Volkswagen, and uglier—scarred from ponderous neck to fluked tail by years of challenges from lesser males. The harems of cows wallowed like huge brown maggots at the foot of their master's throne. Below the cows were the pups. Then, at the pyramid's bottom, the sea lion sugardudies bellowing their brags and challenges, but from a safe distance.

As she watched, one of those young bulls' glands apparently got the best of his better sense and he decided to make good his boasting. He charged through the circle of pups, butting them in all directions, and made for the harem. He started to mount the first young cow he could reach. The big bull didn't even bother to leave his throne. His head went back in a roar so potent that harlequin ducks fell from their nesting holes all the way across the grotto. The roar must have been some kind of kingly command, because immediately a dozen other bulls from his pyramid lurched into action. They were on the offender before he had copped so much as a decent feel off the lolling cow, like LA swats on a Fourth World fanatic. They left the impetuous braggart a pile of tattered fur and torn flippers at the island's bottom, bleeding in the driftwood and kelp.

Alice wondered if she shouldn't hurry back to the elevator and say something to the girls upstairs about the demolished young bull—maybe there was a ranger they called or something—but then the sun sank unseen out on the horizon and the cave was again just a dim mess of smelly bellowing.

She finished her Yukon Jack before she headed back for the tunnel. She put the empty bottle in the trash receptacle at the elevator, being neat by nature. 'It's a wicked world in all meridians,' she remembered Queequeg's words as she waited for the elevator. 'I'll die a pagan. But at least I can be *neat* about it.' Years ago . . .

When the Samurai rounded the little knoll before her motel she was surprised to see three of the movie company's silver-and-blue shuttle vans parked in the fireweed in her vacant lot. The vans were the very latest in the turbo methane models from Mercedes, powered by shit and yeast, she had heard, and cost a hundred grand apiece. So here's three hundred thousand bucks worth of very high-rent hardware, she thought with a wry smile, parked in the same weeds through which our very low-rent Daddy-daddy had crept only a few hours earlier. It was beyond her. How could *any* operation absorb such expenses and expect to make a profit, especially with a dippy little kid's flick about people that never existed in a time that never was? A holomated cartoon flick maybe, but not a real film, with real actors. The charm of the Shoola stories lay in fantasy, not reality. That was why Disney's remake of *The Jungle Book* with real animals had not worked; nobody wanted to relate to real bears or panthers or snakes, no matter how wisely or bravely or slyly they spoke. Real animals were too messy, and people these days had enough mess. Besides, where would some casting director ever find a maiden as clear-eyed and innocent and beautiful as the storybook Shoola? Or as brave and broken as little Eemook, or as quaint as the grandmother? Cartoons, maybe, but not real actors. The sea lion spirit, for instance; whoever they got to play the part was bound to be your usual pumped-up Ramboid, about as real as a McNugget Meatcake.

Yet when she pulled around the last cabin into her courtyard, there they all were, as if they had jumped up out of the pages of the book she had just finished and raced down ahead of her to be waiting. There was the old chief, in a real gutskin parka and caribou boots, and his wives standing on each side, faces obedient, concerned for the pack of little kids pressed about their skirts. There was the crippled hero, a boy about fifteen in a wheelchair, reading a newspaper through shell-rimmed glasses; and there was the sharp-eyed old granny with her pot belly poking through the unlaced parka. Most obvious, there was Shoola . . . sitting on the little wooden sill at the front of Unit 5, in doeskin skirt and blouse and hair braided on each side like Pocahontas meeting John Smith in an old litho. Only more beautiful, her face more authentic—open and broad, with the cheektips dawn-pink like a wood rose, and the almond eyes of Mongol blood. Innupiat, Alice thought. Or Upiak. The real stuff, from somewhere up high and still far, far away.

Alice stopped her car and got out, the pup under one arm, the old dog limping behind. The crowd of strangers watched her cross the yard toward them, but did not move or speak. It was her son Nick who stepped out of the laundry room to greet her.

'Mom. I've been phoning all over town. We were about to start breaking windows.'

'Sorry,' Alice said. 'I had to run up to Sallas' to see about this old mutt. Sorry, everybody. You should have just busted on in.'

No-one answered. They didn't look at all impatient or put out by the wait. In fact, they didn't look like they understood a word she said.

'Some speak English, some don't,' Nick whispered. 'I know for a fact the old woman doesn't.'

'Christ. Unbelievable. But how are they going to speak lines?' She was whispering too.

'We'll have them lip-move and dub in the real dialogue later.'

'Unbelievable. I didn't think there was anybody like this left.'

'We netted the whole cast, from the gimp to the granny

to the glowing girl—is she perfect or what?—in one fell swoop. We found them in the Baffins, an entire family. C'mon, Mom; admit it. Did we land the Shoola show or didn't we?'

'It looks like you got 'em all,' Alice admitted, 'except for the sea lion god. You're not going to find an oddity like that, even in the Baffins. Where do you expect to . . .'

She stopped. Nick was pirouetting in the yard before her, swirling his white overcoat like a cape, shaking his long silver mane. 'Ta-*da*,' he said. 'Ta-*da* . . .'

'Jesus unbelievable Christ,' was all she could answer.

10

O, The Prickle-Eye Bush,
It Grieves Me Heart Full Sore . . .
If I Ever Get Out Of The Prickle-Eye Bush
I'll Never Go In It Anymore . . .

Michael Carmody had been a great round ball even at
birth, a prize pearl of a boyo, especially considering the
size of the poor oyster that produced him. She never
reached forty kilos, even at the peak of pregnancy.

The father that had planted the seed in the little maid's
mollusk was as large as the mother was small. He was an
Olympic single-shell rower named Pull Carmody. He had
won three Olympic golds for Britain before he retired to
the Carmody home in the Scillies, still much in the pink
and very full of himself. There was talk he was *too* much
in the pink, and that the reason he retired was he could
no longer be certain of passing the test for anabol. And
even if the test-blockers worked, he was *such* a brute-o!
Wouldn't look good for the crown, anabol brute like
that.

He looked perfectly *grand* to a timorous young country
girl from the oyster-bedded Cornwall coast, however. She
moved over and opened right up.

But that grain of anabolic sand he planted in her dark
folds seemed to require more than the usual laving of
inner tears. It was nearly a year in the rounding and
finally had to be knifed out, four kilos two. The labor
lasted two days and two nights and scoured the vessel
clean as a jam jar. Not enough scrapings left for a fly
to blow. Nor drop of milk for the babe nor loving light
from a mother's eye. Empty.

The family went home to Steep Cliff as soon as the stitches healed, but something had been sorely strained. The gold-medal rower became more full of himself while the shy young mum became emptier. She was never much more than a shell after the birth. It was as though baby Michael's opalescent emergence into one world had left the world from which he issued hollowed irretrievably, emptied forever of both lives. The young mum's mother and grandmother came to assist, the two of them renting a nearby cottage until such time, they told the landlady, as the poor girl's strength returned. It didn't return. All summer she lay by the window in the cold Cornwall sun, eyes empty, the soft breezes playing across her slack-mouthed vacuity like invisible lips across a flute. When the first chills of fall came she relinquished even her emptiness.

The girl's mother, fortunately, was of stiffer stuff, and the mother's mother stiffer still. They traded off tending the orphaned babe in the old Carmody house until the Olympic champion went sculling off in search of other bivalves, in other oyster beds—then both old women moved in.

The ailing girl now out of the way, the pair were free to bicker constantly. It was so unrelenting that the boy Michael scarcely noticed. This was the natural sound of women, he assumed, like the beak-to-beak natter of gulls on the rocks. When he did begin to notice it, it still seemed a natural sound, however irritating. This was the sound a sailor left home to leave behind. There were easier ways to make a living, he knew, than by sea work. Brighter lads his age were already studying for careers with better futures than fishing could ever again provide. The big blue sack of the sea was less bountiful every year. These bright lads would find better futures surely; they would be chipdish programmers and government barristers and drug counselors, and go home to the spouse and sprats when their day's work was done—*exactly* what young Carmody thought one went to work to avoid. Bad as going home to a houseful of screeching gulls.

While he was away on a three months' tuna run his grandmother choked to death on a scone during the old ladies' teatime bicker. The great-grandmother blamed herself and went into a long decline out of guilt and remorse and melancholy and boredom. She produced an ancient concertina and sat for hours before that sea-view window, wheezing out an endless array of dirges. Young Michael was impressed. He did not know the old gull could do anything with that beak of a mouth except eat and argue. Yet here she was *singing*, and playing a musical contraption to boot! The old crone did not outlast her daughter by much more than a winter and spring, but it was during these months that the lad learned most of the music he was ever to know, and got his first inkling that a woman in the house might be more than just a nattering nuisance after all—might b'god in fact be a bloody actual asset! Forty years and more passed before he was able to put the inkling to the test.

The trouble was, Alice was not a good test subject. It's true she never nattered and also true she never made a nuisance of herself. The hearthful peace which a seaman requires in his shore time was never by Alice disturbed. More often than not she would not even share that hearth, working late at the smokers, then sleeping in her motel. Carmody wondered if it might not be the hearth itself that bothered her. All he had to offer in the way of a home was his lash-up at the muddy end of Bayshore. Perhaps she was embarrassed to inhabit this hearth, ashamed of what her catty Deap sisters might say behind her back. The sound of meows behind the back was known to make his Alice a trifle testy—trifle, hell! she was a damn *dread*nought when she felt she was being maligned—so he shit-canned the shack and built that fool mansion. Not much changed. If anything, she spent fewer evenings under this new roof with its widow's walk and its real cedar shakes than she did under the corrugated plastic of the old one. Carmody was perplexed. For the first time he felt the lack of something in his life. It wasn't the lack of cuddle and cooze (this had never been part of his arrangement with Alice, implied or otherwise; when a Jack needed a little C&C it was easier to chop up to Anchorage for a trip down Meatstreet—cheaper too), it was the lack of company. Man was not meant to live by the by-God hearth *alone*. So he'd rigged his bait and trolled his new boat along easy from Seattle, bay by bay, until he hooked him one, and by Christ she was a peach. Alice was a shipmate, sure enough; a helpmate, and true as a plumb line. But Wild Willi from Waco was a mate of a different stripe. She was more than company. This Texas tomato made him feel a thing he feared to put a name to, because any sailor knows it's the unluckiest jinx can be brought on board. The sea is a jealous old fishwife, and bringing love on board is a four-letter invitation to disaster—bad as whistlin'.

So 'The Prickle-Eye Bush' was the theme song Carmody had chosen for the cruise home. More than his theme song, it became his leitmotif, his opera, the ongoing aria he kept returning to, absentmindedly, all day long, every day. And when he got out his recon whiskey and his old Hohner concertina for his after-supper concert, he usually managed to work 'The Prickle-Eye Bush' into the evening's program two or three times before he passed out.

Not all of it, certainly, Ike and the others were glad to note; the entire ballad could be thirty verses long. The song's story went into all the consequences of passion and poaching and the subsequent pursuit through the pitiless Cornwall countryside. It was a tale of your usual Young Thwarted Lover, driven by poverty to the crime of killing one of the King's Royal Stags, then trading the meat for trinkets to give to his True Heart, then being betrayed by someone unknown but near to him ... and becoming a fugitive, and hounded out and hunted down by the local fatbacked lawman, and captured, and tried, and finally ending up about to be hung from the most terrible thorn tree you can imagine ... where you wait with your hands bound at your back, looking out over the heads of your heartless homefolk, scanning the horizon and lamenting your lonely fate: '0, the prickle-eye bush . . .'

It's the same basic tale, Ike knew, that could be found in a large number of ballads from that melancholy time. The most famous was the Slacky Rope version: 'Hangman, Hangman, slack your rope, slack it for a while, I think I see me mother comin' . . . ridin' from many a mile.' You hope Mother dear is bringing the family silver, to pay the fine for your misdeeds and get you out of this stickery situation. But no; like the rest of the crowd she's just come to see you hang, hangin' from the gallows tree. Then Father, ridin' from many a mile; then Bro; then Sis, and so forth. They've all come just to catch the necktie party. Then, when things are looking their darkest, your True Heart shows up, ridin' from many a mile . . . and *she's* got the silver to get the hangman to slack his rope and set you free, *whew*!

Not so with the 'Prickle-Eye' version. True Heart shows up all right, ridin' from many a mile, but she's ridin' double with Fatback the Sheriff that sentenced you in the first place—she's been in *league* with the sonofabitch all along!—and is just as eager as Mom and Dad and Sis and Bro and the rest of the good law-abiding royalist citizens to watch you dangle to death in the thorns, you low-life deer-poaching weep-and-wailing varlet crybaby!

Another difference: in this grim ditty the wailing does not stop with the hanging. The ballad's narrative continues right out over the precipice, into the void. The trap drops, but your futile vow still keeps on, squeaking out of your stretched neck like a corkscrew squeaking back out of a cork, vowing, even from the black beyond, that if you *ever* get out of the prickle-eye bush . . . you'll never go in it anymore.

Over and over, every day, with whistle, hum or hoot, Carmody's crew was regaled with that refrain. Ike heard the nasal strains of it on the Juneau docks, in fact, before he even *saw* Carmody. He and Greer were carrying Billy the Squid's stretcher across the docks, followed by Archie pushing a shopping cart, when he heard Carmody's tenor cutting through the stinking yellow mists like a sawblade:

251

'—grieves me heart full sew-*wrre* . . .' It was in fact how they located the new boat, moored behind a big trash scow, all but out of sight.

'Mr Carmody?' Archie shouted across the scow at the singing. 'Is that you-all?'

'*Us*-all?' A round pink ball popped up on the other side of the bales of refuse. 'I hope to suck an eel it's us-all! Where have *you*-all been is what I want to know.'

'Well, the last hour we been looking for you, Mr Carmody. How come you're not at our usual moorage, 'stead of parked back here in this, this—?'

'This *dump*?' a merry voice finished for him. Another head popped into sight alongside Carmody's, also round-faced and pink-skinned, but not shaved bald. This was a woman's, her sunny middle-aged face topped by a pile of bleached curls, wild as a tumbleweed. 'We're parked back here in this *dump* with the rest of the old throwaways because we are *hiding out* is why. This old dunk's got the authorities looking for us.'

Carmody chose to ignore this, waving enthusiastically. 'Say, lads, ahoy. I was beginning to fret about you—taking twenty hours to get here from Skag-town. I thought you had a posse on yer tail or something. Afternoon to ye, Isaak . . . Emil. Climb on over and see my sweet new runabout, boys, never mind the unfortunate cargo bucket you got to cross. But I do suggest you cross it at the stern, upwind.'

Picking their way along the scow's gunwales, Ike and his little band circled the load of landfill bales and got their first look at the new craft. Ike and Greer both whistled. It was plenty sweet all right, the latest multipurpose, wide enough for work but built trim enough for speed—all fusionweld steelume like most modern boats. Steelume was impervious to the saltwater electrolysis that eat up other metal hulls. The whole boat shimmered with the alloy's eerie silver-green glow, like a vessel from another solar system. While the multipurpose wasn't exactly new it did look completely unused and immaculate. One hated to imagine getting it all gored up with fish blood and slime and scales, or piling its decks with rusty crab traps.

Carmody had lashed a walk from the flying bridge to the scow's rail instead of using the fishing boat's regular walkway lower down. A plank was all it was, not quite a foot wide, no ropes or railings. Billy raised his head from the stretcher enough to get a look. He groaned and cursed. Greer, carrying the lead end, agreed. 'Maybe we better think about this . . .'

'Psht now, Emil,' Carmody called. 'Haul your old load right on across. Nothin' to it, nothin' at all.'

A loud laugh snorted from the blonde at his side. 'How would *you* know? You haven't hauled your old load acrost it, I noticed.' It was a laugh that should have been derisive, but there was no derision in it. It was as sunny and good-natured as her face. Ike judged her to be about fifty, perhaps older—not anywhere near as old as Carmody's seventy-so, but a good decade or two the senior of Alice. Yet there was something about her that was still quite childlike. She had a lopsided tomboy grin that she held wide open in spite of chapped lips and missing teeth, and there was a bratty twinkle in her blue eyes. A twinkle a lot like Carmody's. Their complexions were nearly identical—a wind-buffed and sun-polished pink. They had the same corn-colored eyebrows, the same pug nose. When Ike saw them side by side, grinning at the spectacle of Billy the Squid being carried precariously across the narrow plank, he wondered if they might not be close kin, perhaps even big brother and little sister. That would explain the hip-to-hip familiarity.

'Welcome aboard, laddybucks,' Carmody said as they stepped down from the plank. 'Stow your kips and secure your wounded. And step lively about it; I'm yearnin' to haul anchor and catch this tide and I really mean *yearnin*'.'

The blonde winked. 'What the old donkey *really* means,' she confided, 'is we got to hightail out of here before the owner of that powerboat by the pumps yonder comes down and sees the hole we bashed in his bulkhead while we was gassing up. And we have *two* posses on our tail.'

Carmody looked hurt. 'He should not've parked the flouncy piece o' fluff so close to the pumps, the stupid gob.'

'Close? I wouldn't call that so close. A container barge big as a goddamn football field steamed in between that sailboat and those pumps this morning, didn't ding a thing.'

'I was seriously undermanned,' Carmody protested.

'You was foolishly overconfident is what you was. Good morning, boys. I'm Willimina Hardesty—' She held out a big pink hand, rough as a reef. 'I'm known as Wild Willimina from Waco, but you boys may call me Willi. I'm hired on as chief software officer for this ritzy high-tech tub.'

'Haw!' It was Carmody's turn to snort. 'Software officer. What do you think, Ike? Would I hire a software officer? Especially a software officer named *Hard*-assy, gnheh-heh-heh . . .'

Ike shook the hand and introduced her to his three friends. Archie flushed. Greer kissed her knuckles and said something in French. Billy just grunted into the metal case he had padded with towels for a pillow. Archie started to explain about Mr Bellisarius' supine condition, but the woman said, oh, they knew all about it—that the gang's daring and spectacular escape on the runaway rail-car had been the talk in all the bars *hours* before Isaak phoned.

'Right!' Carmody added. 'All about it. Now put him down and cast us off, we'll swap yarns later.' He frowned at the two big net bags Archie was carrying. 'What in the hell's all this?'

'One's wine,' Archie shrugged.

'I can see that,' Carmody said. 'A reasonable cargo. But what about the other bag?'

'Books,' Archie answered.

'I can bloody *see* they're books, Culligan. What did you do, enroll in one of those self-improvement courses?'

254

'They're the Squid's books, Mr Carmody. You know I don't read. Mr Bellisarius made us check them out of the Juneau Community College Library. They're scien*tific* books.'

'*That's* what took you so damn long? Lord love a duck. Well, stash the whole shitteree somewhere out from under*foot* if you please . . . because, lads and lady, we are about to foam straightaway home. Nels! Flip us free forward—I'm firing this ritzy bitch up!'

They foamed all right, but not straightaway home. To Isaak's surprise, as soon as they were out of sight of Juneau Carmody wheeled the metal prow left, south, back down the Inland Passage exactly the way he'd just come. 'Evasive action, to confuse the pursuers,' he called from the flying bridge by way of explanation. Then he instructed the woman to key them in a course around Admiralty Island and north up Chatham Strait, which would loop them back to almost the exact spot where they began their so-called evasive action. When Ike mentioned this the old man confided that what he really wanted to do was scope the other side of Admiralty for bears on the beach, maybe pick one off with his new tranque rifle. A half hour later Ike overheard him tell Greer what he *really* wanted to do was 'give this Texas Tootsie a look at An-*goon*. Three years she's been up here and says she ain't yet seen an authentic Indian village.' And a day later, creeping up the strait on auto at no-wake speed, everybody heard him tell the Texas Tootsie herself that what he had in mind was long-lining for some of the legendary sea sturgeon that were supposed to prowl the mud off Hoonah. That's when Ike finally figured it out—that what the old dunk *actually* wanted to do was take just as long as he could getting home.

This was all right with Ike. He had never been in too much of a hurry to deal with Alice in any event, and he had bad feelings about her prodigal son's ambitious return. This was pleasant, cruising leisurely along the calm channel in a deck chair like a tourist on a ten-day special, sipping wine and playing spit in the ocean and scoping the shorelines. Sometimes they put away the cards and trolled off the fantail with spinning rigs and flashers . . . they were cruising that slow. Carmody kept the choice catches to eat—the occasional native coho, the rare sockeye with his neon meat—and tossed the hatchies back. Or sold them over the side to the little pirate processors that winked codes from every cove and cranny.

They cruised and played poker and yarned, and Carmody sang. In the evenings, amid the dirty dishes in the galley, he crooned old love songs, like a young swain serenading his lady. Tin Pan Alley tunes, and sixties stuff, even New Age ballads. But as the nights darkened and the bottles emptied, he always got back to the Old World Traditional, and, at last, to his theme song: 'O, the prickle-eye bush . . .' It was so ever-present it began to seem to Ike that it had been in his head from the moment he was startled from his peaceful slumber by the cat in Kuinak.

Naturally, at first, Ike had tried to get back into that slumberous peace. It should have been easy enough; the crew was certainly in a slumberous mode. Especially Greer. The chemical uplift Greer had been hoping to find in Billy the Squid's briefcase would not be complete until they rendezvoused with the other half of the stimulant's formula in Kuinak. So Isaak's customarily jacked-up partner spent most of his time below decks in a narrow bunk, zeed out. Archie Culligan was no scoot-head, but he was exhausted by his sojourn in Beulahland; he could usually be found slumped against the water heater in the galley, snoring away. The industrious young Nels Culligan tried to remain at least upright, propped against the rail of the flying bridge, stifling yawns while he awaited orders from the captain. But the captain was no ball of fire himself. Never, in the decade they had worked together, had Ike seen the old fisherman so kicked back and languid.

The cushy new boat was part of it; the software in the Loranav pilot was especially programmed for these coasts, user-easy and voice-activated and in constant contact with sea and sky satellites. A ten-year-old with a coastal chart and a mouse could have commanded the course—'Juneau to Kuinak at fifteen knots'—then gone back to watching his Slitman goggles. It was a superb vessel, built when they were still building boats for high-end diversifishing. It had probably been priced originally at a mil-and-a-half or more, back before the Trident leak. Carmody had picked it up for a fraction of that.

But it was more than the new cruising vessel. The old Cornishman had also picked himself up the perfect cruising companion. Wild Willi from Waco might not have been as cushy and modern as the new boat, but she was just as user-easy. It wasn't hard to understand why Carmody had been dawdling along. This was a long-deserved vacation for the old dunker, with a new playmate. Everybody on board enjoyed her company, except for Billy Bellisarius, who was still brooding too deeply about his recent run-in with Greener to have enjoyed anybody. In the days since Juneau they had found Willi to be a good worker and capable sailor, plus she offered them a whole new library wing of dirty stories and ribald sayings—a southern wing. The trip had been a lot of fun, a lot of drinking and laughing and gambling and eating.

Especially eating. It looked to Ike like Carmody had picked out his ritzy new boat as much on the basis of its galley as on its computer-sensor channel-charting fish-finding features. Maybe more. The old fisherman spent a lot more time around the kitchen dials than the computer dials.

'Fish are best eaten absolutely fresh,' Carmody maintained. 'I love fresh fish, by God, right in the galley. All these years busting my butt hauling the bastards in? Don't seem like I remember getting to eat one really truly fresh fish supper. I truly feel I have been deprived, by God I do!'

The size of the man's stomach bespoke otherwise; he had an absolutely enormous midsection, round and pink and wrinkle-free as his shaved ball of a head, and as hard. Carmody's girth was the result of a lifetime of hard labor and good appetite, laced liberally with drink and dance whenever possible. The belly he had produced was the accomplishment of nearly three-quarters of a century's dedicated effort; he was famous for it and proud of it. He used it like a sumo wrestler uses his *kee*, or center. It was his workbench, his fulcrum on the booms, his block and tackle on the ropes. Now, as they hummed along, he had it bellied up against the round cedar table that occupied the center of the galley, leaning on it while he chopped a ten-pound halibut into steaks.

'A fish don't really object to being caught and consumed,' Carmody was explaining, 'long as it happens *fresh*.'

The fish was truly fresh; the glimmer of life had not yet completely left the animal's freakish eyes, and the body was still quivering there on the table, though big slabs of him were already hissing in butter and chopped parsley in the wavepan.

'Fish understand the fishy facks of life. They get et. It's their destiny from the get-go, from the least to the largest, to get et. What a fish objects to is being wasted. "If you need me, catch me; if you don't, let me be." Back in the days we really *needed* whale oil you never heard any whales complaining, did ye? They knew they was greasing the wheels of progress. They didn't commence complaining about it until they found out their oil had become obsolete, progress-wise, and all we wanted them for was food for cats. That's when they organized Greenpeace. Because fish got *pride*. Oiling a gyroscope in a battleship is one thing, feeding the family kitty-cat is another.'

'Whales aren't technically fish, Mr Carmody.' Archie Culligan was now slouched just inside the galley hatchway. He was attending to Carmody's seafood lecture with a bottle of Japanese beer in his hand, a cocky look on his face. Since the experience with Greener, Archie had resolved to be a little more daring in his dealings with authority figures. Isaak couldn't help but grin at the boy; if you needed an authority figure to be daring with you weren't likely to find a better one than Michael Carmody.

'Archie, we're talking fish philosophy here,' Carmody replied, tapping the table with his knife like a professor with a pointer, 'not biology. And whilst I am aware that the whale might have a warm-blooded dick like a *mammal*, he's still got the philosophy of a fish.'

'Not unlike some other mammals I could name,' said the blond woman. Carmody took no offense. He bent back to his cooking, laughing his wicked little laugh—'Gnheh-heh-heh.'

It wasn't that Carmody couldn't be dangerous when dared. Ike once watched him butt a tall tugboat captain called Tex nearly blind for a few chance remarks. The tugger had muttered something about how Carmody shoulda been shipped back to where he came from at the turn-of-the-century census, with the rest of the fuckin' foreigners—leave Alaska to the Alaskans. 'If we had all done that,' Carmody had countered pleasantly, 'then twits like you would be back in jail in Houston or Dallas with the rest of the Texas turds. This whole country would be nothing but Deaps.'

Carmody was a British citizen, being born in Cornwall, and a descendant of the infamous wreckers that worked those waters around the Scilly Islands. Though he had been a fisherman all his life, he still had a touch of that wrecker blood—all coasts were fair game was Carmody's way of thinking.

'And twits like *you*,' the tugboat captain just didn't have the good sense to let the thing sit, 'would be back in limey-land with all them other tub-gutted old English fishermen.'

'Well, sir, I'm not. I'm right here in America, a full by god legal citizen.'

'Well, by god you *would*n't be, if'n you hadn't of got one of them dumb Deaps drunk enough to marry you.'

At that point they were in business. Carmody was a short man, barely five-five. The captain was an easy foot taller. But Carmody possessed a deceptive advantage—

259

his one-hell-of-a-belly. It protruded from his stubby frame like the rubber bumper on the tugger's prow, pooching out just as far and, to the tugger's surprise, just as hard. Carmody grabbed the man's lapels and jammed the belly against him. The tall tugger 'oofed' once and doubled over like a man hit by a rolling barrel. This brought his face into range of Carmody's bald pink head. He was butted five times so fast he thought it was one long sustained blow from a concealed bludgeon. When he came to on the saloon floor he thought he'd lost his sight. 'He *clubbed* me! I'm blind! He clubbed me blind!'

'He butted you,' Ike was kneeling over him with a bar rag full of crushed ice. 'Busted your nose and cheekbone it looks like, so your eyes are puffed shut. You'll be all right when the swelling goes down. If I was you I'd be careful how I talk about a fisherman's wife in the future.'

Now Carmody had taken up with a Texas twit himself, and Ike couldn't help but wonder a little wickedly how that Deap wife was going to react when her fisherman came home to harbor with his new catch. He doubted there would be any butting—since Alice had quit drinking she was a little too modernized for that kind of primitive response—but he could imagine some cutting. A filleting knife was more Alice's style. Many mornings at the cannery, sipping coffee waiting for Carmody, Ike and Greer had watched fascinated as Alice worked one of the thin blades, as delicate as an artist with a brush. But he knew it wouldn't come to that, either. Carmody was too much the charmer, too much the clever clown. Foolish as the old limey might appear, when occasion served he was able to use that round red-rubber head for more than a bludgeon.

'Hey, Greer!' Carmody called up the hatch. 'You guys know the *true* reason I bought this fancy boat?'

The answer came back from Greer and Archie Culligan and young Nels all together—'Just for the *halibut*, gnheh-heh-heh'—in perfect imitation of Carmody's wheezy voice. Carmody didn't care that everybody'd heard the old joke a dozen times in the last week. It was like the old song.

Across the round table from him, Willi looked up from the salad she was chopping. She always was ready with one of her own. 'Hey, Archie,' she called over her shoulder, 'you boys know why the Humane Society passed a law that don't let blind people sky-dive no more?'

'No, Willi, how come?' Archie responded a little cautiously. Some of her jokes had been a little difficult for Archie to understand.

''Cause it gives their dogs heart attacks.'

Archie laughed along with the others, but it was unclear if he really got it. 'Seeing-*eye* dogs, dummy,' Nels whispered to his brother and Archie said '*I* know that.'

'Hey, Willimina,' Greer called down the hatch. 'You know why zey make zee women sky-divers wear zee *jock* strap when they jump?'

'So zey won't *whistle*,' the woman shot back, adding 'gnheh-heh-heh.'

It was that kind of cruise.

There was an electric disposal in the center of the round cedar table. Carmody suddenly stuffed the remainder of the fish carcass down the hole and then swept in what was left of the lettuce and green onions.

'Well.' Willi lifted the bowl out of his way. 'I see the salad must be done.'

'Fish don't wait,' Carmody apologized. 'A minute on each side, then it starts going downhill. Chow's on, mateys! The eating lamp is lit at the captain's table.'

The table was cleaned and swabbed and covered with a checkered tablecloth designed for the purpose. With matching china and silverware and napkins, it indeed did look like a captain's table. The men unfolded their canvas chairs from the cupboard and Greer opened a bottle of Oregon Riesling. A candle in a rusty diesel piston was placed over the disposal trap in the center of the table, and Willi finished tossing her salad by candlelight. Carmody dealt the slices of fish to the places around the table by hand as though they were hot thick cards, then poured the remaining butter and herbs over the chops. Nels filled a plate and headed up the hatch to take it to Billy. The table waited in silence. Carmody liked to have everybody wait until grace was offered. After a minute Nels returned, still carrying the plate.

'The Squid says he's tired of fish. He says he wants a glass of wine and another can of Vienna sausages.'

'That dang Squid has just about et me out of Vienna sausages,' Carmody grumbled.

'He's still stewing about Greener,' Greer said. 'Sausage is a better stewing food than fish.'

'Well, let him stew on an empty stomach. I'm tired of having my crew forever coddling the bleedin' malingerer.'

Billy the Squid's presence on the boat was about the only thing that had cast any cloud over Carmody's pleasure cruise. The old man had not offered any objections when they carried the cot across the plank in Juneau, but neither had he offered any sympathy. He'd never cared for dealers nor cripples, he had let it be known numerous times during the voyage. Neither bloody one. Also, as far as squids went, any fisherman knew what these squirmy characters was best used for: bait.

'I'll take him something,' Ike said. 'Maybe we better open another bottle of wine.'

'He's just about drunk me out of wine, too.'

'Why you miserly old water rat,' Willi scolded. 'Are you forgetting that that poor boy purchased them bottles of wine in Juneau? The sausages, too, as I recall.'

'So?' he said haughtily. 'A galley master don't keep track of where the various parts of his bouillabaisse comes from, does he? It's all his galley, ain't it? Anyways, let's have a grace first, Isaak lad. So the rest of us can commence. A quick one . . .' He laced his fingers atop the shelf of his belly and lowered his pink head a moment in thought, then came up with the quickest one he knew:

'Bless the spirit, curse the skin . . . pin back yer ears and cram it in.'

Ike put two cans of sausages and a pack of saltines in his pocket and headed up the metal steps, his plate of halibut in one hand, two glasses and the half-full bottle of wine clinking in the other.

They were humming along on auto pilot about a half mile off Chilkoot shore, having just cleared into Controller Bay. All afternoon they had been cruising on program, up through the narrows between St Elias Island to the south and the stabbing surf off Suckling Spit to their north, never a hand touching the wheel.

The twilight sky was grey-green and the sea was calm. An easy breeze was blowing out from land. Ike could smell the Chilkoot spruce on that breeze, and the ice of the Bering Glacier from beyond—green and clean and cold. There had been land smell for most of the trip, whether you saw land or not. There were certainly faster and more direct routes from Juneau to Kuinak, but Carmody had programmed the Loranav to stick close enough to land to enable him to duck into a little cove or harbor when the impulse took him—for a little honky-tonkin' if there was a dock and a bar, or a little poker if there was a Deap casino, or to just drop anchor for a little rod-an'-reelin' if there wasn't. He'd probably start looking for a place in Controller Bay to put in as soon as supper was over.

Ike wanted to talk with Bellisarius awhile alone, before the dinner party came topside. Nicholas Levertov was weighing heavier and heavier on his mind the closer they came to Kuinak. He thought he detected the reek of vengeance about this whole prodigal return business, but he couldn't be sure. Billy the Squid was the only one on board who had a smarter nose for that rank reek than himself.

Billy was nested in his pile of books, a long wisp of hair sucked in the corner of his pouty mouth. He was digging in his ear with his diamond cross as he read. For all his clout in the community Billy Bellisarius had never been an easy man to like. But like the bastard or

263

not, no-one had ever doubted his smarts. That was why the Dogs had voted him president. Following the apathy of Ike's declining interest—and the cacophony of Greer's erratic reign—the members knew they needed smarts more than popularity. And while it was probably true that the Squid had made extensive use of the club's networking for his dope dealings, he had as well stirred the organization out of some sticky legal problems. More than that, his cryptic little sneers of wisdom had given the Dogs some solid bones of philosophy to gnaw on. It was Billy who had headed off the Lowlife Movement, just as the encroaching cult of nihilists was beginning to gain a stronghold among the more destitute in the Underdog ranks. He said he didn't give a shit if a delegation went to DC to join the Lowlifers in one of their ridiculous suicide demonstrations; but if they intended to represent the *Under*dogs, then they by Christ better find a better way to do it than drinking those kill-me coolers!

'That stuff is mostly strychnine and curare,' he had sneered to the brothers. 'You don't cash out cool. You go in fits so disgusting even CNN won't show the footage. If you got to end it all at least have the class to *knife* each other or something! Never lose your sense of dognity, even when you cash. Also remember this: Low life is better than no life at all.'

Ike approached softly, the wineglasses tinkling.

Billy's nest was in the lee of the craft's starboard rail. He was still belly-down on the stretcher they carried him aboard on, propped now by an arrangement of pillows and life jackets so he was able to rise to one elbow and read. He was glaring into a paperback titled *The Virtual Effect Effect*. His eyes were glittering. Assembled in an arm's-length semicircle were Billy's demanded necessities—goose-necked glowtube, flyswatter, notepad, cigarette smoldering in a butt-choked ashtray, a box of Swiss chocolates. The steelume case was still cuffed to his wrist, still ticking, for all its use as a lifebuoy in Skagway. Billy claimed that the case's cardkey was in Kuinak, in the possession of some mysterious

Asian who had dropped in one night with a bundle of cash to finance this Skagway run.

Ike pulled a deck chair over and took a seat at the head of Billy's nest. The little man made no indication that he had noticed. He turned to the next page of his book with a vicious flip of his hand, then snatched a chocolate from the box. He stuck it in his mouth and continued his angry reading. Ike balanced his plate of halibut on the railing behind him, then filled the two glasses with wine. Billy took his glass and drank it empty without taking his eyes from the print, then held it back up for a refill.

Ike had forgotten to bring a fork, but halibut is easier eaten with the hands anyway, like fried chicken, and the long sharp rib worked fine for stabbing at Willi's salad. They cruised along without speaking. The water hummed beneath the steelume hull, smooth and tame now that Carmody had relinquished control to the computer. All the channels and currents and banks and depths of this coast were already old news to the Loranav chips in the pilot house.

Billy held up his glass again. Ike emptied the Riesling into it, then hooked the empty over his shoulder. When it splashed sharply behind them Billy looked up and said, 'Good idea! Jettison all crap.' He tossed the book after the bottle. 'Did you bring the sausages? Or do I have to lie here and listen to you crunch your carrots?'

'Willi says you need to eat some vegetables.'

'Willi's from Texas. What the hell could a Texan know about what *I* need?'

Ike fished the two cans from his pocket and handed them down. 'She claims she used to be a nurse.'

'I claim I used to be a doctor. We're probably both liars but at least I'm not from Texas. If a man were made to eat vegetables do you think God would have given him *these*?' Billy craned his open mouth back to give Ike a look at his long canines as he popped in one of the little wienies.

'Yes indeed, Vienna sausages: the *essence* of meat—tallow, tripe and rat-tails.'

To change the subject Ike lifted his chin back in the direction the book had splashed. 'I take it that was your critique of *The Virtual Effect Effect*?'

'That was tripe way worse than anything they pack in *these* puppies, I can assure you. *All* this Buck Rogers baloney—' He scattered the pile of books away from him with a sweep of his arm. '—just science fiction. Kid stuff. It makes me remember why I dropped out of MIT.'

'I thought you said you went to Cal Tech?'

'Same thing.' Billy ate another wienie and stretched languorously. 'Not even science fiction, really. Science *fantasy* . . . cooked up by this big Bunsen burner called *fear*. Fear is all it is. Fear of dark, fear of fire . . . fear of that same old burning brimstone boogeyman. Look at this—' Billy pawed a thin paperback from the pile.

'*Boyle's Law—Can It Be Repealed?* Repealed? When was it ever *enacted*?' The book sailed over the rail. 'You can't imagine how this tripe depresses me, Isaak . . .'

Before Billy could go on Ike cleared his throat.

'Squid? I need a favor. Back in Kuinak there's this guy showed up with the movie crowd. The big albino Greer told you about? Alice's long-lost son?'

'Yeah?' Billy scowled up from his books, suspicious of Ike's tone. 'So?'

'I knew the guy in jail, a long time ago. He kind of idolized me, and I guess I kind of disappointed him. He expected me to be some kind of savior.'

'I can appreciate that. You've always signified that savior thing.'

'Not to him I didn't; he was a shit magnet and I told him so. But he thought I let him down during a beef and he started setting me up to get even. Little things, but it cost me extra months . . .'

'Heroes rust fast. What's this got to do with me?'

'I think he's the other half of your score, and I think he's planning to use it to get even. In fact I think that's why he's brought this movie to Kuinak.'

Billy raised an interested eyebrow. 'To settle some rusty old slammer beef with you?' Billy arched back to look up at Ike full on, both brows lifted now. His purple pout opened in a smile. 'One hardly needs to bring a whole film company along to do that.'

'Not just me. I think maybe he's come home to get even with his mother, his ex-wife, his town—with the whole shitteree.'

'What was it that you did that distressed the fellow so in the first place?'

'I saw him get gang-reamed at the showers, and he saw me see it.'

'Oh dear. Couldn't you summon the guards?'

'Most of them *were* the guards.'

'I see. Still, mightn't you have blown the whistle after your release . . . ?'

'One of them was my parole officer.'

'Ah. And you think that he's still after his getbacks? Isaak, that's some grudge. "After forty years the Bedouin took his revenge." Well, you can just wait your chance and blindside him like you did that bastard Greener,' Billy offered, still smiling. 'But to return to my initial point: I don't see what this has to do with me, *or* my precious cargo. My twin on the other end is certainly not your giant albino, I can assure you of that. He is rather slight, slightly gay, and quite pigmented.'

'That could be anybody in that movie gang he whips around.'

'Unlikely. The two of us put this deal together months ago. I hate to say this, but even Isaak Sallas seems vulnerable to the noids in his dotage. Still, let us entertain the fantasy; for the sake of discussion let us say the other mule *is* part of your vengeful friend's gang . . . what would you have me do?'

'Hold off until the gang leaves town. It's been dry there, Squid.' He nodded at the metal case chained to Billy's thin wrist. 'Whoever controls a score that size is going to swing a big damn whip.'

'You know I can't do that, Sallas. These locks are time-set. I rendezvous with my twin by noon this forthcoming Sunday or I learn to braid my hair one-handed.'

'That's a week away. Maybe you could meet the guy someplace else.'

'What possible purpose would a change of venue serve? Or a postponement? I want this load off my hand, so to speak, as soon as possible.' Billy rolled back to the disarray of cracker boxes and wiener cans and books. 'As soon as possible. I have things to do, tea to drink and thoughts to think. I've got getbacks of my *own* to settle with that Bible-thumper and his cretinous Christian cult. I intend to compose a short broadside to all the state's newspapers for starters, comparing Greener's cult to the cult of the Effect experts—both throwbacks to the Dark Ages: superstitious, simple-minded and wrong. I also intend to initiate personal injury proceedings in civil court. O I *do* have plans . . .'

Ike was waiting for Billy to run down, hoping to appeal to him further to change his scoot rendezvous, but Greer suddenly popped up out of the hatch. His dreadlocks were bouncing like the bells on a black jack-in-the-box.

'Brothers!' he called in a loud whisper. 'Better get ready for a rig-for-rapid-running order . . . because unless I miss my guess I think—whoa! hear dat squawkbox squawk?—we be going to de high level wham-de-*zam*!'

The radio in the galley had been picking up very excited messages, Greer informed them, from a big Korean processing vessel off Middleton Island. There was enough English in the give-and-take to catch Carmody's interest and he was able to figure out that the processor was calling in its fleet. They were all to cease fishing and lash alongside and get cleaned up double mother chop-chop because some big-deal diplomats had just shuttled in from Seoul and the captain was throwing them a big party. Greer was positive they were soon going to change course and foam out to join them. 'Carmody *loves* to crash a party.'

Then Carmody came shoving up the hatch behind Greer and gave immediate orders just the opposite, to heave to and full stop and rig for longlining, right here and now.

'Rig and roll, we're going cod-fishin'!'

Ike was relieved by the command, though he was certain no-one on board possessed so much as a temporary permit for the area, not to mention quota or consignment. They put out a cannonball with a beeper buoy first, for the longshot, then baited a few lines and doled it off the drum. It felt good to stir up out of the tourist mode—move the muscles, get a sweat going. But after a couple of good haul-ins, just as they were finding the depth and getting some prime lingcods, Carmody clapped his hands and called a halt.

'That's a-plenty. Start stowing the lines, rig for rapid running!' It turned out all he wanted was to catch enough lingcod to make a present to the Koreans, who were still restricted from the waters where the spiny fish could be taken. 'The little nippers love lingies. We'll give 'em these for get-acquainted.'

'Don't you mean sell 'em, Mr Carmody?' Nels wanted to know. Nels Culligan was a steady and serious type, unlike his half-brother Archie, and still entertained hopes of saving up enough to buy a few shares in a boat-and-quota of his own some day. Although Carmody was paying him by the week, not by the percentage, it nonetheless bothered him that they weren't up home fishing steady to make some serious money.

'No, Nels, I mean give. "Be ever the goodwill ambassador" is the Carmody creed. "Cast yer bread on the waters and dum-de-dum." I seen these Asian wing-dings before and I b'god tell ya: they do some hard drinkin' and high-steppin'.' He gave Willi a big wink. 'And do they love these nice gnarly fishes. I calculate they might even invite us on board.'

Knowing Carmody, everybody else calculated the same. They decided to leave the cannonball beeping on the bottom and pick it up on the flip-flop—see if they could snag a mystery prize while they were partying. Also, the sounds over the box were getting more exciting and inviting by the minute. They foamed for the processor's signal three-quarters full ahead. They were just

269

finishing getting spiffed up when Middleton Island came into sight. Carmody ordered some colors run up in honor of their diplomatic mission. He wanted a Union Jack topmost but Willi objected—'That'd be like me running up the Texas Lone Star.' They didn't have the Stars and Stripes, or the Alaskan Dipper and Polaris, so the best they could do for homeland colors was Archie Culligan's Kuinak High School T-shirt. He tied it to the sea/sky antenna by the shirtsleeves and let the faded thunderbird flap sideways.

They didn't have the processor's coordinates, but there was ample sign pointing to the festivities. Rockets and starflares and rosy red phosphorous fountains haloed a spot on the evening horizon and Carmody wheeled manually toward the glow. It was the first time Ike had a chance to see what the new turbo-magnetic motors could do, full ahead. It was like riding a race boat without the roar. The wind and spray whipped past so fiercely that you couldn't face forward on deck without goggles; you could have water-skied on the steely surface slicing past beneath the booms. Middleton Island is a good seventy kilometers out to sea from Controler Bay, fifty miles, but it had been less than two hours from when they reeled up their longline rigs to the time they powered down in hailing distance of the processor. At least twenty-five miles an hour: fast for any craft; for a fishing boat, phenomenal.

The Korean processor was a football-field-sized sea-going metal monstrosity. It was shaped like one of those battered iron boxes people used to use to mix cement in—low, flat, and beveled a little at each end. The only way you could tell the bow from the stern was by the name lettered on one of those beveled ends—*Sea Arrow*—with an arrow painted beneath the letters. The arrow had to be pointing forward.

The big brute was anchored about a mile and a half off Middleton Island, wallowing contentedly in a greasy flat of sea. Dozens of little Korean dories were tied in her lee, nuzzled up to her rusty flank like dirty piglets to a big brood sow. Fireworks fumed sporadically from atop a squat boom tower amidships; a godawful cacophony of electric squeals and grunts arose from her guts.

Billy looked up at the bombillating sky with his usual disdain. 'Twinkle twinkle. Phooey. If that damned Greener hadn't grabbed my pyro stuff I'd show them twinkle.'

'That noise is Korean rock 'n' roll,' Greer felt obliged to inform them. 'We pick it up at the Radio Man's.'

'You sure about these Asiatic wing-dings, Carmody?' The rusty processor reminded Willi of the garbage scow they'd hidden behind. 'This don't look so piss-elegant to me.'

'Yeah, Carm,' Archie agreed. 'I don't know which is worst—the sound, the smell, or the look of the nasty thing. I shoulda kept my rubber boots on.'

Archie had dug deep into his locker for his tan-and-ivory saddle shoes, pink shirt and bolo tie, topped by a long-lapeled single-button-roll sport coat; he was feeling a little over-dressed.

'Arch my lad, you ever think maybe it's our task to bring the poor heathen buggers a little touch of *class*?' Carmody had put on a white wool pullover and new red suspenders; he looked like a Santa Claus in the leisure season, coat and beard removed. He dropped one motor into reverse as they swung near the line of dories, and reached for his hailer. 'Look. That plumed peacock staggering around the pyrotechnics? I'll lay that's this lash-up's captain by his outfit . . . a lingcod lover if I ever saw one. Ahoy the *Arrow*! We seen yer lights. We got gifts. You the captain, sir? You savvy?'

'Oh, we savvy,' the figure called back with a hailer of his own. 'Totally savvy. What is name of your elegant vessel?'

'She was called *Lot 49* but I fully intend to re-christen her—soon as the proper handle surfaces.'

'Totally elegant vessel. She looks like a cobra with hood spread. May we call you *Cobra*? For our log?'

'Call me anything but late for lunch, Captain.'

'Then you are welcome, *Cobra*.' He raised a two-liter saki jug. 'Come 'longside and party hard-eee!'

The plumed peacock was a tiny man with thin black eyebrows and an insane scoot-high giggle that kept feeding back through his hailer. He was wearing some kind of full-length ceremonial robe with the Korean yin-yang on the back, white silk hems tucked in his green rubber boots. The plume atop his head was the crowning glory of an antique British officer's hat. It bobbed ludicrously with the captain's stagger.

'That's an old-timey admiral's hat,' Carmody observed a little peevishly. 'Like Nelson wore at Trafalgar.'

Greer was as peeved as Carmody by the unseemly display. 'Got it on backwards, too.'

'Maybe that's the nipper's head on backwards. Nels! Get us a line on one of those dory rears. All hands stand by for boarding.'

Giggling and screeching through the horn, the plumed captain ordered a boom swung out, and lowered a cage. Everybody crowded into the lift except Billy. The Squid wanted no part of their good-neighbor mission, not with that case chained to his wrist. Even Koreans knew what that meant.

'And you tell the little nippers if they so much as land one of those little piss-ant bottle rockets within scorching distance of me I'll have them hauled up in front of the UN for an act of war. I took six terms of international law at Berkeley, tell 'em!'

Nels told 'em when the little party boomed aboard. Not that it impressed the tipsy captain of the rusty hulk. He didn't act all that impressed by anything the visiting Yankees had to offer: the sack of lingcod, the new boat, Archie's sport coat—nothing. When the party was ushered below decks it was clear why not. The interior of the rusty old hulk was as modern and fantastic as the exterior was rundown, a veritable pleasure dome disguised—for who knew what devious inscrutable diplomatic reasons—to look like a sea-going slum. The pompous little captain insisted on conducting an extensive tour of what he called his 'humble vessel,' from the gleaming refrigeration and canning operation on the stern end to the grand salon on the other. The grand salon was an extravaganza as large as a gymnasium, complete with a full-service bar, live music, and go-go geishas in traditional make-up. A disco ball turned and paper lanterns strobed off and on. A hundred or more sailors danced and spun around a parquet dance floor. Some of the geishas were so far out of their gowns that the astute observer could see that the traditional white and red make-up went all the way to the waist. Greer could only stand and stare.

'Hold on to me, *mon amis*,' he moaned. 'I might try to defect.'

As the geishas twirled and danced, they still managed to keep up their tea-service duties; one of these porcelain dolls would swirl past and leave everybody with a cup of hot tea in one hand. Another girl would swirl by and leave a cup of mao-tai rice liquor in the other hand. Carmody and crew were all duly overwhelmed; and their hosts turned out to be more than a little condescending.

'You like ah humble opalation?' the captain kept asking Carmody. 'Eh? Please to follow . . .' He pushed through the melee and cleared a crowded table for the party with a wave of his silk-sleeved arm. 'You like, eh? You savvy?' Then he scurried off to the table that was obviously for the visiting dignitaries.

There was a sporadic blister of explosions from a *fow-tow* toss going on at the edge of the dance floor—a Korean gambling game played by tossing Krugerrands at a packet of silver iodide crystals in the center of a big target mat. The first toss to detonate the packet got all the losers' coins plus the *honorable* antes. These antes were usually pieces of the players' immediate apparel, so the game functioned as a kind of strip poker. The blast of a bull's-eye brought groans from the humiliated losers and gleeful shrieks from the winner, a skinny smiling sailor with old-fashioned steel-rimmed spectacles. This kid had won practically everything off his crowd of challengers except for their Rolexes and their underwear. But none of the competitors seemed that good. After Archie and Greer had watched the gold coins piling up on the mat as the crowd kept missing, Greer judged they could penny-pitch as well as any grinning gook. They talked Carmody into advancing them a handful of hundreds and bought into the action. Before they realized they had been sucked in and suckered royally they had lost all their Krugerrands to the little hustler—plus Archie's coat and tie and saddle-top shoes, and several yards of Greer's jewelry.

As soon as they had slunk back to the table the captain was there, bowing and giggling and shouting above the din of the music in his phony pidgin accent—'You like ah humble sport? Have more tea you forget life's losses. More mao-tai liquor? The real Chinaman 'Gilla, bottled Beijing nineteen sixty foe—best in the *wull*? You Yankees *dig*?'

Carmody kept saying, 'Sure, you bet, best in the world, sir; really takes the cake . . .' but Ike could see the old man was getting a little tired of it. And when the captain strutted over the next time to ask how the Yankees liked the especially rented *dancing* womans —'Rented from Kyoto's geisha school in Japan—best dancing womans in the *wull*. Do they takee the cakee?'—Carmody at last had to take issue.

'With all due respects, sir,' Carmody shouted back in his best British clip, 'they are not the best dancing womans in the *wull*.'

'Ah, *no*?' The peacock's eyes glinted. 'Then *who* are the best, fo' an instant? Who?'

'Well, fo' an instance, *this woman here*.'

'That woman *there*?' The captain turned his glitter on Willi. She grinned and gave him a polite head bow.

'Right-o! This woman here,' Carmody reaffirmed. 'Best in the wull. Takee the cakee.' Then he hauled the grinning blonde out to the dance floor to prove it. Everyone in the hall soon knew a gauntlet had been picked up, and that this timeworn couple seemed equal to the challenge and then some. They did the Twist, they did the Swim, they did the Tango, they even did the Sunfish Polka. The

Yanks could see that their software officer from Texas was a great dancer right away—perhaps not the best in the wull, but a righteous stand-up honky-tonker; she had kicked up those boot heels in many a Lone Star shit-kicking dive. But she wasn't the one that took the cake. It was Carmody that ended up with that honor, alone, in center spot. Carmody's dancing had become so wild that everyone else started backing off. When he had a nice clear working space he went into a hornpipe that was a mechanical marvel to behold, an absolutely astonishing display of rhythm and balance. The band even quit to watch. Ike had seen him perform the phenomenon a few times before, but it had been years ago, and in dim little beer joints—noplace with this kind of dazzling stage, or this magnitude of international importance. It started in a simple heel-toe heel-toe and kick. Sometimes he'd slap the kick with the palm of his opposing hand, sometimes he would clap his calloused hands against his hips or his shoulders. The kicks became higher and the palms flailed wilder. Each time he looked like he was finished he'd lift imaginary kilts and go into a dainty little tiptoe spin-around and come out of it stomping and whooping and hooting harder than ever.

Everyone was completely awestruck, the visiting team as well as the Koreans; it was an amazing display of rhythm and strength and raw jubilation, doubly so for a man of Carmody's years. But what really struck the audience was his gut, his just-one-hell-of-a-belly. When Willi retired exhausted, Carmody danced with his own belly as though the great hard globe were his partner. It was his muse, his very fount of energy, his inspiration. It was the hub of his wheeling frenzy. Yet the belly remained almost motionless, suspended weightless in space about three feet above the dance floor; all the wild flailing and clapping and stamping and kicking went on *around* this floating ball, like a wild sea around an iron buoy. It seemed to remain stationary even when the rest of his body spun clear around. It was a true sailor's dance he did, with a true sailor's balance, built into that gut by years of working a rocking deck on a pitching sea—Carmody's gyroscope; let the waves play as wild a tune as they were able.

He finished with a full forward handspring, landing with both boots spread and his bald head steaming under the disco light. After the ovation the captain walked into the circle of sailors and took off his plumed British heirloom. He announced, first in Korean, then in flawless English, that the Japanese school of dance in Kyoto no longer held the distinction of producing the world's best dancers: 'That honor must henceforth belong to the honorable Alaskan School of Movement, from—?' He waited, the black brows lifted and the plumed hat held high.

'Kuinak!' Nels Culligan's voice was proud and serious.

'—from Kuinak,' the captain echoed and set the hat on Carmody's sweaty dome.

When they exited the ballroom even the diplomats put down their teacups to stand and applaud. The captain refueled the visitors' boat free, as a further goodwill gesture, and presented them with the Korean flag. They foamed away into the brightening dawn, saluted by a full complement of fireworks, as the marquee of the processor's boom tower blinked out a giant K*U*I*N*A*K!

'What was that all about?' Billy wanted to know as the looming bulk of the processor receded over their fantail.

'That was a tribute, Mr Bellisarius,' Archie Culligan told him. 'Won a big one on the road, our team did.'

Dawn was outlining the ragged coastline to the east. Carmody was at the wheelhouse on the flying bridge, silhouetted magnificently. The plume of his newly won admiral's cap was whipping dramatically in the wind— right way front now. Ike grinned and shook his head, feeling his heart swell with pride at the sight in spite of himself. 'Where away, now, Cap'n?'

'Well, me lovelies, I'm thinkin' of perhaps the Barbados,' Carmody answered grandly. 'First Software Officer Hardesty? Set us a course south for the Lesser Antilles.'

276

'South?' Nels Culligan had never been the sort of boy to appreciate grand fantasy. 'But what about the ball and beamer we left out?'

'Oh, bother,' Carmody sighed. He took off the hat and stepped down from the wheel. 'Key us back to the beamer if you would, Miss Hardesty. Two-thirds full. I'm goin' below for a bit of a lay-down.'

Running with the wind, they were back to their starting point above Controler Bay in a little better than two hours. Ike had remained on deck with Billy, feigning interest in the Squid's reading material while the little genius drooled and mumbled in his sleep. About all he was able to conclude was that all the authors agreed the End of the World was just around the corner and that it was Somebody's fault. Somebody else's, of course. The Greens blamed the Burners and the Burners blamed the Breeders—'The bellies just kept doubling and doubling and so did the Protein Producing Acreage'— and the Breeders blamed the Pro-Choicers. 'They interfered with God's Natural Law. "Go forth and multiply," He commanded. Things would have evened out. The Great White Tooth of Famine would have eventually gnawed the problem clean. But the Choicers interfered. And now He's pissed, and *every*body is condemned to reap the fiery whirlwind that those faithless freeloaders have sown.' Finally Ike was tossing the pamphlets over the side himself—save the poor passed-out stressed-out Squid the trouble.

A flashbell atop the wheelhouse rang its bright blue alert and the hum of the motors automatically slowed. They were closing in on the signal. Nels Culligan was the first up the hatchway.

'Them beamer buoys cost upwards a thousand bucks apiece,' the boy explained to Ike in an aggrieved voice. 'Not to mention cannonball and wire.'

The computer had slowed the craft to an idle by the time the rest of the crew were emerging from their bunks. Ike had climbed up to the wheel with his binocs but he couldn't see a thing except the soft Kewpie-crowned sea, rock-a-byeing in all directions. Even if he had sighted the hi-glo flag he wasn't sure that he could have steered toward it. There didn't seem to be any manual override.

Carmody was the last to crawl up from below, squinching his face terribly against the light. 'Any flash of the blessed thing yet?'

A chorus of grunts answered in the negative. Even Billy said no in his fitful sleep. The stern props had slowed to a full stop leaving only the buzz of the little thrusters. In the merciless morning light everybody's face was rutted with fatigue, Ike perceived. All the previous eve's bravado already gullied away. Even Carmody looked whipped. Ike was glad the Korean captain couldn't see them now; he'd have demanded his plumed hat back.

The hum of the motors changed and the boat began to move backward.

'There it is!' Willi was the first to spot the flag, scant yards off the stern starboard. 'I *told* you the damn thing would work. We coulda stayed in bed . . .'

Nels got a pick pole through the antenna loop and hauled it near enough to the back ramp that his brother could hook the buoy on board. He disconnected the beamer and snaffled the lines in a winch. 'Reel 'er up,' Carmody commanded, 'though I never heard of none of these damn long-shot rigs reeling up ruddy squat.'

Long-shot lines had been designed after rumors of fantastic deepwater prizes started circulating through the harbor bars—of giant halibut, and skate, and two-hundred pound bullheads. It was suspected that these giants might be the mutated spawn of the Trident mishap and anti-UN groups had amassed huge bounties for any such abominations captured, dead or alive. Talk was that plenty of prizes had been taken out but that pro-UN lobbyists paid more for them than the antis—which was even a better deal for the lucky dunker. All just rumor, but every dunk who could afford one owned a long-shot rig with beamer. It was more fun by fifty fathoms than the compulsory sports lotto.

Ike stepped aside to let Willi at the topside panel.

She fingered the ten-key and watched the screen. She frowned and touched the buttons again.

'Boys, we are either broke down or hung up. Somebody go below and see what the finder shows.'

Nels was down the hatch like a shot. A moment later his voice squawked on the wheelhouse. 'We got something and not the bottom! Big as a rowboat. Reel it, reel it up!'

Ike levered the winch and saw the wire begin to crawl over the boom wheel and around the drum.

'Twenty-three hundred pounds!' Nels shouted from the comp-screen below. 'More than a *ton* of some kinda somethin' . . . !'

When the some kind of something finally showed they saw it was only a sturgeon, not a monstrous mutant worth millions. A very old and very large sturgeon. Gauging its length down through the water, Carmody announced it to be an easy twelve feet long. 'They say two foot a century so that feller is five or six hunnert years old. Pity we disturbed him.'

But it was too late to change things; the primitive creature was bloated and lifeless. It looked like a big knotty log rolling just beneath the surface. The readout showed it was too heavy for the small longline winch. The Culligan boys were hooking for the lines to transfer the cable to the big pursing drum when Archie suddenly shaded his eyes and leaned out over the submerged form.

'There's something coming out of him, Carm!'

Carmody took one look and spat into the sea. 'Bloody hell. He's full of slime eels! Cut the bugger loose.'

'But Mr Carmody,' Nels tried to protest, 'there's probably still a lot of salvageable meat in there—'

'Cut him loose I say! Agh, ptah, slime eels! I hate 'em, the back-door bastards! What kinda bloody creature comes in through the butthole to eat, I ast ye? No, just cut the poor old bugger loose. What meat they ain't hollowed out won't be worth the messin' with.'

'No, wait!' Billy called from his little nest against the

gunwales, suddenly quite awake. 'I've only seen pictures. What an opportunity.'

The slime eels were far and away the most interesting event of the voyage as far as the Squid was concerned. Their presence seemed to lift the little man's wounded spirit. He managed to drag himself to his knees to look over the rail, his incongruous diamond-cross earring dancing with excitement.

'Look at the beauties! Class *Cyclostomata*, family *Myxindae*, species *myxine glutinosa pacifica*. Literally, "gooey mess." And they are not eels, Mr Carmody. Hagfish is what they are traditionally called—because of that labia-looking mouth-face. Though if they are a fish they are a fish without bones, scales, fins, or sympathetic nervous systems. Actually, no-one has figured out *where* to class them. They have seven hearts and no eyes. They can extract oxygen through their skin, like a prehistoric vertebrate, but they are not vertebrates, and a lot of leading biologists claim they are not even prehistoric. They maintain that hagfish are recent, that they have *de*-evolved, down a different route than the one they rose on. As far as ten thousand *feet* down in some sightings, if you can imagine. They can show up at any depth, anywhere, everywhere. Yet no-one has ever observed them mating or giving birth.'

'Thank God fer small mercies.' Carmody spit again in the direction of the writhing creatures.

'Their sliming mechanism is their most fascinating feature, in my opinion,' Bellisarius went on. 'They are armed with ninety-two slime ducts on each side of their body. A sufficiently stirred-up hagfish can manufacture as much as three gallons of slime—*thirty times its own body weight*—in a matter of seconds.'

'Thirty out of one?' This was a claim too contrary to Willi Hardesty's knowledge of mixed liquids to let pass. 'That's pretty fancy stirring . . .'

'Indeed. Each of those ducts spins a tiny thread of protein compressed into a tight helix. As this thread uncoils, carbohydrate grappling hooks cast out and gather water molecules. These captured molecules web into a thick mucal jelly. The problem is this lethal gel can suffocate and digest its perpetrator as well as its prey if the hagfish doesn't—Look! See that one? It's still too slimed over to swim away. Watch how it cleans itself . . .'

Despite their revulsion the whole crew was compelled to follow the dealer's delicate fingerpoint. A half-submerged eel was struggling against a gooey excess of its own slime, thrashing back and forth in obvious distress. It thrashed far enough back that it was able to work its eyeless face through the loop of its own body. It began to move the knot laboriously down its length, squeezing the slime ahead of it. When the knot squeezed off the tail and untied, the creature snaked down out of sight, leaving a gelatinous ball behind.

'*Glutinosa mysinus,*' Billy grinned at his rapt and reluctant audience, 'an inspiration to ladies and gentlemen alike, as you see, once they are properly appreciated. There are other fascinating properties . . .'

He lowered himself back to his stretcher, looking very pleased with himself. *Genius bellisarius* seemed to be getting his powers to entrance back at last. Everybody waited. He was about to resume his marine biology lecture when a more interesting thought suddenly lit his face. His mouth closed in a wicked smile and his eyes regained their mad-scientist glitter. The eels had brought him inspiration, too.

Archie Culligan was the one who finally caved in to the silence.

'What'd you think of, Mr Bellisarius? Musta been tasty, give you a grin like that.'

'That ancient Moslem saying, Archie, addressing the problem of unwanted slime. They say, "After forty years the Bedouin took his revenge." We modern warriors should be able to take ours a good deal faster, don't you think, Mr Culligan? Especially against slow-witted Old Testament slime?'

'Zam straight, Mr Bellisarius!' Archie Culligan, ever keen to be on the side of the righteous, was jubilant.

'Revenge. I *hoped* that was what you was grinning about. Go get him! Revenge is sweet . . .'

When it was clear that Billy the Squid had said all he was going to on the subject of slime and retaliation, Carmody cut the wire and turned to address his crew. 'Software Officer Hardesty!'

Willi snapped to amused attention. 'Here, Captain?'

'Key us a—what the devil is it?—a "most direct" for home. Three-quarters or thereabouts. I'm going back below and finish my damn lay-down . . .'

'Aye, Captain . . . that's three-quarters speed, most direct route. Right away, Captain.'

She didn't seem to need clarification where 'home' was.

After the dance-night excitement on the Korean mother ship, Ike was still unable to sleep. He padded the bulkhead at the head of his bunk with life jackets and arranged a pinch-neck light so he would be able to pass the rest of the voyage reading. There wasn't much of a selection on the shelves—paperback westerns, boat brochures, skin mags. The craft was too recently in service to have accumulated much of a library. He flipped through a couple of the magazines; nothing caught his eye though he could see the models were trying. At last he reluctantly selected a Louis L'Amour. It was the most dog-eared and spine-broke of the lot so he concluded it had to be the best—at least according to the critical view of the crew: two teenagers and a Texan. Carmody never read for diversion, not at sea. In his cups Carmody could spout long ringing passages from Shakespeare and Tennyson and even Yeats, but these occasional outbursts of erudition must have been the dregs of some long-ago literary passion, for in the ten years of their acquaintance Ike had never seen the old limey put on his reading glasses for anything but charts and reports and boat auction mail-outs . . . and bulletin boards that might have information on the same.

Ike was creeping back between the slumber-filled bunks with the paperback when he noticed a *Kuinak Bay Beacon* in Nels Culligan's guitar case. The little

282

newspaper had apparently been used as a padding to protect the instrument's bridge, and was over a month old. Ike immediately traded the Louis L'Amour for the newspaper—make a better pad for the guitar anyway, all those wide-open spaces.

He climbed into his bunk and made himself comfortable against the humming bulkhead. He quickly skimmed the little sixteen-page paper from front-page headlines straight through to the back-page gun ads and Public Service Announcements of Civic Events. He'd missed the bi-monthly meeting of the Ambience Enhancement Council, he was sorry to discover, not to mention the Pentecostal Picnic. When he finished the back page he went back to front and started again, studying certain articles with a heavy frown, as though something in them indicated hidden truths. Wayne Altenhoffen's editorial essay on the Tyranny of the Majority consumed a full hour of concentrated attention. Altenhoffen was once again decrying the administration's policy in Chile, calling it 'just another megalomaniacal move by the mad Ahab at the helm of our poor ship of state.' The fact that the recent polls showed that ninety-two percent of the American public supported the annexation only added fuel to Altenhoffen's argument. 'A century and a half ago French philosopher Alexis de Tocqueville warned the world in *Democracy in America* that an unenlightened majority could be an instrument more tyrannical than anything dreamed of by European monarchy at its bloodiest. And as our President plays on the worst instincts of Americans to export our national credo—i.e., "The Dumb Is Always Righter Than the Smart Because There's More of Us!"—Tocqueville's warning creeps irrevocably closer and closer to becoming fact.'

Ol' Wayne the Brain, Ike grinned—preaching to the choir. Hadn't Alaska been the only state the Republicans hadn't carried? And Kuinak the town with the lowest voter turnout? Kuinak was the last damn place on the continent likely to coalesce into any kind of majority, Ike thought with a touch of pride—especially not over

283

some corporate claim-jumping dispute clear on the other side of the globe.

Ike read that the parking-lot restoration project was still unfunded, the newt population was still mysteriously diminishing, and that the estate of Frank Olsen had been opened up, the legal sixty days having passed since his Disappearance at Sea. This news made Ike feel bad. He liked newts and, hell, he shamefully realized, he hadn't even heard that old Frank had gone overboard.

On the sports page he noticed that Kuinak High was not to have a football team the coming fall, the tax levy having failed and the campaign for donations falling short of the needed budget. ' "If everybody in town had tossed in just five bucks each we could have fielded a team," Coach Jackson Adams opined bitterly at the press conference announcing his resignation. "Just five bucks, and the poor kids could have played football." ' This made Ike feel bad, too. At the end of the story, the reporter (probably Altenhoffen) made the point that it would have taken more than mere money to field the twenty-two team members required by the ASHA safety code. The male enrollment for all four grades for the forthcoming year was projected at being less than twenty. This made Ike feel worse than ever. He remembered attending a football game the first fall he had come to town; the benches had looked full and prospering. What had happened to the supply of students? Implant contraceptives had all but eliminated unwanted pregnancies, but a simple shot could open up a window of fertility, anytime. Family size had remained constant. So what had suddenly happened to the students? Maybe the same thing that was happening to the newts.

He read and re-read the little paper all night, enjoying a kind of giddy guilt as he rebuked himself for faults ranging from neglect of civic duty to a near-psychopathic disregard for anyone but his own reclusive self. At first light he traded the newspaper for his binoculars and went up on deck, full of resolution to be a better citizen. This little run had been just the ticket! He felt like

284

Scrooge, coming home after that romp with the three ghosts: he would be a better man.

The computer's course routed them around the sea side of Montague Strait, straight past Byling Sound—nearly due north. No more dawdling safe along the ferry lines, or hugging the coast near the coves; if a sea came up they would take it in their teeth. Most of the crew stayed out on deck and watched the whitecaps hiss past. No-one changed out of their festival clothes; home was only a short while away at their speed and course, and they wanted to make an entrance.

Ike was astonished by the excitement he felt at the first sight of the dinky Kuinak glacier. It was like an ivory scrimshaw against the pearly, dove-grey sky. It was early afternoon but a heavy overcast draped over the sun, smothering the light. Ike thought it was incredible that the glacier could gleam so bright in such meager illumination. Criminy, look at it, all aglow like those souvenir pillows the foreign ports always stocked for the visiting US sailors, stitched in neon red, white, and blue—'☆EAST OR WEST HOME IS BEST☆'. Absolutely aglow. Then they rounded Hopeless and Ike saw that the glow did not come from home, or the glacier, or the sun at all. It was the incidental by-product of an enormous array of lights rigged up and down both sides of that magnesium wing-sail. Not decorative, social lights, but huge lights. Arc lights; kliegs! They had cruised right into a major movie shoot. And through his little glasses Ike also saw their home town was totally transformed. Totem poles had sprung up along the bay shore like mushrooms. Painted flats covered all the bay-front buildings, turning these semi-modern boathouses and pumping stations back into the scrubby pine forests from which they long ago came, only now in two-dimension.

The entire western face of the cannery had been transformed into a rugged seashore cliff. This cliff was picketed along the top with dozens of bronze-skinned fishkids carrying spears. Other fishkids were standing in their underwear waiting their chance at the bronzing

285

station, at a screened end of the cannery. A makeup technician with a fruit-tree spray tank was busy creating more natives. The kids were shivering and hopping up and down to keep warm.

The pyramid of lights was directed on a stark and shadowless scene in the bay. This floating set was circled by a ring of pilings disguised as rocks and snags. These were the fence posts for a great seawater pen. A raft with a camera crane rocked wildly in this watery arena, though the rest of the bay was calm. Two sea lions were fighting on the deck of the camera raft. Fore and aft, handlers in two little rowboats were trying to separate them.

No, not fighting, Ike amended as he squinted through the glasses. Mugging would be closer. A big sea lion is mugging the living shit out of a smaller one. The smaller one is trying to escape, to take refuge behind the raft. He is severely hampered in this effort by the life-sized mannequin he has harnessed to his back. This latex effigy is a rendition of a girl, golden-skinned, dazzlingly beautiful, with great wide-set eyes and purple-black hair whipping back and forth. The doll is nude from the waist up, very breasty and lifelike, except one arm has been ripped away. The foam rubber spilling from the armpit hampers the illusion, but the breasts continue to sling from side to side with all the jubilant bounce of genuine young flesh.

Someone plucked the glasses away. It was Greer, eager for a closer look at that breasty bounce. 'Ah, Ike,' he marveled with a happy sigh, 'eez it not *magnifique*? Zee magic of Hollywood . . .'

'Let me see, let me see!' The Squid was struggling to get a look over the gunwales. Nels and Archie lifted one end of the stretcher cot and rested it on the top rail. The steelume case dragged the deck beneath.

'Things have changed some in your absence, have zey not, President Bellisarius?' Greer asked.

Billy reached a hand out for Ike's glasses. But he did not turn them on the melee at the sea lion pen, or on the

286

false-fronted bay shore either. He was scanning the deck of the big yacht they were cruising past.

'*There's* the dink with the other half of my score!'

Ike didn't need the glasses. He could easily recognize the yacht boy by the cerise samurai hairdo and the gleaming white coat. He was still positioned near the mobile wet bar at the bottom of the flying bridge's ladder, his steelume serving tray still staunchly held chest high.

Ike reached for his glasses and eased the lenses along the yacht's deck, sure he'd locate Levertov, or at least that fraternity boy lieutenant of his, Clark B Clark. But the only other man he could scope out was the Asian giant positioned at the top of the gangway. A covey of scantily clad twinkie boys and girls were crowded to the rail, watching the sea lion fiasco. He thought he recognized Louise Loop's pie-dough rear among the harem, but saw no sign of Levertov *or* his flunky. Highly ranked as they were, they probably had better seats at the debacle. Just that big yellow turkey and the glo-haired yacht boy. And that covey of plucked quail.

And of course that trio of caustic crows, squawking over all: 'O, the prickle-eye bush . . . never go in it anymore.'

11

The Trainer Lunged with His Rod
The Beast Arched Backward . . .

EXTERIOR—KUINAK BAY—SEA LION SCENE
HIGH SHOT
Our three-crow CHORUS circles the shoot in progress, cawing droll commentaries down at the
action far below. They are the Three Stooges, they
are Hekyll, Jekyll and Hyde, they are characters in a
Beckett drama: poetic, cryptic, doomed, absurd—in
on things and totally out of it at the same time . . .
yet they are the first to see the pieces of the play
commence to come together . . .

MEDIUM SHOT—CROWS FROM BENEATH
They have been riding the thermal updraft rising
off the big metal sail since the filming commenced.
They are kept from perching on the sail by a spark
wire rigged along the lofty peak—otherwise the
gleaming *Silver Fox* logo would be streaked with
bird shit. But the updraft provides entirely acceptable balcony seating—close enough to the action to
make their sarcasm heard, far enough back to be out
of air pistol range. But now, this unscripted attack
by the wild sea lion against the tame one, tearing
right through the number-nine mesh barrier and
bellowing after that dolled-up dandy from Anaheim
. . . simply too brilliant a piece of improv to enjoy
from a distance.

   The birds break gyre and come gliding down to
watch from ringside.

CUT TO:

INTERIOR—*SILVER FOX*—THE MONITORING STATION—
FULL SHOT

A long windowless room lit by the dreamy flutter of
a score of vidcam images. Beneath a five-foot master
screen two ranked rows of eighteen-inchers show
what is going on outside the yacht, like a double row
of liquid crystal portholes. Each monitor displays
a different off-board scene. MON 1 is backstage
of the cannery/bluff—a lot of FISHKID EXTRAS
dinking around off-camera, being stripped of their
black rubberwear and fitted with leather loincloths,
getting sprayed ethnic brown. MON 2 is the beach
set with its foamade boulder in the Plaztex sand.
MON 3 is a full shot of the frantic melee going on
in the sea lion pool, as viewed from a shoreside
vidcam; this is the shot running on the master.

MON 4 is a parallel POV mounted alongside the
main film camera on the crane; it is interlocked
with the big 70mm lenses to mimic the shot being
filmed. Then three johnny-boat POVs—MONs 5, 6
and 7. Then a view of the parking lot, and the
spectator bleachers, and the main street. There is
even one monitor that displays the whole town of
Kuinak in its shrunken entirety. This overview is
so high-angle that one might think it was being
beamed from a UN satellite, but it comes from a
fixed wide-eye wired to the top of the yacht's big
sail. This is also protected by spark guards.

It's a surveillance freak's dream, this stateroom.
All the essential venues and locations involved in
the Shoola Project have been patchworked into this
double row of images, providing an ongoing electronic tapestry of the whole town. Freeze-frames,
blow-ups and hard-copies available at the touch of
a toggle.

CLOSE SHOT—EXCITED MAN

CLARK B CLARK is scooting crazily up and down this

tapestry in a secretary's chair, tending the network of screens and keyboards and switches like an affable spider. Behind him, hanging head-down and naked on a Nautilex swingboard, NICHOLAS LEVERTOV is lifting hand weights and calling instructions:

'The tandem shot, Wormbrain—Screen 6.'

'Aye, Cap'n. Screen 6 to master—'

A new image jumps to the big screen, very fuzzy.

'Focus, fool! Focus and enhance. This is a *riot*. I want it tasty, I want it now, I want it fucking *zam*!'

'Yowzah, Boss—tasty and zam it is.'

Clark B had never seen Levertov like this before. The albino had been his usual remote self all morning, moodily watching the monitors, hanging upside-down like a bleached bat. Levertov never liked to go up on the set when Steubins was making one of his hambone appearances as the Great Director. He claimed whoring was always boring, even if it was performed for public relations. But when that big wild sea lion bull broke through its corral to attack the trained eunuch, Levertov's interest took a marked upswing. He dropped the weights to the mat to towel the sweat out of his eyes; a look of inverted glee spread across his face. When the beast ripped the arm from the eunuch's mannequin, Levertov had erupted into what had to be a form of actual laughter. It was like the bleating of a wicked goat. Clark B Clark had been at the beck and call of Nicholas Levertov for years—ever since the initial work-ups on the Shoola/Kuinak project—but had never heard his employer make a sound remotely like it.

'Now the crane POV, Dipstick. The one parallel to the 70-millimeter. Now now *now*!'

'Aye, Cap'n,' Clark called back, 'crane POV it be.' He swiveled the chair and keyed in the instructions. The master screen surged full of frothing fur and teeth and eyes.

'Too tight. Pull back one-third.'

The mass became the large sea lion. He was now

completely out of the water, thrashing furiously on the plank deck. His enraged effort to destroy the doll-carrying degenerate had bellied him all the way up on the camera raft. The degenerate was cowering in the water on the other side of the big float, trying to hide behind the crane's scaffolding. It couldn't dive for safety because of the foam-filled Shoola strapped to its back.

The raft was entirely awash with the weight of all the trainers and handlers and assistants that had swarmed on board to intervene. The handlers and assistants were huddled in an uncertain wad behind their leader, the head trainer—a slight-shouldered man wearing a dove-grey angora sweater, with fleecy long hair and beard to match. He was cautiously advancing on the wild bull, his cattle prod held before him in a formal fashion. He looked as though he were preparing to knight the animal, not subdue him. But the sea lion did not seem that interested in ceremony. Every time the trainer got within knighting distance the big bull lurched for him with an incredible fury, forcing the trainer and his followers sliding and stumbling backward. On the third lurch the pitch of the raft tossed the trainer to his butt on the wet planks. He dropped the cattle prod and it slid over the side, sizzling and sparking. The trainer was in danger of sliding down the slick planks after it when an alert first assistant reached out to him. What the first assistant reached out with was *his* prod. Both men arched backward like cheerleaders and the prod flew twirling in the air like a baton. The upside-down Levertov laughed until he had to stop for air.

'How about some audio, you frat-house fool? Let's *hear* this action . . .'

Clark B had forgotten the sound, so completely was he swept up by Levertov's glee. 'Audio it is, *sir!*' He spun a knob and the amplified roar of the debacle filled the long room . . . the fuming crash of wood and water, the deafening bellow of the outraged sea lion, the unconvincing threats from the other handlers: 'Back, you

291

savage thing . . . get back in the water or such a shock you're going to get!'

Then, from very near camera, a bellow even louder than the sea lion's:

'E-*lectrocute* the mother, lads! Go on, zap him. Let's see what he's made of.'

'That's Gerhardt's voice,' Levertov chortled. 'Switch to the rowboat remote but leave his mike up. Let's see what *he's* made of.'

Clark B punched up the cam on the johnny-boat nearest. But the master showed nothing except boat bottom and bilge water, and a pair of open-toed Top-Siders tucked beneath the thwarts.

'My gawd, it's a *camera person*,' Levertov groaned. 'Mr Clark, one of our Affirmative Action twinkies seems lost in limbo-land. Would you please be so kind as to tell the little lady to either raise her camera up and shoot this action like she's being paid to do, or find other employment.'

'Gotcha, Chief. Shoot up or ship out.'

Clark B Clark scooted to the monitor displaying the shot of the boat bottom. The camera operator's name was written on a piece of tape below the toggle.

'Marygold, honey—?' The image jumped. 'Your purple toenails are cute but Mr Levertov would like to have a look at Mr Steubins. Okay?'

The camera swept up to the figure strapped in the crane chair. The high perch was being whipped crazily to and fro, like a crow's nest in a pitching sea.

'This is choice,' Nick said. 'Tell her to give us a big juicy mug shot, Mr Clark—up close and nasty. When that stony composure starts to crack I want a record of every hairline fissure.'

'Zoom to full face, Ms Marygold. Mr Levertov is concerned for the well-being of our venerable director.'

While the flustered camera operator was fidgeting to get a steady lock on the close-up, Levertov swung the board upright so he could step free. He swirled a terry-cloth robe over his shoulder and stepped in front of the master screen, his expression eager. But the enlarged face of Steubins was a disappointment. For all the turmoil and tossing to and fro, the old director's craggy visage appeared quite composed. The weathered brow was still leaned intently to the 70mm eyepiece, tilting the huge camera almost straight down at the action below.

'E-*lectrocute* the brute, I say!' Steubins' voice roared again. 'Only for chrissake do it this time at his *ass end,* out of the shot. We're getting some terrific footage here, buckos. If we can keep it unobstructed I know we'll find a place for it. Okay, now . . . *zap* 'im!'

Clark B Clark was already swiveling to the next logical shot: the parallel of Steubins' 70mm. Its monitor showed the old man was right, he was getting some terrific footage. The trainer lunged with his prod. The beast arched backward and crashed full length in the water, sending a geyser of foam almost up to the lens. Terrific stuff. Clark B's hand hovered over the switch but Levertov didn't call the shot to the big screen; he was still studying the zoom of Steubins' face. Finally he sighed and stepped back from the screen.

'If there's one thing I have never been able to stomach, Mr Clark, it's stony composure. Boring, stony-faced composure. Know what I mean?'

'Indeed I do, Chief.' He was sorry to hear the wild glee ebbing out of his boss's voice. 'Grace under pressure and all that rot.'

'Precisely. All that same old boring rot. Okay, cut the sound and give us a channel scan, see if anything else is interesting. I'm drug with this.'

While Levertov toweled himself with the robe, Clark B Clark keyed all the other remotes up on the master, one after the other. He went through the main scene pots first. There was the terrified eunuch, mewling gratefully as the handlers coaxed him back into his cage at the docks. There was the wild bull, stretched full length on

293

his back. Johnny-boats were stapling floats to the flippers to keep the inert beast from sinking. It was impossible to say if he was alive or dead. Levertov didn't seem interested one way or the other.

'There's more where he came from. Keep scanning what's doing in town.'

Most of Main had closed down so the shopkeepers and waitresses and office workers could all observe the heralded sea lion-riding scene. It was supposed to be the most spectacular sequence in the film—the big final climax. Publicity pass-outs had advised the people that director Steubins wanted to shoot the climax early on, out of sequence. 'To get it in the can while the weather holds,' the press release had explained for the benefit of untutored outsiders.

Of course, Clark B Clark and the insiders knew that the real reason was to get the scene in the can before the trained sea lion feebled away and died. The animal had been going downhill since the day the chopper flew it in. All this threatening expanse of sea and sky and shoreline had come as a harsh shock to an animal that had spent all his life in a refrigerated pool in Anaheim. He had lost his appetite and was beginning to look very haggard and homesick—and this was before his wild sea lion double had been shipped in and started bellowing insults at him day and night. That made him even more twitchy and distracted. For six years he had been training for this role, rehearsing with live riders and dolls, and now that it was time for his big scene he seemed to be stricken with stage fright and jumpy nerves.

Main Street was empty. Cook Boulevard was empty. The porch in front of the Underdog House was empty; all the members were down at the shoot working security. The whole club had been contracted as Foxcorp deputies.

There was plenty of action at the bowling alley, but it was all bureaucratic activity. Foxcorp and Louise had finally talked Omar Loop into renting them the place for the central production office. The wooden alleys were lined with computer stations and filing cabinets.

294

Dozens of secretaries were hurrying up and down the lanes. Levertov sighed again, watching the young men and women.

'Maybe we'll go down there some afternoon and bowl us a few lines.'

Levertov showed a little more interest in the shot in front of the Searaven Corporate Casino. A pair of ancient Deaps were busy turning laminated Foamglass logs into totem poles. The old men were using battery-powered carving knives, whacking the traditional totem features out of the foam logs as easily as one might slice up a Thanksgiving turkey. The foam dust was flying. The shot's background was also picking up the two longhairs brought up to laminate the synthetic planks. They were professional surfers who ran a custom board shop in Malibu. They wore shorts and tank tops and neon stripes of sun block across their noses and cheeks, though it was quite cloudy.

'Burned-out beach bums and worn-out Indians,' Levertov observed in his ironic purr. 'Striving together side by side for art's sake. No business like show business, eh, Mr Clark?'

Clark B nodded enthusiastically. 'Like no business *I* know, Chief. Look! They've even got the Indians using sun block. Oh, yes, only in America.'

Clark zoomed in tighter. The two old men had streaked their cheeks with the colored oxide. They looked like fat caricatures of warrior braves, cast in some kind of gaudy musical comedy. The sight gave Levertov a bit of a chuckle. So did the view behind the cannery, where the Underdogs paraded in their new silver Foxcorp Security jackets—at the ready should the brown-sprayed tribe of fishkids go on the warpath. A bit of a yuck. But it didn't look to Clark B Clark like anything was going to bring back the giddy flush of delight that the sea lion attack had set off. He kept scanning. Levertov had put the robe around his shoulders and announced he was about to retire to his quarters for a shower, just as Clark B happened to pan seaward with one of the dockside remotes. A glimpse of something silver flicked the water.

'Wait! What was that? Pan back and scope in!'

Clark fingered the keys. The prow of a big steelume fishing boat flowed into focus. The starboard rail was lined by a row of faces. Clark frowned. 'Who the hell could that be? I swear, Boss, we radioed orders, absolutely no unauthorized—' Before he could finish, that wicked goat sound bleated again.

'*That*,' Levertov laughed, clapping Clark on the shoulder, 'is the good guys coming to the rescue. Just like in the movies! Let me get some clothes on, this next scene has to be seen out in the real world. In 3-D All-around, up close and nasty. You understand, Mr Clark?'

'Right!' Clark B Clark nodded in ardent agreement. 'Out in the real world, up close and nasty!'—his neck prickling with pride and enthusiasm whether he understood or not.

EXTERIOR—KUINAK—HIGH SHOT

Back at their vantage point in the thermal the crows can see the whole town, too. They can watch the rear door of the Crabbe Potte should one of the Crabbes get around to throwing out the compost. They can see the offal drop out the secret and illegal trapdoor in the kitchen floor of the Fisherman's Wharf Bar and Grill; they can witness Laralee Jerome should she decide to slip up to sun-bathe on the top of Laralee's Beauty Shop. And it's all in 3-D. And lately their little stadium has been lively with more action than even the most curious crow could have hoped for. Right now, for example— there's Alice Carmody teetering around in a pair of emerald-green high-heel spikes the likes of which no woman has worn in forty years—dolled to high heaven and riding for a fall. O yes, they have to agree, circling satisfied in their wry gyre . . . only in America.

Alice was fuming around in the oyster shells of the motel yard, trying to button a man's heavy plaid work shirt over a voluminous silk blouse. The blouse gushed from the shirt's collar and cuffs in a peachy froth. Word had just come in over her CB: boat sighted. Big steelume multipurpose steaming into harbor. So she had dressed up. Sort of. The blouse was a fave; the shoes a statement; the work shirt a practical afterthought.

The motel yard was empty except for Old Marley and Little Worthless. Everybody else from the motel was already down at the docks for the big shoot. She had been glad for the chance to stay home and try to do some sketching, forgo all this fake sea lion action. But the sketches hadn't worked. The lines wouldn't come. It made her think of past periods of barren effort. Which made her wonder if she had lost the touch. Which somehow made her think of Carmody and the rest of them, which started making her mad. So against her far better judgment she had mixed a pitcher of morning margaritas. If Carmody didn't get home pretty quick it looked like she might relapse all the way back to the Angry Alice of old—the Alice that drinks when she gets mad and gets mad when she drinks. When the news about the incoming boat came squawking in over her C-band the margarita pitcher was nearly empty.

'Carmody, goddamn you, that *better* be you, you bloated old dunker son of a!'

She was so flustered with the news and the tequila that, in truth, she had barely noticed what she was putting on. Pawing through her closet she couldn't decide whether to go with cotton and comfort or with flash and itch. She couldn't decide whether she was pleased by the news of the new boat bringing the prodigals home to port, or pissed, or what. Then, when she was finally clothed and outside and saw that those damned Eskimo movie stars had borrowed her van again and left her nothing but a kid-sized go-ped bike to ride (in a stupid skirt and heels?), she made up her mind: pissed it was.

The bike of course hadn't been recharged. She plugged

297

the fucker in and strode back and forth, cursing and kicking the shells at Marley and poor worried Worthless while the battery quickamped. Marley ignored the tantrum, but the pup knew the woman was upset about *some* dog that had done something bad, and she was fawning hard at the woman's high heels to make sure it wasn't her. Alice stomped and kicked and cursed the entire ten minutes it took to charge the machine, and she didn't leave anybody out, not even pathetic puppies. She was still muttering when she pedaled out of the yard to the path through the vacant lot.

Pumping hard, Alice made it through the fireweed to the road to town, then motor-coasted on the pavement, to catch her breath before tackling the grade up to the bridge. The road was deserted and she sincerely hoped it stayed that way; she knew how she must look, green heels hooked over the pedals and knees nearly to her chin every time she pumped the damned runt motorbike. But there wasn't a soul in sight as she coasted down off the bridge on to Second Street. The whole downtown looked vacated. She decided to stay off Main, though, and try the old board footwalk through the alley. The gate was usually latched to discourage this very sort of two-wheeled shortcut to the docks, but of course this wasn't a usual day. The shops were too deserted for anybody to be concerned. Everybody was down at the shoot. She saw the gate was unlatched and pedaled for the narrow opening.

What Alice did not see (though the crows did) was another go-ped, pumping hard up the narrow wooden walkway from the other direction. Alice swung in the open gate just as the other cycle was about to swing out of it. The two bikes clashed handlebars like a couple of young elk trying out their antlers.

The overall maneuver was spectacular. When the crows stopped cheering and held up their score, the cards proclaimed a 9.6, a 9.4 and a 9.8 for Alice. For the other rider, three perfect tens. Difficulty points was what swung it. For one thing, the girl had clearly never ridden a go-ped before; instead of gripping the hand brake at the sight of impending collision, she had squeezed the throttle full open. For another, she was riding with nothing on but a beaded doeskin skirt and shower thongs. Even Alice's ridiculous high heels and silk-blouse-and-work-shirt combo was no match.

'You ringy *twit*!' Alice shouted, her voice fiery in her throat. 'This isn't the wild Arctic wilderness, you know.'

'I know,' the girl said, appearing much chagrined but in no way seeming to feel obliged to cover her nakedness. She was on her knees, still astraddle the humming machine. 'I very sorry.' She did not raise her eyes to Alice.

'This is a civiliz*ation*, in case nobody has informed you,' Alice ranted on. 'Not much of one, but we try. See that sign on the gate?'

'Yes,' the girl said. She still did not raise her face. The long hair almost covered her nakedness, like a rich purple shawl.

'Well, can you read?'

'It says "No Vehicles by Order of the Kuinak Association of Greater Downtown—"'

'Okay. You can read but you can't ride. Are you okay? Anything busted or should I say bruised?'

The girl shook her head so meekly that a pang of remorse suddenly cooled the fire from Alice's throat. After all, she thought, the collision had been as much her fault as the girl's. More. She at least knew about the No Vehicles rule; in that summer of the Rollerhoard Alice had been one of the businesses that petitioned to get the rule put in. She stepped free of her bike and reached out a hand.

'Get up, then. What the hell's your story, anyway, pedaling around topless like this? Christ all Friday, look at you; you're humongous. You're lucky you didn't have that whole mangy pack of Underdogs after you, like hounds on the tail of some—' Alice paused, searching for a kinder comparison than the one she had in mind. The girl finished the phrase for her.

'Some bitch in heat?' she offered, at last raising her eyes

to meet Alice's. 'The thought did cross my head. But them Underdogs, they got other fishkids to fry. Nobody notice me slip away.'

Alice was still tongue-tied by the sight before her. She had never really looked at the girl before. Now she couldn't draw her eyes away. Cosmetics accounted for some of it—the makeup artists' highlighting and underscoring—but what was being highlighted and underscored was already there. Alice knew she would henceforth never see the girl as anything but beautiful, with or without cosmetics or clothes. 'I'll just *bet* nobody noticed,' she finally replied.

'It's true! Everybody was busy watching those sea lions. I've seen sea lions before, so I borrow this bike and just slip away, *shoof.* And that's my story. Okay?'

'Okay by me,' Alice conceded. 'I imagine it must get tiresome for you, standing in front of all those people with, with your—'

'My tits sticking out naked?' The girl looked down at herself and shrugged. 'I've sticked out like this since I was nine years old—on account of that UN-Spam the nuns served for school lunch, I think.' She pursed her lips, musing. 'No, what is tiresome for me is now that the doll got ripped—you understand about the doll of me they're using?—they are going to want to make *another* mold. They had to crack the first mold to get the doll out. I don't know why. All I know is it takes this Hollywood guy ten hundred hours to plaster it on me and twenty hundred hours for it to set and it itches all the time like a million mosquitoes and pulls out lots of my body hairs. And that's my story.' She gave the bikes a penitent look. 'You think these little gonids will go again, or shall we have to shoot them like ponies with broken legs?'

The girl's on-running rattle was so captivating that Alice threw back her head and laughed. 'Oh, they'll pull through. Nothing's wrong with your steed except a bent shoe, and all mine needs is a new front leg and it'll go good as ever. Shut yours off, we'll leave them where they lie. But I mean Jee-zus, *look* at you! Here.

Put this on. Maybe your attire is suitable for the Baffins or Beverly Hills, but if you're going to be traipsing around my town you need to be a bit less provocative.' She pulled Carmody's frayed plaid shirt off and held it out.

'Oh, no, Mrs Carmody! You were in a hurry to some important business. You take my machine and go on. I will be fine. All I need to do is slide back up to the motel and hide out awhile; I will be completely okay.'

'I suspect you will,' Alice allowed, 'but you put this on anyway. Had any breakfast? Let's see if we can find a place that's open. Then maybe we'll both slide back to the motel and hide out.'

'Slide and hide,' the girl said, wrapping the shirt around her. 'What's first?'

'First is getting some of the grease and blood cleaned off. Follow me.'

Main Street was still completely deserted. There weren't even any loafers at the Tomb of the Unknown Wino. Most of the shops were locked and grated with signs out. Only the door to Old Lady Grady's little store was ajar, which didn't surprise Alice. Here was one citizen who wouldn't be deserting her post to go down and see the big movie action, or any other action, for that matter. Iris Grady was legally blind, from a lab accident. The old woman had been a trim red-haired young chemistry teacher at Kuinak High when Alice had attended, with quick green eyes. But after school on one well-publicized extracurricular evening, something had gone wrong in a test tube. Her strung-out meth-head brother, Jimmy Grady, was the cause, the story went, forcing Big Sister down to the high school lab to try to stir him up a little relief. The ether had ignited, and all the sprinklers in the school had gone off. Brother Jimmy ended up in the Icehouse. Red-haired Iris was cleared in view of her and her brother's reputations, but both corneas had been too damaged to allow her to continue teaching. She bought the Novelty Boutique and Antique Clock Shop with her insurance money, and learned braille, and got fat. She could still see a little, but her eyes looked like destroyed rifle targets, so she wore a gingham sleeping mask in public. Ragged eyeballs were not conducive to novelty and notion sales. Miss Iris trusted her customers to make their own choices and tally their own bills and make their own change while she waited behind her gingham mask. This was one of the reasons Alice bought a lot of her clothes at Miss Iris' Boutique. She could indulge her terrible taste in clothes without worrying about some snooty sales clerk watching her.

'Afternoon, Miss Grady.'

'Good afternoon, Alice.' The woman was perched ponderously atop a padded stool, where she had been contentedly listening to her collection of antique clocks. She looked like an overstuffed doll, but her voice was trim and light, as from a proper young school-marm. 'What can I do for you?'

'I'm not shopping, Miss Grady. We're just strolling up Main for a snack and need to spruce up a bit. Care to join us for lunch?'

'How considerate, but I had better stick to my post. You know where the washroom is, Alice.'

When she heard them come back out she asked, '"We" who, may I inquire?'

'Just me and my young friend—what *is* your name, anyway?'

'Shoola,' the girl answered.

'Shoola? Don't be giving me any crap, girl, I mean your real name.'

'Shoola's what everybody is calling me, and I like it better than my real name. My real name, you know what it means in Innupiat? It means Walks in Muddy Snow and Cries. How would you like to be called Walks in Muddy Snow and Cries? I would rather have a make-believe name. Good afternoon, Miss Grady.'

'Good afternoon, Shoola,' Miss Grady said in her diminutive voice as she slid down from the long-legged chair. 'I've heard of you, the beautiful Eskimo movie star. Pay Alice no mind, she's a scissor-tongue.' Hand outstretched, the old lady felt her way across the store

302

to their voices, then ran her fingers lightly down the girl's cheek and torso. 'Goodness, child. What size are you, offhand?'

'Offhand, I do not know, Miss Grady. But Mrs Carmody here, she estimates me to be huge-mongous.'

She said it with such innocence that Alice didn't realize she was being kidded until she heard the girl and the old schoolteacher laughing. 'C'mon, movie star,' she said. 'You need sustenance to carry all that around.'

'Sustenance?'

'Food.'

'Yes, I do. I am hungry like a walrus. Pleased to meet you, Miss Grady.'

'Have a nice time, kids,' Miss Iris called after them. The old woman waited until she heard her front door close, then climbed back on her padded stool behind the counter, like a dropsical doll returning to its shelf. Her shop was again filled with the friendly sound of ticking clocks.

They left the two damaged go-peds commiserating together against the alley wall, and turned up Main, away from the tall metal sail. The girl fell in alongside Alice on the deserted sidewalk, and for a while walked briskly along in silence.

'All the cafes look closed,' Alice remarked, motioning at the street ahead. 'I was born and grew up in this town and I never saw Main so empty, not even in the middle of winter. I don't see but four dogs and one wino.'

'Where I was born and grew up, four dogs and a wino is a crowd. To me, I find it all very full and wonderful, Mrs Carmody. Everything in Kuinak is like the summer carnival the nuns took us to in Dundas Harbor, to me—just wonderful.'

Alice was quiet. She didn't know what to say about Kuinak being called wonderful.

'I was raised Jesuit,' the girl went on, 'by the New Jerusalem nuns. You was raised Orthodox, I can tell. Kim, the cripple boy, he was raised by Russian Orthodox. That's why he always acts so pissed off.'

Alice felt her face burning again. 'Do I always act so pissed off?'

'Like a mama bear with a missing cub. I mean why are we walking this fast, for an instant? We in a hurry for something?'

Alice slowed her stride. 'No, we are not in a hurry for anything,' she realized; she was no longer in any foaming rush to get down to the docks to greet a boat full of returning dunkheads, all jacked up on testosterone. 'Walking fast through this wonderful town is a habit I developed for my nose's sake. I like to get through the smell of dog shit fast as I can.'

'See? That's exactly what I mean. The Jesuits say slow down, smell the flowers; whereas Orthodox say hurry up so you don't have to smell the dog shit.'

'Is that right? What if there isn't anything *but* dog shit?'

'Then the Jesuits say plant flowers. Hey, isn't that an open one across the street down there? I'm hungry like a wolf. These movie people get you up too early, then they never give you breakfast. Jelly doughnuts and coffee is all. I can't handle coffee—us English are tea drinkers. Herbal is what I like. Mint Zinger or chamomile. But no caffeine.' She suddenly pirouetted into the street in Carmody's half-buttoned shirt. 'So, what you think? Am I presentable enough to take into a Crabbe Potte?'

Alice looked hard to see if she was being ribbed, but again she was so dazzled by the girl's beauty that it was impossible for her to assess what lay beneath. What a damn picture! she thought—the classic pagan female. Far more female than any of Rubens' yeasty nymphs or Modigliani's sprawling strumpets, more primal even than Georgia O'Keeffe's labial lilies. Because the girl actually *was* that overblown nymph of wildness that Rubens had tried to imagine, not the model meant to transmit the ideal . . . *was* the wide-spread lily, not some senile old broad's tempera symbol. What a pity that such a blithe spirit had been shanghaied aboard this sham, far from the familiar shores of home and at the mercy of every

304

tawdry trick and flashy flimflam. The poor kid was doomed to go for some ball-brained hunk-o sure as shit, hook, line and sinker. You could see it in her eyes. In ten years she'd be just another single mother with a substance problem and jugs down to her knees. Less than ten years.

Alice had not graced the Crabbe Potte with her presence since the blowup with Myrna Crabbe the night of the reopening. But she was reasonably sure her old school chum would be down at the set, gobbling up the movie glitter. The street door to the lounge hadn't even been unbolted, and the diner section looked as deserted as Main Street.

One of the Crabbe girls from the other side of the family —the Eastwick side—was alone behind the counter when Alice and Shoola swooshed through the automatic screen. She was leaned against the coffee urn, whining into the celefone. Her name was Diana but everybody called her Dinah—Dinah the Whiner. Lowest in seniority, it had been Dinah's lot to stay at the 'Always Open' Crabbe Potte Grill and Lounge while all her cousins got to go down and be seen with the Beautiful People. Poor Dinah was ugly as a mud clam, even if one overlooked her adenoidal whine. Her hair looked like a deck mop left to dry on an overturned bucket. Her eyes were sullen pits. Her chin dribbled away like a melting vanilla cone. Dinah Crabbe and Iris Grady were probably the only shopkeepers in Kuinak still minding the shop, Alice mused—each the other end of the stick from the other. One couldn't see worth beans; the other wasn't worth seeing.

'How's it goin', Dinah? They left you at the helm, bar and all?'

'I'm too young to barkeep, you want a menu?'

Dinah wasn't into small talk, Alice immediately perceived, so she didn't bother introducing her guest. She took two of the crab-shaped menus and led Shoola toward a corner booth with a view of Main. Anybody coming up from the docks would have to pass the Crabbe Potte, especially Carmody. It wasn't his favorite hangout—he preferred the Tail House out on Airport Road, where they had a dance floor—but he'd want to be dropping by the Crabbe Potte today. The Crabbe Potte Grill and Lounge was the afternoon watering hole of Kuinak high society. Anybody who was anybody in Kuinak could be collared in the Crabbe Potte during happy hours. If that new boat report was true, Carmody and the boys would come here first, all wild-and-wooly from their high-sea adventures and aching for an audience. They were going to be disappointed, Alice thought with a smirk, to find nothing but women—one an Eskimo, one a whiner and one a grouchy wife.

'You can start us with two coffees—no, one coffee and one herbal tea for my English guest. No caffeine.'

'We got coffee, Mrs Carmody, but not no teas, herbal or otherwise. The cook is down at the movie with everybody else. They left me with one urn of coffee and one crockpot of chili and one of chowder, and *that's all*.'

'All you have to do is put the kettle on, Dinah. You can do that, can't you? Boil water?'

'The cook is down at the *docks*,' Dinah repeated, turning up the whine. 'All I have is coffee and chili and chowder.

'Coffee is okay,' the Innupiat girl called in a bright voice. 'And any of that other.'

Dinah glowered a moment at the girl—*another* person younger than her having a better time! 'That other what? Chili or chowder?'

'I'd go with the chili if I were you' was Alice's whispered advice. 'The chowder fluctuates. And you'll have to lend me some cash; I left home without my purse.'

The girl pulled a ball of hundred-dollar bills from a pocket of her doeskin skirt. 'I got plenty. I get per diem every day whether I take off my shirt or not.'

The coffee was tepid and the chili burnt, but neither of the diners raised any complaint. They were too busy talking—or talking and listening, to be more precise. Alice mainly listened and smiled and nodded, or frowned and shook her head. The girl talked on nearly nonstop, right through repeated refills of coffee and chili beans and biscuits and a wedge of coconut cream pie so outdated that Alice wondered if Omar Loop hadn't missed his weekly pickup. When the girl was finished with her piece she asked for what was left of Alice's. Alice could not think of anybody besides Carmody who could get as much pleasure from the simple comings and goings of food and talk across the lips.

The girl's mother was a half-dozen years dead—a suicide—and the father had disappeared south on a snowmobile before she was born. The two old Eskimos in Unit 5 actually were her grandparents, though the girl could never clear up whether they were her grandparents on her mother's side or her father's side, or one from each. She figured it was probably one from each or they would have been more forthcoming. These damn bloodlines got a little hazy up far north, she begged Alice to understand; too close an accounting wasn't too good an idea in the too-close quarters that you had to live in, up Far North.

The screen swooshed and three fishkids came in wearing their inner-tube burnooses over their brown spray jobs. They sat at the counter, where Dinah offered them menus and a few guarded whispers, then went back to her phone. The fishkids seemed more interested in studying Alice and the Eskimo girl in the counter mirror than in their menus. The door opened again and in walked the two not-so-young surfboard makers from Malibu. They were riffing about the LA Raiders' upcoming season. When they spotted Alice and Shoola their eyes shined with excitement. Alice couldn't imagine the surfers knew who she was, but Shoola they probably knew. Shoola was the star.

The pair exchanged looks with Dinah, then took the booth nearest Alice and Shoola. They had come to listen. The Eskimo girl could not have helped but notice the pair's obvious eavesdropping, but she didn't let it slow her down. The go-ped collision, the chili, all this coffee and all these attentive ears really had her bubbling.

To Alice's dismay, the next pair through the door was the other half of the totem pole factory—the two old

307

Deap brothers Walter and William Barrow. Their dust masks were on top of their heads like little yarmulkes and Foamglass chips mantled their shoulders. The lascivious old scamps sat right down with the surfers, grinning like they'd just scored a ringside seat at a high-five event. They had come to rubberneck, too. The old farts ought to be spanked with kelp, the way the tribes used to deal with dirty old men.

After the Barrows the door barely ceased swooshing as more and more people continued to fill the long diner. Alice was convinced Dinah was the one sending out the call, but why were so many responding? Maybe they were hoping to see the babbling starlet bare her bounty again.

Shoola just kept sipping and bubbling, undeterred by the audience. She was a dam-burst of observations about her new world. She had questions and thoughts and opinions about everything. What would the fishermen be when the season closed? Why did the high-school girls pluck their eyebrows? Basketball interested her especially. She had been studying the half-court games on the deck of the *Silver Fox* and had become an avid, albeit unenlightened, fan. Why did the mob of players suddenly cease their wild scrambling and become orderly and pensive, allowing one man to shoot free? Why did they slap each other after achieving a basket? And why weren't *girls* allowed to join in the play? 'Is it because some of the players must play without shirts? I'll play without shirts.'

'I'll bet you would,' Alice said. She could feel the surfers in the neighboring booth aching to make some crack or other. 'I'll bet you would get to shoot free a lot, without shirts.'

When the girl's caffeine jag led her toward things she'd overheard about the sexploits of the film crew, Alice decided to rein her in, if only to frustrate the hungry ears. Especially the Barrow brothers in the next booth; they were too old to be exposed to these steamy stories.

'All right, we can do without the gossip. There's something I've been wanting to ask *you* folks about, anyway, about this story you're shooting. The Isabella Anootka story? I assume you're able to read.'

'Jesuits can read *circles* around Orthodoxes. I know the Shoola stories from before I was in grade school.'

'Okay. So what do you think of this so-called Northwest Indian tale we're doing? From your far-up-north primitive point of view?'

The girl was a while answering. 'I know it isn't no authentic North People story; it is way too dolled up. But I guess it is a all-right story.'

'Did you know Isabella Anootka was an old maid from New Jersey who never went north in her life?'

'So? It's still a all-right story. Do you hold it against the story that a round-eye wrote it?'

'No. I like the story,' Alice answered. 'It's better than most real native stories because it *is* dolled up. It has a *plot* and makes a *point*, which is what it takes to make a movie. A real Indian story would be too meaningless for Hollywood.' Now she could feel the old Barrow brothers wanting to make a crack.

'Meaningless?'

'Yeah, meaningless. Pointless. Indian stories, they just don't have any points to make; like, say, *Pinocchio* makes, where if you lie your nose gets longer. Or in Aesop, where the greedy dog loses his bone by biting the bone's reflection in the water. You think Hollywood would send all this money up here to shoot a real Indian story? What would be the point? A real Indian story would be as useless to Hollywood as, say, a real totem pole.'

She knew it was a low blow, but elders like the Barrow brothers were supposed to show a little more class than eavesdropping and ogling—especially in public.

'So what I was wanting to ask was how do you and your folks, your *grand*parents, honestly feel about doing this kind of dolled-up styrofoam story instead of one of your own? As both native *and* artist, I'm curious . . .'

Alice waited. A low blow and an accurate one. Not so much as the sound of a coffee sip came from the booth beyond. In fact, the whole room was leaning in

309

their direction, listening. They must be pretty starved for titillation, to be tempted down to fare as bland as this.

When it was totally quiet the girl drew a slow breath and spoke. 'Pointless?' she asked.

A little taken aback, Alice nodded. She noticed that the beautiful face across the table had darkened ominously, and the big black eyes were narrowed to sharp slits. The girl drew another slow breath, wagging her head back and forth strangely as she did, like a dotty old woman. When she spoke again the voice was throaty and measured:

'One morning . . . my brother did not come back from his trap line. All day I waited for him to come back. But he did not. All day. It was very cold. I knew he would not survive the night outside in such cold, so I put on my furs and went to look for him.'

Alice was completely surprised by this strange recital. She had half expected her dig about the uselessness of authentic native literature to provoke some kind of protest—from the Barrow brothers, perhaps, even from the girl—but not this sudden non-sequitur narrative. This was off the far wall.

'I came to the first trap and it was sprung but there was nothing in it . . . and my brother was nowhere to be seen. I came to the next trap but it was also sprung with nothing in it . . . and of my brother there was not one sign. Trap after trap the same—sprung; no brother. It began to grow dark. I was very cold. Then I came to the last trap. It was not sprung. And hanging from a branch just above the trap was my brother's leather pelt-sack. I reached up and untied the cord, and from out of the sack fell my brother's head.'

'Your brother's *head*?'

'Yes. And green fire was coming out of the neck and green fire was coming out of the mouth.'

'I see. Green fire . . .'

'Yes.' The girl's voice dropped lower still, like a winter wind beneath a drafty floor. 'And he was gnashing his teeth and he was biting, like he was very hungry.'

'So what did you do?'

'I backed away. But the head began to roll after me . . . with green fire coming out of his neck, and green fire coming out of his mouth. So I pulled off my mittens, and I threw them to the head to chew on while I ran for home as fast as I could. Then I heard something behind me. It was the head, rolling after me, gnashing and snapping his teeth . . . and green fire was coming out of the neck and green fire was coming out of the mouth. So I pulled off my left hand and threw it at the head. The hand wrestled the head and the head began to bite the hand. And I run and I run. But pretty soon I hear this gnashing and snapping behind me and it's the head, rolling faster and faster and closer and closer . . . and green fire is coming out of the neck, and green fire is coming out of the mouth. So I take off my *other* hand and throw it, and it fights the head and I run on. I run and I run. But pretty soon there it is again, the head, right on my heels, hungry-looking as ever. What can I do? I take off my right foot and throw it and the foot *kicks* the head, and *kicks* the head . . . and *keeps* kicking it, right across the snow to the ice and right across the ice to the water and right into the water. And the head sinks in the sea . . . green fire still coming out of its neck and green fire still coming out of its mouth. Me, I hop all the way back to the cabin on one foot.'

'Good for you.' Alice meant to sound flip, but her mouth was dry and that winter wind seemed to be blowing up the back of her neck. She shivered. 'I'm so relieved to hear it.'

'But, you see, the cabin door was latched and tied . . . and I could not get it open, because I had no hands. And I could not climb up the ladder to the smoke hole because I had only one foot.'

Alice waited, feeling irritated that she was the one who would have to ask the question. None of the other listeners were going to do it, that was for sure.

'Okay, I'll bite. *Then* what happened to you?'

'I froze to death.'

Alice groaned. 'See? That's just what I mean about these damned half-witted Indian stories. What the hell's the point of *that* one?'

'The point of that one is "Don't lose your mittens."' Then, abruptly yet smoothly, artfully, the low voice changed back to the light trill of a teenager. 'So, this is a good lunch place, don't you think? So friendly and quiet. Allow me to pay, please? You are plenty kind to take me, a wild primitive savage girl, into your town for all these treats and coffee. I am in your debt.'

'What for?' Alice laughed and took a hundred from the bundle the girl held out. 'It's your money.'

'But it's your town.'

Another dozen customers had tiptoed in during the story, Tommy Toogiak Senior and some Underdogs in their Foxcorp Security jackets, and some of the Teamster roadies—and more were coming. Alice saw the Crabbes' pink Lexus van pass by the window and turn into its parking spot on the bar side. Was *that* what had drawn this big crowd so quick? Were all these rubbernecks gathering in hope of watching Myrna the Crabbe and Alice the Angry Aleut get it on again? She hoped not, for godsake. She was way out of training for any big catfight. 'Shall we?' she said to the girl, and waved the hundred at Dinah. But before she could slide out of the booth there was a stir among the spectators and she saw her own van pull up and stop across the street, right at the fire hydrant. She assumed it was the rest of the Eskimo family, on the way back from the canceled shoot, stopping by to spend their per diems.

'Leave it to those relatives of yours to park in the only red zone on the whole damn street. Why should they worry? By the time the ticket comes in the mail, you'll all be back up north in your igloos.'

Then Alice saw it wasn't Shoola's relatives at all. It was Greer at the wheel; he came skittering out the driver's door in that skimpy little crazy-quilt vest he wore to show off his recklessness. He'd rubbed cocoa butter on his face and his skin gleamed like an island idol.

312

'It's the lads home from the sea,' she told the girl. 'That dark dandy is Emil Greer—our local ladykiller. Watch out for him.'

'Haw,' the girl said.

Greer bounded around the front of the van to the passenger door and held out a chivalrous hand. A round pink head swung into view, followed by an even rounder belly.

'And that,' Alice explained, 'is the so-called important business I was on my way to: my Mr Michael Carmody.'

Mr Michael Carmody disembarked without taking the offered hand. Greer continued to hold it out, waiting. The side door slid open and a load of passengers began stepping forth into the street. All the faces were suntanned and wind-whipped and robust.

'That slimeball with the suitcase is Billy Bellisarius, our local scooter. That's Archie Culligan, works for us, a nice kid. And the Greek-god guy with the Elvis Presley eyes is Isaak Sallas. Damn, would you watch those bozos strut. God only knows what manly mischief they've been up to, sailing around this long. Just *look* at them.'

'I am looking,' Shoola said in a voice gone suddenly very weak. Her face was leaned close to the steamy window. 'And I think he looks just beautiful.'

'You mean Mr Carmody?' Alice kidded. She knew that the girl was speaking of Greer, with all those grand, penny-ante gestures and dramatic dreadlocks and jewelry. 'Nice of you to think so, but the old dunk is mine, such as he is.'

'No, not Mr Carmody, though he does have a happy look about him . . .'

'Then I guess you must mean the teakwood face with the springs for hair: Mr Rasta. I was afraid of that. But I tell you, watch out.'

Greer again held forth the chivalrous hand. As they watched another took it, and a blowsy blond head ducked out the door into view—a woman as tanned and robust-looking as the rest. She gave Greer a smile of thanks and he bent to kiss her sunburned knuckles.

'See? Greer's a Casanova, always got one blond twink or another hooked on to his snaky black arm. Though he usually manages to hook them a little younger not so—'

Alice stopped. The woman had freed her hand. This particular blonde was not taking Greer's offered arm—

'No, no,' the girl kept on, unmindful of Alice's sudden silence. 'I don't mean Mr Carmody *or* Mr Casanova . . .'

—*this* blonde was hooking on to *Carmody's* big pink forearm, like a tug to a barge! Alice heard the crowd behind her draw a single happy breath. Ah. So here was what they'd all hustled up to the Potte to witness, not some Eskimo doll doing a topless, not some fat old Myrna Crabbe clacking her claws. Here was a high-five encounter with *miles* more potential. Alice felt her neck and shoulders burn beneath all that anticipation at her back.

'I mean the other guy?'

'Other guy . . . ?' Alice asked vacantly, watching the little band crossing the street toward them. 'What other guy?'

'The Greek-god guy,' the girl crooned, sounding now every inch a teenager, fourteen and completely smitten—hook, line and sinker—'with the Elvis eyes. I never seen such a beautiful man, not even in the soapdishes. I love him, Mrs Carmody. I will be his girlfriend forever.'

'Jesus H Christ,' Alice said. She slumped back into the booth, drained at last of madness and margaritas and frustration and fascination and all. 'Jesus H upside-down Christ.'

314

12

Looking Back Through Scratched Crabbe Glass

The first sight of the *Silver Fox* had impressed everybody, even the dour-mouthed Billy. Isaak had been worried that Carmody might be a little deflated when he came storming into home port eager to show off his grand new multipurpose, only to find all his thunder stolen by a gargantuan yacht. But the Cornishman had not seemed at all jealous of the magnificent craft with her towering magnesium sail. He made only one comment as they hummed gently past the gleaming vessel:

'Them lower decks would be useful in a big tuna strike, I'll grant ye, but they'd be a bleedin' bitch to hose down after.'

They pulled into the slip that had accommodated Carmody's previous boat and left young Nels aboard to secure and stand watch. Billy had cut enough of his cast away that he was able to stand, even walk a little. He looked like a pathetic old redcap, forever stooped by the weight of that infernal suitcase. The ramp to the dock was so steep he was afraid to descend forward in his condition. He began slowly backing down, a few doddering inches a step, until Carmody got so impatient with the spectacle he ordered Ike and Greer to make a cross-hand cradle and carry him.

The moment Ike touched solid ground fatigue began to wrap around him like a heavy wool blanket. He hadn't been able to relax in days; now, suddenly, he was sleepy. It was like he'd been on a good old-fashioned week-long wire run and was finally, mercifully, spiraling down. He hadn't really had a full run since he and Greer flew out, more than a week ago. Longer, actually—not since the yacht—no, not since that cat in the bottle had pumped him full of adrenaline. Then that run-in with Greener, another big jolt of juice, and more still from that roller-coaster ride down the White Pass to splash down in the icy Yukon waters . . . enough jolts to wire anybody. Also, all those toasts of hot tea the night before on that processor? If some of those cups hadn't been laced with scoot or Korea-crank, or whatever this season's designer upper happened to be, then he'd eat his rain hat. Now he was coming home and down at the same time, and so abruptly that he found himself weaving around the parking lot like he was seasick. He hoped he could get his land legs long enough to get him back up to the dim morgue of his trailerhouse with its narrow slab of a bunk. Just keep a steady course, sailor, he advised himself—steady and slow and you'll soon drop anchor in the sweet haven of oblivion.

The rest of the landing party had other plans. Willi and Greer wanted to leg it right over to the movie hurly-burly they'd seen sailing in; Carmody wanted to hit a bar first, to get in the spirit. Archie needed to go by his mom's triple for some more clothes and some decent shoes; he was damned if he was going to make his home-coming appearance in a pair of floppy old gum boots. Ike said flatly that none of the social possibilities interested him one bit; all he intended to do was drive straight up to the trailer, check on Old Marley, then hit the sack. Greer reminded him his Heftyvan was clear out Bayshore at the airport where they had rented the plane, and that he was likely going to have some tall explaining to do about the Otter before Herb Tom let him drive away with the van.

Billy Bellisarius insisted he had quite a number of extremely pressing meetings that he had to make: with the mule of the other suitcase; with Goldstein the lawyer and with the Kuinak Clinic radiologist for some X-ray evidence . . . with the lap-fax at Altenhoffen's newspaper so he could begin his letter-to-the-editor lambasting of Greener and his Beulahland Buchenwald . . .

'Hush, Squid, hush.' Carmody had his binoculars trained across the lot. 'I see Alice's six-wheeler nosed in among those movie-star trailers unless I'm mistook. What say a couple of you stout lads stroll over and quietly commandeer the dear buggy for a while? Alice she won't miss it with all this Hollywood *hoop*-de-do.'

Willi said, 'Who's Alice?' but Carmody was at his glasses again. Archie said he positively was *not* going over there in these rags and gum boots. Greer shrugged philosophically, then hitched up his crazy-quilt pants. 'Join me for a little grand theft auto, Pardner?' Ike declined with a weary shake of the head and Greer started strolling along across the tarmac, hands stuck casually in his hip pockets. In the little lull Willi wondered again, 'Who is Alice?' looking from face to face, at which point Ike suddenly changed his mind and decided to join his partner after all. In his sleep-starved state of mind, he reasoned, a little simple car-stealing would probably be easier than a lot of complicated question-answering.

Ike was glad for all the hurly-burly going on around the camera raft. It allowed them to stroll up to Alice's van unnoticed, and he had no more desire to confront the woman right then than Carmody did. There was no card in the ignition, but Greer knew an old hot-wiring trick. Using his jackknife to pry the panel off and a foil Gumgo wrapper in the wiring, Greer bypassed the chipware and got back down to battery-to-starter-motor basics. He started the engine quietly and backed the machine around; it idled away from the other studio vehicles as though on tiptoes. They scooped up the rest of the crew and drove Billy to the yacht, taking care to keep the imposing hull between them and the movie crowd as much as possible. Carmody and Willi got out to have a look at the strange vessel while the Squid headed for the gangway to take care of his business.

The giant wouldn't let Billy come on board, refusing even to switch open the gate at the bottom of the ramp. Billy was forced to call out his pleas like a wharf bum importuning a tour boat. It didn't take long for this indignity to bring out the wrath of the Squid at its eye-burning inkiest. He stood at the gate, with his stringy hair and his suitcase and his tortured scoop-backed stoop, and cursed the big guard with such seething, unrelenting eloquence that he attracted a nice crowd of admirers to the yacht's rail. Not the least among these was the goggle-eyed first mate, Abu Bul Singh. When Billy's diatribe finally had to pause for air, Mr Singh cut in masterfully and informed him, in the deadly and deprecating voice of a British naval officer, that the seaman about whom he was so stridently inquiring was at present attending to his assigned ship-board duties and would continue to do so for another—the eyes goggled down to check an enormous chronometer on his wrist— '—ah, twenty-three minutes. It will be my pleasure to tell him where he might meet you, sir, if you wish . . .'

Billy was dumbstruck by the man's command of a style that he had always considered his own—a cold, condescending, superior snottiness wrapped politely in proper English. He was too tongue-tied to name a meeting place, even if he could have come up with one. Billy Bellisarius had no home of his own, properly speaking, but roamed from motel room to hotel room to the bedrooms of occasional girl- or boyfriends as the mood or the moving orders happened to take him. He couldn't even remember where his bedroll happened to be unrolled at present.

'Somewhere, please?' First Mate Singh prompted with a delicate nastiness. 'Take your time . . .'

That was when Carmody had hollered from where he and Willi were strolling back down the dock. '*Tell the bloody admiral where the Crabbe Potte is, Squid, so's we can shove off.* I'm fairly sufferin' for a mixed cocktail at a real bar with real barflies. Even if it ain't real hooch no more. How about you, Prairie Chicken? Care to sample the syrup at one of Kuinak's quaintest little pubs?'

318

'Long as there's real ice cubes,' Willi answered in her sunny voice. But when she climbed back into the van Ike noticed that a puzzled cloud seemed to have settled across the sunny face. Carmody must have hedged his way around that prickly question about the sudden and mysterious certain somebody called Alice, or ducked it entirely. The old bounder was turning out to be a slicker-tongued Fat Jack Falstaff than Ike had been giving him credit for.

They drove first to Dorothy Culligan's triple-wide out Bayshore and Archie grabbed a windbreaker and a pair of his brother's penny loafers. Dorothy was a widow of a drowned king crabber and the town's only CPA and notary public. She also peddled homemade pastry on the side. She carried a sack of fresh-baked thimbleberry muffins out to the van and made Greer promise to save at least two for Nels back at the boat. She said hello to Carmody and gave the tousled blond stranger seated next to him a long, inquisitive look. Nobody offered to introduce her.

Ike stuck his warm muffin in his pocket as they headed back toward town. 'For Old Marley,' he explained. 'I'm a little anxious about him, alone up there all this time. Why don't you guys just run me on home first? I can do without the cocktail, ice or not . . .'

'Now don't be anxious, Isaak.' Carmody twisted around to grin his big grin. 'We'll just pop into the Potte for half a mo' . . . to cruise the bulletin board, you understand.'

Though he didn't believe Carmody's reason, Ike did understand. The bulletin board in the Crabbe Potte Grill and Lounge was where all the important maritime trans-actions and activities were listed —bankruptcy auctions, pleas for financial bail-outs, cryptic announcements of back-outs and give-ups. One could sometimes pick up a blue-chip quota dirt cheap from some disillusioned dunker by cruising the Crabbe Potte bulletin board.

'Cap'n Carmody's right, Ike. A Kuinak man he must cruise de Potte, no matter what.'

'Hey, Greer, it's your dog.'

'Sallas—' Carmody twisted around again, his face practically in Willi's hair, '—if Alice said she'd feed the dog then she fed the dog.'

This time the question didn't have to be voiced; the silence was articulate enough. Then they turned off Bayshore up Main Street, and everybody was so amazed by what they beheld that Willi's wonderings were forgotten. The squalid little street scene they were accustomed to had been totally transformed, as though a team of makeup artists had been flown in to do a face-lift. The shabby planking of the buildings had been covered with primered siding. Composite shingles of the same flat tan shade replaced the rickety cedar on most of the roofs. There was new red and white molding around the windows and doorways of the shops, like fresh gloss on the lips of business. Ike saw that somebody had even leashed a banner over the carved Underdog sign that usually swung above the clubhouse porch: SILVER FOX-HOUNDS, the banner said, like an engraved dog collar in silver and black. In fact, silver-and-black banners were displayed everywhere. It reminded Ike of the way some of the valley 'burbs around LA used to deck themselves out when the Raiders were in the Super Bowl. Probably no damned accident, either, it occurred to him, that the colors flown by these invaders from Orange County were the Raiders' silver and black.

But the banners and the new tan siding weren't as disconcerting as the street itself. The very pavement had been scrubbed as clean and clear as one of those make-believe Main Streets in Disney World. There were a few parked cars along the curbside, but only new ones, neat ones—none of the familiar junkers that had been abandoned for so long they had become moldering landmarks. There were no beat-up pickups with their load of tools and ropes and beer cans and dogs. More astonishing still: no dogs. Not a sign as far as Isaak could see. He wondered if the dogs had been towed off like the junkers and pickups, stored in some big pen somewhere built special for impounded eyesores. And the dozen or so drunk

Deaps that were always stationed on all four corners of Main and Pine, rain or shine, like diligent sentries armed with bottles in brown paper sacks . . . what the hell had they done with them? Found a part for them in the flick, too, probably, along with the rest of the town. What had Clark B Clark said? Make everybody partners? Maybe these Hollywood hustlers were truer to their word than he'd imagined; maybe they *were* going to cut the whole town in on the action, make everybody rich and famous. Ike still didn't feel at all good about it. In fact, he was surprised how much it all annoyed him. He'd been looking forward to coming home to the Kuinak he knew and, if not loved, was at least comfortable with—the scruffy, rundown, ramshackle little North Coast fishing village with its traditional reek of bum carburetors and rotting fish and dog manure—not to some candidate for the *Sunset* Magazine Urban Beautification Award. It was another damn jolt, and he'd had enough jolts. All last night he'd been thinking about getting home and getting some sleep and then getting back to life as usual. But home, he thought wryly, frowning out the window, was never like this. Home is never this neat. The only mess in evidence along the whole street was in the little plaza in front of the First Deap Bank of Alaska, where a pair of half-finished styrofoam statues were stretched out supine on sawhorses amid a clutter of tools and beer bottles and resin cans.

'Might've been first-rate poles,' Carmody observed in a gloomy voice as they cruised slowly past, 'had they'd of used cedar. First big blow'll rip them phonies to flinders.'

Greer was, of course, delighted by the little town's sudden sprucing-up. 'Whoa! lust *look* at these old digs— polished up slick as snot. We could have our own little Mardi Gras parade up here, make New Or-*leans* jealous, not to mention dat tourist trap Skagway.'

'Skagway,' Billy amended from the backseat, 'is a trap for more than tourists these days, as I plan to soon make brutally clear.'

'Slick and then some,' Ike said, to keep Billy from carping about Skagway. 'Can you believe all this? Even the broken glass swept out of the gutters? You'd think *this* was the movie set.'

'Yeah, you old fibber.' Willi elbowed Carmody in the side. 'You had me believing we was coming home to some kind of dirty dead end. This is an adorable little burg . . . and I for one think it's admirable that folks have polished it up so nice. What's wrong with a little urban renewal?'

Carmody's red-rimmed eyes continued to stare gloomily out the window. 'Spit-shine job' was all he answered.

'And whoa damn zam look over *there*!' Greer pointed across the intersection at Omar Loop's bowling alley. 'Even old bowling nut Omar be sucked into the scene.'

Omar's famous filthy front windows were scrubbed clean as all the other shop-front panes and a long silver and white bunting was draped over the LOOP LANES marquee on top of the building. A glaser print on the front door announced that the establishment was now the SHOOLA/FOX PRODUCTION OFFICE and open to AUTHORIZED S/F PERSONNEL ONLY.

'And him making all dat noise he *never* rent his alleys,' Greer snorted.

'Bowling nuts have their price, too,' Carmody remarked as they passed the building, attempting to sound philosophical. Ike could see the old Cornishman's mind was not really on the rented bowling alley or the passing street-front, either, for all its shined-up change. Like Billy fretting about where he'd just been, Carmody was fretting about the troubles that lay ahead. That was the real reason he'd insisted on the Crabbe Potte, Ike suddenly understood, instead of one of his usual hometown haunts—not because he wanted to check the board or have a drink and a brag with the barflies, but because the Potte was the b'god last place in all Kuinak where one was likely to run into Myrna Crabbe's old enemy, Alice. Everybody in town knew Alice had not been to the Potte since her last ejection, years ago. Yet, moments later, when Greer stopped the van and set the brake, Ike looked out the sliding door and saw that there she b'god was, big as life in a diner booth, her black eyes aimed out a window right at them—like a brace of drawn pistols. In fact there was a whole damn fusillade of eyes leveled at them, Ike saw, from all the diner windows.

Carmody was so eager to get out of the van and wet his whistle he never noticed. He steered full-steam for the cafe across the street, his Texas Tootsie by the hand. By the time he saw the audience in store for him it was too late to change course. The prideful old rogue didn't even slow down, let alone make any attempt to disengage himself from the pink-nailed hand hooked in his arm. He swooshed through the Potte's front door and waded right into the complete salvo, his loyal crew washing along apprehensively in his wide wake.

'Well, now, by God! Would you look at this mess of stump barnacles. Glad to see they ha'nt scraped the old harbor *completely* clean. Bill Culbertson! I'd of thought you'd be down selling them movie stars tidal-wave insurance. Hey, Will Barlow! Walt! You must be the *artistes* carving the foam poles, eh? It ain't too heavy a work for ye, lads, is it? Mr Toogiak! How's the Searaven real estate responding to all this new Kuinak look? Hello, Culligan; I bet you just talked to yer sis-in-law, didn't ye? And Alice! Goodness me, Love, what are you doing here? Emil, I thought you told me Alice was *involved* some way with this movie show. Held a *position.* But it looks to me like she's languishing in the wings with the rest of the riffraff . . .'

Greer raised his shoulders in their bony shrug and said nothing. Alice put down her coffee cup and leaned her chin on her knuckles. 'I'm not languishing in the wings.' Her words were to Carmody but her eyes were on Willi's tousled hair and freckled face. 'I hold a quite prestigious position—First Unit Artistic Consultant—and I am at present doing lunch with our leading lady is what I am doing here.' The eyes slid down to the pink fingernails. 'So. What have *you* been involved with?'

Willi withdrew her hand from Carmody's arm, it finally dawning on her who it was they were confronting. Carmody clutched the hand again, never blinking an eye.

'Don't be shy, girl. Let me introduce you ladies. Alice, this is Willimina Hardesty. She's from Texas. Willi, this is the missus, Alice Carmody, about whom I've told you so much . . .'

'About whom he has tole me exactly squat,' Willi said, pulling free of Carmody's clutch again, quite emphatically. Grinning hard, she said, 'Missus Carmody,' and, fearing that a handshake might be rejected under the circumstances, made an awkward little bow.

Alice nodded back. 'How do you do, Miss—? Mrs—?'

'Oh, it's Missus,' Willi laughed. 'Definitely Missus, more Missus than I care to remember.'

'One's been enough for me,' Alice said. She turned to the girl. 'Shoola, this is my husband, about whom I've told you absolutely nothing, either—Captain Michael Carmody, and his intrepid crew.'

'I am very glad, Captain Carmody, to make—and don't believe your wife! She told me of you often— that you have a new boat? And that you are like me a British subject by birth, eh? And perhaps other things that I don't recall with all this coffee and lunch we been having—to make your acquaintance. *All* your acquaintances!' she added with genuine warmth, beaming about at the Carmody crew. It was on the face of Isaak Sallas alone that this steamy beam finally focused.

Ike was rocked from his torpor first by the force of the girl's gaze, then by the girl herself. She was wildly beautiful, like one of those implausible sprites that romped through those posters so popular at the turn of the century—kitschy pics of wanton innocence in sylvan woods primeval. She didn't look real. Her skin was a polished, pliant, translucent amber—you could see right down into it. The untamed bloom of hair framing her face looked like the rich fur from

324

some rare animal—a black wolf, perhaps. Her smile was just as wolfy and wild. It could devour a heart in one gulp. Without actually releasing Ike from her hold she turned and resumed her irrepressible chatter to the others. The breakneck way she sailed through an unfamiliar language made him think of a light little sloop skipping along in a gale.

'Or should it be "this lunch we been *do*ing," like Mrs Carmody said? For correct English-talking grammar? You must excuse my English talking, Mr Carmody; we still talk most of the time Innupiat at our home up Far North. I would like to express myself much more full after I been here awhile in civilization—but right now, like they always say at Herky's store, the express lane is closed.'

Carmody gave her his big grin. 'You express yourself full enough for this Englishman,' he told her.

'Full enough and den some, mon!' Greer was beginning to detect the treasure chest Alice had hoped to bury beneath Carmody's old shirt. 'Neverdeless,' he continued, 'if our visitor from the up Far North would like de private tutoring in the *new*-ances of our local tongue—whoa!—den I be humbly at you service. Emil Greer, *all*-so Englishman.'

'Also a Frenchman, an American, a Rastafarian, and a con man,' Alice explained to the girl, 'depending on which day you happen to talk to him.'

Greer was indignant. 'Hey, I am born in Jamaica in the Hospitalia Santo *Jorge*! Christened in the Royal Church of England by a lay minister from Edmonton, *Scot*land! That's as British as it gets, you know, down in de islands.'

'Alice was raised Russian Orthodox,' Shoola said, turning her smile on Greer, 'but she's not no Russian.'

They were all still standing, impacted at the booth by the curious crowd. They were unable to sit or proceed on down the length of the counter to the door that led on into the cocktail lounge. The attention in the packed diner was carnivorous. Ike was glad that the girl kept up her ebullient prattle. It was a relief from the looming tension—a postponement, anyway. But it was making him feel more and more hemmed in and uncomfortable, this tableau: the Steamy Virgin; the Wronged Wife; the Other Woman; the Ridiculous Old Rake Caught Red-handed; the Circle of Nosy Neighbors with their bloodthirsty tongues hanging out, wishing for the worst. And wishing this worst mainly for Alice, it occurred to him quite suddenly. Not for lovable old Carmody or his frowsy floozy, certainly—a buck has got to have a little fun *some*day, don't he—but the worst for Alice. For angry, uppity Alice . . . pull her down a peg or two, do the bitch good.

His thinking exactly, a couple of nights back.

'All right, let's break this up,' he clapped his hands loudly. 'Carmody, let's have this damned drink if we're going to—some of us want some rest. Look out, Culligan, Mr Toogiak, you guys. Clear a path.'

'You can't go in the lounge half, Mr Sallas,' Dinah said. 'It's locked. I just spoke with Aunt Myrna and she says I'm to keep it locked. I'm underage.'

'Well, you better get somebody above-age, Honeybucket,' Carmody commanded, sensing an escape route out of the tricky predicament he had inadvertently let himself get cornered in. 'You phone Aunt Myrna right back and tell her this piddlin' little half o' Potte is liable to bust its hinges unless the other half gets unlocked. You tell her Michael Carmody says so. Folks, we are accustomed to fancier consideration than this, I tell ye. Why, last night, we was the guests of honor on the Emperor of Korea's royal by God *flagship*.'

While Carmody regaled the crowd with his version of the party on the processor, Dinah poked petulantly at the phone buttons. Alice and Willi glared menacingly at the back of the old philanderer's fat neck. Greer fidgeted with his hair and Billy the Squid leaned his elbows on the counter to give his back a rest. Ike gazed out the window, trying to look cool and collected. But he didn't feel cool or collected. What he felt was that girl's unrelenting attention wrapping around him like steam in a sweat lodge.

Everyone in the room was relieved when Dinah put aside the phone and stepped to the portholed lounge door, shaking her key ring for attention.

'Aunt Myrna says them that wants can go on into the bar and wait,' the girl announced in a put-upon voice. 'She says she'll get here soon as she gathers up all her wine carafes they been using at the catering. Until then, we got coffee and we got soft drinks and we got chili and clam chowder.'

'What about hard drinks?' Carmody insisted. 'Me and these lads been at *sea,* ducks, bearing the salty burden of the sailor's life. We need grog. I mean, look at poor droopy-tentacled Mr Squid here; he's been bearing the burden so long he's dehydrated! We need solace for the soul, not no damn clammy chowder!'

'I can't *serve* alcoholic beverages,' the girl whined, 'I'm under*age.* Aunt Myrna will be here soon as she gathers all her carafes. She takes a lot of pride in them carafes. They're real crystal. Besides, I don't know nothing about mixing drinks.'

'I do,' Willi said. She could recognize an escape route as well as Carmody. 'I've tended bar coast to coast, border to border. I mix up a Long Island Iced Tea that'll make you think that ocean out yonder is the At*lantic.*'

'They don't have tea here,' Shoola let Willi know. 'Just coffee and soft drinks and chili and chowder and more coffee.'

'Tea be damned!' Carmody bellowed. 'I want an Irish coffee. Willimina, you're hired. Ring the gong, girlie; we are a-boozin' and Michael Carmody's a-buyin'!'

'You're hired!' the crowd cried. This was what would bring this watched pot to a boil—booze! Even recon booze. 'Hired, hired, hired!'

The bar bell dinged the old Alaskan signal that somebody was buying a round and Ike was gradually swept into the lounge by the enthusiasm of the throng.

Willi was already behind the bar, taking orders. Carmody had resumed his account of the party on the Korean processor, describing how he and that there Texas

Tornado had defended the round-eye honor by dancing the little nippers right off the dance floor and out the scuppers. Greer was at the man's side, his eyebrows shooting up and down as he avowed to the accuracy of Carmody's every exaggeration: 'Yes! It be true, people, every word!'

Ike hung back by the bulletin board and read a few announcements. Looking back out through the scratched glass of the Crabbe Potte porthole he saw Alice and the girl were still in their booth, alone now except for Dinah. Alice had ordered more coffee and was sipping it stubbornly. The girl was watching the lounge door like a big-eyed pup. Before thinking why, Ike swung the door open and called across the empty booths.

'Care to join us in the bar, ladies?'

He regretted the act instantly. It sounded like something Greer would say, even to the lascivious lilt he gave to the word 'ladies.' He hoped his eyebrows hadn't shot up and down.

'Not me, no,' Alice answered. 'And the lady with her mouth hanging open there is too young to go bar-hopping.'

The girl snapped out of her thrall with a start. 'Why, I am not, Mrs Carmody. I always go bar-hopping when my uncles go into Totting Bay. I'm the one who drives the snowmo home. Once I had to bring my uncle's ear home in a snowball so we could sew it back on. We gave him a lot of medicine shots but it fell off anyway.'

'That reminds me, Sallas,' Alice said. 'I gave your poor low-rent mutt a couple injections of prednisone. He's walking better.'

'It's Greer's poor low-rent mutt, not mine.'

'Yeah, well, it's Greer's low-rent rear, too, but it seems like it's always somebody else having to look after it. Usually you.' She touched the girl's arm. 'Mr Sallas here, Shoola, rooms with Mr Greer up on Sanitary Landfill Terrace. They have one of those quaint antique tin trailerhouses from the previous century.'

'Oh, I know the kind very well!' the girl exclaimed. 'They have many of those quaint antique tin trailerhouses

328

on Totting Bay. They fill them with dirt and line them up for a sea wall.'

Alice shook a finger at Ike. 'So *that's* why you trailer twins have been collecting all that dirt. I knew there had to be some reason . . .'

'You went in my house?'

'If that's what you call it, yes I did.'

'Alice, I appreciate you taking care of Old Marley, but I don't see why you needed to go inside my house to feed an animal you knew was living under it.'

'He wasn't living under it. He was living in it, along with a dozen or so other four-legged guests. The door was wide open.'

Ike groaned. 'Oh no, the bastard. I didn't think he was strong enough to bang that door open anymore.'

'Maybe he was assisted by a hard-charging cadre of coons. Looked like about a dozen.'

'The old bastard,' Ike said again.

'Maybe he missed you too much,' the girl offered. 'And was looking for you.'

'That's it,' Alice said. 'Loneliness and despair lent him super-canine strength. He broke in the door, then *phoned* up some company was what happened. But he's cooled out now, Sallas. I got him a little partner to play with. They been having a great time together, over at my motel. Marley looks much better and so, incidentally, does your home.' The bar bell rang again and a loud cheer came through the door. 'So. Aren't you planning to kick the gong around in there with the others?'

'I'd better go see to that dog—'

'Haven't I told you? I've already seen to your dog. Go on back in there and slosh it up with the rest of your crew.'

'I've sloshed enough.' Ike was surprised at how his voice sounded. 'I'll just walk on over to your motel.'

'You won't walk on over to anywhere the way you're weaving around. Besides, that dog might rip a chunk out of you if you just suddenly show up and try to drag him back to that cheerless hovel of yours. I tell you what, Sallas. You pay for all this coffee and pies Dinah has tallied up against us and I'll give you a ride to your precious dog and your precious trailer both.' She handed back the hundred she had taken from the girl. 'Here you go, Sugar. You got to learn not to be so free with all these riches. They won't last. Dinah?'

'A ride in what? I thought you two were afoot.'

'Isn't that my van parked across the street? Don't I always keep a cardkey hidden under my plastic Jesus?'

Ike stood at the lounge door, uncertain.

'Come on, Mr Sallas. Ride with us, please.'

'Yeah, don't worry about those other intrepid Argonauts—something'll show up for them. Let's go.'

The something showed up before the three of them had made it across the street—Herb Tom's six-door rent-a-limo. The tinted windows were rolled up, guarding the identities of all the passengers save one: Louise Loop. She was standing on something so she was halfway out of the open sun roof, like some kind of dignitary in a one-float parade. A fluffy coiffure of gold-green hair wafted about her head, and her face was garishly sculpted and tinted by some very sadistic makeup artist. She was draped in a billowing array of diaphanous paisley scarves and blouses and wraparounds. They continued to billow about her even after the limo had come to a complete stop. Ike realized it must be the vehicle's air-conditioning system that was creating such a dramatic whirlwind.

'Isaak Sallas!' Louise called from her whirl of chiffon. 'Welcome back to the unreal world. How do I look?'

Ike said only, 'Hello, Lulu . . . looking good.' She looked just the opposite. He was reminded of those new gene-spliced wonder flowers that they force-bloomed to win all the county fair shows. Lasted about a weekend, then shriveled and died. Lulu was a nitwit and a nuisance, but it annoyed him to see her mocked like this; she thought she was being dolled up when she was really being put down.

330

The door swung wide and Nicholas Levertov ducked his silver head out into the milky afternoon sun. 'Slamboy!' he called to Ike. 'And our dear mum, too? Even our lovely little starlet? Outstanding—all the principals of our pageant scuttling out of the Crabbe Potte together like this. You make quite the trio.'

'Hello, Nick.' Ike realized the women on each side of him had each slipped an arm into his at the appearance of the limo.

'And look at our little Shoola's new outfit—casual, cute, and uncannily clashing. Mother, only you could have helped her pick it out.'

'The poor kid needed something,' Alice said in a defensive voice.

'I like it,' Shoola said. 'I think I'll wear it to midnight Mass on Sunday.'

'You will be the jewel of the ceremony without a doubt. Well, Slam, your rescue mission was quite successful, word has it. I'm not a bit surprised.' He called over his shoulder at the open limo door. 'Didn't I keep telling all you nervous nellies: "Who needs hired muscle when Isaak Sallas is on the job"?'

'Indeed you did, boss!' came the reply. Ike could see the suntanned surfer's legs of Levertov's lieutenant, knee-to-knee with a pair of white deck trousers seated opposite. A metal suitcase just like Billy's was situated across both laps. This was what Louise was standing on.

'Who needs hired muscle!' Louise echoed like a zoned owl. 'Who who who . . .'

Levertov ignored her. 'Now I believe that my man Cato has a bit of business with your man Bellisarius.'

'He's in the lounge,' Ike answered, 'but he's sure as hell not *my* man. He's just our club president.'

'Mr Clark? Would you be so kind as to dip into yon pot and spoon out the illustrious club president?'

'Incapacitated here, boss. Supporting the stage . . .'

'Lulu my lovely. Stop flapping and fluttering like a gypsy flag. Come on down and show these ladies what high Hollywood fashion is these days.'

331

Singsonging 'Flapping and fluttering, flapping and fluttering,' Louise stepped from the suitcase and sank into the big car's cushioned interior. She came out the door rump-first. The manifold layers of airy material did little to conceal the fact that she wore no underclothes. She turned and faced them with a little curtsy. 'Frederick's of Hollywood,' she said.

'You look beautiful, Miss Loop,' Shoola told her. 'I see what Mr Levertov means about high fashions.'

'It's true, Louise,' Alice was quick to agree. 'You look like a cover off the latest *Cosmopolitan*.'

'Mrs Carmody, that is the nicest thing you ever said to me.' She spread her arms and survived a precarious pirouette. 'Who woulda thought? Dumpy old town, dumpy old street, dumpy old Lulu Loop, all prettied up courtesy of our Nicky-wick. Admit it, Isaak Sallas: even you got to be impressed how Nicky's changed things.'

It didn't look to Ike like she was particularly drunk, or zammed out, or zoned; she just looked overwhelmed, addled by events. Louise reminded him somehow of the women he'd seen up at Greener's commune.

'Yeah, Lulu,' Ike said, 'I'm impressed. Especially by the change down at Loop Lanes. I didn't think old Omar would ever get up off his bowling jones, even for one night.'

'Nicky can be very pro-suasive,' Louise said proudly. 'Who woulda thought?'

'We offered Papa Omar a first-class round-the-world on an *Island Princess*,' Levertov confided to Ike. 'The one with the new gyro hull? It has, along with billiards and bocce ball, a six-lane bowling alley. Everybody knows bowling is a staple in the life of Omar Loop, right? So we made him an offer he couldn't refuse.' Levertov gave his long hair a deprecating toss. 'The price of the tour ticket was about ten times what those dilapidated old lanes are worth, but Papa needed the vacation and we needed the office space. Excellent! Here comes Clark B and the other mule. Won't you swingers pop back in the Potte with us for a quick one? Mother?'

'Isaak is itching to check on his trailerhouse—'

'Valuable antique,' Ike put in.

'—and Shoola and I need to take a shower and relax. We've had a busy afternoon.' They watched as Billy followed Clark B into the limo. He gave no indication he'd even seen Ike. The door shut, then the sun roof rolled closed.

'How about a ride, then? This business shouldn't take long.'

'We're fine,' Alice said. 'That's my van. You might ask some of the rest of the dauntless crew in the lounge there, though. About six drinks from now they're going to stagger out and find they don't have wheels. Let's go, Sallas. I've enjoyed enough of this fashion show.' Then she turned back to add: 'You do look real cute, Louise. Real nice.'

When they had loaded the two go-peds into the rear door of the van and were turned around and headed back across town in the direction of the motel, the girl commenced again her tumbling talk—observations and ruminations, questions that were more musings aloud than inquirings because she didn't seem to expect an answer. In the backseat by himself, Ike was content to lean back and let her chatter. It was relieving and relaxing, like lying near an easy stream in a sunny meadow. He didn't doze, exactly. Once, on the way back down Main he heard the girl's monologue mention the Crabbe Potte. He looked up long enough to see Billy the Squid and the Japanese boat-boy bustling across to the limo, their mutual burdens bumping between them. He shut his eyes and sank into the current of words. A meadow stream was just the right metaphor, he thought—wash things clean. Needed a shower himself. He felt covered with a layer of grime not from the week's boat work or the fishing or the grimy offshore air they had been sailing through, but from the town itself. There was something dirty beneath this cleanup. When anybody comes into a place with plans to clean it it's usually because what they have in mind is taking that place over.

When he heard the wheels on the oyster shells Ike snapped awake. He thought it was his yard. But out the window there was milky sky where there should have been garbage mountains, and a half-circle of white cabins where there should have been surrounding spruce and fern. The girl's rose-brown face was in the van's doorway, mooning down at him. 'You snored right off, Mr Sallas. Alice sent me out with this blanket.'

The blanket was a quilt, but Ike didn't argue. He asked something about Alice and the girl said something about laundry and driers. He was too tired to give a shit . . . and as he drew the quilt under his chin a line from an old Dylan classic came to him: 'My weariness amazes me, I'm branded on my feet . . .' He saw activity out the window in the motel's courtyard—units arriving, units departing and units entering units—like characters in Virtual game-goggles.

'Wake up, Sallas.' This was Alice's voice. 'We're going to need some space for the sisters.'

'Sisters?'

'Sisters. They're bored. They want a ride.'

Ike stirred himself from under the quilt. Marley was already in the back, wide awake and grinning at him. Out the sliding door he saw Shoola come bustling across the motel yard. She was carrying one little sister on her hip and had the other by the hand. Following came an old Eskimo couple. They looked like they'd walked right out of one of those National Geographic specials, gut-skin parkas and all. The woman wore eyeglasses but the old man's eyes were obviously still sharp; they sliced out of his brown face through the thinnest of slits—as though years of squinting against the polar glare had carved him a pair of permanent snow goggles. Both old people were grinning with excitement, as snaggle-toothed as old Marley.

'They thought the girls might be interested in those hogs up at your dump.'

'It's not my dump,' Ike told Alice.

'I know,' she said. 'And it's not your dog or your hogs, either. Just make some room, is all I ask, and try to act a little neighborly for a few miles. It's not going to kill you.'

The old couple stood waving. Shoola plunked the two girls in with Ike and resumed her shotgun seat beside Alice. It seemed she liked to be able to turn around and moon at him face on, as they drove. The two little girls kept giggling at their sister.

Alice didn't think it was funny. 'Shoola, stop all this staring. It's not polite to stare at poor ragged old sea dogs no matter *how* much like Elvis they look. Turn around.'

As soon as her big sister was no longer watching, the middle-sized sister hopped right into Ike's lap and hugged his chest. He let her stay. Ike thought the child had fallen asleep but when they left the last scattering of outskirt buildings she raised her cheek from Ike's chest and looked up at him. 'They kids here?' she whispered secretly.

'What?' Ike whispered back, surprised; her English was uncertain but it was clear. 'Kids where?'

'This town? They kids live here?'

'In Kuinak? Sure . . .'

'Kids like me?'

'You mean your age? I'm sure there must be kids your age.'

'They good kids?'

'Yeah, they're probably good kids. Most of them . . .'

She waited awhile before asking the important question. 'They play with me?'

Ike felt something cold pinch him, under his ribs. 'Sure, Honey. They'll be glad to play with you. Any kid in the whole world'll be glad to play with a doll like you.'

She studied his face until she was satisfied he was telling the truth, then leaned back to his chest. He closed his eyes, shutting out the lurch of the van, the hazy sun, the garbage smell—everything except that hot little cheek against his ribs and cold pinch beneath. Not fair, he

335

thought, not fair at all. One side says it's running down, then the other side says 'Oh *yeah*?'

When the shells crunched again it was his own yard.

'Rise and shine. You're home. No, you keep the quilt. It's probably infested with God knows what breed of sea flea by now. Hush, you girls. It's not polite to giggle at poor mangy wore-out old sea dogs, either.'

He slid the door open and stepped out on to the shells, drawing the quilt about his shoulders. Old Marley followed, right over the backseat, surprisingly supple. Whatever treatment he'd received had done wonders for his aged limbs. 'Thanks, Alice. I owe you one.'

'Keep that one, too,' Alice said, 'whatever it is. But close that damned door. I don't want to go dribbling girls out all the way back to town.'

He started back to the idling van to slide the door, then he saw the stakes—driven everywhere, heavy-duty lath, all sizes, some of them five foot high or more, driven upright into the driveway and along the turnaround, among the ferns and salal that bordered the trailer's little clearing . . . into his shell-covered yard itself! Each stake was tied at the top with a colored plastic ribbon— red, yellow, green—and the taller stakes had numbers written along the rough lath.

'What the hell are these?'

'Those are stakes, Sallas. Didn't you notice them all over town?'

'I thought they were part of some kind of road business.'

'They're part of some kind of movie business,' Alice explained. 'Location markers. Maybe they need some footage of your trailer for a prehistoric dwelling scene. Be sure they pay you for any footage they take. The cannery's getting about two thousand dollars a minute just to look like a cliff. Okay. Shut my door and go in to sleep, I've got other sea dogs to see to. Shoola, you and your sisters can come back to earth now. The Greek god has disembarked.'

The six-wheeler cramped around and headed back down toward the pillars of smoke above the dump, leaving him standing in the clearing, alone. Nothing but dry weeds and empty oyster shells and an old dog. Except for those stakes. Those stakes worried him. He tried to recall what the status of the property was. He leased his little chunk from Omar Loop, but he thought he remembered that the county actually owned the bulk of the area—the lot the water tower was on; the dump. They surely couldn't be planning to clean up the dump, could they? That would take the Army Corps of Engineers. But you could never tell. Look how they had taken that little snarl of rundown saloons and hippie hot-dog stands down in Skagway and turned it into a Knotts Berry Farm version of . . . not the famous Gold Rush of 1898, exactly—it had always been that, with its paint-peeling little landmarks like Soupy Smith's barbershop—but a *version* of a version of a Gold Rush town, some advertising agency's version, pruned and simplified so the image could be cleanly communicated on one of the cruise ships' dish commercials—'Gateway to the Gold Rush'—then that forty-foot gold-plated statue of the Lone Prospector kneeling with his spotlighted pan of pump-fed water pouring unendingly out into the goldfish pond while his upraised face squinted toward the peaks lifting above the town. Not fair. The whole illumination stripped of sweat and frostbite and hunger and despair, of all quirks and complications that had made those long-gone stampeders such potent symbols of American optimism in the first place. Stripped and cleaned and simplified, then blown up big as a house, so the actual bulk of the thing diminished it, belittled it, so the treasure that had once been alluring and just out of reach, else what's heaven for? had been devalued until those still drawn by the old allure were forced to stretch down, bend over, cramp the back and humble the neck, to reach for the prize where it lay, like a diamond dropped in shit, like a star knocked into the mud—so that even victory was a debasement.

'Well, they haven't got to us, have they, old dog?' Ike said. 'Not yet, anyways.' He jerked up the stake that was driven into the yard directly in front of him and carried it up the aluminum steps. The door opened on a scene as transformed as the main street of the town. The walls were scrubbed, the rug wet-cleaned and vacuumed. All the spider webs were gone. The dishes were washed and the countertops scoured. The windows were shined, inside and out, just like those panes along Main. It even looked like the pillowcases had been laundered. When Ike saw that the bookcase had been dusted and the sauce stains wiped from the postcard he had never sent to Ojo, he felt a thin, cold rage rising in his throat, making his sleep-starved head spin, his ears ring. 'Shit!' he said and headed back for the door. He broke the stake and flung the pieces into the brush. Three crows flushed up, screeching indignantly. Marley jumped to watchful attention, his ears perked though he could not hear, his eyes scanning the yard though he could not see. Damn that woman and her prednisone! 'This yard is worthless, fool!' Ike told the old dog. 'Why the hell watch over it?'

Watching, the old dog answered, 'Seems to fill the space between what's now and what's to come, sir, like sniffing old tracks and scratching old bites . . . It seems to pad out the hard, unupholstered relentless space just a little . . . sir.'

13

To the Ships of the Sea
and the Women of the Land

Wild Willi the Waitress from Waco was still running the Crabbe Potte bar when Carmody walked out. *Snuck* out, more's the truth, strolling, trying to be inconspicuous, his round head lowered in what he hoped would pass for an appearance of drunken distracted concentration if the inconspicuous shot proved unsuccessful.

He hated to leave the convivial atmosphere—the barroom was just beginning to roar comfortably, like a well-stoked fireplace—but the wise maneuver, he had reasoned, would be one of self-denial and discreet retreat. Especially with the way Willi had been looking at him. More's the blinkin' truth *not* looking at him; she took his orders, served his sauce, made his change, but the smile she afforded him was just the generic gin-mill grin, same as she offered all the other squareheads. He could feel her rebuke lurking behind that smile, like a bulldog behind a hedge of flowers.

He checked first out the lounge door porthole to make sure that the coast was clear and then pushed on through, not looking back at Willi at all. Didn't need to. The image of that big blonde hung like a saloon painting right inside the smokey bar of his forehead: the body secret and suggestive, the face sunny-bright and busy (too busy to have to mark his lily-livered departure) and O, with that corn-colored curl stuck to her sweating brow and the good-natured gleam of those Easter-egg eyes in that nest of sunny wrinkles! A darlin' girl, and as born a barmaid as ever pulled a dark one.

It was that very gleam had first attracted his admiration

339

in Juneau—the harbor-light twinkle from the eye of an honest publican, beaming out into the cold wet treachery of night a signal saying 'Come on in, Sailor Jack; you'll be treated fair and warm.' O, what a gleam! Better'n any red-light lass, or holy-glow nun, even: the honest barmaid's beacon, soothing and steady as Polaris. And more ruddy comforting, far. Because any Jack knows the waters most treacherous he most often must cross is the bars. That's when, safety statistics show, he's most likely to get stove in is while crossing the bar. And the one nearest home, at that. Just like statistics say how most automobile accidents happen practically at the driver's front door. So a bright honest keeper-of-the-bar oughter be a star in any sailin' community's cap, Carmody re-assured himself. So I harpooned us one and towed her back. Who's to find fault with that?

That was his reasoning and he found it sound, but he still was in no great hurry to head on around the bay home. Though Alice would not likely be out there (besides her motel and smokehouse chores, it appeared she was involved in these movie-show shenanigans after all), he was worried she just b'god might. Or she might catch sight of him driving by on Bayshore and follow him out to the house, confront him, make him do a lot of tedious explaining. And Carmody did not feel quite capable of repeating that line of reasoning he had just worked out—not in a confrontation situation, and certainly not until either he got sober or a deal more bloody boiled. So he mumbled to whoever it was behind the wheel of whatever it was that had gathered him up from the heaving street in front of the Crabbe Potte and was driving him to wherever he wanted to go that if it was all the same he would as lief be ferried back down to his new boat, thank you . . . see to those tedious shoreside duties to*morrow*, under a calmer sky, mumble mumble . . . ease down, mark the log, let the cradle of the bay rock them worries away.

Fortunately it was one of the Wasp cops he was mumbling these requests to. Other pilots of a more sporting

340

and less rule-bound nature would have driven Carmody home by *way* of the motel, hoping to see the cuckolded Alice in angry action. But this courteous and obsequious peace officer ferried him straight back to the boat just like the drunk dunker requested, helped him climb the gang, then wisely split. A wise Wasp cop knows to avoid any situations that might lead to domestic violence; those reports are the most difficult of all to fill out. Still, the officer kept one hand on his side mirror so he could adjust it to watch the boat behind him as he drove away; a wise Wasp wants as well to avoid any situations involving tipsy citizens tipping into the bay.

Michael Carmody was aware that he was being observed. He positioned himself on the deck accordingly: the image of a master, proud and statuesque, one hand on the rail, the other in a fist at the small of his huge back . . . legs spread dramatically for balance though no waves rolled and the decks heaved not. When the patrol car was across the lot out of sight, the old man gave up the posture and hugged his bare elbows; he was shivering on the empty deck. More and more of late, it seemed, he found himself shivering in the emptiness. That was the other reason he had not wanted to go out to the house. Alice well might not come out at all, nor anybody else. Quite the opposite of Ike Sallas' desire for solitude, Michael Carmody had of late longed more and more for company.

The boat creaked mournfully against its rubber bumpers. The stereomiser alcohol thumped against Carmody's shaved temples like polluted waves, thick and listless as shit. Blast this recon booze! Saves yer liver but gives you no lilt. No lift, no glow! Suddenly he realized he had allowed himself to get shivering so hard he could scarcely stand. 'Up *out* of that, Michael!' he rebuked himself. 'Hullabaloo belay!' then attempted a quick little jig across the metal decking, singing:

> Loo-wee was the king of France
> Before the rev-o-loo-shun
> But Louie got his head cut off

Which spoiled his con-stee-too-ooo-shun—
Hullabaloo be-lay me boys, hullabaloo belay.

The shuddering ceased. Satisfied that he could not only
stand he could b'god *dance,* Carmody felt he was ready to
face his crew. He rubbed his numb nose hard and called,
'Nels! Yer captain is aboard.' Nels did not sing out. Nels
did not come sprightly from below. Carmody felt that
lonely shiver starting. 'All hands on deck!' he called
again, more loudly. 'Or hand, as it were. Mr Culligan!
Look lively!'

The boat rocked on the gentle rolls coming in off the bar
like mercury. The Korean flag hanging from the antenna
waved slightly. Carmody was beginning to deeply regret
leaving the tavern, wisest maneuver or no. What's a captain without a crew, however grand and new his blaggin'
boat? He was filling his lungs for a full-scale command
when a deep drawl up the hatch stopped him short.

'Your boy's not aboard at present, Captain.' A grey-
maned head with a black eye patch appeared in the frame
of the hatch, stooped lower than you'd think necessary just to duck up past the hatch-top head-knocker.
'Ah been standin' his watch.'

'Who the hell goes?' Carmody demanded of the patch-
eyed apparition. 'Stand and identify yourself, sir! What
do ye mean, boardin' us without permission?'

'The name is Steubins, Captain, and I apologize for the
unauthorized visit. I *did* ask your young man if it was
all right to come aboard. Naturally, he was interested in
particulars. When I told him I was one of the big brass
on this big movie if that was the particulars he was
interested in, he gave me to know he was *extremely*
interested—not to mention a tad put out being given
guard duty and denied the chance to check the action
personally, especially the *star*lets. So I confess I took the
liberty of telling him to sashay on over, be my guest, that
Ah'd take the watch.' His explanation complete, the tall
man resumed his climb up the narrow stairwell. 'You
understand I am a skipper myself.'

'Not on these decks, you ain't!' Carmody proclaimed, his indignation rising rapidly as he appraised the long grey form that just seemed to keep coming up from the hatch's gloom, like a big bony fish breaching in slow motion. A loose grey twill draped the man like a tailored shroud, matching the silver mane. Even the man's weather-worked face and neck were silver grey, like old cedar shakes. Instead of the usual ruddy burn of sailor skin, it seemed as though the sun itself had agreed to the color scheme. '*I'm* master here,' Carmody felt obliged to add.

'I can see that.' Steubins' voice was as studied as his appearance—an oily drawl on troubled waters. 'And I swear I'd salute you, Captain, but for having both hands full.'

Carmody noticed that the man held a bottle in one sun-greyed fist and a pair of ice-filled tumblers in the other. The tumblers looked like real depression glassware, the kind once found free in oatmeal boxes and now practically priceless; the bottle looked like an authentic heat-distilled fifth of Old Bushmill's Irish whiskey, outlawed worldwide by UN sanctions. A golden liquid flashed seductively in the famous square bottle.

'I can see that you have,' Carmody said, reining back his indignation somewhat; a visitor bearing such get-acquainted gifts as bootlegged Irish whiskey and depression glass to sip it from oughter be given the benefit of the doubt no matter *how* long and grey and unauthorized they might initially seem. On the other hand, protocol and appearance had to be kept up. Carmody changed his stare to a glare. 'But a handful of how-d'ye-do don't give a man license to dismiss off duty a sailor he ain't in command of.'

'No, Captain, you are right. It does not.' Then Steubins bent low again, furtive. 'My only defense is that I have never been able to resist the siren's call of a well-built lady of the waves. The minute I clapped eye on your beauty I had to motor over and take a peek.'

'There's a difference between peeking and prowling,' Carmody growled, watching the liquor sparkle.

'Again you're right. I should not have gone below, never would've if you'd had ice in your topside coolers. But I much prefer my Irish on the rocks, don't you? as befits that poor land's rocky past.'

'Is that actual Bushmill's,' Carmody wanted to know for certain, 'or reconstitute?'

'The actual McGilla, smuggled out of Galway by these actual hands.' Steubins straightened back up to dart his eyes back and forth over Carmody's bald head, scanning the docks. 'May Ah propose we step around seaward the wheelhouse, out of sight? Unless you want every blessed Irish Extract with a dry throat up here seeking to share our bounty.'

Carmody maintained his glare. There was something bloody well fishy here—in the man's furtive glances, the muted hat-in-hand voice—something to keep a suspicious weather eye on . . . Then that bottle flashed again like a golden beacon and Carmody could not help but swing his big bow after it.

The first shot was sipped in respectful silence as the two men leaned side by side against the port side of the wheelhouse. When his glass was empty Carmody found his suspicions had considerably abated. It was Irish, sure enough—the real McGilla. Carmody rattled the ice and held his glass sideways. 'What say to another, sir?'

'Most certainly, Captain,' Steubins answered in his decorous drawl. He clinked the neck of the bottle against the rim of Carmody's glass, then filled his own. 'May I propose we lift this one in a toast?'

'By all means,' Carmody agreed. They lifted their tumblers to a distant line between sea and sky as Steubins intoned a solemn dedication:

> To the ships of our sea
> And the women of our land—
> May the former be well-captained
> And the latter be well-manned.

344

'Sir, amen,' Carmody said and they drank. He wondered how Willi was making out down at the Crabbe Potte.

The glasses were refilled again. The second toast was by tradition Carmody's:

Here's to the foolish extravagant queen;
Here's to the housewife that's thrifty;
Here's to the maiden of fitful fifteen;
And here's to the fishwife of fifty.

This time Steubins responded—'Amen indeed, sir'—and they drank, in reverent silence, listening to the clank of the water against the alloy hull and the busy murmurous gossip of the oldsquaw ducks out toward the bar. When Carmody was ready for his third refill he decided it was time to look this gent he was drinking with over. He rolled away from the wheelhouse so he could challenge the ashen apparition face-on.

'You're Gerhardt Steubins, is it then? I've heard a impressive by God lot about you from my crew. I don't go to the movies myself anymore; seats got too damn narrow on me.'

'Gerhardt Steubins it is,' the tall man answered with a nod.

'The very son-of-a-gun responsible for these wonderful changes taken place in my hometown while I was to sea?'

Steubins flipped up the black patch. 'The very son-of-a-gun,' he smiled. He clinked the neck of the Irish against Carmody's glass again, his eyes holding against Carmody's as the liquor flowed. 'At your service.'

'Also that crazy business with the sea lions we witnessed pulling in? Cameras and crew and all?'

Steubins nodded.

'Well, if you'll pardon me fer speakin' frankly, *Cap*tain Steubins,' Carmody continued his challenging, 'you simply don't look, ah, *sprightly* enough to command all this vast fleet of enterprises.'

'Captain Carmody—' Steubins leaned even closer toward the round head, becoming intimate, conspiratorial. '—let me also speak frankly, for I feel we have

something in common, we two . . . Ah *ain't* sprightly
enough. The only thing I command in this fleet of enterprises is a certain . . . I guess you'd call it ceremonial
respect, and scant fucking little of that. Another?'

Carmody held forth his glass, sighing loudly. Whatever righteous outrage he had built up drained away
on that resigned sigh. He realized that this grey-browed
ghoul looming before him was about to become a bit of
a bleedin' buddy if he didn't watch out. A shipmate.
Cradling the glass, he rotated his tight denim rear end
back against the wheelhouse, alongside the slack drape
of Steubins' trousers. The pair leaned in silence again for
awhile, sipping and squinting at the gentle teeter-totter
of the horizon. Carmody was the first to speak.

'They tell me you was a famous film director.'

' "Was" is the word, all right,' Steubins said. 'And you,
Captain? I've heard a by God lot about you, too, from our
executive producer. Who I take it is your stepson?'

'Nicholas Levertov? I would not go so far as to call
him my stepson. I only met him oncet before. He flew to
Hawaii when Alice and me was on our honeymoon. He
gave us a stone fish-poaching pot that was carved to look
like a yellowfin—cracked the first time I tried to cook in
it.'

'Nick tells me you are a kind of famous fisherman in
these waters. A highliner, I think he said?'

' "Was" is the right word in my case, too. Highliner,
eh? Well, sir, that there quaint moniker was always just
one of those playground distinctions anyway . . . like
kids use until they grow away from it? Or it from them,
in this case. Nobody can be a real highliner anymore,
not like you used to could. There's not enough fish left
in the ol' barrel. The best a hustling dunk can aspire
to *these* days is, I guess you'd call it a "bottomliner."
A bottom-of-the-barrel scraper. Still, it's honest work,
fishing; it's kept me out of the employment halls. And
you, Mr Director . . . what you been up to since your last
job of honest work?'

Steubins gave a low laugh, acknowledging the taunt.

346

'I've had sporadic employment. Have you seen that ad of the crag-faced captain with the Vandyke doing the pitch for Princess Tours? That face is mine. The beard and the eloquent voice belong to the ad agency.'

'I seen that ad. You smoke an old clay churchwarden.'

'That's mine, too. But, to be candid, my last job of directing was a decade or more ago. A swishy swash-buckler dog called *The Dark Loves of Sinbad*.'

'Not a big-time winner, I take it?'

'Hardly. It was the big-screen big-budget big-dollar loser of the year. We shot it with all the African Miss Universe contestants au naturel, all up and down the Gold Coast. The hero was a steranoid twinkie with lip implants. It lost the studio close to a hundred mil.'

'And you got the sack?'

'I'd cost them too much to be sacked. They made me Presiding Figurehead.' Steubins unfolded to his full imposing height and struck a pose, eye patch down. 'I can still cut a dashing figure in dress whites when the studio wants to impress investors. I make appearances, do lunches, promo their little PR specials on the return of the Brazilian bald seagulls . . . crap like that.'

'Looks like that would depress a fellow of your obvious top-lofty cut.'

Steubins laughed again, a sound both taut and sub-dued, like heavy crosslines being strummed in the hold of a big freighter. 'It's a way to keep afloat and stay aboard. You see, Captain, I have a terminal sailing jones. I'm a wind junky. Incorrigible! I'd sign on as the lowest rat in the hole if that was the only berth I could get.'

Carmody rubbed his red nub of a nose; it was still numb and cold. His arms were chilly too, but he wasn't shivering anymore. 'And that's what you reckon us two got in common I suppose: sailing?'

Steubins shook his head. 'Naw, what you got is a *fish*ing jones. I can always tell a fisherman from a sailor, by the eyes. A fisherman's eyes is kind of set certain, because he always knows what he's after and when he gets it—or when he don't. A sailor never knows.'

347

'Not both sailors then? All right, I'll grant ye that quick enough. I did some yacht work as a lad and cared not a bit for it. Sissy business. I'd rather haul in a halibut than haul down some rich son-of-a-gun's mainsail, any day. The ol' barrel may be nearly empty, but leastways it's still connected to the main gut of life—fishing is—whereas sailing is nothing more than a hobby. Like sword fighting or typesetting. So if it ain't that we're sailors . . . then it must be age.'

'No,' Steubins said thoughtfully, 'it isn't age we have in common, either, Captain—though I'm flattered that you might think so. Just how old are you?'

'Late sixties,' Carmody lied.

'And what would you guess me to be?'

'Mid-seventies or so, I'd calculate.'

'Try the late eighties. I'm easy twenty years your senior, Captain, not that that's all that ancient. I come across rich son-of-a-guns every tour older than me. Anybody can pile up the years if they're lucky enough and wealthy enough. Naw, it's not age, it's *the* age. We're both anachronisms. We don't belong anymore. We're out of place in this time, this society—'

'Because we both still like to sail and fish and sip traditional booze? Tommyrot!' Carmody felt the Irish spirits rising to the occasion. 'I don't know about *you*, old soak, but I'm still considered a very vital part of *this* by God modern society!'

'I can see you are, Captain,' Steubins answered mildly, 'just by the lines of your new vessel here. I was wrong. I apologize for trying to lump you in with an old fossil like myself.' His deep voice was so conciliatory that it once again took all the wind out of any argument Carmody had been hoping for. The long grey hand gestured vaguely at the stretch of empty water before them. 'Perhaps what we share is simply this, the sea, nothing more than this damned old ocean that we both—Wait! Listen!' The hand stopped, lifted in the haze as though it were an extra ear. Then Steubins suddenly bent back over, lower than ever. 'Don't you hear that?' he whispered.

348

At last Carmody heard it, a sound like the mechanical pacing of a big wooden horse, with wooden horseshoes. It was coming up the dock toward them on the other side of the boat.

'That's the Jap giant,' Steubins breathed in Carmody's ear. 'That's them riser clogs he wears, as though King Kong needs risers. Now listen; the next sound you hear will be that neutered nincompoop Clark B Clark. We better finish off this bottle right now, Captain; we're gonna need all hands free for action.'

The clogging came right up on the gang ramp without so much as a by-your-leave. Outrage began pumping back into Carmody's round form. He was about to call out just who the devil did that mysterious clogger think he was, clogging up on *his ramp*—! when a second sound stopped him:

'Mr *Stooo*-bins . . .'

It might have been one of the oldsquaws calling on the soft breeze, it was so murmurous and insinuating.

'We know you're here, you sly old fox, you. The Culligan boy spilled the beans. Come out, come out, wherever you are.' The voice was a little like the Wasp cop's, only more obsequious. Friendlier. Carmody hated it at once.

'Seriously, Gerhardt; nobody's upset about those stupid sea lions. It wasn't your fault and it's no big deal. We can make another dummy. And that big bull isn't dead after all, haven't you heard? Merely zoned. The zap the handler gave him was probably good therapy for the nasty bastard, like lectroshock. Nobody's upset the *slight*est, Gerhardt, honest to God; but we *do* have a very important social obligation scheduled for this evening, if you'll recall. You're dining on sockeye salmon and Cambodian millionaires—one a prime minister. Gerhardt? Permission to come aboard?'

There was the squeak of tennis shoes on the metal ramp. Carmody puffed up rounder and redder than ever—*another* cheeky bloody boarder.

'Also, if there's a Mr Carmody within the sound of my

voice, his wife is looking for him. Ahoy? Halloo? I'm coming aboard, gentlemen, ready or not . . .'

Carmody felt Steubins give his arm a squeeze. 'Been a pleasure to get to know you, Captain,' he whispered. 'Now if you'll excuse me, I'll be saying so long.' Still bent like a half-closed knife the tall figure went tiptoeing to the gunwales. With an air of finality he swung a long twill pantleg over the rail. Carmody bounced after him.

'Wait a minute, man, don't go bein' the fool—!' Then he saw the grappling ladder hooks over his railing, and when he looked over the side saw the tiny twin-hulled Zodiak that the ladder led to. '*That's* what you motored over in?'

'My seagoing getaway car,' Steubins admitted.

'Looks more like a seagoing coffin you ask me.' He heard Clark B Clark calling down the hatch. 'But I'm blast if I intend to stay aboard and fend off yer foes and woes while you abandon ship. I've already got myself into more fending than I care to contemplate. Climb on down out of my way. I'll drive.'

'I don't know about that. I'm the one's familiar with this craft.'

'I'm the one familiar with this *coastline*. Climb down out of my way, damn ye. Let me show you how a *fisher*-man navigates!'

He took the seat at the rear, beside the outboard. Steubins untied from the ladder and Carmody let the buoyant craft drift with the tide and bump along forward, floating out from under the steelume bow of his boat. He was bent low, like Steubins. 'Sit tight. We won't start the motor till we drift into the current. By then they might not even notice.' The Irish was making him feel reckless. He grinned at the man hunched on the seat in front of him. 'What are we making this getaway from, anyway?' he whispered. 'I forget . . .'

'I'm getting away from a very important social obligation that I just don't quite feel up to at present. I don't know what *you're* getting away from, but I must say I'm grateful for your company.'

350

'I maintain a comfortable retreat over across the bay,' Carmody said. 'We can hide out out there if you don't object to illegal moose and homemade beer.'

'Not at all. But won't the whole town see us out on the open bay? Clark B and his boys will have the speed launch after us before we're halfway across.'

'We're not going across, Mr Steubins—' Carmody pistoned the cardkey in and out of the slot three times to be sure it had a spark, then touched the starter button; the little engine fired on the first turn. '—we're going around.'

When he tried to throttle the engine up it was still too cold and it died; and when he tried it again it backfired. The exhaust pipe happened to be riding clear of the water, and the sound rang across the empty bay like a shot from a signal cannon. Carmody turned to look over his shoulder. Back down the dock he saw the giant give a yap and a jump, as though the cannonball had whistled just past his head. A moment later Clark B Clark appeared on deck and scrambled to the roof of the wheelhouse, shading his eyes in their direction. Then he was clanging down the metal steps of the ramp after the giant, toward the limo.

'Here they come,' Steubins said.

The motor caught. Carmody swung back forward, grinning. 'And here we b'god go!' He gunned the little boat hard to port into the wrinkled green current, full throttle, out to sea. The tide was ebbing hard and the light craft rode it like a surfboard, straight across the bar. The channel bucked beneath them but the hull was designed to flex and flow with the surface. It stuck to the bucking water like a featherweight bull rider to a two-ton Brahman: the two men grinned into each other's faces and let 'er buck.

They came off the bar and whirred and popped across the rumpled water for a while without speaking; then old Steubins bent forward toward Carmody. His eyes were bright as galvanized rivets. He was still whispering.

'Ah, Gawd, I do love it, Carmody, you know? Fucking love it!'

351

'I am not sure what yer talking about, Mr Steubins.'

'Don't you know I'm talking about the *thrill,* man? the thrill of clearing a new bar, of cruising across new waters, of being driven by the whim of new winds to a new landfall? Look at it: here we are free as young squirts in the salty spray! Off to our port the open sea! On our starboard an absolute cliff of sapphire-blue clouds, heaved there thousands of feet high by God knows what meteorological phenomena! Aye, Jesus, man, the *thrill* of it!'

Carmody didn't answer, but the muscles in his cheeks stretched his grin wider than ever.

Steubins slapped the inflated hull. 'That's the spirit. You know what I'm talking about: the thrill of being *called,* summoned to adventure on the high sea. Romance! Mysterious islands! Ride the strange tide and spy the unspied! Aye gods, man, can you tell me you don't *love* it?'

'Can't say as I do. I've took too many waves across my bow to regard it as romantic.'

'Well, I do.' The wind was tossing the silvery hair like foam. 'Capsizing, foundering, dismasting . . . all of it! The chances and challenges of it! Can you beat off a lee-shore blow in bad weather? What's your speed windward? How's she outfitted? Is she shipshape Bristol fashion? You know the yacht has *always* been an instrument of statecraft. Henry the Eighth's royal warship the *Henri-Grâce-à-Dieu* is a good example. You *must* have seen the pictures of her in some limey library somewheres: a floating palace, all gilt and grandeur?'

'Probably,' Carmody conceded, knowing exactly the litho Steubins was describing.

'That ship gave Henry a throne with some *teeth* in it, unlike his armchair back at Buckingham. Henry's "Palace on the Sea" was the true ship of state of the time, more useful to the realm than any damn castle on the land. Probably smelled better too.'

'Probably correct about that,' Carmody agreed again. 'I smelt some of them castles.' They were passing the *Silver Fox,* many hundred yards landward. A man in a

352

white uniform was shouting something at them through a hailer. Carmody knew this was what had this old grey ghost coming on so.

'Louis the Fourteenth's yacht for another example . . . now she was so richly ornamented in her raised platforms that she was too top-heavy to be seaworthy. She went belly-up from the frill she flew. What could be more French? I mean, why do you think it's called a fo'castle? Because it's the castle *before* the mast, raised so it can be under the royal gaze of the chief of state who stands back in the *after*castle, flying the colors and representing the realm. Vessels of statecraft, do you see?'

'Sort of.' Carmody tilted his head in the direction of the big metal sail. 'But out of curiosity, what realm does that freakish grand vessel of *yours* represent? What are her colors? Stars and Stripes? The Union Jack, the Rising Sun? I'm curious . . .'

Steubins refused to look toward the yacht. 'It's true she flies no flag of any realm, but that freakish grand vessel is an instrument of statecraft just as sure as you're sitting there. I just no longer know what state.'

'Seems to me a captain ought to know who he's sailing for.'

'I told you, I'm just her figurehead. I stand the wheel now and then, but only for show. That starched-up prick screeching at us with the hailer—no, *don't* let on you see him!—that's First Mate Singh, the *real* honcho. And I don't think *he* even knows who he's sailing for. His orders come in over one gadget and he types them into another gadget which passes them on to the ship's computer. The ship's computer charts her course, tends the tiller, even sets the sail, and Mr Singh he works the keyboard. They tell me he can type twenty-two hundred characters a minute. I'm doing good if I can button my *fly* in a minute.' He spread his knobby hands and gave a mournful shrug. 'Yep. Just her silly old wooden effigy. My only sea duty is keep my nose to the wind, my keen eye forward, and get good and shellacked at these important social obligations, to prevent cracking.'

'Then why do it? You're bound to have enough chips stuffed by to keep a roof over your head . . .'

'Because I like to *sail*, man. I told you.' Steubins squinted past Carmody. 'Whoops, I was afraid of that. They're lowering the speed launch. Well, sir, I hope you know someplace we can duck into.'

'I do. And if you're the keen-eyed effigy you claim to be, turn round forward and peel 'em. We'll be looking for the ribs of a wreck along that sandbank yonder. Peel 'em forward, I say!'

'Aye, Captain.' Steubins gave a little salute and swung around to look, shading his eyes with a long grey hand. A dashing figure sure enough, Carmody warranted, watching the man's angular profile—all the blagger needs is a parrot.

Steubins was the one that spotted the ribs of the wreck. Carmody would have missed it; the rusted tips were sticking out of the sand now. The channel had shifted, running out of the low dunes to the north of those bones instead of the south, and shallower, so shallow it looked like water from a car wash running over a curb. Carmody went at it head-on and full-throttle, tipping the prop of the outboard out of the water at the last instant. They skipped across the sand like an otter over a mud bank. When they reached the sanctuary of the little bay Carmody cut the engine; the launch would not be able to see them from out on the channel, but it might have a dish for sonics. As they bobbed along in the stillness Steubins began again to talk.

'Before I was a sailor I was a Merchant Marine, back when being a Merchant Marine meant something. A fella running the Mississippi garbage barge I drove Cat on put me on to it. I was just a peckerwood teenager he called Jimmy the Hick. He had been a card-carrying USMM since before that war with Hitler. Man, he could spin tales about adventure in every deepwater port in the world—Rotterdam, Liverpool, Sydney . . . and of course ol' Frisco. San Fran was where he got his dick tattooed, round and round with a spiraling red ribbon.

354

In repose it wasn't much, I admit, but in full rampant glory it was a damn barber pole!'

He was quiet a moment to give Carmody opportunity to appreciate the image. The oldsquaws murmured and the Zodiak nodded in the gentle water.

'I was very impressed by the old merchantman's yarnin', and that's putting it mildly. By the end of that garbage run my mind was made up: the life of the sea was the life for me. He gave me some letters to influential acquaintances from his seagoing days and I was on my way. In less than five years young James Hicks, the peckerwood from Tennessee, was graduating from the New York Maritime College at Throgs Neck— qualified to work any American merchant ship in any port in the world. Trouble was, there was hardly any work left on the American merchant ships by this time. The old Yankee fleets were being sucked up by the Dutch-Asian lines like so many woodchips sucked up a bilge pipe. What was that little wreck we passed back on the sand-bank, by the way? The remains of one of your previous expeditions into these waters?'

'I don't know what she was,' Carmody answered. 'Those bones were sticking up there already when I first discovered this little gutter, twenty years ago or so. Iron ribs, they are, from something big and ancient. I reckon she was one of the casualties of the '64 quake; nothing but a tidal wave could have druv a boat with a draw that deep up a gutter this shallow.'

Steubins nodded in somber agreement, then resumed his maritime history. 'I spurned yacht work as sissy business at first, just like you. I spent months hanging around the Eastern Seaboard looking for ships—mostly getting forklift work on the RO/ROs. I disliked that duty nearly as bad as bulldozing garbage; not only was it tedious, it was downright dangerous. Those big clumsy containers were always tipping off the fork. Turned my hair grey as ashes inside of six months. Then one weekend in Charleston I seen a ad in the classified that somebody needed a replacement to finish captaining some rich

Spanish museum curators around the Horn on a *his*tory ship—which is what they were called before the appellation "fantasy yacht" . . . a *young* replacement captain, the ad specified, preferably from New England with an aristo*cratic* background. That's when it occurred to me that if I aimed to have any kind of career as a sailor I would have to make some changes in my image. I shelled out my last dollar on a used yachtsman's cap and blazer at a St Vincent de Paul, hiked down to the boat, and they hired me on sight. There was even a name tag in the breast pocket—Capt G Steubins. But it was the premature grey hair that turned the trick, I've always suspected: I *looked* like a Yankee yachtsman, for all that I'd never sailed a stitch.'

'Must've made you a mite nervous,' Carmody conjectured.

'A mite, yes. I ordered the first mate to take us out under diesel, I'd go below and rest myself for tomorrow's rigors on the open sea. All night long I drunk mah whang tea and tried to figure out old Bludsoe's *Fundamentals of Sailing*. When I took the wheel the next morning I barely knew one sheet from the other, let alone the lines. Luckily, the entire crew was made up of seasoned Portuguese hands. They barely understood a word of English so it didn't make any difference what command I sung out; they went ahead and did what they'd been doing successfully for three months and three thousand miles. They knew I was a sham, of course, but they never said anything. And the millionaire Spaniards could not have been happier. Apparently the old skipper had been some kind of born-again Captain Bligh who saw to it that the crew dressed in proper naval attire in all weathers and never fraternized with the passengers. By the time we rounded the tropics some of the lads were working the rigging in no attire whatsoever and there was fraternization going on like blue blazes. And by the time we rounded the Horn *I*, by the powers, knew how to sail! I been working the wind ever since, and my home's been one captain's quarters after another. Speaking of which—' Steubins shaded his ˈ

eyes again, peering toward the brushy shores—'you claim you have a domicile on this miniature bay somewhere?'

That was the signal to restart the engine.

'It's on the other side of that high bank with all the Scotch broom,' Carmody told him. 'On the main bay. Just a shack.' Carmody's grin widened, anticipating Steubins' reaction. For the first time since he'd given the carpenters the go-ahead Carmody was glad that he'd insisted on that worthless widow's walk around the stone chimney. 'It ain't any castle-on-the-sea but I think even a tall order like you'll find it adequate to stretch out in.'

But when they had beached the little Zodiak and climbed over the narrow windswept esker that separated the gutter from the main bay, and Carmody pointed proudly to his property down the beach, the house was gone! Stone chimney, widow's walk and all . . . flat gone! There had been a trade. In place of Carmody's mansion stood a native longhouse—the biggest and the fanciest that Carmody had ever seen, even in the old explorers' sketches. The front was an enormous frog design, with great green eyes where his widow's walk had been—that high!—and outspread green knees instead of his carport and smokehouse. The frog's long open oval of a mouth was the longhouse's lone window; the dark slot where her spotted thighs joined, the door.

'Holy bloody hell,' Carmody declared in a drained voice. Steubins was laughing, his face now the one with the bright pucker of mischief and Carmody's slack and grey, as though the expressions had been traded, just like the pair of houses.

'It's just a flat, Captain, a painted front set so our long shots wouldn't pick up a modern house in the background. Your wife's the one painted it, in fact. They'll pull it down soon's we finish the exterior shooting across the bay.'

'Why bother? have 'em leave it up!' Carmody decided that the best thing was to take it all in philosophical

357

stride. 'It looks better'n the set I had built and that's a fact. Let's go see what this big frog's got in her fridge.'

They were met by a ball of ragged orange fire erupting through the slot of the frog's spraddle to accost them. It was a one-eyed one-eared stub-tailed Manx cat, very fat and very impatient. The animal wasted no time on cordialities. It positioned its ugly bulk right in front of Carmody's feet and launched at once into a yowling condemnation of the delinquent fisherman.

'What we got here,' Carmody introduced the cat, 'is my old tom, Tom-Tom.'

'Tom-Tom sounds a trifle peeved.'

'Don't he? He always gives me bloody what for when I been gone, but never *this* severe. Tom, what's ailin' ye? Look at the crazy varmint. I bet that three-story frog is what's upset him, squatted like this right in his favorite sandpiles. Tom-Tom! Stow it! This here's a guest, be *nice* to him! I wouldn't try to shake hands just yet, Steubins, till he takes in a little sail. Tom's like a old prizefighter, still hearin' bells; he can be a little hair-trigger if you approach him from his blinky side. Years of being the only tomcat on a dock full of dogs has left the old fella kinda punch-drunk. *Tom!* Calm yourself for decency's sake! You're embarrassing me.'

Tom had come about stern to fore and was rubbing a pair of balls big and yellow as boiled egg yolks up and down Carmody's pant leg, meowling grievances all the while.

'He still appears dangerously fit,' Steubins complimented the cat. 'He must have been a rip-roarer in his prime.'

'A by God *gale* is what he was! A regular cyclone of teeth and toenails. I seen him peel a big wooly Bedlington balder'n me one time while we lived on the *Columbine.* Some blockheaded drifter looking for work didn't believe me when I advised him he'd best tether his pet on the dock. He wouldn't listen. And that dog had no more than set one paw on board when Tom came sailing down off the wheelhouse and was tilling up the poor brute's topsoil like one of them Weed Weasels you see on garden shows. When he was satisfied with his work, damn me if he didn't sprang about and light into the brute's fool master the same way! If Blockhead hadn't been wearing a rain hood Tom woulda peeled him too.'

The cat's poisonous green eye was set in a massive, battle-scrolled head and the head in an even more massive fat roll of neck. He enlarged on this way to shoulders, ribs, and a rump big as a basketball. But there was nothing slack or slow-looking about the animal's obesity. When Carmody pulled his pant leg free and stepped through the slot in the fiberboard flat so he could get to his real front door, the cat bounded through after him, feather light, then raced around the corner of the house like a road rocket. By the time the fisherman had managed to dial the door open the cat was in the hall ready to resume his diatribe.

'Nobody's ever figured out how he does that,' Carmody bragged. 'When I had the place remodeled I in*sisted* the carpenters had to make it absolutely bear-, coon- and possum-proof—on account of past problems with intruders. But they weren't able to make it Tom-proof. Come in, come in. But let's leave the door open for some new air and a bit of illumination. Wheh! It's dank as the belly of a frog in here for *some* strange reason . . .'

Carmody led the way, switching on light fixtures and lamps. Steubins saw that the house's interior was as much a facsimile of a bygone era as the false front of the native longhouse outside. The ceilings were high and dim and heavily molded; the windows double-draped. The walls were walnut wainscoting, then lumpy floral wallpaper above. The furniture was ancient but completely unworn, as though a time pirate had looted it new out of some upper-middle-class harbor-town home a century earlier. Tiffany floor lamps leaned over the shoulders of matching Chippendales, like attentive butlers. A weight-driven grandfather clock with a gold-plated pendulum ticked somberly, waiting to toll the hour, and a brass-bound barometer on the wall beside the clock politely pointed out that the pressure seemed to be steady and holding and would stay that way.

In the dining room a tall china closet displayed Buffalo bone china behind cut glass doors. There was a complete service already set out at each end of the cherrywood dining table—silverware and folded napkins and all, ranked in patient attention. But a deep build-up of the pearly Kuinak dust revealed the lack of diners. This room had not been used in years. There might have been an invisible chain across the room's sliding doorway, Steubins thought, with a DO NOT TOUCH EXHIBITS sign hanging from it.

The kitchen had no such invisible chain. This was a functioning room, bright and busy with gadgets. Coffee-cup rings patterned every countertop. Pots and plates were still piled in the dish drainer and the range was decorated with burned-in stains. The refrigerator door was cluttered with notes and the glass-front freezer packed with butcher-paper packages. The packages were carefully marked with grease pencil, exactly which cut of wild game was inside, where it had been bagged and when it had been frozen. Without a word Carmody commenced pawing through the frozen packages until he settled on two he wanted. He set them humming in circles on the microthaw, then began pawing again, this time through the cupboards and drawers. He finally found what he was pawing after on the topmost shelf of a walk-in pantry, behind the pickles. 'Yreka!' he cried, carefully climbing down off his stool with a two-liter jar of a liquid that was as green and ghastly as the old tomcat's eye. 'I knew I had the beat of that Bushmill's buried away somewhere.'

'Looks potent, Captain. What you aim to do? Strip some of the varnish off your walnut heirlooms?'

'You wait,' Carmody grunted, twisting at the jar's rusty lid. 'Yer about to find out that yachtsy-totsy movie directors ain't the only nabobs with access to exotic forbidden treats.' He pointed to one of the butcher-paper packages.

360

'I'm but a simple fisherman but I doubt you ever had moose-nose scrapple before, did ye? The Deaps call it Power Meatloaf. I doubt as well you ever had polar-bear liver fried in mandrake oil—a combination to put *two* leads in a fella's pencil, so Great-Granny Wong who gave me the recipe claims . . . and I'll lay a copper penny to a pound sterling that for all your worldly wanderings to Galway and such you *never*! lapped a *lip*! over the likes of *this*!'

Carmody held out the open jar in triumph. Steubin hooked his nose over the emerald liquid. 'Licorice' was his analysis. 'It's just a murky old Pernod . . .'

'Hah! It ain't licorice—it's anise, for yer information— and it ain't "just Pernod," neither. What we got here is absinthe, real 'Gilla absinthe, with *wormwood*. The bitter falling star itself. I traded a Romanian root-woman up in the Barrows forty-nine bear-dick bones for a crate of these jars clear back, oh, before the turn of the century. She claimed it was the last of the world's supply, squeezed from the last survivor of the con-demned *Artemisia* species, and what you're holding right there is the last of that last. Go on, try a sip. But carefully, man, and re*spect*fully . . .'

Steubins squinched his eyes in a frown, drew in a small mouthful, and swallowed it. After a moment a look of sweet relief filled his face. 'Damn, that *is* a treat. That Romany woman must have had considerable need for those forty-nine bear dicks.'

'She did a fortune-tell in the rear of her root shop, and one of the oracles she used was the China-Eye Jing. You know? with the bundle of yarrow stalks? I think she reasoned that forty-nine bear dicks would put her in closer contact with the primal powers of the Barrows than forty-nine little hippy sticks. Woop, there's the buzzer on my thaw. You'll have to excuse me for awhile, Mr Steubins; I got Power Meat to prepare. Through that curtain yonder is my pitiful excuse for a gentleman's den. I shouldn't be surprised if you can find you a siphon and a couple of snifters. You high-class swells prefer taking your refreshments outen glasses rather than the uncouth bottle, I seem to recall. The light switch is on yer portside.'

Steubins pushed through a thick maroon curtain into a dark cavern redolent with manly scents—gun oil and cigar smoke and boot polish and bay rum. He found the switch and a trio of green glass lampshades poured light down into the aquamarine-green pool of a full-sized snooker table. Not pool, *snooker!* with all the diminutive red balls racked and ready in the table's green felt center.

'Pitiful excuse the mischief!' the director chuckled to himself as he looked around the room. 'This old British beer barrel is deeper than he looks.'

He decanted the liquid out of the jar and poured two handcut glasses full. 'Do we sip this precious elixir straight up or dilute it down?' he called at the curtain. 'I'll bring you in a glass if you tell me how you fancy it . . .'

'Watered, no ice,' Carmody called back. 'But don't come in. I'll pop over for mine in 'alf a mo. Ye want something to do, set up that card table by the sound rack. Or play the radio or put on a record or something, but don't come in. Hot grease is a-flyin'!'

Steubins tried a sweep through the main bands, but Carmody didn't have a new-enough discriminator; all the director was able to pick up was the gobble of overlapping stations. The black-market glut of new, cheap, long-range macrotransmitters had made radio broadcasting available to any turkey with the urge to gobble, on just about any frequency he chose to gobble over. The UN regulators weren't able to develop jamming fast enough to keep ahead of these frequency pirates. They were into every lane. Even the sacrosanct Greenwich International wavelength was becoming polluted with rifrap and nut rock evangelists. The big shipping lines had their private systems, but the only way a small-time navigator could be sure of a clean time fix or weather report was with a secure code you had to phone for from one of those private systems; very spendy, and if your plastic came up insufficient it didn't matter to the system if you were lost in a storm or sinking with a boatload of babies—you got no code and no fix, though they *would* pass your problem along to the closest 378 the Coast Guard had in the area. And the radio pirates were already beginning to crack into *these* so-called secure systems, just like the video vandals were popping up on the major network dishes. Right in the middle of a tender episode of 'As the World Turns,' some pimply raghead would suddenly be spraying your screen thick with spit and politics. It was the age of electronic graffiti.

The only voice Steubins could bring in clear was that same stuttering Australian that he picked up all around the dial of his old Zenith—Dr Beck. Beck's signal overrode most of the competitors because it was local, Steubins figured, and because the oddball was using one of those huge old transmitters that used vacuum tubes, like the Zenith. He sipped his drink and listened awhile to Dr Beck's discourse dealing with the distressing de-decline of den-den-dental health d-down under, then switched to the record player.

Carmody's taste in music ran mainly to the traditional Celtic—drums banging and pipes squealing and ballad-eers bewailing lugubrious fates—but there was also a small collection of old American jazz. Steubins chose the Miles Davis classic *Porgy and Bess* and dropped it in the slot. The mewling funereal cry of 'Buzzard Song' drifted darkly out of the high-ceiling speakers, like the high-sailing bird itself. Steubins drifted around beneath, studying the den's decorations.

There was only one window in the pine-walled room, an octagonal affair located up some steps in a little loft, near the ceiling. A telescope was mounted there, and a padded stool for the viewer. Steubins stepped up to look but the window was dark, blocked by the side flat of the longhouse facade no doubt.

'Right! That there's my little keep's peekhole and watchtower —for privacy's sake.'

Carmody had popped in, as promised. He was beaming

wet-faced up at Steubins, bearing a large platter of candied kelp and melon rind. He was wearing a lace doily tied around his fat forehead to keep the sweat out of his eyes, and a frilly print apron.

'When I hear a visitor approaching I can scoot up there and scope 'em out, whether they be approach by land, sea or sky. Come on down and try some of the appetizers.'

Steubins stepped back to the floor in one storklike step. 'What do you do after you've scoped 'em, I'm curious to know. Raise the drawbridge? You don't strike me as a recluse . . .'

'I ain't a recluse, but I can get pretty choosy about the company I keep ashore. It comes of being jammed in with all those square-heads when yer out to sea, cheek to jowl, month on month, whether ye like the darlins or not. Ashore, you got a choice.'

'I thought you had a wife?'

'I *did*, till an hour or so ago. But she never has cared much for staying way out here; that's why the decor don't have what you'd call the feminine touch. She's got her own motel business in town, plus her own damn taste in decor. That big fat frog she painted is the most home decorating she's ever done out here.'

'Yes I *did* notice,' Steubins teased playfully, 'a distinct lack of the quote feminine touch—except for that fetching little apron thing of course. There's your drink on the highboy . . .'

Carmody scooped up the glass and ducked back through the curtain, too busy with supper to be distracted by teasing. Steubins resumed his examination of the room: the gun cases; the trophies; the wall full of framed pictures, enlarged photos mainly, of bygone boats and crews and hunting buddies. No, no feminine touch whatsoever. Not even any little girlie pics on the calendars in the gun cases. It was as though there was a kind of anti-dress code in effect, laid down by that powerful Big Green-Eyed Presence—the sea. Steubins was familiar with harsh rules of this jealous martinet; she had never allowed him to put up any girlie pics in his quarters either.

The meal was amazing. The moose-nose cakes were as good as any scrapple the Pennsylvania Dutch had ever put up, and prepared perfectly—crisp on each side and sprinkled with capers and orange sauce. The bear liver had been sliced pencil thin and stir-fried with ginseng root and shiitake mushrooms. A steaming couscous provided a welcome padding for the two heavy main courses and a fiddlehead salad rounded out the fare. Dessert was fresh red huckleberries that Carmody had noticed out back while he was gathering the fern tops for his salad. He sprinkled the berries over yogurt and served them with espresso. When the coffee was finished Steubins stood in sincere tribute.

'Captain, to say I'm impressed would be way too weak a statement. I've dined at every five-star hotel and hashhouse in the known culinary world, but have *never before* enjoyed anything the equal of this here feast. You say you're only a simple fisherman, but I swear you cook like you studied under a grand *saucier*!'

'I did,' Carmody confessed, with a lowering of his pale eyes. 'I studied at the Cordon Bleu in Paris. Well, now . . . if you're finished with your java what do ye say we get back to the wormwood? And I'll show you what a simple fisherman can learn in *Liver*pool if he hangs around enough snooker halls. What do ye say to a dollar a point for starters?'

Steubins' rutted features spread into a long loose smile. 'Bless your heart, Captain Carmody. I suspect you might be just the tiniest bit of a hustler.'

'I'm a whole heaping big bloody *bunch* of a hustler, Mr Steubins, and I must say it's a rare treat to come across a fella with taste enough to appreciate it. Yer the guest, you break.'

Halfway down the decanter of green liquor the pair got into a lovely brouhaha about a disputed shot. It was jubilant and juvenile. They called names back and forth across the table that went all the way back to the earliest grade-school invective—'Fart-snapper!' 'Bugger-suck!'—with Tom-Tom yowling under the table and the *Boys from the Loch* banging away in the Celtic background. A very *rouser* of a rhubarb, so absorbing and satisfying that neither man knew of the brief rogue windstorm that struck the coast that midnight, not until hours later, when they went outside for a break from the cigar smoke and the green table and the greener bottle.

The front of the longhouse facade had been torn free from its smaller side wall and blown flat. It lay facedown over the whole of Carmody's front yard, peaceful and shimmery with pools of rainwater between the struts. Blinking and peeing, Carmody had no idea what he was looking at at first, or peeing into. It looked like his front lawn had been converted into an elaborate complex of fish-breeding ponds. He didn't object; the lawn had been a failure from the git-go. But what *kind* of fish, he wanted to know. Steubins had to set him straight.

'Not fish, Captain,' the tall man drawled, peeing into one of the other lumber-banked pools, 'frog. Don't you remember the three-story froghouse? No? Well, there you are: neural alcohol syndrome. You Brits never could handle your liquor . . .'

'Handled it well enough to snooker you eight games out of ten, I remember.'

'That's because you play with those little bitty balls. Who would play with little bitty fucking balls like that but a *Brit*?' They had been drinking together for close to twenty-four hours now, and were allowed to say things like that.

'You want bigger balls? Let's drive to town and I'll *bowl* the bejesus out of you. No, I forgot; the bowling alley's one of your holdings nowadays . . .'

'You also forgot we have no car,' Steubins reminded his host.

'Billiards!' Carmody clapped his hands. 'If it's size you need, that table of mine con*verts*.' He zipped shut and bounced back up the steps, happy as a boy with a friend over for the weekend—that new boy, from out of town. It was good fun, and far less trouble, too, having a boyo for a playmate. Those girlie friends can drive a bloke barmy.

14

Straight from the Pole
Sudden as a Spear

That Kuinak midsummer-night blow had blown straight down from the Pole, narrow and sudden as a spear. A complete surprise. The satellite scans did not even register it as a wind; the weather experts interpreted the data as another aberrant ion storm, a tiny needle pricked up by unusual sunspot activity. When that tiny needle stabbed huge holes in jetties and sewed up ports along a hundred miles of coastline the experts decided it was time to re-evaluate the data.

The strange wind came shrieking out of the northeast, made a little hop over the Aleutians, then banked hard left. It cut across coastal towns with such keen delicacy that many of the anesthetized citizens never noticed they'd been cut. It sliced down a street in Cordova leaving a row of demolished triple-wides on one side and a row on the other side without a window broken. Survivors of the rash of Texas twisters say a tornado can slice like this when it so chooses, the funnel point ambling along in an aimless scrawl, then suddenly, for a few thousand feet, becoming precise as a scalpel. There didn't seem to be any preamble to this polar wind. It was grim and steady and purposeful all the way, like a warplane on a midnight strafing run. The memorial grove of Sitka spruce in Dillingham Park, for example, was completely leveled by a devastating barrage of 70mm hailstones. Some of the stones were buried four inches deep in the wood, like armor-piercing slugs.

By the time the wind reached Kuinak Bay it was out of heavy ammunition. The best blitzkrieg it could deliver

was a stinging yellow mix of sea foam and grey grit—
and only a couple of minutes' worth of this. Scarcely a
squirt. But it was enough to smear all the new-washed
storefronts along Main with grime and cause a lot of
fender-benders among the boats moored in the marina.
Carmody's new craft lost its ramp. The Boswells' processor lost a boom.

The *Silver Fox* secure band had advance warning
enough to give First Mate Singh ample time to instruct the
computer to crank down her sail and spider out four of her
six pontoon feet to steady the pitch. The hunkered vessel
rode out the brief blow so smoothly that the Cambodian
millionaires never spilled a drop of the Noble Rot they
were sipping with dessert. A few lights flickered was all,
in the saloon; they were back on steady within seconds.

In the levels below, the yacht's backups weren't as
important or as prompt. Greer was moussing the tiny
dreadlocks of his beard when the lights blew in one of
those lower-level staterooms; these lights didn't come
back on for four hours. He never did find out exactly
which of the flavors he was moussing with: Russian,
Scandinavian, or that new taste from the edge of Asia—
Soy Shi.

In the back office of the partitioned gloom that had
once been her papa's open-all-night bowling alley, Louise
Loop was alone when it struck, plugged into the Virtual
Dildrama the studio provided. She was feeling kind of
blue and homeless. She didn't want to be on the yacht
anymore, with all those snooty beauties looking down
their noses at her, and she didn't want to be up at the Loop
house with all those snouty sows, so she had slipped in
the back way with the old Loop code the studio must have
overlooked. She didn't know that the old code had been
left in on purpose, or that her activities were on display,
and beamed all the way to the yacht. All she knew was
that the device was designed to respond to the subject's
alpha needs, however blue. When the brief storm hit the
machine went off at the same time that she did, so Lulu
missed the phenomenon of strange wind as well.

Billy Bellisarius was wide awake when it hit. Wider. His face was stretched broad and his eyes wide and popping like a pair of old-century spark plugs. He had been working with Wayne Altenhoffen in the stuffy editorial office of the *Bay Beacon* all afternoon and evening, drinking hot tea and dictating hotter messages for Altenhoffen to key into his authorized media faxlines—fiery letters to senators and anchormen and other news editors. Wayne's poor brain had become severely drained by the strain of working with the high-wired Bellisarius, and he was now passed out on the mountain of rival rags that arrived weekly from around the globe: the *Manchester Guardian,* the *New York Times,* the *New Pravda* from St Petersburg. 'Gotta keep on top of the competition,' Wayne had explained when he crawled up on the mountain of newsprint to catch a few zees and recharge his batteries.

Billy's batteries, on the other hand, were just beginning to crank. With that nervous newshound out of the way at the AP faxline, the Squid could let his bitter ink squirt hot and black. His most devastating diatribe thus far was scalding its way that very instant to the Canadian Immigration authorities at the Royal Mounted headquarters in Vancouver, All Eyes Urgent:

> . . . Allow me to say in closing, gentlemen, that while it is within the pale of reason that you busy bureaucrats might conceivably overlook a few illegal aliens farming an insignificant tract of land in one of Her Majesty's Royal Parks, and that you could possibly have become so deadened by the travesties and tribulations of our terrible time that you no longer consider the practice of black magic and white slavery to be the proper concern of modern border patrols—that, too, is understandable—but one can in no way fathom how *any* educated Englishman in service to the Crown could tolerate the dissemination of such fallacious drivel (see enclosed Beulahland brochures) from a commonwealth with such a heritage of rationality.

Read the 'expert scientific proof' in the so-called 'educational materials' entitled *Sanctuary in the Clouds*. This shameful screed is not science and it is certainly not proof. These 'experts' are nothing more than the customary chorus line of Chicken Littles in the current musical comedy revival of *The Sky Is Falling, the Sky Is Falling.* Of course, the good Reverend Greener plays the part of Foxy Loxy, kindly proprietor of that cloudy sanctuary.

And you gentlemen are allowing this tripe to be transmitted postage free as educational material? As *science*? What would your ancestral scholars think? Outraged corpses from Francis Bacon to Marshall McLuhan must be spinning in their sepulchers!
[Signed:]
A Friend of the Crown and a Guardian of the Truth.

Billy was composing his next letter, to the secretary general of the UN, when the sudden wind shook the office and cut off the fax. His eyes glowed above the dark screen for a moment; then he leapt up with a glad cry. He ran out into the alley, his teeth bared and his hair whipping in the icy wind: 'Fire next time my skinny wop *ass*!'

Clark B Clark wasn't wide awake but he was conscious, tucked into one of the hanging berths in the speed launch's cabin, half listening to the emergency Coast Guard band. One of the *Fox*'s able-bodied lackeys hung in the cocoon berth on the other side of the cabin— an ex-hydro racer. Clark B had been the one to suggest that they anchor offshore on ready watch, in case word came in and they had to suddenly resume the search for the two senior delinquents. The racer didn't like the idea and Clark had phoned the yacht. Levertov's dulcet voice on the celefone sided with his lieutenant but added, 'Stay out if you want, but not to worry. There's no weather and the water's calm. They're just adrift, out of gas and out of danger.'

The polar blow changed all that. The launch was suddenly pitching between its anchors like a terrified mustang lassoed head and heel. The radio was roiling with voices full of confusion and incompetency. Clark B was on the celefone to Levertov again, immediately.

'Adrift in calm weather is one thing! Adrift in this is disastrously different. I think you better call in a complete search-and-rescue.'

'Calm yourself,' Levertov told him. 'Nobody would look for them until it gets light. This blow might even bring the dumb old duffs out of hiding. And if it doesn't—?' Clark could almost see the white shoulder shrug in the celefone's pause. '—then it was by the duffer's own dumb design, right? Whatever comes down. Go back to sleep.'

Clark B replaced the phone, his face now peaceful in the bucking cabin. The ex-boat racer had finally managed to worm out of his berth. His face was pale. 'What's he say, head for port? I told you. This baby's not made for rough seas . . .'

'He says it's by their own design, go back to sleep,' Clark B reassured the worried sport. 'What a mensch, huh?'—and didn't give the situation a whit more worry.

Search choppers came in from Bristol Bay at daylight. The weather was calm and they were sure they'd spot the raft right away. When they did it was empty, way out on Hopeless Rock. By the following night the Coast Guard communiqués were beginning to sound somewhat pessimistic, and by noon of the second day everybody but Clark B and his boss was beginning to lose hope. Rumors were rife. Press was everywhere. The converted bowling alley was frantic with secretaries and assistants yelling into all the phones in a dozen different languages. Three code-lock radios were squawking at once—one from the air search, one from the sea search and one from the UP wire service demanding a statement. Headlines were on every newsdish: 'WORLD-RENOWNED DIRECTOR GERHARDT STEUBINS CARRIED TO SEA BY FREAK STORM WITH FISHERMAN. MISSING TWO DAYS . . . CAPSIZED ZODIAK FOUND ON ROCK CALLED HOPELESS . . . FOXCORP SPOKESMAN FEARS WORST. DETAILS AT ELEVEN . . .'

Alice was in the dim laundry room at the Bear Flag folding cold sheets and listening to her CB. She was hard-dialed into the cacophonous turmoil down at the production office. She'd been down there in the flesh most of yesterday and this morning, keeping abreast of the rescue reports. But all that press in that converted bowling alley had become noisier than she could stand—an absolute din, louder than any all-lane tourney that old Omar had ever dreamed of. She pinched a code card and headed home to her CB; she'd know as much by listening to the cacophony over the little speaker as she would by enduring it firsthand.

She still wasn't exactly worried, even after this long. Just attentive. Waiting. Since yesterday's report of their boat found on Hopeless, there was only one thing else to know, one simple fact, with two possible faces: they would either find them alive, or they wouldn't. She could fold sheets and listen to the radio and wait for that piece of news by herself, in peace.

She hung up her press dress and went down to the laundry room in panties and a crimson suede pullover. But the laundry room chores afforded her none of the usual solace. For one thing, the sheets had been left in the tumblers until they were damp and uncooperative, petulant about being neglected; and for another she was becoming increasingly aware that there was something *more* than that piece of news, that simple fact with two faces, that she was waiting on. Something else. It galled her as time went on that she couldn't put her finger on what that nagging something else could be. It was like the hazy anxiety you get playing solitaire before you realize the deck is light. This soon became a more vexing mystery to Alice than the whereabouts of her missing husband. She did not for one instant believe Carmody was drowned. Fat and foolish as he might look, she knew Michael Carmody was no clumsy Alexis Levertov. Oh he was a drinker, all right; but he wasn't clumsy. He wasn't a sinker. She remembered Hawaii, when he couldn't even sink in a hot tub, the big ball of blubber. Yeah, marooned somewhere Michael Carmody might well be, and very likely in another one of his sticky predicaments, but not drowned. Never drowned. Missing was all, off where somebody who knows his ways will eventually look and find the tub-gutted old—

She stopped, furious and amazed: it *was*n't a some*thing* else, it was a goddamn some*one*! And what *really* fucking galled was having to gradually begrudgingly admit that that someone was probably the *only* one capable of finding and fetching those missing marines. Somebody was going to have to drive up to the dump and activate that damned someone, and since Greer could not be located, and the Culligan boys were in jail drunk and Bellisarius was scooted to high heaven and babbling in the streets, it became ever more exasperatingly evident who that somebody was going to have to be.

She pulled on the short suede skirt that was the other half of her heirloom disco outfit and set about stirring up another pitcher of margaritas, to work up some steam. She hated asking anybody for anything. And Ike Sallas? If she was overboard in a typhoon she'd rather drown than ask him to throw a line. But she wasn't the one overboard.

She poured the pitcher in a fruit jar, screwed on a lid and slammed out the laundry room screen. On her way to the car Shoola confronted her in the courtyard. She was holding the hand of her six-year-old sister, Nell, who was holding the hand of the youngest. All three were wearing silver and black.

'Where you goin' now?' Shoola was frowning at Alice's crimson clothes and travel stash of green margaritas. When Alice told her where, the girl wailed, 'We want to go. We can help at something . . .' Her voice trembled helplessly with a naked longing. Alice fought back a wicked impulse to laugh. Sympathetic the dickens, she realized; *jealous* was more like it—green as the juice in this fruit jar. Our little Eskimo has *also* guessed that somebody is going to have to drive up and activate the beautiful Greek hero. How long had she been waiting for that screen door to slam so she could come out armed with her sisters and demand to go along? Imagine! Passions this primitive in this day and age, and over what? A worthless burnout with a nice nose and sorrowful eyes. Alice felt a little pinch of shame, confronted by the girl's unabashed infatuation; she couldn't get *this* intense about her own damn *husband*—missing at sea plus having an affair with a Texas tart though the dear old walrus was.

'You girls must be able to find better things to do. You can keep track of the search news on my radio if you want to be helpful.'

Shoola was having none of it. Still scowling, she released the sister's hand she held and waved both little girls away. 'What if there's another phone call?'

'Tell the caller I'll be right back,' Alice answered. 'Punch in Save, if you think the call's important. I won't be long . . .'

'But I want to go *too*,' she stamped. 'Please, Mrs Carmody . . .'

'Not this time,' Alice said and got in the van and drove away, her fruit jar of green drink getting warmer and her little pinch of shame getting colder. Why hadn't she invited the poor smitten girl to come along? To avoid complications? To protect a helpless chick from the heartless hounds? Oh, come on! Isaak Sallas was a dog guilty of a lot of aggravating vices, but chick hunting was certainly not one of them. Let's be straight, here . . .

Alice was so involved with her self-castigation that she forgot completely about her drink on the drive through town. She didn't remember it until the smokes from the garbage heaps were scorching her throat. Slowing the van to a crawl she rolled up her window and took the bottle between her bare knees. Her hands were sweating so she could barely unscrew the lid. She guzzled a third of the drink with one long swallow, sighting down the jar toward the red trailerhouse as though along the barrel of a bazooka. That calmed her a little. She was able to idle along and drink the second third of the concoction in a more leisurely and dignified fashion.

Marley was on guard beneath his old bush at the yard's

edge, but he recognized Alice's slow-moving van and came out grinning to greet her. She would have preferred a few barks for announcement's sake, but the animal only licked her hand when she stepped out into the oyster shells. She walked to the trailer door and knocked. Nothing. She knocked again. More nothing. Fuck this, she said at last, and stepped inside.

The tubelike interior was still dim as a submarine, even with the windows washed, and she could still smell the musky fume of accumulated man sweat for all the two bottles of Pine-Sol she had used. Balls! She'd thought herself quits with this junk heap *days* ago. Now here she was, already back in it, and the mess was already returning. A trail of strewn clothes led her all the way to the bedroom. As she stepped into the sleep-filled cubicle that first guzzle of tequila hit her so hard she had to sit down on one of the bookcases. When her eyes opened she saw the sleeping man across the narrow space from her. It took a giddy moment to remember who he was, turned to the wall like that, with his tousled hair and his skimpy, frayed quilt clutched over a shoulder like a pathetic toga. He was dreaming. His bare back twitched and his ribs heaved in and out in fitful whimpers. Some white knight, Alice observed with wicked pleasure; stripped of his shiny armor he looks like a little kid on the run from some nasty nightmare.

'Sallas,' she said. 'Wake up.'

The form spun over violently, throwing back the quilt with a sweep of his hand. Alice was confronted by a naked man and a long-barreled pistol, aimed right where that second round of margaritas was just starting to go off. The unexpected sweep of motion made her feel a little ill, but she kept completely still, right where she sat, and watched the gun. She remembered a recent article in *Parade* which emphasized that thirty-seven percent of all of today's accidental—no, not accidental—thirty-seven percent of all today's mis*taken* shootings happen at sudden awakenings. Because of the prevalence of hand-guns and scoot hangovers, the article theorized, the best thing was to keep completely still in these hair-trigger situations.

Comprehension finally trickled into Sallas' face.

'Alice, what's this mean?'

'You mean does it mean I'm here to clean your room again? No, it does not. Get dressed. Carmody's missing. Two days ago he and Gerhardt Steubins cruised out to sea in an inflatable raft and never came back.'

'The movie director?'

'That's right. Like a couple of kids: got into a little hot water at home, run off to sea . . .'

'Carmody's not about to run off to sea in an inflatable raft, Alice. Don't talk screwy.'

'Hey, there's been some screwy stuff, Sallas. You been asleep two days. You missed a very screwy polar blow . . .'

'Has anybody checked his place on North Bay?'

'Of course somebody has! The first day after the blow the Coast Guard S&R chopped out and found it locked and dark. And this morning they spotted the Zodiak driven up on the rocks at Hopeless. Which means they cruised south, not north. You can put your weapon down, by the way; I promise not to hurt you.'

Sallas slid the .22 back beneath the pillow and stood up, trying to keep the quilt around him. Alice waited on the bookcase, feeling a little feverish. She noticed her heart was pounding, too. Hard. She feared it would be heard in the tight quarters.

'Which way did the wind come from?'

'A polar blow? Which way do you think it came from? Are you dense?'

'Then the Zodiak could have been driven south,' he said.

'From Carmody's house? That's ten miles out the bay and around to Hopeless. More than that . . .'

'Not if you don't come out the bay,' Ike mused, mysterious. 'Okay, I'll come. Get out and let me get dressed. Go doctor the dog or something.'

Alice left him there clutching his skimpy wrap. Outside, she sat on the van's bumper and poured the last of the cool liquid down her throat, hoping to quiet that fever-ish pounding. She wondered if she hadn't picked up some kind of sentimental virus from that trembling Eskimo teenager, some extinct pestilence carried down out of the Arctic cold storage to infect the emotion's immune system. Where was her angry army of antibodies? Deserted? Flustered into frightened flight by nothing more than the sight of a little manflesh in a toga? No, no, it wasn't the meat; she'd done enough charcoal studies of that stuff in art classes to inure her for life. She'd sketched male models with bodies smooth as Michelangelo's marble— delicious-looking dudes, a lot of them moonlighting from stud bars—sketched them for days on end yet never drooled a drop. Sallas certainly wasn't a match for any of those beefsteaks. He wasn't bad looking, but he was nowhere near hunk enough to get work jock-dancing, or modeling, either—even if he'd been so inclined. That was another thing no-one ever accused Ike Sallas of: of being any sort of exhibitionist anymore . . .

Sensing Alice's fretfulness, Marley left his guard post and walked over to lay his grey muzzle on her knee. Alice leaned down and gave him a grateful hug.

'I can't believe myself, old mutt,' she laughed into the dog's coarse mane. 'I cannot believe I'm even *think*ing this shit.'

The screen door scraped open and Sallas came down the steps, buttoning his shirt. It was the Old Hickory she'd found rumpled on the floor and hung in his closet. A dark nausea was beginning to churn deep inside her. She pushed the dog away and headed for the shotgun seat.

'Okay, Sallas, this time *you* drive,' she told him. 'While I doze.'

'Drive where? The Coast Guard station?'

'You know Carmody's not at any damn Coast Guard station. Drive out to Herb Tom's and rent a plane.'

'Herb Tom's not going to be too likely to rent me another airplane.'

'Drive, damn you. I'll rent it, you fly it. Aren't you the famous rescue flyer? If you can find drab little pissants

377

like Billy Bellisarius surely you can locate a big pink buoy like Michael Carmody. Drive.'

The keen edge in her voice sounded dangerous. Ike backed around and headed the six-wheeler down the road. Alice tossed her empty jar at the first pig they passed.

'You probably think I'm drunk, don't you, Sallas? Yeah? Dumb drunk at a dumb time?'

Ike shrugged. 'Practically everybody's drunk these days, Alice . . . practically all the time.'

'You think I'm drunk because I'm despondent with worry that I might be losing my old man. Well, you're wrong. It's going to take more than a polar blow or a Texas tornado to drag Michael Carmody under; he's got too much cork in him.'

Ike didn't answer. He had to swerve out of the ruts to go around a sow nursing her sooty litter. The sow mothers often preferred suckling their brood in the brushless open of the roadway, Ike had noticed. It must make it harder for the boars to sneak up and snatch one of the little smokey links for an appetizer.

'Slow down!' Alice commanded; the journey around the sow and litter was making her more nauseous. 'And roll up your window. I paid for all this fancy filtering so I wouldn't have to smell the passing pig shit.'

He obliged her without comment. They jounced back into the road and drove on more smoothly, sealed in their padded cylinder. But the unspoken approbation was finally more than she could endure.

'God *damn* you and your sanctimonious silence, Ike Sallas! Just because you dropped out of the race doesn't give you the right to be so self-fucking-righteous . . .'

'Race? What race?'

'The *hu*man race,' she hooted, 'the human mother *race*!'

To her surprise, the dark nausea was miraculously dissipated by the old joke, and in its place flowed a kind of sardonic giddiness. Her brief fever fit suddenly seemed laughable and ludicrous. 'Jesus, look at you in that raggedy hermit getup. Smell you! You ever hear of a laundromat? Open these damn windows back up,' she commanded. 'I guess I would rather smell pig shit than beefcake!'—then collapsed in laughter against the van's padded doorpost, delighted at her joke. The trouble was, Ike Sallas didn't get it. She saw his face in the sideview and it was filled with concern. The poor goon mistook her giddy paroxysm for *grief*, of all things! He thought she was *crying*. This made her shake even more with mirth, so terribly that he finally had to extend the hand of sympathy. And since the shoulder was heaving too hard to invite consolation, the hand had no place to land except her thigh. Her skin tingled at the shock. He drove on, left-handed, and kept both eyes forward on the road. When the shaking at last began to subside he gave a quick, crisp squeeze—what he probably hoped would be taken as one of those *brotherly* gestures—and once again gripped the wheel with both hands.

'Why was Carmody out motorboating with Gerhardt Steubins, anyhow?' he asked after a time.

'Nobody knows. Nicholas says Steubins was ducking out of a business dinner. Carmody probably just went along for the ride, in my opinion.'

If Sallas had other opinions he kept them to himself and drove on the rest of the way in silence.

The porch of the Underdog House was packed with beer-drinking Dog Brothers. It looked like they had been given the day off from their security duties. Some of them somberly raised their cans to the van as it passed, but Alice did not acknowledge the show of respect. When they turned off Main to Bayshore Alice saw the crowd in front of the bowling alley had increased by at least two network dish crews. Ike slowed to gawk at the throng and Alice jerked back away from the window.

'Keep going, dummy, keep going! Do I look like a woman in any shape to do a bunch of stupid interviews?' She kept her face averted, toward the bay. She knew her eyes must look red and terrible, the way they were burning. Not only that, her damn thigh felt as hot as her

379

eyes! She imagined if she glanced down she would see the shape of a hand burned there. For the second time today she cursed herself for wearing that stupid suede outfit with its crack-high miniskirt. She should have him swing by the motel, at least put on a set of hose. Easy and quick, rush in and rush out. But god*damn* if she would give the bastard the satisfaction, she decided. That had always been another of her troubles— she was not only gifted with exquisitely bad taste, she was adamant about indulging it.

She tried the car radio but the cacophony was worse than ever with all that media fighting for the frequencies, so she turned it off and they drove in silence again. Sallas spoke once, as they passed the swampy flat where the fishkids camped. At the edge of the welter of tires and lean-tos and crates a gleaming cyclone fence compound had been constructed around a thicket of moonbroom. From this brushy green enclosure arose a desultory baying and barking.

'I wondered where the city council put the poor miserable mutts,' Sallas said. 'I should have guessed.'

He kept driving, right on past the airport. When Carmody's place came in sight Alice wondered what had become of her longhouse front. 'Must've blown down. I designed this canvas flat, see, to hide the house, but the wind—'

'I see them,' Ike interrupted, cupping his eyes toward the ungainly house down the graveled road. 'Hanging out on the porch. Didn't I tell you?'

In answer, Alice began to cry, this time for real— distractedly tugging at the suede hem of the skirt and letting the hot tears roll, red-rimmed eyes be damned. God *damn*, she hoped that handprint would be faded by the time they got there, imaginary or not.

So just like Nick-o predict-o, it worked out fine by its own design —was Clark B Clark's evaluation of the two-day debacle. It turned out the Cambodian millionaires had been far more impressed by the missing Gerhardt

Steubins than they ever would have been by eating supper with the old bone pile in person; they signed on for a sumptuous slice of theme-park stock. The developers were impressed by the way the little bay had weathered the rogue storm (other coastal towns not far distant had been ripped to merry shit); the studio reps that had sea-jetted up from Los Angeles in a corporate panic went home happy about all the publicity and pleased with the footage their famous director was shooting for them; and clever bossman Nick had milked more media time out of this one little fuck-up in the backwater of *no*where than a PR firm could have pulled off with one *hundred* catered ho-hums in all the major cities on the globe.

Clark B had been positioned at the bank of monitor dishes they had installed in one of the bowling lanes when the media uplink aired. Suddenly, there the boss was on every major network, bigger than life and sure as shit, Hollywood's freshest Young Lion, presiding live in his official capacity as Foxcorp spokesman—minister plenipotentiary, chargé d'affaires, ramrod—*Bossman*!—Nicholas Alexandro Levertov! And the masterful way Boss Nick handled the situation?—tasty! It made Clark B Clark swell so with pride he feared he might pop, like a burr-headed balloon. Whatever the turn of the question at the press conference, Nick could put a reverse spin on the answer, like some devious dervish. When Steubins was asked by a certain priss from *People* what he was doing out in that little Zodiak anyway, Nick adroitly spun the query on to the pot-bellied fisherman by telling the reporters that if it hadn't been for the superb seamanship of Michael Carmody their great director probably would not be with them this afternoon: 'Tell them how you were able to steer the raft to refuge, Captain Carmody.' When that same prying priss asked Captain Carmody what *he* was doing out in that inflatable, then, since Mr Steubins wouldn't answer, Nicholas Levertov spun it over to Alice—his own mother, he makes sure everybody knows—by asking her if she was ever worried about her husband's mysterious absence.

'Carmody floats like a cork,' was Alice's answer, looking right at the *People* woman. 'You couldn't sink him with a torpedo.'

Masterful, Clark B Clark remarked again to himself as he stood in an attitude of casual reverence before the array of screens, watching the press conference fumble on to its frustrated conclusion. Nick wound it up with a lengthy listing of all Steubins' previous picture credits and awards; and if anybody had *fur*ther questions for the principals of this scary adventure with its Thank God happy ending, they could ask them later on the *Silver Fox* at the reception which the studio was even now preparing for the media, *all* of whom had been so patient and considerate and understanding—open bar and *very* fresh sushi, gratis to anybody with a press card. Everybody cheered and began to mill around smiling, fulfilled and expectant both, like a dismissed self-esteem seminar. Just masterful. Use 'em, abuse 'em, but never bruise 'em. Nick was a genius of the hidden agenda, of the will behind the veil. The invisible whip in the smiling lip. And who was it first appreciated this genius of the Silver Deal? This Prince of Quid Pro Quo? Clark B-as-in-Believer Clark, that's who. From the first day young Nick showed up in the studio cafeteria with his chrome-plated charisma and his bag of chemical tricks I appreciated him. A lot of the lower-echelon execs gave him nothing but the Fuck You Friend Grin back then: just another flake dealer — high today, gone tomorrow. Now most if not all of that bunch are *ex*-execs. They learned Nicholas Levertov was no flake; he was a stayer, a sticker, a stirrer-of-pots. Especially teapots. The scoot he was dealing wasn't just prime zam, it was *both bags*, green *and* black. That was back when you *never* ran into a mule that carried both sides of the mix. There might be green mules and black mules thick as flies all up and down a shared turf like, say, La Cienega, but a very violent tradition advised that each bagman stick to his color's side of the street. That's why the cartels used the Thuds and the Humps for so long; those lads were already trained in that kind

382

of one-street-two-sidewalks system. So if you needed a refill you always had to deal with two different donkeys, usually a Mex-Asian and a German, each more unreliable than the other. Nothing's more exasperating than having a gross of German green tea bags burning a hole in one pocket, the other pocket languishing empty for days, weeks, *months*, while you wait on some Slant-Eye from T-town to show up with your gross of black. How Nick was able to arrange connections to both sides of the scoot operation nobody ever managed to find out. 'There's no place like jail for contacts' was the only explanation he ever tendered to the adoring fans who were soon sidling by our fax room a couple of times a week, 'and no place like ChemAnon for networking.'

Well now, it so happened, that one of the fax mates on our floor was *never* going to become a fan of young Nick. Maybe this savory anecdote will give you an example what I'm driving at. She was a sprouts-and-spring-water bitch with a bone up her butt about impure additives in general and scoot in particular. The sticker on her Gucci said, 'Life is Natural; Death is Artificial.' She was a USC film grad from one of the old Jewish film families, and she was dedicated to keeping the Dream Machine *unsullied*, if you can imagine. She started ragging on Nick from the first moment he made it up to our level. He'd accumulated enough rep to rise fast up the gofer ladder and this Gucci bitchie has obviously heard of him: the Great White Mule every teahead in the studio's been talking about. I've just shown him his station when she pops over her half-wall and aims a red fingernail at him. 'You! Coffee! And I don't mean this Mr Dishwater. I mean fresh-roasted from the deli on Vine—cream, no sugar.'

I was a consultant's second assistant at the time, also in one of those half-walled offices, except mine was way at the rear and my folks weren't Jewish, just union pooh-bahs from Pomona who still had a few strings to pull. I knew I wasn't going to rise in the business. This old-family bitch wasn't going to rise, either, but she

383

didn't know it. Or maybe she did. Maybe that's why she chose off on Nick so quick.

'You,' she'd bark. 'More coffee. And use the cafeteria mug from now on. Styro particles destroy ulia in the lower intestine.'

It's about the third day of this. He comes back carrying *two* cafeteria mugs. One is coffee, cream and no sugar, and the other is hot water with a pair of tea bags already steeping in it.

'I worry about all this caffeine you're taking, Miss Meyer,' he tells her, polite and subservient. 'Why don't you sample a little of this herb tea instead? You might enjoy it—'

'Not on your brass chain, Goychick.' She dumps the hot water and tea bags into the hallway wastepaper. 'You're not getting *this* woman on your wavelength.' She then starts slurping down her mug of fresh-roasted—cream, no sugar. Nicholas Levertov digs me watching this action and raises up his prescription shades. What a wink he gives me. Made my heart go hippity-hop.

Well, so a half hour later the silver-spoon bitch is yipping and yowling all over the place like a Mulholland coyote with the rabies. When the parameds take her away their hands are all bloody where she'd snapped them. Not a thing showed on her urinalysis, either. Many meaningful months later, when I was *his* gofer, we were reminiscing about that incident. He confided that, unbeknownst to many, there are certain *passé potions* that do not register on the tests if you only use minute amounts.

'Purple Haze, for example. And some people are already out on the edge enough that all they need is a minute push. Haze is made out of blighted wheat, by the way. So it *is* natural . . .'

But wait, wait, don't jump to conclusions. By her own design, you see; all of them dealt by their own design. Zachary Zant, if you need another example. He was this I-Luv-It golf nut, as well as being another silver-spoon Old Family turd type. *Horrible* to do a back nine with.

Things like trying to distract you on your upswing with lame little tricks like suddenly offering advice on how to improve your form. Was it Nick's fault that Zachary put his fat mouth in the path of a nine-iron follow-through? Yet another example: Mr Action Thriller Saul Manley? The boot-fetish and sky-dive enthusiast? He was always getting Nick and me to drive him out to the airport and jump with him. When the chutes opened and we three were floating in he had manlier thrills still that he kept trying to get Nick to consider. Footsie free-fall thrills. It wasn't Nick's idea. Nick wasn't the one that unlaced his boot on the fall. Nick wasn't the one pulled off the sock. And no-one was ever able to show evidence that Nick pulled his cord prematurely, either. The guy simply couldn't stop sucking that heavenly toe jam. The spine isn't made to take that kind of jolt.

So you heed what Clark B is telling you about appreciating Nicholas Levertov, and about what happens to those turds that *don't* appreciate. It's all by their own design as you soon shall see.

The photo op's over. Everything's back on. The town's in its warren, the snail's on its thorn.

Clark B Clark is behind the wheel of the rented stretch limo, smiling beatifically. He's chauffeuring his boss and Ike Sallas through the darkening streets. Levertov had insisted on giving Sallas a ride home after the press conference finally broke up. 'Least we can do, Isaak, for the hound that found our runaway relic. Besides, I haven't had much chance to talk old times with my main slambro.'

If conversation was what Levertov was after he didn't get much of it on the drive. He did most of the talking. Sallas was content to sit against the door on his side of the insulated interior and let Levertov's garrulous purr wash over him. Clark B adjusted his rear-view to study this famous slambro. The face was handsome but guarded, private, and a trifle dangerous . It was clear why Nick would be fascinated by a face like that; there was a challenge in the implied incorruptibility of such a face. 'You remember Sweets, Isaak?' Levertov was prompting. 'Deputy Sweets? The big Mormon with the gap in his front teeth that was always beefing on the Bloods?'

'I remember Deputy Sweets.'

Levertov leaned forward to include the driver in his reminiscence. 'Deputy Sweets, you understand Mr Clark, was one of the worst pigs on the farm. Your basic brain-locked bigot. He always wore his holster even though guards weren't allowed to have guns at honor camp. Talk was he had gut-shot several black kids back in Texas or Arkansas or wherever he hailed from, just to watch them wiggle. He still referred to them as *Nee*-groes . . .'

'Sounds sweet all right,' Clark B said into the rearview.

'He was also a fanatic for a surprise piss test. The black prisoners were the only ones he tested—which wasn't all that off-center considering that ninety-nine percent of them were in on sub abuse of one kind or another. No, what was off-center was that none of the guys he sampled ever got hauled in for testing positive. *None!* Everybody in camp knew that most if not *all* of these Homebloods had either been shooting or scooting ever since the first day they checked in! Those county camps were a regular pharmaceutical bazaar. So why no positive results from the lab?'

'It's a mystery to me,' Clark admitted happily.

'It was to us, too. Quite the mystery . . . until our famous Bakatcha Bandit solved it. Tell Mr Clark what you did, Isaak.'

Isaak shrugged. 'I was in charge of packing the shuttle van for the weekly run to Sacramento. I noticed the stuff in the sample jars wasn't quite the right yellow so I took a sniff. It was colored water.'

'Right! And what do you think Deputy Sweets was doing with all that *Nee*-gro piss, Mr Clark?'

'I'm afraid to speculate,' Clark B answered.

'Isaak Sallas wasn't,' Levertov declared. 'Isaak Sallas speculated so loud the press got the story and the sheriff was forced to mount an investigation. The lab records

386

showed there hadn't been piss in the bottles since Deputy Sweets took over as abuse counselor. The dear deputy stonewalled through it admirably. The county chemist, he testified, was unreliable, so he had been running his own private titrations in his camp cabin. He showed the inquiry squad his own cute little chemistry set and everything. He stone-walled everybody but Slambro here. Tell him, Isaak.'

'It's not one of my prouder moments.'

'Isaak slipped down to Sweets' cabin one night, torched a trash can and yelled, "Fire!" When the deputy ran out to deal with the burning trash Isaak slipped in for some search-and-seizure. The next morning Sweets is on mess-hall watch. Isaak Sallas strolls over to his table and sits down and says he's sorry for any trouble he caused. Sweets says, "Get back to your own area." When Isaak leaves he leaves a little surprise in that empty holster, unbeknownst to anybody until he spins around in a crouch in the center of the hall and yells, "Slap leather, Sweets." What Sweets whips out of his holster is this baby bottle, still half full of yellow liquid. The pig's eyes go *zang zang zang* and he *wigs*. They haul him off in a restraining jacket. The whole camp stands at the barracks' window and waves a victorious goodbye, expecially the Bloods.'

'Victorious?' Ike made a face. 'The replacement guard they brought in popped about three dozen junkies his first week and shipped them back to maximum. Some victory.'

Clark B Clark had to take issue with Sallas' dour appraisal. 'But they weren't being degraded by some racist perv anymore is what Nick is saying. I call that a victory . . .'

'I call it a crock,' Ike said. 'Slow down. Up around that next garbage pile a sow was nursing her litter in the road this morning.'

The sow was gone but some of the piglets were still lounging in the ruts. They scattered before the limo's honking. Two big boars were fighting lackadaisically back up one of the dump's little inroads, disputing the right to a deer carcass that had been dragged free of the smoldering heaps.

'Oh look, CB! There's where Isaak and I had that heartfelt little reunion I told you about. With wife Louise and papa-in-law Omar and other attending swine? Odd, isn't it, Isaak? How we can't seem to get away from the pig farm?'

Before anybody had a chance to respond to Levertov's coaxing purr a wild shape erupted from beneath a clump of roadside salal, sleek and sudden as a black torpedo. It was aimed dead at the limo's front right tire. Clark B Clark wrenched the wheel left, lurching up out of the ruts and into the scattered trash. The fuel tank shrieked across a reef of broken glass and gravel and Clark B had to gun it over, like gunning a boat off a sandbar. Then that crazy thing was around on *his* side, attacking the other tire, hazing the car back over another reef and into the road ruts again.

'What the hell was *that*!' Levertov wheezed through his teeth when the limo had coasted to a halt in the oyster-shell yard. The cant was gone from his voice.

'That's just Marley, Greer's old mutt,' Ike told him. 'He's real old.'

'Moves very well for an old mutt.' Levertov threw back his disheveled tresses with an irritated toss of his head. 'If you'd keep him tied up he might get older still.'

'I haven't seen him jump out at a car like that in years,' Ike protested. 'It's that medication Alice gave him, some new prednisone stereomiser.'

'Money makes the world go round,' Clark B Clark sang, 'but dope makes it jump up and down.'

Levertov was not amused. 'Get out and distract the brute,' he told Clark B. 'I'd like to look over my old cellmate's current accommodations if I don't have to get bit by a wild dog to do it.'

'He's tame and he's toothless,' Ike reassured them and popped his door. The milky afternoon haze blinded him after the tinted gloom of the limo's interior. Ike felt the dog muzzle up under his hand so he could scratch his ears. 'See?' He noticed his Heftyvan had come home. It was parked nosed into the brush with the rear door agape and bedding spilling out over the bumper—just like it looked at that 'heartfelt reunion,' as Levertov called it.

Clark B Clark was sliding cautiously out the driver's door. Marley bounced toward him. 'Wait wait wait,' Clark B commanded in an unconvincing voice, 'there's a nice doggie.' Marley only wanted to smell the hand lotion and get more scratching. 'The brute is subdued, Boss,' Clark B called over his shoulder. 'You may safely disembark.'

The door of the trailerhouse scraped open and Greer stepped out, squinting in the hazy glare as he buttoned up one of his see-through shirts. In his haste he had started the buttoning wrong by two buttonholes; the wide lime-yellow collar jutted crazily, one point down toward an armpit, the other out over a bony shoulder like a dragonfly wing. The squint cleared. 'Hey, Ike man . . . folks . . . anything happ'nin'?'

'Hey, Greer. We missed you at the big media doings.'

'I was doing my Rasta show; but I kept up on ol' Radio Man's shortwave. You come across like the real reluctant dragon, Pardner, you be glad to know. Hey, Mr Levertov! *You* on de other hand came across like God's own Bes' Boy. Mm! Well, get on out, we won't bite. Hey Mr Clark B Clark! I'm not clear on you yet, you know. Is you de *show*fer or is you de *go*fer?'

'I'm de Bes' Boy's best boy,' Clark answered.

The door of the trailer squawked again and a debauched female face peeked into the light. 'Hey, this isn't what it looks like,' Greer was quick to protest when he saw the sensation caused by his guest's ravaged appearance. Her hair looked like the gaudy topknot of a carnival Kewpie. Magenta streaks drained from both eye sockets like diseased tears. The penciled eyebrows were off almost as bad as Greer's misbuttoned shirt and the lipstick wandered around the outskirts of the mouth as though lost. If not for the butterfly tattoos she could have been a total stranger.

389

'Louise is here because she is beside herself with worry. That's all.' The Bob Marley accent was gone. 'The Northdish news ran a sky shot of some wreckage on Mount McKinley and she's worried it could be her brothers' Piper Hyperhol. That's all, wasn't it, Louise?'

'It was black and *blue*!' Louise wailed, reminded suddenly of the cause of her concern. 'Just like Oscar's. And Papa on that tour and Mama at her mama's, you were the only folks I could turn to. My neighbors . . .'

'Louise, *all* the ethenol Pipers are blue with black trim,' Ike tried to reassure the woman. 'The company issued them that way so fuel-pump attendants wouldn't make the—'

His explanation was cut off by a blood-curdling bay; it was Marley again, leaping incredibly all the way across the limo's hood. Levertov had at last stepped out of his door and was just straightening his hair when the howling animal struck him full in the chest. He went down screaming, the dog all over him. Ike and Greer both were instantly on the animal and had him off the man in seconds. It was fortunate all those years of rock-chasing had worn away the points of the dog's big canines, or those few seconds would have left Levertov throatless.

'I *never* see him do that before.' Greer was holding the animal by his bushy mane; Ike had him by the tail.

'You better never see him do it again,' Clark B Clark said. He was holding an Uziette in both hands, its tiny black muzzle leveled at the dog's grey one. But the fit of fury had apparently passed as quickly as it had begun. The old dog was grinning and twisting to get at Ike like a playful puppy.

'He's not usually like this,' Greer apologized.

'Of course not,' Levertov said in his ominous purr. He was on his knees brushing the shells from his sides. 'It's the medication. Put it away, Mr Clark. No harm, no foul . . .'

The gun vanished as mysteriously as it had appeared; small though it was it did not seem possible that Clark

B could hide it anywhere in his hide-tight shorts and T-shirt.

'Git, Marley!' Greer shouted into one of the ragged ears until the dog's eyes hazed over with disbelief and hurt. 'Git!' Greer shouted again and kicked a blast of oyster shells after the tucked tail. The old dog slunk pathetically back to his salal-bush outpost at the entrance to the clearing, like a sergeant stripped of his stripes. Levertov smoothed back his hair and smiled at Louise, atop the trailer's steps. Her hand was still lifted in an ossified attitude of greeting, like one of those plaster lawn boys with the paint all peeling. 'My little lily of the landfill. You look positively ravished.'

The ring-heavy hand fell back like a rock and Louise began to cry, soundlessly, washing both cheeks with a seemingly inexhaustible downpour of magenta. 'This is not how it looks,' Greer repeated. He had an eye on Clark B, trying to figure out where the hell that deadly little Israeli squirt gun was holstered.

'Come on in,' Ike said at last. 'I think we've got some beers.'

The beers were gone. Alice must have drunk them. Anybody else would have left the empties. Ike boiled water for coffee while Louise sobbed out her tangle of troubles in the breakfast nook. She had forgotten her brothers and was now troubled by problems of a more personal nature. Nobody liked her down at the *Silver Fox*. She was a joke to those ritzy bitches. She wasn't even a good twinkie. She was a bimbo! She'd move back home but for the fact that her mother was filing for divorce and her brothers were off somewhere she couldn't remember and she was *not* gonna stay up here all alone with the goddamn bears and boars! Also she'd got the goddamn yeast from somebody! And—what else was it?—O, right, she'd made a phone call to the Princess Tours and her papa was nowhere *aboard*! 'He never even showed up at the *shipping* office,' she sobbed.

Greer patted her hand, making the rings clink against the formica. 'He's just tomcatting around with his old bowling cronies somewhere, Lulu—Anchorage . . . Juneau . . .'

'That's right, Louise,' Ike added. 'Old tomcat on a spree. Look how long Carmody was AWOL.'

'But he never even cashed in his ticket for the *re*fund,' she wailed. 'That's not like Omar Loop. Is it?'

They agreed it was not and Ike poured the coffee. They let her cry herself out. Levertov promised he'd find her someplace nice in town. Greer had crawled in his bunk. Clark B was nodding out in the breakfast nook's corner, lips loose and eyes rolled up to flickering deities on the wide screen of his dreams. When Levertov finally rose to walk Louise to the limo Clark B leapt to attention as though he'd never left. 'All aboard women and white men first! Clark B-as-in-Brass-Hat's got the helm.'

'Not this time,' Levertov told him. 'Give me the card; I'll drive. It's your turn to console the inconsolable Louise.'

Clark B thumped the rubber heels of his deck shoes together smartly and sprung to take Lulu's other arm. Isaak followed them out into the yard. Good thing, too, Clark realized. He was the only one saw that senile sonofabitch crouching to attack again. Nicholas was looking the other way, his rear flank vulnerable. He and Clark B had their hands full with Lulu. She hung between them by her armpits, her head flung limply back. Upside-down, the makeup was beginning to streak the other direction, across her forehead. Her eyes were radiating magenta beams in all directions now. Clark B and Ike were maneuvering her toward the limo door like you would handle a big puppet with its strings tangled when Isaak Sallas shouted, 'Watch it!'—or Nick could have got his back broke. Nick never flinched. He was so cool one might have thought (except *he'd already decided to drive!*) that he *knew* that hound was going to come after him again. What was it dogs had against him? The hair, maybe? But if he had already decided to drive he didn't need a second offense. In fact the second offense *was* a surprise. That's why he hung around in the yard yacking goodbye with Sallas so long, while me and the nutso doll waited in the backseat . . . to give the offender time to get back into position under the bush. By their own design. And when Sallas went back to the trailer and Nicholas got behind the wheel, no more was said about the crazy mutt. Not a word. Nicholas, he played it straight ahead, just driving. He never swerved to hit anything on purpose: he never swerved to miss. Fair's fair. Pure and simple. All he had to do was to keep doing what he was doing and not buckle under to all the little tyrannies society uses to push your button, jerk your chain. Look neither right nor left. Know neither fury nor mercy. Vengeance is fine, sayeth the Big Enchilada— if you play it straight ahead. Vengeance is easy, vengeance is simple. Barely a bump under the floorboards of that cushy old heavy-metal cruiser. Barely a little bump. Left front then rear. Didn't even let on he noticed, let alone slow down. What a guy.

15

Should We Give Our Hearts To a Dog to Tear?

The Underdog Cemetery is sprawled up a steep and seepy five acres of beargrass and boulders located at the top of Cook Street. Cars and four-wheelers and six-wheelers are nosed several deep at the ragged end of the street's pavement, go-peds and three-wheelers and Harleys tucked in between. Scattered clots of mourners meander in a stately stroll all up and down the slope, with more mourners arriving on foot all the time. The meandering is so slow and measured that a vidcam monitor might assume the scene is a loop, running at quarter-speed—until the monitor notices the one incongruous figure with black bow tie and two notebooks and eight shiny glass eyes, spinning from clot to clot like a spider in triple time.

Wayne Altenhoffen was in newshog heaven. When he zaxed and circulated Greer's two hundred black-bordered handbills the evening before, it had been as much in jest as in earnest. He never really expected more than a dozen or so to show besides club members. Certainly nothing like this. The timing all synched, for one thing. A fair-sized fleet of fishermen were lying at anchor, awaiting tomorrow's opening of the midsummer purser session. The movie wasn't working until sets could be repaired, thus the Underdog security force had a free afternoon. The daily crowd of spectators had been turned out of the shoreside audience area so the union grippies could move the bleachers to the next shoot site. These spectators could have hung around and rubbernecked from the parking lot, but declined in favor of this event

394

on the slopes; a dog's funeral up in the wildflowers might not be much, but it would be better than hanging around watching the Teamsters work. More action.

The Loyal Order of the Underdogs had purchased the five-acre parcel of land back in their salad days, when the enthusiasm to build the Home for Lost Puppies was still scooting high. The piece of land had always been considered completely useless by bankers and builders—even by the buy-anything, build-anywhere Asiatics—but the Underdogs were more visionary. They saw the rocky slope as the ideal site for their much-heralded puppy project. The top third of the acreage angled into the ragged treeline of the Pyrites, where the poor orphans would have a nice wilderness to romp in. There were year-round seep springs for drinking and mud-rolling. For sniffing and digging there were lemming burrows in complicated crisscrosses among all the big basalt boulders, and there was a clear, wide view to the southeast and northwest where you could sit and howl at the moon when she rode by in full bright gallop. Mainly, the parcel was cheap. Conveniently close to the town's center though the location was, no real estate hustler had ever sought to develop it. Too steep and unstable. The only structure in the clearing was the town's original wooden water tower, and over the years the repeated mudslides had made it possible to step directly on to the catwalk at the rear of the big barrel, though the ladder at the front was still a climb of some twenty rungs. That unstable. True, the site offered what would have been a top-dollar bay-window view, but a homebuilder would have had to cantilever the front door twenty or thirty feet higher off the ground than the back door to have the floor level. Young dog legs, on the other hand, needed no level floor; and the tilt of their orphanage would in all likelihood prove beneficial, the club conjectured—*exercise*-wise. So they bought the place outright and had enough cash left over to begin their dog shelter of mercy.

The rocks were the first obstacles to thwart their noble intentions. These jagged outcroppings were lots harder to move than anyone ever imagined. After breaking two cats and a backhoe, Mrs Herb Tom observed, 'It's like trying to grub out one of those Easter Island stone heads and finding out the body is attached belowground.' The whole club spent all one Labor Day weekend laying a gravel road between the jagged abutments so they could at least drive the supplies from Cook's End up to the building site. The result of their labor was a poor excuse for a road. It zigzagged like a broken, dirty snake through the immovable rocks; but it could be driven. Then the night after the road was finished a little tremor twitched down the flank of the Pyrites. A 3.6 or 4. Nothing. Except the next day's dawn revealed that the road was gone. It had been completely returfed with bright green grass and salal. Everything above the road had simply slid down to conceal the unsightly gash.

By the end of that summer the Underdog enthusiasm had scooted away. Naturally, nobody wanted to buy the piece back from the discouraged club members, so it became, eventually and just as naturally, the final resting place of the Underdogs' deceased. At first it was only for the four-footed, but one June day it opened up to also include members that had once walked upright but had died too down-and-out to afford better accommodations.

A poor cracked-minded mute called Slobbering Bob Spitz was the first two-legged member that was honored with interment in the hallowed ground of the Underdogs, though to say that he walked upright would be a ways from the truth. Slobbering Bob had no toes, his knees were locked in a permanent half-crouch, and his spine was ossified from his ribs down. When he walked he bent so low that his matted beard sometimes brushed the ground. The catastrophe that had cracked his mind had done the same to his back and knees. No-one ever found out his real name. A 'Bob' was located on the collar of his tattered T-shirt, and his bristly beard and sideburns suggested that he might have some Spitz blood. No-one learned his history, though the pitiful way he whimpered whenever he saw a big king-crabber heave into sight, piled high with its precarious towers of crab pots and pounded raw by the icy Arctic seas, gave the members a pretty good idea what had happened to the man. As the king crab had become scarcer, the waters the bug-hunters had to work had become fiercer. Survivors of crab-boat tragedies weren't hard to spot. The spine is shattered by a falling tower of ice-heavy pots. The kneecaps go as the boat heels over. The toes freeze and swell and putrefy and crack in the days adrift in a survival pod. It's easy for whatever mind that's left to soon follow the broken body.

Nameless and penniless, there was no place for Bob Spitz in the Rest Haven Cemetery grounds. None of the Deap or Catholic charities would claim him. President Sallas decided the club would handle the funeral and burial, permits be damned. The members nailed Spitz in the packing case that the club's fireplug lectern had been shipped in from Taiwan (a regular coffin would never have held the crooked corpse anyway), then they bore him defiantly from one end of town to their cemetery at the other. They buried him at the foot of one of the massive grey blocks of basalt. With a routing tool they etched his name into a flat surface on the monolith: 'Slobbering Bob—Spitz—He Looked Up To Everything'—just like they had etched the names and breeds of dozens of other departed dogs on other obelisks. The fact that the poor wretch had been so nearly on all fours anyway was probably what persuaded the authorities to let this unauthorized cross-creature burial pass. But he was only the first. Two Deap members were next. Drunk on a mutual bottle of Mad Dog 50-50, they had shot and killed each other with a .270 Magnum they each had a mutual half-interest in. It seemed right that they share the same hole. When both the native and Round-Eye authorities flatly denied the request, the Dog Brothers dug their own double-wide grave. It was quicker, cozier, and much cheaper.

The Wongs, who owned Rest Haven, saw a trend in the making and launched a vigorous legal battle to stop it. They were about to triumph in the courts when something happened that made them surrender their fight: their youngest adopted son got blown off the deck of a processor during a stormy drinking bout. The boy's body was never found, but his sea-bag revealed a journal. The last entry in the book recorded the boy's dearest wishes. More than anything else in the world, he wrote, he wished to become an Underdog when he attained legal age, to run with the mangy pack all the rest of his days, then be buried with his Dog Brothers up on the stony steep among the boulders where the moon goes galloping. The Wongs took it as a last will and testament, and the club inducted the lad posthumously. The act became rather fashionable for a while in some of the suicide-prone high schools around the area. In the years since the Wong boy's honorary induction, the Loyal Order of the Underdogs had pledged, initiated, inducted and then buried no fewer than five other defunct aspirants—three of them under thirteen. 'So, in a weird and rather wonderful way,' Wayne Altenhoffen wrote in the three-by-five notepad, 'the rocky slope has become a sort of Home for Lost Puppies after all.' Sets the old bean spinning.

But this was no callow pup they were planting today. This was no honorary inductee. This was—as Sergeant-at-Arms Norman Wong tearfully put it in his opening invocation—'a real damn boney-fed Underdog *old-timer*!'

Perhaps the oldest of us all, Altenhoffen mused, dog-year-wise. Marley had been around from the very beginning. He had attended that historic Holy Confinement beneath the rock 'n' roll bleachers in Seattle, where the tender seeds of the club first found root. Marley had in fact been one of the principal causes of that confinement, Altenhoffen recalled. Before the show, in the hot rear of the parking lot where the will-callies shoved and idled, one of the Dreadful Great's high-strung old ladies had started it. She had sicced her high-strung brace of purebred Dobermans on Marley because Marley was relieving himself on the front right fender of her pearlescent limo. At her command the Dobermans had exploded out each side window like blood-seeking missiles. They homed in on the big amiable collie mongrel from both sides, making a hellacious racket all the way. Slow to anger, Marley tried backing away and reasoning. Land for piss, he grinned. He was even willing to roll over and expose himself to the pair's hysterical haranguing, rather than do battle. But when they rudely went so far as to actually *snap* at his yielded privates—an act against all codes of canine civility, worldwide—Marley was left with no recourse but to roll back up to all fours and reluctantly break both their purebred but uncivilized necks.

'So this is no lightweight wag a-burying,' Altenhoffen scribbled; 'this is one of the founding fathers of the Loyal Order of the Underdogs, as well as a citizen held in affectionate high regard by the rest of the Kuinak community.'

This was evident by the unprecedented crowd that had gathered for Old Marley's graveside ceremony. Altenhoffen could think of only one other departed Loved One who had attracted this large a crowd—Great-Grandfather Toogiak. And that had been an event with such extensive history and hype that it wasn't a fair comparison. Great-Grandfather Toogiak had been around the area one hundred and six years previous to cashing in his chips, then another fifty-four days longer before his ceremonies were finished. As per instructions his Deap relatives from both moieties had marinated the toothless old shaman for two full moons in a carved dugout full of eulachon oil. It didn't take long for people to get wind of an event like this, even from a considerable distance. When they at last torched off the rank finale of these rites in the parking lot behind the Searaven First National, three major dishworks were there to cover it, and Deaps and Deap lawyers and Deap-lickers from as far away as Washington DC had choppered in to pay their respects.

There were nearly as many in attendance this afternoon for Old Marley's last rites—and he had lain in state less than a day. All the Dogs were present, with the traditional white paper bags they carried to toss into the grave. A lot of them had even changed their Foxcorp Security jackets for shirts and ties. Most of the fishermen that still lived in town were there. Marley used to be a popular dock-hound, famous for the big friendly grin he always had for the guys on the returning boats. There was a cluster of the Main Street crowd, clerks and merchants and barkeeps who fondly remembered him for the pacifying effect he'd had on the other latchkey mutts that roamed Main. Back on the edge of the crowd was a shadowy contingent of fishkids, most of whom likely only knew the animal by reputation—'Ike Sallas' dog . . . ate a Dreadful groupie'—and farther back still a small but respectful delegation from the movie. Altenhoffen recognized Nicholas Levertov and his lieutenant, plus director Steubins, plus assorted mixed twinkies. This decorous delegation had even eschewed their limo, they were so respectful; they had all walked up the hill in somber silence. But they were all costumed so elaborately for the occasion that it was hard not to see their presence as a kind of send-up. The spectral old director was decked out in a grey silk eye patch with matching ascot. Clark B Clark was without his gum and was wearing full-length trousers instead of surfer shorts, and the twinkies had all been outfitted in identical mourning attire, black suits, black felt hats, face nets and all.

But it was Levertov's costume that pushed the line. The black armband he had tied around the sleeve of his white overcoat was several yards long; it dragged behind him in the dirt like a tail. There was something explicit in the untrimmed oversight, Altenhoffen thought. Even more so in the overcoat. Altenhoffen changed one pair of eyeglasses for a closer focus and eased around the rock to see if any of the other Dog Brothers had flashed to the send-up Levertov and his lackeys seemed to be putting on. Ike Sallas might not be in a mood for any campy graveside humor from these clowns. Not from what Greer said. When Greer had dropped by the *Beacon* office the night before with the copy for the funeral announcement, Altenhoffen's nose for news had picked up something juicy.

'I'm worried for my man Ike, Poor Brain. I fear he's gettin' the shaky noids. He ain't scootin', he ain't shootin', he ain't tootin', but he gettin' 'em anyway.'

'Isaak Sallas shaky? Seems unlikely, Emil. Isaak Sallas has always been a veritable Gibraltar.' Lowering his voice, Altenhoffen had pointed toward the back room where Billy was firing off his latest fax. 'And compared to *some*, Ike's Mount Everest. How*ever*,' he took out his notebook, 'the noids such as? If we can be specific . . . ?'

At Altenhoffen's professional prompting, Greer had recounted various misgivings that Ike had expressed about Levertov and the action he was laying on his hometown—that Ike had a sick suspicion the motive behind all this was not movie-making, or even money-making . . . it was revenge-taking! Wayne's brain spun not. That wasn't news. Lots of people had had those misgivings, himself among them. Then Greer had told about Ike tweaking when they found the dog. ' "Levertov done it!" he yells. I never hear him yell like that before. He also thinks Levertov popped Omar Loop and the twins—rubbed 'em flat *out*.'

That had set off some bells. True or not, that was the kind of lead that had spin on it. 'MOVIE MOGUL POPS PAPA-IN-LAW! Reliable Source Fears Worst.'

This was what had set him printing and distributing the handbills with such dispatch, and had him up to the cemetery with *both* notebooks, spinning around like a hungry spider. He loved gossip, and came by his love naturally; Wayne Altenhoffen was heir to a line of veins that had pumped the ink of journalistic curiosity around Kuinak for nearly a century. *Real* curiosity, not the feigned interest of the ambitious reporter on the rise. The Altenhoffen family had put out the *Bay Beacon* since the first nosy ancestor from pre-Holocaust Germany had ended up in Kuinak with an Olivetti. The first *Beacons* were typed, over and over, with five carbons. They sold for one cent and always began with the biblical quote 'As Cold Waters to a Thirsty Soul, so is Good News from a Far Country' at the top of the page as the paper's credo. The *un*written credo that the generations had handed down was closer to the point as well as to the heart of the Altenhoffen family philosophy: 'False or True, Gossip is the Glue That Holds a Hometown Together.' And *this* showed promise of being indeed some sticky stuff: 'Local Cult Hero Links Entertainment Entrepreneur to Disappearance of Prominent Prize-winning Bowler.' Spin and glue both.

Altenhoffen slipped on his medium-close-range lenses and peeked around the basalt rock beneath which Marley's grave yawned. He couldn't tell if Isaak Sallas had noticed the arrival of Levertov and his costumed contingent or not. His face was as impervious as a profile stamped on an old coin. All one could deduce from Ike's expression was that he was as impatient with the overlong ceremony as everybody else. Norman Wong's eulogy seemed to go on forever. For close to half an hour he had sobbed out stories of every dog he could remember, all the way back to his first springer spaniel. *Every*body got antsy, but not antsy enough to argue with a seven-foot crying jag packing a .44 Colt. Then Greer did a Rastaman prayer that was so ethnic nobody could tell what language it was in. Now, Mrs Herb Tom was toiling through a lugubrious version of 'Old Shep.' President Bellisarius was waiting to wrap it up. He held a copy of the club's chapbook that he glanced into from time to time with a kind of begrudging attention. The pages fluttered in his thin fingers like leaves in a winter wind. The little man seemed so wan and wasted that Altenhoffen found himself fearing that if Mrs Herb Tom didn't speed it up they could end up burying more than one member.

Mrs Herb Tom finally finished and folded away her Casio. Billy closed the chapbook and stepped to the graveside. He frowned into the hole, his face looking more feverish than funereal. Everybody waited. But the Squid seemed sunk in such deep and raging thought that all he could do was glare into the ground. He stood so long without speaking that the crowd began to mutter and fidget in the still afternoon light. Sallas was the one that finally prompted him from his reverie.

'Say your say, Squid. We've got other things to think about.'

The troubled face rose from the ground, like a mushroom opening. 'I don't really have a say,' he snarled. 'And I, also, have other things to think about. I liked Old Marley, though. He was decent. He got old. He had a last romp. He died. I did come up with a bit of doggerel that seems apt.' He took a last glance in the book, then raised his face to the rest of the crowd. 'Here is what a nineteenth-century poet had to say on the subject— Englishman, named Kipling. "The Power of the Dog." And these are words of warning, Dog Brothers, as much as mourning.'

He closed the book, and after another long frowning silence began to recite from memory:

> There is sorrow enough in the natural way,
> From men and from women, to fill our day;
> And when we are certain of sorrow in store,
> Why do we always arrange for more?
> *Brothers and Sisters, I bid you beware*
> *Of giving your heart to a dog to tear.*
>
> Buy a pup and you think you buy
> Love unflinching that cannot lie;
> Perfect passion and friendship, fed
> By a curse as well as a pat on the head
> *Nevertheless it is hardly fair*
> *To risk your heart for a dog to tear.*
>
> When the short term of years which Nature permits
> Is ending in asthma, or fever, or fits,
> And the vet's unspoken prescription runs
> To lethal chambers or leveled guns
> *You'll find it's also your affair*
> *And that you've given your heart to a dog to tear.*

When the thing that lived at your single will
With its whimper of welcome, is still (how still),
And the spirit that answered your every word
Is gone, wherever it goes, for good,
You will discover how much you did dare
When you gave your heart to a dog to tear.

We've debt enough in the natural way
When it comes to burying two-legged clay;
For treasures aren't given, but only lent,
At compound interest of building percent,
And though I've no firm figures I firmly believe
That the longer they're borrowed, the deeper we
grieve

Yet, when debts come due, for right or for wrong
A short-term loan seems as bad as a long
So why in hell, before we're called there
Should we give our hearts to a dog to tear?

The ol' Squid still had the stuff, Altenhoffen noted
with pride. The poem left everybody as seepy as the
slope they stood on. Big Norman Wong was baying like
a heartbroken hound.

The eyelids lifted; the sulky little man kicked a few
clods into the hole, then hurried stiff-backed through
the crowd toward town, without another word. After the
doggie bags were tossed in, Norman Wong proffered
the silver spade and Isaak Sallas started shoveling the
moist purple dirt back into the hole. Altenhoffen snapped
a quick cover shot with his Fuji and the crowd began to
disperse. That did it for the funeral. Filler copy. Public
interest, but not very. Altenhoffen strolled around the
boulder to stand beside Sallas, his notebooks at the ready.
It was Ike got in the first questions.

'What's with the four sets of glasses, Poor Brain?'

'I scrounged them out of Grandpa Altenhoffen's rolltop.
My eyes got so cooked with that brew Billy brought back

I can't wear my contacts. Stiff stuff, Isaak. A pot'll stretch forever . . .'

'Is that what's wrong with the Squid? He looks like death stretched out to dry.'

Altenhoffen shook his head. 'The poor Squid is badly spooked, Isaak. A lot more spooked than stretched. This morning's *Victorian Mail* reported the Canadian government came down heavy on that place of Greener's last night—about twenty tons' worth, it sounded like.'

'Why should that spook Billy? Wasn't that the point of all these broadsides you two've been firing off?'

'Because the Good Reverend got away is why. Nobody knows where he is.'

'And now the Squid's afraid Greener's going to come all the way up here after his ass?' Ike laughed. 'That's just scoot fantasy, Poor Brain. Everybody knows Billy's always been a little paranoid. Greener, on the other hand, he's a very *big* paranoid. A *mega*lomaniac. He's got way bigger worlds to conquer than our crummy little Kuinak.'

'You mean unlike your friend Levertov over there?'

'What are you talking about?'

Altenhoffen avoided Ike's sharp glance. 'The Squid told me about the "fantasy" you ran by him out on the boat. Your suspicions about Levertov's plans for our crummy little Kuinak? Now Greer tells me you think the man ran down your dog, not to mention *other* souls. Ike Sallas, the poor brain boggles—'

'Bellisarius had no right to pass on that kind of dirt. Neither did Greer. Especially to a goddamned nosy newshound.'

Altenhoffen was stung. He changed his writing specs for his mid-range horn-rims—the horn-rims lent him a look of scholarly indignation, he felt—and said in a wounded voice, 'I wasn't *just* being nosy, Isaak; I was also being Brotherly.' He shoved the small notebook into his shirt pocket, the larger one into his belt, then held up his empty palms. 'This is all off the record unless you say otherwise—Dog's Honor. You know me: I want to know what people think. I *like* dishing the dirt; publishing it is incidental. So dish nosy old Brother Poor Brain up some dirt, Isaak. Please.'

Isaak took the newsman by an elbow and steered him away from the others, up the slope. The rock they stopped beneath was Slobbering Bob's.

'I don't have any dirt, Poor Brain. Not a speck. Greer was right. All I had was a flare-up of old-fashioned paranoia. I mean, there was bear sign in the mud all around the carcass. But did I see any *limo*usine sign? Not a speck.'

'What about old Omar and the Loop twins?'

'What about them? I don't even have the luxury of a corpus delicti for that fantasy. So drop it, Altenhoffen. I have.'

'That doesn't sound like our old Bakatcha bulldog of all these wild years past. I remember speeches so hot people—'

'Maybe all those years finally taught an old dog to drop the bone *before* he gets his tail in hot water, trying to avenge crimes he can't, ah, prove—'

'That so?' Altenhoffen was on the lie before it was all the way out, like an oyster-catcher on a kelpworm. 'Then why do I detect dark thoughts still seething beneath this cool exterior?'

'Drop it, Poor Brain—or you might find yourself bopped on your butt in that hole with Old Marley.'

'O, I don't think so,' Altenhoffen grinned. 'Isaak Sallas would never bop a man smaller than himself, especially one wearing four pairs of eyeglasses.'

He would have pressed further into Isaak's fretful fantasies about malevolent movie people if their little off-the-record tête-à-tête in the cemetery had not been interrupted.

'Hey, Mr Isaak Sallas! We have some things for you.'

It was the Eskimo teenager, right behind them. She was standing barefoot in the soggy bear grass, holding her baby sister's hand and a fat husky pup under her arm. She was wrapped in some kind of flowery South Sea sarong that could only have come from Alice's wardrobe.

'Mrs Carmody sent you up a letter.'

She pushed the little sister brusquely forward and the child handed Ike a wadded pink ball. Unwadded, it became a sheet of Bear Flag Inn stationery. Both girls' eyes remained unblinking on Ike's face while he read the message out loud.

'"Sallas: Carmody plans to shove off with tomorrow's tide and anchor out at the boundary. He wants you and Greer at *Cobra* at sundown. Alice."' Ike looked up at the older girl. 'So the Carmodys are speaking again?'

'On the phone machine. He come round last night and Mrs Carmody and Mrs Hardesty squirt him with fire squirters. The letter isn't all we bring you.' She was studying Ike's face so intently that the veins in her brow were pulsing from the effort. She held up the sleeping puppy; it wobbled and drooped over her hands like a fluffy doll filled with jelly. 'Mrs Carmody says you can have Worthless, she's a fine puppy—to take place of your dog you lose.'

'It wasn't my dog. Greer!' he yelled over the head of the girl. 'You ready for a replacement for Marley?'

Greer stepped back from the hole and wiped imaginary sweat from his eyes. 'We don't even got the old one cover up yet, mon. Dese t'ings dey take time, y'know . . . de propah period of mourning. Let's think about it a few days, y'know?'

'I'm afraid we don't have that luxury. Carmody wants us at the boat at sundown. Sounds like he's ready to try his new gizmos.'

'O my; O me—' Greer wearily passed the shovel on to Susan Boswell and started up the hill toward the group, shaking his tasseled head with exaggerated fatigue— 'de whip of de sea.'

The girl paid Greer's theatrics no attention, continuing to hold Ike's face in the ferocious grip of her gaze whether he let himself look down at her or not. When Ike didn't take the pup she thrust it into her sister's arms and stepped more directly in front of him. She stood there, raw and defiant, her bare brown feet planted wide in

407

the turf, her bare arms crossed beneath the sarong's flowery bosom, too beautiful to bare. Altenhoffen had never thought of himself as a woman-watcher—far from it—so he was surprised and mortified to hear himself moan half out loud at the picture she made there in the afternoon glow. For the first time he appreciated what Greer and the town's other eyeballers meant by 'off the tootsie scale.' Here was a treasure so rare that it could not be assessed by conventional measurements. The legs were far too short to model stockings, the hips and chest too broad and confrontational for a centerfold. The face was wide and flat as a summer sea, and the dark islands of the eyes were set so far apart you needed a compass to sail from one to the other. But the whole unlikely composition worked, like a great painting. In fact, the way she stood with her arms crossed beneath that abundance of flowers made Altenhoffen think of Gauguin's island girl bearing that platter of fruits.

'What with you, Mr Isaak Sallas?' the girl demanded. 'The soaps say all the time, "No man is the island." Don't you want no life's companion like they talk about?'

The offer was as naked and undeniable as a slap. Mr Isaak Sallas gave her a fatherly look—the kind you keep ready for kids with crushes. 'Shoola, honey . . . that stuff is just soapdish crap. Nobody lives like that anymore. Right, you guys?' He turned to Greer and Altenhoffen for verification. They each nodded, each trying to clothe the girl's naked offer with the whole cloth of their own shabby smiles: 'Right . . . absolutely . . . soapdish crap.' Then the girl's eyes were brimming with angry tears.

'You people are . . . *crazy*.' There was an awe in her voice as she realized this. 'Nobody up home would say no to a nice fat pup like this. If she don't work out for a life's companion we can always eat her or something. *No*body would say no. But you people . . .' She looked from Altenhoffen with his slanted bow tie and his four sets of eyes, to Greer's ludicrous ogle, like a lascivious lingcod ogling out of his kelpy lair of dreadlocks, to Isaak Sallas' threadbare excuse for a fatherly face . . .

then around wildly at the group of citizens strolling like sleepwalkers among the huge stones . . . wildly, wildly, until the angry tears came skipping down her cheeks: 'All of you people. Crazy. I'll be glad when I go home.'

16

The Ways of Man Are Passing Strange
He Buys His Freedom and He Counts His
*   Change*
Then He Lets the Wind His Days Arrange
And He Calls the Tide His Master

—was the theme song Carmody had chosen for their purser shake-down. It might have been composed especially for this session, for this very season, but Carmody claimed he'd learned it from a last-century folk trio called Bok, Muir and Trickett. He heard that Bok had adapted it from a fisherman's lament from the century before that. Some things only change by getting more and more the way they've always been.

The chorus was so universal and timeless it might have been wafted on melancholy breezes across any forlorn fishing village anywhere, all the way back to the first crude dory-shells in the dim dawn of time:

> *Ah, the days; ah, the days*
> *Ah, those fine long summer days—*
> *The fish come rollin' in the bays*
> *And I thought they'd roll forever . . .*

The second verse, however, had a more regional ring to it, a more contemporary tone—and was getting more so every day:

> *But the days grow short and the job gets old*
> *And the fish won't come where the sea ain't cold*

And if we're gonna fill the hold
We got to go way out to find them.
Ah, the days; ah, the days . . .

When the session bell sounded at dawn most of the
fleet went foaming full-throttle across the boundary line,
their gear still stowed, their underwater fish-finders re-
tracted to reduce drag. A lot of the pursers had already
cased the near-shore waters; all anybody had spotted
were a few meager blips of hake and eulachon, sprinkled
here and there in the blue-green buzz of the display
screens. 'Got to go way out to find them.' So way out
they went, as fast as their sea-splitting, diesel-guzzling,
bankrupting boats could carry them.

When Carmody's ultraspeed *Cobra* pulled far enough
away from the pack that they were out of sight, he throttled back so they could lever out the little finder dishes
on each side of the keel. There weren't even any hake
blips on the screens. He scanned along at trolling speed
until he saw the riggings of the pack approaching, then he
pulled in the pair of underwater eyes and foamed farther
out. All day they did this. Once, for two hours, they
chased a promising signal of something on the starboard
screen. The blip dodged and dipped before them until
it finally turned up an alley of kelp and vanished, like
a street gang eluding the heat. They never did find out
for certain what it was. 'A school of South American
skipjacks,' Greer had guessed, 'skippin' dey school and
come north for va*cation* . . .'

The sea was flat and the sky clear enough they were
able to cruise and hunt all night. But the pack kept
catching up, and all those blinking lights and beeping
signals finally got on Carmody's nerves.

'These disturbances are scarin' the fish, is my thinkin'.
What d'ye say, boys? Let's go where the blinkin' blaggars
ain't. I know a little spot off the mouth of Pyrite Creek . . .'

He wheeled the vessel in a wide burbling turn to the
port and struck a course to the southeast, through
the dark. Carmody suggested they take advantage of

411

the time by studying the manuals on the new purser equipment; then he put the helm on auto and cracked out his concertina. 'The Ways of Man' provided him the ideal text for the evening's theme. The song had pathos. It had pertinence. And while it may not have been as obvious to him as it was to gloomy Isaak Sallas or the tangle-headed Emil Greer, the song also had a nice dark undercurrent of irony:

> Ah, you tides; ah, you tides
> Ah, you dark and you bitter tides
> If I can't have her by my side
> I guess I'll have to leave her.

Greer was so glad to be cruising shoreward he didn't mind Carmody's serrated tenor slicing up the silence in the wheelhouse. And it gave him a chance to chew the breeze with Ike without the old Cornishman listening in. He was a little worried with the way his friend had tweaked after finding the dead dog, and more than a little resentful about Ike's attempts to try to stretch his suspicions to cover the whole Hollywood show. Those movie people had been nothing but nice, Greer insisted. 'They's just folks, Pardner, lighten up. Under all dat flash and zam, dey's all just folks.'

To try to distract Isaak from stewing about wrongs and retaliations, Greer kept the topside scuttlebutt steered in another direction whenever possible, toward a subject that as far as he was concerned was ten times more enticing than the most voluptuous vendetta man ever stewed up.

'There's a t'ing young sea lionesses dey *do*, mon' was one way he steered into the subject, 'when dey get too randy, y'know? Waitin' for dere turn on top de rock with the big bull-daddy?'

'What sea lionesses?'

'Sea lionesses I used to watch when I was fishing the Oregon coast around Wakonda. Whoa! You'd see 'em cruisin' the surf line, see, all lounged back and lonely. What they do is keep a *hind flipper* hoisted out of the water, you know, mon? Like a signal flag for any young sea lion jack who be on the lone and horny *too*. Jack can tell as soon as he sees that flipper: she cruisin', mon; she's got on her high-heel fuck-me flippers and she is *cruisin*'!'

Greer had done one of his shows for The Radio Man after they got back from Skagway—'Masta Rasta, Mouf de Souf!' His accent was still strong on him.

Ike didn't look up from the purseware manual on his lap. 'Greer, I don't know what the hell you're talking about.'

'Ain't I talkin' about *romance*, mon? Birds-and-bees *basics*? I seen the way that hot little Eskimo Pie offer herself up to you yesterday. Dat's sweet as it gets, *mon confrère*. My advice is go ahead and sink your long yellows in it even it drag you to your doom . . .'

Ike seemed relieved and scandalized all at once. 'That *girl*? Jesus, Greer, not even you would take that kind of advantage.'

'Advantage? I am to laugh, ho-*ho*! Dat girl she swallow *three* of you with fries and de Coca-Cola it comes to taking advantage. She is a *wild* thing, mon.' Greer went into a reggae scat and soft shoe, right where he sat: 'Wild *Thing*! . . . uh uh *uh* uh . . . you make my *ding sting*!'

'Belay that!' Carmody called from his swivel stool at the control board where he had been eavesdropping. He had just finished his second fifth of Irish and was ready to have another go at the concertina. 'If there's to be any profane songs sung aboard this bucket, I'll by God be the one sings 'em.' He and his instrument wheezed together:

> *Polarpussy's a fantastic creature;*
> *Dark, and covered with hair.*
> *It looks like the face of a preacher*
> *And smells like the ass of a bear.*
> *Ah, the nights; ah, the nights*
> *Ah, them long dark winter nights . . .*

We romped and rolled in the Northern Lights
Till the ice thawed from beneath us.

Greer was sorry to note that the glum Isaak didn't even smile.

They made landfall just as first light was showing over the Pyrites and got a reading on the finders as soon as they put them out. All three men were gathered at the com in the wheelhouse, studying the signal.

'They're probably just silvers, boys, and piddlin' damn few o' them at that, it looks like; but they're all we've seen. Let's stow these damn manuals and do a set. I want to try this fancy new foofaraw afore it rusts. Stations, all! And step sprightly.'

One of the features hyped by the builders of Carmody's new multipurpose was the boat's ability to perform all the tasks of any eight-man fishing operation with a crew of two, though the manuals recommended having an extra hand on hand until the hard- and software became familiar. It was taken for granted that Greer was that extra hand. Zipped as usual in his cumbersome survival suit, he couldn't be expected to step too sprightly. But Carmody had wanted him along instead of one of the nimbler Culligan boys; the sea-fearing fop might not make much of a sailor but he was the best mechanic Carmody had ever seen perform, especially when something went blooey in a deep-water situation. Terror seemed to guide the long black fingers the way divine Providence guided the idiot savant at the keyboard. Greer could repair machinery he couldn't see, and that he'd never seen before, in gales that would have blinded most machinist's mates.

Luckily, the summer waters were still holding smooth, because it turned out they needed all the divine guidance they could get with Carmody's fancy foofaraw. That boat's fish-finder system was supposed to beam out beneath the surface, bounce back information about pockets of potential prey, then steer you there. Then all you supposedly had to do was push a button to initiate the drop. The boat's brochures claimed the whole procedure—hunt, drop and haul-in—could be accomplished by two men in well under an hour. But for some reason the autopilot seemed very circumspect about following fish signals this close to shore. It kept buzzing for compass verification and veering off the chase, and Carmody would have to go clanging and cursing back to the wheelhouse and take control of the helm manually, leaving Ike and Greer to work it out on the afterdeck.

One man would toggle the roboat and run the command panel above the net; the other would assist from a work cage where he could lean out and make sure the floats fed off properly by prompting them with a peavy pole. Naturally, Greer wanted the task of maneuvering the remote-controlled cylinder around in its clever circle, but it was evident from the first that he was completely without talent at the ten-toggle. The roboat just would not obey him. After the second try Carmody called down on the squawk box: 'Another waterhaul! Greer, damn ye . . . next time you handle the picker pole and the floats and give Ike that roboat gizmo. Leave the remote-control stuff to a skilled pilot. Now, both of ye—haul in and load for another drop. Let's see if we can't get at least *some* of our by God forty minutes' worth!'

Like all legitimate pursers the drop readouts were monitored by strict international regulations; times and positions were outlinked directly to UN stations up and down all the fishing grounds. A seine had to be dropped, circled, set and closed in less than forty minutes, and out of the water in under an hour. One minute longer and a UN warden would be chopping his way to your coordinates. You could have your whole lash-up confiscated. It was another right idea being enforced on the wrong people; everybody knew that Chinese drift-subs were still putting out miles of their lethal web illegally, but the United Nations wardens found it easier to hassle the smaller operations.

After two more sets they were beginning to get it right.

Carmody carried down granola bars and two quarts of milk. 'We'll have something hot later. Oh, they are here, boys. I can smell 'em.'

On the next set they drew the string on a swirl of small silvers, not many, but Carmody got so excited by this first success that he throttled backward too fast and caught the rising purse in one of the props. The fish shimmered away through the tear. Cursing, he boomed the net on deck, where Greer was able to patch the hole with a heat spindle. It would hold until they got back home to the web-weaver. But Carmody was a little depressed by the mishap. 'It don't bode well when you rip your new net afore you get one by God fish. Not your best omen.'

He looked west, scratching his belly. The sun was sliding fast toward the unbroken horizon.

'Let's drop the hook, lads. We'll have a nice supper and recharge our willy-works, get a proper spry start in the mornin'. Because they are here, boys, and they'll still be here tomorrow. Then watch us lay into the finny devils!'

He was right about the bad omen but wrong about the fish. The next day they roamed all up and down the ten-mile stretch of coast without a signal. They tried some blind sets for practice, and were getting smoother and surer at their position. But each time the net came up empty except for a few jellyfish and kelp fronds in the top of the purse. The following day they boated one haul of assorted bottom-fish and one meager haul of hake—then more empty sacks. Each set took them a couple of hours, even with the forty-minute pull-up. The automatic web folder was nowhere near as automatic as the brochures claimed, and the roboat didn't seem to like slipping back into its waterline slot. It bumped and veered in the running swells until Ike was cursing and Greer was laughing at him. 'This skilled pilot ain't so hot in tight places, Cap'n,' he called toward the squawk box. 'Maybe some hair around de hole would help.'

Carmody got so he could hold the boat perfectly with the little side turbines, keeping the prow into the swell.

Greer would fork off the gaudy orange floats as Ike maneuvered the cylinder out in a long, whirring loop, then back beneath the bow. Greer would hook the roboat's trailing line with his pole and pull the line into the slide ring on the boom winch. Ike pushed a button; the roboat's deadeye would release the line and the little remote would be momentarily free, bucking in the swells like a silver wienie in a boiling kettle, until Ike maneuvered it into its teflon slot. They were all getting good at their tasks. All they lacked was the fish.

They picked up a lot of other stuff. Seaweed. Porpoises. Once they thought they'd finally struck it, but when the purse surfaced they saw they had only bagged an ancient driftnet snarl—a huge ball of Molecumar web and fish skeletons that took an hour to pick free of their purse. The reports over the marine frequencies were almost as snarled—a dozen dialects and languages at once. All they could be sure of was 'Zip . . . de nada . . . diddly squat, squeak, squawk.'

They were also picking up some Tinkerbells on the deck. Greer spotted the first one. 'Fuck Mary, mon, I *told* you! *That's* one of the unholy mothers . . .'

Greer was pointing at a spot of light on the deck near the aft hatch. It was a gently fluttering figure eight, each loop of the intersecting figure about the size of a mayonnaise jar lid. It fluttered a moment, then vanished. Ike had not really believed in the phenomenon until then. 'I wonder why they got named Tinkerbells?'

'Because they looks like Tinker's squashed *spirit*, mon' had been Greer's forensic interpretation. 'Like Captain Hook he *stomp* the bitch!'

Carmody had yet to see any of these phenomena. He was in the wheelhouse most of the time, furiously trying to get the hang of the craft's complicated chipware. Whenever they spotted one of the little lights it was always gone by the time he made it out to see what they were hollering about.

'A fluttering figure eight, ye say? *I* say it's either a little spot of St Elmo's or too much of that Squid tea.'

417

On their fourth day out Carmody had them curled around south of Pyrite Cape, checking a little cove. It was an unlikely spot because there wasn't any freshwater outlet. Carmody was getting a little desperate, trying such a location. The weather was still calm, the sky was a foreboding dark blue. The water looked sluggish as tar. A breeze coming off the land was so warm that Greer decided to peel out of the sweaty neoprene suit. He was half out when Carmody's voice barked over the intercom.

'I've got a feeding swirl! Huge one! This is it, lads. We're homed and running. Stand by to drop at my command . . .'

'Oy vey,' Greer yawned and pulled the suit back up over his shoulders. Ike stepped to the panel and pushed OPEN. The cover over the fantail rolled back with a metallic yawn. The net lay in neat gossamer folds, floats loaded on the spring gun like day-glo orange doughnuts on a big pogo stick. The roboat's bullet nose could be seen protruding from its firing tube. Greer hooked the line in the deadeye. Ike took the remote from his parka pouch and switched it on. The roboat's antenna slid up, winking. Greer snapped a tether belt around his waist and took his place in the work cage.

'Ten and counting,' Carmody called from the speakers. 'This is the McCoy, boys. I mean bloody *vast*! Let's get it right. Three . . . two . . . one—*drop*!'

Carmody set the siders on auto and came out of the wheelhouse to look things over. 'This is the bag we been looking for, lads,' he said, rubbing his stubby hands together. 'I can feel it in my bleedin' bones.'

All Greer felt was sweaty and sleepy as he watched the tarry surface. When the timer on the panel showed ten minutes, Carmody left them and bustled back to the wheelhouse. The autopilot was supposed to keep a steady heading, but he'd seen boats swamped before, trying to haul up an overload. He wanted to be ready if any maneuvering was needed. At the last minute he gave orders to close the purse. 'Reel 'em in,' came the voice over the speaker. 'We got 'em this time, by God.'

418

Ike pulled the lever on the haul-in and the web began to roll up over the big drum on the boom. Right away Greer could tell the old fisherman was correct. The winch motor whined and groaned; the deck tilted in a steep slant toward the boom. Suddenly wide awake, Greer dragged at the floats with his picker to help the laboring apparatus. As the heavy purse began to rise, so did his excitement. 'Mm! When Peter and John pull up dey net from Jesus' side of de boat,' he paraphrased to Ike, 'dey say, "Whoa, shit, damn, look dere! Fish forever!"'

As the catch rose more and more into view, Ike found himself as astonished as those Galilee fishermen—not at the amount so much as at the variety. There seemed to be some of practically everything in the monofilament reticule. He saw salmon and albacore wriggling cheek-to-gill with Pacific cod and Arctic whiting. He recognized barracuda and sablefish, an endangered rarity in these waters. There were harlequin flashes of red snapper and orange rockfish scattered through the writhing collection. He saw long-nosed skate and some starry flounder. Even a couple of the vacationing skipjacks Greer had joked about. He was about to call the news up to Carmody when the sight of something beneath the surface stopped him.

'What do you see, damn it?' the com called. 'Sing out, somebody!'

Greer expected Ike to answer, but Ike stood speechless, staring at the water. 'A prime load, Carm,' Greer called back at the squawk box. 'And a very mixed one, too.'

'Load of what?' Carmody's voice was cracking like a kid's. 'Tuna? Albacore?'

'Albacore and tuna and more, mon. I mean a *very* mixed bag! Salmon and cod and snapper and just about *ever* t'ing else got fins and gills. I mean, whoa! What kind of convention all dese fish been *attending*, way off here in dis little two-bit puddle?'

Then he saw the thing. No wonder Ike was struck speechless. At the very bottom of the rising bag was the body of a human being, naked, hanging upright, back to them. It had to be a man's body, by the huge girth of it.

419

The torso was enormous, big as the force-fed wrestlers on the Sumo dish. Bigger! As full-packed-looking as the pendulous bag that held him! His weight had pulled him almost free of the net. He had slipped down to his armpits through the hole they had tried to patch. The monolar was stretched so tight around the back that it was embedded in the swollen flesh. The arms and shoulders and head were still out of sight up inside the shuddering mass of fish.

The man was without clothes but not without wraps. He had been wound in rolls of clear mylar superseal, completely and carefully, though it looked like the mylar had shrunk or the man had gained considerable weight since his wrapping. The huge torso was literally bursting out of the tough film; plastic tatters dripped about his purple flanks like windings from some kind of failed attempt at modern mummification. From the hips down the mylar had been clawed at by crabs. This meant the corpse had been on the bottom—weighted. As the purse slowly rotated, the two men saw the weight that had anchored him down there. Attached at the corpse's crotch was an iridescent red globe, slick and translucent as a salmon egg, bigger than a man's head. The heavy red ball dangled there, obscene and ridiculous, from a thin twist of stretched flesh. At the sight, Greer felt something boiling up his throat so hellish he couldn't tell whether it was hysterical laughter or hot vomit. Before he could find out, Ike's voice stopped it cold.

'You still think Marley was popped by a hog or a bear, Pardner?'

'There's more than one bowling ball like that,' Greer answered at last, staring at the dangling globe. 'Bound to be . . .' Not a trace of Jamaican dialect remained.

'Not in this neck of the woods there isn't,' Ike said. 'And just look how cleverly they hooked him to it. What was it that Clark B said? Bowling was a *staple* in Old Omar's life?'

'This guy is too big to be Omar Loop,' Greer tried to insist, 'far too huge around.' Then, as they stared, a gentle groundswell swung the pendulous load against the corner of the bow. The bump wasn't hard, but it was enough to jar the stretched twist of flesh free from the body. The ball dropped back into the sea with a satisfying plunk, carrying organs and hair down with it. From the mangled opening a fresh abomination began to pour forth, like a living rain. It was a struggling brown trickle at first, then a writhing downpour, then a mucilaginous deluge.

'Slime eels,' Ike said, as though he'd been expecting them all along. 'That's why it didn't look like Omar. Suffers a sea change, poor Papa Loop do.'

'What's going on down there?' the voice on the intercom wanted to know. 'Why ain't you got that load swung on? Damn your eyes, I'm comin' down!'

The sack of skin was shrinking like a deflated balloon. The eels continued to gush back down to the sea in a lashing, unbroken brown river.

'Remember the joke about the rummy and the spittoon?' Ike asked matter-of-factly. Greer nodded, frowning to recall. 'Rummy threatens to drink out of the spittoon if somebody at the bar doesn't stand him one. When he gets no takers he hoists the brass bucket and starts guzzling it down. The patrons are nauseated. "Stop, stop! We'll buy! We'll buy!" The alkie keeps guzzling. They throw money, begging him to stop. He keeps guzzling. When he's finished and takes the spittoon from his mouth they demand to know why he didn't stop. He tells them he couldn't: "It was all of a piece."'

Greer shuddered. 'One of the most disgusting jokes of all time. Well, move over, Mistah Spittoon Man; here's one be even worse.'

The cadaver's chest and neck were deflating now. The mylar wrap had held off the crabs and the fish long enough to give these back-door boys time to do a real job inside. The lungs and heart must be gone. Larynx . . . tongue. Suddenly the collapsed torso lurched and pulled free of the bag with a thick sucking sound, like a boot pulling free of a bog. Greer was near enough he might have hooked the corpse with his pole. But it was so damn awful. He shot a quick look for advice and was grateful that Ike felt the same way he did. Just too nasty, too sticky. Besides, what would it prove? The hot stuff was boiling up again in his throat. He knew now it was laughter. 'All of a *piece*, a-yuk yuk yuk.' He would have preferred vomit.

Carmody charged down the steps behind them just as the thing sank beneath a cascade of escaping fish. 'What happened to my *catch*?' His eyes bulged with disbelief at the emptying purse. 'We had forty-seven hunnert pounds in the air by my last readout. More than two ton.'

'That was the problem, Mike,' Ike explained. 'That patch we sewed ripped off.'

'Couldn't you've swung *any* of the buggers aboard?' Carmody wailed. 'Just from there to *here*?'

'They didn't look right, Carm,' Ike answered. 'There were a lot of hagfish, too.'

'Slime eels?' He turned to Greer. 'I thought you said we had a prime haul.'

'I was wrong,' Greer answered penitently. 'I got all excited. It was eels, mostly, eels for miles. Maybe that's what greased the hole.'

'Eels!' Carmody spat over the side. 'They used to be but an occasional repulsive rarity in these waters, but now—bloody shits are everywhere!' He was about to say more when a beeping interrupted. Carmody took a celefone from the pocket of his overalls and held it to his ear as he stared into the water. Greer was sure it must be Alice or Willi but, after a moment, Carmody passed the caller on to him. Greer worked it into his dreadlocks.

'It's Altenhoffen!' Greer's eyes went white around the hardwood irises. 'He says we're needed at the Dog House. Isaak—?'

'Another full moon already?' Ike asked. 'Time flies when you're having fun.' He gazed away north, musing. 'Well, tell him that the Squid can handle the scout meeting this time.'

'He says Billy has disappeared again.' The celefone was squeaking frantically beneath the black braids. 'And Poor

Brain says this is no scout meeting. It's important. He says the issue on the floor tonight is the Dog House itself. Foxcorp has got Searaven to sell their half and tonight they're going to make us an offer.'

'Us?'

'The Underdogs. And everybody. He says the whole town needs to be saved from making a terrible mistake.'

'Waste of time,' Carmody snorted. 'Tell him we're fishin' and fishin's more important.'

Greer found himself hoping Ike would agree, even if it meant more dreary dunking around pulling in waterhauls. But Isaak was still gazing away north, and his damn Greek jaw was getting that locked look.

'Aw, what the heck,' Ike suddenly relented. 'Let's haul on in, Carm. Maybe we can mend that net and save the town both.'

17

Mistreated Mammals
Enlarging the Pool

Leonard Smalls, the first-unit animal trainer with the baby face and the Grizzly Adams wild-animal bush of beard, was an Old Green. Admittedly, even somewhat proudly, an Old Green. He still had a laminate and some vintage *Green Gazettes* with his name and his Anaheim address, to prove his membership to doubters and nostalgoids. He also had Emerald City hologram invitations to several of those sumptuous underground benefits that were all the rage back when movie stars and sports celebs still proclaimed support for the outlawed cause. Isaak Sallas had even spoken at one of them. No mementoes after those awful terrorist connections came to light, though. He drew the line. Playing poison politics was one thing, poisoning politicians was another, especially those bi-vi sister senators from Colorado joined at the spine. Leonard had canceled his membership after watching the televised trial. And not a moment too soon. When The Hague declared the whole organization was guilty of 'flagrant societal infractions' and its members were 'nothing more than biological Bolsheviks,' all Hollywood turned against the Old Greens, and movie workers that had not already renounced their membership were blackballed for life.

So Leonard had disposed of all but a few mementoes of his activist period—right down the dumper—but he had kept his wild-animal beard. For Leonard Smalls had really always been more animalist than activist. He loved animals, and was desirous of being by animals loved. Facial hair should help accomplish this desire, he always reasoned. Smooth skin must seem quite queer to most animals; what animal can relate to a creature that skins its own face? Of course, there are also some women trainers, exceptional ones, and of course, they are smooth-faced; but an animal can see that these are *she*-faces, and that they are naturally naked. This womanly nakedness might well even heighten rapport, Leonard suspected. Cases in point: Fossey and her gorillas; Mara Bethelozi and the psychopathic baboon pack. Bare female face hath charms to soothe, so to speak. Whatever it was, it seemed to work for the girls. It was most assuredly working for this Eskimo adolescent he'd been instructed to tutor at the pinniped pens—he had observed *that*.

Every afternoon since that savage business between the wild sea lion and his tame one, she'd come down to the pens as per studio instructions, to familicate for an hour with Harry. Harry was the tame pinniped. Leonard had raised Harry since the neutered pup was brought to the studio pool in Anaheim more than six years ago; now Levertov had ordered him to act as interlocutor between Harry and the two young Eskimo stars of the movie. Every afternoon he was supposed to get the girl, the cripple and the timid sea lion *com*fortable with each other. The first afternoon the girl showed up, grimly chewing gum as she waited to be let into the compound, but no crippled companion. Leonard suggested they should wait—he had a little introductory lecture prepared—but the girl shook her head.

'Eemook's gone. They wrote him out and flew him home this morning.'

'Wrote him out? I thought he had the lead.'

'Not no more. Mr Clark says a cripple isn't any good for lead, in a movie or a dogsled race. Is that my chair where I sit? Tell me when the hour's up.'

From the very first he could see his interlocution was not going to be heeded or needed. He might as well never have bothered with the introduction he had composed; theories of totemism and primal relationships were clearly going to be wasted on this gum-chewing mope.

Not that she was in any way *backward* or il*literate*. Quite the contrary. He knew she could speak English more than adequately; he'd heard her on the set. Sometimes, amid a shoal of her fishkid peers, she was a veritable *avalanche* of words, crashing and careening through thought processes that would have made a lot of Hollywood High rifrappers swallow their tongues. But that first afternoon at Harry's poolpen, all she did was chew gum and watch the horizon through the cyclone fencing. She wouldn't even do him the courtesy of feigning interest in his expertise when he tried to tell her about pinnipeds. She just sat in the chair, far-gazing. Even when he stepped right in her line of sight her wide-set eyes remained fixed on some distant puzzle that she seemed to see right through him. He'd seen caged wolves' eyes far-gaze exactly the same way: acknowledging your presence yet dismissing your importance as they concentrated on deeper considerations—such as revenge, fear, hunger, blood. Who could be sure what such a look meant?

That evening he dropped by the production office at the bowling alley to hear the gossip and learned of the girl's crush on the town hero. That was what the look was. It was love, fierce and forlorn and unrequited. So the next afternoon he just let her in and retreated to his tent, intending to leave the familication assignment to herself. What could be gained by driving poor depressed Harry out of his den to deal with her? Or her to Harry? Not a thing . . . just heartache compounded. He resolved firmly to maintain a disinterested distance and observe, in a clinical, scientific, dispassionate way, the subjects before him.

Yet after two days of this dispassionate observation— watching poor Harry's depression deepen; watching the pining Indian maid with her wide brow as troubled as a field of wheat under a threatening cloud—Leonard Smalls felt his emotional side getting the better of his scientific.

'I'm going to put the sea lion in the pool now,' he announced to her on the third afternoon.

'Okay by me, mister,' Shoola shrugged. She was tilted back in the low lawn chair, practicing her bubble gum. It was one of the Round-Eye skills she seemed still determined to master. 'I thought he always ready been in the pool.'

'Technically he is. But he's shy. He's ensconced back in his cave. He's been afraid to come out and face things ever since that humiliation he suffered with the other sea lion. I'll drive him out and close his door so he can't duck back in.'

'Why is it we have to do this business?' Her eyes remained fixed on the faraway sea, but the wide brow lifted slightly. 'I forget.'

'You are supposed to establish a rapport.'

After waiting long enough she prompted, 'A rap or what?'

'I mean an affinity, a *friend*ship. So when we shoot the scene where you climb on his back you won't be afraid of him.'

'Haw,' she said.

'Very well, so Harry won't be afraid of you. His well-being is my responsibility. I raised him, from a suckling babe. Six years of my life I have given to him.'

She turned to give Leonard a fierce appraisal. 'I bet you did, Mr Whisker; just *look* at you.' She seemed to see his face for the first time. 'Are you the Santa Claus for sea lions or something?'

'He's always been shy,' he repeated defensively.

'Drive him in!' she decided with a wave.

She barely glanced at the animal when Leonard poled it from hiding and locked it in the open water. The sea lion swam to a far corner and remained there, whimpering pathetically and blinking its great eyes. At the other end of the pool the girl practiced blowing hi-glo pink bubbles.

When the hour was up and Leonard Smalls unlocked the gate to let her out, he told her not to worry about Harry's rejection. 'Tomorrow I'll let you feed him some salmon cheeks.'

Again she gave him that penetrating appraisal. 'More haw. This sissy sea lion of yours does not want fish cheeks, Mr Santa Claus. He does not want anything. Maybe tomorrow I will make him want something.'

The next afternoon when she unrolled her gum she also unrolled a second piece. She placed it beneath her chair near the water, then turned away to watch the horizon and practice her bubbles. After a while Leonard saw the sea lion leave its simulated cave. It cruised across the pond, growing more fascinated than afraid. Harry might be a sissy, Leonard Smalls observed with no small amount of pride, but he was a sissy with curiosity.

The sleek head zigzagged closer and closer to the pink prize, careful to stay as much behind the bubble-blower's line of sight as possible. As he cruised he was eyeing the gum and the girl *both* in a way that was entirely uncharacteristic for the timid beast. A bit menacing, even. The lips kept drawing back from the teeth. Leonard Smalls had never seen Harry act this way before. Suddenly concerned, he reached under his army cot for the spranque prod he always kept close. Who *really* knows what's going on in the minds of these hothouse home-growns? Everybody in the business had a horror story about some trained subject or another unexpectedly cracking: 'Never seen a more docile old gamma wolf until that morning those Camp Fire Girls came in the backyard with those chocolate-covered cherries.'

The sea lion skulked closer to the reclining girl. Leonard activated the prod. But just as he was about to charge from his tent to intercede, the girl turned and snatched away the second piece of gum and popped it into her own mouth. Harry surged away and vanished in a confusion of foam.

'Now he wants it,' she said.

The next time she let him capture the prize. He dived away to the bottom with it. When he surfaced at the other end of the pool he appeared to be chewing. Actually chewing bubble gum! Before the end of the hour he had edged near the girl again, and appeared to be trying

428

to *mimic her lip movements.* The girl was whispering soft encouragements. She rolled out of the chair and got down on her knees and elbows poolside, for some intensive vis-à-vis information exchange. She was *coaching* Harry!

Leonard watched from his tent in such a passion of excitement that he began to feel like a voyeur. Tomorrow he would requisition a vidcam to document this unprecedented intercourse. Not that he expected to get disk of an actual *bubble*—don't be ridiculous. The labiadental dexterity of the pinniped was not adequately evolved. But a vidcam record of this relationship would be *more* than sufficient basis for a thesis, perhaps even a Barry Lopez grant. No-one had ever studied anything like it! Such rapport, so fast, so *close* . . . Then he saw something else. No, to be more precise, he *didn't* see something else. For the pair had gone suddenly completely motionless. They seemed frozen, eye to eye, a scant dozen inches separating the animal's face from the girl's. The something he did not see held them frozen. Both had ceased chewing, their jaws hanging open, the wads of gum lolling out. They seemed mesmerized, locked in a kind of mutual thrall, like dedicated data computer sharing a chipwell. For an irrational instant Leonard imagined he could actually hear the doubled humming of hard drives, swapping whole ROMs of information. Then, abruptly, the hook-up broke down. The girl jerked back and moaned. Harry answered, rolling away with a motion huge and graceful and profoundly tragic, and disappeared under the surging water. He surfaced beside the latched door of his den and waited there, bubbling the water, not looking back.

Both pieces of masticated gum lay on the drenched poolside planks. The girl picked them up and walked to stand at the gate. Leonard Smalls ducked out of the tent and hurried over with his cardkey. The girl was absently rolling the two wads into one pink ball.

'I trust you're not planning to chew them both.' A light attempt at humor to mask his amazement. 'Who knows

429

what you might catch from Harry, him from sleazy LA and all . . .'

The girl didn't laugh. She turned toward him, the motion also graceful and profound. Her face swung up to him, her eyes to his eyes. And Leonard saw they were gemstone brown, as brown as cut garnet and wonderfully mysterious. Then across this exotic brown he saw flow another, more familiar brown, the scum brown of Southern California, the brown of the Orange County sky oozing through the scummy palm trees, staining the patio tiles, the succulents, the knuckles and neck of the pool maintenance man scumming the pool . . . all walled in brown rails and brown stucco and no horizons . . . no depths, no heights, just chopped squid in the rusty brown bucket. The sun the moon the red rubber ball? All the same ball of brown, rolling and rolling, round and around, repeating the same silent grievances over and over, like a loop of bleak brown magnetic tape.

Leonard Smalls shook his head so hard his beard snapped. When the dreadful vision was dissipated, he found himself alone. The gate was open wide; the girl had let herself out. He shaded his eyes until he saw her on the dock. He followed her with his eyes across the crew lot and watched her start a go-ped, then watched from beneath his shading palm until she was out of sight around the sea cliff facade that fronted the cannery.

Back at the pool Harry was still bubbling, waiting to be let into his fabricated sea den.

'I'm sorry, old friend. I didn't know. How *could* I have known?'

Harry waited at his gate, offering no opinions . . . the great convex mirrors of his eyes enlarging the pool to the whole boundless water beyond.

18
Destry Rides Again

As soon as the point of Pyrite Cape was off their stern, Carmody heaved a resigned sigh and slipped in the dedicated homing chip. The reptilian bow of the craft swayed a few degrees harder northwest and settled on course. The engines phased into a happy hum; you could almost see the big machine's foamy-toothed steelume smile: 'Mmm, these chips are *good*.'

Ike was also happy that Carmody had plugged in the chip. It wasn't just that it meant the fastest, most efficient passage home; something cumbersome and heavy had at last been cut loose, relinquished, given up on. Like the way Carmody had at last admitted that all this bloody damn modern chipshit nonsense was beyond him; and if Carmody couldn't learn it he could never hope to best it, and if he couldn't best it, fuck it. 'Go to total auto. We'll just ease back and see what the piano roll plays.'

'That's the spirit.' Ike tried to look on the bright side. 'Frees the piano player up for dancin'.'

Ike had to admit he was beginning to feel up for a little dancin'. Sometimes, when a noble but hopeless cause at last gets confessed as lost, there's a kind of reckless energy passed back to you through the little confessional window. It's a compensation one wants to make the most of.

The three of them were out on the deck, reclined on float chairs in the lee of the wheelhouse, sharing a fifth of Steubins' Irish and a quarter of a tiny Dall lamb Carmody had traded for in the spring and pressure-smoked. The meat was as tender and rich and wickedly sweet as Old Norway's cream cheese; you could slice it with a

431

cracker. The Bushmill's was even wickeder. Ike had to keep reminding himself to go light on both items. He could ease back now but knew he was going to find some tense business to attend to when they got back to Kuinak. He could not have said what that business was, or how it would be handled, but he was resigned to do what had to be done. He had kind of gone to total auto himself. The moment he saw that telltale red bowling ball he knew he was going to cut loose any hopes he still harbored that his suspicions about Levertov might just be fantasy. No, this dirt mama was real. Dolls were being set up, and being knocked down. The situation was in progress, and in dedicated lock; it couldn't be blinked and it couldn't be ducked. Fortunately, it was a situation for which he had his own dedicated program. All he had to do was plug it in. His program was surely outdated, but he knew he could trust the old chipware to guide him into correct position and action when the chips were down.

The boat had quartered them into a sluggish, lackluster sea. Long mud-blue swells were straggling down from the Aleutians. They looked limp and lifeless, like old Irish fishwife hair, strained wet through the family comb. Ike thought about sharing this Celtic image with Carmody, for companionship's sake—but decided to remain silent. He didn't feel like small talk.

All three men seemed content to cruise along in their private thoughts. Ike knew they were essentially musing along the same lines he was: about getting home and tending to business. In Carmody's case the business was surely the tangle he'd left his shore life in; did he have two fish on the line, or none? Or was *he* the one that was hooked, with two hooks, gill and tail? Greer was still struggling with the implications of that dreadful apparition they had pulled from the depths. Whoa! It meant giving up such sweetmeats o' the mind! It meant admitting that this great gossamer genie that had swooped into town with its magic teapot and its seemingly bottomless cornucopia of delights was not only not 'folks,' as he had been assuring everybody, but was actually *anti*-folks; and

432

that he, Emil Greer, personally, was very likely very high on the list of folks that this evil genie was *most* anti towards. *Mm!* Equally as troubling was his worry that his main soulbro and roommate was now on his way to town to get *involved serious* with that genie. Greer'd seen that resigned look in Isaak's face before; it usually meant rash action was being contemplated. Nimble feet might be needed. So he held up a prudent hand the next time Carmody offered the bottle.

'I'm close to my edge, Carm. We got to keep our composure. We don't be wantin' to drink ourselfs clean out of it.'

Ike was still drinking himself into it. The sight of that bloated doll at the bottom of the purse had left him resigned that he was going to have to make some sort of move, and experience advised him that in these kinds of situations there were only two possible moves: full strike against the bastards or back off and bide your time. Full strike is generally the best tactic, if you can muster up the dash for it. The juice. So when the bottle came by again he took a long, deliberate pull. 'Sometimes,' he gave Greer a reckless grin, 'we need courage more than composure.'

It wasn't really courage he was looking for in the Irish spirits, it was decisiveness. He wanted to get to it and do it, like with Greener. No more wordplay, no more show biz, no more fancy Bakatcha shots off the far-left cushion. Go straight for the tomato can. And what he needed for this was Teddy the .22 Bear. How many times had he lain awake in jail and kicked himself for not driving straight on up to boss Jason 'Cog' Weil's ritzy digs overlooking all the Weil Produce Estate and unceremoniously blowing a hole in the fat prick's tomato can? Simply *skipping* all those hot-dog stunts with the spray plane. It would have saved a lot of trouble, and statistics suggest he would have served less time. And so what if Boss Weil was only a cog in a bigger wheel in a bigger machine for some ritzier biz somewhere? His tomato can would have sufficed. You can't get all stymied with concern that you're not getting to the true, the main, the *Top* Fat Prick. The Fat Prick Directly Above You is adequate.

When they rounded Hopeless the three men got unsteadily to their feet and folded away the chairs. Carmody began policing their lounging area so it wouldn't look quite so much like they were returning home from another pleasure cruise. Greer swept up the lamb bones and broken crackers and tossed them to the little welcoming party of crows and gulls. Ike slipped the newly opened bottle of Irish out of sight into his sea bag, should his resolution begin to waver.

When the boat cleared the bar and passed the last data buoy a soft female voice began calling from the wheelhouse, 'Course accomplished, awaiting instructions. Further instruction, please?'

'How about kissin' me ruddy ass for starters?' Carmody called back and went clanging heavily up the wheelhouse steps. As soon as he was gone Greer glanced furtively fore and aft, then stepped close to Ike at the rail.

'Talk to me, Pardner. I don't like this gunslinger look come over you. You aren't contemplating some kind of vigi*lante* play, are you? Remember how quick that Clark B bastard pulled that Uziette outta his ass?'

'Not contemplating a thing, Greer. Just waiting for what's next.'

'I don't like it for you to drink like you been, man. It cause you to grin all shit funny . . .'

'I been thinking some funny shit, Pardner.'

'I don't like that, either. Maybe you oughta just go straight up to the trailer soon's we hit shore, let Vice-President Emil handle this meeting.'

'One of the very things I been thinking, Ol' Veep: straight up to the trailer soon as we hit shore.'

Carmody broke wake speed so he could hurry in and see if he could find an open slot near the fuel house to tie up; he was still determined to be gassed up and ready to head back out as soon as they could get the web changed in the morning. He might as well not have hurried. There were plenty of openings, but there wasn't a worker to be found at the pumps, or anywhere up and down the pier—though there was still plenty of daylight left in the work day. The only person they saw in the whole west end of the marina was Altenhoffen. The journalist came careening across the lot to meet them in a bandaged forehead and a brand new Caddy slide-top. Carmody was impressed.

'They must be paying paperboys better.'

'It's a loaner from the insurance company,' Altenhoffen explained. 'Two days old.'

'What happened to your poor head, Poor Brain?' Greer asked in an unfamiliar voice. His accent still hadn't recovered from the shock of Omar Loop. Altenhoffen had to change glasses to be sure who it was asking.

'The same thing that happened to the car, Emil: vandals took the handles. Darlene Herky phoned in the middle of the night and tells me some cars are around back of the newspaper office, and guys in bandanna masks are up on the roof. I drive up just in time to see Great-Grandfather's plywood beacon come toppling down right on top of me. Demolished the Chevy, knocked me cold as a cod.'

'Fishkids!' Carmody declared.

'I thought so—until I went in and found they'd been hammering on my press.'

'Your *new* press? That big bird-looking thing? Whoa!'

'My new Heidelberg Glaserflow, yes. But the whole operation is steelume blimped, right? They barely dented that armor. The keyboard and screen were ruined, of course, but the Squid and I jerry-wired in the ones from the Mario dish. It gives me periodic little Italians on the screen, and no italics on the printout, but *excelsior*! You can't stop the press!'

With a flourish he produced a crude, makeshift tabloid, full of clashing fonts and sizes. The editorial was headlined on the front fold: SILVER FOX IN SHEEP'S CLOTHING.

'It's a follow-up on my last Friday's bombshell, MAKEOVER OR TAKEOVER? That was the night the vandals took the handles.'

'Come on, Poor Brain,' Greer jeered, for Ike's benefit. 'You don't mean you think the *movie guys* busted up your paper?'

'Either them, or guys in *cahoots* with the sneaky varmits,' Altenhoffen answered jauntily. 'Just like in the classic westerns, huh, *compadres*? Crusading Journalist Bushwacked by Land Baron's Henchmen. Billy maintained it was Greener's work, naturally. That's why the Squid lit out and holed up.'

'I still say it's fishkids,' Carmody insisted. 'Did you call the cops?'

'Darlene Herky says one of the cars *was* the cops, Mr Carmody.' He tapped the side of his long nose and winked. 'Mount up, pilgrims, Fort Underdog is under attack!'

Ike tossed his sea bag in the backseat beside Greer and stepped in after it. 'How about first dropping this pilgrim up home, Poor Brain? I'm not sure I'm up to another public event. Brother Greer can handle the club's affairs.'

'Great Scott, Isaak; this is the Showdown at the Underdog Corral! It's *volatile* up there. You need to make an appearance if only for appearances' sake. Talk to him, Mr Carmody. Greer?'

Carmody said it *would* be a pity to miss the showdown. Even Greer chimed in. His worry that his partner might do something impetuous was now overshadowed by the prospect of chairing a volatile Dog meeting without backup. He took Ike's elbow. 'We *do* need you, my man . . .'

'Poor Brain said that, but I'm damned if I can imagine what *for*. Sounds to me like what you need is a real-estate counselor—'

'We need you to talk, Ike,' Altenhoffen said.

'Talk? Damn you, Altenhoffen—'

'To speak. Orate. Address the issue. Rouse the rabble. I caught your act a couple of times, Mr Demosthenes. You didn't know that, did you? I saw you once at Shoreline, then at that debacle in front of Sproul Hall that they teargassed us. Remember that one?'

When Ike didn't answer Altenhoffen turned to Carmody. 'Our laconic lad was once quite the orator, Mr Carmody, if you can believe it. You should have seen him. He could rouse the rabble to some out*rageous* heights.'

'I believe it, Mr Altenhoffen. I do. And you know? I *would* like to *see* it.' He took Ike's other elbow. 'C'mon, Ike lad. Let's pop by for a bit of rabble-rousing while the glow's still on us. Aye? For Auld Lang Syne?'

'Yeah, okay. But I still want to swing up past the trailerhouse for clean clothes, and . . . incidentals.'

'You look *fine*.' Greer had suddenly guessed what the incidentals was that Ike had wanted from the trailerhouse. 'You look all rugged and earthy, the way rabble likes it, right, Poor Brain?'

'Right!' Altenhoffen cranked the little turbine to a higher whine. 'And we bottom line simply do not have time for any side trips, Isaak, the rate this thing's been snowballing. I shudder to imagine what's been going on up on that porch while I've been absent. Things change fast, wait until you see!' He backed around and headed across the lot, sliding the top closed as he drove.

Ike did not believe he was likely to see any changes in the town more startling than he'd seen on his last home-coming, but he was wrong. Main had been completely redone *again* . . . back the way it *was*. In less than a week the spruced-up street had returned to almost the same old scruffy, neglected low-rung Kuinak look it had originally sported. Almost. Storefronts that were dazzling white just days ago now were boarded with planks so weather-worn and time-silvered they almost looked like they'd been weathering there since before the invention of paint. But again: almost. Almost. The word made Ike think of a limerick from his Navy days:

> *There once was a lass from the coast*
> *Who had an affair with a ghost*
> *At the height of orgasm*

With this pallid phantasm
She said, 'I think that I feel it . . . almost.'

Carmody was especially confounded by this artificial authenticity. 'I don't get it, by *God* if I do!' The renovation of the little town had seemed to him a task futile but certainly understandable, what with the sudden transfusion of new cash into the communal bloodstream, but why they should want to return it to its original ramshackle state was beyond his comprehension. 'What the dotty hell are they about *now*?'

'I'll show you.' Altenhoffen turned abruptly at the intersection so his headlights shined into a wide thermoplate window. It took a moment for Ike to recognize that it was the front window of the bowling alley. Or had been, he corrected himself. Here it seemed was the one set piece of the whole downtown that had not been redone to match its original. The neon BOWL 'N' BEER sign was gone from the wide window, as well as the fly-specked legions of bowling trophies. In their place was the cartoon map. The map was now mounted on a fancier stand than had displayed it in the Fox's salon, and there was another transparency flipped over. Altenhoffen eased the car across the empty sidewalk until the map rose directly in front of their hood, like a hologrammized landscape in front of a dish-game ride. He threw open the slide top.

'Does this boggle the brain or what?'

The south jetty had been extended twice its length and was crowded all along with happy hologram tourists—rock-fishing, skin-diving, kite-flying, bird-watching. Their many-hued faces and ethnic attire made it clear they had journeyed from every part of the globe to enjoy this revitalizing experience.

'It looks like one of those Small-World-for-Christ Sunday cartoons' was Greer's appraisal.

There was a hologram ski lift carrying smiling cartoon faces to the top of the glacier, and a hologram toboggan run thrilling them back down. Cartoon faces hung from hang gliders and bungeed from helicopters.

They skimmed on water skimmers and buggied in dune buggies. They thronged the rustic cartoon Main Street loaded with souvenirs and prizes, happy as marks on an oldtime carnival midway.

'Gaw, what a pipe dream!' Carmody'd seen enough. 'How the blazes do they think they'll be getting all these big spenders *in* here anyways, and the only deepwater port a hundred miles away?'

'Why, how about by *air*port, Mr Carmody? Major *air*port?' Altenhoffen nodded back toward the map. A hologram Concorde was coming in for a landing, the pilot's face out the window smiling to the airstrip below. The strip was across the bay, where Carmody lived.

'So *that's* their game. They think they'll get their hooks into my property? Not bloody likely!'

'No, no, this is some completely undeveloped acreage *past* your property, along the Duck. The Army Corps of Engineers team is out there this very PM, taking seismics. All quite proper . . .'

Carmody snorted and shook his head. 'Just a pipe dream, I say, but the notion of it does make me thirsty. Isaak, I seen you squirrel away that bottle. I judge we need a shot of courage all around.'

As the whiskey made a circle Ike studied the map. On the overlay he finally located that last little finger of the road pointing up past the water tower. The finger was now paved and polished—manicured—and the flat toward which it pointed was swept clean of the mountains of refuse. A condo resort crowned the ridge instead.

'They missed your place, Michael,' Greer observed gloomily, 'but it looks like they set right down on top of Isaak and me.'

'I still maintain the whole business is just so much smoke in a bottle, but let's go raise some devil for the fun of it. Full back, Altenhoffen! Where's all these het-up rabbly throngs we was promised?'

But as they approached the Underdog House they saw no throng at all, rabbly or otherwise. The wide plank porch was deserted. This brought a big grin of relief to

Greer's face until they passed the double screen front of the big hall. Then his face fell along with his spirits. The throng was already inside. The din of a dozen tumultuous arguments poured out the screen doors and over their open car like waves over a dinghy.

The presidential parking place was already occupied by a stretch limo. It was not one of Tom's renters. It was a new Tornado, smooth and silver as a satellite tender. Even the windows were silver.

'Squeeze right in next to the bastard,' Ike commanded. 'You can make it.'

Altenhoffen gave him an anxious glance. 'Isaak, that happens to be a Grand Emperor Tornado—the most expensive turbine Toyota makes. The *Pope* has one . . .'

'Go on, you can make it. Scrape him if you have to.' The cartoon map and that last shot of Irish courage had Ike feeling like dancin' again. Greer was right; he didn't need anything from the trailerhouse. The tongue can be as wicked a weapon as the hog leg. 'Make some Hollywood hotshot think twice about taking the Underdogs' presidential parking place!'

'That's the spirit, Ike darlin'!' Carmody was getting more and more worked up himself, what with the thought of airplanes landing on his gutter. 'Full speed ahead and damn the Tornadoes.'

Altenhoffen squeezed between the big car and the porch with scant inches to spare. They couldn't open any of the doors, but they could climb out the slide top; how the limo passengers were going to manage would be somebody else's problem. On the porch they all had another round before Ike capped the bottle and zipped it in his shoulder kip; it had been years since he'd done any serious rabble-rousing, and he might need more nips of courage before the evening was over.

Norman Wong came out on the porch to meet them, a miserable hangdog look in his yellow eyes.

'I couldn't keep 'em out, Ike,' he lamented. 'I tried and tried. Everybody in town showed up. The mayor said I had to let 'em in because it's the only place big enough to hold a full town meeting. And Lieutenant Bergstrom said if I shot my pistol one more time he'd be compelled to have the Wasps take it away from me.'

'Don't worry about it, Norman,' Ike told the dejected sergeant-at-arms. 'Just get us up front.'

Even before they were inside the clamorous hall Ike could detect the presence of Billy the Squid's score. The room was a din of frenetic haggling and wrangling on top of the talk Herb Tom was trying to give at the lectern. The air was sour with sweat and adrenaline, and scoot vibes writhing around near the ceiling like invisible snakes. The clamor quieted noticeably when Norman ushered in the new arrivals.

Ike followed in the big man's wake feeling like a fighter being escorted to the ring. Altenhoffen was right. It *was* like those big Rabble Rallies, when tens of thousands would fill the parks, eager to be inflamed by the Eco Movement's ranting firebrands. The Bakatcha Bandit's rant was always expected to be one of the day's fieriest. Because in those days Ike Sallas was no talk-circuit environmentalist with a collection of cold scientific facts, no starry-eyed tree-hugger or toothy politician trying to get just the right sound-bite on the evening news. Ike Sallas was a warrior with battle scars and stripes, a decorated veteran railing against the same flag that had honored him with the Navy Cross. The Monster had struck him a random, circuitous blow, as it had so many others—but Isaak Sallas had struck back, with deeds of daring and words of fire! And had kept striking back until they finally locked him up to cool him off and let the fire go out. But it wasn't the joint where Ike Sallas started cooling off, nor the work camp. It was the halfway house, a mini-secure facility outside Modesto where the prisoners were allowed conjugal visits. The halfway house wasn't more than an hour from Fresno, but no visits ever happened, no conjugal privileges were ever exercised. Ojo Bravo came to see him that once, from Yuma. He was wearing dark glasses and a drooping, lopsided handlebar and he instructed Ike that his name was now

Emiliano Brando, *por favor: Ojo Bravo es muerte.* Had Ojo seen anything of Jeannie, Ike wanted to know, before he became *muerte*? The moustache drooped more lopsided than ever: *Nada,* Eye-zack; the bean, she has jumped. Two days later his second and only other visitor showed up: a young legal aide with downcast eyes and a folder full of divorce papers. That's when the firebrand really started sputtering out. Ike hadn't believed it could ever be rekindled. Now here he was, bound for the podium and burning to go—just like old times.

Norman was right; it looked like everybody in town was here, plus a lot of foreigners. And a lot of them in costume! Mr and Mrs Wong were wearing ornate Chinese robes, though the closest they had ever been to China was Grant Street in San Francisco. Their big brood of adopted boys ranged around them like woebegone samurai around an imperial couple of the Mandarin court. A large percentage of the Deap contingent was wearing traditional robes and button blankets. They were gathered to one half of the room where Tommy Toogiak Senior and the other Searaven executives had established a kind of office area with laptops and brief-cases. The Underdogs were packed on the other side. Those that were Deap and Dog both had tried to slip into an ambiguous position out in the aisle, between the two factions. There was Old Boswell and his wife, rarely seen off their tender, and the city council, and most of the Kuinak High teaching staff. Fishermen and pilots and RO/RO men ranged along the walls, hands in jacket pockets in their customary attitude of waiting.

Ike saw no sign of Levertov but he caught sight of his flunky, Clark B, tipped back against a wall with a beep-board on his suntanned knees. He saw Willi Hardesty at the back with the two Culligan boys, near the door they had just followed Norman through. Along the same wall, standing on a bench, was the Eskimo girl. The girl gave him a quick wave, then began whispering to a little gaggle of fishkids gathered at her bare feet. Ike was glad she seemed to be over her fit of infatuation. On the opposite side of the doorway Alice was seated atop an antique brass fire extinguisher—the soda-and-vinegar kind, which had to be turned upside to activate. Alice had found it somewhere and cushioned it with her folded jacket to make it comfortable. She wasn't looking at the crowd or the speaker or anything. She had patiently folded her arms and leaned back to study the ceiling. Maybe she could see the scoot snakes writhing around up there, too.

Herb Tom was winding up his prepared statement. As nearly as Ike could make out it was some kind of rickety reasoning constructed to link tradition with exclusivity; Herb had always been the only rental agency in town and apparently felt the tradition should continue. There was a token spattering of applause when he finished and the next up was Charlie Fishpool. Charlie said *he* thought what was most important was that everybody stick together and be aboveboard and out-in-the-open. This set the Underdogs growling. Dog Brother Marge Boswell demanded to know why, then, had Brother Charlie gone along with Searaven when the sneaky sonofabitches had got together on the sly and sold half the club-house? This got the Deaps stirred up. They called for an explanation of the conditional rider the Underdogs had attached to *their* side of the deal—that they would relinquish their half of the property only on condition that they would serve as security for the forthcoming theme park—*exclusively*. Marge responded with a barrage of questions of her own. 'Didn't Searaven write in a clause you guys'd be the only ones allowed to deal Deap artifacts and souvenirs? So what's your problem with us being the only ones to deal security? We been dealing it very well for a month now.'

'Exactly my point!' Herb Tom agreed with a shout, jumping back to his feet. 'Tradition comes first, it all comes down to that: keeping tradition.'

It was beginning to dawn on Ike that what most of this wrangling came down to was that everybody wanted to make sure that when this juicy new pie was cut up they would be guaranteed the same slice to which they had been traditionally accustomed, or maybe a bit bigger. He began to have some misgivings about this talk Altenhoffen had roped him into. He'd come steaming in to argue against a sellout; now he wondered if any such argument might not already be moot—that the pie might be already sold, and the only issue left was how to cut it up.

Before he could dwell on this Norman Wong rapped for quiet and motioned Ike up to the podium. 'Sit down, Charlie. Hush, Marge. Let's hear what our founding father has to say. Ten minutes, Isaak.'

Ike took the podium, his head lowered in thought. He didn't speak for a long minute as he appeared to agonize over how to begin. The buzz of room talk subsided, curious. This long agonizing was a trick he used to use—a way to let the drama build and at the same time get the house settled. Because he already knew exactly how he was going to begin, with his old tried-and-true opening. Back in high school he had memorized a few paragraphs from an American history text. He had won the Junior Toastmaster finals in Sacramento with his recitation—two hundred bucks plus a goldloy plaque that he promptly sold. He couldn't remember what he'd done with the cash. But he never forgot those paragraphs. He had used bits and pieces of them to begin almost all of his rally speeches. It was surefire. When the room was quiet enough, his face rose:

'*Ye . . .* are a crowd con*fused*, wavering at a *critical crossroad*!'

The voice that tolled forth was almost as great a surprise to him as to his audience. He was glad he hadn't finished that Irish after all; he was right on the edge and then some.

'Ye that oppose independence *now*, ye know not what *ye* do: ye are opening a door to *eternal tyranny*. I say to *you*: To talk friendship with those in whom our reason *forbids* us to have faith, and our affections wounded through a thousand pores *instruct* us to detest, is madness and folly. And can there be any reason to hope that as that

444

relationship expires the affection will increase?'

His eyes raked the astonished room. He raised an arm and pointed at the wall where Clark B Clark and his cadre of lawyers sat staring.

'*Ye* tell us of harmony and reconciliation—can ye restore to us the time that is past? Can ye give to prostitution its former innocence?'

He turned to the Searaven crowd.

'There are injuries which nature cannot forgive; she would cease to be nature if she did. As well can the lover forgive the ravisher of his mistress, as this continent forgive its ravishers.'

Then to the Underdogs, who were looking a little ill at ease about the way their famous founding father was carrying on.

'The Almighty hath implanted in us these inextinguishable feelings for good and wise purposes. They are the *guardians* of our hearts. They distinguish us from the herd of common animals. The social compact would dissolve, and justice be extirpated from the earth, were we callous to these touches of affection. The robber and the ravisher would escape unpunished, did not the injuries which our tempers sustain provoke us into justice.'

He drew a deep breath so he could boom the grand finale toward the very rear of the room where Willi and the Culligans and the fishkids listened with rapt, dumbfounded faces. Alice wasn't studying the damn ceiling anymore, either.

'O ye that love mankind, that honor the earth and respect the gentle denizens thereof! Ye that dare oppose not only the tyranny but the *tyrant*, stand forth! Every spot of our world is overrun with aggression. Freedom hath been hunted round the globe, roped down and by the smiling tyrants of *greed* most cruelly raped. O, stand forth against these tyrants, receive the hounded fugitive, and prepare an asylum for mankind—an asylum for *all* mankind—*not* just for some fucking phony-baloney elitist amusement park bullshit built by the very assholes that got rich raping us in the first place!'

445

At this point Ike was accustomed to pause to allow the applause and cheering to calm down before he segued on into the more contemporary portion of his diatribe. But this time no hands clapped, no inflamed voices of support were lifted. Instead, an unanticipated silence smote him in the face like a cold wind.

'Those are some words from Thomas Paine,' he explained, 'one of our *real* founding fathers.' It sounded more like an apology than an explanation. Didn't anybody remember who Tom Paine was anymore? He was about to say more about the great American revolutionary when a voice from the crowd interrupted him.

'What have you and Carmody been *doing* out in that boat, Sallas? . . . And where can we get some of it?'

A roar of relieved laughter erupted. Ike felt his face reddening, but he took it with a grin, trying to see who had asked the question.

'Yeah, Ike . . .' This was another voice, from the other side of the room. 'I don't personally get what you're driving at.'

This was Bob Mowbry, the welder. He was standing against one of the peeled pine columns of the hall with his thumbs hooked in the leather bib of an old-fashioned blacksmith's apron. He wore no shirt and his arms and shoulders were as tanned as the old leather; he must have been taking melanin injections since Ike last saw him—big ones.

'What I'm driving at, Bob, is I think everybody's about to make a big mistake.'

'Amen to *that*!' Carmody concurred.

'A big mistake *how*, for example?' Bob demanded in a forceful voice . . . and he had always been such a *mealy*-mouth, trying to worm his way into the club. '*Where's* this mistake?'

'The way they've got you *out*fitted, for example, Bobby. Do they provide you with a spreading chestnut tree, too?'

Mowbry took his thumbs out of his apron to give everybody the benefit of his arms. It appeared he'd been mixing a few roids in with his melanin. 'What's wrong with the way I'm outfitted? I got as much right to be traditional as Herb Tom does, ain't I? Or them damn Indians? And I'm gettin' paid more a week than I used to make in six months.'

'Whoa, is dat *right*?' Greer's accent was finally returning. 'Jes' to dress up all cute an' blacksmiffy like dat, they pay you? Mmm, where I get me one of dese dress-up jobs, *Bob*?'

'It ain't just dress-up, butthole,' Bob Mowbry flared, raising a big fist. He looked like a pro wrestler doing a promo: Black Smith! 'I'm *still* a working welder, damn you! I'm *still* doing a man's job!'

'My, my, yes,' Greer was quick to agree. 'I can see you are, *Bob*.'

'Fuck you!'

'That's the spirit, Mowbry,' Carmody applauded. 'A bloody *man's* job.'

'Fuck you and Greer both, Carmody. And Sallas, too. You assholes are *out of touch*. Sit down and let the rest of us get back to business .'

Ike sat down, maintaining the grin but feeling more a fool than he had in years. What had he been *thinking*? He should have known the pearls of Paine's rhetoric would be wasted on this pork-barreling throng. Mowbry was right. We're out of touch.

Norman Wong hammered the podium and called the next speaker, Betty Jo Gohappy. Betty Jo was curator of the Daughters of the Deap Museum and she announced that she wanted to address the issue of Ethnic Authenticity. She was concerned that she did not see much Ethnic Authenticity in any of the plans she had studied for the proposed theme park, and she wanted to read a prepared statement clarifying that concern. Betty was a Chugach history scholar of some renown in the anthropology departments of most major universities. She had an intense, bird-thin face and a reputation for honest, dedicated devotion to the preservation of the area's native heritage. Even Alice held Betty Jo Gohappy in high regard. Unfortunately, Betty also had a bird-thin voice. She could not command the same attention in the Underdog hall as she was used to in an anthropology seminar. In less than a minute after she started reading her statement of concern the hall was once again abuzz with little pockets of discussion about concerns more mundane: Who runs the resort? Who builds the public restrooms? After a few minutes of this Carmody leaned over to Ike and Greer and whispered that he felt he'd participated in enough civic action for the summer; he thought he'd slip off to the Crabbe Potte for a little drinkie-drinkie and hanky-panky. But *tomorrow*, he reminded them, bright and early, they'd trade that torn web for a fresh one and head back *out* to that nice hot hole of theirs—do some dunking in bloody earnest! He grinned at the murmuring crowd, his face impish and conspiratorial. 'Not a word where we was, though. *These* chowderheads aren't like to stumble on to the hole, but boats out of the other ports won't be so starstruck. So six bells at the *Cobra* and not a b'god word. You hearin' me, Mister Greer?'

'Hearin' fine, Mistah Carmody,' Greer saluted. His anxieties were ebbing now that Ike's move had been made, and survived. 'Not carin' so much about it, though. Whoa! Six bells.'

'Isaak?'

'Don't worry about me, Carm. I've had my fill of civic action, too.'

Carmody pushed his way back through the crowd the way they'd entered. They saw him pause to say a few words to the Culligans and Willi, then slip on out. After a moment the big blonde followed. Ike couldn't tell if Alice even noticed, leaned back on her aloof perch at the doorjamb.

A few minutes later Greer told Ike he thought he would take advantage of the liberty he had left, and headed for the front door, veering aside enough to enlist Marge and Susan Boswell as accomplices. Ike ached to follow, but he couldn't bring himself to run that gantlet—not after the fool he'd just made of himself. For years this crowd had been waiting to see the famous Bakatcha Bandit flash the famous fire and talk the terrible talk. Now they'd seen and heard and ho-hum. He had signified and he had bombed. And even if he could have screwed up his courage and braved the gantlet, there was still Alice, right by the damned front door like the bitch twin of Cerberus. Good old razor-tongued Alice would be bound to have a couple of cutting comments. There was a fire exit along the north wall, but it would set off an alarm. The hall had no back door. The Grangers that had built the place a hundred years ago had never anticipated the need for a retreat to the rear.

Then Isaak remembered the storage closet—a narrow hall-space behind the podium, where the Deaps kept their bingo prizes. The tiny door to the storage space was hidden behind the flag and was always kept locked by the Deaps, but it was a code punch lock and the Underdog president was entrusted with the code, in case of fire. Ike edged that way. Kneeling behind the piano he lifted the flag and fingered the lock buttons. He wasn't surprised to find that the code had not been changed since his term in office. Who wants to steal what they're planning on winning?

He ducked through the panel at a particularly tumul-tuous moment in the meeting's wrangling and slid it shut behind him, unnoticed. The only illumination came in through a vent grating near the ceiling, above the door panel. He waited while his eyes adjusted. The space was narrow and cramped, with shelves along both sides making it narrower yet. The shelves were stacked with prizes: blankets, cookingware, cuckoo clocks, Kewpie dolls, microwaves, dishmen, chipmen, celefones. He couldn't see it, but he knew at the other end of the dark hall was a bolted door that opened to the alley. He was easing carefully in that direction when a sulky buzzing voice spoke, right at his ear.

'The Jimmy Stewart impersonation was boffo, Isaak. It reminded me of Destry. But it didn't turn the trick, did it?

These people are too far gone even for Destry. The only dude can turn the trick now is the Deuce.'

'Squid? Is that you? Jesus, man, what are you talking about?'

'You mean Deuce? Or Destry? Destry was the reluctant gunslinger that Jimmy Stewart played in *Destry Rides Again*. With Marlene Dietrich? He tried the inspirational exhortation tactic, too, but he was finally forced to break out the old six-shooter . . .'

'Where the hell are you, Billy?' The voice sounded more than just close, as though that sulky hornet had escaped his bottle only to end up in your head.

'The Deuce, on the other hand, is the famous Deuce X of Greek drama. Deuce X Machina, don't you get it? Not to worry, not to worry. About any of it. You did your best, Isaak, but we are past the point of inspirational exhortation. Far past. Yet do not dismay; Deuce X is on the way. The fan, you see, is catching up to the shit.'

'God damn you, Bellisarius, I can't see a thing!'

'Some say fire—' Inches from Ike's cheek a bright blue flame sparked from a green lighter, like a tongue from a lizard. '—but ice will suffice. Good evening, Isaak. Do you have any real alcohol? You do, don't you? When I heard you out there I thought you sounded boiled. I said to myself, "I never knew Isaak Sallas to get so boiled. And so *el*oquent! I bet he has some real McGilla and I bet he brings me some." Isaak, this little Squid's ink sac's about empty . . .'

Ike noticed the green lighter was trembling desperately. He drew the Irish from his hip and held it into the blue butane glow. The last quarter still shimmered at the bottom of the square bottle. A thin hand came first into the light and took it; then Billy's face appeared, in strict profile. It was stark and sharp, like a glyph on the wall of a limestone cave. The face tilted to drink, which wasn't easy; Bellisarius was lying on one of the plank shelves, a slot hardly more than a foot wide. Ike had to help him hold the bottle.

'What are you doing here, Billy? People have been looking high and low for you.'

'Don't I know,' Billy said. 'Especially *certain* people.'

'You mean Greener? Snap out of it, man, why would Greener be after you? *Me,* maybe, if he's got a score to settle, but why you?'

'Because he knows I *know,* Isaak. He knows I'm the only one able to see the flaw in his fantasy. He's selling hellfire and I'm seeing ice. Have a drink with me, Ike, for Old Dog Tray's sake.'

Ike took the bottle and swallowed and handed it back. Through the gloom he was able to discern that Billy had made his little shelf as comfortable as possible. Blankets were spread as a pad and rolled for pillows. He had a water jug and a plastic bag of trail mix. Books and notepads were piled at the shelf's head and an extension cord led to an old-fashioned gooseneck incandescent. There was also a cup-sized hot plate and a metal cup. Spent tea bags littered shelf and floor both, always two bags twined together.

'Yes, ice. Those mammoths found frozen with fresh buttercups in their mouths? Instantaneous refrigeration! As the rain forests are burned, the air at the equator gets hotter and hotter, correct? Rising faster and faster and higher and higher, pulling the cold air down from the poles to fill the vacuum. Same principle as butane flame refrigeration. Faster and higher, higher and colder, until the gases are separating into liquids. Hailstones of oxygen. Hydrogen sleet. Can't make a fire without causing a *Hindenburg.* Ice storms breaking the sound barrier. Mercury plummeting. Hydroelectric power stopped at the turbines. *Ice* age, Isaak, any day now.'

Ike had to admire the delight the little man took in his paranoia. 'Sounds like you've got a lot to look forward to, Billy. Why not come out in the open so you can enjoy it?'

'Ah, you're sweet, Isaak, to be concerned for the poor Squid. The truth is I *like* it in here, hiding; I've been enjoying some high-IQ meditations.'

'You can't hide in here forever.'

'Oh, I don't know. Forever? I just hope it gets here before *Greener* does. I don't fear random doom; I would rather be an insignificant casualty of a random catastrophe in an indifferent system gone in*sane* than risk salvation at the hands of that Bible-thumping Monster from Beyond the Locker Room. Because he *will* be coming, Isaak, and I don't possess your kind of cowboy backbone. More mind than spine is the Squid.' He held the bottle near the flame. 'Here, Brother, the last corner is yours. Please. I know we have never been friends—why should I make an exception with you? I *have* no friends—but I have always felt we were actors in the same movie.'

The green lizard sucked back its tongue and the room went dark again, signaling the oracular interview was coming to its end. 'In my movie Destry *Hides* Again. But not to worry. The townspeople will escape the clutches of the villain, regardless of our actions, Brother Isaak. For the very Deuce is coming.'

'I could care less about the townspeople,' Isaak said into the dark. 'Fuck the whole moronic mess of them. I mean, Squid . . . everybody's gone crazy.'

The buzz at his ear was gentle, almost tender; charitable; compassionate: 'It was the only place left to go, Isaak.'

Out in the last lingering twilight of the alley Ike listened until he heard the bolt slide tight on the other side of the narrow storeroom door, then set out for the rental yard. He walked still a little cramped over, from the storage space. The thick sky overhead seemed to be heavy-laden and close, pressing down, like that dark shelf full of bingo prizes pressing down on that poor addled fugitive back in the closet.

Ike knew he was weaving a little in his crabbed walk, but he was confident of his steps, feeling quite drunk but strangely clear-headed. This trashy old alley was just what he needed—smelly, uneven, haphazard, shamefully cluttered. Stacks of empty shipping crates and overflowing garbage cans and discarded machinery. At least you

452

knew this was *real* trash, *real* garbage; if you'd been out on that insane Main you could not have known for sure; it could have been prop trash, like that studied clutter of simulated trash in Pirates of the Caribbean.

At the end of the alley he looked both ways, then turned up the empty sidewalk along Cook. Before he got to the top of Cook a footpath shortcut would take him overland through fireweed and salal and Scotch broom, then back down to upper Bayshore to the rent lot. A walk along Bayshore itself would probably have been shorter than the shortcut, but he didn't want to risk having some nosy good Samaritan pull over and give him a lift and a lot of flack about his unfortunate return to public speaking. It happened anyway. He was almost to the footpath when a sudden glare of headlights swung on to Cook way down behind him. The lights sent his shadow stretching out over the ruts and potholes all the way to the Underdog Cemetery. He didn't turn. He kept up his crab-legged striding until the vehicle pulled alongside. It was the new limo they had crowded next to. A window whirred down, like a sheet of silver melting.

'Hop in, Isaak. See what you think about my new wheels. Our old rental mysteriously picked up a *wobble* in the left front.'

He climbed into the back alongside Levertov, but he didn't say anything. The limo's interior was as thick as the sky. The silver flowed back into the window space but the vehicle didn't move. After a few moments of silence Levertov asked, '*Quo vadis?*'

'Back down to Bayshore, I guess. I was going to take a shortcut, but I don't think your new wheels better try it. Unless you want to risk picking up another *wobble*.'

Levertov spoke into the dark and the big car made a noiseless U-turn back toward town.

'I'm pleased we are getting this little opportunity to talk, Slam-boy.' Levertov's words were weighted with sad courtesy. 'Because I have a bit of a bothersome bone to pick with you. I don't think I care for what you were implying with your stirring speech back there. No, I don't.

Beneath all that high-and-mighty doubletalk you were ranking me quite *viciously*, I thought, and without cause.'

'I didn't notice you at the shindig, Nick,' Ike said.

'The night has a thousand eyes.' Levertov must have touched a control, because three monitor screens fluttered on behind the driver's seat—two angles from the hall's interior and a high long shot from outside. One was from a ceiling corner, static. One was a hid-vid, probably Clark B's beepboard. The exterior long shot had to be from someplace up very high, higher than any building Ike could think of in town.

'It's from the top of the wing-sail,' Nicholas answered Ike's unspoken question. 'Neat, huh? But you have never appreciated these modern zim-zams, have you, Isaak? You're probably wise. Just toys.' He flicked the screens back to dark. 'Now, can we talk? No zim-zams, no flim-flams. Slam to Slam, all wounds open. I honestly don't know *what* I've done to offend you, Isaak. I realize what an insufferable conniving snake I am, of course, but that's just the nature of the beast, nothing personal. Yet I get the distinct feeling that you think I've done something to affront you *per*sonally?'

Ike was sure then about Old Marley, and positive that Levertov knew he was sure. So why all this ballroom courtesy? Was Levertov trying to needle him into taking a shot, or was he just gloating? Ike had an angry urge to answer the taunt with the truth, and toss in the grisly hole card they'd come across off Pyrite Cape—he'd bet the thousand-eyed night didn't have a spy eye out *there*—but decided quickly against it. No sense in tipping your hand too soon. Besides, it would have gone against the protocol of the situation in some way. This wasn't a game. This was a kind of psychic dance that Levertov had maneuvered them into doing, and the proper steps had to be observed.

'Why, no, Nick, I can't think of anything personal. Like you say, it's just that you're an insufferable conniving snake. I said what I said at the meeting because I'm still slam-smart enough to recognize fried ice cream when I see it. And that's what this town's getting served: fried ice cream by the shovelfuls, Nick, by the shovelfuls.'

'Apparently they don't see it that way, Ike.'

'Punks never do, Nick. Never have. Why they're punks. But if it will ease your mind any, let me say this: You're not going to hear any more rank-job speeches out of me. I'm nowhere near as concerned about what kind of ice cream this punkhole goes for as I was an hour ago.'

Levertov tossed back his long hair and bleated with delight. 'Ike, I love you. You're a treasure and that's the truth. They need one of you in the Bureau of Standards. Where were you bound? Why don't you come out to the yacht and we'll do a couple of shovelfuls of our own, for old slam's sake?'

'I guess not, Nick. If you want to give me a ride, my van's still out to the Tom Rentsa-Lot, and I'd like to grab it while Herb's still at the big meeting. He's got a bone to pick with me, too. I'll just kind of sag back, if you don't mind. I'm tired. And go ahead and turn the zim-zams back on if you want; I'm about half interested, in a spectator sort of way.'

They continued the rest of the way out Bayshore in silence, watching the three video points of view of the Dog House. Wayne Altenhoffen was at the fire-hydrant lectern, reading his scathing editorial, but no-one was listening. Everybody was talking. Groups had grouped up and deals were going down. When they reached the bay moorage, Ike pointed in the direction of his van and Nick said something into a ring mike. The big car wheeled soundlessly on to Herb Tom's lot. When they got to the spot where he'd left his van weeks ago, it was gone. In its place was the Jeep. Greer had somehow beat him to the van again, revitalized as he was by the Boswell girls and the return of his Jamaican dialect. Ike grinned to himself and got out of the limo without mentioning it to Nick; if the Jeep failed to start he'd get that chance to take his solitary walk after all.

Before he closed the limo's luminous door he leaned back in—'No don't worry about any more shit-disturbing out of me, Nicholas; I've decided to leave it all in the hands of the Deuce'—then shut the door before more could be said.

The Jeep was still warm and started easily. He let the limo get out of sight before he backed up and swung out of the lot back toward town. He felt free and giddy. He was glad to be driving the topless old rattletrap. It was comfortable. The bayside air whipping his cheek was mysteriously ripe with the smell of smoldering garbage, as though the stink was being piped in from the dump all the way on the other side of town, just for him. It wrinkled the nose, but it was still a better air than that ionized atmosphere in the limousine.

He turned before he reached town to avoid Main and came into his road just below the water tower. There were three big earthmovers and a hydro-cat hunched in the sodium glow beneath the metal tower. The machines looked very devout in their stillness, like pilgrims that had come to worship at the site of a prophesied miracle. The buildings of the Loop place were just as dark and devout. When he turned up the ruts toward his place and the Jeep's headlights swept the flat, the mystery of that ripe bay air was solved. The smoldering mountain range of garbage had been removed. Scraped clean! Only the scraps of a few foothills remained. *That* had been the smoky stench he'd smelled from across the bay; they were using the dump as landfill for the new landing strip. The *bas*tards! Then Ike reminded himself, so what? So the hell what? It's their land and their landfill; they can put it where they please. And it's *my* trailerhouse, my castle keep—bought and paid for. I hauled it in here and I can haul it out of here. Fuck 'em.

He was about to drive on when a gaudy figure came spinning into his headlights like a disheveled dervish. It was Louise Loop, her variegated locks and paisley silks flying. Mascara was draining from her eye sockets down her sweaty cheeks again.

'Help me, please, oh help me-e-e.'

He should have known as soon as he saw that abomination in the net—it was going to be one of those vooshaw days.

'They're trying to kill me, Ike. They put me alone up here on zoners to kill me, but I spit them out.'

'Who's trying to kill you, Louise?'

'The hogs and the bears. They are starving without the garbage. Hear them out there?'

He could, actually; there were hungry snorts and grunts all up and down the hillside. 'What about your dog? Nerd'll protect you, Louise.'

'Nerd is drowned, don't you remember? O, Isaak, there's just me . . .'

She sank to the dirt like a rainbow deflating. Ike had to drag her into the Jeep, then carry her to Greer's bed at the back of the trailerhouse. It would be a colorful surprise for the Masta Rasta if he came home later.

He took three aspirin, and a warm shower, and three more aspirin. Finally, sitting in his bathrobe in the dim undisturbed air of his bought-and-paid-for castle keep, he couldn't help but wonder: what's next? Come on, goddamn it, what's next? In eventual response came the ricocheting bounce of headlights through the trailer's windows, bouncing brighter and brighter, then the scrunch of a rig in his oyster-shell yard. Out on the steps, he shaded his eyes against the headlights' glare.

'Sorry if we disturb you, Mr Sallas. We are just some fans. We heard you at the meeting . . .'

It was a big balloon wheeler, its electric motor grinding. There seemed to be three in the front and three in back. He was glad the .22 was still in the hanging planter, within reach. He held the planter with his outstretched hand, as though to steady his balance.

'You were kick-ass, Mr Sallas. Posolutely zam.'

'Yes, Mr Sallas, you were. A lot of us thought so. But we didn't want to draw attention.'

He realized then they were all kids, just kids. That first voice sounded like one of the Culligans, or younger, even, and the second was a girl. Perhaps the Eskimo. He thought he could make her face out in the dash glow. Beside her, behind the wheel, was somebody with a fluffy grey beard. But the face was still the face of a kid.

'We just wanted to let you know, Mr Sallas,' the girl's voice went on, 'you got comrades you don't know about. Allies. We can say no more. Good night.'

He was sure it was the Eskimo; he remembered the husky voice she was using that afternoon at Marley's funeral. As the balloon wheels backed around, it suddenly occurred to him he was being very inhospitable. 'Hey!' he called. 'I been thinking about that pup—'

They were already bouncing back on to the flats, trailing conspiratorial whispers like streamers from a midnight float. Ike stood listening until they were out of hearing, then went inside. He discovered he was carrying the .22.

'Hope you don't have any more visitations, Mr Zam,' he scolded himself. 'You're getting a tad trigger-happy.'

19

Rave Like a Madwoman
Don't Pussyfoot

Alice stuck it out at the meeting much longer than she had
intended or anticipated. Speaker after speaker ascended
to the podium and spent their precious ten minutes,
fumbling out the words like coins into the slot of a
gambling machine, hopeless and resigned—*clearly* the
damn thing was never going to pay off. For hours now,
since early evening, each word-fumbler had watched
his predecessors try their luck to no avail. No jackpots.
No big misses. Not even so much as a few little teaser
enticements to keep the suckers coming. Enticements
weren't expected and teasers were unnecessary. This
was a slot one played not for fortune, luck, chance of a
long shot or a killer pot or the like, but to be able to say
at those scenes afterward, when the future got together
to chew over the past, 'I put in *my* two cents' worth!'

No big misses, that is, except that one of Ike Sallas'.
That was a miss so vast and reverberating that the whole
room was shaken by it, fumblers, gamblers, kibitzers and
all; and for a number of spins afterwards the speakers
could be seen spending their little roll of allotted words
more shrewdly, with some feeble flickers of what was
half hope; because, hey! such a big fizzle *has to* indicate
the potential of a big flash, they reasoned. But that flicker
soon faded, and the speakers lapsed back into their spirit-
less spending of talk and time.

It had been obvious from the beginning that the game
was rigged, had been rigged for months. Years, probably, and no-one had noticed. It reminded Alice of that
FOR SALE sign in the lot full of fireweed and broken

machinery next to the Bear Flag. The sign had been poking up out of the lot's trash for so long that Alice could not remember when the SOLD sticker had been stapled across it. She had not noticed. Both sticker and sign were bleached dim now. And it wasn't until the Cat crew pulled in yesterday to start pushing the trash into a pile that she was moved even to inquire who had paid for that SOLD sticker. The crew foreman was a bright-eyed go-getter fresh from Georgia Tech with a corporate beepboard and a silver hard hat. He cheerfully informed Alice that he was not yet at liberty to divulge the identity of his employers nor what their plans might be for the property. 'It's a *secret*,' the boy beamed. The plans might be a secret, Alice had thought, but that fox-head decal on the boy's beepboard and hard hat left little doubt as to who his employers were. No, this was no cheap fly-by-nightie carnival wheel they were up against; this was a high casino caper, big-time owned and big-time rigged. And the fact that these small-fry citizens had been given the opportunity to put in their two cents' worth was something of an honor, whether any of them had a snowball's chance of coming out winners or not. And it was an honor that had better be appreciated, in full public ceremony. You wouldn't want these new owners of the gaming house to get the idea that you might be one of those un*grate*ful sorts of sports, would you?

So Alice had stuck it out for the novelty of the spectacle, enduring one display of futile verbosity after another with a kind of perverse pleasure. When Carmody stopped by to tell the Culligan boys to be ready for a full run tomorrow, that they'd located a hot spot with fish so thick they ripped the net and he was on his way to make some phone calls for a replacement, Alice thought of getting up and going along. When she found out where he planned to phone from she changed her mind.

'Join me, Mrs Carmody? for a champagne and chateaubriand at the Crabbe Potte?'

'Why, Mr *Carmody*,' she answered in a voice that came

out far too harsh and loud, 'I'd be afraid I might cramp your style.'

He backed away, stung speechless.

As soon as he was gone she bit her tongue in self-recrimination. Everybody at the back of the room had watched; now she was pinned down by all the attention her reply had attracted. After a few minutes, when Willimina Hardesty got up and ambled out after the barrel-gutted old scamp, she bit it again, hard. This must have caused her to make a hell of a face, because the girl Shoola got down from her bench and came over to offer a few unsolicited words of wisdom:

'Blame the moon, forgive the man.'

'What?'

'Blame the moon and forgive the man. Sister Poor Clare used to say it to us girls in catechism.'

'What does a Jesuit nun,' Alice demanded angrily, 'know about a man?'

The girl shrugged. 'As much as that old Orthodox priest of yours knows about women, I guess. Every time after Mass he keeps telling me, "*Falsus in uno, falsus in omnibus.*"'

'Meaning?'

'Meaning he thinks I'm either improperly dressed or that this isn't all *me* in here. You want to go over to Tire City and hear some guitar singing?'

'I'd be the one improperly dressed, then; I didn't bring my inner tube.'

And when the girl left a little later with her new bearded boy-friend and the others, Alice knew she had allowed her stubborn goddamned pride to make her miss *another* opportunity for a dignified escape.

The crowd continued to thin as the speeches droned on. Well, if she felt pinned down, imagine what that poor mortified Sallas must be feeling. While Wayne Altenhoffen was reading his scathing editorial from the makeshift *Beacon*, she looked for Ike's red face and noticed that he was no longer at the bottom of the podium steps. He had been stuck there since his talk, like

461

a man in a sinkmire avoiding any move that might mire him deeper; now he was nowhere in the hall. He must have crawled by on his belly, poor devil. She had been enjoying a certain sardonic comfort, realizing that their predicaments were similar. Now even that comfort had somehow slipped away. When she was certain he was nowhere in the hall she tipped down from the fire extinguisher and went pussyfooting across the crowded porch and down the steps, her face a mask of careless disdain.

In the privacy of her office above the laundry room she dropped the mask and took herself severely to task. What a hypocritical hussy she was under that carved nonchalance! What a clown! Why had she always been the puppet to this clumsy handful of hometown opinions? She hadn't worried about opinions in San Francisco, where such puffed-up ragbags as she was acquainted with were certainly more critical; and she hadn't worried about opinions in the little cul-de-sac in La Jolla. Only here, in this cultural backwater! She had to make a show of treating Michael Carmody like a cad when she honestly wasn't angry at the old rip at all. She really held no brief with him about this big blonde. Willimina Hardesty was no more a home-wrecker than Michael Carmody was an unfaithful husband. As a married couple, Mr and Mrs Carmody had enjoyed a better-than-average partnership, primarily because it was understood from the first handshake that this marriage was founded on the practical; it was bureaucratically beneficial, and anything else was gravy. Their businesses had prospered and their excesses had ebbed. Carmody had stopped dropping big poker wads every time he got the blue lonelies; Alice had stopped fueling her wraths with nightly stokings of alcohol. Their lives and lifestyles had certainly mellowed, the town had been gratified to note—especially Alice the Angry Aleut's. But there it was . . . *there* it was: still the homecoming runner-up, parading for the gratification of the hometown band.

'God damn me,' she cursed herself and the band both;

'I need a drink, I don't care *how* angry it makes me. Better to rave like a madwoman than pussyfoot around like a pansy.'

The tequila was gone as well as the last of Old Norway's mead. The only thing she knew of on the premises was the bottle she had found earlier in the week in the laundry room—some absentminded Deap's Mad Dog Jack. She had never been able to stomach the cheap port taste, even during her hardest-drinking times. You had to draw the line somewhere. But with Herky's closed and signs of a rough night ahead, it was any cheap port in a storm.

She threw down the first few swallows with her eyes clenched, as though to shut out the taste. It finally started to hum a little and she put the bottle back on the shelf with the detergents and went back upstairs. She kicked off her shoes and peeled out of the square-dance outfit she'd worn to the town meeting. It was a red thing with white checks on it, like an old-fashioned tablecloth, and the skirt stuck stiffly out to show the myriad ruff and rustle of petticoats. She had picked it up at a Pioneer fundraiser in Ketchican as a joke; she had worn it to the meeting as a defiance.

After a shower she pulled on her floppy warm-up pants and wrapped one of Carmody's old plaid flannels about her. The shirt was worn to a frazzle at the cuffs and what buttons it still had left were useless in the frayed-out buttonholes; but it was voluminous, the measure of Carmody's girth. The shirttails could be overlapped more than halfway around her narrow waist in each direction.

She opened a Gatorade and cross-legged herself on her mattress with her back to the wall and her legs bent so she could study her bookcase. She had old acquaintances on these shelves, trustworthy friends who had accompanied her through many a rough night before. Sassy Zora Neale Hurston had been especially helpful on those first nights kicking the hard juice. And Eudora Welty, with her good ear and her clear amused eye; she was always a stimulating companion on a dark passage. But this night was going to need someone more classic.

More timeless. She selected *Helen in Egypt* by Hilda Doolittle. After a few pages of the chipped-ice verse about the antique antics of Helen and Achilles, Alice went downstairs to fetch Worthless for cozier company. After a few more pages she admitted that neither warm puppies nor cold poetry were going to cut it, and she went down again for the Mad Dog Jack.

She had been reading and drinking and petting the pup's sleeping head for nearly an hour when she heard a rig pull into her court. It must be the Shoola girl, being dropped off by one of her gang of admirers. After the Eskimo girl had recovered from the crush she had on Isaak Sallas, she had become quite the deb of Kuinak's teen scene. Down at the set she was always chattering away at the center of some circle of fishkid extras. Even such local luminaries as the Culligan brothers were squiring her around, and they were pushing twenty.

Alice listened to the young voices calling goodbyes as the car backed around and went spinning away down the street. The motor's whine and the teenage calls were somehow touching and melancholy, receding into the overhung night. When they were gone Alice put the book down and hugged the sleeping ball of warm fur up tight beneath her chin, to melt the cold lump there. Ah, Sister Poor Clare was right: the moon was to blame. She hoped Michael Carmody had found himself a cozy harbor for the night. If ever a merry old dribbler deserved one, it was he. He had never complained about the increasing number of nights she'd left him alone out at his gothic absurdity across the bay. She knew he valued her company. *Any* company. Carmody liked to have a face across from his coffee cup in the morning, and an ear sympathetic to his opinions about the b'god bloody Christ-killing world-dish news at night. Yet he never protested when she headed for town in her van. He had always honored her need to be by herself, and it shamed her to tears to think how, when the other end of the stick came around, she had given him such a loud load of shit over his need for a little glandular camaraderie. She took another swallow

464

of the hundred-proof and tried to dam back the tears by burying her face in the Worthless pup's fur.

It was in this pitiful position that the native girl found the native woman.

'Hey, Mrs Carmody, you all right?' The wide eyes peeked into the room from the round stairwell. 'I saw your reading light . . .'

Alice wiped her eyes on a frayed shirtsleeve. 'Come on up, sweetheart,' she hiccoughed. 'What you see is what you get: Helen in Egypt, drinking in bed, weeping in bimbo despair.'

'I was worried for you. I knew you felt ashamed for that way you acted to Mr Carmody. It wasn't very civilized . . .'

'I know, I *know*!' Alice hiccoughed again, a sound between a boozy sob and a tipsy giggle. 'But you know what really shames me, girl? Not that I acted uncivilized but that I acted so fucking *trite*! Like one of those wronged wives on a damn *soap*dish cliche. I *hate* being trite! I like to think of myself as a lady of taste and learning. I've got a master's in *art*, you know. Ah, how can I be so smart and act so dumb at the same time, God *damn* me!'

That was the damn that broke the dam's back. Tears came in torrents. The girl climbed on up the stairhole and dropped to her knees on the mattress. She put her arms around Alice—pup, book, bottle and all—and rocked them for a while, humming a tuneless nasal tune.

'What you must think of me now,' Alice said when the sobbing had subsided.

'Just what I thought of you then,' the girl assured her. 'I thought, Oops, that Alice Carmody has got her mouth full of feet again; she'll be looking for something to wash it out.' She took the bottle and examined it, frowning. 'I did think a lady of your taste and learning would be able to come up with a better brand of mouthwash.'

Alice laughed aloud, shaking her head in amazement at this precocious wonder. Scant weeks ago Alice had considered *herself* the counselor and comforter, the world-wise protector of a kind of naive naiad that went pedaling around bare-nippled in a world of sharks. How things

changed. 'Mogen David's worst,' she said, taking back
the bottle. 'It's what I deserve. I turned *down* champagne and *chateaubriand*, if you'll recall. I hope Mr
Carmody had better sense.'

'I think I heard him down at that yacht a while ago,
partying with Mr Steubins, I think.'

'Heard him?'

'It was dark on deck. But you could hear Mr Carmody
ding-donging like a bell buoy. He was the light of the
party.'

'Ah. A yacht party. I'm glad. Who else was there?'

'I don't know. We were not actually *at* the yacht party
except, well, a little bit. We just went by to drop off
Leonard. You remember?'

'I remember Leonard,' Alice told her. She had the
distinct feeling the girl was hiding something from her,
and that fanned the hot tongue of anger in the ashes again.
It wasn't so much that her old man was philandering, it
was that somebody would do her the insult of trying
to *hide* it from her. But she bit her tongue. 'Leonard
seems a harmless enough Hollywoodie. Did you have
an interesting evening?'

'Very interesting. We all went first down to Tire City
where some fishkids sung street-corner. Then I tell some
stories for a while. Then we had the idea to drive up to
tell Mr Sallas how we liked his talk tonight. No, don't
think the wrong thing; my heart is over that business. It
was Leonard that had the idea to drive up there.'

'Mr Sallas must have been most gratified.'

'I don't know about that,' the girl frowned. 'He looked
most lonesome and sorrowful is what he looked. He said
he might want Worthless after all.'

The girl rubbed the sleeping pup's round belly for a
thoughtful moment, then smiled into Alice's face. 'So
anyway . . . I just came to say goodnight and sleep tight
and don't worry that you say dumb things that hurt
your husband. He's not the one those things hurt, he's
having a fine time, I think. At least he's not sorrowfully
lonesome.' She rocked back to her heels and stood, her

466

face twinkling between innocence and mischief. 'I hope you don't think me out of base, Mrs Carmody, popping in unannounced and saying stuff like this?'

Alice would have liked to counter with a mischievous rejoinder of her own, but all she could get out was 'Not at all. I'm glad you came.'

'Goodnight and sleep tight.' She bent to give the pup's head a final pat. 'Goodnight, Worthless. Maybe somebody will get you and Mr Sallas together sometime.'

Alice took another swallow of the fortified wine as the girl's soft footsteps descended the metal steps and crossed the laundry room. When she heard the door to the girl's cabin close across the yard she stood up. She slipped her feet into her moccasins and carefully negotiated her way down the spiral of stair, carrying the half-awake animal and the half-empty bottle. She kept going on out to her six-wheeler without giving deliberation a chance to start. The thick, chill drapery of a ground fog parted to let her through.

By the time she had reached the water tower the fog was gone and the cloud cover was unraveling in long black tatters. A full moon swam in and out of sight, splashing the treeline luminous blue. In this lambent haze the stark flat voids where the garbage heaps had been came as a shock; the scraped earth seemed a sight far fouler than when it was mountained with rotting trash. Smoke rose from hot pockets of ash and hungry pigs ran scattering from her headlights. At the end of the road the trailerhouse was dark. Just as well. Then a porch light came on before she could back out. She switched off the van and sat awhile, listening to the motor tick cool. She swallowed as much of the sweet liquor as she could without gagging, then got out. He was already on the top step, his terry-cloth bathrobe steaming a little in the blue moonlight.

'Ike Sallas!' she commanded. 'I heard you were lonely so I brought you some company. Were you asleep?'

'Alice? Well, not quite. Just out of the shower. I thought the night's visitations were over . . .'

'Well, not quite,' she echoed. 'But this won't take long. Can I come in?'

'Sure.' He pushed the twisted screen wide for her and switched on a light. He smiled when he saw her pair of burdens. 'Which one's the company—the pup or the Mad Dog?'

'Take your pick,' she said, holding both forward. The bottle was now nearly empty; the pup was fully awake and struggling. She tried to clasp it back against her, but it struggled harder, pawing at her shirtfront.

'I better take the pup,' Ike said in a low voice, 'before she disrobes you.'

'I've been calling her Worthless.' She pulled the flannel back around and tucked it in her warm-ups. 'But you can name her what you wish.'

'Worthless is fine.'

'Why are we whispering?'

'Because I've already got some company, it just so happens. Louise Loop is zoned off back in Greer's bed. Or I guess I should say Louise *Levertov*.'

Alice answered, 'Suit yourself.' Her whisper seemed a trifle cold.

'I found Lulu raving in the dark about an hour ago,' Ike hurried to explain, 'looking like a little girl with a monster after her. She said she feared she was being set up for slaughter, was what she said . . .'

'She did, did she?' Alice's eyes were on Sallas' face. 'Poor Lulu. All those Hollywood hair jobs must have bleached out what little brains she started with. Set up by who?'

'As near as I could make out, by her husband. Your wonderful son. Like I said, she was raving.' He watched her raise the bottle to tight lips. 'Good God, Alice! If you're actually going to drink that stuff, at least let me get some mixer. And some hors d'oeuvres. Have a seat, I'll be right back.'

He tiptoed out of her sight, toward the other end of the tubular dwelling. She remained standing, her hip against the harsh edge of the formica tabletop. She realized she

468

was seething beneath the plaid flannel. Bite your battle-ax tongue, she commanded herself; he's just trying to do the chivalrous thing, the *gentleman* thing. Oh, yeah? Then what was that 'wonderful son' dig about? And that vitriolic diatribe at the town meeting, come to think of it; what was he driving at with *that*?

Isaak returned carrying a round wooden cutting board arranged with glasses, Perrier, crackers and a block of Swiss cheese. He made no move to slide into a seat, either. He put the makeshift tray on the table and mixed the drinks. The sparkling water *did* help the Mad Dog a little. She watched him snap open his buck knife to slice the cheese.

'I hope that's been washed since the last fish belly it cut open.'

Ike smelled the blade. 'Fish guts wash off easy. It's the corns and bunions that sometimes leave a stink.'

When she didn't smile he went back to his slicing. She tried to warn herself again about her battle-ax tongue, but she couldn't stop the seething. He thinks he's playing all this so cute and close to the vest. Hors d'oeuvres and mineral water from France. We'll see about *that* crap . . .

'Okay, Sallas; I think it's time we lay our cards on the table. What did you mean by that "wonderful son" slam? No more pussy-footing . . .'

He finished slicing the cheese on to the crackers and stuck the knife in the cutting board. He divided the remainder of her bottle in their two plastic glasses again and topped them with mineral water. He stepped back so he could lean against the wall opposite the fold-out table, facing her.

'I mean Lulu thinks they're trying to murder her. She says they filled her full of downers and left her at the Loop place alone, with all the doors open.'

'What for?'

'So the bears would eat her. Or the pigs. But she upchucked enough of the drug to keep conscious.'

'No, fool, I mean what in the name of God *for*?'

'For the property, for one thing—'

'The *property*? Oh for the love of Jesus and all his—
Listen, Lulu has been stashed up here alone at the Loop
house so she can dry out and tighten up a little! Everybody in town knows that. She was getting too damn loose.
You know what I mean, Lautrec? Too loose?' When he
didn't say anything she went on. 'I mean, what would
be the point? Lulu is Nick's best hope for getting a chunk
of Papa Loop's land. Old Omar doesn't care for Nick
any more than you do. If Lulu got murdered it would
be bye-bye son-in-law freak.'

He waited before answering, frowning down into the
bubbles in his glass. She barely heard his whisper.

'Old Omar's already murdered, Alice. Greer and I saw
him in the purse this afternoon.'

'Drowned?'

'Yeah, drowned.'

'Then how the hell do you jump to the conclusion that
he was murdered? Omar was never known as a steady
sailor, and that old tug he used for his gut boat was just
as chancy.'

'He was wrapped in mylar filmseal, Alice. And he
had a bowling ball stapled to his dick. Nobody's that
unsteady.'

'There's still the heir-apparent brothers.'

He shook his head. 'I don't think so. No-one has heard
from them since they flew off weeks ago—on some
mysterious mission for Foxcorp. I think that heirline is
crashed and burned.'

'Honestly, Sallas . . . you've let yourself get as loony
as Lulu.' Her whispering was becoming sweeter, softer,
though the mad glint in her eyes was hard as obsidian.
Couldn't he hear, for the love of God? Couldn't he see?
Didn't he notice the deliberate way her hand set the
empty glass down beside the cutting board?

'I don't know, Alice. Honestly. I *do* know Nick could
get very bitter and very vengeful when he was in jail. And
more than a little scary. He was always saying he'd been
getting abused and misused from before he was born, and
wouldn't rest until he got even.'

'We *all* can get very bitter and very vengeful,' she pointed out. 'And with good reason. Look at the bag of shit our predecessors left us holding. Who wouldn't get— And come to think of it, look at all that stuff *you* used to pull! What was that about if it wasn't vengeance?'

'Damn you, Alice, that was about my kid!'

'And this isn't about mine? Listen, Sallas, I've taken a lot of gouging from you over the years—about the way I run my affairs, my marriage, even the way I fucking *dress*—but I never expected you to start saying stuff about how I—'

'Alice, I have never said one word about—'

'You don't need to *say* anything; I'm not blind. But I *never* expected you to rank me about how I raised my son!'

'Shhh. I *wasn't* ranking you. All I—what I meant was ... Christ, woman; it wasn't your fault that Nicholas was born like he is, or where he was, or that he didn't have a fa—'

She was on him before he could finish the word, right in his face—hissing and clawing just like that cat out of the bottle. And *stabbing*, he realized. He saw the buck knife come down against his collarbone, twice, so hard the whole side of his ribcage went numb. Luckily it came down handle first; she was so rattled in her Mad Dog rage she didn't know if she had grabbed the weapon blade-up or blade-down.

'*Alice!*' He managed to catch the wrist before she could strike a third time. The other hand got a fistful of his cheek and ear. 'Alice, you insane bitch, if you—'

She stopped him short again, her knee glancing savagely off his hip into his stomach. When he doubled over she tried to sink her teeth into his scalp. He shook free and was able to straighten up enough to bend her backward against the tabletop and hold her there, thrusting his thigh between hers to keep her from kneeing him again. He held her wrists wide and squeezed until the knife fell back among the scattered slices of cheese. The two faces were so close and intense their eyes might have been points in carbon arc.

'Nicholas did have a father.' The words came through her clenched teeth like bacon frying, but she was still whispering. In fact, neither of them had raised their voice above a whisper. 'He had the same degenerate Russian son-of-a-bitch father that *I* had!' She waited until she was sure this had sunk home before she went on. 'So who's abused and who's misused, you tell me?'

He pulled back a little to regard her face. There were curls of his hair between her teeth and her nose was bleeding; she must have cracked it against his skull. 'I'm sorry,' he told her. He let her raise up a little but he didn't release her wrists. 'I never knew.'

'Neither did Nick. What was the sense of telling him? Ouch, damn, my kneecap's busted. What was that hard thing I hit, anyway? That was that fucking gun of yours again, wasn't it? Do you always arm yourself for visitors, or just me?'

'So Nick . . .' Ike couldn't get over the shock of what he'd just been told. 'Did anybody else—?'

'Ever know?' She could hear her heart's heavy beat even through the heave of her breathing. 'No, just the son-of-a-bitch. Only him.'

'Was he drunk?'

'Every time.'

'Jesus, Alice.' He had dropped his eyes. 'I'm sorry, I truly am. He must have been some son-of-a-bitch. No wonder you got such a gripe against guys. I always assumed—' He stopped, his eyes still lowered.

She looked down and saw what had stopped him. Their struggle had pulled the frayed shirttail from the waistband of her warm-ups. The faded plaid flannel was parted like a shabby curtain on one of the Meatstreet strip-dance stages. The comely pair of dancers on stage seemed aware of the effect they were having on their audience, and were heaving hard to the beat. Before Alice knew what was happening her hips had joined in with a little involuntary heave of their own.

472

Their eyes raised back to each other's. Ike's face was flaming with embarrassment. 'Okay, Alice . . . if I turn you loose will you give me your word you won't try some mad attack again?'

'I don't see why I should,' she teased. She suddenly felt quite amused and a little flattered by the radiance of his blush. She arched back just to needle him, he was such a comical prude. 'I *am*, after all, a madwoman.'

'Hush,' he said.

Her hips throbbed again and this time she thought she detected an answer. 'Besides, you've always got that big old pistol in your pocket if things get out of control—'

'Just hush. Please . . .'

But she just could not. She felt drunk with mischief. Her mouth had a mind of its own and was on a roll, one sharp rejoinder after another. She might have gone on needling him all night if he hadn't stopped her mouth with his. The port in the midnight storm went magically calm and bright. Beacons and bells. That's when she realized it wasn't mischief she felt drunk with.

'Hey, Alice—Jesus, lady, I didn't mean—'

This time he was the one needing hushing. Beacons and bells sure as hell. Trite but true. It was comical, all this enchantment. The aluminum ceiling an exalted dome. Even the sound of the bears and pigs in the hungry night: a blessed choir. Absolutely comical. But she wasn't laughing. With her wrists released she was able to lean back on the tabletop with her elbows for support, but the formica was too cold, and the cheese and the cuttings were going to be a problem, enchantment or no.

'Okay, Sallas; if we're going to go through with this we've got to get more comfortable. We're too old and out of practice for acrobatics.'

They had to move the pup.

Before sleep gathered her up and carried her away, Alice saw the elongated dome of the Galaxxy come alive with rippling forms of light. A Kandinsky phantasmagoria was taking place where the man's silhouette had been.

473

Geometric flowers, fountains of jewels, shifting jigsaw shapes cut from flame. Cerise snakes squirming contentedly among paisley lime polyps. Things and half-things and things on the verge. She saw crimson chimeras and magenta manta rays and the fleeting plumage of flamingo-pink flamenco dancers —all waltzing wildly to the tune of some invisible fiddler, all *over* the inverted dance floor of the trailer's aluminum ceiling.

At first she wondered drowsily if this might be the fabled fireworks of love, lighting up her life at last—but that was just *too* trite to be true, except in Harlequin Romance fantasies. The next thought was that Sallas must have dosed her. A little Purple Haze in her plastic glass? It would have been easy. But she quickly conceded that was an explanation as fanciful as the first. Isaak Sallas could no more dose you to get you into the sack than love could light up your life with a disco show on the ceiling. Finally she concluded it had to be the big sun storm the weathermen had been predicting, producing an unseasonal aurora borealis—explosions of charged particles funneled by the magnetic flux above the pole and projected against the screen of the earth's atmosphere, like those picture tubes in old TV sets. The cold fire of excited atoms. It must be reflecting up from the faceted mirror of Sallas' mother-of-pearl yard, through the trailer's window.

She remembered reading that oxygen atoms produce the reds, yellows and aquamarine greens, and nitrogen makes the violets and the neon blues and those languid dribbles of electric lime. She was somewhat disappointed at her rather unromantic solution to the mystery—just agitated atoms in the dreary domain of physics. Then she recalled another, a more *classical* interpretation. Just before sleep swung low and claimed her she remembered a mythology lecture she had audited at SF State. According to Viking folklore the northern lights are the reflections from the golden shields of the warrior-maiden Valkyries as they escort the souls of heroes through the heavens and across the Rainbow Bridge, to their reward in Valhalla. Ah, solutions classical! Better than pills purple or fancies Harlequin, certainly, or chilly physical facts from the upper atmosphere. Truer, too, in their primal mythic way, the way Cézanne's vision is truer than Wyeth's, or Pollock's than Picasso's, Chagall's than Hopper's . . . until a three-alarm scream through the dreaming drowse abruptly rebutted all the theories—physical, fantastical, romantical, mythical:

'*Eeee-ee Jesus*, I *told* you! They burned my papa's *slaughter*-house down!'

20

Look Out Shit
Here Comes the Fan

They called her—because she was endowed with that certain heart-jerk charm that unbudded waif-types always possessed in those old black-and-white I-can't-pay-the-rent-you-must-pay-the-rent melodramas—Nell.

She was Shoola's middle sister, the one that that Isaak man had reassured: yes, I'm sure they'll play with you. She was six summers old and her real name was a maze of glottals and vowels and fricatives to tangle the nimblest tongue—even up home. And the name's meaning didn't make any kind of sense, even to her: something about a flounder fish and ice worms and being late for the launch to church, all some way involved. So the Movie People called her Nell and as far as she was concerned, that was just fine.

Besides the nice motel rooms, the Movie People had provided her and her family with a kind of Movie Stars' waiting place in one of the empty wings on the middle floor of the old cannery. They said it was a green room though it wasn't much of any color at all. It was big and wooden and starkly unpainted. There was no floor covering on the old pine planks and no wallboards on the studs. The pipes and wires were right out raw, like the veins and sinews on a skinned seal. But none of the family complained. There was a bathroom and cook thing and cupboard full of food. There was a nice big corner where foldouts had been set up for napping and soapdish-watching. There was video poker and blackjack. It was *plenty* more comfortable than their house up home. The house up home was wooden, too, handmade by the tribesmen so they would keep their aboriginal status and the UN grants that went with it. But her people were not very good wood carpenters. Snow was more their material.

Nell liked the soapdish, but only for so long. It didn't make her stare-drunk like it did her uncles and cousins and grandparents. She watched some of the morning musics on it sometimes, before the old people started on their soaps. Then she would go outside on the plank walk. A plank walk ran around the cannery building on three sides, at each of the three floor levels. Attached to the outer railings of these walks was the great huge long wall of struts and canvas and chicken wire and papier-mâché that the movie builders had erected and painted on the other side. It was supposed to be the sea cliff in the Shoola story. On the other side of this wall was where the movie story was being filmed. You couldn't see much of the action from behind the fake cliff, but there were peek-holes here and there disguised as oyster-catcher nests and hummocks of cliff grass. You could watch the scene they were filming if you were on the right level of walkway and guessed the right hole. If you didn't guess right you still had to stand where you were and wait. First they buzzed Warning and then they rang the All Quiet bell. Once they started shooting you were not allowed to go clumping along the walks or up and down the wooden stairs at each end, making noises. If you did Security would shine a red dot on you and then you had to move back to Tire City with the rest of the outcasts. Nell had seen it happen three times. She would never go clumping after the All Quiet. Not one clump.

This meant you had to guess real good about your spot, and get there early enough to claim a place. This was easiest before the musics were over. A lot of the fishkids didn't leave the dishes until the musics were over. Sometimes the warning buzzer came early and they were still in the dorms and waiting rooms. Then you had a chance to get one of those good spots with a view of the shooting. Nell never got one of those spots, even when she left early before the Warning buzz. Fishkids could go right over the rails to the walk above or below, nimble as lizards in their black rubber briefs. The top level had the best peek-holes, and they were always there by the time she made it up the steep, slivery pine-plank steps. It was disheartening.

So this day, when the musics were coming to an end, she thought, I'll go down.

A lot of her fishkid friends were surprised to see her barefooting down the steps as they came up. 'Hello, Li'l Nell. Where you headed? You can't see nothing from down there ground level. There's no peep-holes.'

'"I'm a one-eye cat, peepin' in a see-foo store."' It was the song that had been showing when the Alert buzzer bleated. 'I'll find a hole, I bet.'

On the bottom walk she saw what they meant. No holes nowhere. This was the facade's foundation, and it was doubly crammed with supports and weights and reinforcements after that big blow. It was like a long wooden cave, all the length of the building—and not a shaft of peep-hole light the whole way.

At the corner of the old cannery she saw that more steps led down into the dark. She was sure she was at the bottom of the building, but there the steps were. A signboard hung on a chain at the top step, but she could not have read it even if it had been lit. She knew some good French words from the nuns' day center, but the only English words she knew for sure were Men and Women and Off and On.

She ducked beneath the chain and continued on down, her bare feet finding the same sliver-thick steps. The purple gloom of the walkway faded above her. At the bottom she felt a grate and pushed it open. A cool emptiness sucked at her and she could hear the lapping of an unseen sea. Her toes found water and she paused. The lapping echoed away into a cavernous dark. She was in some kind of vast basement beneath the cannery. This dank underworld was a place utterly mysterious to her, yet not the least frightening. She could smell old pilings and old machinery and brackish, stale water. It was inky black, but the lapping echoes she heard described the void for her like a radar fathometer, from wall to distant wall, from the creosote-treated wood above (which had to be the bottom floor of the cannery) to the invisible hulks of obsolete boilers and steam engines . . . even to the big pine pilings. She was confident she could see the whole dark grotto in her head, clear as a dollhouse.

Nell took another step. Her bare foot found bottom, not much more than ankle deep. It was smooth flat stone, that concrete stuff, and it wasn't slicked much at all. This was not water where slick things grew. It smelled a little like water in a sno-mo battery. She stepped in with both feet. It was fine. Besides, she had that dim purple light from outside, slanting down the top of the stairs like a safety line.

She started walking, her fingers spread feeling before her like eyestalks on a banana slug. She walked and walked and walked. She walked all the way to the concrete wall at the other end and felt along it until she was satisfied; then she turned around and walked back, sloshing along bolder and bolder as she became convinced of her visualization of the place. It was easy. Except for one little sort of uncertain place, she didn't even need to hold out her hands anymore. She knew right where to turn, this way and that, to avoid things. She didn't stub her toe against any of the machines, she didn't bump into any timbers. It was exactly as she had seen it in her head, she complimented herself when she made it back to the steps; she could have done it without that purple safety line of light. She'd bring some of those fishkids down here and show them that her big sister wasn't the only Eskimo with special eyes.

But when she was back through the slatted door and up under the hanging sign to that floor-level walkway, she suddenly saw that, oh! she had done a very foolish thing. Wandering around down there in the dark all this time, now she didn't know if the All-Quiet had sounded or not! The realization of the dilemma paralyzed her. She didn't know what to do. If the All-Quiet *has* sounded and is still on I can't go clumping back up and must wait. But if I wait and the All-Quiet has *not* sounded, then when they *do* ring it, it will be for On and I will think it is for Off and start walking and get shined with a red dot. Oh, oh, oh. I am in a strained land and I have missed a signal and now I don't know what to do!

It was neither Off nor On. It was still on Alert. Clark B Clark had turned it on in hopes it would hustle things up before Boss Nick got any hotter under the collar. Clark B was covered with a fine shine of sweat all over from hustling so hard to get the shoot on line before Nick got hotter. Especially in that sea lion suit. Everything was running very behind-ish this AM, the understandable consequence of all those unfortunate, ah, *flare*-ups that had followed the big town meeting. But when you have social fireworks like those last night you've got to expect some sparks to drift loose. The town's brave brigade of volunteer firemen had to chase around after hot spots all night long—sirens and bells and blinking lights and brave deeds going on simply everywhere. An extravaganza! Then all the *questions*. Wasp cops could ask questions better than any other breed—as if the talent was *born* to them, complete with notepad and pencil. So was it any wonder that it was nearly noon before they were set up for their first take? Or that no-one had noticed the big metal sail yet?

Clark B was the first to notice it. He had climbed up on the crane scaffold and raised his hailer to call for the All Quiet when he saw the graffiti. He could only stare, dumbstruck. Levertov wanted to know what the holdup was. He followed his lieutenant's wide-eyed stare and began at once to curse the outrage. This attracted the attention of the ADs and the script coordinators and the camera crews—finally even the teamsters. When Steubins saw it he tried to get the crane operator to swing around so he could get a 70mm of it, his low laugh strumming in his chest. Gradually everybody saw it. They were all amazed—not so much that it was there but that it had to have been there during all those hours of prep and setup and cop questions, plain as that leftover moon in the sky, and just as unnoticed. They were all *so* amazed—so completely stunned; flabbergasted—that Leonard Smalls' announcement about the escaped sea lions hardly registered. It seemed minor.

Alice and Ike didn't notice the altered image right off either, though the distant marina and the big silver sail were now in plain sight with that mountain range of garbage removed. You could see the whole bay front. It was indeed going to provide a spectacular vista, Ike had to admit, for the guests of that proposed resort. He and Alice didn't get much opportunity to appreciate the view; they were trying to keep an eye on Lulu. She had run, clad only in her butterfly-embroidered bra and mini-slip and the few last straggling scraps of silk, straight across the glass-strewn flats barefoot. By the time they had dressed and caught up she had reached the smoldering ruin of the Loop estate.

Nothing remained but bed shapes, table shapes, scorched appliances—all still exactly where they had sat, in a precise floor plan of ashes.

'It must have been gone in minutes,' Ike speculated. 'I can't believe that somebody somewhere didn't notice a blaze this big.'

Alice didn't say anything. She was beginning to get the knack.

Ike kicked at the outline of ashes. 'I wonder what torched it?'

'Could it have been caused by all that hog lard in the wood somehow?' Alice ventured.

This got a hysterical laugh out of Louise. 'All that lard? All that *lard*?' She glared at them, eyes as burnt-out-looking as the house site. 'Jesus, Alice, get real! It wasn't the lard, it was *this* fat that was supposed to get fried in there—' She shook a handful of flaccid hip, setting the butterflies jiggling. '—and the Hand of Evil was what torched it off! Did I tell you or didn't I, Mr

481

Isaak Sallas? Wasn't I right? *This* little piggy didn't want to stay home tonight, did she? She knew what was the next target on the slaughter line . . .'

'Yeah, Louise. You were right.'

'Hold on, now,' Alice still tried to defend her son, 'let's not jump to conclusions.'

'That's easy for *you* to say, "Hold on, now," Mrs Mama Two-Shoes! But you wait. You're on the line, too. You too, Mr Slamboy. Also Mr Greer and Mr Carmody—*every*body that ain't for him is on the knock line.'

This got Ike thinking about the pistol in the pocket of the terry-cloth bathrobe. 'Let's go back to the trailer, Lulu. Your feet are bleeding. It's my turn to stick some bandaids on you. C'mon, I'll give you a piggyback.'

They washed and bandaged the woman. Alice was just getting her calmed and into one of Greer's tie-dye jumpsuits when a patrol car pulled into the yard.

'It's the Wasps!' Louise squealed, diving for Greer's closet. 'Hide me! Hide any of my butterfly stuff! All these new Wasps are working for him! Everybody's working for him . . .'

Alice thought it was just more hysteria until the young officer that came into the trailer began almost immediately to ask about Louise Loop. Alice told him they'd seen no sign of the woman.

'No sign, you say?' He started to glance around but was distracted by something at his feet. The fluffy pup was licking at the oxblood polish on his shoes. 'You mean, I take it, you were over at the scene of the fire?'

They both shook their heads innocently. 'I mean no sign of her *here*, Officer,' Alice explained. 'We've been here all night . . .'

'I see.' The implication of Alice's answer sent a ripple of distaste across the young man's clean-shaven face. 'And you were entirely unaware of a nearby fire of such magnitude?'

'Oblivious,' Alice assured him.

'What about an ATV buggy full of fishkids? I take it you were oblivious to that as well.'

Alice smiled and nodded. 'No ATV, no fishkids.'

'Ma'am, Officer Deerborne and I just saw balloon tire tracks,' he warned, 'right up to your yard. Deerborne's outside taking tread impressions. These may be suspects, and if what you—'

'What I want to know,' Ike cut in, 'is why nobody in *town* saw a fire of such magnitude. What were you guys doing down there?'

'We were busy, Mr Sallas, with other fires. At least three of which were definitely the result of arson.'

'Uh-oh, where?'

'An abandoned boathouse, and a tool-storage shed on the north breakwater—'

'That old shed? That shed's been empty for years.' Ike was relieved. These didn't sound like targets of the Hand of Evil.

'—and the newspaper office.'

'Uh-oh. Is Altenhoffen all right?'

'He's at the clinic with epidermal trauma to the face and forearms. He was injured in a foolhardy attempt to save a typewriter. He said it was an heirloom. Very well, no sign.' He closed his notepad. 'Should you receive information regarding Louise Levertov, or the juveniles in the balloon wheel, Lieutenant Bergstrom would like you to phone the office immediately. Get out of the way, puppy—'

'Wait!' Alice stepped in front of him. 'Has anybody seen Michael Carmody?'

Again that subtle sneer of distaste. 'Relax, Mrs Carmody. Your husband steamed out at dawn. If *you* hear from him, however, tell him there are some questions we would like to ask. Also, if I may, a word to the wise': He paused in the doorway and let his hand drop to the gunbutt at his hip. 'You would be well advised to send your animal to an obedience school. Kuinak's days of undisciplined dogs running around unlicensed and unleashed are over. Be prepared and be warned.'

Ike was. He told Lulu to stay in the trailer with Worthless and bolt the door from inside, and this time, when he headed for town following Alice's van in the Jeep, he had the loaded .22 concealed in his shoulder kip. A word to the wise was warning enough.

They stopped side by side at the gap where the *Kuinak Beacon* had stood. The old newspaper office had been extracted from the line of buildings as neatly as a troublesome tooth; Foxcorp workers were already repairing the scorched walls of the adjoining sno-mo dealership and Iris Grady's boutique.

'Poor Poor Brain,' Alice said. 'He didn't deserve this from anybody.' She backed out and headed on up Spring Street to the clinic. Ike followed, glad she hadn't said some lame thing about accidents or fishkids. There's a time when even mothers have to get up off their prerogative.

The nurse at the clinic told them that Wayne Altenhoffen was still woozy from the sedative but in no danger. They had needed to glaze on only one small patch of skin-jelly. 'He burned the end of his nose off.' Altenhoffen was propped against a bank of green pillows. His head was wrapped in a white turban bandage, and his nose was protected by a wire-mesh guard that had been cleverly created out of a tea strainer. The lack of brows and lashes made his eyes look weaker than ever, but his smile was bright and cocky.

'Got me again, Isaak. The poor old bean has to wonder at all these vicissitudes I'm putting it through.'

'Maybe it's time you gave the old bean a break, Poor Brain,' Isaak suggested. 'It's probably not as indestructible as your famous Heidelberg.'

'We may never know. Because they *took* it this time, you know? They must have rolled it out the rear door before they had their little marshmallow roast.'

'Took your new press and burned your old building?' This touched Alice far more than Louise Loop's loss. The *Beacon* had been coming out of that same little office since before her mother was born. 'I'm sorry, Wayne.'

'I saved Great-Grandfather's Olivetti,' he said proudly. 'The press never sleeps.'

Back outside, Ike was surprised when Alice climbed into the Jeep with him. He had assumed she would drive on out to her motel. He didn't know what to say, after last night. He wanted to sort stuff out. He wanted to be able to attend to his business with Levertov as the opportunity presented itself, without interference. That was maybe why she came along, now that he thought about it; she suspected he had something up his sleeve without even knowing about the gun in his bag.

They didn't talk. They couldn't look at one another. They jounced along in the slow old open-topped vehicle, looking intently about at *any*thing else, in fact. So you would have expected at least one of them, Ike had occasion to think later, would have noticed the amazing thing that had happened high up on that silver sail. But it seemed they had other marvels on their minds, that were more amazing and much, much nearer; within arm's reach.

Downtown was nearly deserted; today was supposed to be another attempt at the big sea lion transformation scene. When Ike reached the marina he saw his van, parked at the empty slot where the *Cobra* had been moored. Across the lot was the camera crane, lifted above the movie set like the cocked neck of a huge heron. He was dismayed by the jam of cars and trailers and film workers and spectators milling around at the foot of the crane. He would have preferred to get down to business with Nick under more intimate circumstances—Slam to Slam. Levertov would feel more free to talk without witnesses around. To gloat. But witnesses or not, Ike was determined to procrastinate not one hour longer. It was to-it time, as they say. Call the bastard out and bring up the bones *he* had to pick. He'd be able to tell. Even if Levertov's responses were inhibited by a whole crowd of onlookers, he'd be able to tell. If it was Nicholas Levertov's slimy white hand pulling the strings on these fires, or on Omar Loop's kinky drop job, or even Old Marley's broken back, Isaak Sallas would be able to tell. Nicholas Levertov would not be able to resist strutting a little if he was the string-puller. There would be the hidden simper, for a slamboy's benefit. The cleverly coded confession. And as soon as Judge Ike heard it the trial was going to be over and the sentence would be put into effect, then and there, Slam to Slam, with no circumspection—just the way he should have done with old Cog Weil. Pull out the sword of Justice and go down swinging. He just hoped he could swing it before Clark B Clark popped out of hiding and sprayed a lot of loose lead into innocent bystanders.

'It looks like they're taking a break,' Alice said. 'There goes old Steubins and some twinkies in a slide-top . . .'

Ike veered the Jeep across the lot after them. 'Maybe Nick's on the yacht,' he hoped.

The twinkies weren't twinkling; they filed somberly up the gang without a word. One young quarterback type had his palm on his brow like the game was already lost. Steubins, however, was in great spirits. When they told him they needed to see Nicholas about a couple of matters, he let out a loud guffaw.

'A couple matters with Mr Levertov, you say? Wellsir, kids: the boy wonder ain't aboard the *Fox* at present . . . but you can *see* him yonder.' Grinning, he aimed a long finger at the shooting site across the lot. The melee seemed to be getting more and more agitated. 'See that fur suit on the office trailer roof? That's him. Beg pardon, ma'am, but that's our cool cucumber Nicholas Levertov. I don't think this is the ideal time to talk to him, but if you-all are determined—?'

'I'm determined,' Ike said. 'What's he going so nuts about?'

'Well, Isaak, for one thing, a lot of his precious location stakes turned up floating in the drink this morning. For another, he just found out that somebody let his sea lions go. *Both* of the bastards! The tame bugger was wearing the brand-new mannequin, too—about a two-and-a-half mil's worth of robotics and cosmetics.' Steubins laughed again. 'But those ain't the insults that's *really* twistin' his little white weenie.'

He flipped the eye patch up and grinned from face to face until Alice asked, all right, then, what exactly *was* the insult?

'Neither of you noticed it either, did you? That's because they done such a smart job of it—aloft, and in the dark, too! Look.'

This time they followed the finger up the swoop of the looming windsail, to the second section from the top, where the black-and-silver Foxcorp logo had provided a ready-made outline for the bull's-eye. All that the toplofty graffittists had needed to add were the target's famous red and yellow concentric circles, then the final black splat. It had been slung against the target, it looked like; something thick and viscous, like liquid rubber. The spidery blot had drooled clear down out of the circle into the next section of the telescoped sail, and appeared to still be drooling.

Alice couldn't help but throw back her head and laugh with Steubins. It was too many jolts in a row for Ike to find humorous. He had to hold the gangway rope to keep from reeling over backwards. It must have taken some tough stones to wire-walk way up there and rig that bosun's chair and sling that bucket of black. Who were these jokers, tossing their hat into his ring? Could they know what this meant? Here? *Now?* How could they, it wasn't possible. On the other hand, how could they go to this much trouble and *not* know? By God, maybe it wasn't as essential for him to go down swinging the solitary Sword of Judgment as he imagined. Maybe there *were* allies out there, he ventured, some kind of third-rate Fourth World fifth-column nobody even dreamed of—with a sixth sense.

Steubins draped a hand over Ike's shoulder. 'We still got that poker game you promised me, son. How about tonight? I think the movie business is gonna be slow tomorrow, so we could play the clock out. What do you say? Straight stud, one joker, a couple of your Dog friends? I got a Jack Daniel's you can still taste the redneck sweat in . . .'

'Carmody would never forgive us if we had a poker night without him.'

'Speak of the devil, did you happen to encounter my old rounder last night?'

'Our courses did intersect, ma'am, yes. I attempted to corrupt him, too; but he claimed he had to get down to his boat. He'd done found the hole of *holes*, he claimed, fisherman-wise, and was raring to get back to it. He and your Rasta sidekick and some others were away on the dawn tide. Now pardon, gentles all'—he glanced again toward Levertov—'I have learned to steer clear of turbulence and temper tantrums. It's me for the hammock.' He flipped his patch back down and stalked on up the ramp, toward the rocking sail. Riggers were already stringing line and tackle to raise scaffolding to the violated emblem. 'Been interesting,' he called back without turning.

Ike and Alice watched the shock of grey disappear over the gunwales, then got back in the Jeep and drove on to the crowd of cars. They had just parked when a cry jangled the air.

'She blows!' The voice came from atop the goosenecked camera crane. 'Tits ahoy, Boss, about a half-mile toward that Hopeless rock. I see our doll breasting the waves, positive sure.'

Ike trained his Zeiss glasses on the crane. Okay, that's where Clark B Clark's stationed. He looked like a Malibu Beach lifeguard in his burr cut and binocs—a lifeguard with an Uzi in his shorts. Ike followed the man's line of sight until he focused the glasses on the lewd rise and fall of a female torso on the rollers.

'Are you *sure* you're positive?' Ike swung the glasses to Levertov's strident voice. He saw a shaggy half-human, half-sea lion makeup job, snarling at a nervous collection of underlings. 'Is there corroboration? Does anyone else see what Mr Clark says he sees? Does anyone else have *any fucking binoculars*?'

Teamsters and trainers and ADs and best boys all shook their unionized heads; union regs did not allow members to carry hardware categorized outside the range of their job description. Levertov raised his loudhailer toward the packed bleachers.

'Anybody up there see the mannequin?'

Twelve tiers of faces turned to study the sea, then shook their heads.

'I *saw* it, Boss, I did,' Clark B protested. 'Ask Sallas over there; he saw it, too!'

Levertov shaded his brow their direction. The animal makeup brightened at once; the cool came back. He climbed down the trailer ladder and came walking across the strip of tarmac, smiling.

'So, it's Slam and Ma'am. What a pleasant addition to our little dockside debacle.'

'Having an interesting day, Nick?' Ike asked.

'Invigorating. Night, too. Various little imps seem to have been quite busy. Perhaps you noticed?'

'We saw the sail,' Alice said. 'Isaak had nothing to do with it.'

'Of course not,' Levertov purred. 'Never suspected him for a moment. Of the freeing of my sea lions, either. Did you scope anything that looked like a million-dollar doll on a worthless mammal, by the way, Isaak?'

Lying was never a thing Ike had been able to accomplish with much success. 'Maybe,' he hedged. 'I might have seen something out toward Hopeless—it could have been a loose crab marker—'

Levertov turned and was shouting through his hand-horn before Ike could finish. 'One thousand—no *five* thousand dollars to the man that brings back that dummy,' he called toward the bleachers. 'I don't care about the sea lion. *Shoot* the fucking sea lion; we can strap the dummy on a fat skin diver. Make it a nice round ten thou, Dead or Alive. What do you say, Kuinak; anyone interested in joining a posse?'

The spectator bleachers emptied with a cheer. 'Wonderful, the feeling one gets,' Levertov smiled, 'seeing the community all pitch in for a common cause.'

'Let me borrow your phone a second, Nicholas,' Alice said. 'I want to see if I can raise my old man.'

'Certainly, but don't expect much. The phones have been fritzing all morning like everything else. Isaak, why are you looking at me like that? My costume? Nothing says class like a Saks Fifth Avenue fur, I always say.'

Ike didn't answer. Alice punched in a number and bent to listen, her screen of black hair providing her with a little privacy while she waited. 'Carm often keeps it switched off,' Ike told Alice. 'You know how he is.' Alice finally folded the phone shut and handed it back to her son. Levertov touched the antenna to a shaggy brown brow.

'If you two charmers will excuse me?' He swirled around with a flourish of his fur cape and headed back across the tarmac, shouting through the horn again. *Warm up the big cigarette, Mr Clark, bring it around! Bring that spot-sight thirty-thirty and the twelve-gauge also if you would. The game is afoot—or in this instance—*' he added to Ike and Alice, over his shoulder, to give them the benefit of his wit under pressure, '*—aflipper.*'

In the distance Clark B's horn could be heard—'Looks like a wrap, people!'—and from farther still the first burble of boat motors firing up in their moorage behind the camouflaged flat.

Ike stood at the Jeep, wondering what to do next. Two scents tickled his nose, one up each nostril: a waft of Levertov from one side—hair spray, jasmine and adrenaline, and camphor off the fur cape—and from the other a sweet, singular fecundity; a fragrance he had completely forgotten about until a few hours ago. Now it was so close and commanding it gave him a kind of vertigo. He was grateful that Alice was sensitive enough to offer a respite.

'Maybe one of us, me, should drive up and check on Louise. In her state she could be a disturbing influence on an impressionable child like Worthless.'

'Good idea. I'll drop you back by your—no, I can take Greer's van over there, I mean *my* van, then you can take the Jeep and go—' He stopped. He had no idea *what*

490

he was going to do, where he was going to go. All the familiar ports of his life's routines seemed to be closed by unfavorable conditions—fire and flood and turmoil and entanglement. His captain was gone, his berth and boat. His homestead blooming into an open house. A fat puppy rolling where his old dog used to snore . . . a bed suddenly too narrow and a fragrance suddenly too close.

'Pick up some steak and eggs at Herky's,' Alice suggested. 'Bring 'em over to the motel and I'll cook 'em for you. I'll take the Jeep.'

They parted in the middle of the parking lot without a glance, like children avoiding each other's eyes after sharing a forbidden delicacy. Ike walked across the tarmac and climbed behind the wheel of the van and sat there. The door was still open. Everything was blooming with bright change. The grey old scene through his windshield—cement; sea; sky—was now so bright and steely sharp it hurt his eyes. The naked threat of a whetted knife. O, the prickle-eye bush. O, the foolish heart that leaps into the air to put its neck in a noose. Because there's your trouble, your ache, your dilemma: that these bright blooms always hide the sharpest thorns. What is changed is new and what is new is harsh. There's no ducking back into safe old soporifics for comfort, for those are now the harshest. Your favorite pillow is filled with foil where there once were Grandma's feathers. Your favorite meditation has been recalled by the factory for adjustments. And that spot where you could always go for solace? That private place, upholstered with rich mildew? That's now the place where you find solace most lacking. Like it wasn't losing the baby that broke Jeannie; it was losing the Bible. She had held that doeskin book like cupped light between her palms, praying out of it from the day she saw that naked spine, that obscene wedge of boiled purple cabbage under the hospital light, to the very day when the feebly smiling object of her prayers ceased to breathe. Then that soothing doeskin became as flesh of the poison toadstool to Jeannie. The words within were nothing but lying whores; the prophets just ass-kissing

491

suck-ups trying to get in better with Mr Big; the apostles a dozen degenerate pervs! That was when Jeannie said fuck it and traded book and belief both in on a hash habit and a Nasty Nineties attitude—just as both of *these* solaces were coming to an end. The hash went first. Genetic spray flights were already introducing the unisex recombinants by then, setting off a botanical chain reaction that was so successful it rendered all dangerous vegetables fruitless within a few years. After that the only specimens left were what was kept alive officially—wizened bushes nurtured by archivists in the Vatican and the UN. Cannabis for the public was over. And Jeannie never was able to get behind any of this designer shit, any more than she'd been able to get behind the Reader-Friendly Paraphrased Version of the old King James. Jeannie was a trifle twinkie-ish, perhaps, but she knew there was no magic without poetry, and poetry can't be manufactured, or modernized, or paraphrased—it's all of a hung-together ongoing event-of-a-piece, like that brown river of eels torrenting from old Omar Loop's spill-chute.

Ike looked out the open door. The saw-toothed ridges of the Pyrites gashed at the low sky. Out the other side he saw Levertov's posse of boats fuming away after the escaped sea lion and its kidnapped doll. Ten thousand bucks, dead or alive. He saw trawlers with poles upraised like fixed bayonets. He saw gillnetters foaming like a pack of mad dogs. Ah, the long sweet laid-back days of the old fishing village were over, it appeared to Ike, and he had to admit he was going to miss them. He had never thought of it before, but he was fond of gentle dawns when those trawlers waltzed gracefully to and fro with their arms outspread, like stately old ladies at a pioneer dance. He was fond of the decorous disorder of the bow-pickers in gillnet waters, waiting like rodeo contestants in a grumpy line for their chance to throw a loop. Ah, the days, over and done —swept away by the winds of special-effects change, by American Anarchy, the New Disorder of the Ages. Into the firepit and gone for good.

He was moping along in this melancholy mood when an amplified voice hailed him.

'Ahoy, Ike Sallas! We've picked up a message might be of interest to you. Damned odd.' It was Steubins with a hand horn, calling from the fantail of the silver yacht. The old director was waving something. *'From the Cobra . . .'*

'Be right over,' Ike called back and shut the door. The van's interior also reeked of sweat and fecundity. And fish. But no flowery fragrances. At least Greer and the Boswell girls had the sense not to mix their scents.

By the time he parked the van Steubins was already waiting at the top of the yacht's ramp, holding a strip of pink toilet paper. The cadaverous old man was panting hard and more grey-faced than ever after the run from the fantail.

'Happened to be on the head . . . scanning . . . the dial of my old Zenith. Heard this godawful bunch of buzzes . . . just about blanketed the whole two-four single-band frequency—used to be the old emergency band, you know?—and I says to myself, "Say, this is Morse code," and jotted it down.'

He lifted the eye patch to better read his penciled notes on the flimsy paper. The letters were smudged and over-sized, like the work of a child practicing the alphabet.

'"S-O-S-O-S," it reads. Then "H-E-L-M-G-O-N-E-C-O-B-R-A." Then a T and a N-K and some L's and an S, followed by stuff I think was static. Then the word "A-L-O-V-E-R-U-S."'

He handed over the fluttering message. Ike studied it a moment and looked up. 'Nothing else? No coordinates?'

Steubins shook his grey mane. 'Another couple SOS's maybe, then static and buzz. I'm sure them first three words was "Helm Gone Cobra." I don't know what that middle word is. I haven't done Morse in half a century.'

'That middle word is "Tinkerbells," Mr Steubins. It says "Tinkerbells all over us." Can you drive this big flashy mama, Captain? I know where they are if you can get us there.'

Nell had made herself comfortable on the next-to-the-top step to think what to do next. After a while she fell asleep with her cheek on the plank walk. She slept there until a high, grinding, itchy buzz awakened her like a swarm of mean mosquitoes. She sat up and rubbed her eyes. She *still* didn't know was it All Quiet or All Clear in the world above. But that wasn't the movie buzzer that had awakened her, she knew that. This itchy buzz was coming from *down* the steps—and she saw that now the purplish light was coming from down there, too.

She didn't feel so brave as before, but she made herself creep back down and look into the echoing cavern. The huge basement was now gently illuminated. A grape-green glow showed she'd been right about just about everything she had visualized—where the big wooden posts were, and the walls, and the rusty old wrecks of steam machines and stuff that time had left behind. The thing the glow was coming from, though—that was not one of the things she had been able to place in the pretend world in her head. This was what she had felt in that *uncertain* place, and it wasn't like any of the other machines. It wasn't old, it was real new, and it looked like, well like . . . a big machine *seagull,* with spread-out metal wings and metal sides and a yawning maw of wide rubber rollers where its head should have been. Or its tail. The thing was too big to have come down the steps. It must have been dropped down into the darkness from a hatch door in the wooden floor above. It lay half on its side, supported by a submerged wing tip. Big rubber caster-wheels were tilted up helpless on one side, and plug-in wires dangled in the air. It must have been there a day or so by the way the water was scummed up against the wheels, but not long; there wasn't a spot of rust or dust on the metal body anywhere. Instead, it was covered with little loop-the-loops of shimmery grape-green light. They were fluttering over every part of the thing except for

494

its rubber rollers and casters, like a cloud of butterflies. The itchy buzz she had heard was their teeth, chewing, gnawing away, grinding away.

Nell ran clumping up the plank steps and all the way down the empty wooden walkway hard as she could run and up the next steps, and the next. She didn't care if it was All Quiet or All Clear or nothing. She didn't care if they shined a red dot on her and sent her out to Tire City to live with the fishkids or not. Fishkids weren't so bad, when you got used to the smell of that black glue.

They had been locked into a tight little circle at no-wake speed for so long that six porpoises had joined in, circling along behind in single file, their glistening black backs appearing and disappearing, rising and falling, like steeds on a seagoing carousel. Porpoises weren't uncommon in these waters, and were frequent welcome entertainers for the tour boats—but Carmody had never heard of such follow-the-leader behavior as this from the quaint creatures. Of course, the creatures hadn't likely come across such quaint antics in a boat, either, round and round in the same tight pinch like a merry-go for three jolly hours. It even sounded like calliope music was playing accompaniment somewhere overhead! All afternoon a queer damn wind had been moaning and whistling up there above the dark silk canopy of the sky, though not a breath below. Carmody remembered the very sort of wind from his boyhood on the Scillies. The Wrecker's Pennywhistle, Great-Gran called it. 'Ye can't feel it, but ye can *hear* it,' the old hag would cackle. 'It be saying, "Bad blow coming, bad blow coming." And Mike me bye, a Wrecker's Pennywhistle is a harbinger of doom and gore. It means wrack and ruin for some, pick and plunder for others. Soon . . . soon. A-woo, a-woo-o-o. Bad blow coming.'

The old crone was usually right with the blow-coming part, anyways. It usually didn't take long for that dreadful harbinger of itself to claw down through the cloud cover and play merry hell all along the Cornish coast. The queer thing with *this here* high-altitude keening, though, was there was no cloud cover! Not mare's tail nor thunderhead. Just the darkish purple sky, like the extra eyelid over a seal's eye. The sound was up there in that, someways. Bloody unnerved everybody, what with the boat controls gone and those cursed light things *every*where . . . had just about give poor spookish Emil Greer the screamin' meemies.

'Mayday! Mayday!' Greer screamed. 'Send out ships! Send out ships! Do you copy, come back . . . ?' The dreadlock-draped face was bent over a hand mike, desperate with fear. 'This is the *Cobra*, this is the *Cobra*, send out—whoa! *Cobra* my black butt, this is *Emil Mother Greer*, vice-president of the *Loyal Order of the Underdogs* and first communications officer under *Captain Michael Carmody*! Is there anybody *out* there, come back? For the blood of *Jesus*, come back!'

The screaming would then pause a few moments while Greer scanned the radio through the bands. Everybody would lean toward the squawk box and listen. Nothing. Nothing but a brain-dead radio hum and the steady burble of the starboard stern screw, screwing them in a steady circle—and of course that cursed calliope of wind high overhead, moaning and droning as though some twisted Phantom of the Opera had commandeered the keyboards. Archie Culligan maintained it had to be the voice of either the Avenging Almighty or the Beast with Seven Horns, as Greener had foretold. Carmody didn't know so much about yodeling angels or beasts and horns but he *did* know he was not happy with the way the racket was scarifying his crew, what*ever* was making it. As skipper he knew that the morale of the crew came first in troubled waters. He raised his cannonball of a fist and shook it at the noisy sky.

'*You* up there, damn yer moanin' mouth! If the game is to blast us to bits then have at it if ya got the stones! Foul Faggot from Hell! Ya overblown puff adder! Enough of this cat-and-mouse. If it's gonna come down *let it come buggering down*! Aye, Windbag? Anything? Nothing. I thought so. All moans and no stones . . .'

'Easy, Boss.' Willi stepped to the rail beside him, her hand slipping under his elbow. 'It don't do to tempt you-know-who.'

'Yeah, Mr Carmody.' Archie Culligan figured that whatever wrath God had in store was going to be fearsome enough without adding the Devil's to it. 'Don't go tempting *any*thing!'

Carmody grinned around at them. 'Aagh, he's all bluff. Watch. Hey, Windbag—bag *this*!' In a show of burlesque braggadocio he turned around and bent over and farted at the sky.

Everybody but Greer gave up and laughed at the old fisherman. Greer was in too serious a state to be distracted by devil-baiting or braggadocio; he was signed on as communications officer aboard this doomed bark and he had some serious communicating to do. He leaned again to the CB set by the hatch, looking like a parrot in his hi-glo survival suit and his natty black braids, and resumed his screeching.

'This is the *Cobra*, out of *Kuinak*, adrift off Pyrite Point without helm! Don't know coordinates. Tinkerbells fried the Loranav. No instruments, no controls, computer pilot down. Send Out Ships, Send Out Ships, send out *any*thing—airplanes; submarines; Mormons on bicycles! Hello, *any*body? Come back . . . ?' He let up the thumb switch on the mike but even the buzz from the speaker was breaking up. He glared at the radio. 'Ah, will you look at that. We don't even show numbers on the channel scan anymore. Hey out there, *some*body!'

'Try that code stuff again, Communications Officer Greer,' Willi suggested. 'I like it better than the hollering. Anybody ready for a drink? A boilermaker seems appropriate . . .'

'I am,' the Culligans held up their hands. Greer declined so he could concentrate on his Morse. Willi turned to Carmody. 'You want one, Skipper? To drown the worries?'

'Why not? I've tried everything else, from kickin' the equipment below to cursin' the heavens above. A boilermaker might be the very spanner to turn this nut. Maybe some of that big blatwurst in the fridge, too, ma'am, if you'd be so kind? To keep the lads' peckers up.'

She gave the exposed bulge of his belly a playful slap and hurried away swinging her hips. Greer stepped aside and let the big blonde down the galley steps without looking at her; his black brow was knotted terrifically as he buzzed out dots and dashes with the mike's thumbswitch.

'That's the spirit, Mr Greer,' Carmody called encouragement. 'There's bound to be some other blaggar out there knows Morse.' Carmody's voice was jaunty and confident for the lads' sake. In fact, he felt pretty good. He chocked his gut against the rail and reached to feel where she had given him that sweet little slap. The dear bird's palm was so work-roughed he half expected to find his skin scraped, like a nutmeg by a grater. A rough old Sheila right enough, he grinned. Boilermakers indeed. And that flip of the hip? Talk about tempting the you-know-who. Well-O-Wailey and hey-nonny-non . . . if this be love he was glad he'd brought it on board, jinxed luggage or nay.

The boat went round and around. Archie Culligan began muttering his Beulahland litanies, hoping to offset any blasphemies that Carmody might have committed. His brother Nels was beginning to get embarrassed by the display. 'Gee, Archie, whatever happened to those prayers Grandma taught us? What's the matter with "Now I lay me down to drown; the sea will rock me till I'm found"? That used to be your favorite.'

'Leave your brother be, Nels,' Carmody chided gently. 'My great-gran used to tell me a prayer's as good as a laxative, only on the other end. And I'd rather have ye prayin' than befoulin' these nice new emergency rompers. They cost me three thousand bucks apiece. You keep on prayin', Archie boy.'

All except Greer had on mylar pumpsuits, the very latest in survival gear. They looked like baggy coveralls until water activated them; then they would puff tight with lumafoam. They could be drained and refilled when the crisis was over, but they frequently puffed so snug you had to cut them away. Carmody's suit still hung at half mast, the empty sleeves tied above his gut. He'd heard of the things activating prematurely and he didn't want to be spraddled out like a marshmallow man should things get busy.

The boat went around like a bagpipe droning. The beat of Greer's Morse grew more insistent, and Archie's low mutter and the high wind's singing more dolorous. Carmody saw no reason not to join in. He drew the concertina from behind the float-chair and took a seat.

> *She's a fair-weather ship and a low-water crew,*
> *We should keep to the coast but damned if we do,*
> *We was sick of the beach and our money was gone*
> *So we signed on this packet to drive her along.*
> *Now, blow ye winds westerly, westerly, blow—*
> *We're a starvation packet; God damn, let us go!*

Archie lifted his face from prayer, intending to petition again for a little more reverence in view of their predicament, but a distant flash caught his eye. He shaded his brow until he was sure. Yes! A flash of silver above the ridge line. 'We're *saved*, praise Jesus! It's the yacht!' He pointed with one hand and pounded his brother's back with the other. 'Are there any doubts about the power of prayer *now*?'

Carmody lifted his binocs; the bowsprit of the yacht was indeed coming into view around the cape. 'Certainly no doubts from this old clam-brain, Archibald; you prayed us up a salvation by God! It's the *Silver Fox* and she's coming about. And I believe that's our Isaak on point and Admiral Steubins himself back at the wheel! Good work, Signalman Greer. I told you there'd be some duffer out there old enough to read code, didn't I?'

Greer didn't answer. He was so drained he couldn't

even raise his head to see what he had summoned. He collapsed against the bridge wall and let his face hang between his knees like an exhausted balloon. Willimina came bustling up with a tray of drinks and sausage sandwiches.

'Saved, did I hear? Then we don't have to drown our worries after all; we can celebrate our salvation.'

'Yes, by God, the *Silver Fox*.' Carmody was still leaned into the eyepieces, pivoting his girth against the rail as he compensated for their craft's slow circling. 'And himself at the wheel, eye patch and all. By the powers it's just like some old Errol Flynn character swashbuckling to the rescue. Hooray for Hollywood, I say! Everybody: hip-hip-hoo-*ray-y-y*!'

The thin shout reached Steubins across the smooth water. He didn't shout back. He had other matters on his manifest, like having to answer to First Mate Singh every time that bullfrog face jumped in front of him on the binnacle monitor.

'Is that them?' the face wanted to know. Steubins said that it was. 'You're not mistaken?' Steubins swore he wasn't. The face jumped away and the screen went back to the Nav-graph display with its scroll of twinkling coordinates. This display mode always made Steubins think of coded financial reports scrolling beneath a stockmarket dish, arcane numbers and symbols that only the privileged elite were allowed to interpret. Steubins spit a gob of his cold cigar at the screen. He knew it all meant plenty to Frog's Mate Singh and his nav staff, tending their punchboards in the comroom half-light below, but all it meant to him was that it didn't mean a damn thing. He'd barely been able to get the hang of how the old-fashioned Loranav worked! And that was data from only three coordinates—two fixed sea levels and yourself. This new navigational chipware was always factoring in at least two more fixes: a sea-floor beacon and a sky eye. Nav-graph experts claimed they could chart a course from the bottom of the Aleutian Trench all the way to the highest ice peaks of Neptune, never scrape a sunken tree stump or ram a roaming asteroid, either one. Well, Gerhardt Steubins had never rammed into either one, either. As a yachtsman he'd always had an eye for signs of submerged-tree-stump sorts of stuff—a brief glimpse of an erratic swirl of foam; a wrong-way riffle in the starlight—and as far as asteroids went he could give a wharf rat's ass. What had asteroids to do with seafaring? It was all just advanced starcade fantasy as far as he was concerned, the inevitable growth of rich little dishgame assholes into bigger ones. And Singh was one of the biggest. For one thing, the asshole was richer than bat shit. He'd grown up hanging around the poshest starcade halls India had to offer. For Abu Bul Singh this boat must be just like one of those third-level goggle games you heard about, only ritzier. More zams, more variables. Singh belonged to an elite New Delhi starnet game club that plugged together every Sunday at eleven AM Greenwich, religious as clocks, members from all over the world. God alone could follow what they were playing at behind those toggle boards and helmets—and even He probably wouldn't be interested enough to follow it very far.

The face flashed back on. 'Hail them, Mr Steubins. Try to explain that our task will be vastly simplified if they would terminate their elliptical circling.'

'Shouldn't *you* explain it, Mr Singh? You're better at this technical talk . . .'

'They're your friends, Mr Steubins, and *your* problem' was all the screen explained. Then it jumped back to graphics and scroll-by numbers. Pompous little mongoose, Steubins thought; he's on to me. He knows my lie sure as shit floats. He must finally have got through to Levertov. Well, that's it, Stewbrains, you old fraud: you're history for sure, now . . . He reached around the wheel for the binnacle's handmike.

'*Ahoy*, Cobra,' he called in a morose voice. '*This is the Silver Fox.*'

He heard a voice come back at him across the waters,

distinctly British: *'Do ye say so for a fact?'* It cheered him up.

'Belay that circling, Cobra, and heave to so we can come alongside.'

'Would like to comply, Silver Fox,' the answer came back. *'Dearly would. But we ain't able to belay bloody fuck all!'* It was Michael Carmody, in some kind of mylar bag from the armpits down. His cueball of a head shined in the strained sunlight and he was hollering through a plastic cup with the bottom poked out. *'We been at this beastly business for three hours now, like a squirrel in a wheel! Driven some o' me crew a bit daft, I fear!'*

The blonde at Carmody's side waved gaily. *'Afternoon, Mr Steubins. Willi Hardesty? Awful nice to see you-all.'*

Two other bag-shrouded forms echoed her sentiments. Behind them something was trying to rise from the deck. It looked to Steubins like a collapsed carnival tent.

'Afternoon, Miss Hardesty . . . Captain Carmody.' They were close enough now he could put away the mike. 'What put you folks in such a predicament, may I ask?'

'It was the arm of the Avenging *Almighty*!' declared one of the bags .

'I wouldn't go *that* far, Arch,' the blonde amended; 'to *me* it felt more like the Fickle Finger of Fate.'

'Pipe down, both of you,' Carmody ordered. 'It was just some kind of freakish storm, Mr Steubins. Spot of sheet lightning gave our electronics a power surge.'

The face popped back on beneath the binnacle compass, froggier-looking than ever in close-up. 'There have been no storms in a two-fifty-kilometer radius from this point in the last thirty-six hours. I'm afraid your friends have been drinking, Mr Steubins, or worse. If they can't control their craft that is unfortunate. Inform them we will not risk collision. They shall have to ferry themselves to us.'

'Can you put a dinghy over?' Steubins called across the water.

'Negative,' Carmody answered. 'Dinghy bay is seized up like everything else; otherwise we'd have put ashore long ago and let this blasted tub of troubles go to blazes. Hate to be a bother but I'm afraid you'll have to come to us.'

'Quite impossible,' the frog face said. 'Both launches are up north on the search—as *we* should be. Mr Steubins, inform your quaint friend if he cannot ferry over the best we can do is signal their location to nearest Coast Guard. This is *their* responsibility. Ours, Mr Steubins, is to return to port and await orders. Please convey this information and prepare to come about.'

This was just too warty to swallow. 'You goggle-eyed little turd!' Steubins exploded. 'You can't leave men on a floundering ship. It's against maritime law! There'll be a UN investigation.'

The face was noticeably taken aback by this possibility. It turned and consulted with an off-screen presence, then turned back. 'They could swim to us . . .'

'They could *drown*!'

'They have flotation gear.'

'They could be swept away! And one of them is a *lady*!'

'Why, thank you, Mr Steubins.' Willimina pinched the quilted mylar at her hips and dipped a curtsy. 'I used to swim varsity for the UTEP Tigers but I'll take that as a good-ol'-boy compliment.'

Ike had made his way from the forward lookout to the wheelhouse. 'What's up?'

'The game,' Steubins whispered behind his hand. 'I think Abu Bullfrog Singh's found out we lied to him about Leyertov. He's gonna head back. He says he won't steer us closer to them and we got no launches.'

'What about the Zodiak?'

'Out of the question!' The face apparently could hear whispers behind hands. 'Exposing flimsy inflatable material against moving metal? Far too dangerous. I will not allow any of our crew to take the risk.'

'I'll do it,' Ike said.

'Well of course *you* would, Mr Sallas. We've all heard about *your* daring exploits. But you may rest assured I do

503

not intend to risk our only remaining boat-tender *ei*ther, Mr Sallas. That would be *also* against the maritime law.'

The face waited. And Steubins. Ike gave in with a careless shrug. 'Then I guess they've just got to swim it,' he said. He gave Steubins a wink and turned to head back forward. As soon as he was on the other side of the wheel out of sight of the binnacle vid-eye, he turned. 'Where is it?' he mouthed silently. Steubins blinked, uncomprehending. 'The raft,' Ike mouthed again, then began pantomiming a hand of cards. 'Tell . . . me . . . where . . . it . . . is!'

'Ah!' Steubins' deep chuckle hummed in his chest. 'So long, Mr Sallas. See you level *trey*! Passage *three aces* and a *deuce*! And that bay door's a natural blackjack.'

Ike whispered 'Gotcha' and sprinted for the nearest hatchway. Steubins smiled down innocently at the face in the binnacle. 'Yankee poker slang,' he explained. 'Means "Better luck next deal." But see here now, Singh; it's time for us to get to articles. You can write it down as insubordination if you have to—you're the *patron* here— but I'm *damned* if I'll order those folks into the drink. You're going to have to come up here and take that on your*self*. That's my bottom line.'

The face started to protest but Steubins turned and strutted away to the aft rail, arms folded and his back stiff. The screen called after the rigid back for a while, then finally said, 'Oh, *such* a spoiled peacock!' and switched back into sonar menus and numbers. The big teak wheel continued to make its precise adjustments back and forth, though no hands held the varnished handles.

Ike slid down the narrow stairwells, barely touching anything but the polished rails. The third-level corridor was more crowded than anybody would have ever imagined, this far below decks. Everybody seemed quite busy with their duties, bustling from doorway to passageway with beepboards and sketches and stacks of film cans. It was a little eerie, Ike thought, all these people carrying on so collected and cool in their little blue-and-white outfits, not a notion of what was up up above. It reminded him of those mysterious legions the archvillain always seemed to be able to surround himself with in old James Bond thrillers—soldiers who seem bright, brave, busy and not quite human. They could always be counted on to be entirely oblivious to the hero in dirty mufti strolling through their uniformed activities.

The last door off Passageway 5 was Door 21. This was far to the stern. One noncom was buffing the floor, singing along with his earphones. He kept right on singing while Ike pried off the lock with a fire ax.

Inside he found a narrow launching bay slanted at the slapping water. The Zodiak was waiting, nosed up against a locked grating at the water's edge. The lock pried apart as easily as the other one, and the grating swung open to the sea. Ike rolled over the inflated side into the boat's bottom and with one ax chop at the cinch strap he was launched, bobbing away beneath the fantail. The cardkey was in the ignition but the motor was cold and wet. He was still trying to start it when he drifted from beneath the fantail. First Mate Singh was on deck admonishing Steubins at the rail when the raft bobbed into his pop-eyed sight.

'Sallas! Stop at once! Return that property in the name of the law! Security! Security to Level 3 aft! Get a hookline on this man. Mister, I'm warning you. Get away from that engine! I'll be forced to call for weapons. Sallas! This is an order.'

Ike grinned up at the face thirty feet above him: a bullfrog for sure and *that* was giving the sucker the benefit of the doubt. 'Fuck you,' Ike called pleasantly and bent back to the motor.

'She's flooded, son,' Steubins volunteered in his decorous drawl. 'Spin 'er over twice with the choke full out, then twice with it shut.'

'That does it, Steubins! That goes *beyond* insubordination.' First Mate Singh stepped tight up against Steubins, eyes popping with indignity. 'In my country you could be executed for mutiny.'

'In *my* country,' Steubins looked down at the outraged

face at his elbow, his drawl still polite and genteel, 'you could fall overboard and bang your head and get et by the bald eagles. They like the *eyes* first, I'm told . . .'

On the fifth spin it caught—just as two security men appeared in the launch slot, grappling hooks swinging at the end of their hairy arms. 'Stay there, fellows,' Ike waved. 'I'll be right back.' He throttled away in a tight bank starboard, face in the wind, spray in his teeth. Yes, those trumpets were blowing that old fool fanfare for sure, now; there he goes, fans, steaming straight off to hell in a leaky bucket once again.

'But at least I'm enjoying the ride,' Ike told the trumpets.

When he reached the circling multipurpose they already had a ladder over the side. 'Wouldn't I have better luck approaching from the stern?' he called to Carmody.

'More negative, Ike boy. We can't put the ramp down. You'd be coming right at the screw. Come 'longside starboard, outside our course; see if you can't latch on to the ladder.'

It took him two complete turns around the liquid carousel, with the five passengers and the six dolphins urging him on. Even after he caught the ladder Ike had to rev the Zodiak and keep it revved to maintain orbit; the big boat was circling faster than it appeared. The ladder strummed and flapped between boat and raft until Ike got it right. 'C'mon, Willi,' he finally called up at the row of faces. 'Ladies first.'

Greer rushed into view. 'No, wait, wait, wait!' He shoved the woman aside, his face ashen. 'Not her, not yet.' For a moment Isaak thought the fear of a watery death had finally drowned out all the better angels of Greer's nature, his best one in particular: the charming cherub of chivalry. But he didn't seem scared exactly. 'It's going to be too hard for Ike to work ladder and rudder both.' Greer's voice was steady and commanding. 'Nels, you go first; you can belay and control the slack. *Then* Willi.'

Greer was right. The string of narrow rungs was whipping all over the place as Nels climbed down. The boy

506

had to hang beneath the stretched ropes while Ike fought to control the ladder with one hand and the outboard with the other. If the nose of the Zodiak got outturned too far it could be swamped; too close and the little boat could be caught against the *Cobra*'s hull and rolled under. When Nels finally flopped into the inflatable, Greer called again for Willi to wait. He said the raft ought to have a second line from the *Cobra*, played from farther forward to give it towing stability. He sprang to the line cabinet before anyone could debate the issue. Carmody beamed at his dreadlocked crew member with pride.

'You never know just which Jack is going to rise to the occasion.'

With Greer tending the second tow line it was a little easier holding position. When Willi came over the side she also flipped beneath the ladder but was able to keep her feet in the rungs. 'Just like stirrups on a upside-down bronco,' she reassured Carmody. She tried to dismount too soon and her rump dragged in the water, activating the lumafoam. By the time she was aboard the Zodiak her suit was swollen tight and glowing bright green. 'I feel like an eight-months-along country girl,' she laughed, 'with the bloat.'

'You next, Archibald,' Greer ordered from his position forward. The boy didn't stop mumbling his liturgies until he was alongside his brother in the raft. 'See!' he said. 'Prayer works.'

'Now you, Emil,' Carmody said. 'You've done first-rate. Tie your line off and let the boys below handle the slack. Over ye go . . .'

'Nosir, Captain,' Greer shook his coxcomb. 'Now you.'

'A captain is expected to stay with his ship to the last, Mr Greer. Cardinal rule of the deep. Traditional . . .'

'A gentleman is expected to stay with his lady.' Greer nodded toward the blond head sticking out of the glowing suit in the raft. 'A cardinal rule of a whole lot *deeper* tradition, mon, and it's high time you heeded it.'

Carmody opened his mouth but he could not think of a rebuttal. It appeared Greer was going to be the winner of their old debate about chivalry after all. Carmody tapped his brow in quick salute, then zipped up his suit and swung on to the ladder. He was so heavy he hung right against the hull, bringing the Zodiak directly beneath him, and dropped in easily. He elbowed himself a place alongside the inflated Willi on the raft's middle seat, chuckling at her pneumatic plight.

'Perhaps a little less leavening in the dough, if I may make so bold?' Her arms were pumped up so tight that she couldn't even elbow him.

At the stern Ike was having to give the little motor more throttle; the prow of the heavy-laden raft was half submerged against the push of water. 'You're chocked to the gunwales,' Greer called. 'Head on out and unload. I can wait.' He cast free the forward line before Ike could protest, and the inflated bow swung away; there was nothing Ike could do but turn loose the ladder.

'Okay, Pardner.' Ike tried to sound cheerful. 'I'll be right back.'

'I'll be right here,' Greer waved.

Ike throttled viciously away from the boat, his concern and foreboding revealed by his abruptness. 'He'll be safe as Moses,' Carmody turned to reassure him. 'God looks after fools.'

Willi wasn't able to turn around. 'Especially chivalrous fools,' she added straight ahead.

Ike had banked on the success of his daring rescue to change the attitude of the *Fox*'s first mate. When he nosed the Zodiak up to the ramp grating at the bottom of its launching bay, he saw he had misjudged Mr Abu Bul Singh. The man was waiting with two more hairy-armed security officers with hook lines. The hairiest of the four had a huge side arm strapped at his hip. Ike tossed an end of Greer's line to this gorilla before anybody got any ideas with the hooks. 'Belay us, mate, until we get the woman off.' Of course everyone else had to disembark before the woman could work her inflated way forward. As soon as Ike saw she had made it on to the corrugated bay-ramp he cast loose his end of the line and gunned the motor

508

in reverse. Singh's face looked as though it might swell up and burst over this latest affront to nautical protocol. '*Sallas!* If you continue to jeopardize our vessel I have no other recourse but armed intervention! You understand me, mister?' Ike kicked the outboard into forward and heeled away into the spray.

'Very well, Mr Sallas, very well. Mr Smollet? One across his bow, if you would . . .'

Faster than Ike thought possible for hands so crude and hairy, Mr Smollet sent a pistol shot whistling through the bow's spray. Ike kept throttling. 'Ah? That's your answer, is it Mr Sallas? Then, at your will, Mr Smollet, at your will . . .'

Ike dived for the webbed bottom—not that the inflated hull would offer any armor. But no shot came. Instead, he heard a startled curse ring out above the outboard noise, followed close by a yelp and a splash, then more cursing. Ike peeked over the stern and saw Mr Smollet slapping water and drifting away under the fantail's overhang. In the side bay Carmody seemed to be apologizing to everybody and getting in everybody's way at once.

Back at the *Cobra*, Greer disdained the need for a second line; the ladder would be enough for him, he assured Ike: 'I used to eat these monkey glands in Belize.' He was out on the quivering rungs before Ike could argue, his duffel looped round a shoulder of the neoprene suit. The glands must have been potent. He scrambled aboard the Zodiak nimble as a gibbon. Ike swung clear. But this time he didn't throttle up. He cruised along so they could catch their breath. He wasn't in any hurry to take the medicine waiting for him back on the *Fox*, and Greer looked like he could use some easy cruising. The man's usually colorful face was still ashen as he situated himself on the raft's middle seat, facing backward. He was staring over Ike's shoulder at the receding *Cobra*.

'I saw it come, Isaak. We were about to put out the purse. I was in the cage and just happened to look up. I saw it come out of the north, I saw it veer, and pass over us, and I saw it disappear out to sea. It was no mother electric storm, either, my man. Trust me.'

Ike nodded and kept quiet. There was a strangeness in Greer's voice he had never heard before, in all the years of accents and dialects.

'There was no lightning, no thunder. Not a sound until it was gone by. Then it sizzled for a while, as it faded out. Sssszzzle . . .'

'What do you think it was, Pardner?' Ike hadn't been able to get much out of the previous load of passengers. 'What was it like?'

'Like bacon frying.' Greer glanced at Ike to see how this was being received. 'Like a strip of purple bacon five hundred miles long and five miles high. Thin sliced. Sssszzling . . .'

'Did anybody else see it?'

'Everybody else saw some of it, they just won't cop to it. Completely understandable; the experience was paralyzing.' He tilted his head at Ike, curious. 'How come we're putting along so slow, man?'

Ike explained the subterfuge it had taken to get the *Silver Fox* out to their distress signal, and how he had commandeered the raft. He described the reception he had just received from First Mate Abu Bullfrog Singh, and Carmody's tactics with the security personnel. He expected this to get a laugh out of Greer, but his friend barely nodded. He was staring again over Ike's shoulder back toward the *Cobra*. After a while he asked, 'You ever unwrap a stick of gum and get a little piece of tinfoil in your mouth?'

Ike told him sure, everybody had.

'You know the way it feels when the foil hits a filling? Like something's got cross-wired?'

Ike nodded and waited, but Greer didn't elaborate. They putted along in silence, coming up on the yacht. Ike could see the side bay yawning at the waterline, inevitable. 'Well,' he sighed and glanced down at the chronometer and compass mounted atop the motor housing, 'it looks like it must be time to face the music.' He reached for the throttle, but Greer stayed him with a raised palm, whispering:

'Sacred Mother of God, Isaak—'

Ike realized then what it was that was strange about his friend's voice: it had not only been washed clean of any affected dialects—mannerisms; self-mockeries—it had also been ironed. It was as flat and grey as his face, as two-dimensional as a hieroglyph.

'—here it comes again.'

Ike didn't look right away. Something was happening to the compass needle. And when he finally made himself raise his head, to follow Greer's eyes, he didn't see anything as fascinating as that compass—at first—only the ragged mountain range and that purple shell of empty sky. Nothing more, nothing unusual. Except . . . far away . . . he thought he glimpsed a streak of another purple—a ripe-grape purple that was darker than the sky and at the same time brighter, more intense. It was just a tiny thread spooling out of the northeast low on the horizon, barely above the distant mountain-tops. If the streak had been white it might have been dismissed as a vapor trail from one of the Concorde hops over the Pole. Or you might think it was a beam of the northern lights if you saw it after dark. Except it's moving too fast to be either of those phenomena, he realized, watching it grow from a thread to a string to a ribbon. It had to be zooming. Greer was right about the weird silence. The gulls went silent, the murres, the oldsquaws. The wind. It's like the silence that preceded an eclipse of the sun. He and Jeannie drove to Mexico to watch the last total eclipse of the twentieth century . . . everybody pulled over to the side of the road, drinking and jiving, watching the sun across the sagebrush being eaten away like a big cookie . . . Then just before it goes total a thing happens. It's called the Ripple Effect. Sheets of grey light suddenly come fluttering across the ground toward you, like butterfly wings going a thousand miles an hour. Waves of cold grey flame. Even when you have prepared yourself by reading about the Ripple Effect, and halfway understand that it's caused by Einstein's bending of the sun's rays around the moon so they synch up on the earth with other yet unbent rays—Gravity's Rainbow—you still are not prepared for the Effect's impact. Nobody is prepared. No thing. For miles around every entity sucks in its breath and goes dead quiet. Singers, drinkers, birds, donkeys, dogs; the cells in the flesh and probably the charged particles in the cells. Dead quiet. An awe beyond theories and explanations. And, now, this purple ribbon snaking down out of the north was more awesome far. It looked like a diaphanous plastic shower curtain being pulled along a zigzagging curtain rod that was mounted all along the Pyrite range. Like a sheet of grape-candy glaze. A Running Fence. A pane of glass a mile high. The edge of a crystal sword! At the last instant, less than a quarter-mile away, it broke hard right where Pyrite Cape petered into the surf, then stretched away west-by-northwest in the direction of the Aleutians, out to sea.

Ike couldn't remember if the thing itself made a sound. It seemed that it should have. Your mind told you anything that vast traveling that fast veering that sudden should have emitted some groans of inertia, some squeals of friction. But he couldn't remember. The curtain of transparent residue it left behind certainly made a sound—a furious hiss of sputters and snaps.

'Like a big strip of purple bacon,' Greer reminded Ike solemnly, 'frying.'

'Some flash,' Ike said. 'But it doesn't look like it did much damage.' He decided not to mention the compass needle, turned end for end.

As the curtain gradually faded from sight the sizzling cooled to a murmur. It had almost raveled away to nothing when they noticed something was happening to the water in the cove.

'Didn't do this before,' Greer's flat voice observed. 'But the other one wasn't nearly this big . . .'

The surface of the water was beginning to dimple and hop, not in waves but in moire patterns, the way wine in good crystal hops in patterns when the edge of the glass

512

is set to ringing, or like water in a big galvanized stock tub when the metal side is kicked by a beast. And that huge yacht in front of them was having spasms. All six pontoons were extending in shuddering starts and stops. The radar sweeps and satellite dishes on the flying bridge were spinning out of control, but the roiling prop-wash behind her screws had stilled completely.

That was when Ike noticed that the little outboard under his hand was stopped . . . had been stopped for a while, it seemed. Behind them, the *Cobra* was pitching with far greater violence than the dimpled swells against her hull could have provoked. Her motor had also been killed, and the trance that had held her circling was broken. But she wasn't drifting. The sleek craft was bucking and tossing like a wild mare on jimsonweed. This was too much for the dolphins; they stampeded in six different directions, their infatuation with the merry-go-round business finished for good.

The *Cobra* was becoming brighter as she bucked. Incandescent. Ike raised his Zeisses and saw that there were swarms of those intersecting circles of light flickering along the *Cobra*'s alloy flank like a plague of stinging flies. You could hear them. The stricken boat was trying to shake them off, but they were getting thicker, crueler. Both men watched without comment, deeply touched by the vessel's torment. A call across the water interrupted their silent vigil.

'Look sharp, boys!'

Carmody's warning came too late. The Zodiak was struck portside-on by something, a very solid something that had not been there moments before. The impact knocked Ike to the boat bottom and tossed Greer end-over-end high into the air like a clown off a trampoline. The thing that had struck them was one of the pontoon feet of the yacht's spider-legged outrigger system. All six legs had suddenly extended to their full length. The little inflatable had been booted by the left rear pontoon, like a football by a big metal foot.

Greer splashed down alongside that foot and spread

513

out splendidly on the dimpling sea in his neoprene suit. He resembled one of those paper pellets that blooms when dropped in a bowl of water. The Zodiak was bouncing away in the direction it had been booted. 'Swim for it, Pardner!' Ike shouted. Greer continued to float spreadeagled on his back, his face looking beatifically at the empty sky. 'Can't swim, Pardner,' the face answered. 'Never could.' 'Then just roll over and *grab on*, for chrissakes! The pontoon's right there.'

There were even metal handles for just such grabbing. Greer was able to pull himself up on the hollow pod without difficulty. The Zodiak was drifting further aft of the big yacht still. Ike was spinning the starter wheel on the outboard, but to no avail.

'Now *you* swim, smart boy,' Greer called. 'You can make it here.'

Ike shook his head and continued to spin the wheel. 'There's going to be need for this boat,' he explained.

'Then check the cardkey,' Greer called from his perch on the pontoon. 'See if it's all weird . . .'

Ike plucked out the plastic card. Its magnetic strip had become a twisted moire design. 'Yeah, it's screwed up.'

'So was the one on the *Cobra*. Okay, there's a vise grip in my duffel. Rip that slot panel off so you can get to the wires.'

A sporadic clanging from the scaffolding high up the metal sail gave testimony to a stiff upper breeze, though the air at sea level was still dead calm. Ike knelt in the inflated bottom with the tools, hunched over the motor. The Plaztex housing peeled up easily once the vise grip had torn a start.

'I got the wires,' he shouted without turning. 'Now what?'

'How many?'

'Five, six . . . *eight*!'

'Lawd perfect us. Okay, twist any of them that are the same color together. Then you gonna have to trial-and-error what's left against the starter motor—'

'Give the damn thing up, Ike lad,' he heard Carmody's

voice call from above him. 'Jump for it while you can still swim safe to us. You ain't even wearin' a life jacket . . .'

Ike turned to grin up at the bright round face leaning over the rail. The distance between them was clearly increasing. 'I'm not so sure you folks are much safer off, Carm, the way you're blowing. You might not clear those rocks.'

Beyond the yacht the southwestern tine of the cove's fork was protruding darkly into the sea, a tarnished line of rocks and waves. The big yacht was beginning to crab slowly toward it over the uneven water, sideways.

'Great God, he's right!' This was Steubins' emphysemic baritone, out of Ike's sight up at the wheel. 'Our tops'l's bringin' us about! If that wind drops on down it'll have us abeam and drive us straight up on them rocks. Singh! Mr Singh! Where the devil's the bug-eyed mother now we could use him? Ensign Tenboom, where's the Grand Pasha first mate? We got us a priority situation here.'

'Mr Singh is back in the comroom,' a starched young voice answered. 'Indisposed.'

Ike bent back to the bundles of disconnected wire. He didn't need to see the owner of that voice. Though he had never heard it before in his life it was nevertheless completely familiar to him.

'The first mate instructed me to inform everybody,' the voice went on, 'that he is extremely displeased and refuses to come out until reparations are made.'

'Re*pairs*? The booger thinks we can someway *fix* this?'

'He doesn't mean *repairs*, I don't think, Mr Steubins—' It was the kind of voice you become familiar with in any institutional power pyramid; the terse tone of the aide-de-camp, staunchly making the announcement to the group wing in the ready room that the commander was 'indisposed' and the group would just have to 'wing it'; the uptight twang of the rookie screw having to march into the waiting block to tell the men weekend visit had not been cleared because some maggot had poisoned the sheriff's Rottweiler and, owing to his understandably distraught condition—'All of you knows how much he

515

cared for that animal'—the poor sheriff had neglected to process the paperwork. It was the voice of the lowest lackey of the top circle, of the stooge left holding the bag and still trying to keep a straight face:

'—I mean, I think Mr Singh means more like apologies.'

'Great God*amighty*! What you really mean is he got just as zapped as the rest of his fancy machinery, didn't he? I ain't surprised. They don't prepare you for unprogrammed events like this in them starcade schools. You, yonder! Sing out down them hatches: All hands on deck! On the double! And tell 'em bring up all the one-inch line and block they can muster. And ladders! Sledges! Acetylene torches! Do we even *have* a machinist's mate on this nut-bucket anymore? Clivuses and linchpins, tell 'em. Lag bolts, C-clamps, come-alongs . . . *any*thing! And tell the best boys to load the hand-held 35mm with Fuji Crystalchrome; if we're doomed to go down we'll by the powers go down shootin'!'

Red to red, black to black, green to green. Still no jiggle on the amp needle. Ike felt a taut line of air begin to strum the back of his neck, surprisingly cold. Behind him he could hear feet pounding down corridors and up hatchways, and the scaffolding clanging more and more insistently.

'Now *you* there,' Steubins' voice continued to toll, 'alongside the girl in the makeup smock! Lay hold of that flippin' rope and hush that damn scaffold. Right. Now lash it to the rail if it'll reach. Go on, give him a hand, honey, don't be shy; your manicurin' days are done. *All* of you pitiful bleached-out bilge rats . . . line up and let's have a look at you. Come on, come on, snap to! Jay-sus, at least *act* awake.'

Ike didn't need to raise his head to see *them,* either. They were the witch's castle guards set free by Dorothy's spell-breaking bucket of wash-water, somnambulists shaken from their unnatural dreams. He put yellow to yellow and the needle twitched. Now, what to do with the leftover unmatched white and orange and blue?

516

'Cap'n Carmody ol' hoss?' Steubins called. 'While these poor tykes are getting the *sleepy* rubbed out of their eyes how would you like to lay some of that muscle to this wheel with me? The rudder's just a leetle stiffish without all them servo-amps and so forth.'

'Be more than proud to, Cap'n Steubins. Anything elset ye need, be assured you can count on my crew here. We're a starvation packet but we *are* full awake.'

'Much obliged. I don't reckon any of you all have *tops'l* experience? We're going to need somebody with four hands and a tail, up that high in this wind . . .'

'I used to eat monkey glands,' Ike heard a flat, matter-of-fact voice answer coolly. 'And the higher from the water it gets, the better I like it.'

Ike was still grinning about this when the starter whirred the little outboard back to life. It was the very last one that did it, the blue one. He raised his head from the wiring and was surprised to find that the yacht was nearly a football field away. The repartee had been coming to him courtesy of that strand of cold air, like voices over a kid's can-and-string telephone. Now he could feel that string beginning to tremble and whip, and hear his line of communication start breaking up.

'Come on, *I-I-Isa-a-a-ak*—' He raised his glasses. The shout was from Greer, already up ninety feet of rope and balanced on the swinging scaffold. '—you can *ma-a-a-a-ay-yay-yay* . . .'

The words went whipping away.

'*Negative, Pardner!*' He probably didn't have to shout; the chill wind was still carrying his voice straight toward the rocking metal sail. '*Go on ahead. You guys look like you're outward bound, and I still got business back home. Bon voyage!*'

There were more garbled shouts, but he didn't have the time. He throttled up and started swinging around into the rising wind, intending to try to make shelter behind Pyrite Cape. He came about landward just in time to see the stricken *Cobra* literally pop apart at all the fused steelume seams, like a spring-loaded toy. The

517

scattered sections sank immediately in the foam, dragging the fluttering loops of light down with them. The gouts of foam and the boat's flotsam went skipping away before the rising wind, free.

A sudden vicious gust sliced in beneath the Zodiak and nearly flipped the raft over backward. The prow was riding too high and light. Ike had to come about and run before the gale until he was able to get Greer's duffel and the raft's emergency locker stowed forward for ballast. He lay down on his back so he could put his head on the canvas seat amidship and get the center of gravity as low as possible. With his shoe off he was able to steer the outboard with his foot. He brought her back around into the wind and held her there at about a sixth throttle, making just enough way to have some helm. He leaned back into the stretched canvas seat and let the gale buffet the back of his head. Past his bare foot he could just make out the silver sail of the yacht disappearing through the whipping spray. It looked like they were going to clear the headlands and have nothing but open water in front of them. He reached behind him and dug one of Greer's Guatemalan sweaters out of the duffel and tossed it over his foot. Might as well try to get comfortable. You never know how long the End of the World is liable to take.

21
Blackjackatcha!

Father Pribilof should have been seated at his tonedisk, face to the little musical altar for afternoon vespers when the bolt came hissing past. Instead, he was slumped on the edge of his swaybacked bed in dingy underwear and slippers, staring at the patch of sky through the solitary window of his quarters, telling himself if he didn't trim his lilacs he soon would have no sky.

He wasn't surprised at the Miracle he witnessed. He wasn't alarmed that a slice of light came smiting through the town, steely blue as the sword that goeth out of the Mouth of the Lamb. For months he had detected signs of its coming. Yea, for decades. Yet when it came he was just as inadequate to the occasion as he had always feared he would be. It blasted him straight over backward on the bed like a carnival doll in a baseball toss.

He lay with his eyes closed, listening to the hiss. He wasn't hurt anywhere, it seemed, except in spirit. At ninety-four he was still durable in the flesh, but failing in spirit—and at the very hour when spirit was most sorely needed. As he'd heard the fishkids of his flock occasionally put it, this was to-it time.

'If you get *to* it, and cannot *do* it, there you sure are—uh!—*aren't* you?'

Yea, if ever a flock was going to require a steady hand on the staff and a clear eye to guide them through the Valley of the Shadow, this must surely be that time. His hand hadn't been too steady in half a century, though; and, as far as *vision* went, well, he was not only congenitally colorblind but cataract-prone to boot—his old eyes had been scoured of scales so many times they looked

519

like the pitted headlights of a dune buggy. This well-worn lamentation about his inadequate eyesight was followed by a sudden, soul-jarring afterthought: steely *blue*? He had never known the color blue before in his life, steely or otherwise. How then could he have known what color that sword was? Because it came from the heavens? No, that wasn't it. A great number of things from the heavens were not blue—rainbows round the throne, for instance; spirits like unto emeralds . . . Yet he knew this was *blue*! He knew it as well as he knew he was a feeble old man bowled over backwards on a swaybacked bed.

He sat up and raised his flimsy eyelids. He saw chaos. Such meager focus and acuity as the cataract operations had preserved seemed to have been smitten asunder by that blue bolt, shattered into luminous smears. But those formless smears were in *color*—predominantly of that same slicing blue, but shot through now with trembling ribbons of red and black. How did he know that was red alongside those swatches of black? Because it made him immediately think of Stendhal's *Le Rouge et le Noir*, the colors of the cloth of the man of the cloth, trembling before the blue vault of heaven. *The colors of the cloth*! Giddy with excitement, Father Pribilof slid from the bed to his bare knees on the floor. He knotted his waxy fingers at his throat. Lifting his face to the blurry radiance coming through the window, the old priest drew a rattling breath and began to speak. The supplication he spoke into this celestial smear was not in his mother Russian tongue, or his adopted English, but in the classic Latin of Rome and might be translated as 'Very well, Show-off; this is Your good and faithful servant, still praying half-blind. And I say unto You: let me see or let me be!'

Waves of blue chaos came billowing by, above and beneath.

Straight overhead past the wind, barely a few dozen yards above the raft, the sky was still clear. The waves were bobbing higher but without much force or direction. Ike found some consolation in those forceless waves. The crazy wind that followed that crystal sword of light had continued to rise in velocity, but it was coming off the near shore. There wasn't distance enough for it to rally the waters into joining its fanatical pursuit. It was getting stiffer, though, and thick with cold, blue-grey vapor. Ike could no longer see much of the mountains and nothing at all of the metal sail. He was surrounded by banks of whistling mists, and such sky as he could see above gave him no bearing. The sun must be hours from setting but it was smothered in those mist banks. One direction looked no brighter than another.

It was wet in the ribbed bottom of the boat but not swamped. A scuppervalve at the end of each of the inflated troughs let the raft bilge itself with the wave action. A clever enough feature for a run-about hauling Hollywoodies around in the near-shore scenery; for a lifeboat it might not be so clever. It might well need that water in the bottom for ballast. If he got blown out into some heavy stuff this inflated toy was going to be just a rubber duck in the paws of the sea. But for now, Ike was grateful for the scuppervalves. At least he was semi-dry. The temperature was falling fast. Wet, without a survival suit, he could easily die of hypothermia before those paws ever got a chance at him.

The gale kept rising. He had to sit up and crank the throttle to keep her nose in the wind. Exposed for a few seconds, his back and neck were peppered with a stinging grapeshot of ice. He tried to reach Greer's duffel in the prow but the ice cut at his face like blowing glass. He had to roll back around and squirm his way beneath the canvas seat along the inflated ribs. He reached the rope of the duffel and pulled it facing him. He felt through the sport shirts and trousers until he found the wrinkled rubber of a rain parka. He tugged it out, along with one of Greer's knitted Rasta caps. As he rose on one elbow to pull the parka on, the wind found the open hood. It ballooned the parka like a sail and the Zodiak sheared hard about. Shielding his face with his arm, Ike sat up and revved the outboard around in an attempt to regain his heading. He was rebuffed by the gale. He tried again with the same result. Each time he tried to bring the raft about, the wind would catch it broadside and hurl it back. The uptilted nose of the craft was too light to hold against such buffeting. He gave up and let it swing; slowed the engine and jacked it into reverse; as long as the waves didn't get any bigger he could get better helm with his heavy end forward.

He had to trade feet on the steering handle. It wasn't that his toes were too cold; the tension was cramping them into claws. He kicked the second shoe off and slipped his foot up the other sleeve of Greer's sweater and gripped the tiller with his toes. It was actually steadier maneuvering screw-forward into the icy wind, the way a front-end drive is steadier on an icy highway.

He lay back again and pulled the drawstring of the parka's hood in a tight oval around his face. Savage gusts of wind still came ripping right up his nostrils. When he wiped his face his hand came away red. Those grapeshots of ice were drawing blood! This was starting to piss him off. He felt up under the hood and pulled the cap all the way down over his face. You couldn't see much through the wool, but what was there to see? Dark blue above and smoking wind on all sides. There was no need of visual bearing anyway. The wind itself kept the raft correctly aimed landward, like a feathered arrow.

The knit of his cap exposed in the tight oval began to ice up. He could see the crystals webbing together right before his eyes. He might need that ice. He was alarmingly thirsty. Adrenaline-induced cottonmouth, probably. He used to get cottonmouth so bad on tense Moth runs that he'd bite on his tongue tip until he got some saliva flowing, or some blood. But he didn't feel that tense. This aridity seemed to be coming from without. His lips felt as though they had been freeze-dried and his thirst was becoming mind-numbing. He pulled the emergency locker near. There was a three-gallon tank of spare gas, some hand flares, a chemical flashlight, a sea anchor and another little compass with its needle spinning crazily. But no water.

522

He raised a hand to deflect some of the ice balls strafing past, but they stung his palm like hornets. He found a deckshoe and slipped his hand in it like a goalie's mitt. He was able to deflect some of the whistling crystals to the chest of the parka. He lifted the wool to examine them. They were cherry-sized burrs, barbed geometrically. When he picked one up it was gone in a smokey instant, leaving on his fingers a familiar odor that took him a minute to place. It was the smell of a dental office, and the spacey sweet taste of nitrous.

The lacerated blue above began at length to drain of light, turning more and more purple. There was still no glow in any direction to indicate where the sun was setting. This seaward wind was his only bearing—if it hadn't changed. It had certainly grown more and more savage. He estimated it must be hitting sixty or seventy knots, but he knew he could be wrong by half that in either direction. It was like no other wind he'd ever felt, so flat yet so fierce. It came screaming over the water like one of those thin plazlucent conveyor belts in the cannery, cranked to maniacal speed. Stars could occasionally be glimpsed through the thin fury of it.

After it had been dark a long time Ike switched on the flashlight to check his watch: it was ten-thirty AM yesterday, and the second hand was spinning crazily counterclockwise. Like that spinning compass needle. It's probably not that hard to figure out, he reassured himself. The positive and negative have exchanged residences, like wealthy execs from New York and Miami. He remembered Jeannie trying to explain the principle of moving polarity according to the Chinese Book of Changes. The yang lines tend to get more and more yang and the yin lines more and more yin until they have to *switch through*, to obey the laws of balance. Through the looking glass, *crack*. The totem pole flips, low man now on top. And that switch-through has to happen almost instantly. There's no *place* for gradation between plus and minus, on and off, up and down. There's no *time* for gradation; or evaluation; or judgment, especially that musclebound Old Testament kind of judgment that Greener was trying to peddle. No heavy hand from heaven. No, this was just the adjustment of a minor glitch that had to be periodically alleviated. Just an impersonal physical phenomenon. Yeah? Then why do I *feel* like it's so personal?

The thin shrilling of the wind was the only answer he received. He stretched beneath the seat again, out of the blast. Except for the raking thirst he wasn't that uncomfortable. The boat's bottom had dried and so had his clothes. He switched his steering foot every few minutes and kept the stern steady into the gale. If the wind had maintained direction he was still on a general heading landward, though he was almost certainly losing ground. That couldn't be helped. To try to gain against this wind, especially butt-first, would have been a waste of fuel. All he could hope was to maintain heading until the moon showed or daylight came.

He heard the engine sputtering empty sometime before dawn and pushed the protective wool up from his face. He quickly unwound the blue wire. The engine kept sputtering. Shit. That had to mean the blue lead was just for ignition. It should have been unwound as soon as the engine caught. By now the solenoid was probably fried. He had to get some fuel in the tank before the engine sputtered out completely! Holding the flashlight in his teeth, he was able to slosh enough gas in to rescue the dying motor. He then made a funnel out of the sea anchor and emptied in the rest of the can. The wind was so cold and dry he couldn't smell the gasoline until he was back in the bottom of the raft.

When he saw the somber blue wash of day returning he loosened the parka and cracked the crystallized wool free from his face again to look around. Nothing much had changed; the wind was still strafing the water with a withering fire of ice. The motor still churned in cranky reverse. The view in any one direction was exactly like the other three. 'All right,' Ike said to the dawn, 'what's next?'

He looked at his watch. The date claimed it was still yesterday (that would be the day before yesterday, now) and the second hand had stopped. He thought of taking off the worthless timepiece and throwing it into the teeth of the wind just to show things where he stood. But the time might come when he would need that watch (the time might come, right) for bait, or barter. He pulled the cap down and lay back in the bottom of the boat, looking up through the crystal weave at the damned dawning blue blue blue.

This blue dawning was what aroused Father Pribilof to the fact that he had been kneeling on the floor all night. He was hoarse with muttering and there was no sense of life below his waist. He untangled the pious knot of his fingers and felt down a bare leg. It was cold as kelp, and numb, and dripping wet. What a silly, stupid Simple Simon; he prays the whole night long for blessed vision, on a cold floor on old knees, and of course ends up with exactly what to show for it? Two numb legs, a leaky bladder, and his stupid eyes not one mustardseed better! Everything still an ungodly smear. 'Scribe visum et explana eum super tabulas, ut percurrat, qui legeriteum—*Write the vision plain on tablets, that the worker may readeth it running.* Was that not the way You instructed Habakkuk, chapter 2, verse 2? What about worn-out old workers too numb to *crawl*, Godforbid run? Do such loyal workers not deserve a plainer tablet than this?'

The smear got a trifle brighter, but no clearer. He wiped his hands on his undershirt. He knew he should try to get a washcloth to clean himself but he would never make it. He strained back to grasp one of the cold porcelain bedposts behind him. After a long wheezing struggle he managed to pull himself on to the bed. His legs lay like a pair of dead eels. He drew each side of the quilted bedspread around the sorry things, and felt along his nightstand until he found the glass of Listerine he soaked his teeth in. He drank as much as he could, then leaned back and turned his pitted stare again toward the window glow. 'Bonum certamen certavi, fidem servavi —*I have fought the fight and kept the faith* but if You think I have finished the course You are mistaken. I am resolved. I am hurt in the thigh, as Jacob that wrestleth the angel, but I am resolved; and unto You I swear this: I have You in my *headlocked*, and, like Jacob, I swear my hold will not open until You surrender the blessed *key*! Are You there? Do You hear me?'

The void remained blue and without form, and surrendered nothing. Father Pribilof sighed. Without turning his eyes away from the light he felt again for the glass and drank the rest of the Listerine.

Alice slowed the Jeep so she could check the time through Miss Iris' Boutique window. None of the dozens of antique clocks had identical times, but they all agreed it was nearing noon. The Radio Man came out of his tower every day at noon, to read any communiqués and talk-show snatches he had picked up on his shortwave. Most of the town's citizens would already be up at his shortwave tower. As she drove along Main she saw ten or twelve roaming strays. The compound out at Tire City must have been liberated. The few people she saw on the street were hired guards, the majority of them Dogs, too: Underdogs, still in their Foxcorp Security jackets. When the city council learned that Bergstrom and his Wasp Patrol had slipped out of town on the RO/RO, the Brotherhood of Bowsers somehow seemed the only logical replacement. Several of them called out as she passed, asking for the time. They had seen her stop at Iris' window.

She saw Mrs Herb Tom sitting on a crate outside the open door of Herky's. Now here was an interesting Dog Brother. The sharp-chinned little woman had a big shoulder holster strapped on over her jacket—a far more potent badge of authority than the Silver Fox logo under the holster. She stood and waved at the Jeep.

'Hey, Alice, what did the clocks say?'

'Eleven-forty-five or so,' Alice answered, slowing the Jeep. Mrs Herb came walking over in her steel-toed boots.

526

'You're headed up to Dr Outbeck's, eh? Well, I guess we could all use a little news.' There was an embarrassing hunger beneath the woman's gruff voice. 'If there's any word from outside, I'd appreciate hearing about it. Even nonsense.'

Alice assured her she'd bring back whatever, one way or another—and drove on, shaking her head. Any word, however absurd the message, however ridiculous the need. Desperately trying to keep contact with the outside world the way everybody was still trying to keep track of the time. Sure, time had been a long fun game but it looked to Alice as though the game had been called, for lack of universal Greenwich time codes. When that bolt from the blue passed over, all of the timegame's quartzware timekeepers had suddenly stopped, short, never to go again. All that was left were the old mechanical windup jobs, like those in Miss Iris' window. When those run down we can wind them again but how will we know which one to set to? Will it matter, if the timegame's over? Probably about as much as The Radio Man's fractured messages mattered. It looked like time codes and talk shows were both about to become passé here in Kuinak's quaint little crack at the remote end of the world—a prospect as appealing as it was terrifying. As their Delphic Eskimo had remarked this morning over the last can of Diet Pepsi: 'From here on up it's all downhill.'

When the engine finally sputtered quiet Ike noticed that the wind seemed to be running out of fuel as well. The keen whistling seemed softer; the grapeshot ice balls had shrunk to BB size. His drymouth, though, was worse than ever. He had never known such thirst. His tongue felt like a dried herring. He dug again into Greer's duffel and came up with a tube of rum-flavored toothpaste, black Jamaican. It might as well have been green spearmint for all his tongue could tell, but it soothed his cracked lips and got a little spit going.

He put out the sea anchor to keep the raft from spinning helmless across the water. Sure enough, the wind was falling. The wave action seemed to be kicking up, however. It was that same up-and-down dimpling action he'd seen in the cove, only greatly magnified. The bright blue peaks of the waves were now ten and fifteen feet above the darker valleys, but the water didn't seem to be rolling anywhere—just pumping up and down. No dangerous breakers or combers. And the dry-ice cold was easing off rapidly. All right then, he encouraged himself, this isn't so bad.

That's when he saw the squid.

Tommy Toogiac Senior discovered the body when he unlocked the storeroom to see if there might be a stash of flashlight batteries among the Deap bingo prizes. Flashlight batteries had already become scarce and dear as people recognized the need for canned electricity. Tommy saw no reason to share these ancestral riches with the Round-Eyes.

When he saw it on the shelf he thought at first it was some kind of big carved doll, a prize for one of the grand bingo quinellas. It was that emaciated. Even when he lit a rolled-up bingo card for a torch he couldn't figure out what the hell it was. Then he saw the teabags, hundreds of pairs, black and green, twisted together and tossed everywhere to dry in woebegone wads, like evanescent tide-pool creatures that had expired after the singular thrill of their mating. There was no odor—the doll was apparently as desiccated as the dry teabags—but Tommy Senior had to grab his nose and back his way out of the storeroom, deeply shaken.

'This is a job for Junior and the rest of them damn dogs.'

So the helpless old priest was discovered when a delegation of them damn dogs walked out to the church to ask the Good Father to do a funeral. He was still flat on his back, his face toward the window, expectantly praying. He ceased his supplication at their knock and turned to stare in the direction of their voices. As they spoke he smiled and nodded. They went on and on. Tommy Toogiak Junior's voice was explaining 'Usually, Father, our president does them but in this case, you see, this is our president,' when, without fuss or warning, Father Pribilof began vomiting a thick slurry of bile and Listerine down his chin. They carried him to the bathroom so he could finish in the sink, then they found him a quart of milk that hadn't quite turned. They warmed water on his butane range and toweled him clean and found fresh underclothes. He thanked them each by name, by the sound of their voices, and tried to touch their hands. The Dogs thought the old bird seemed pretty perky, all things considered. And he absolutely refused to be moved to the clinic.

'C'mon, Father,' Tommy Junior pleaded. '*Please*, for God's sake.'

'Help me back to my own bed if you would, Thomas,' the priest croaked. His throat was now as abrased as his eyes. 'I shall be fine. A funeral. This departed soul you speak of? Was he Catholic?'

'He was an Italian,' Norman Wong answered.

'I see. I shan't be going to town but if you will bring the remains by, I will do what I am able to give them unction.'

'That's a long way to carry a body, Father,' Tommy Junior pointed out.

'The same distance you would have had to carry me to town, Thomas. And I doubt if this old body would fare the journey as well as your president's. Now, if you kind people will excuse me? I'm deeply involved in a rather demanding project. Good day.'

He was back to his staring and muttering before the last of them had backed out of the cramped cloister.

Alice found a spot at the edge of the crowd beneath The Radio Man's tower. She backed the Jeep in. She was close enough to hear any bulletins announced but far enough away to avoid having to deal with people pestering after rides. Greer's Jeep was one of the few rigs that still started. Yesterday people had pressed her so hard to be a taxi service she had been forced to move the sleeping pup so Ike's .22 could be seen. All the other clunkers parked around her had weapons displayed in one way or another. Most of the citizens were showing iron, too. Only three days (or was it five?) and the town was already as bare-fanged and skittish as a coyote convention. So far, though, not a shooting, not a robbery, not even a fight. Well, it was still early. This wily convocation was still sniffing and circling.

The Radio Man's station was in the town's original water tower on the steep slope at the top of Cook—an oaken barrel on a circle of pressure-treated poles. It was this seepy slope and these wooden poles that had prompted the town to build the new metal reservoir on the other end of town a quarter-century earlier. Federal inspectors had warned them that wooden poles planted in damp ground like that would inevitably rot and collapse and send the big staved barrel barreling down the hill like a ten-thousand-gallon water bomb. But it was the new tank that had collapsed and exploded, last week during the ice wind, blown right off its metal legs. Now there was talk of trying to get this old barrel going again. A civilized community *must* have water pressure, the city council agreed; you can't go on indefinitely hand-hauling buckets from Kuinak Creek. And who knew how long it might be before machinery and material were available to rebuild the metal tank? Of course, resurrecting the old tower would mean rooting out the Australian ham operator and his tangle of equipment and moving it someplace else. The damned wombat would not listen to reason! He vowed he would not reassemble the complex hookup if they took it apart. 'You touch so muh-much as one tube and I'll let you wire up your *own* prodding earache. *Then* we'll see what the community reckons most necessary: your precious WC that flushes, or radio contact with the rest of the wuh-wuh-*world*!'

The disbarred Australian doctor in the wooden tower had not been happier his whole life long. He had never enjoyed medicine—slicing sun cancers off some sheep herder's snoot; flushing out some Sheila's lower after she plugged it with too much Zonex. He had often suspected that his disbarment might have been the grand turning point of his life. After the halls of healing were closed to him he could devote himself to his true calling: radio! When his stutter stopped him from making it as a deejay he sought to become a sound engineer, taking an apprentice position in Adelaide. When he couldn't master the new comchips he stole all the equipment he could carry from the station, sold it, bought a passage to as far away as a bloke could get, the antipodes of Adelaide: Alaska. He arrived in Anchorage with just enough cash left to buy his antique short-wave. He chose Kuinak because it was the only town of its size without a radio station. He skimped and scrabbled for fifteen years, living mainly off the money he got for his Sacred Healing Skins. 'Imbued with authentic Eskimo balm! Just give the affected area a bit of a rub twice a day.' The FCC tried to shut him down but they could never pinpoint the transmitter. He had survived, he was prevailing. He was *The* Radio Man, now, who cared a futter about a little stutter? 'Anybody on this wuh-wavelength?'

Until the transistors or the celefone satellites started working again, The Radio Man had them by the hairs. He was right. They wanted news more than running water. More than anything anybody could think of, they wanted word from the world beyond. For this holy word they were willing to pee in the streets and mill around the base of the rickety tower for hours—days!—like religious fanatics at the sacred minaret of their cult, waiting.

An occasional word was about all they were getting, too, these last couple days. The broken messages coming in had become increasingly infrequent, or meaningless, or in a language The Radio Man had to guess at. 'German!' he would call out through the barrel's window. 'I just picked up something in German on the muh-marine band. What does *"verboten boot"* mean, somebody?'

'Dangerous footing,' Wayne Altenhoffen translated and scribbled in his pad.

Altenhoffen was daily more diligent at his journalistic duties; now that the network dishes were empty the good

531

old reliable American newspaper was going to have to serve up the dirt, even if he had to serve it on typewriter carbons headlined by letters made out of spuds.

At first there had been stations coming in on all the shortwave bands, snippets and snatches from a scattering of ham hobbyists all over the globe. A radio boy on a tanker off Costa Rica had bleated hysterically over the ship's set for exactly twenty-four hours, in English, Spanish, and a tongue The Radio Man called Scared Shitless. As the fear increased the boy talked more and more to his parents in Yuma, Arizona, about things he should have done *diff*erent—you know, Mom, things like, oh, stayed in school like Dad advised . . . got that engineer's license, never wrecked the Merc—

The message cut off in mid-bleat at midnight and never came back on.

The best reports had come from an evangelical station in Quito, Ecuador. Two young missionaries from Cleveland, a bus driver and a hairdresser, had taken the church assignment expecting it to be a pleasant tropical vacation. Now here they were, alone together, atop Mt Quito in a rickety station tower called God's Perch. The Radio Man had even been able to talk to the girl for a while. Her name was Doreen and she said that from what they could sort out from the transmissions they'd been receiving on their exalted church channel, praise the Lord, it was the same everywhere: all magnetic memory systems deleted, tape and disk, mainframe and backup; all digital chipware scrambled; all nations in turmoil, all people in godless despair. As time passed the girl began to wax rhapsodic: 'though verily the radiant throne of *jasper* and sar*dine* stone shall soon appear, and the four and twenty *elders* with their luxuriant crowns of flowing *gold* and their *glo*rious—'

'Can it, Doe-reen,' the bus driver had to interrupt, 'we're inna disaster, for chrissakes, not some beauty parlor down on Prospect.'

The transmissions from Quito had dwindled fast on the third day. Only occasional quick updates of their own dwindling contacts. No more oracular oratory.

'We are all runnin' out of battery,' The Radio Man had explained. 'I'm at the bottom like a drunk Abo in a gully. We need a generator what can put out direct current.'

There were dozens of diesel-powered alternators around town, and some of the older motors could still be started. But they would not crank out a current, direct or otherwise. As the radio news had grown dimmer day after day, the crowd on the slope had become larger and ever more skittish. That was another reason why Alice parked for quick getaway and always kept one eye on the crowd in the rearview.

In front of her was the town, and the tranquil sweep of sea between the jetty and that week-old wall of fog. The panorama was as serene as an old scallop shell. Those first days the bay had been frantic with activity. Every developer and foreign investor and studio flake in town was scrambling after anything that still could be made to fly or float. Fortunes were paid for fifty-year-old bowpickers. Herb Tom traded three Israeli real estate attorneys his oldest Piper for an envelope full of diamonds. They claimed they were worth eight million. A seat on the old rundown RO/RO hightailing for Seattle went for a Rolex, so *what* if they no longer kept time. The few trawlers and gillnetters that had been able to straggle back from the big sea lion safari barely had time to gas up before they were booked full of passengers and off again. Anywhere! So *what* that the Loranavs and automaps didn't work. You didn't need any fancy stuff to find your way to civilization—just keep the continent off your port and Polaris over your stern. Kick the passengers off the first place that suits them and head home. With a little luck a dunker could come back with a fortune—make more in a short week than he could in a whole long life of fishing. Of course, so far, no-one had come back.

Nor did the *kind* of civilization they might find seem to be a concern to the escaping flakes and dream-developers. All they knew was that they wanted to get away, right away, and far damned away. Sure there was probably king bastard end-of-the-world insane *hell* going on in Seattle and San Francisco and, Christ knows, Los *An*geles, but at least it was hell in a place with some class. Who in his right mind would want to spend the end in this retro rinky-dink nowhere?

The day after that first frenetic exodus Boswell's ancient processor steamed into the bay towing a line of dead-in-waters a quarter-mile long. He and his girls had stayed to patrol around Hopeless and round up such straggling boats as they could find still afloat. The others had been blown out to open sea or on to the rocks or swamped. Some of the flakes that missed the initial exodus offered to richly reward the old tugger if he would keep on towing them south. Boswell refused. 'What would a floating fishgut factory do in San Francisco?'

Down the slope Alice can see some boys on the high school football field, tossing a yellow Frisbee. The weather has warmed up so much they are playing without shirts. Their shouts drift up the sunny distance, incongruously carefree and bright. She notices that her old mural on the side of the gymnasium is looking pretty shabby by comparison. All the colors have gone wrong except the red. She had mixed that hue herself, boiling pine resins and linseed oil and adding crushed cinnabar for pigment. The school board had tried to get her to use commercial enamel, insisting her mixture looked too much like dried blood. She told them this was the red of her ancestors, the true red of the old burnt earth, the *angry* red of the mother of Quicksilver. It was the red she was going to use or they could send the grant money back to Washington. Now, she was gratified to see that it was the only color on the mural that still worked.

She saw Wayne Altenhoffen's bandaged nose approaching in the rearview. 'Paper, lady? Read all about it.'

Grinning like a newsboy, he handed her a sheet of white bond filled with dim print on both sides. Alice saw it was a carbon copy with a masthead added in blocky green ink:

534

'Altenhoffen, you are a case,' she conceded. 'Incurable, too, it looks to me.'

Altenhoffen beamed with pride at this compliment from the Angry Aleut. 'I can crank it out in runs of up to six—an original and five carbons. The block letters I carved from potatoes. That'll be ten bucks.'

'Ten *bucks*?'

'Potatoes are a buck apiece at Herky's,' he explained. 'Uh-oh, look! The Radio Man is about to give out the morning's wire-service report. Keep the *Beacon*. I'll send you a bill.'

He bustled back up the slope, notebooks fluttering. Alice folded down the Jeep's windshield and sat up on the dash to listen. The Radio Man was leaning out the barrel's single opening holding an FCC logbook. He was a strange-looking little creature, spiny-haired and chinless, blinking at the unaccustomed sunlight like an echidna flushed from his burrow. He cleared his throat and began to read from the log.

'Eight to nine AM, quote: SIMPLE THINGS RAILS BLOCKED PORTLAND WITHOUT SOMETHING IS HAPPENING HERE WHAT IT IS AIN'T EXACTLY CLEAR BREAKER BREAKER THIS IS BOOGER RED COME BACK THIS IS BOOGER RED LAYTONVILLE WE EAT THE MUH-MUH-MULES. Unquote.' He turned a page. 'Nine to ten AM, quote: CHOLERA CHOLERA HELP HELP HELP JUST KIDDING HAW HAW HAW SEND BROADS . . .'

Alice stood as much as she could, then decided the words just were not worth the wait and the frustration. She slid back beneath the wheel and put in the clutch. The Jeep began to roll. It wasn't that the battery was low; roll-starting just seemed to have become one of those things one did.

Back at the motel she was confronted by the entire

Johanssen family except for Shoola. They were lined up outside their three units with all their bundles and boxes, just as they had appeared on that distant-seeming day a month before. The six-year-old they called Nell stepped forward to state their case.

'We check out, Mrs Carmody. The rooms are clean like the Negro's hull.'

'I'm sure they are, Nell. But why are you checking out? You are all welcome to stay as long as you like.'

'Grandfather says we must get back to things is why.'

'Precious, tell your grandfather I sympathize. A lot of us would like to get back to things. I fear, however, that you may have a hard time finding anybody interested in making a flight up to the Baffins.'

'Oh my goodness, Mrs Carmody, Grandfather knows that! He knows we are more-ooned like everybody. He is going to find a place here. He is going to find a place on the shore where he can put some lines out and see how the animals live.'

Alice smiled at the girl. 'I may know just the place: lovely big longhouse, right on the beach. The owner is away at present, though you may have some problems with the cat. Tell them to pile in, we'll drive out and see if it'll do. Should we try to find your sister?'

The girl shook her head. 'She's not with us no more. She's went to live at the church.'

'At the *church*? I thought the church was closed since Father Pribilof's collapse.'

'That's why she went there. Hey! Hey, everbody!' She headed across the courtyard, clapping her hands and clucking instructions to her relatives, quarrelsome as a little hen. *'T'alsoo san-san!'*

While the Johanssens are loading their bundles and boxes into the Jeep, Alice takes the opportunity to skim Altenhoffen's little news sheet. There is a list of the unaccounted-for boats and crew members, and a feature story about the most newsworthy of the missing:

**NOWORD FROM
CELIBRATIES!**

The whereabouts of World
renowned movie direct-
or Gearhardt Stuebins,
and famous environ-
Mental activist I-
saak Sallas remain
unknown as of
Tuesday the 3rd. Al-
so missing are
prominent highliner,
Michael Carmody, Arch
and Nels Culligan and
erstwhile native son,
producer, Nicholas
Levertov-

Mental Activist and Native Son. Alice smiled. Wouldn't they both get a kick out of *that*? Also Mr Prominent Highliner. She tried to laugh but the sound stuck in her throat, burning. She bit her lip to make it stop but it burned hotter. At length she drew a shaky breath and turned to glare across the courtyard at the hooded sea. Her eyes were brimming with rage. *You slimy Bitch have you finally got your cold hooks into all my poor doomed misters? All? Father, son, husband, lover and fucking all? You blue-bosomed slick-thighed widow-making whore, you can't snow me with that old Sea Queen masquerade, I don't trust you and never have. You are no queen I'll bow before for all the glories hincty poets hang on you, I know your true face and if I ever get close enough, you sloe-eyed slut—*

'This up-and-down action is not that amusing anymore —and you, you damn grampus, you're not making the situation any funnier!' The giant squid had been bobbing up and down alongside for hours now, eyeing Ike. The eye was the size of a hubcap, and from what Ike had been able to see the creature measured at least five times

537

the raft's length, tentacle to tail. It seemed to intend no malice; it just hung around off his starboard bow and watched him sideways with that big forlorn pleading orb. 'What you looking at *me* for, Hubeye?' The words came out cracked and bleeding. 'You think if I had any answers I'd be out here bobbing up and down? Back off!' Knock knock. 'Hey Father?' A girl's voice. 'Can we come in?'

Father Pribilof's answer was a long groan. Ever since the Underdogs had found him he'd been plagued with well-wishing parishioners, interrupting his concentration every time something exceptional seemed about to come into focus. The knocking continued. 'Oh, very well,' he groaned, 'come in if you must.'

He smelled liver and onions and rubber. The familiar signal of fishkids bearing nourishment. He knew the group. They were the black rubber sheep of his flock. The ebullient girl's voice, though, was not something he recognized.

'Hey, Father, God bless you. Me and these friends we come here to help you out.'

'Please. I'm fine. I've been brought ample sustenance. I very much need to be left alone, is all . . .'

'Sure. We heard that. We mean help out in your *church*. Sell the candles and do the little window. I can give a good catechism if you don't mind Jesuit. First, let me have a look . . .'

Before he could protest warm hands cupped both cold cheekbones and he smelled a sweet breath, inches away. He could not see her eyes but he felt them somehow rope his roving stare and rein it in. The pitted irises converged and narrowed.

'Uh-oh, Father. It look to me like you and the bear been circling each other. You better eat some of this meat just in case. We'll go out and do the candles.'

She folded the waxy fingers around a slice of fried flesh still warm from the skillet. When the visitors had left the room he raised it to his mouth and sucked on it pensively. She was right. The meat helped. So did that reining thing she did. The colors were becoming clearer, the crisscross

538

more distinct. It was forming into a distinct silhouette—a crucifix, most certainly. Or a totem pole thunderbird with wings spread. It was not really important which. The silhouette was merely the display rack. It was the pair of *pictures* congealing at the spread tips of the cross that were important. He sucked harder at the liver. The pair of illuminations seemed to be symbols of chance. Cards. Yes, most assuredly. Card designs. Nor did it matter that he knew not what the designs represented, or what game. He had never made the swing when Deap poker nights became legal; the only cards he had ever played with were bingo cards. It was all right. What mattered was not the *meaning* of the illuminations—that was the mistake the picklock mystics always made. No, what mattered was the clarity.

The two images snapped into focus, clear and sharp as icons in the outstretched arms of that sacred shadow: a big red

on the right hand side and a

of some kind on the left. Hail Mary hallelujah and keep it coming. This was *worlds* more exciting than bingo.

The forlorn orb was still alongside as the sky purpled once more toward night. Sometimes the creature got so close it rode the waves in sync with the raft. Usually it stayed far enough off that it would be going up when he was going down. Even when it was on a peak and Ike was way down in the gully, it kept its baleful eye on him. Ike was no longer afraid that it would snag him and swallow him down, but he was worried that it could fall on him from one of those liquid pinnacles. They were still getting bigger. Even when it grew too dark to see the waves he could feel them continue to build. Sometimes when he was in the very center of a crater he could feel the steep nearness of a wall of water all around him; next he would be rising fast and faster, until he was tossed into breathless space, like a Deap kid being tossed in a blanket. An eternity would seem to pass before the raft slapped back to the surface.

Worst of all it went on and on, even more unrelenting than that roller-coaster ride down the White Pass. At least *that* tail-twister had been in the daylight; you were able to see the dips and dives coming. In the dark they could only be imagined.

He tied Greer's duffel beneath the boat's front seat and lay face-down with both arms wrapped about it. There were moments when the slope he was riding was so steep he could feel himself standing on his feet, or on his head, straight up or straight down. More than once when he came shooting up out of the bottom of one of those craters he was certain the boat was tossed in a complete somersault. That he always fell back to the water right-side-up was an unexplained miracle to him until he became aware of a heavy bulk at his side in the boat bottom. It was the motor, flipped free of its mount by the water's violence. Here was the ballast he'd been needing.

Waves of nausea began to rise and fall in concert with the black sea outside. It had been years since he'd been seasick; a minor laser procedure on the inner ear had all but eliminated motion sickness. These waves were obviously more powerful than that procedure. He'd forgotten how miserable the malady can make you. He could feel his gorge rising. Then the retching started and he remembered he didn't have any gorge to give up. His heaves were as dry as his mouth. He retched until his ears rang and blue sparks boiled around his brow. His whole tormented body seemed to be trying to escape through his throat. He would gladly have let it go if he'd known how; he was too sick to want to live.

One choking paroxysm followed another until he was faint from lack of air. He lay on his face in the boiling sparks, unable to get up, unable to draw breath. For a long, agonizing time he tried to breathe, then he stopped trying. The agony left him. He had suffocated in that blue boil. Dead at last, dead at last! Great God Amighty I'm dead at last. Should have done it years ago saved everybody a lot of grief they say the man that seeks revenge digs two graves and I should have jumped in the second the second one was dug. A whole life wasted trying to get getbacks—just as bad as Levertov. A man with slam smarts should know better than to take things so personally. Except. It *is* personal damn it! Are apocalypses any less personal than dead babies and gang rapes? Vengeance is Mine sayeth the Lord. Oh yeah, says who? When your doom ain't right a man has to try to straighten it out even though the attempt dooms him. Oh yeah, except. A doomed-if-you-do-and-if-you-don't-both kind of dilemma. It's too bad St Nick and I never took the opportunity to dig into this interesting paradox: we might have learned something. Now I am dead in the water and all his carefully constructed getbacks are blown with the wind. We might have got deep, Slam to Slam, philosophically.

Levertov was alive but in neither mood nor condition to talk philosophy. He was slogging along behind Clark B Clark across an exposed brown bottom of slimy silt. The tide had dropped so far during the night that bottoms unseen since the '94 tsunami were again laid naked. They could walk off their little sandbar. They had been pinned down out there ever since the speed launch had evaporated beneath them in a fizz of Tinkerbells. The Asian giant hadn't made it to the sandbar; he'd been posted as lookout on top of the wheelhouse and had put on his lumafoam suit. It was custom-made for his size. The manifold rolls and wrinkles of the loose material made him look like one of those Chinese dogs with rolls of loose skin. When the launch came apart he hit the water and the suit puffed up big as a four-door sedan. The giant went skidding away west like an enormous beach ball. There were times, marooned on the little windswept spit, when Levertov acted as though the giant had been the lucky one.

Levertov had become ominously quiet since that first afternoon. He had lost his glasses and his face was pinched into a continual searching squint. The crimson smile had begun to look strained and unpredictable, dangerous, like a wounded beast. Everything in his carefully constructed world had come apart at once it seemed, just like the launch, and Nicholas Levertov was at a loss where to lay the blame.

Clark B Clark was worried about his boss's unfocused silence, and he didn't care for the way that squint kept casting about this direction and that. He didn't want those barbed eyes looking *his* way, hooking into *his* sunny California countenance. So Clark B tried to keep up a lively chatter as they slogged across the exposed channel bottom, not really caring what came out. The chatter was more for self-preservation than conversation.

'I told you we'd make it, Boss. Fate can be cheated just like any mark. There is a something that shapes the some-thing of something, Shakespeare says. Or something like that. Pasadena Playhouse, *Henry the Fourth, Part One*. I was one of Falstaff's crowd of cronies. They made me wear a kielbasa in my tights. That was when I first flashed that it was *fool*ish, right? playing a fool's fool? No place for advancement, you see? Better far to play the *villain's* fool, or the madman's, or the monster's fool. Long shot with those roles anyway . . . chance at the *beeg* time. But what's the best fare a fool's fool can look forward to? Pie crumbs and banana cream is about it . . . meringue you get to lick off the old clown's phisog. Hey, *Igor's* even got it

542

better than that, up at Frankenstein's: do the circumcise, Igor . . . all you can eat plus tips ho ho. So don't for one instant think, Boss, that I am in any way downhearted that our rigged deal got busted by some kind of sneak raid from the elements. Because the game ain't over, merely interrupted. For the deal isn't done, as I've heard you say so many times, until the pot's right. The hand is still up for grabs until the pot's right, right Boss?'

'Be quiet,' Levertov said. He had stopped just at the edge of the silt, where the dry beach started to rise. He stood squinting, his head tilted. 'What's that?'

'That smell? Why, that has to be all that garbage they trucked down for fill, wouldn't you say? Which means that brushy ridge ahead must be where they been building the airstrip which further means the bay is just beyond. I *told* you we'd make it—'

'Hush. I don't mean the smell. Listen.'

With his chatter stilled Clark B heard them immediately. They were scattered all through the Scotch broom and blackberries that grew from the ridge down to the beach. The whole hungry bunch, from the sound of them. 'They must have followed the smell. Is that incredible or what? All this way. They sound a little salty, the poor confused brutes, and who can blame them? How could they have guessed that after such a long journey their old larder'd be paved over when they found it?'

A huge hog came grunting through a moonbroom bush to study the men with his ravenous little eyes. His snout was bloody from trying to root through the paving to the graded garbage. He grunted again and more pigs started coming out to look. They all had damaged snouts. Then the men heard a jubilant roar above all this grunting. On top of the ridge an old grey she-bear had reared into view. She stood swaying and sniffing with both forepaws lifted in an attitude of happy surprise, like a grandmother being surprised by a birthday cake.

'Maybe we better look for an alternate route, chief.'

'Not on your life, Mr Clark,' Levertov purred. He sounded as pleased as the bear by this unexpected

543

encounter on the beach. 'Not on your boot-licking life. I *own* this piece of property, and I don't take kindly to trespassers.'

Clark B Clark's heart jumped with joy at the familiar purr. The wounded smile looked like it was rallying, and Clark B saw that that searching squint had finally found a target to focus on. Look out, you swine; back off, you bears; Nasty Nick is back in the saddle and he is one bad hombre . . .

A piercing alarm of sunlight roused him from the raft's bottom. What a difference a night makes. The sea was flat and shining and the warm air heavy with vapor. It felt like the air in one of the rain-forest domes. Maybe he'd been blown all the way to the tropics.

It took a lot of groaning effort to get his aching body up from beneath the seat to sitting on top of it. He ached from stem to stern. He hadn't felt so totally hammered since boot camp. Or so thirsty. But it was now just thirst, ordinary old-fashioned, miserable thirst—not some newfangled freeze-dry experiment perpetrated by strange liquid gases.

His giant traveling companion had deserted him some time during the night and he was alone. He had drifted into an arena of sunshine ringed round with a beetling wall of inky blue mists. The wall looked ten or twenty stories high—it was hard to estimate—and the ring perhaps a mile across. An island of sunny calm in the middle of who knew what misty weirdness.

He peeled off the parka and cap and let the sun's warm rays massage his shoulders and back. He was becalmed, like the Ancient Mariner: 'as idle as a painted ship upon a painted ocean.' As his head and eyes cleared he unfolded his Zeisses to study his walled circle of sunny water. He discovered the outline of a dark green patch a few hundred yards off the raft's starboard bow. A patch of seaweed, in all likelihood, gathered off the bottom by those bobbing waves. It was better than nothing.

He tried paddling toward the dark patch with his hands, leaning first over one side, then the other. All he did was wobble the raft back and forth and break a sweat. He noticed his hands weren't cramped with cold by the water. Could he have really been driven to the tropics in such a short time? Not unless that wind had been driving ten times the speed limit.

He slipped over the stern into the tepid water, crossed his arms through the motor mount and began frog-kicking at an easy pace. A half an hour later he felt himself enter the patch and climbed back into the raft.

The mass was mainly seaweed, uprooted cables of kelp tangled together and stinking with dead sea creatures; but as he drifted farther into the miniature sargasso he discovered it to be rich with treasures that only a cast-away could appreciate. The stinky green tangles were bejeweled with a splendid collection of flotsam: crab floats, foam cushions; light bulbs and bottle corks and gas cans; wooden slats and planks and staves and poles. He retrieved a twelve-foot polished banister with a piece of teak decking still attached to one end. It had to have come from one of the big tour cruisers, wood like this. With the banister he was able to pole and scull his way about in the green mass, and pick and choose from the treasure. He found scores of lidded jars and bottles, most of them empty. Some still showed a corner of whatever the container had originally held—sweet pickle juice, salad dressing, Vicks 55 respiratory syrup, Angostura bitters, Canada Dry mixer. He tried not to bolt the liquids down but they started him heaving again anyway. The two inches of Canada Dry seltzer was what saved him. It slaked his thirst and there was still enough carbonation to settle his stomach. His best find was the apple. It was big as a hardball, shiny as life itself.

He was still nibbling at the core when his slow poling brought him on to his worst find—a land creature this time.

A young man in a life jacket lay back among the tangled ropes of kelp, arms spread casually as though he were reclined in a green hammock while he watched a show on an invisible dish. It must have been a comedy show, by the lad's expression; his head was thrown back and he looked as though he were laughing, uproariously, through a broad purple grin. His throat had been opened from jawbone to jawbone in a single efficient slice. For a while Ike tried to convince himself to search the body. Maybe the kid still had the knife on a cord somewhere, the way a lot of dunkers did: a knife could come in handy. He finally shook his head and sculled rapidly away. Deaps claim a suicide blade is cursed. He could use broken glass if he needed to cut something.

As he poled through the flotsam he became aware that the floating island was rotating. He could tell by the circling sun and the shadow he cast. This gentle turning didn't concern him until he noticed that his little sargasso was wheeling toward another *bigger* wheel—and that sucker was hauling!

He began to scull in earnest to avoid the impending swirl, but it was slow going; he had foraged deep into the tangle. Even so he might have made it out if he hadn't taken a side trip to a promising bottleneck he spied winking at him from one of the little kelp-locked vortices. He lifted the bottle into the sunlight and saw that it was more than half full of a sparkling clear liquid. He had just wrenched the rusty cap free with the vise grip and taken a triumphant taste (gin! wonderful, earth-scented, juniper-tainted gin) when he heard a steamy hiss behind him. That other vortex had been wheeling along faster than he thought. It was colliding with his! The stately circling of the kelp-and-flotsam swirl was no match for the opposing force of this new maelstrom. The collision of waters at the rims braked the kelp swirl almost to a stop. Ike realized that he might have been better staying in the middle of the kelp circle. He had reached its outer rim just in time to be sucked into another orbit and swirled away in the opposite direction. He found himself prisoner of a carousel that was far faster and weirder: this dizzying swirl was loaded with land creatures, quite a number of which were still very much alive.

The turning gyre widens. The colored things fall apart,

their center cannot hold. But Father Pribilof knows it is more than mere anarchy loosed upon the world this time, more than just your run-of-the-mill rough beast slouching his way through another remake come around again at last. This is a *new* falling apart, turning and turning in a newfangled gyre that webs together even as it widens. This way, one can *not-know* what it means, the way one must *not-know* grace, or *not-know* the Holy Ghost. How else can these Divine States be made available and kept inviolable at the same time?

Cut loose from the bottom-bound anchor of the need for meaning, the priest's liberated vision goes flying free through the breaking waves of color and space into the heart of chaos, yea, the very beating heart of it, completely unafraid—*Bitch blood is really going to fly! You're not dealing with some Celtic Crone this time, Queenie, some dour old dishrag resigned that her Riders-to-the-Sea were delivered into the clutches of your cold pussy by the holy pimp of fate. You are dealing with a Third-and-a-half-World Squaw here, Bitch, and the only bowing I'll be doing is when I piss down your throat*—completely comfortable. Let it fly.

LOOP HEIR DONATES FIRE TRUCK

Louise Loop does not
see herself as an angel.
But that is how she looked to
Robert Mowbry when she came
driving up to his burning
welding shop Monday morning
in her father's familiar green
tank truck.

 'All I had was a bucket
until Miss Loop showed up,'
Mowbry stated. 'She jumped out
and threw the sucker hose
into the water. The thing
gulped it up like a water-
spout. I couldn't believe

547

my eyes. Then she handed me
the hose and showed me how
to use it. "It blows as good
as it sucks," she told me and
she wasn't whistling Dixie.
I had the fire out in a minute.
I told her I would have lost
shop and all without that truck
and she says keep it, just like
that.'

Mowbry, a volunteer fireman,
said that the truck would be
modified for use as a substitute
until the regular fire engines
can be started.

The truck is at present still
parked at the dock behind Mowbry's
Metalworks where it is being cleaned,
inside and out. Volunteers are
needed.

This one was an immense dish of spinning liquid
metal, like a long-play laserecord: rainbow chrome on the
tops of the grooves, specks of cobalt and jade sprinkled
on the bottoms—along with a multitude of other specks,
swimming for their miserable lives. At first I don't think
much about these swimming specks; I'm too blown out
by the dish itself. A four-hundred-meter track would fit
inside its foamy rim. It's turning so fast that the center
is funneled somewhat down from the rim. The raft flies
around the grooves like a test car on a banked track. I
sit down amidships, trying to use my banister as a tiller
to keep the raft heading straight on the merry-go-round.
Then I feel things at my feet. I'm being boarded. Dozens
of my fellow go-rounders have already stormed up the
motor mount into the raft and hundreds of dozens more
are swimming hard to join them. I tilt the mount out of the
water but this doesn't stop the bigger ones from clawing
hold of the rail-rope that runs around the inflated sides

of the raft. They can't quite pull themselves all the way up, but the little ones are using them for ladders. Before I can get the rope untied and pulled free of the loops, scores more of the tiny pirates have made it on board, as well as two of the larger ones. On both sides I can see the larger ones still, veering their way across the grooves to intercept me. Sallas, you superstitious sissy: before this ride is over you are going to wish to hell you had that kid's knife, however cursed.

BOIL KUINAK CLINIC EMPHASIZE

'Boil, boil, boil,' Paramedic
Dorothy Culligan told the Beacon's
health and welfare desk Monday.
'Even fresh creek water should
be boiled. Chlorine and alcohol
will work but we ought to save
these. We'll need them. So, boil,
boil, boil!' *Bitch, Bitch, Bitch,* Alice raved through her office window. *It takes one to know one I ought to know.* She had tilted back in her swivel chair and kicked off her shoes so she could be comfortable at her raving. It was something of a relief, having a nemesis the size of the sea; here was a target worthy of her wrath. Benedicta tu in mulieribus Shoola made the candle flame quiver et benedictus fructus ventris tui Jesus you'll swamp me! Out, out, out! And the rest of you back off, off, off! GASES DETECTED MT LASSEN LITMUS STATION The Radio Man writes dutifully. HYDROGEN METHANE   AMMONIA   NO CONCLUSIONS ANYBODY OUT THERE? He likes to leave the spaces, gives the citizens a sense of how sad and spare these signals are, cryin' out in the wilderness, so lonesome-like. OTHER FINDINGS INDICATE   OZONE OFF THE SCALE ANYBODY   so angry for so many years RELATIVELY SMALL AMOUNTS SULPHUR so busy fighting them off   ALL THESE SOGGY RODENTS? and tossing them over *bored stiff with all this forever trying to blame everything on men.* They're simply

549

too puny to serve as fair sport. Too boring. A sporting woman as it were finally has to take aim at a tougher target; and you are it, Big Mama.

Ike was not aware of the next whirlpool until a long black shadow came stroking past the raft. He looked over his shoulder and saw the shadow was being cast by a Sitka spruce, uprearing a moment in splendid limbless despair, then tumbling away out of sight. He couldn't see the pool itself but it had to be the mother-in-law of all maelstroms by the noise it was making. A sound of terrific momentum was coming to him from beyond the rim, like the high-pitched rush of a speedway. Beneath this he could hear a deeper sound, a muffled rumble of thuds and thumps, coming from far below the surface. Some very big items were knocking around down there—barrels, trees, boats, buildings. The next time his wheel carried him around past the rim of this adjacent maelstrom he saw one whole wall of a dockside fuel station come cartwheeling into view. A basketball backboard was still mounted on the wall, the basket crammed with ribbon kelp. The next spin around he couldn't see anything. The rims of the two whirls were beginning to collide in a steaming thunderhead, billowing and piling to blot out the sun. Ike frantically tried to scull away from that impending cloud, but the powerful current kept wrenching the end of his pole loose. Once it cracked him hard across the bridge of his nose, setting off that familiar boil of sparks. He locked the pole under his armpit and leaned into the work. If he could get past this collision of wheel rims *one more time* then maybe—the banister gave way with a sharp crack. He went down, cheek-first against the motor. The cloud took him then. Kettledrumrolls of doom were the last thing he heard. The last thing he felt was a scrabble of tiny paws all over him. The last thing he thought was, *Isn't this sweet the patter of little feet, at last? I would have preferred a warmer family if we if we had had . . . It might have worked you know, woman? Our whirlpool romance? I know it was skimpy but that little taste was certainly sweeter*

than revenge and you know it might just have floated
then he went under for good *Bitch? Are you listening?*
Don't think that I don't know you for what you are, you
you hear me, Mrs Carmody? *You're not asleep You're
never asleep* You awake? *not even on the nicest night
of Your nasty life . . . and* now *with all these* hot flashes
ooo Mama *You must be boiling in Your bed* We are loaded
as ready as we can get Mrs Carmody—' The little girl's
face was showing at the top of the stairwell, flushed with
anticipation. '—if you are awake?'

'I'm awake.' Alice followed the girl down the stairwell
and out to the Jeep. It was incredibly overloaded and
none of the family were even on board.

Sinking into his pillow, the old priest was at last content to turn loose the wild pinwheel he had hooked into.
He felt both drained and fulfilled. He was satisfied with
the meager fruits of his week-long vigil. Things were
clear, however incomprehensible. Clarity is the key and
the door. He was blissfully asleep when Shoola crept back
into the room to check on him.

'Hey Father?' she whispered into the gloom. A healthy
snore answered. The face on the pillow looked peaceful—
unshaven, toothless, slack with fatigue, but profoundly
pleased with things accomplished. It was the face of one
who had made it through the heart of the storm, the eye
of the needle and the crack of the looking glass, all in
a single wave-wracked voyage. 'Blessed art thou,' she
whispered more softly still, tiptoeing out backwards for
fear of waking the exhausted priest. There was no need
for her to be so worried. He didn't even wake up when
the antique Bell helicopter came gonging and racketing
down into the churchyard, so close to the old man's
bedroom that the rotors gave his unkept lilacs a neat
green flat-top.

It took Alice two trips to get all the Johanssens and
their packs out to Carmody's mansion. She had to load
off most of the bundles for the first trip. The girl explained
to the family that Mrs Carmody would drive back for the
rest of their stuff. It was quite a pile. Alice didn't recall

551

them arriving with such a pile of plunder a month ago, all these hide bundles and basket traps and bentwood boxes. She had the girl tell them climb aboard, not to worry, the pup would guard their valuables. They all piled on, laughing, except the grandfather. There was one prize he refused to leave behind: a big flat-drum. The drum was a yard across or better, made of raw elkhide pulled tight around a narrow band of white pine that had been steamed and worked into a perfect circle. Nell climbed on top of the hood with the drum and Alice belted her to the windshield. The little girl rode out there, grinning into the wind and holding the drum by the cross of the braided rawhide at its back. Even without a drumstick the taut hide hummed and sang all the long bumpy drive, like a throaty country crooner. It seemed appropriate: the face of the drum had been rendered with an Innupiat-style painting of a very saintly-looking Elvis.

'Whatever was on your grandfather's mind,' Alice shouted over the windshield to the six-year-old, 'hauling that damn thing all the way down from the Baffins? Did he think he was going to Graceland?'

'Oh, this drum? Grandfather didn't bring it, he builded it. He did it while we was waiting around that green room all the time. You cannot get nice wood like this in the Baffins no place.'

The longhouse facade had been blown down again. They unloaded the Jeep right on top of the flats and Alice headed back to pick up the rest of the family's bundles. She had just reached the pavement when an ancient gold-sprayed helicopter rose from the town and came coughing over her head in a whirl of oily smoke, north, up the coastline. A visitor? She couldn't recall ever seeing the battered old eggbeater around Kuinak before, and it wasn't a sight one was likely to forget. She must have missed its arrival during the bumpy ride out with the Eskimos and that drum-throated Elvis.

Altenhoffen was sitting on one of the hide bundles when she pulled into her motel yard. He was bent intently over a lapful of books and notes with the pup

552

asleep between his feet. Neither one of them looked up at her arrival.

'What was with the golden chopper, Poor Brain? That's the first visitors we've had from the real world, why'd you let 'em get away?'

'No stopping 'em,' he told her, keeping his bandaged nose lowered to his work. 'They were armed and unreasonable. It was Thad Greener, accompanied by three handmaidens with high-powered handguns. The *Beacon* of course was more than anxious to hear any news from the world beyond but they refused to be interviewed. Greener said *he* would ask the questions, fuck you very much.'

'Reverend Thump Greener? The asshole Bellisarius was hiding from?'

'The holy hole himself. He couldn't believe the good Squid was dead until we took him to Boswell's walk-in and showed him the poly-wrapped mummy.'

'Good God, why hasn't he been buried?'

'That's the same thing Greener asked. Because we've been hoping Father Pribilof would rally from his collapse in time to do the rites. The moment Greener found out there was an opening at the pulpit he seemed to lose interest in the mummified Squid. He climbed back in his golden chariot and chopped straight up to the church. I have not yet had the opportunity to find out why he left without taking the job. Overqualified perhaps? I can't imagine any of those kids at the church standing up to him. I tell you, Alice'—he lifted his glasses to give her a look for emphasis—'the big steranoid was just as scary as the Squid described him: three hundred rippling pounds of born-again psychopath. He didn't *need* a handgun. His eyes were like looking into a twelve-gauge double-barrel. All right, look.' He held up the notebook he had been working on.

'I copied this out of a pile of code signals The Radio Man received that first night. He couldn't remember his Morse well enough to translate the stuff. It might have lain forever forgotten were it not for the *Beacon*'s intrepid newsman. I found the pile in what would be called a dark corner, except The Radio Man's tower *has* no corners.' He held up a 1964 Boy Scout Manual. '*This* I found on one of Iris' rare-book shelves. It set me back a cool one hundred shekels and made me wonder if Iris isn't some kind of closet kin. Your part starts there at my checkmark.'

She took the open notebook. It was two pages of dots and dashes on every other line. The letters were filled in above the code marks in Altenhoffen's hurried printing. She could almost hear the halting beeps and buzzes as she read.

'—THIS IS E GREER COBRA OUT OF KUINAK AK COBRA LOST CREW PICKED UP BY YACHT S FOX OF DEL MAR CA M CARMODY W HARDESTY A & N CULLIGAN ALL SAFE ON FOX I SALLAS DID NOT MAKE IT THIS IS E GREER COME BACK—'

She reread the last line, then closed the book and looked across the courtyard toward the shimmer of water. 'You Bitch,' she said softly. 'You couldn't resist, could you, you rotten Bitch—'

'I beg your pardon.'

'No, Poor Brain, I don't mean you. Forgive me.' She caught his soft little hand between hers, grateful to have something to laugh about. 'In fact you have turned out to be a prince and a pal like I never would have imagined. A *warrior*.' She squeezed the hand hard. 'But stay away from the ocean until this nasty period's over, will you, warrior? We can't afford to lose our best newsman to some madwoman's menopausal mood-swing. Who would report it?'

Altenhoffen laughed along although he could barely fathom what Alice was talking about. It was obviously some kind of mad-woman in-joke—too primal for him. Too *Deap.* Made the poor brain blush.

He tried to help her load up the rest of the Johanssens' belongings until Alice told him he was more underfoot than the pup and ran him off. By the time she got back out to Carmody's it was getting late. The sun was depositing itself in the fog bank like a big copper penny.

The Johanssens had made a tight little beach fire out of some of the broken longhouse struts. Nell was seated beside the firepit on a striped blanket, stirring a tilted cookpot with one hand and playing rollball with the toddler with the other. The pot she was watching was the authentic brass spittoon from Carmody's den and the balls were red snooker balls. She waved a wooden spoon at Alice. 'We are down here, Mrs Carmody. You want some *oot-oots*?'

Oot-oots seemed to be a kind of limpet the women had gathered from a tidepool. Alice had never seen their like in all her years wandering these shores. The girl showed her how to bite the top off the bean-sized mollusk and suck out the meat. They tasted vaguely of nicotinic acid but that could have been the cookpot and she was warned *never* to eat the speckled ones.

'Grandmother and the aunts they are in the bathtub. They heated it with hot rocks. Grandfather and the uncles and the mean cat they walk around to see what's the noise they hear over there.' She aimed the steaming spoon across the water. 'I think it's monsters, what do you think?'

Alice listened. A fiendish skirl was coming from the leveled bank across the toe of the bay. She told the girl she hated to disappoint her but she didn't think it was monsters. She'd heard something similar one night last week on the other side of town, and she was pretty sure it was the same bunch. 'Boars and bears arguing over garbage. I find it kind of musical. All those soprano squeals and baritone growls? Sounds a little like they're singing romantic opera. Aw, shit.' A dreadful woe was clawing up her throat. She fought it down; she wouldn't give the old Bitch the satisfaction. 'Shit, shit, *shit*!'

'What's the matter, Mrs Carmody, that's making you so sad?'

'I'm all right, sweetheart. For a moment there I was reminded of old memories I almost had. The moment passed. Look out! Your *oot-oots* are boiling over.'

On the way back to the Jeep she ducked in Carmody's

house to gather up her canvases. She could imagine St Elvis working his way into her studies of plump nudes in no time at all. She also grabbed some books and all the booze she could find. The air was steamy. The smell of bubble bath was all through the house, and the splash and giggle of women at play could be heard through the bathroom door. Must be like a steamy Third World Rubens in there, she imagined, modern and classic and primitive all at once. She chuckled over the mental picture all the ride back around the bay.

This time it was coming on dusk as Alice bounced the Jeep up on to the abrupt pavement of Bayshore. She wondered vaguely what time this might be. Midsummer dusk like this, ten or eleven was probably a good guesstimate. Alaskan twilight. The cool evening air coming over her windshield was rank with the smell of fireweed and fennel, the way air was supposed to smell at this time of day, this time of the year. The extreme mood swings must be about over, she thought, the chills and fever passing.

She swerved sharply to miss a black Labrador retriever loping across the road. His coat shined with prosperity and health and his tongue was flapping over his shoulder like a red silk necktie. He was heading for the path overland to the Underdog Cemetery, for a drink at the seep spring. As Alice watched him lope away up the path she saw a pair of figures coming down. In their tubewear attire they were as shiny black as that lab. The young man wore a kind of serape patterned with a sunburst of ventilation slits. The girl had on a big apron affair fashioned so the shoulder straps served also as blouse and bra. Each of the figures was carrying two five-gallon plastic jam buckets on each end of a shoulder yoke. The yoke collars were made from a slice of tire with a hole cut to stick the head through. It was the frostback couple, the Navidads. Alice could tell by the girl's voluptuous gait that they were soon going to be more than a couple.

She put the Jeep in four-wheel and angled right up the embankment the way the dog had gone. The young couple seemed to know that Alice was driving up to give them a ride. The boy helped his wife unhook her load, then lifted off her collar. They were waiting side by side when she drove up. *'Buen' noches,'* they said in unison.

'You kids *stayed* here? Jesus, I thought you'd be in Mazatlán weeks ago. Now you're stuck up here with us left-behinds.'

The boy's diffident face reddened but his voice was steady. *'Sí*, Mrs Carmody . . . we are stuck.'

Alice appealed to them all the Jeep ride down to Bayshore to come back to the Bear Flag with her. 'You two are going to need a nest and I happen to have a vacancy. I'll let you have it gratis if you'll give me a hand around the place now and then.'

They both said they were eager to lend a hand, anywhere, anytime, but they politely declined her offer of a cabin. They were working on their own little nest, if she would like to see. So Alice found herself driving down to the bay flats again, this time down a neglected side road toward the smokey black battlements and tepee triangles that were the skyline of Tire City.

The graveled ruts stopped at a gate swung between two tall black obelisks. These pillars were made of sportscar tires stacked in ever-diminishing sizes up a pair of planted brailer booms. The topmost tires must have come from wheelbarrows and toy wagons. The gate was a weave of heater hoses.

'Gracias, this is fine,' the boy said when he saw Alice was looking for a way through. 'They don' open the gate, just on special occasions.'

'Okay, but I'll carry the young mother's water. Show me how to get into this yoke contraption.'

'No, no, please,' the girl protested. 'Our hub is not very far. I will be fine.'

'I expect you will, girl,' Alice said. 'But you let me carry those buckets or me and this Jeep'll *make* this a special occasion. *Sabe?'*

'Sí, Mrs Carmody,' they both answered with lowered smiles. 'We savvy, *gracias.'*

The compound was divided into four areas called hubs. These little boroughs were delineated by neat lines of tires planted upright in the sand. Each area had its own central cooking pit, with huts and tents and lean-tos of every size, shape and material crowding the fires. There were RO/RO boxes stacked like blocks, overturned hulls, car hoods welded into hexagons and octagons, tepees on tripods of broken trawler arms . . . yet there was a harmony among all these conflicting forms, owing to the one essential material they all had in common: black rubber. Quilts of glued inner-tube pieces covered the tepees. Squares of treads shingled the boxes. Sections of balloon tires were fitted to make tile roofs. Igloos of tires, domes of tires, yurts and hives and pyramids of tires, all softly polished by time and weather and trimmed with evening firelight.

Spectral figures worked over the smoking cookpit grills and kettles while others lounged on contrived benches and ottomans. Many of the villagers had put on the simple one-piece affair that fishkids wore against the evening damp—a half-circle of inner tube that buttoned at the throat, creating a simple hood and a short cloak. It made them look like devotees preparing for formal ceremony.

A big firepit smoldered in a space between the four hubs. This was clearly the town square. Long sausage strings of stuffed tubes had been arranged to make a tight little amphitheater of seats, focused on a speaker's podium. The lectern was a handsome stack of bicycle tires with the rear of the stack cut away to allow the speaker entry. It was oiled and polished and quite handsome.

'Looks like everybody's getting decked out,' Alice observed. 'What's on the program this evening, the Royal Tire Choir?'

The girl giggled. 'We don't have a meeting this night, Mrs Carmody. Everybody is getting ready to go to town for the Underdog fireworks.'

'Good God, it's the Fourth of July! Fancy that. What makes them think there's going to be a display? The Squid's shipment of fireworks got scuttled in Skagway.'

'The Dogs found some of last year's, I think I hear—in the belongings of Mr Bellisarius.'

'Incredible.' Alice laughed. 'The rockets' red glare from beyond the grave. Long may it wave.'

The Navidads' nest was in the newest section of the city. There weren't any baroque battlements and most of the dwellings looked recently begun. The boy unhooked his buckets, then helped Alice. They watched nervously as she walked around their little domicile. It was circular with a parasol roof; about half of the structure had been covered with overlapping fronds of tube rubber. The shape of the thing was familiar. 'It's going to be a palapa hut!' she realized. 'It's nice. You can sell *cerveza* and nachos, just like the beach cabañas in Baja.'

'It is nothing.' The boy gave the structure a deprecating wave. 'But it will keep off the rain. Excuse me, please. I must take two buckets to the kitchen.'

'Stay and have supper, Mrs Carmody,' the girl said in a rush. 'Everyone will be so honored. Look. We are having red meat.'

Alice could see supper on the cookfire spit, golden brown and sizzling. A mouth-watering aroma of rosemary and garlic drifted with the smoke of dripping fat. 'Smells tempting, I'll admit. Somebody poach a nice young deer?'

'A Rottweiler,' the girl said. *'Muy gordo* and *malo.* We voted on him last night.'

'I always knew they'd be good for something,' Alice said.

She tried a little of the sample slice the boy brought, just to show she wasn't above eating dog. It was as good as venison, she conceded, and juicier. But she told them she better get back to her place: she had her own mutt to see to. She asked if they would like a ride in to the Fourth of July celebration. The boy shook his head.

'Perhaps if it was the Cinco de *Mayo,'* he added in an awkward attempt at frostback humor. They escorted her back to the gate, one on each side, with their black hoods up.

559

There was already a line of hooded figures trudging alongside the dirt road. Quite a few greeted Alice by name as she drove past, but no-one was interested in a ride. They wanted to walk. Some of the walkers carried odd little twisted candles that spit yellow sparks and smelled like fish burning. These hooded forms and their candles could be seen lining out across Bayshore and flickering away up the footpath to town. All they need to do is learn 'Ave Maria,' Alice thought.

After checking by the Bear Flag and feeding the pup she headed on down toward the docks. She saw Myrna Crabbe come out of the lamplit Crabbe Potte and pulled the Jeep over to see if she wanted a ride. The woman grunted and slid her huge rear into the seat. The two rode all the way down Main to Spring and across the empty marina lot without speaking. They could hear some of the Underdogs howling feebly from the dock. A bottle rocket squirted a few yards into the sky, then fell sputtering to the water.

'Nothing works.' Myrna grunted with disgust. 'Especially Underdogs.' Beneath the disgust Alice detected a note of reluctant affection.

'In high school you used to say nothing works but the *women*.'

'That was in high school. Now nothing works period.'

Alice found a good viewing spot close to the shadowy action on the dock's south end. Myrna scooted out and glared in the other direction, toward the sparky gathering of candles near the cannery. 'Thanks for the lift. I'm gonna check those fishkids. My niece Dinah, she's took up with them. I'm aggravated.' She waddled away toward the gathering.

Alice got out and climbed on the warm hood of the Jeep. She leaned against the windshield and wrapped the plaid shirt around her bare knees. Before her on the dock, a string of awkward silhouettes stood against the porcelain shimmer of the bay. They looked like a clumsily cut chain of black paper dolls pasted to a mother's refrigerator door. Alice couldn't help but feel a little affectionate

560

herself. 'The Loyal Order of the Underfoot, still working to keep the old flag flying. Well, Myrna,'—she smiled after the grumpy woman—'when nothing works you have to admit it keeps on working.'

From her right another bottle rocket scratched the sky and fizzled out. She saw now that that first fizzle hadn't come from the line of Underdogs after all. It came from the bleachers the studio had built for the citizens. By the hoots and boos the bleachers sounded full. Another rocket squirted out of the dark seats. This one at least made it high enough to pop its little flash in the dark. The citizens' next launch was one of those prop jobs—flying saucers, she thought they were called. A light breeze flipped the little spinner upside down and it whizzed into the water right at the stern of Boswell's processor. It burbled around on the surface, then boomed up a bright geyser.

'Say!' Boswell's voice called from the dark hump of his afterdeck. 'Say there now—!'

'There now!' answered a chorus of scattered wags. Someone called, 'Do you surrender, Herr Capitán Boswell? If so, strike your colors—'

'Herb Tom, is that you?'

'—or hoist your daughters.' Boozy laughter rose from the bleachers.

'I know your voice, Herb Tom,' Boswell shouted. 'How much to rent your wife this week? I got some places need rubbed.' 'Oooh,' the crowd encouraged from the dark, eager for more.

This rising irreverence was stopped abruptly by a stupefying blast of serious weaponry. Revealed in a glaring muzzle flash was Sergeant-at-Arms Norman Wong, his official .44 Colt aimed at the sky for order. When the blast finished echoing Norman had the whole town's complete attention.

'This is the birthday of our great nation we are celebrating here.' The big man's voice was shaking with emotion. 'As well as the passing of a noble president! Have a fucking care and govern yourselves accordingly!'

561

'Damn straight, Norman!' Boswell's voice agreed. 'Tell 'em if they can't keep their rockets out of trouble keep 'em outta the air. This ain't the place for amateurs. The Squid never endangered no boats and gas tanks.'

There were no more *espontáneo* displays. Someone began to chant, 'Squid . . . Squid.' Everybody picked it up. 'Squid . . . Squid . . . Squid . . .' Not in impatience, Alice realized, but in a kind of dawning reverence. The chant went on until it had the ring of practiced ceremony. Then it changed, at the sight of something, into a heart-breaking howl. Alice turned and saw the approach of a cluster of those spitting candles: the candlebearers were escorting six men carrying an old wooden dinghy on their shoulders. The procession crossed the docks to the last slip and put the boat in the water. Norman dropped a candle into the stern and an oily fire popped to life. The howl rose with the flame. Running hard along both sides of the slip, the Underdogs propelled the dinghy out into the bay. It rocked away over the flat water as the fire crept forward. Thirty or forty yards out, the boat bottom began to erupt in a holocaust of ill-aimed pyrotechnics. They had been sitting upright around the mummy until that running shove made them keel over backwards. A bombardment of fire and color belched shoreward— whistling, whizzing, booming and star-bursting. The chain of paper dolls dived for cover. A ball of orange fire whooshed right past the Jeep's hood and bounced across the tarmac, stampeding fishkids and citizens both. It exploded against the side of the cannery like a galactic spider.

The oily fire in the boat's bottom burned past the over-turned displays and the upright star-shells began going off correctly: into the sky. But the recoil of that initial bombardment had swung the burning dinghy broadside. It was coasting back toward the docks. The first sea breeze in a week was lending a hand.

'Shoot it, Norman, shoot it,' Boswell screamed. 'It's headed for the fuel shed.'

It was headed more toward the jetty than the fuel shed,

but Boswell's alarm had a nice ring. 'Shoot it, Norman, shoot it!' the bleachers agreed. Norman Wong pulled his official gun but was reluctant to fire it. He couldn't remember anything regarding this in the club rules. Some other citizen's pistol cracked the dark, kicking water across the burning boat. Dozens more immediately joined in, and, at last, Sergeant-at-Arms Wong. Norman had the bigger bore and the better aim. His first shot ripped away the old boat's bow. The second slug caught her at the waterline and the dinghy began to take on water. Just before it listed under the floating pyre's magazine fired off one last sky-climbing shell. The shore battery ceased its pistol fire to watch the fuse of this pyro-technic cannonball. It rose lazily, fizzing and tumbling high into the stars until it stopped and bloomed huge, like a satellite flash camera photographing the entire town. A bowel-loosening thud followed, reverberating off the glacier to the bank of mist, then back across the town. Everyone waited for the expected display, faces lifted. But apparently that was all. The sky stayed black. The shore battery resumed their sporadic barrage on the stricken dinghy, a kind of drowsy popping and cracking, slower and slower . . .

Alice jumped with surprise when she discovered the girl Shoola seated alongside her on the Jeep's hood, holding one of those little spitting candles.

'You Kuinak people put on a good show, Mrs Carmody. I'm happy to be here.'

'We're happy to have you, Miss Shoola. I noticed you're carrying a Tire City taper; when do you get your rubber hood?'

The girl laughed. 'Oh, you don't have to worry. I learn to appreciate colors too much from my fashion teacher. I like these candle things, though. One of the kids in the city is a scientist; he makes a powder and then rolls the hooligan in it.'

'You mean "eulachon," I'll bet. Candlefish. I *thought* I smelled something familiar. My people used 'em for eons. Ours never burned this well, though.'

'He says the spark is from iron dust and the yellow is flashlight batteries. You want one? They burn and burn forever . . .'

'Sure, light one up. It looks like our fireworks are finished for this Fourth.'

The dinghy had disappeared and a bent, burning shape was all that remained afloat, like a cocoon spun from threads of flaming plastic. The shape was beginning to sizzle in a golden glow, just like that Rottweiler, but the aroma was not mouth-watering.

'I drove your folks out to Mr Carmody's empty house around the bay. They said they needed to get back to things.'

'I heard so from Mr Altenhoffen when he came up to Father Pribilof's. Thank you again for all you have done.'

'Poor Brain was curious why Reverend Greener hadn't muscled in as priest. Apparently it is the kind of job he's usually interested in.'

'That big helicopter man? Oh, he was plenty interested. Even after we told him Father Pribilof was resting just fine he kept being interested. He's a stiff-neck man, and I did not like the way he was being to my friends. Here you go, Mrs Carmody, six of them. We will light one now and you can save the other five in your pocket.'

Alice accepted the little bundle of dried fish; they were like the nasty twisted cigars that Carmody called crooks. She pulled one free and held it to the burning stub of the girl's light.

'It was *you*, wasn't it, that ran him off? What did you say to him, you imp?'

'Say to him? Nothing. I just said that Father Pribilof was okey-dokey was all. Hold still, please, they are hard to get burning at first; but when they do they burn and burn—'

'All right then, do. What did you *do* to him?'

Alice's dried fish was sputtering to life. 'I did nothing,' the girl answered. Her husky voice was sincere and innocent. 'Nothing.' To emphasize this she raised her eyes to

Alice's. The combined candles flared between the two faces like a medicine man's fire. The gazes intersected—a cat's-cradle string game, performed with webs of copper between a pair of hidden hands, everything else darkening away in the game's concentration, stringing away, until nothing remained but the single shining speck of intersection. It twinkled with tiny firepoints of color, like Sirius the Dogstar, on a clear dawn horizon.

She was alone when she woke, in the Jeep's driver's seat, wrapped in a cloak of cloth-lined rubber. The docks were deserted. She didn't have to turn her head to know the bleachers and the parking lot were empty as well. A damp breeze was coming in across the bay and her wrap was weeping with condensate. So was the Jeep's windshield. She unsnapped the latches and leaned the flat glass to the hood so she could watch the colorful speck as it labored its way across the drab fetch of water. It *could* be Old Norway. It took forever but she was not impatient. Marvelous wonders don't have to happen of a sudden, the way they do in the *Arabian Nights.* They can also take a long time, like crystals growing, or minds changing, or leaves turning. The trick is to keep an eye peeled, so they don't slip by unappreciated.

When the variegated spectacle got close enough she got out of the Jeep and walked to the dock's edge to wait. She still had the black blanket draped about her shoulders though she wasn't cold. The sun was breaking clear of the Pyrites behind her, warming her back and shoulders to a sweat; but she was amused by the picture she knew she must be making: the seaside glyph of woman waiting, stark and somber and colorless—especially compared to that peacock rowing homeward home out there!

Greer's duffel had bloomed all over on the raft's bottom like an exotic vine. Blossoms of purple and vermillion and variegated hybrids and cross-colors were twined everywhere. An unzipped tie-dye jump suit was hoisted as a sail. The rower had a pastel linen dress shirt arranged on his head Arab-style, with a sleeve tied round his face. Only a narrow eye slot was left open to the elements, like a Bedouin in a sandstorm. He was seated amidship, rowing forward. His oars were two halves of a cracked pole tied to the oarlocks. A scrap of wood was still attached to the end of the starboard oar and a deck shoe tied to the end of the other. As he neared the dock she saw that his craft was loaded with an impressive complement of passengers. At the pointed prow of the inflatable was an excited crowd of squirrels, moles, possums, gophers, and chipmunks . . . along with a pair of young raccoons, a white-tail fawn and a mass of other immigrants too small to identify.

'You look like Lawrence of the Ark,' she called to him. 'How's the life-saving business?' Tiny soggy rodents were already springing overboard and swimming for the docks.

'Not too bad. I count a hundred and thirty-four souls saved.'

'Pretty fair haul for an out-of-shape savior.'

'One-thirty-five was a crippled ptarmigan.' Ike unwound his face, gingerly, letting the raft coast. 'I cooked her with Greer's lighter and had her yesterday for supper. The fawn was going to be next.'

He unlashed the oar that had the deck-shoe paddle and reached it up. She caught it by the toe just as the coons led the stampede for shore.

'Good thing you guys sent up those rockets,' he told her. 'Me and the gang here were a little lost in that fog.' His face was a welter of purple bruises and sunburned blisters.

'Kuinak is always eager to attract tourists to our quaint little cove. But my, *look* at your get-up! *We* never expected such a fashion statement. Colors must be in this season.'

He wasn't able to think of a comeback. The fawn hopped past him, on to the dock, and pranced stiffly after the others. Ike was even stiffer, stepping out, reaching to her for support.

'No, stay away from me! Keep away! I swore to myself I wasn't going to bawl about this, one way or another. Stay away I say, you clam-headed, ball-brained . . . Aw, *damn*, Sallas; you look good to see.'

'You too, woman. You look posolutely zam.'

The crows circled, cheering hoarsely. Mejack, the youngest, took the opportunity to swoop down and pick up a six-pack of Soggy Rodents, to celebrate the victory.

Appendix

The North Pacific is where an in-depth examination of Kuinak ought to begin, in the open sea, down under the offshore zone termed *Oceanic Environment* by the Marine Biologists and the Geologists and the Federal Zone Termers. This is the big blue anvil where the beginnings of the life-chain are forged, in links as infinitesimal and myriad as the anvil is vast and singular.

Because of its peculiar location, the waters off Kuinak are still comparatively unaffected by the Trident Rupture. Diatoms and phytoplankton still thrive near the sun-fed surface, copepod and zoo-plankton flourishing feverishly deeper down. The detritus off of all this microscopic action drifts eventually to the black bottom, termed the *Abyssal Environment*, to mix with minerals and mud. This nutritious murk is then up-welled shoreward into the next zone, the *Neritic Environment*, becoming breakfast for bacteria and protozoa and shrimp larvae. These are lunch for the fry and the fry in their turn serve as supper for the larger fish—the pollock, the black cod; the Pacific herring and Pacific perch; the flathead, yellowhead and rockhead soles; the sculpin, the halibut and the turbot—and, of course, for those shining stars of these waters—the Pacific salmon.

Even these stars are separated into castes. At the bottom of the ladder is the lowly chum salmon, also called 'dog' salmon because it was once dried and fed to the dog teams, before the snowmobile retired the dogs to the backs of pickups.

Next rung up is the silver salmon, or 'coho.' In the old times the silver was taken in steady quantities off the coasts of Oregon and Washington and British Columbia, commercially and for sport. In those days most Alaskan fishermen used to spurn this fish as a waste of effort. Even today Old Norway the Gigger throws them back when he hauls one into his rickety outboard.

'Hey, me I don' mine for silver,' Old Norway steadfastly explains; 'me I chust mine for gold!'

The gold comes in three varieties: the pink salmon (also called 'hump-back' or 'humpy'), the chinook salmon (called 'king' and looks it: an overpowering majesty of a fish, often go fifty pounds, with the fight and fangs of a finny lion and the heart to match) and the fourteen-carat treasure of them all—the sockeye or 'red' salmon. The iridescent meat of this prize is so esteemed by the fish-eating world that it rarely reaches the American table anymore; it is contracted almost completely to the Japanese sushi dealers or bid up by the Israelis before the delicacy is even caught. At the Anchorage Auction a prime red can go for thirty dollars an ounce—fifty-seven hundred bucks for a twelve-pound fish!

You can see how it would interest Hollywood, this last bastion of lox.

LITTORAL ENVIRONMENT

The third and last sea-zone. This near-shore shallows is the home of chitons and sea urchins and sea stars and bitter-stars and starfish, king crabs and tanner crabs and Dungeness, marine worms and comb jellies and sea cucumbers . . . of all the little things that crawl the slimy bottom.

There used to be an abundance of clams, but the 1994 earthquake tsunami brought down eight inches of new silt and clogged the suckers' suckers. No clams since then. The balance is delicate.

On top of this water are the dabbling ducks and the divers, the oldsquaw and harlequin, the scoter and scaup, the flocks of pintails and mallards and golden-eyes, the courts of king and common eiders, the colonies of black-legged kittywakes and horned and tufted puffins, cadres of pelagic and redfaced cormorants; common and thick-billed murres; dapper sandpipers and ruddy turnstones . . . and groups and gobs and gangs of gulls, glaucous-winged and otherwise.

Up the surf and across the rugged rocks run red phalaropes, oystercatchers, least auklets, fulmers and shearwaters, also storm petrels, ancient murrelets and contemporary grebes.

Moving from the seashore into the land: now there can be sighted savannah sparrows, Lapland longspurs, grey-crowned rosy finches, white thrushes, black-capped chickadees, white-winged crossbills, olive-sided fly-catchers and piliated redheaded woodpeckers that look exactly like Woody. Sing like him, too—ackitty-*ack*-ack, ackitty-*ack*-ack! It is the only place on the continent where they still fly wild. They were gradually eliminated in the lower forty-eight, coincidentally with the old growth. Woody was traded for pulp-board speaker cabinets made in Korea.

Moving higher you find spruce grouse and jays, hawks red-tailed and hawks rough-legged, owls short-eared and owls great-horned, and white-tailed ptarmigans, both willow and rock. Higher still sail peregrine falcons and gyrfalcons, osprey and cliff swallows. At the very top, as befits his commissioned rank, reigns the bald eagle. His ranks are actually on the rise; he has learned to battle for his breakfast in the not-so-sanitary land-fills, right along with common crows and gulls.

In the freshwater streams and lakes roam rotifers, flagellates, ciliates, flatworms and crawdads. Freshwater clams and snails slide and syphon. Waterskippers skip and backstrokers stroke. Dragonfly larvae and stonefly larvae and mosquito larvae bustle and dart among the reeds, all impatient to metamorphose into their blood-thirsty maturity.

Feeding on all this larval largess are lake trout, golden trout, rainbow trout and Dolly Varden; Arctic grayling;

blackfish, whitefish and cisco fish; northern pike and pigmy pike; sticklebacks with three spines and sticklebacks with nine spines; the worthless chub and the double-ended helldiver; and the freshwater catch claimed to be the very tastiest by the knowledgeable native—the Arctic char.

Moose can still be confronted, muddling in tundra marsh. On the riverbank and mountainside beaver and muskrat still abound. You can still see occasional lynx and mink and land otter. In the bush, short-tailed weasels vow never to become ermine and Arctic hares still cock their ears for the diving rush of feathered doom. In the high tundra, diehard wolf tribes still stalk the Dall sheep. Musk-ox, which were thought finished in the 1800s, have waded back from near-extinction until now more than a thousand exist in protective incarceration.

And then there are the bears. The bears. What about the bears? Let this suffice: while visiting the tin-and-tarpaper shack of an old native carver of outlawed ivory, I noticed that many of her carvings were of bears, terrible bears, doing terrible things to people—stalking them, chasing them, rending them literally limb from gory limb. I asked why she always depicted bears in such cruel combat with the helpless human. She gaped at my stupidity:

'Bears,' she explained, thrusting both brown palms toward me, jagged fingernails hooked inward to emphasize the obvious, 'are *monsters.*'

SOILS

The topsoils occurring on the bulk of these slopes of the Aleutian Range are largely of one kind: gravel. Coarse gravel at one end of this very narrow spectrum; well-drained deposits of sandy ash at the other. We're talking grit here—constant, grey, grindy grit.

TERRESTRIAL SUCCESSION

This is the term used to describe how life naturally comes back into an area after a full-scale natural devastation. Say, volcanic. The black ash of the caldera slopes leaches to varying shades of brownish grey. Wind and rain erode minerals from the cliffs to form sand. Lichens gain toeholds on barren ridges and begin to chisel hairline fractures. The lichens die and form thin layers of organic matter that mixes with the sands, composing soil enough to give mosses a beginning. The mosses lay a bedding for the first tiny fiddleheads of fern, and so on. Eventually the fire-blasted desolation is transformed once again into a lush community of floral associates, waving and blooming in happy innocence of the dark joker that nature had got around to dealing. Terrestrial Succession used to be the way nature hedged its bets, a trick of putting things back like they were. How long does this putting-back normally take? Forty million years? Forty thousand? Not at all. In less than forty seasons this can happen. But that's *normal* seasons, in good old four-four time—spring; summer; fall; winter.

FLORAL ASSOCIATES

—are divided into eight categories:

1. *Wet Tundra:* horsetail, pondweed, bur reed, wild flag, mare's tail, rush, fir club, quilwort . . .

2. *Moist Tundra:* herbs, grasses and sedge rooted in mosses and lichens, flowers, hairmoss, reindeer lichen; goldenthread, which sparks the saliva glands like a touch of herbal electricity; monkshood, marsh moss . . .

3. *Bottomland Spruce:* white spruce and balsam poplar

on a lush rug of ferns, like patterns on a carpet; rose, oakfern . . .

4. *Low Brush-bug Muskeg:* fibrous peat in stratified silt loam; heath, northern water carpet . . .

5. *High Brush:* littletree willow, green alder and birch, twinflower, naked fern, bluejoint . . .

6. *Lowland Spruce:* tamarack, birch, aspen and poplar, at the base of which flourish an understory of cranberry rooted in sphagnum moss; Arctic dock, sidebells, pyrolax . . .

7. *Upland Spruce:* is white on the southern slopes, black on the northern exposures; dwarf birch and milk vetch; fireweed, basket grasses that can grow a foot in a week in good seasons, feltleaf willow . . .

8. *Alpine Tundra:* blueberry, bayberry, crowberry, thimbleberry, lupine, aster, cinquefoils, alpine azalea, Arctic willow, mountain avens, cow parsnips, saxifrage, yarrow, fescue, mountain timothy, rockbrake, and a nasty damn thing called Devil's Club that looks like an innocent little fiddlehead but can fill your palm with microscopic thorns if you so much as brush it.

Lots of plants, not many big ones. The soil isn't deep enough to support them. As I say, delicate. It doesn't take much. Most of the similar slopes south of Kuinak are already stricken or wounded at this story's start—festering along road cuts, choked by thick air, cooked and confused by the Anarchy of the Age.